The Collected Supernatural and Weird Fiction of
Mrs G. Linnaeus Banks

Through the Night

&

Mrs Alfred Baldwin

The Shadow on the Blind and Other Stories

The Collected Supernatural and Weird Fiction of
Mrs G. Linnaeus Banks
Through the Night
&
Mrs Alfred Baldwin
The Shadow on the Blind and Other Stories

Twenty-Four Short Tales
to Chill the Blood

Mrs G. Linnaeus Banks
&
Mrs Alfred Baldwin

LEONAUR

The Collected
Supernatural and Weird
Fiction of
Mrs G. Linnaeus Banks
Through the Night
&
Mrs Alfred Baldwin
The Shadow on the Blind and Other Stories

Twenty-Four Short Tales
to Chill the Blood
by Mrs G. Linnaeus Banks
&
Mrs Alfred Baldwin

First published under the titles
Through the Night
and
The Shadow on the Blind and Other Stories

Leonaur is an imprint of Oakpast Ltd

Copyright in this form © 2016 Oakpast Ltd

ISBN: 978-1-78282-517-3 (hardcover)
ISBN: 978-1-78282-518-0 (softcover)

http://www.leonaur.com

Contents

Through the Night   7

The Shadow on the Blind and Other Stories   317

Through the Night

Mrs G. Linnaeus Banks

Contents

Prefatory	11
A World Between	13
The Pride of the Corbyns	45
Wraith-Haunted	69
The Piper's Ghost: A Legend of Elvet Bridge, Durham	84
St. Cuthbert's Cup: A Legend of Hell-Kettles, Darlington	107
The Fairies' Cradle	133
My Will	164
Judgment Deferred	174
A Dour Weird	199
The White Woman of Slaith	222
Larry's Apprenticeship: An Irish Fairy Legend	242
The Fate of the Fosbrookes	257
A New Leaf	272
The Plainbury Mystery	295

Prefatory

It is the fashion nowadays with one section of the community to decry all allusion to the supernatural as remnants of bygone superstition; another section, rushing to the opposite extreme, professes power as potent as the wand of Prospero to commune with the spirit-world, and summon the long-departed back to be heard, and seen, and felt, through the night of the dark *séance*; a third, and much larger proportion—in which may be included the writer—holds a midway position, admitting the; possibility that disembodied spirits may haunt certain places and certain people, but that it is by no means an assured fact.

Science, which has driven so many a beautiful myth from our nurseries, and driven the childhood out of our children at the same time, has done much to depopulate Fairyland. The elf and the hobgoblin only linger in green nooks untrodden by the proverbial schoolmaster; and he has shaken his rod at the wraith and the banshee.' It is an age of scepticism; men—aye, and women too—walk abroad and with faces unabashed avow their disbelief even in Deity. Can we wonder that the same scepticism mocks at ghosts, and all that a belief in them implies?

Is it not, therefore, an anomaly that the era of hard science and scoffing unbelief should have given so many mystic and ghost-stories to our literature?

Can all these be wholly imaginative? Nothing of the kind. Some scrap of family history, some waif of confidential communication there may have been, which crystallized into a story, vivid with life, and form, and colour, at the point of the author's pen. And not a few of these may have been given to the world by professing cynics, who laugh lightly at their own work, lest a shadow of suspicion of belief should expose them to society's ridicule.

Not so the author of this book, who, in the course of her long life, has come in contact with so many persons both of credibility and culture who have assured her that either they or their friends have been visited by apparitions, that in spite of a rebellious will, and what is called common sense, she has been forced to the conclusion of Hamlet—

There are more things in Heaven and earth, Horatio,
Than are dreamed of in our philosophy;

. . . .and it is upon such personal narratives that these stories of shadows flitting through the night have been founded. She excepts, of course, the old North-country traditions, and the fairy lore, with one or two others which are wholly fiction; and in the appendix at the close of the volume may be found her authority, oral or otherwise, for aught which may seem incredible.

It may be objected that such shadows flit only *through the night* of superstition, but she holds a theory that disembodied spirits are around us everywhere, the messengers and ministers of Almighty God, and that it is possible He may either, in His love or wrath, for reasons inscrutable to us, permit certain eyes to be opened to behold that which is dark to others. But that such revelation is common, or that the spirits of the dead can be summoned up for vulgar exhibition is too monstrous for credence.

In George Cruikshank's amusing brochure on ghosts, he makes merry over the *ghosts of garments*, the "ghost of a stocking," and so on, but *if* spirit does take a visible shape at all, why not take the shape of a cloak or a stocking, or a suit of armour, as readily as of the discarded body?

And so long as those mysterious affinities exist between kindred souls, which herald the coming foot, the coming letter, or awaken simultaneous thought, so long as the thousand-and-one premonitions and coincidences of our daily life remain inexplicable, so long as the historian and biographer chronicle visitations from the world of shadows, the self-sufficiency of utter incredulity is inadmissible. And so the author trusts no apology is needed for these stories of fays, and wraiths, and phantoms, who are said to have come as messengers of good or ill, whether in the gloaming, or through the night, the night which surrounds the living and breathing world; or for her title, since elves and spirits, tricksy or solemn, shun the garish day, and, like the stars, be only visible *Through the Night.*

A World Between

Mt father's will had left me master of Tarnbeck, and sole guardian of my half-sister Amy, the child of a second marriage; a light, laughing, fairy-like creature, all song and sunshine.

Fashion did find her way to Tarnbeck occasionally in the train of Lady Clevedale and others, and had trifled with skirts and bonnets; but never dared Fashion lay a ruthless hand on Amy Beckton's glorious flaxen hair. So it rippled in light curls to her waist at nineteen freely as when the buoyant schoolgirl of nine chased butterflies in the green lanes, with her tresses floating on the wind.

The Becktons of Tarnbeck had held their own when a strong arm, a strong will, and a strong hold were the three requisites either for the acquisition of power or its maintenance.

Alas for the degenerate scions of those warlike ancestors, whose armour shared with antlers and other trophies of the hunting-field the honour of decorating the entrance-hall! Sword and halbert, gun and pistol, hunting-horn and hound, had given way before the followers of William Caxton. The cannon on the battlements could not be trusted to fire a birthday salute, the strong-room was the library, and for three generations the owner had been a confirmed bookworm.

The castellated mansion was peculiarly situated. It was built of coarse grit-stone, on an elevated knoll, at the junction of two rapid streams fresh from the hills, which, on their marriage a hundred yards or so away down the valley, assumed the dignity of a river. In wet seasons, when the becks, swollen by heavy rains or melting snows, overflowed their banks, the water crept upwards like an insidious enemy on all sides, until the house stood isolated on a raised island, calmly defiant above the threatening waters, which never passed the vanguard of firs, however close and angry might be their advance. An array of mediaeval windows, and the Gothic entrance with its nail-studded door, opened northwards, towards the hills and recesses of Clevedale, where the tumbling becks supplied water-power for one or two woollen mills; the cottages of the operatives looking like flocks of dingy sheep on the distant hillsides.

This was the original front of the buildings; but Amy preferred the modernised back with its southern aspect of green pasture lands, straggling plantations, and the impetuous streams which chafed and fretted before they blent and rolled away placidly under willows and sedges, a respectable river. A fierce semi-circular-fronted tower, having two unequal wings, pierced with loopholes for defence, had Tarnbeck been in its fighting days, before the ivy crept over it, and the baron's hall in the central tower had been converted into a spacious drawing-room, with three lofty windows at the embayed end. Over this was the library, our room of rooms, triply lit in correspondence with the apartment beneath, but teeming with well-bound, well-bought volumes on shelves which occupied every available space.

Amy had had full liberty with lace and muslin, gorgeous satin and damask, to brighten up the dark nooks of Tarnbeck, so long as she left the entrance-hall and the library as our good father had bequeathed them to us. So the thick old Turkey carpet still preserved silence beneath the foot; dark and cumbrous ancestral chairs and tables served as depositories for tomes as cumbrous; the summer sun shot his rays through heavy crimson velvet drapery, and fell with a ruddy glory on the large, elaborately-carved, old oak cabinet, which, black as ebony, had faced the windows and defied the sunbeams to pierce its secrets for many generations.

There is no doubt I am a bookworm, as my father was, but I have not reached the age of mustiness: perhaps Amy has dusted the cobwebs off her studious brother Charlie; perhaps Amy's friends have helped to preserve some of youth's freshness in the student whom she twitted with old bachelorhood at thirty.

Yes, Amy's friends, all Amy's. The laughter from the croquet lawn, the music from the drawing-room, the whiffs of cigar from the terrace, all indicate the friends of my beautiful, lovable little sister; the pet of Clevedale society, the *fiancée* of Frank Fairclough, whose father is head partner of the firm owning the chief mill in Clevedale. Have I no more than a brotherly interest in her friends? Ah! well, we shall see.

I suppose I am naturally too shy and reserved to cultivate friend-ships. At all events, I have never had more than one *friend*, Oscar

Bergheim; and he went away—to place a world between us. Oscar was the son of a Swedish merchant, sent to England for education; and we met when mere boys at a public school, both boarding with the same master. There are few animals more cruel than the untrained schoolboy; and this native savagery drew together Oscar and myself, in spite of our utter dissimilarity.

I was a pale, slight boy, more inclined to pore over a book in a corner than to join in rough games in the playground; I was soon dubbed "Miss Charlotte," and marked out for persecution. Oscar, though three years my junior, was stout, muscular, dark-browed, fiery-eyed, impulsive, with a capacity for loving and hating rare amongst men. His ignorance of English, his foreign accent and manners, made him also a butt for the bullets of ridicule and practical joking; but he went in for a tussle with one of the bullies, and gave the ruffian a grip which served for the whole squad. Still in speech they had him at a disadvantage, until I (who from my father had picked up a smattering of many strange tongues) became interpreter for him, and he became champion for me. "Damon and Pythias," "Orestes and Pylades" were among the wordy brickbats hurled at us; but they fell like feathers, and our friendship grew with our years.

There were no home-goings for Oscar; he was too far away. It saddened me at vacation time to see his efforts to hide his home-sickness, his longings for Sweden's streams and mountains. At my earnest entreaty he was invited to spend his holidays at Tarnbeck; and his rapturous admiration of the picturesque old place won my father's heart at once. Then Oscar had a store of genuine Norse rhymes and ballads, which made him free of that tabooed chamber, the library, and set my good father corresponding with half the antiquaries in England.

Amy was then a blue-eyed, flaxen-haired child, with speech as imperfect as her slave Oscar's. She was the veriest tyrant to him. Putting her sash for a bridle in his mouth, she would mount his shoulders and drive him on all-fours as inexorably over the hard gravel as over the smooth lawn; throw ball or hat into almost inaccessible places, and demand their recovery, and would go to sleep in no arms but Oscar's. One vacation he fished her out of the beck into which she had fallen; another, caught her runaway pony; and finally pounded Frank Fairclough (then home for the holidays) almost to a jelly for throwing duck-weed on her new muslin frock and calling her contemptuously "a wax doll."

When, at seventeen, Oscar Bergheim was hurriedly recalled to

Carlscrona, with no leisure for leave-taking, the nine-years-old damsel wept bitterly, and she was scarcely consoled by the large box of Swedish toys he sent over as a souvenir to his "little sweetheart."

At nine we weep with the eyes. At twenty we begin to weep with the heart. And so I wept my one friend Oscar's removal. He had been my sole companion and confidant, and, despite my seniority, my patron and protector. I never got into, a scrape he did not champion me through, though it occurs to me now that, but for his leadership I might never have got into the scrapes at all.

Letters and summer visits to Carlscrona bridged over the sea. My father's death changed everything.

I was appointed sole guardian of Amy, who was in her seventeenth year. Then I had the conditions of my father's will to carry out. The entailed property was unencumbered, but the personal, was weighted with so many legacies as to embarrass me considerably. I was, moreover, charged with my sister's care and maintenance until her marriage or majority, when I was enjoined, to deliver up the title-deeds of certain properties, her own mother's jewels, and securities for moneys in bank and funds to the value of £15,000. All of which were lying, and were to lie in the family depository known as the "Palmer's Scrip."

This was one of those receptacles so ingeniously contrived within the recesses of the old carved cabinet as to defy suspicion, or search, and doubtless dread secrets had been consigned to the Palmer's Scrip in times gone by. The knowledge of it was held as a sacred trust, only to be passed from sire to son in the hour of extreme peril, and the master-key was only permitted to drop from the owner's dying hand into that of his successor.

My father, who had no mysteries of his own, had been wont to leave the outer doors of the cabinet open for convenience; and, having full trust in me, had initiated me into the secrets of slides and springs ere I was five-and-twenty. Yet it was with no little awe that I approached the cabinet the week after his funeral, holder of the little key and all which it represented. There were two entrances to the library, one on each side of the cabinet which filled the space between; I not only locked the one, but tried the lock of the other, which, leading principally to guest chambers, was kept fastened and rarely used. Noiselessly and reverently I cleared from the table the books and papers which had been my father's latest studies. There was a solemn hush in the house; my footsteps made no sound; and yet as I put the curious little key into the ornamental key-holes, I felt as if the room were peopled with shadows of dead and buried Becktons, all striving to prevent intrusion on their dead-and-buried secrets.

As the doors flew open I thought, too, of the now cold hand which had last opened those leaves; and, overpowered with emotion, sank on a chair unable to proceed. The cabinet had three outer doors; within were several smaller ones closing on pigeon-holes and drawers. There were also two carved figures in niches, but only one affects my narrative. It was a Palmer, with hat and staff and scallop-shells and scrip complete. The scrip, notwithstanding the will, was an innocent immovable bit of wood-carving, but on pressing the least prominent button of his "sandalled shoon," when the outer doors were unlocked, the entire figure revolved, and displayed a cavity behind, at least a foot deep, divided by three shelves—on each of which lay papers yellow with age. But it was not until the lowest shelf was pulled forward that the true scrip was revealed by the retirement of the adjoining nest of drawers. When these moved back a lid held down by them flew open, and the box it covered was the Palmer's Scrip.

The title-deeds, the money securities, and an old case of trinkets were there. The chief of the latter were a set of sapphires, another of emeralds, and one of garnets, by no means so antique as the casket.

Closing the cabinet on replaced notes and parchments, I stepped downstairs to the drawing-room, casket in hand, hoping by the display of her mother's jewellery to divert the current of Amy's thoughts, and so for a time lighten the sorrow which seemed to press so heavily on her fair young head.

My entrance was arrested by a strange voice, low, grave, and musical, a voice which thrilled me as nought had ever done before. By nature somewhat reserved and shy, I hesitated, with the door in my hand, whether to face the enemy or beat a retreat. Amy's prompt "Come in, Charlie. I want to present you to Miss Proctor," decided the question for me. And decided a much more momentous question at the same time.

There was nothing in the serene eyes or the calm gravity of the young lady to whom I was introduced to daunt any man; yet my embarrassment was painful. I coloured to the roots of my hair, and it was not until Lucy Fairclough smilingly put her hand in mine, saying, "What have I done to be overlooked this morning?" that I recovered my self-possession.

Lucy Fairclough was an average specimen of northern England's maidenhood; but the daughter of Mr. Fairclough's partner was something more. She was scarcely above the middle height; there was nothing marvellous in her brown hair or mild hazel eyes; her features were not chiselled to absolute proportion; yet there was such an air of fitness and harmony in face and figure, so much that was womanly in her manner, so much reposeful grace in every movement, that I was hopelessly fascinated on the spot. Not even in her garb was there a tint to startle us in contrast with Amy's sombre crape. Both she and Miss Fairclough were dressed in complimentary mourning, the effect of which was more soothing than gloomy.

"What curious specimen of antiquity have you there?" asked Amy, to break the first pause.

At the mention of the talismanic word "jewels," three pairs, of eyes sparkled simultaneously; but I saw a quiet smile gather on Miss Proctor's face at the eager persistence of her friends to have the casket opened.

Conquering a strange foreboding of evil, I yielded to their entreaties; and we clustered round a small table near the middle-window for their inspection. This brought me into close proximity with Miss Proctor; and as, case by case, the sparkling gems were displayed, and as I compared her calm appreciation of their beauty with the demonstrative admiration of Amy and Lucy, the ice of shyness thawed rapidly.

I was in no haste to retreat with my charge, but joined Amy In her solicitations that the young ladies should remain at Tarnbeck and dine with us. On my volunteering to send a messenger to Fairclough House, and to be their escort should Mr. Frank not be at liberty to join us, Amy looked amazed; but they consented, and I retired to fulfil the first part of my promise, and to replace the casket, little dreaming how bitterly I should regret their exhibition in the future.

Frank Fairclough responded to the invitation with an alacrity, I neither comprehended nor appreciated at the time; and notwithstanding our recent bereavement, which, of course, had subduing influence, the hours flew by so rapidly and satisfactorily that Lucy's frequent reminders of their flight and the propriety of moving homewards seemed to fall on deaf ears.

That was but the precursor of many social evenings, to which, as our sorrow wore away, other guests were admitted; but I never left my beloved books so readily as for our pleasant quintet parties, of which Miss Proctor made one. All happiness has an end. Mine terminated when Miss Proctor went back to Leeds at the expiration of a three-months' visit.

Other friends came and went; notably the Faircloughs, but I shut myself up in the library, rarely quitting my shell, whilst Amy visited and received visits alone; until Lady Clevedale read me a sharp lecture on the impropriety thereof, and suggested a companion or chaperone for my pretty half-sister.

Frank Fairclough (who had long been forgiven his contempt for "wax dolls") frowned, and Amy pouted, at the proposition; but Aunt Lydia had not been at Tarnbeck two days before Amy danced round her, declaring she was "a dear old darling," and clenched the assertion with a hug and a kiss which the genial old lady reciprocated.

Aunt Lydia was certainly an acquisition. She relieved me of much anxiety and responsibility in the care of my sister; then, she guided the reins of household management without taking them from Amy's hands, and was to the blithe little beauty just the companion, confidante, and wise counsellor the motherless girl needed.

When Amy was eighteen. Lady Clevedale carried her off to London in triumph, not without many misgivings on my part, and expostulations from Frank Fairclough, whose interference I felt at first inclined to resent.

Yet his warmth and vehemence took me somewhat by surprise, and his manly earnestness impressed me more in his favour than years of previous intimacy.

It was my first glimpse into his heart, where I clearly saw Amy enthroned, though never a word said he of an interest in her welfare deeper than that of a true friend. And he might have shaken my resolution but that my promise to Lady Clevedale was already given.

During her absence my solitude was broken in upon, to my great content, by the unexpected arrival of Oscar Bergheim, whom I had not seen for more than two years. He, like myself, had lost a father in that interval, and having no taste for mercantile pursuits, was about, so he said, to retire from the firm. Business connected therewith had brought him over.

His stay was short, and I half fancied Amy's absence had something to do with it. We talked over old times, visited old haunts, played chess together of an evening; but he had evidently outlived our quiet life, and I felt as if an imperceptible, impalpable film was spreading between us and our old friendship. To bear him company, I smoked and drank more than was my wont. It occurred to me that Frank Fairclough, from his larger intercourse with the world, might assimilate better with him—but lo! I brought a lighted match to gunpowder.

There was an explosion, and Oscar Bergheim departed from Tarnbeck the next morning.

He did not leave England, however, so soon as I expected. Amy's artless letters to Lucy and myself told of meeting him in society, then of his frequent visits at Lady Clevedale's, and his brotherly attention to herself.

The day following the receipt of this last communication Frank Fairclough was summoned to London on unexpected business.

More than a year had flown. The woods were dressed in their fullest robes of green; the sombre firs put forth pale fingers with which the sunbeams toyed; hill and dale and garden were glorious with summer's crown of flowers; the air came up the valley from the south, and through the open windows filled the rooms with the sweet scent of new hay from the meadows. Soon the sun turned towards his western couch, the starlings flew home to their nests on the battlements, and twittered their vespers ere they tucked their heads under their wings, while the grasshopper and nightingale, on the alert, answered from below.

I was imbued with the fullest sense of all this sweetness, bat I felt rather than saw or heard these country time-keepers. I sat, from, habit, by the fireless grate (which a fluffy haze of some fibrous material veiled), studying neither nature nor books, but human hearts.

Alicia Proctor was again at Fairclough House. Aunt Lydia and Amy had driven up the dale to greet her. I, who had been longing for a sight of her as a parched Arab for a desert spring, had not dared to join them. And there I sat, taking myself to task for my timidity, asking myself over and over again what there was in the pale shy bookworm of thirty to attract so perfect a sample of fresh womanhood as Alicia.

I had nursed my love in solitude and silence until it had grown almost too big for my heart, yet the "dear Alicia" of my dreams was only "Miss Proctor" when we met; and I had small reason to hope she had penetrated my secret.

A sharp rap at the room door put to flight my cogitations. My "Come in!" was followed by the entrance of Amy, in an airy azure robe and jaunty hat trimmed to match, with a flush on her face as if fresh from her drive. She was accompanied by Frank Fairclough, whose arm (or I was mistaken in the twilight) encircled her as they passed through the doorway.

I was not left long in doubt.

I usually sat with the side of my chair inclined towards the windows, so that the light should fall on my book or paper; it fell now on the faces of the pair as they came together round by the cabinet, and Amy, kneeling on the footstool at my feet, threw her arms round my neck, and whispered, "You love me very much, do you not, Charlie dear?"

"You know I do. Amy," I answered, smoothing her radiant aureole of curls with my disengaged hand, as the other held her close.

"And you would like to make me happy?"

"Are you not happy, Amy?"

"Ah, yes; but very much happier, I mean, Charlie."

I glanced up at Fairclough's manly face before I replied. It wore a look of anxious expectation.

"I would lay down my life. Amy, to secure your happiness."

A moment's hesitation; a tug at a tiny glove; then, in lower and more tremulous tones, as a sparkling ring was revealed: "Frank has placed this on my finger, Charlie. May I wear it?"

Frank, who had been silent hitherto, interposed.

"Charlie, may your sister be permitted to wear that ring as a token of betrothal until I replace it with a plainer one?"

Amy clung to me, and Frank looked out of his clear grey eyes, alike entreatingly. An overwhelming sense of responsibility overpowered my utterance. I paused to reflect. I think the form of Oscar floated before my eyes, obscuring my vision.

Frank was the first to break the painful silence.

"Charles Beckton, you *must* have seen that I have loved your sister for many years. My father, though fully approving my choice, imposed silence upon me. But for that I should have declared myself last year, when I trembled for my hopes, and for my love, consigned to Lady Clevedale's fashionable coterie. My business in town was solely to watch over our darling. I felt that my presence was needed, Charles." (He did not say why.) "Our firm takes me into partnership this week, and that change in my position sets my tongue at liberty. You see I use my freedom to forge fresh fetters. I have Amy's promise. Surely, old fellow, you will not withhold yours?"

I had risen, and buried my head in my arms against the carved old mantelpiece. From time to time vague suspicions of this had flashed across my mind, to be as instantly dismissed. I had regarded Amy as a child, and had other views for her maturity. The crisis had come all too soon, and my daydreams were dispelled. I felt Amy's hand creeping up to my shoulder, and a plaintive murmur in my ear.

"Charlie, are you sorry for this? I thought you knew that I loved Frank, and would be glad to give me to one you knew so well—so good a man."

She touched me there. I did know him for a good and true man, firm and self-reliant, the very one to guard and guide my darling. I was not so sure of Oscar's principles; yet had I, without warranty, built up an aerial castle in which he and Amy were to reign blissfully together.

I was roused by Frank's voice—somewhat husky in its tone.

"Come, come, old fellow, I did not expect this! Amy and I have been picturing a pleasant surprise, a cheery welcome. You should not have left us so much together had you not looked forward to this with satisfaction. Was not love inevitable?"

I turned round.

"Yes, yes, Frank; you are both right. It is only I who have been blind. Now kiss your bachelor brother, Amy, and go to Frank, with my best blessing. I believe you have chosen better for yourself than I should have done for you. Frank, give me your hand."

Chapter 2

Frank was in Leeds when, a week later, Oscar Bergheim took us by surprise as before. Ours was a quiet household, and, except now and then a quaint old antiquary, we had few male visitors staying with us. His sudden advent would have put Aunt Lydia in a flutter, had it not been a whim of mine to keep Oscar's room: (in which no other friend was ever lodged) always aired and in readiness. He, too, was the only one to whom the library door was unreservedly open. It had been so in my father's days; it was not likely to be otherwise in mine.

How tall and handsome he looked as he grasped my hand in the ancient entrance-hall with all the heartiness of bygone times! How courteously he acknowledged Aunt Lydia's old-fashioned curtsey, and how eloquent were his soft dark eyes as he held Amy's small hand in a tenacious clasp, and said, "I trust my little sweetheart is glad to see me again!"

I saw the colour mount to her face, and so did he; but we put different constructions upon it. I sighed to think that he might, like myself, have indulged hopes not to be realized; and, observing her continued embarrassment, was glad that Miss Proctor and Lucy Fairclough were spending the day at Tarnbeck.

How much more at ease was he than I! I envied his graceful self-possession as he took Amy in to dinner, whilst my arm trembled under the light touch of Alicia. So charming was his manner, so fluent and sparkling the conversation with which he enlivened the repast, that my own awkwardness impressed me painfully in the contrast. It was never so with Oscar Bergheim,

And so it was throughout his stay. He shone conspicuously, and I, nowise loath, sank into the shade. We had, all unconsciously, fallen into our old positions. I admitted his superiority by my tacit acquiescence in all he proposed; in fact, I bowed down to the hero I had created.

He had a fine voice, well cultivated. He opened the piano, and we revelled in song and music for a space. He longed to breathe the fresh air, and we were straightway strolling under the firs, or among the flowerbeds, and, like children, pelting each other with young fir cones and roses, or plucking blooms for general presentation. He proposed cards, and Aunt Lydia responded on the instant, produced the cards, and helped him to arrange the table. But he appointed the game, and we novices were duly initiated.

He expressed his desire to renew his acquaintance with the neighbourhood, and immediately we found ourselves arranging boating-parties, croquet-parties, sketching-parties, picnics, rides and drives, with a zest unknown to Tarnbeck.

Lucy Fairclough, Aunt Lydia, and I were alike carried away by his impetuosity and enthusiasm; but I noticed that Alicia was graver than her wont, and that Amy shrank from his pointed attentions.

I observed also, with a thrill of delight, that when he pressed forward to hand the ladies to their carriage, Alicia calmly placed her hand in mine, quietly ignoring his proffered assistance.

His presence created quite a revolution in Tarnbeck. The magnet drew other friends into the circle, and one pleasure-party succeeded another in rapid succession. But, whether at home or abroad, Oscar always attached himself to Amy with a kind of protecting devotion which she could not resent, and which gave me pain to witness under the circumstances.

I resolved at length, out of my great love for both, to acquaint him with the fact of Amy's engagement; but the task was not left to me.

In the mountain limestone, about seven miles up the dale, was a natural cavern, known as the Hermitage. It was screened from observation by larches, pine, and mountain-ash, and only accessible by a narrow zigzag footpath cut in the steep face of the rock. This terminated at a green plateau in front of the cavern, close by the side of which gushed a stream of the purest water. It had worn a runnel for itself across the platform, and fell in foam over the crag to be lost in hazel bushes, brambles, and bracken at the foot of the hill. This was a favourite resort for gipsy-parties; and Oscar, remembering the spot, had pitched upon it for our picnic.

Our party numbered just a dozen, including the vicar's two un-married daughters, the Rev. John Smiles, the curate, Dr. Halgarth's son James, in all the flush of newly-acquired honours as M.R.C.S., his sister, and a student friend, who kept very close to Miss Halgarth. The rendezvous was Fairclough House.

Amy and Lucy, being capital horsewomen, were mounted. So were Miss Halgarth, her brother's friend, and Oscar.

I, being but an indifferent rider, presented myself as Jehu of our basket phaeton, containing my bosom's secret idol and Aunt Lydia, whose youthful heart and spinsterhood were voted sufficient qualifi-cations for our party. The vicar's carriage, thrown open, held his stately daughters, the curate, and James Halgarth.

Jock, our groom and ferryman, was in attendance. Hampers had been sent on by servants in advance.

The drive proved delightful. The morning air was fresh and exhila-rating; the September sun shone, if not with a scorching glare, at least with sufficient warmth to brighten up the grey stone houses of the overgrown village, and to gild the spire of the ivy-covered old church.

In my supreme content, I neither observed the equestrians before us nor heard the sound of hoofs rapidly advancing from behind, until Aunt Lydia, in the seat at our back, exclaimed:

"I declare, Charles, here is Mr. Frank Fairclough!—I understood you would not be able to leave Leeds for a fortnight?"

This latter was an interrogative addressed to that individual, who checked his horse to shake hands with us all.

"So I thought," was his prompt reply. "But you see there is an all-powerful magnet to draw me hither."

"And I thought," murmured Alicia, in a tone meant only for his ear, "there was no magnet potent enough to draw Mr. Frank Fair-clough from duty to pleasure."

"Thanks for your good opinion. Miss Proctor. I am drawn to duty and pleasure both on this occasion," was the response, given with more emphasis than I saw any reason for at the time.

He raised his hat from his wavy brown hair, urged his glossy chest-nut horse forward, and in less than two minutes was by Amy's side.

We were near enough to perceive that his appearance in our midst was unwelcome to one of our party. Oscar Bergheim's palpable start, as Frank saluted Amy, caused his horse, a frisky bay, to swerve and plunge, to the additional annoyance of the rider, who, unused to the saddle, had not too firm a seat.

The episode was soon over, and we drove on, little recking how dangerously Oscar chafed at the want of self-command which he had exhibited before Amy and his cooler rival, and which the sudden exhilaration of the fair lady's spirits did not tend to subdue.

I was assisting Miss Proctor and Aunt Lydia to alight when they dismounted, or I might have trembled as Amy did on seeing Oscar's black brows come down over his flashing eyes, when, with a smiling "Come, Frank!" she put her arm through her lover's as a matter of course, to be helped up the rough pathway, so long, at least, as it would hold two abreast. The vindictive look sobered lively Amy on the instant. Would that I had had the same warning!

The ride and the fresh air had sharpened us for luncheon. The three equestrian Graces came forward, in their closely-fitting jaunty jackets, to help Frank and myself to unpack delicate comestibles with which only feminine hands could deal. Oscar, Halgarth, and his friend Jackson ran to and fro between the hampers in the cave and the table-cloth on the grassy plateau, where Aunt Lydia presided over the arrangements.

Gradually we fell into our places, with little confusion but much laughter. There was a popping of corks, a plopping of wine into glasses, a rattle of cutlery and crockery, small talk and badinage, and all went merrily.

Oscar, who sat between Miss Halgarth and Amy, was apparently more than usually buoyant and agreeable; but he drank an unusual quantity of wine, and I, sitting opposite, by the side of Alicia, observed that he visibly winced whenever Amy addressed Frank, whose place on the grass was in close proximity.

Luncheon over. Aunt Lydia retired to the cave for a nap on a pile of carriage cushions; baskets, satchels, and hooked sticks for pulling branches within reach were appropriated, and the party, in straggling pairs, strayed down the path to the copse below, ostensibly in quest of hazel-nuts and blackberries.

A natural affinity seemed to draw Alicia and myself together. I was carefully guarding her down the rocky path, when the voices of Oscar and Frank in loud altercation above painfully arrested our steps.

"Resign the lady, sir!" thundered Oscar Bergheim.

"Not to any man; certainly not to you," was Frank's emphatic reply, in which evidently lurked a covert sarcasm.

"I have the prior claim—"

"And I have the authorised right."

There was the sound of a blow, followed by a scream from Amy.

The nature of the path had retarded our return. We reached the platform to see Aunt Lydia (roused from her nap) and Amy, white as snow, wringing their hands, and the two men struggling as for life or death on that limited arena.

Jock and his fellows, apparently benumbed, were afraid to interfere.

They were locked together, swaying to and fro perilously near the cliff.

Once before, in bygone years, those two had fought, and Oscar had won an easy victory. Now they were better matched. What Oscar had in size and weight, Frank had in agility and nerve.

They held each other in a vice-like grip, regardless alike of Amy's piteous appeals or my entreaties. Backwards and forwards they swayed, when to our horror the treacherous earth gave way under Oscar's feet, and he fell, crashing through the light branches of a giant elm which towered above the copse, and swept the face of the cliff dragging Frank with him, and scaring a pair of crows from their rugged nest.

There was a moment's awful stillness. Amy had fainted. Lucy was speechless with terror in the copse below, whence distant voices answered ours.

"Thank God! They have not fallen to the foot of the crag!"

I ventured to look over. A jutting shelf of rock, overgrown with rank vegetation, had providentially broken their descent midway; and there they lay motionless, Frank uppermost.

Were they dead?

Whilst we on the platform above were consulting how to reach them, Alicia, with the help of Jock, had loosened the cords from our hampers, and knotted them into a stout rope; but it was not sufficient to peril another life upon. To scale the precipitous rock was still more hazardous.

I was slight and lithe of limb, and, though unskilled in athletic games, could climb a tree or scale a cliff with any man. I saw that the large boughs of the grand tree through which the foes had crashed still overhung the rocky ledge.

It is a marvel I kept my footing as I flew down the unequal path to gain the tree below. In an instant coat and hat lay on the ground, and

26

my limbs clasped the great bole of the tree. It was a tough ascent, but I mounted steadily to a strong arm above the level of the ledge. Along this I crept as far as it would bear, then grasped it with both hands, and with a swing landed by the side of my prostrate friends.

My example was infectious. I had barely ascertained that both were living than I was thankful to find Halgarth at my elbow.

"Fairclough is reviving," said he. "The sprinkling of that tiny cascade has done the poor fellow a service. Your friend Bergheim's case is more serious. I wish we had some brandy."

Brandy, thanks to Alicia's forethought, was being lowered from the cliff. The stimulant restored Frank to consciousness; but on Oscar neither water, brandy, nor the removal of Frank's pressure had any visible effect.

A welcome emissary from below in the person of Jock. He bore one end of a thin line by which we hauled up a stronger one, then cart sheets and blankets (from a farm close by) already formed into hammock litters. Into the first of these we placed Frank, whose ascertained injuries were a broken wrist and a sprained ankle; and, by using the giant bough as a crane, we contrived to lower him to the anxious group beneath.

We had a much more arduous and hazardous task with Oscar, from his weight and utter helplessness, placed as we were on a ledge where there was barely room for the three to stoop or stir. A groan, as we lifted him into the second litter, was the only token of sensibility he gave.

How different was the slow, sad procession homewards from that which had left Clevedale in the morning! My agony is not to be described. We were bearing back my guest, perchance to die beneath my roof; my sister's lover lamed and injured; my tender-hearted Amy scarcely in full consciousness; and I seemed to hold in my breast the pain of all.

CHAPTER 3

Oscar did not die, though for very many days he was delirious, and life trembled in the balance. Above all his injuries there was concussion of the brain. And no wonder: he had gone down with all the force of Fairclough's superadded weight; and, but for the mosses and weeds which covered the providential rock like a cushion, he must have fractured his skull. As it was he had escaped by little less than a miracle.

We had hired a nurse from the village, and Jock and Thomas shared alternately with me my constant watch by Oscar's bedside during his delirium. Aunt Lydia also was the best of good nurses. Yet, as the fright had thrown our darling Amy also on a sick pillow, I was glad when Alicia Proctor said, "You will be worn out with your double duty. You must suffer me to relieve you occasionally. Between Mrs. Fairclough and Lucy, Mr. Frank is likely to be spoiled with over-nursing."

I know not whether she did more good to our patients or to myself. Her presence to Amy was more than medicine. Her sweet voice, her gentle tone and manner, acted on the girl's shattered nerves as a soothing charm; and before the week was out her remaining languor gave way before a drive to Fairclough House.

Frank's sprained ankle was a much more tedious affair than had been prognosticated; and before he was able to reach Tarnbeck his rival was gone. It had been well for him that he was himself invalided, or Amy's pity for Oscar, who in his delirium raved constantly of her, might have changed the destiny of three lives.

It was early in October when Dr. Halgarth first permitted his patient to take possession of a small sitting-room which adjoined his chamber in the west wing, and was almost on a level with the library. He was soon able to sit up and walk about the room, and to propose cards and other games as a relief to the tedium of the hours.

One afternoon I was called downstairs to a tenant whose premises had been considerably damaged by high winds the previous night. I left Amy playing chess with Oscar in this sitting-room. She wore a dress of dark blue silk, relieved at the wrists and throat with lace, and as I glanced back I thought she had never looked more lovely.

Perhaps Oscar felt so too. I had barely closed the door, when he, oblivious of the game, laid his wasted hands on hers and looked steadfastly in her face. Possibly the ring on her finger, sparkling as she moved the pieces, arrested his attention, and was more significant to him than it had been to me.

"Amy," said he, with forced composure, detaining the hand she would have withdrawn, "I have a question to ask you: Did Fairclough speak truth? Have you promised to marry him?"

Amy trembled. A flush rose to her forehead, but she answered, unhesitatingly, "Yes."

His brow contracted as if with pain. After a pause he asked, in a low impressive voice, "Do you love him?"

His manner quite precluded evasion. She felt constrained to speak truthfully and openly. "Mr. Bergheim" (she had ceased to call him Oscar), "you should not ask me that. But since you have done so, I will answer you, I love Mr. Fairclough with my whole heart."

"Incredible!" he muttered between his teeth, as if to himself. Then taking her other hand in his to keep her on her seat, for she was rising, he resumed, impassionedly: "Amy, that whole heart was mine for years. True, you were then a child; but I had hoped to find it mine still; and mine it shall be, in spite of that mercenary wretch, who seeks not you but your dower."

Amy rose indignantly.

"Nay," he urged, "you know how devotedly I love you; you see to what that mad passion has reduced me. Have you no pity?"

"Oh! Mr. Bergheim, you forget yourself. I gave you my answer in London. It Is not honourable to speak to me now in this way. I cannot listen—"

"Not honourable! Talk of honour to men consumed by love and jealousy!" he hissed. "But if I may not love, I can hate; and my revenge shall touch your lover where he is most sensitive!"

I met Amy flying along the gallery in a passion of tears. Alarmed, I drew her into the library, and after a time succeeded in calming her, and learning the cause of her emotion.

At once I sought Oscar, whom I found in so dangerous a state of excitement that I was compelled to postpone my remonstrance.

Reaction left him so prostrate that he had once more to be carried to bed; and three more days elapsed before Dr. Halgarth permitted him to return to the little sitting-room. After that he seemed to doze away the hours, and want no company.

Feeling at liberty I walked to Clevedale to inspect the injured premises, and give orders for rebuilding the shattered chimneystack, repairing the roof, &c., and on my return went to the library to put the builder's estimate with other papers.

As I opened the door I thought I heard a rustle, followed by the click of a lock, and a draught of wind upon my face. There was no one in the room; the windows were closed, the cabinet doors open, as I usually kept them. So impressed was I that I even tried the door beyond the cabinet. It was, as usual, locked.

Not convinced, I stirred the fire, which had gone down through inattention, left the room, relocking the only door I had opened, and hastened along the gallery to Bergheim's apartment. I found him lying in a doze on the sofa, as I had left him two hours before. Inquiry did not solve the mystery, and I was compelled, reluctantly, to ascribe to a freak of the imagination the supposed closing of the door. How my senses could have deceived me was perplexing.

On the following Tuesday, as we sat by the drawing-room fire, with the lamps lit and the amber curtains drawn, Oscar, who had not regained his composure, but followed Amy's movements with moody eyes, announced his intention to leave us. Aunt Lydia put up her hands in surprise. Amy pursued her tatting in silence. I remonstrated, on the ground that he was unfit to travel.

He met my objection with the plea that he should regain vigour neither of mind nor body at Tarnbeck; that the atmosphere of the place was unwholesome to him. His glance sought Amy as he spoke.

What could I say? I was loath to lose my friend, unwilling to let him travel until he was thoroughly restored; but I felt that the man whose passions could so transform him was not the Oscar Bergheim I had clung to; and my heart ached as it acquiesced in his decision that it was best he should go.

I drove him myself to the little station some four miles away, packed him snugly in a first-class carriage, extorted a promise that he would travel by easy stages, and would write when he reached London. But I drove back brooding over his renewed insinuations that Frank Fairclough was mercenary, and only sought Lucy to prop a failing business with her money. I felt that the imputation was false; but for the life of me I could not shake off the fear of the possibilities it engendered.

In less than a week the following letter came to hand:—

Liverpool, Oct. 19, 186—.

Dear Charlie,—I have consulted a physician, who advises a sea voyage, change of scene and climate, as my only chance for either brain or heart. The chain which drew me to these shores has been rudely snapped: I sail for Australia this afternoon. When next you hear from me there will be a world between us. A word from Amy might recall me. She will never speak it, and I have a presentiment we shall never meet again in this life. I know I leave an enemy at your elbow; but neither time, distance, detraction—nay, not even *death*—should sever a friendship such as that which has existed between Charles Beckton and his old schoolfellow,

Oscar Bergheim.

"Thank heaven, the scoundrel has gone without doing more mischief!" exclaimed Frank, glancing from his arm in the sling to the bandaged foot lying on a cushion before him, when I called at the hall to report. "I shall not regret the price I have paid to be so well rid of him, though I am tied by the leg at a most unfortunate crisis. There are damaging rumours afloat respecting the stability of our firm (whence originating no one knows); but the consequences may be serious, and I ought to be up and doing."

My mind misgave me somehow, as I attempted the defence of Bergheim. I think the remembrance of Oscar's conversation on the way to the station somewhat tempered the warmth of my manner, as I replied: "Frank, I cannot listen to such an epithet as 'scoundrel' applied to my old friend. It is true he made a savage attack on you; but the successful lover should make some allowance for one with an impulsive temperament, whose jealousy at the sudden overthrow of life's hopes overpowered his reason."

Frank had cause for chagrin at his lameness. The report that the firm of Fairclough, Proctor, and Fairclough was "shaky," running through the commercial world, seriously affected its credit and stability; and, had not its available resources been equal to the demand, the old house would have gone. The first use Frank made of his restored power of locomotion was to trace the rumour, if possible, to its fountain-head.

He spent the evening prior to his departure at Tarnbeck. I had discreetly left the lovers to themselves, and was busy poring over *Gary's County Atlas,* with *Grose's Antiquities* by my side, when Amy's light tap at the door heralded her entrance. Her flaxen curls contrasted well with her purple dress; and I thought she looked bewitching as she came coaxingly towards me and put her arm round my neck, as was her winning way when she had a request to prefer.

"Charlie, would you mind letting Frank have just a peep at my mother's jewels? I do so want to let him see how I shall look in them."

I pretended to be grave and solemn, and put on my studying cap before I answered:

"Well, well, my love! go back to Frank, and I'll see presently, I'm busy just at this moment."

The business was a fiction. No sooner did the door revolve on its hinges, than I left my books, and turning to the open cabinet, touched the button on the Palmer's sandal. The figure duly turned, exposing the three shelves. I pulled the lowest. Back went the adjoining drawers, and up flew the released lid of the secret Palmer's scrip. My hand went down for the casket.

The casket was gone! Gone, too, bank-book, securities, and the

31

title-deeds of Amy's property!

I stood aghast, paralysed, incapable of speech or motion. I could not even think.

I have no remembrance of closing the rifled receptacle, or of sitting down; yet I must have done both; for when Amy, impatient of delay, again tapped at the door, I was seated on a chair by the fire, with my head in my hands bowed down to my knees. She tapped several times before I was roused to consciousness. My own voice, as I bade her come in, startled me. No wonder that Amy, as she beheld my crushed figure and: haggard face, stood for a moment in blank alarm, before she rushed towards me with a faint cry.

"Charlie, what is the matter with you? Are you ill?"

She had supplied me with a plea—I was ill, and I answered: feebly, "Yes."

"Shall I send for Dr. Halgarth?" she asked anxiously.

"No, no! I shall be better presently. A sudden dizziness seized me, that is all. It will soon pass. Go back to Franks that is a dear girl, and take no notice."

She obeyed me in part. She went back to Frank (jewels forgotten), but only to communicate her alarm, and bring him and Aunt Lydia to the library. I endeavoured to rally, but in vain. The shock had been too severe and sudden. It must have marked its impress strongly upon me, for, notwithstanding my remonstrance, Jock was despatched in all haste for Dr. Halgarth.

The old doctor could only shake his large head, look wise, talk of some shock to the nervous system, and prescribe doses of medicine.

My malady was as great a mystery to him as the empty Palmer's scrip was a mystery and terror to me. I had no disease, only the shadow of a dark cloud over me. I sat alone more persistently than ever, but I never read; or, if I took a book, my mind wandered from the page to brood over the abstraction of the jewels, the title-deeds, and other securities.

It was not the mere loss of so much property that troubled me, although that was considerable. Had it been my own I could have borne its loss like a man. But it was a *trust* confided to me. My sister's dower, which I was bound to produce and surrender on her marriage morning. The nature and values of the several money securities were duly set forth in my father's will; the jewels I had prematurely exhibited; and there was no replacing them by substitution, any more than the old parchments. Then the bare fact of the theft proved that the guarded secret of the Palmer's scrip was known. But to *whom?* Few entered, the library save those near and dear to me. Strangers were rarely left alone in it. Never with the cabinet open.

Brooding over the matter brought me no nearer to its solution. I sought our family lawyer and confided in him. His perplexity equalled mine, but he suggested that which I had shrunk from—application to the police. I took the next train to London. When I spoke of the pillage of a secret receptacle, which I could not lay bare, to a detective even, an incredulous smile stole over the official's face, as if there was either a doubt of the tangibility of the property, or of the robbery. Nevertheless, the machinery of Scotland Yard was well oiled and set in motion. Bankers were privately communicated with, pawnbrokers' searched for the missing jewels. As well might we have dredged for them in the Red Sea. I returned home more dispirited than I went, only to isolate myself as before, and brood over the impenetrable mystery, which daily assumed more formidable proportions.

Amy's wedding was fixed for the fifth of January. December stepped onwards with brisk strides, and the tower was as blithe with preparations for the *trousseau* as the master's melancholy would permit. As I sat day by day looking into the fire, until the flames went down, and the red died out disregarded, all that Bergheim had said of Frank's mercenary disposition flashed across my mind and took unfair possession of it.

I had a keen presentiment of Frank's incredulity—he knowing how religiously the secrets of the cabinet had been preserved from generation to generation. I felt that the odium of the robbery would attach to myself, and I should stand condemned as a treacherous custodian who sought to deprive his half-sister of her lawful inheritance. As residuary legatee the law compelled me to make good all trusts, and this I was willing to do to the utmost of my means. But this would not save my good name. There was no second key to the cabinet; none had the secret of its springs but myself.

One gleam of thankfulness shone through the gloom. For the first time I was thankful that my deep love for Alicia was unspoken, and, as I imagined, unsuspected. I must be content to bury my hopes among my books, and let the name of Beckton die out in my old bachelorhood. Once my library had been peopled with intellectual companions; now I sat solitary. Authors no longer spoke to me through their works. The very skies wept in torrents, as if in pity for my misery. The swollen becks rushed on; the river rose higher and higher, until it encircled the knoll, and Tarnbeck was as isolated as its master. Yet wedding preparations went on merrily downstairs, Alicia and Lucy, who were to be bridesmaids, braving the rough ferry in coming and going, to confer on knotty points of feminine adornment.

There was a servants' ball at Fairclough House on Christmas Eve, to be followed by a family party the next day. All our domestics, except Thomas and Hetty, had gone thither in glorious array for the occasion. Frank had borne off Amy to share the general festivities, after vainly endeavouring to "drag the hermit from his cell," as Amy phrased it

I had a pleasant fire, closely-drawn curtains, and a well-lighted room. No outward accessory to comfort was wanting, yet I sat there gloomy in the midst of light and warmth, my eyes fixed on the old cabinet, racking my brains how to discover the thief and the missing valuables, tormented by suspicions of those around me, and by the penetration of a stranger into the family arcana.

I had declined supper, and had sat with my head on my hands for hours. The antique Nuremburg clock above the mantelpiece roused me to the flight of time by striking twelve in quick vibrations. The last wave of sound yet lingered in the air, when a loud pistol-shot, and the whiz of a bullet past my ear, caused me to start from my seat and rush to the curtained window whence came the sound.

No one was there concealed. The glass was uncracked! The bright Christmas moon lit up a wide waste of waters, and the wintry grounds, where no assassin could lurk in concealment. I turned to the other windows with like result.

I examined the cabinet against which the bullet had apparently struck. There was neither mark nor indentation!

Amazed and perplexed beyond measure, I examined the scant household. I found Aunt Lydia toasting her toes on the fender-stool in the cosy parlour, and trying her eyes over the *Leeds Mercury*. Though that apartment so closely adjoined the library, and had the same outlook, she had heard neither shot nor footstep.

"You have been dreaming, Charles. My ears are good, and I have not heard even a leaf rustle in the ivy, all is so still." So said my aunt. But I denied the dreaming.

Downstairs in the kitchen I found Hetty concocting egg-flip for Thomas, who sat with his old limbs stretched out, his pipe in his mouth, the very impersonation of calm enjoyment, by the hot fire, where a great Yule-log, lit from last year's brand, was sputtering and blazing cheerily. The cat had made a cushion of Jock's favourite terrier, and both were dozing comfortably on the hearth. It was evident they had heard nothing.

"Shot, measter? I heerd noa shot. And whoa could get anigh Tarnbeck ta fire oather gun or pistol, wi' th' watters out, an' th' boats a' on this side?"

"Thomas is right," assented Aunt Lydia, who had followed at my heels. "Nothing but a kelpie could approach the Tower through this flood without a boat, and kelpies are not supposed to carry firearms. My dear Charles, you sit alone until you grow morbid and fanciful. Who should seek to injure *you*? Besides, no shot could reach you from outside in the middle of a room so elevated."

"But I *heard* it, Aunt, and felt it stir my hair."

"Now, do be sensible, Charles, and don't look so absurdly obstinate. Suppose," she added, "to satisfy yourself, you and Thomas take a survey of the grounds. Hetty and I will go over the house."

There was no one hiding—there was nowhere to hide—the bushes were bare, and the evergreen wall half under water for the first time within memory.

A small looking-glass hung by the kitchen dresser, and as I passed through, burthened with a second mystery (for I was unconvinced), I saw reflected within it Thomas, behind my back, tapping his forehead significantly with his forefinger, and nodding towards me, as if to intimate to Hetty that my wits were wandering.

CHAPTER 4

Without giving offence I could not absent myself from Fairclough House on that special Christmas Day. But if I was present in body I certainly was absent in mind. Not even the gentle voice of Alicia could restore my old self. I joined in games and dances, but I felt as if I were a marked man.

The glare of lamps, the music, the laughter of children, the very life and motion, distracted me. I crept away into the billiard-room, now deserted, and began to knock the balls about as vacantly as I had taken up the cue. I cannot tell how long I had been playing there alone, when a light step, crossing the tessellated hall, stopped at the door, causing my pulse to quicken and my face to flush. A mist came before my eyes, and I struck my ball unsteadily, as, after a moment's hesitation, Alicia came forward and slightly touched me on the sleeve.

The subdued intonation of her voice, no less than the touch, thrilled through me, as she asked, with real concern in her face:

"Mr. Beckton, why do you desert your friends? Has anything annoyed you?"

"No. But like Dr. Johnson, I am not a gregarious animal. I feel myself out of place in a crowd," was my evasive answer.

"I know you only as a cheerful and intellectual companion," she returned. "Tonight you seem gloomy and abstracted. The free comments I have heard respecting your absence have given me pain; therefore I have come to seek you, and carry you back. Unless," she added, after a fluttering pause, "I myself have incurred your displeasure."

"You! Alicia—Miss Proctor! You displease me! Good Heavens! If you—I beg your pardon—I am out of sorts. Pray excuse me. I am not fit for company tonight."

"Will Mr. Beckton forgive me if I use the freedom of a sincere friend?" Her delicate hand again fell lightly on my sleeve, and her serene eyes met mine with an eloquent look of entreaty as she continued:

"Your friends fear you are not fit for your own company; that some secret is preying upon you which you are afraid to divulge. And, oh, Mr. Beckton, all the whisperers are not friends; there are slanderous suppositions abroad."

I felt that the bolt had fallen before its time, yet I could not speak a word. She went on earnestly: "I myself know you to be the soul of honour and chivalry. If there be a weight on your mind, it is from some outer cause. That you had had a shock I heard from Dr. Halgarth. If you have a painful secret, can you—will you—entrust me with it? It is true I am but a woman, and my counsel may be of little worth, but I have sympathy, and even that may help to chase some clouds from your sky."

Overpowered, I had fallen into my solitary attitude, and buried my face in my hands, leaning with my elbows on the billiard-table. If ever angel spoke to mortal, Alicia was one that night to me. I loosened the fetters on my tongue, and threw the burthen off my soul in confidence to her. Though not at liberty to lay bare the *arcana* of the cabinet, I told her how mysteriously Amy's dower had disappeared from the thrice-guarded depository—of my inability to trace the thief, or to replace either documents, book, or jewels in their integrity, even if I made monetary restitution, which I was preparing to do through the medium of a mortgage on a portion of the Tarnbeck estate.

Alicia followed my narration with marked and sympathetic attention, only interrupting with an exclamation of surprise, or a question here and there. But when, in answer to her natural query, "Why did you not at once make the theft known?" I told of my hesitation lest I myself should be branded with their abstraction, and Frank Fairclough should reject the hand of my darling sister, she drew herself up in noble defence of our friend.

"What grounds have you for suspecting Mr. Frank of such baseness? He could not possibly doubt your integrity, notwithstanding the mystery of the case, and he is too upright and honourable to break off his engagement to your sister, even had there been a leaven of Mammon in his choice, which there is not. Someone must have poisoned your mind against him."

In fealty to my boyhood's friend I said nothing of Oscar's Insinuations, but, deferring to Alicia's unbiased judgment, resolved to throw myself upon Frank's generosity on the morrow. Engrossed in the subject, neither of us had heard how often Time had flapped his wings, nor yet the closing of the door, which someone, conceiving ours a tender interview, must have shut quietly.

The inference was natural but mistaken. No word of love had been spoken; yet when Amy tripped in with the sportive exclamation, "What are you two arch conspirators plotting, whilst a disconsolate sire is wailing his missing daughter?" both started and blushed with self-consciousness; and we left the billiard-room to take our places in *Sir Roger de Coverley*, sensible of a new link between us, with hearts that beat in unison, and hands that thrilled to each other's touch.

Mr. Proctor went back to Leeds by the first morning train, and Frank drove Alicia over to Tarnbeck in the afternoon to remain with Amy until the marriage.

After dinner I bore Frank off to the library, and, though not without considerable nervous hesitation, laid the whole facts before him. He listened most attentively, and questioned minutely, but I could see that from first to last no doubt of my integrity crossed his mind, and he was cooler than I had expected.

"It was a stupid trick of your governor to consign so much valuable property to the keeping of a private cabinet, however well guarded by secret springs. Woodwork is proof neither Against fire nor crowbars, and might well tempt burglars." After a pause for cogitation he resumed: "You say you are bound by oath not to disclose the secrets of the escritoire. Should you feel equally bound to prohibit my unassisted examination. Someone must have penetrated it, and why not I?"

I gave my assent willingly, and thereupon Frank began to pull and push the carvings wherever a prominence caught his eye. He made one or two unimportant discoveries, but the insignificant little button escaped detection. Still he persevered. Suddenly a bright thought struck him, and he sat down in the chair opposite to me.

"Beckton, were you ever a somnambulist?"

I saw the drift of his conjecture, and answered readily, "Not to my knowledge."

"Nor any of your family?"

"Nor any of the family."

"Well, this is altogether unaccountable. Depend upon it, someone else has had access to this room, with ample leisure to try the cabinet, as I mean to do before I give it up." He rose as he spoke, and turned again to his task, over which he had spent two hours, just as the clock was on the stroke of midnight.

As it struck, a cry burst from my lips. Oscar Bergheim stood by his side at the cabinet, with a pale face, and a red spot on his broad shirt-front. At my cry Frank turned round.

"What ails you, Beckton? You look as scared as if you saw a spectre!"

"Oscar," I cried rising with outstretched hand. "Oscar, my dear friend!"

There was no response. The figure passed to the unused door and was gone, the door remaining closed. I saw Frank watching me in amazement. No doubt I looked bewildered.

"Frank, did you not see Oscar Bergheim standing there?"

His eyes followed my pointing finger.

"Oscar Bergheim? Nonsense! He is in Australia by this time. I saw nothing and no one."

I shook my head. "But I did!"

"My good fellow, the fact is you have brooded over this unfortunate theft until your brain is teeming with morbid fancies. You had better go to bed and get a good night's rest. And make your mind easy. I want Amy herself—neither her jewels nor her money. Her real property will not run away, and there is little fear of a claimant coming forward whilst bricks and mortar hold together. And now I must be off; there will be black look& when I get home for keeping the servants up so late—or, rather, early."

Frank came again in the evening, after the mill was closed and dinner over; and, dismissing the groom, announced his intention to remain the night, as he said, for the pleasure of a long chat, but as I suspected, in reality to watch over me.

Under the pretext of a headache, which music increased, I stole away to my retreat soon after his arrival. After a long gossip with the ladies he came to the library as if to say "goodnight." But he lingered; again sounded the dumb cabinet—the Palmer never opened his scrip. But precisely at twelve Oscar Bergheim stood there again, with the red spot on his breast, to disappear as before, unseen by my companion.

This time my tenor was palpable. Perspiration gathered on my brow, and a tremor shook every limb. I feared some accident had befallen the friend of my youth. Frank laid his cool fingers on my pulse in evident perturbation, sought Aunt Lydia for a sedative to still my nerves, and would not leave me until he saw me in bed and asleep.

I found him with Alicia and Aunt Lydia in full conclave the next morning. The conversation broke off abruptly on my entrance, and after ordinary salutations we sat down to breakfast.

It was not until afterwards that I ascertained that Frank and Aunt Lydia had exchanged mutual confidences respecting my declarations—the alleged shot on Christmas Eve, Oscar Bergheim's appearance on the 26th and 27th, and, finally, the missing treasure. The two came to the conclusion that study had turned my brain, and that even the loss of the dower was a delusion. Only Alicia maintained a belief in my sanity.

That night Alicia claimed my assistance in a troublesome translation. How every fibre quivered as she sat by my side at the table, and occasionally our fingers met as we turned over the leaves! Amy came dancing in and out, until an arrival below found her more agreeable occupation, and we were left in quiet—quiet so profound that I heard our hearts keep time with the ticking clock. Still we plodded through the book; but I have no remembrance what we translated. All at once—I know not and care not how—in turning a leaf my hand closed upon hers. I flung my arm round her, and strained her to me with & passionate clasp, only to release her instantly, and sob, rather than say, "Heaven forgive me, Alicia; I could not help it. I love you more than my life."

"And I love you, Charles," was the quiet, unexpected answer, which, at the same moment, stilled my nerves and set my heart aflame. All my prudent calculations, all dread of the paternal Proctor, vanished as I held her in my arms unrebuked, and laid my kisses on her brow and lips.

In the unlooked for excitement Alicia lost sight of the purpose with which she had come to the library (I need scarcely say the translation was a fiction). The striking clock broke in upon our dream of bliss. Simultaneously we turned expectant.

The cabinet doors flew open, and there stood the semitransparent figure of Oscar Bergheim in his summer suit of grey tweed, with his finger on the button of the Palmer's scrip. Then he glided to the door, looking back, as if inviting us to follow. For a moment he lingered, a yearning look in his eyes.

"Let us follow," whispered Alicia, clinging to me. It was evident the apparition was visible to her also. She had more nerve than I. Lifting a small reading lamp, she advanced, still holding fast my arm. I had to open the door through which the figure had passed. It was standing in the archway of the west wing as if awaiting us. It moved onwards to Oscar Bergheim's chamber, the door of which stood open. We followed in silence, the palpitation of our hearts being audible in the stillness. Our lamp barely dispelled the gloom around us, yet Oscar's form stood clearly outlined as it stopped at the wide fireplace (closed and fitted with a modem stove) and laid one hand on the central medallion richly carved in wood above it, the other over the red spot on his breast.

Ere we could advance another step Oscar's semblance was gone, and with it a sense of light and companionship, however dread.

As if by mutual agreement, yet without a word, we hurried together from the west wing along the dim corridor and staircase to the lighted drawing-room below.

Aunt Lydia was nodding on one side the fire; Frank, lounging on an amber satin settee, with Amy on a low stool by his side, was toying with her silken ringlets.

The light of another world must have lingered on our faces, the pair started up so appalled. Aunt Lydia was aroused. Alicia was the first to tell what we had both seen. Frank looked incredulous, but there was no more thought of my insanity. Alicia, at least, was not a dreamer.

Poor Amy's teeth chattered with fright. Frank threw his protecting arm around her, and, remembering she had been kindly kept in ignorance, told her, with all the brevity of a business man, of the mysterious events which had made my life miserable. Long before he had concluded she left Frank's arm to put both her arms round my neck, and lay her bright head on my breast, reiterating the words, "Charlie,

Charlie! as if I cared so much for money or trinkets!"

Alicia suggested that there must be some connection between the apparition and the missing valuables, and proposed that an instant search should be made in Oscar's chamber. All agreed to the general proposition, but Amy and Aunt Lydia demurred to its immediate attempt. "Why not leave it until daylight?" they both cried in a breath.

"I think the sooner your brother's mind is relieved the better," put in the thoughtful Alicia, and I thanked her with a pressure of the hand which no one saw.

"I think so too," assented Frank, with decision, but Amy, who had gone back to her lover, looked up beseechingly in his face, and he wavered. We had been standing grouped around the fire. Aunt Lydia resumed her seat, and one by one the rest sat down also. There was no thought of going to bed. Amy would not hear of Frank leaving us.

The fire was replenished, the lamps retrimmed. Jock, who was sitting up to ferry Mr. Frank and his horse over, was sent to his repose. In a body we made a raid upon the larder for refreshment, even Alicia not caring to visit the dark and unknown regions alone. Frank and I brought wine from the dining-room, and we prepared to wait for the slow daylight, in a sort of shuddering, anxious expectancy, somewhat allayed on my part, by the new happiness I had found in Alicia's love. We sat next to each other, and I think my arm stole along the back of her chair. Once I caught a surprised glance from Frank's eye, followed by a merry twinkle, and a demure expansion of his closed lips, as if well satisfied.

Conversation was carried on in whispers, and when general was of a weird and ghostly character.

With morning came courage, which baths and breakfast strengthened. What the domestics thought of our sitting up I did not inquire.

About ten o'clock we went together to Oscar Bergheim's room. The light streamed in through the Gothic windows, and fell on the bed where he had tossed so wildly in his delirium. Frank was for raising the stones of the hearth. Alicia would try the medallion where the shadowy hand had rested. For some time it baffled our efforts, but at length the whole panel slid downwards, and there, in a deep recess, lay Amy's dower—casket, bank-book, parchments, etc.

Who shall tell the deep thankfulness of my heart at that moment? What had I not recovered besides! An avalanche seemed to slip from my life and leave me sound and free. I could now look up to Alicia unimpoverished, unsuspected. I was too happy to do more than

41

wonder what had befallen Oscar, and why he had been permitted to return for my behoof.

Amy's wedding was an event in Clevedale annals. The vicar offici-ated, and Mr. Smiles assisted. The bridal dress, of white silk and lace, looped here and there with orange blossoms and jessamine, was the gift of Lady Clevedale, who herself shone graciously upon the occa-sion, and the wondrous loveliness of the bride was the theme of all the strangers present.

But the revelation made after the breakfast, when I resigned my trust and surrendered Amy's dower, furnished a topic of after conver-sation for miles around.

When I had given Amy a parting kiss, and wrung the hand of Frank, as he stepped beaming into the carriage which bore them to the station, I invited the awful Mr. Proctor into the library. When we left I was accepted as his son-in-law.

The bridal tour was over; the young couple were fairly installed in one of Amy's own houses, four miles up the dale, which old Mr. Fairclough had furnished for them handsomely; Hetty and Aunt Lydia were turning the Tarnbeck Penates upside down in anticipation of another wedding, when the mail from Australia brought the following letter with its enclosure:—

Melbourne, December 26, 186—.

Sir,—It is with pain I convey to you the melancholy tidings of our passenger Mr. Bergheim's death, the more so that he died by his own hand. His manner throughout the whole voyage had been peculiar—at times hilarious, at others moody. Yester-day (Christmas Day) we sighted Melbourne at midday. The sun was glaring hot, and its rays pouring down melted the pitch on the steamer's sides. Mr. Bergheim paced the deck with his head uncovered. I warned him of the risk of sunstroke; a passenger remonstrated with him, but he only laughed. In about an hour he went down to his cabin. An hour and a half later (precisely at 2.30 p.m.) the sharp report of a pistol-shot rang through the vessel. Your friend Mr. Bergheim had shot himself through the heart. The enclosed lay on the desk before him. As we were almost in port, the remains were carried ashore for interment. His papers supplied your address.

I am, Sir, yours respectfully,

James Stevens, Commander of S.S. *Naiad.*

If I read this with emotion, supernaturally prepared as I had been, how much more was I moved by the terrible enclosure!

Steamship *Naiad*.

My Dear Charles,—I dare not call you friend; you will reject the title when you know all. Yet I must unburthen my conscience before I go mad outright. Charles, you know how much I loved your sister, even from her infancy. Not until my father's death was I free to marry. Then I sought Tarnbeck. Amy was in London. Without a word to you, I followed. I found ready entrance into Lady Clevedale's circle. Amy had grown into a lovely woman—lovelier than my dreams; but she did not recognise me. I followed her everywhere, but my attentions annoyed her. I avowed my love, and she rejected me—gently, but firmly.

Still I did not despair, until Fairclough came between us. I saw her smile on him, and it maddened me. Wheresoever she went, there was he as her shield—quiet, unobtrusive—but there. And, looking back, I know that he loving her well, was justified. I had disgraced my father's name, and Fairclough knew it. I was going headlong to the deuce, and he knew that too. I was not worthy to marry your pure sister, and he knew that, and told me so to my face. Baffled, but not despairing, I presented myself at Tarnbeck when Fairclough's business should have kept him away.

Fool that I was, I thought that I had your sanction, and so set up a claim to her. He came between us again at that accursed picnic; and, in my unspeakable agony, I struck him. You know what followed. To me there was a blank, and then the torment of the lost Amy's gentleness led me to tempt my fate again. Good heavens! it was only to hear her avowal of love for Fairclough! Then the demon of jealousy fired my soul with revenge. Charles, do not wholly hate and despise me. During the last vacation I spent in my youth at Tarnbeck I sat alone in one of the library windows. The heavy curtains hid me. Your father entered. He unlocked the cabinet; I watched him touch a spring and pull a shelf, and saw the result. The shelf and figure went back to their places.

When he left the room the cabinet door stood open. I stole from my lurking-place and tried the spring, and I had mastered the Beckton secret. You have only one key to both the library doors. There were two. I abstracted the one. Your father—unsuspicious soul!—never, to my knowledge, observed its loss. You will ask why I took it. I cannot tell; unless from a desire for power and mastery. My principles were at a low ebb even then. You will have missed all that your father left secure for Amy. I took them—I, your trusted friend. Not for their value—they were useless to me—but for revenge.

I was mad. I thought that Fairclough would abandon s, portionless girl, and leave me a future chance. He may have done so—I know not. I had not taken them an hour but I was stung with remorse, and remorse fought with revenge. I was a thief. I parleyed with my conscience, and quitting the Tower, left the things behind me, where no Fairclough can ever find them. My torment was not over. If I hugged myself with revenge at first, I have suffered tortures since. Not till we were fairly at sea did the consequences of my act to you, my more than brother, dawn upon me. Oh, that I could undo the past. It cannot be. I have blighted all I loved. I can only atone with my own blood. There is a world between us as I write—there will be another world between us when you read.——Farewell—forgive me if you can.

You will find the accursed things hidden behind——My—I cannot—Fairclough would—

Jealousy and revenge had clearly overpowered remorse. A red splash was the only signature to the incomplete letter. But the fatal shot had carried its message instantaneously to me, though a world lay between us; and who knows but repentance came even as the spirit fled, and hence the apparition we had seen.

We kept all knowledge of Bergheim's fate from Amy. She would never have worn her jewels without pain had she known what they had cost. But I showed the letters to Alicia and Frank. It was not until then that he told me he had traced the false reports, which had shaken their firm, to my friend Oscar. He had been only silent lest he should grieve me. And I did grieve. But when my dear Alicia came to rule at Tarnbeck, we closed Oscar's room with all its memories, though we never saw his remorseful spirit again after Amy's dower was recovered.

The Pride of the Corbyns

Death stood knocking at Archibald Corbyn's door—not at the door of Corbyn Hall, but at the door of the Corbyn heart; and when that had ceased to beat, one of the oldest, wealthiest, proudest, and most aristocratic families in Barbadoes would be extinct.

It was a boast of Archibald that the highland district in the north-west, of which Mount Hillaby is the centre, owed its name of Scotland to the loyalty of the first Corbyn, who, settling beneath the shadow of those conical hills, first cleared away dense forests of the bearded fig for the better cultivation of cotton.

He was one of those nine British merchants who, in the reign of Charles I., landed and built Bridgetown as a commercial depot, each having a grant of a thousand acres, contingent on the payment of forty pounds of cotton annually to Sir William Courteen, the original founder of the colony. Tracing down the family history, Archibald would tell with a glow how another Corbyn had introduced the sugar-cane into the island, in spite of troublous times, and how he erected the first primitive windmill to crush out the sap, when he had only open-air boilers in which to crystallize that sap into golden sugar and golden coin.

Riding home from St. Andrew's church on one of these occasions, with his old friend and shipping agent, Matthias Walcot, by his side, he pointed to a mound, below which two streams, rushing right and left of Corbyn Hall from the mountains, there met at a sharp angle, and ran on to join Church River until that ended in a lakelet known as Long Pond, partially barred by sand and vegetable wash from the sea.

"There, Matthias," he said, "the first Corbyn roof-tree stood just where that group of *courida*-trees now casts a shadow over the grass. It was but a rude wooden shed with palm-leaf thatch—old Cuffy has

45

a better now—but young colonists have to rough it, and if a man has pith in him, what matter?"

As they turned from the white mountain road into the long avenue of sandbox and cocoa-nut trees, and neared his handsome two-floored, square, stone mansion, with pillared piazzas and overhanging balconies on three sides, overgrown with creepers and standing picturesquely against a background of white clay-tipped, rugged, dark brown rocks, variegated with waving cane fields, he told how he owed the substantial abode before them to the spirit of desolation which, riding on the wings of devastating hurricanes, had in two successive centuries swept homesteads and plantation into one indiscriminate wreck.

"That was in 1780, when Jamie Corbyn, my grandfather, was the owner. *He* was a man with pith in him, was Jamie; and when he saw his plank walls flying about like so many palm-leaves, he just made up his mind to build under a sheltering nook of the hills; and since stone came almost as handy as wood, he built a house that should stand during his lifetime and his son's after him."

"Well, Mr. Corbyn, it is an ill wind that blows no one good," Mr. Walcot put in. "It blew the Corbyns a house that will last."

Archibald's mood changed; he sighed heavily. "Ay, friend Matthias; it did blow the Corbyns a home to last—a home sacred from intrusion. Our dead were washed out of their graves, and my grandfather, horrified, planned and built yon solid half-sunken mausoleum at the extremity of the wood to receive the ancestors the hurricane had unearthed. And there he too lies, with his sons and daughters in niches by his side; and there I in time shall be laid, with no child nor relative to mourn or follow me. My dear brother Charles lies under the sea, and I am the last of the Corbyns," with another sigh. "He built a home for the living and a home for the dead, to serve for many generations to come; but I am the last of my uncontaminated race, and when the mausoleum doors close upon me they will close for ever."

Uncontaminated! Ah, there the full pride of the Corbyns spoke out. No drop of Indian or negro blood flowed in Corbyn veins. He was pure white as his first English ancestor; could stand the test of any hotel in the United States, and draw his fingers through his hair without showing a tinge of blue in his oval nails, or the slightest "kink" in his flowing locks—a grand distinction this in Barbadoes, where so few even of the wealthy planters but had a taint of the Creole in their composition, however infinitesimal. And no West Indian could more fully appreciate the value of the vaunt than Matthias Walcot.

But Death knocking at Archibald Corbyn's door was growing clamorous, and black blood or white would be all as one within the hour.

Dr. Hawley and Matthias Walcot stood by his bedside, and Dinah, his old negro nurse, readjusted his disordered pillow or wiped the heavy dew from his clammy forehead with gentle, sympathetic hands, and watched his wasted fingers pick the counterpane with sad forebodings.

With quick intelligence she caught the meaning of a glance from the doctor to Mr. Walcot, and escaping from the chamber by the open window, with her big black hands before her face, she leaned over the edge of the balcony to sob out of sight and hearing.

Yet her own ears were alert for any sound from the sick-room, and presently the faint voice of her dying master attracted her attention. True to negro instinct, curiosity arrested grief. She crept nearer to the open window.

He was saying, in feeble gasps, "Will in my desk—I've left you—sole executor, Matthias. I know I can trust you. Use my slaves well, and—no whipping, Matt!"

There was a pause. The doctor administered a stimulant; Archibald evidently revived.

"And, Matthias—I—charge you—leave no stone unturned—find a Corbyn to inherit—Charlie's dead body never found—may be after all—I—not—last of the Corbyns. Mausoleum close for ever—Corbyns extinct—pure race—"

The voice was lost in indistinct murmurs. There was silence.

"He's gone!" whispered Mr. Walcot; "hush"

The doctor placed a finger on his lips, and with the other hand checked Dinah's impulsive return to the room.

"Matthias—England—advertise—I have—last Corb—"

Close the jalousies: exclude the light. The master of Corbyn Hall can neither see the sunshine nor hear the universal wail that from every corner of that wide estate follows his soul to the gates of heaven and pleads for its admission. Archibald Corbyn, too proud of birth to do aught unworthy his pure blood, has been a master without peer!

There was a small grating in the thick door of the mausoleum, which was reached by a descent of four or five steps. This entrance, which fronted a bye-road, was bricked up. The mausoleum itself was a solid stone structure, with little or no attempt at ornament; externally about fourteen yards square, with a domed roof rising not more than four feet above the level of the road; the ground on all four sides sloping downwards towards the building. It was consequently in a deep hollow, and was further sheltered from high winds by the hills which rose steeply above the road on the other side, and by the wood of *manchineel* and sandbox trees, which had marched up to its three sides like a protecting army of giants. Here and there might be seen rotten stumps of cocoa-nut trees, destroyed by a general blight long before Jamie Corbyn made his Machpelah among them and brought the dead to the dead.

Though they were clothed with parasitic verdure, they had a weird aspect on a moonlight night, these ghostly skeletons of forgotten forest-palms.

It was midday. The ripe pendulous pods of the thorny sandbox tree burst one after another, and scattering their seed-rings to earth with sharp reports, as if a platoon of distant musketry proclaimed the fall of each. But another ripe seed was ready to be "sown in corruption," and a louder report proclaimed that.

It was the invariable gun fired through the unbricked grating, to dissipate noxious gases generated within, lest the opening of the vault for the dead should let out pestilence on the living.

A night had passed. Intelligence had flown swift-winged over the little island. The vault was purified; the door stood open. From all parts of Barbadoes planters and others had assembled to show their respect for the dead. Rising and falling with the undulations of the hills, a long procession of carriages and pedestrians marked the white road with a line of black for half a mile or more. Slaves and friends, bond and free, white, Creole, *quadroon, mulatto,* and black, were there with sable suits and white headgear; but of all those hundreds, not one relative to hold the pall or shed a tear over the silver-mounted black coffin as it was borne to its niche in the sepulchre with solemn funeral rites; and the door was closed on hospitable Archibald, the "last of the Corbyns."

"Brick it up close, Dan," said centenarian Cuffy to the labourer at work; "nebber be opened no more. Massa nebber rest in him grave if a drop of nigger blood be berried with him. An' I'm 'fraid, Dan, there be no real white massa to come after good ole massa."

"Fraid not, Cuffy?" questioned Dan ruefully—for Cuffy was the oracle of the plantation—adding, "Ah, him proud gemp'lman, but him berry good to black man. Wonder who be massa now?" A momentous question this to a slave!

Cuffy extended his withered arm to an opening between the distant foliage, where a glimpse of the shining Atlantic might be seen three miles away.

"Ib dat hungry sea swallow up young Massa Charles, I much Afraid, Dan, Massa Walcot will be. *He* got a splash ob colour in him, but his heart no so warm as our poor massa's for all dat;" and old Cuffy turned away mournfully, shaking his head.

Corbyn Hall had got a new master. The will which made Matthias Walcot sole executor made him virtually proprietor.

All that stood between him and absolute ownership was the very improbable chance that Archibald's younger brother, Charles, had escaped when the *Mermaid*, in which he had sailed from Bristol seven years before, foundered off the Irish coast, and not a soul was known to be saved. There was also the remote possibility of his having left a legitimate heir on dry land; but as no echo of wedding-bells had ever wafted to the brother in Barbadoes, this was as improbable.

The brothers had parted in anger; and Archibald had never been his own man after the *Mermaid* went down. He was only forty-eight when he died; and his will was full of mournful regret. Matthias was enjoined to spare no cost, neglect no means to find a rightful heir; but if within ten years no claimant could be discovered, then—and not till then—Matthias Walcot and his heirs were to possess the Corbyn estate, with all its living brood, in perpetuity.

Matthias Walcot passed as an honourable man amongst men; had been esteemed and trusted by the dead; would have resented the charge of dishonesty. But the temptation was great, and *he* was *not*.

Prompt to take possession, he was not prompt in measures which might eventually oust himself and his. He made languid official inquiries at first; sent occasional advertisements to an English newspaper; and persuaded himself, and tried to persuade Dr. Hawley, that he had been very active.

Chapter 2: The Walcots at Home

I said Corbyn Hall had a new master; I should have said a mistress and three masters, a younger lady being thrown in. There was Mrs. Walcot, dominant, of large dimensions and lofty pretensions; there was Miss Walcot, slight, languid, listless, and intensely fashionable; and there were two sons, William and Stephen, the most bumptious of all bumptious Barbadians.

What a revolution their advent created in that hospitable, free-and-easy bachelor household! The will interdicted unnecessary change until heirship was determined. But Mrs. Walcot was disposed to read its provisions liberally. She did not sell or destroy plain or old-fashioned fittings: they were simply huddled into a lumber-room out of her way, and replaced with the very brightest and newest importations from Europe, before even the dogs and horses had well learned to recognise the new mastership.

Matthias himself forgot he was only executor. He turned his shipping agency and his stifling office on the wharf over to his tall sons, and settled down comfortably at Corbyn Hall as proprietor and planter. But Mrs. Walcot was fond of society, and was not content to dwell for ever ten miles from town and two or three from their nearest neighbours; so their old house at the Folly was retained, ostensibly for the convenience of William and Stephen, and the lady rejoiced in a town-house and a country-house, and became a very grand personage indeed. She oscillated between the two houses, paid and received visits, went shopping, and ransacked the heterogeneous stores of every dealer in Broad-street, to the intense disgust of Scipio, her mulatto charioteer, whose lazy life was at an end.

Nor was Scipio the only grumbler on the estate. Flippant lady's-maids invaded the sanctity of Chloe's kitchen and Cassy's laundry. Will and Steve in house or stable were as ready to use their riding-whips on the shoulders of valet or groom as on the flanks of their steeds. There were sharp overseers in the boiling-sheds, on the rocky slopes amongst the waving yellow canes and the changeful fields of Indian corn, and among the bursting cotton-pods. The change sank into the negro heart, and from Chloe in her kitchen to Cuffy in his distant hut, there were sunken spirits and low-voiced murmurings. If a "boy" carried his dish of cuckoo to window or door sill, or squatted on mat or ground outside to eat his dinner at ease, he was sure to become the centre of a group no longer shaking their fat sides with laughter, but shaking their woolly heads mysteriously, and comparing the present regime with the past.

Dinah—or Aunt Dinah, as she was called—who had nursed the infant, sick, and dying Corbyns for two generations, and ruled supreme in Archibald's time, had been deposed, and the poor old thing fretted much, as might any other prime minister in disgrace.

It was none of Mr. Walcot's doing. Had he been consulted, he might have remembered her presence in the planter's death-chamber, and from motives of policy left her to govern her coloured brood as of yore.

Yet even he knew not what she had heard, nor how it had worked in her brain. As it was, she brooded over her dying master's words, and felt their import greater than reality.

Old Cuffy—still the nominal head-gardener—she made the depositary of her knowledge, and the pair held frequent and solemn conference. From these twain, no doubt, the first faint murmurings against Walcot rule went out like a breath, as soft and unsuspected. And now aunt Dinah was troubled with ominous dreams, and Cuffy grew portentously prophetic.

Meanwhile Mrs. Walcot, blessedly obtuse, prepared to give a grand ball before the rainy season should set in, with one matchmaking eye for Laura and another for William, who had set both his on a lovely orphan heiress, then the ward of the Rev. John Fulton.

Vainly Matthias, with due regard to appearances, urged that it was "too soon." Madam was wilful, and issued her invitations to the cream of Barbadian society, with a select few of her former Bridgetown friends, whom she hoped to overpower with her grandeur.

Mourning was all but discarded: a gauzy black scarf for herself, a black sash for Miss Walcot, were all that memory could spare for the late master of the mansion whose family diamonds they wore. The coloured attendants were arrayed in the gayest of tints: brilliant turbans, kerchiefs, and petticoats, flashing striped trousers and light jackets, fluttered everywhere, like swarms of black-bodied butterflies, to which every guest-bringing phaeton added its quota, either in driver or lackey.

Odour of fruits and flowers and wines, flash of glass and gilding, wax-lights and mirrors, sparkle of eyes and jewellery, flutter of satins, gauzes, and hearts, patter of feet and tongues, melody of piano, guitar, and song within.

Banjo and beating feet, the rollicking song and the dance, a babel of laughter and gabble without; and Cuffy and Dinah sullenly aloof in the shadow of a *manchineel*-tree—the only two to whom Mrs. Walcot's magnificent ball had brought neither pleasure nor occupation. The hooting owls in the sandbox trees were scarcely such birds of ill-omen to the Walcots as were these two, brooding over that festival as being an indignity to the memory of their dead master.

Song, and dance, and rippling laughter, flushing cheeks and fluttering fans! A shrill scream, like that of the Shunammite's son—"My head, my head!"—and with one hand spasmodically raised to her brow, Laura Walcot fell back into the arms of her partner in the quadrille, speechless and gasping!

In vain ladies proffered scent bottles and vinaigrettes, and gentlemen darting through the open casements brought back clusters of soft; sandbox leaves to bind on her throbbing forehead, as antidotes to pain. The dark green but served to show how deathly was her pallor; and Dr. Hawley, brushing in through the crowd from the card-room, could do little more than shake his head gravely, and say "No use, no use! Too much excitement!"

Mrs. Walcot shrieked in hysterics; Matthias sat with bowed head like one stupefied; the haughty brows of William and Stephen lowered in presence of the grim intruder—Death.

Startled visitors departed, or remained for the ceremonial of the morrow. An awful hush fell over and around the mansion. The negroes, strangely unlike themselves, indulged in no noisy demonstrations of grief. They were silent, save when whispers of "Doom" and "Judgment" passed from mouth to mouth in stifled undertones.

As the white coffin of the maiden was being carried into the house, Cuffy, standing under the *piazza*, heard William Walcot give Dan instructions for the opening of the Corbyn mausoleum.

Uplifting his head and his bony hands in superstitious horror, he clasped them as they dropped before him, and ejaculated: "There! Berry young Missy Walcot in Corbyn grabe! Nebber. Old massa's flesh creep in him shroud if dat blue-nailed missy laid inside there!"

The tall old man, venerable with the grayness of his hundred years, drew a long breath, then stalked unbidden into the presence of Matthias and Dr. Hawley, and stood before them erect, with fiery eyes, much as Elijah must have stood before usurping Ahab.

"Massa Walcot better not berry him dead with the Corbyn dead. Sure's you live, Massa Arch'bald nebber 'low it!"

"Not allow it, Cuffy! What do you mean?" said Mr. Walcot testily, looking up amazed and annoyed.

"Massa Corbyn leave him hall, leave him plantation, leave him money to him friend; but him keep de Corbyn maus'lum for de Corbyn *only*. If"—and undaunted Cuffy laid special emphasis on the "if"—"if no heir, an Massa Arch'bald *be* last ob de Corbyns, den dat maus'lum be closed till Judgment-day!"

"Cuffy, you presume on your gray hairs. I shall lay my poor child where I think fit. I do not suffer my slaves to dictate to me. Your mind is wandering. Quit the room; this is no season or intrusion."

Dr. Hawley listened in silence. Cuffy still maintained his ground.

"Massa Walcot, de 'mighty God above send Cuffy to warn yon. Dere am *doom* on dis house till Corbyn heir be found, and de first thun'erbolt fell last night. For own sake, Massa Walcot" (Cuffy never said "*massa*" only), "berry pretty missy in de churchyard!"

A similar scene was enacted upstairs.

Dinah, arranging the folds of the fine muslin shroud, and the fan-shaped face cover to stand stiffly up until the last moment, made way for the bereaved mother to kiss the pallid lips ere it was folded down. She ventured to ask the place of interment.

Being told, she bent her aged knees, and implored her mistress to change her plans, or evil would be sure to come of it.

Mr. and Mrs. Walcot were alike obdurate and indignant. Cuffy and Dinah were declared crazy and superstitious, and cautioned to make less free in future.

Bat though they laid their daughter's corpse in the Corbyn mausoleum, in spite of premonition, for some innate reason they did not place it in any one of the unfilled niches; it was left on the floor in the centre of the sepulchre.

And then the Corbyn vault closed for the first time on one of another name and another caste.

Chapter 3: The Mystery of the Mausoleum

It is not customary for Barbadians to court the heavy noxious dews and the bloodthirsty mosquitoes by being abroad after nightfall; but the unwonted events of ball and burial on two consecutive days had brought to that lonely plantation a concourse of people, some of whom were detained by the claims of friendship, others of business, to a late hour.

It was close upon midnight when Dr. Hawley and another friend shook hands with Mr. Walcot under the portico of the Corbyn mansion; and stepping into his light cane phaeton, he bade his black Jehu "Tear away home."

Once clear of the sombre avenue, where accommodating fireflies hung out their tiny lamps, the white marly road shone like a streak of silver in the bright moonlight. They spun along rapidly, to the drowsy music of their own wheels, in concert with the droning trumpet of obsequious mosquitoes, and the thin metallic pipe of an occasional cicada, to which their pony's hoof beat time. Otherwise the stillness was unbroken, save by Sambo's involuntary ejaculations to the steed.

As they neared the point where the road branched off to the sea-coast, passing the mausoleum on its way through Corbyn Hall Wood, a shrill scream was borne up the bye-road on the clear midnight air.

The pony stopped involuntarily, quivering in every limb.

"Golla, massa! what am dat?" cried Sambo in a fright.

Before Dr. Hawley or his friend could reply, a second scream, louder and more piercing, smote upon the ear, and was followed by a succession of unearthly yells.

"Quick, Sambo! Turn to the left. There is some foul play going on down this road. Quick! or we may be too late to prevent a tragedy."

But Sambo's white teeth chattered, all the more because the pony obstinately refused to obey the rein—willing to bolt down the road home, but determined not to turn to the left for either man or master. As he snorted, reared, and plunged, threatening the slight vehicle with destruction, and the shrieks still continued, the doctor and his companion leapt out, and ran at full speed down the road, athwart which sparsely set *palmetto*, or cocoa-nut trees cast spectral shadows.

A faint sea-breeze met them, laden with the mingled perfumes of fruit and flower, but with it came more hideously the strange discordant noise. Then two or three wild dogs darted past them, howling as they went. Then with garments flying loose and eyeballs glaring, a negro woman, blind with terror, ran against the doctor. A man, little less excited, was close at her heels.

"Hallo! what is the meaning of this outcry?" demanded the doctor, grasping the man by the arm, under the impression the negress was escaping from ill-usage.

The man—who proved to be the undertaker's foreman—could only gasp between his chattering teeth, "Dre'ful! Dre'ful, doctor; dre'ful!"

The woman—a seamstress whom the foreman was gallantly escorting home—had continued her flight,

"You black scoundrel, what have you been doing?" cried the doctor, giving him a shake.

The man's protest was drowned by a fresh outbreak of the same appalling cries.

Dr. Hawley, exclaiming, "Again! What is that?" released his arm, convinced that he at least was not the peace breaker.

"O! doctor, dre'fdl down dere! Dead man's fight."

"Pish!" "Rubbish!" from the doctor and his friend; and they rushed forward, drawing reluctant Cicero back with them.

But they too stood aghast as they approached the mausoleum. The noise—a demoniac compound of blows, groans, shrieks, and howls— evidently *issued from the bricked-up sepulchre!*

It seemed, indeed, as though a desperate combat raged within the closed-up tomb; and the blood of the spectators curdled as they listened.

They were not the only auditors. A neighbouring planter and a sturdy sea-captain, named Hudson, on their way inland, had been arrested on' their journey likewise, and seemed rooted to the spot with a mysterious dread.

Could anyone imagine a scene more terrible! The mausoleum, worn with age and weather, overgrown with moss and lichens, sentinelled by sandbox trees and blighted cocoa palms, whose shroud-like drapery of creepers gave them the aspect of ghosts of dead trees keeping watch for ghosts of dead men; and scared by the unearthly din, owls and monkeys screeched and chattered, to make if possible a greater pandemonium.

"I have seen the ocean in its fury, heard the winds break loose, and the artillery of heaven rattle, but never did I hear anything so terrific as this. It makes my very flesh creep," said the captain, addressing Dr. Hawley. "Can you, sir, offer any solution of this mystery?"

What Dr. Hawley might have said was interrupted by a final burst of triumphant yells, followed by a peal of still more discordant laughter, which died away in feeble cachinnations, till silence scarcely less awful fell on all around.

A harmless snake then uncoiled itself on the mausoleum steps and dragged itself across the road, a pair of green lizards crawled over the dome of the mausoleum to bask in the moonlight; and the unaccountable noises having ceased entirely, the party drawn together so singularly moved away in a body.

As a natural sequence, conversation turned on the place they had just quitted, Archibald Corbyn's funeral, and that of Laura Walcot; and so much was Captain Hudson interested, that when they shook hands and separated at the fork of the roads, he had promised to call on Dr. Hawley at his house near Kissing Bridge before sailing for England.

Seven persons (including Sambo) went their several ways surcharged with the story of a horrible mystery.

What wonder that the succeeding midnight brought a crowd to the spot, to test, verify, or ridicule, as might be? Notwithstanding the previous shock to his nerves, Dr. Hawley made one. With him was Stephen Walcot, much concerned by this commotion over his sister's grave; and on the extreme verge of the assembly they saw a group of old Corbyn servants huddled together like a flock of timid sheep, with Cuffy and Aunt Dinah at their head.

The doctor had lost no time in making Mr. Walcot acquainted with his nocturnal experience. Matthias had only curled his lip, shrugged his shoulders, and said, "Were I you, doctor, I would not repeat this nonsense. Your patients will not care to consult a medico who takes too much wine." He had spoken to the sons. William laughed outright. Steve, subdued by his sister's loss, gave their informant a more respectful hearing, and, in spite of his brother's banter, volunteered to watch the tomb that night with the doctor, little surmising how many would share that watch.

Twelve by Dr. Hawley's repeater! The silent expectant crowd shrank back with affright as, without one moment's premonition, the air was rent with a volley of shrieks and yells, which wakened the echoes of the hills, and a chorus from owls and monkeys drove the raccoon from his bed, the pigeons from their nests, and sent batwings from the shadows to flutter in the moonlight.

For one whole hour the noises were unceasing. If superstition drew the crowd together, fear dispersed it. Only the most daring of the auditors remained, and amongst these were Cuffy and Dinah, who stood apart with hands upraised, as if invoking unseen protection.

Bearing Cuffy's adjuration and previsions in mind. Dr. Hawley—well acquainted with negro subtlety, and anxious to find a natural solution for the phenomena—drew the centenarian apart, and, with Stephen by his side, subjected him to a fire of cross-questions.

"Know nuffink 'bout it, doctor; 'cept Massa Corbyn not rest. Him angry; all him dead family angry," was all they could elicit.

Yet, in spite of his genuine trepidation—for every nerve seemed to quiver—there appeared some reservation, of which the doctor took a mental note for question at a fitter time.

Mrs. Walcot was frantic. Sorrow for her daughter's loss was reduplicated by this scandal over her very grave. Mr. Walcot and William repudiated all notion of the supernatural, and ascribed the strange phenomena to a plot between Cuffy and his colleagues. Stringent orders were left with the overseers that no slave should quit the plantation after sundown, or approach within a given distance of the mausoleum, under penalty of a flogging.

But that did not quell the nocturnal riot. Matthias brought his own eyes and ears to the test, had the place examined by day, placed a cordon of military around, but all to no purpose.

For five nights the supernatural warfare continued. Trafalgar Square and the Bridgetown ice-houses were thronged with thirsty gossips, and Barbadoes throbbed with superstitious fear to its very fingertips.

Then it ceased. The excitement gradually died out, business resumed its sway, the Walcots were condoled with, and the dead reposed in peace.

Still superstition held the haunted mausoleum in dread; and argent must be the business and hardy must be the man that should travel that road by night.

Even over the Corbyn mansion crept a sort of eerie atmosphere. There was less laughter, and more whispering in secret corners. Every figure in mourning robes seemed to cast a shadow of death, on the hearth. A cloud deeper than that of grief rested on the brows of Matthias and his wife; and the infection spread to the white tenantry on the estate.

Chapter 4: Obeah!

A fortnight later Dr. Hawley rode out to the hall. It was purely a friendly visit, so he said; but ere he went away he asked his host how he was progressing in his search for a legitimate heir, adding that a friend of his, a Captain Hudson, of the barque *Adelaide*, would readily undertake any commission in furtherance of that end in the mother country.

Mrs. Walcot bridled up, and Matthias, reddening, answered stiffly, "Thank you, doctor, but I can manage my own business without the intervention of strangers. I need no reminder of my duty. A sea captain is scarcely the person to institute inquiries of this nature."

"Perhaps not," assented the doctor dryly, with a peculiar smile, as he took his departure, much like one who has but done half his errand.

Had their voices wafted to Cuffy through the open casement, that he should quit the jasmine he was pruning by the portico to hurry to the avenue? Whether or not, he stopped the pony under shadow of the large trees, and whispered earnestly and mysteriously:

"Dr. Hawley, you good man; you lub ole massa. Him spirit angry; all de Corbyn spirits angry. Last night Dinah dream—dream of Massa Charlie. He wet an' white upon the steps; he ask to come in, and

Massa Walcot shut the door—an' Death come in instead! Doctor, dere be nudder Corbyn *somewhere*, an Massa Walcot no try to find him; an' spirits *berry* angry. Cuffy work Obeah charm tonight, to keep de evil doom from de black boys and girls dat lub ole Massa Corbyn!"

"I would advise you to have nothing to do with Obeah, Cuffy. It may breed ill-feeling and do mischief," said the doctor, as Cuffy loosened his hold of the reins, and Sambo cracked his whip.

In Corbyn Hall Wood, remote from the hall itself, close by a mountain streamlet which ran down to join the river, was a bubbling boiling spring. The spot was lonely and sequestered, shadowed by the *palmetto* and the *manchineel*. Gourds and squashes trailed along the ground and hid the iguana, the green lizard, and the spotted toad. No pine-apple or banana grew beside it; no seaside grape spread its branches low to the ground, hanging thick and ruddy clusters under every branch, glossy with leaves of green; but all that was dark or rank grew there.

It was a dismal spot. Yet hither dusky forms came stealthily in the middle of the night to watch and share with Cuffy in the dread rites of Obeah incantation. To his fellows he was known as a Mandingo priest, and the hold he had on their superstitious souls was strong and terrible. His hut was near at hand, and in this weird corner of the plantation had he been wont to concoct healing balms, philtres, and the yet more potent Obeah, whose spell, wrought in secret, was supposed to work in secret, And set human skill and precaution at defiance.

Dinah was there—a fitting priestess of these mysteries—and Dan and Scipio, and Chloe and Cassy, with others whose names are unrecorded.

There was a fissure in the ground close to the boiling spring. To this Cuffy applied a light, and instantly a jet of flame shot up, and the poor dupes bowed down to the fire-spirit. From a hollow tree was produced an iron pot. Half filling this from the boiling spring, it was suspended on a triangle of sticks over the natural naphtha flame, and the weird rites began.

There was a low monotonous chant in a strange tongue, a dance around the seething pot, which in the lurid light was half demoniac; and Cuffy, swaying to and fro, muttered words unknown even to his confederates, as one by one he threw into the pot snakewood from the trumpet-tree, sap from the deadly *manchineel*, a snake cucumber, the poisonous sandbox leaves and rings, a living lizard and a toad, a turtle's egg, the root' of the cat's-blood plant, a bat, a young owlet, a dead man's hair, pernicious scum from Long Pond, and other venomous ingredients with and without a name.

It was a horrible compound—a deadly poison; and as it bubbled in the pot, white teeth and eyes gleamed out from midnight faces, hideous from their own imaginings.

The charm wrought out, the mixture poured into a calabash bottle and closely stopped, the refuse buried in the ground, the pot restored to the hollow tree, the magic flame extinguished with wet sand, Cuffy dismissed his impish brood to their huts, and bore away his revolting decoction, to be buried the ensuing night under the threshold of the hall. The doom hanging over Corbyn would then fall upon the fated mortals who should step across it first; and thus, Obeah satisfied, his followers would be protected.

Be sure there were early risers among the initiated, and sharp eyes to watch the threshold under ban, and warn off unwary footsteps.

Mr. William Walcot was the first to leave the house; but months went by, and still he came and went healthily and haughtily, in spite of Obeah; and he was more frequently at the hall than either his father or Stephen liked, the Folly being his home proper. The father considered that Will interfered too much on the plantation, to the neglect and detriment of his shipping agency; while Steve, aware of the comparative proximity of the hall to the parsonage, regarded him as a dangerous rival.

The fact was that the elder of the twain had determined most fraternally to "cut his brother out" of the favour of Miss Wolferstone, if the clergyman's rich and lovely ward had any leaning in that direction, and altogether comported himself as if be were his father's natural and certain successor on the estate.

But Mrs. Walcot sickened: an inexplicable disease, which caused her lower limbs to swell painfully, marred her enjoyment, and made her splendid mansion little better than a prison, although stately Augusta Wolferstone and lively Mary Fulton came like sunbeams now and again to brighten it up. Then Matthias grew aguish and shivery. Finally Steve, diverging: from the wood-path on his way from the Parsonage one Sunday at the hour when son and moon looked each other in the face, fell over a fern-covered boulder and broke his leg.

Cuffy and Scipio, out after dark on some occult errand, directed by his groans, found him lying amidst the rank vegetation, just over the spot where the Obeah refuse lay buried. "A coincidence," the old man observed to his companion; with the *addendum*, "Sorry Massa Steve hurt: him best cane of bundle."

Cuffy moreover showed his sincerity by binding cooling herbs, on the broken limb whilst Scipio ran for a litter, and by setting, the said limb skilfully as a surgeon, long before Dr. Hawley could be found.

Superstition regarded these untoward circumstances as so many visitations of warning or admonition. Indeed, so freely did Barbadian society discuss the Walcot succession to the Corbyn property by the light of Walcot ill-luck, that Matthias found his bed of roses invaded by gnats stinging worse than mosquitoes, to say nothing of the private thorns planted by conscience under the rose leaves.

From the morning when Dr. Hawley entered his office like a spirit of evil, to tell how his dead child's rest was disturbed, his own rest had been disturbed by nightmare memories of Archibald's death-bed. The dying man had trusted him. He had ill-deserved that trust. He had not meant to defraud the heir, if there was one; he had only been luke-warm in his efforts to find him. But was there one? He thought not; and so advertising was only waste of good money. Besides, it might tempt some knave to worry him with fictitious claims. However, some day he would send Will or Steve to England to make inquiries; and there was time enough.

And so he tried to salve the conscience that would not be salved; especially as Dr. Hawley now and then gave it an unexpected prick, and Cliffy and Dinah looked unutterable thorns.

The rainy season had almost passed. Steve's leg was nearly well; he could move about by the help of crutches; and Scipio had more than once driven him, very gently, over to the Parsonage, to be especially petted, both by Miss Wolferstone and Mary Fulton, the English parson's English daughter.

It was Will's turn to be jealous. He "could not see why a broken leg and a pale face should be so devilish attractive to a woman. They didn't attract him!" It went to his heart to see Augusta Wolferstone place the easiest cane chair in the verandah ready for his brother, and adjust the softest cushions to his special need. He was exasperated, too, that business should keep him so much at the wharf, and an accident clear the way for Steve to woo the girl in his absence.

So persistent were his grumblings that Mr. Walcot, for the sake of peace, went back to his old office to lighten Will's labour and give him an occasional holiday. On one of these days, William, who slept chiefly at the Folly during the wet season, rode from Bridgetown to St. Andrew's, calling in to see his mother on his way. He there learned that Stephen, taking advantage of a fine day, had gone before him, and was then at St. Andrew's Parsonage.

This roused his domineering temper; and with scarcely a civil word to his ailing and querulous mother, and a very uncivil cut with his riding-whip to the Creole groom who held his horse, he set off neck-or-nothing, resolved to try whether he or Steve had the best of it before the day was out. So vicious was he in his brotherly love that he cut at his horse as if it had been Stephen's self, and dismounted in front of the Parsonage, little improved by seeing Stove on a couch under the verandah holding a skein of purse-twist for Augusta, whilst Mary read aloud to both.

His first remark was a sneer at his disabled brother's womanish oc-cupation, his next a rude retort to Augusta's defence of Stephen. A bad beginning this; and his consciousness that it was bad only paved the way for further discomfiture.

Later in the day, he demanded, rather than solicited, a *tête-à-tête* conversation with Miss Wolferstone, and with little delicacy and less tact urged his suit as one whose claims were imperial—urged it as Steve's elder brother, and heir to the Corbyn estate.

Whatever claim he might have had on the young lady's regard he lost in that interview. His rudeness and unbrotherly feeling were so palpable, she felt impelled to resent both.

"I have no desire, sir, to marry the heir to the Corbyn or any other estate; but I do choose to marry a gentleman. I must therefore decline the honour of your alliance;" and she swept from the library as she spoke, without giving him a chance for another syllable.

Without a word of *adieu* to the ladies he darted from the house, almost too impatient to wait for the saddling of his horse; certainly too much irritated to accept the genial invitation of Mr. Fulton to remain the night, even though the weather had changed, and the rain was the rain of the tropics.

A sane man would have remembered that previous rains had flooded lowlands, had swelled mountain runnels to rivers, and rivers to torrents, and, so remembering, have taken the safer high-road by which he came, however circuitous.

But he, blinded by passion, disappointment, and jealousy (had he not left his silken brother behind him?) dashed homewards the near way, across Church River and through the wood.

Over the bridge he went safely enough; but when he reached the Corbyn rivulet, fed from Haggart's spring, he found his way stopped by a formidable stream rushing tumultuously on towards Long Pond.

In no mood to hesitate, he madly urged his reluctant animal to attempt the perilous crossing.

He must have either missed the ford, or the horse lost its footing, and been carried down by the force of the water. His body was found the following day at the entrance to Long Pond, blue, swollen, and swathed in a shroud of the poisonous green scum of the pond.

Chapter 5: On the Wings of the Wind

Once more orders were given to open the Corbyn receptacle for the dead.

The preparatory gun was fired into the vault; the brickwork was removed, the door opened for ventilation, then for preparation; and lo, the place was strewn with coffins and wrecks of coffins, skeletons and fragments of skeletons; and old Archibald's black coffin lay across Laura Walcot's white one, which was itself dinged and battered as if with heavy blows.

Scared out of his senses, Dan ran, as the crow flies, with his strange tale to the mourners at the hall.

Incredulity faded before the fact. Matthias was staggered and terror-stricken. The air was sultry, even for sultry Barbadoes, and that left no time for fresh arrangements. The solemn ceremonial *must* proceed.

The hearse had reached the mausoleum before the disordered coffins could be replaced, or the debris collected and cleared into a vacant niche.

Then, with many misgivings and intensified anguish, Matthias saw the white coffin of the unmarried young man deposited by the side of his sister's, and the creaking door closed upon both.

And as he and Steve, now his only son, were driven back to the hall, he saw how great a horror had fallen on the funeral guests one and all.

Nor did the horror end there.

Again scuffling, wild yells, and shrieks made darkness terrible for five successive midnights; and then the haunted mausoleum sank to silence like a common grave.

And now there was a lull. The calamitous storms of fate and the season seemed alike to have spent their fury. The earth was green, the sky was bright, and Matthias steadfastly put the past behind him, refusing to look back. Like Pharaoh of old, he hardened his heart, unwilling to "let go" his hold of Corbyn,

Not so Stephen. His bumptious front had lowered when his sister was stricken down in the very midst of festivity. Old Cuffy's prophetic warnings had not fallen on deaf ears. He appealed to his father to remove the remains of sister and brother from the Corbyn mausoleum, and to take prompt steps to find a living heir, if such existed. Matthias was obstinate; so was he, and a *little* more conscientious.

He conferred with Dr. Hawley. Judge his surprise to find that the Captain Hudson, whose services his father had rejected with so much asperity, had eight years before picked up at sea a woman lashed to a spar, who supposed herself the sole survivor of the *Mermaid*, in which husband and son had both gone down. The *Mermaid's* destination had been Barbadoes, and the woman's name was *Corbyn*. Shortly after, happening to hail a passing schooner, the Boyne from Cork to Bristol, he transferred the rescued lady to that vessel, his own *barque* being outward bound.

"And, my young friend, as you appear anxious to see justice done," added the doctor, "I may tell you I have already guaranteed Captain Hudson his expenses in the prosecution of a search for that lady."

A hearty handshake at parting sealed a cordial agreement between the twain, and Steve set off for the parsonage with a lighter heart than had been his for many a day.

The season rounded, bringing with it a prospect of Steve's marriage with Miss Wolferstone when their term of mourning expired.

Long before that, fresh sables were called for.

Mrs. Walcot's unaccountable disease, aggravated by grief and her exclusion from society, had terminated fatally.

An altercation again arose between father and son respecting the place of sepulture. It ended in orders for the opening of the mausoleum under Mr. Walcot's own eye.

The sight he beheld was enough to chill his blood; but it never turned him from his purpose. Scientific men discussing: the phenomena had talked of gaseous forces; but he spoke only of conspiracy amongst his black slaves to bend his will to theirs.

Again the battered and broken coffins were replaced, and the fragments hid out of sight; again he laid his dead among the Corbyn dead.

Again the Corbyn dead arose at midnight to protest against intrusion; again the night was hideous with discordant cries; and, as if the free spirits of the air were leagued with the captives in that tomb, the rising wind howled and shrieked in unison.

Fiery Barbadoes could not remember more oppressive weather. The louring clouds, the stifling heat, the sultry heavy atmosphere had boded tempest, and at midnight came down the rain in sheets, driven by a breeze from the north-east which grew and strengthened to a tremendous gale. Then there was a treacherous calm, and then suddenly the winds ran riot; and from three to five o'clock mad hurricane swept the island from end to end, flashing lightnings forth to trace destruction by.

Daylight broke on August 11th, 1831, upon ruin and desolation. Houses and huts were blown down, fields laid waste, trees uprooted, valleys inundated. Wreck strewed the coast. The Government House was unroofed, the Custom House blown down, churches were damaged; the verdant paradise was a wilderness.

Amidst the general wreck, Corbyn had not escaped; yet the hall itself stood firm, though the windmill sails and cap were torn to shivers. But the Walcot House at the Folly had disappeared, and with it much valuable property.

The coast had its black chronicles. A ship had been driven on the rocks in Long Bay, and only one of her crew was washed ashore. He was the second mate, a fine young man with light wavy hair, straight nose, ample forehead, and blue eyes. He had been borne on the crest of a wave, and cast on a rock with just strength left to scramble a few yards beyond the range of the swooping billows, and to thank God for his miraculous preservation.

He was bruised, ragged, and destitute; yet in the universal ruin his wants were all but disregarded. A compassionate negress gave him a draught of rum and a piece of corn-cake, but her own hut was dismantled, and shelter was far to seek.

On all sides he saw desolation and trouble. Dispirited, he turned to the highway, in hopes of gaining a shelter before nightfall. Some unseen hand led him in his helpless friendlessness to take the road William Walcot had traversed in his frenzy. Now, as then, the little stream was swollen to a great one; but the sailor was a good swimmer, and having daylight to his task crossed in safety where the other lost his life. The path through Corbyn Wood was blocked in places by fallen trees, which made his progress slow and perilous. There was no lack of scattered cocoa-nuts and other fruit to stay his hunger, but night fell as he slept the sleep of exhaustion on an uptorn tree-trunk.

He was awakened by loud shrieks. Following the sound, he emerged from the plantation on to the open road, and soon reached a low windowless building, across which a large sandbox tree had fallen. As he neared it the shrieks were overpowered by loud hurrahs, which somehow made his chilled blood tingle with a sensation akin to a shudder.

People like himself, cast adrift; by the hurricane, were on the else-avoided road. In answer to his questions, he was told that the nearest habitation was Corbyn Hall, and that low-domed edifice, the haunted mausoleum of the Corbyns.

"Corbyn?" echoed the sailor; "did you say Corbyn? My name is Corbyn, and I have an uncle Corbyn living in Barbadoes!"

"Was your nucleus name Archibald?" asked a passing gentleman on horseback.

"Yes; and my name is Archibald. My father's name was Charles."

"Is not your father living?"

"Alas! no. He was drowned in the wreck of the *Mermaid*, on his way to Barbadoes, when I was only twelve years old.

"H'm! And where were you at the time, young man?"

"Shipwrecked too, sir, and my mother also. I clung to a hencoop, and was picked up half-dead by the skipper of the *Boyne*."

"And your mother?"

"She too was mercifully saved, as I have been this day; but as Providence willed it, the captain who had picked her up sent her aboard to us, his own vessel being bound on a long voyage; and we had reason to be thankful for it, or we might never have met again in this world. But"—impulsively—"are you my uncle, sir? You ask so many questions."

"No; Archibald Corbyn has lain for eighteen months in yonder tomb. But I knew him well. I see you are in a sad plight, and in no condition to walk a long distance; so I recommend you to present yourself at Corbyn Hall—no matter the hour at this awful crisis. I do not suppose you will be a very welcome visitor to Mr. Walcot. Executors seldom like to disgorge; and if you can prove your identity as old Archibald's nephew, yon are heir to his estate, and my gentleman will have to turn out. In any case, should he treat you as an impostor—as it not unlikely—any of the old negroes will give you food and shelter, if they have it. Your name will ensure *that*."

"I thank you, sir," was all that Archie in his weakness and bewildering whirl of emotions could utter, as he bowed and turned as directed towards Corbyn Hall.

"Stay!" cried the stranger, wheeling his horse round. "I am a clergyman and a magistrate—the Rev. John Fulton, of St. Andrew's. There is my card. Show it. Should Mr. Walcot reject you, call upon me tomorrow; or upon Dr. Hawley, of Kissing Bridge, Bridgetown. We will see you are not wronged. My business is urgent, or I would accompany you now."

Bareheaded, barefooted, ragged, sea-stained, weary, footsore, and bleeding from sharp stones and sharper thorns, the famished, shipwrecked heir dragged himself slowly to Corbyn Hall, to sink exhausted on the very threshold.

There he was found by ever-wakeful Dinah, whose screams, "A ghost, a ghost!" roused the whole tribe of woolly heads, from the mats on which they slept—and blown-down huts had filled house and *piazza* to overflowing.

"Massa Charlie's ghost!" from a chorus of tongues reached the chamber where Matthias lay shivering with ague. Watchful Stephen leaned over the balcony to seek the reason of the uproar.

Quick as thought he was in their midst, supporting the fainting youth in his strong arms. Little need to ask his name: the likeness to a picture in the house told it without voice.

Archie Corbyn was carried within; and while Scipio was despatched post-haste for Dr. Hawley, he was restored, refreshed, and tended with an assiduity no Walcot had ever been able to command. The previous day's hurricane had not created a greater commotion than the finding of the fainting sailor it had blown amongst them.

Matthias Walcot, however, was not disposed to receive Archie Corbyn on the strength of a likeness and his own *ipse dixit*. He put upon him the onus of proof, in the secret hope (hardly confessed to himself) that difficulties might arise and his own position continue intact. At all events he would remain master in the interim; and—but that he feared a rising amongst his slaves, headed by his own son—so much were his principles demoralised that, in the face of conviction, he would have compelled Archie Corbyn to seek other quarters until his rights were indisputably established.

Steve stood by the heir gallantly, though his coming did close the prospect of succession to a fine domain. So did Dr. Hawley and the Rev. John Fulton, his first adviser. Cuffy and Dinah worshipped him. But he had no warmer champions than Mary Fulton and Augusta Wolferstone, with whom, no doubt, it was more a matter of feeling than of legal right.

Dr. Hawley and Steve had opened their purses to him, and once provided with means, he dressed, and looked the gentleman he was.

Archie's first care had been to write to his mother, begging her to leave England for Barbadoes without loss of time, armed with all necessary credentials.

Scarcely three weeks after the despatch of this letter, Dr. Hawley sought Stephen Walcot at the wharf.

In less than an hour Sambo was driving a party of four in the doctor's phaeton as fast as the unrepaired roads would permit.

They alighted at Corbyn Hall.

Archie Corbyn was at the parsonage.

Steve was always glad of an excuse for a visit there. Resuming his seat, he was whirled thither, carried off Archie without a word of explanation, and left the young ladies excited and curious.

In the drawing-room of Corbyn Hall Archie found, to his joy and amazement, his mother. With her was Captain Hudson, to whom he was indebted for her appearance on the scene before his own missive was half-way over the ocean. The sea-captain had proved too good a seeker for Matthias Walcot, who sat there nervous and fidgety, with one arm resting on a side table, on which he kept up a spasmodic tattoo with his long finger-nails.

What further credentials were wanted than certificates of birth and marriage, and magisterial attestations, and Captain Hudson's testimony?

Corbyn Hall was once more in the hands of a Corbyn, and from Cuffy the news spread like an electric flame.

Archie Corbyn was magnanimous. Setting Stephen's heartiness against his father's tardiness (he called it by no worse name), he offered both a home until their own house at the Folly could be rebuilt; and he did not call on his executor to refund the moneys so lavishly expended out of the Corbyn coffers.

Yet Matthias had another bitter draught to swallow before he returned to his shipping agency and to the Folly.

The midnight outcry at the mausoleum had never ceased since Mrs. Walcot laid therein. The hurricane had torn away the newly-plastered brickwork, and now it sounded as if heavy hands were beating down the door.

Dinah took care that Mrs. Corbyn should not remain uninformed; and ancient Cuffy gave to Archie his version of the mystery with fervid impressiveness.

"It Cuffy's 'pinion, massa, dat Massa Arch'bald nebber rest till dem Walcots be cleared out. Him berry proud ob him pure white blood, an' dem Walcots hab got berry mixed blood under dere white skins."

Archie took counsel with his friends, Steve among the rest. The result was the removal of the Walcot coffins to a vault in St. Andrew's churchyard. They were found, strange to relate, wedged together close to the door by the coffins of Archibald and Jamie Corbyn.

Quiet fell on the mausoleum after that—a quiet in nowise disturbed when, after the lapse of some three or four years, the elder Mrs. Corbyn was placed there reverently by her son.

In saying the elder Mrs. Corbyn, it must be understood that when, proud of her generous lover, Augusta Wolferstone gave herself and her money to Steve Walcot, Archie Corbyn took to wife without a fortune the fair English girl, Mary Fulton, whose heart he had won as a poor shipwrecked sailor before it was proved that old Archibald was not the last of the Corbyns.

Cuffy and Dinah lived to see slavery abolished in the West Indies, and to watch the toddling feet of more than one young Corbyn, into whose undeveloped minds they did their best to infuse the old Corbyn pride of race and pure blood.

Wraith-Haunted

"Yes, Helen?"

The speaker, a tall, elegant woman, in whose every lineament beauty yet lingered, as if loath to accept from Time his seventy years' notice to quit, looked up interrogatively at her niece, a blooming matron, busy writing invitations for a juvenile party.

"I did not speak, aunt."

"Did you not? Nor you, Mr. Birley?"

Mr. Birley, engrossed in his evening paper, looked up somewhat vaguely.

"Eh, what?"

"Did you call me?"

"What, I? Certainly not."

"Strange!" murmured Mrs. Carson, involuntarily glancing at the ormolu timepiece ere her eyes bent down once more on her interrupted sewing. The fingers pointed to *ten minutes before nine.*

Click, click, went her needle steadily through the seam; Mrs. Birley's pen made a faint sound as it traced the pink paper; and Mr. Birley studied the "share-list" and "markets" with more than ordinary assiduity. A spaniel coiled up on the hearth dozed in a dog's paradise, in the glow of a ruddy fire, which lit up every corner of the crimson room, and was reflected cheerfully by glass, gilding, and polished furniture.

Presently Mrs. Carson's head was raised again.

"Well?" said she, glancing alternately from niece to nephew.

"What?" questioned both in a breath.

"One of you spoke this time—I heard my name distinctly."

"Indeed, Aunt Marianne, I have not uttered a syllable; I have not lifted my eyes from my desk since you addressed me last."

"Nor I from my newspaper. Mrs. Carson," continued the gentleman, "Dash is snoring most melodiously; possibly you mistook his

69

utterance for mine. Not very complimentary if you did, I must say."

"Indeed I did not" returned she, with more emphasis than the occasion seemed to warrant. "I certainly heard myself called by my Christian name."

"Nonsense, aunt; I am sure no one spoke. You must be dreaming."

Again Mrs. Carson's eyes sought the timepiece on the mantelshelf: the index had advanced five minutes.

"Maybe so; old people do dream sometimes," replied she quietly, resuming work with a sigh as if to dismiss the subject.

With a light laugh Mrs. Birley dipped her pen into the ink, and Mr. Birley sought his lost paragraph.

Had either husband or wife cared to listen, there might have been heard a beating heart keeping time with the sharp click of the needle and the steady tick of the timepiece. But there was only one listener, and she, seemingly occupied with her needle-work, sat with lips apart and head bent in mute expectancy.

The hall-clock gave warning. With a first stroke of nine her work dropped; she grasped the arms of her chair and rose. Her face was blanched and rigid, her brown eyes were wild and wandering. For some moments she stood thus, then with a groan sank nerveless in her seat.

Her companions, alarmed, were by her side in an instant.

"My dear aunt, what is the matter?"

"Are you ill, Mrs. Carson?" and Mr. Birley as he spoke made a movement towards the bell.

The old lady, recovering, arrested his hand, "Are you sure neither of you spoke to me?"

"Quite sure," was the simultaneous reply.

"Do you think any of the children called me?"

"Why, Aunt Marianne, what *are* you thinking of?—the children have been in bed two hours." "Did neither of you hear anything?"

"I heard nothing."

"Nor I, save the scratching of my own pen and the rustle of James's paper."

Mrs. Carson looked from one to the other as if incredulity struggled with a foregone conclusion; then in answer to their inquiries, said seriously, "I distinctly heard my own name, 'Marianne,' called thrice, with an interval of five minutes between each call, although *I saw nothing!*"

"Saw nothing! Why, what did you expect to see?" asked Helen, much perplexed.

"Bosh!" muttered Mr. Birley between his teeth as he resumed his seat and study.

"*What* I expected to see is not easy to say; but I heard a voice I have not heard for thirty-five years. It is a solemn, warning."

"Of what, aunt?"

"Of *death!*" was the low and measured response.

Mr. Birley laughed outright; his wife fidgeted nervously.

"James," said the old lady, "I know you think me a superstitious old fool, and are laughing in your sleeve at my supernatural forebodings; but if you have patience to listen to an old woman's story first, I will then tell you what I believe is foreshadowed now—you can laugh afterwards, if so inclined."

Mr. Birley yawned and compared his watch with the clock; but there was a grave dignity in the speaker's manner which awed him into something like attention. His wife's curiosity was already aroused; she drew her chair to the fire, and with a gesture and grimace meant to call her spouse to order, said—

"Well, aunt, we are listening."

"Well, Helen, I suppose you know, if James does not, that when your grandfather Denton was in business he was for many years his own traveller; and as there were no railroads, few stagecoaches, and those only on main roads, he used to travel with a horse and gig. On one of his journeys he met at a roadside inn a Mr, Lavery, from Bristol, likewise travelling on his own account, although in a different line.

"The two had met before on the road, but on that occasion he found Mr. Lavery not only invalided but crippled by rheumatism. The women of those days were of a different type from the present generation, and your grandmother was not only an excellent nurse but possessed a valuable specific for rheumatism; so being a man of impulse, without even a letter to announce his return—for a letter would have been longer on the road than himself—my father brought Mr. Lavery, wrapped up in blankets, to his own house, and placed him under my mother's care. For months the patient remained an invalid guest, tended by my mother, his wife being sent for after a while.

"Out of these services rendered and accepted grew a very warm friendship, one token of which was Mrs. Lavery's declared inability to dispense with the society of one or other of the Misses Denton. I, however, was the favourite, my visits generally extending over many months.

"I was about two-and-twenty when my last visit to Bristol was made, and—I may say so now without vanity—I was known as the beautiful Miss Denton; perhaps one reason why Mrs. Lavery was so proud to have me with her. Fond of dress and company herself, she was glad to have an attractive companion, and introduced me into much gayer society than my own mother had thought well for her daughters.

"I had been in Bristol nearly nine months, when the first of those peculiar occurrences which have marked my life stamped its indelible impress on my soul and memory.

"Mr. Lavery was away. Mrs. Lavery and myself had been to a card-party, which, as was customary in those days, broke up about ten o'clock. There had been music as well as cards, and I having then a very fine voice—"

"*Then!* You had a fine voice when I knew you first, twelve years ago," interrupted Mr. Birley.

"Well, James, perhaps so; but I *had* a good voice *then*, and naturally was pressed to exercise it. One of the guests, Mr. Carson, whom I saw that night for the first time, apparently had neither ears nor eyes for anyone else; he seemed literally entranced by my singing, and whispered as much to me as he handed me to my sedan-chair when we left.

"Neither admiration nor adulation was new to me, yet at the one compliment of this young Scotchman I , flushed with a strange pleasure such as no flattery had ever called up before. The words lingered in my ears all the while I was carried home; even his peculiar intonation had an unwonted fascination for me; and indeed, when I retired to rest, I found myself still dwelling upon those incidents of the evening in which the handsome Mr. Carson had the most prominent place. I am afraid I answered Mrs. Lavery's remarks somewhat at random, and went to bed with this stranger's parting words floating through my mind as I fell asleep.

"I mention this, my dears, merely to show that there was no possible link of connection between my thoughts and that which followed.

"The bed assigned to me was an old-fashioned four-post, with heavy moreen curtains and full valances, the curtains suspended from brass rings which ran upon iron rods. Mrs. Lavery, in her husband's absence, always slept with me.

"I had been asleep some time, when I suddenly awakened with a start, hearing myself called. I sat up in the bed affrighted. The curtains at the foot were slowly undrawn, the rings jingling as they slipped over the iron rods, and there, in the aperture, distinctly visible in the frosty moonlight, stood the form of *my mother* in her night robes. She was thin, and ghastly white; but a smile of ineffable sweetness parted her wan lips, from which issued slowly the words 'Marianne, Marianne, Marianne!' Raising her hand as if in benediction, she melted away, as it were, into the moonbeams.

"Terror for the moment held me fast. When I recovered my self-possession I roused my bedfellow. She had seen nothing, heard nothing, and was therefore sceptical. In vain she strove, like you, to persuade me I had been dreaming; *the still open curtains refuted that*, for she recollected closing them with her own hand as she got into bed. She then suggested that the maid had played me a trick; but we found the door locked, with the key inside, as we had left it.

"'Oh, Mrs. Lavery,' I moaned in an agony of apprehension, 'something is wrong at home—my mother is either ill or in trouble, perhaps dying, and wants me. Oh, that I had never left her!'"

"'Now do, my dear child, go to sleep; you have had the nightmare, that is all. It is not much more than a week since you heard from home; all was well then,' said Mrs. Lavery, trying to soothe my distress.

"'Oh, that was ten days ago,' I argued. 'It is a fortnight since the letter was written. What may not have happened since then! I must go home at once.'

"There was no response from my friend; sleep had overpowered her sympathy. Neither my terror nor distress had fully roused her.

"For me there was no more sleep that night. I sat up shivering in bed until the piercing cold compelled me to lie down. I watched the still open curtains and the retreating moonbeams as they marked on the wall the passage of the silent hours; but although my mother's pale face and languid voice haunted my memory, the actual presence came no more.

"Night shadows linger long in December, and I was afraid to rise until daylight, but the first streak of dawn found me astir collecting my scattered possessions; and by the time Mrs. Lavery bad got up I had almost completed my packing, for I had determined to go home, and knew that the 'Royal Mail' coach would start that very day for Manchester, and, if I missed it, I must wait three days for another.

"Mrs. Lavery's astonishment is not describable; the episode of the night had left no impression on her sleep-bound faculties. She tried raillery, banter, persuasion, to induce me to abandon a 'foolish whim, the off-spring of a dream.'

"She changed her tone when the sluggish postman called out to the deaf servant 'a letter for Miss Denton, and a shilling to pay!' in a voice which penetrated to the breakfast-table, and my trembling fingers almost refused to unclasp my purse or break the seal, which, however, was *not* black.

"Well I remember the tenor of that letter. It told that during my father's absence from home some rollicking fellow with that in his head which was *not wit* had knocked loudly at our door in the middle of the night when all were asleep, and then run off. My mother, always a light sleeper, had started up under the impression that your grandfather had returned unexpectedly, and in her hurry to reach the door before he, in his irritable impatience, should knock a second time, caught her foot in the coverlet and fell heavily against a carved oak coffer. There she was found in the morning with her collar-bone broken. The fracture was reduced, but she never fairly rallied, and I was summoned home, her symptoms being alarming.

"We were yet discussing these sad tidings when Mr. Carson was announced.. He called, he said, not only to inquire after our health, but to offer his services in conveying either message or package to my friends in Manchester, whither he was then bound. (You need not smile, Helen; it was a common practice at that time to burden travellers with friendly letters and parcels, until their delivery at the journey's end became quite a tax.)

"'You have come quite opportunely, Mr. Carson,' Mrs. Lavery answered briskly; 'you will relieve me from a sore dilemma. Miss Denton's mother having met with a severe injury, our young friend is summoned home hastily. She has never travelled alone in her life, and I was debating how I could trust her so far without a guardian. Will you undertake the charge? I know I can rely upon your care.'

"I saw a flush of pleasure light up his clear eye and handsome face as he answered earnestly, 'If Miss Denton will graciously accept my humble services, I shall only be too proud of the trust.'

"In my eagerness to depart I had lost sight of the dangers: and discomforts of the long journey to an unprotected girl, but the picture drawn by Mrs. Lavery to deter me from quitting Bristol, as she then thought, needlessly, had made the prospect something formidable. There was no disguising my satisfaction when a protector offered himself so unexpectedly; and if I thanked him quietly, I know it was sufficiently.

"Mr. Carson's place had been booked the day before—outside. He hastened to the coach-office to secure an inside seat for me, and to transfer his own. A fruitless errand; every inside place was already secured. There only remained the hope that some male passenger would surrender his inside seat in favour of a lady.

"A vain hope. The 'insides' were all long-distance passengers, and to a man resented any infringement on the right of 'number one,' expressing their personal opinions more freely than courteously.

"'Mr. Carson,' I whispered, 'do not let there be any altercation on my account' (he was waxing warm). 'I should dread being penned up with those coarse men for two days; I would much rather sit outside with you.'

"An incautious speech, but the grateful look which answered it sent my blood tingling with very shame to my finger-ends. He answered soberly, 'I do prefer the outside in all seasons; but, then, I am hardy. You are not fitted to brave the inclemency of a midwinter frost. Only the urgency of life and death should tempt you to make the experiment.'

"'It is the urgency of life and death,' I answered. 'But I am not afraid of a little cold; my pelisse is warm, and my fur tippet protects my chest.'

"I bade my weeping friend 'goodbye.' Without another word Mr. Carson assisted me to mount the movable ladder to a seat at the back which held two, and fronted the guard's solitary post. Just then a messenger, despatched by Mrs. Lavery, came up laden with a rug and shawl.

"With much care Mr. Carson placed the rug beneath my feet, and adjusted the shawl around my knees. I felt at once that I was in good hands, though in my ignorance I considered the precaution unnecessary.

"The leaders' heads were released, the coachman cracked his long whip, the guard blew his horn, a final 'adieu' was said, and I had started on the most momentous journey of my life.

"Rightly judging that my emotions were not less deep because they did no more than well-up into my eyes, my new protector entered into a conversation with the guard to divert his attention, and left me to my meditations. Sombre enough they were. I could not quit my kind friend without regret; but what weighed heaviest on my heart was the presentiment that my mother was *dead*, and that I had seen her *passing spirit*. More sorrowful and gloomy became my thoughts as one by one the milestones were left behind on the turnpike-road, and notwithstanding my wrappings I began to feel a little chilly.

"I need not weary you with the details of that long and miserable journey, only rendered endurable by the unremitting attention of my protector, for such in truth he was. Not only the scenery, but the weather and temperature varied with the districts through which we rode. From hard black frost we passed to a region where snow lay thick on the distant hills, like a shroud on a dead giant, and in light patches here and there by the roadside or on the trees, which tossed their skeleton arms in the breeze and played at snowball with us as the coach swept past. From falling snow we made an advance under a canopy of weeping clouds—first a drizzle, then rain, soaking, persistent, pitiless rain, rain without intermission, rain which would have penetrated a plank.

"No wonder, then, that notwithstanding the plaid which Mr. Carson had stripped from himself to fold round me during the chill of the first evening (using as a substitute, when too late, a horse-rug obtained from an ostler at a fabulous price)—no wonder, I say, that several hours before we reached our destination I was drenched to the skin, and utterly worn out both in body and mind.

"When the steaming horses drew the miry coach up before the Bridgewater Arms, I had lain for some time in a state of insensibility on Mr. Carson's shoulder, utterly unconscious of his supporting arm, or of the anathemas vented by the sympathising guard on the stolid 'insides,' whose victim he clearly considered me to be.

"Uncle Bancroft was fortunately in waiting, for I had to be lifted from the coach-top, and my generous friend was himself too cramped and benumbed to render further assistance. Brandy was poured down my throat, and as soon as a hackney-coach could be found I was conveyed, not to my father's house, but to my uncle's, Mr. Carson never leaving me until I was safe under the roof of my friends and showed some signs of returning animation.

"My shoes, stockings, and upper garments, sodden and saturated, had to be cut from my swollen limbs; but of this I knew nothing, for a fever had supervened and blotted out everything.

"Evasive answers were given to my first inquiries for my mother, as I was too weak to bear the truth; but when I approached convalescence, I was told everything. *She was dead when I commenced my journey—had died on the 23rd of December, close upon midnight.* Her last inquiry had been *for me.* Glancing feebly around from one weeping relative to another, she had said: '*All here? All! all except Marianne, Marianne, Marianne, Marianne!*'"

"Helen, there could be no question that my mother's parting spirit had visited my bedside. The impression made was thenceforth ineffaceable."

"The coincidence was certainly remarkable," said Mr. Birley; "still, I incline to think the whole a dream."

"There was something very awful about it, even if it was a dream; you must own that, James," put in his wife.

"It was *no* dream; but my next revelation took place in broad daylight—*that* could be no dream," said Mrs. Carson sadly. "I have called my journey momentous, and justly. It influenced my life. My friend in his care for me had sacrificed himself. Hardy as he was, inflammation laid its hot hand upon his chest, held him down, and only let him rise with a spot marked like a target for the shaft of death. Gratitude and pity rose to heart and lips when I first saw his altered face. That journey had indeed fused two souls into one.

"Whatever impressions our first meeting had made, my sufferings and his self-sacrifice had confirmed. What I had found him during our long and miserable ride I found him ever, and loved him as such large-hearted, self-denying men should be loved. There was no talk of marriage between us for at least eighteen months; but there was no doubt whither we were drifting. Every moment he could spare from business was spent with me; and I think it was principally on my account that he induced his uncle in Glasgow, a muslin manufacturer, to engage a traveller and give him a permanent agency in Manchester, opening a ware-room for the sale of their goods.

"Shortly after that I became his wife, with the full approbation of friends, and with every prospect of happiness. He had furnished for me, simply but well, a house in Hanover-street, then a thorough Scotch colony, and my father's house being in Cannon-street, I was not more than a quarter of a mile from home. As was then the custom, we were married on Sunday, it being likewise my birthday, the 21st of December, and at once took possession of our new abode.

"The twenty-third was signalled by one of the fiercest conflagrations Manchester had known for years. A cotton-mill at Ancoats had taken fire whilst the hands were being dismissed. Some were in the upper-stories at the time; the narrow staircase was crowded, and many lives were in danger. Attracted by the glare, Mr. Carson was quickly on the spot, forgetful of all but the duty before him, and to his heroic efforts three girls at least owed their lives. They came to thank him a week later. Alas ! where was he? His hair was singed, and so was his coat, from which the tails were dangling loose; he had been wetted through alike with perspiration and water from the engine, but he waited until all danger to others was over, and when he reached home his clothes were apparently dry. He kissed me, apologised for keeping me waiting tea, and sat down to describe the incidents of the fire. Of his own exploits he said little; but on the plea of fatigue excused his sitting down to tea in the plight he then was. After the meal, he dozed off, which I attributed to his recent exertions and the heat of our own fire. It was only on going to rouse him that I discovered his clothes had been wetted, and I was too inexperienced to calculate the consequences.

"The following day I had promised to spend with my father and sisters. William was to join me on closing the warehouse. Being a bride, 'twas, of course, an object of special attention, made more of by my relations than at any other period of my life. I found there a perfect levee of aunts and cousins, discussing the bride's cake and future prospects with equal freedom. In the midst of our lively chat time fled fast. There came a sharp *rat-tat-tat* at the street-door.

"Why, that is William's knock; what brings him from the warehouse so early?" exclaimed I, running to anticipate the servant in opening the door. Without another word than 'Marianne,' strangely spoken, he passed me by, never stopping to kiss me, as was his wont.

"I confess he had spoiled me. I pouted, petulant tears welled to my eyes, and I lingered with the fastening of the door before I turned round.

"'Marianne!'"

"He was calling me from behind. I dropped the latch and followed him, as I thought, into the room I had just quitted.

"'Where is William?' I asked, looking round but not seeing him.

"'He has not come in here.'

"'Marianne!'

"The voice seemed to come from the room on the opposite side the hall. I ran thither, anticipating the loving embrace he was too reserved to give before strangers.

"*He was not there,*

"'William, dear, where are you? don't hide from me!'

"There was no answer. I ran into the back parlours—upstairs— downstairs, calling his name. *He was nowhere to he seen.*

78

"By this time the house was in commotion. Sisters and cousins alike had heard the knock, but no one had seen my husband or heard his voice.

"As they looked from me to one another for an explanation of that which is inexplicable, I having protested that Mr. Carson had passed and spoken to me in the hall, a sudden light flashed over and appalled me. I remembered *seeing the hall-panelling through his figure!* With a startling shriek, I rushed bareheaded from the house, tore across Cannon-street, along Sugar Lane, and up Shude Hill, like a mad woman, nor paused till my grasp was on the handle of my own door,

"That was ajar. A bad omen. I found my beloved husband extended on our bed, a doctor by his side vainly trying to bleed him—*the blood would not flow.*

"Inflammation—the result, no doubt, of his overnight's wetting and fatigue—had seized him suddenly.

"On his way home he had called on his doctor, who never left him again in life.

"Before night fell on the earth, the night of Death had fallen on my idolised husband, and my soul was in eclipse.

"Maid, wife, widow in a week, a widow all unconscious of her widowhood. A dumb, dreamy, statuesque automaton. I lived and moved, but that was all.

"I was taken home. When the funeral was over, the house in Hanover-street was given up. I was incapable of managing it.

"In this state I remained until my boy was born. Then the ice at my heart thawed, and tears came to my relief. The babe lived, and I lived for him.

"How I idolised that boy! I watched him night and day with more than a mother's care. He grew up a fine strong youth, the image of his dead father, whose name he bore. His father's uncle would have taken the entire charge of him; but I would not part from Willie, so we were summoned to Glasgow together, and there lived until the death of old Mr. Carson, when Willie was sixteen. The old gentleman left considerable property behind him, much of which was bequeathed to my son.

"Having no ties in Scotland, I came back to the old home, from which two of my sisters had gone away to homes of their own.

"Between myself and his grandfather, Willie stood a fair chance of being spoiled. He grew a tall, athletic man, not over-fond of business or study, but much given to all manly sports and pastimes; in which he was encouraged by his grandfather. As for me, I saw no harm in his pursuits, and never dreamed of danger.

"Willie had a friend close by with whom he often put on the gloves, or practised fencing and single-stick.

"One day, towards the close of the year—my sorrows have always come in the midst of other's rejoicing—I set reading by the fire; my father was playing his favourite game

Of backgammon with my sister Sarah; you, then a child of three yeas, sat nursing a kitten at your mother's feet; she had brought you to spend Christmas with us.

"My father, I most tell you, had then given up business, and our garret was filled with old lumber from the warehouse, several open baskets or 'wiskets' containing waste 'cops,' spindles, and other refuse amongst the rest.

"Our quiet was broken, and the rattling dice drowned by a loud clash and clatter upstairs.

"'Someone has left that garret-window open again, and the cats the making fine havoc with those cops, I know; hark how they rattle!'

"'Go upstairs, Sally, and shut the window,' said my father, pausing in his game.

"Sarah went. All was still.

"'The window is fast enough, and I saw no cats,' said she, as we sat down again to the board, "Again the clash and clatter, as of metal, clear and distinct.

"'Helen, do you go up. Take my stick, and rout the intruders out; I'd swear the cats are there.'

"Your mother went, and came back with the same report—nothing there; all silent.

"Again the self-same clash and clatter, louder than before. I, haunted by old memories, felt my heart sink.

"'Here, Marianne, lass, lend me thy arm; thou and I'll go up and see what all this din's about; but don't thou look scared.'

"We mounted the first flight, he leaning on my arm. All at once the clatter ceased.

"'Mother, mother, mother!' came floating like a breath down the stairway, and while we paused to listen—for my father heard it also—the figure of Willie brushed past us, with one hand pressed upon his heart.

"I trembled and grew faint. *I had seen the balustrades through the form.*

"My father chuckled outright. 'Ah, the young dog, so it was Willie playing tricks upon us, after all.'

"I said nothing until I reached the parlour. As I rightly conjectured, no Willie was there.

"'Father,' said I, clasping my hands in anguish, 'that was not Willie, it was his wraith. I have been *wraith-haunted* all my life.'

"My father looked dazed; my sisters, perhaps with a good motive, rallied me on my Scottish superstition, much as you have done; but ere their laughter had well subsided, there was an imperative knock at the street-door.

"We were summoned to oar neighbour, Mr. Neale's; an accident had befallen my son.

"He lay on a couch pale and bleeding, wounded in the chest, the room in disorder, foils upon the floor. He had barely strength left to press my hand, and say 'Mother, do not weep; Tom could not help it—the button came off his foil. Mother, forgive—' and I was childless.

"I was spared all the agony of the inquest, for there was another long blank in my memory; and during my mental oblivion your grandfather died, borne down by the double sorrow.

"You see, I have good reasons for saying I am wraith-haunted, and for knowing that the voice I heard tonight is a call from the spirit-world to me."

Mr. Birley and his wife both looked perplexed and serious.

"I do remember something about a ghost in grandfather's garret when I was a very little girl. But how is it I was never 'told of the warnings' you think you have had?"

"They were hushed up lest my grief should be re-awakened. And now let us go to bed—it is late. The issues of life and death are in higher hands than ours."

The morning broke—clear, sparkling, exhilarating. Mrs. Carson made her appearance in her ordinary health, a little paler it might be, but that was all.

Mrs. Birley had hesitated whether to issue her invitations, but finally resolved not to disappoint the children, and so they were sent.

The nursery-doors were thrown open, and all hands, big and little, summoned to the task of decoration with evergreens and holly.

In the midst of it all a carrier brought a large box, inscribed, "Aunt Carson's Gift." The old lady had made her purchases the day before. There was a general rush to wrench open the lid, and make a raid on the contents. Books, dolls, workboxes, a desk, toys noisy and noiseless, were there, each labelled with the fortunate recipient's name. Flushed and elated, the youngsters rushed hither and thither displaying their prizes. Frocks and pinafores filled to repletion dropped their contents, until the little ones might be tracked by straggling Shems and Noahs, cups and saucers, whistles and drumsticks.

The box had been removed, the litter cleared away, the stray waifs collected, when Mrs. Carson descended the stairs after her customary nap. A wee round toy, the colour of the staircarpet, had been overlooked; she stepped upon it, and fell from top to bottom, striking her head against the balustrades.

There was a rush through the house to where she lay stunned on the oilcloth. Reverently and sadly she was earned into the nearest room,—the one occupied overnight. A messenger was sent on horseback for a surgeon and for Mr. Birley.

Shocked beyond measure, the latter gentleman hastened home in time to hear the fiat pronounced.

"An injured spine—concussion of the brain—no hope whatever."

A physician summoned hastily confirmed the surgeon's decision.

The weeping children were huddled from the room.

"How long may she linger?" was Mr. Birley's question.

"She may go off any moment, the shock to her system is so great; she may last two or three hours."

"Do you think she is conscious?"

"I am afraid not."

Mrs. Birley, sobbing, whispered to her husband, "James, do you think aunt did hear anything supernatural last night."

Two days before he would have said, "All bosh!" now he answered, "God only knows! It is most mysterious."

"If she did she will not die until nine o'clock."

"At nine!" murmured the dying woman; "at nine."

She was evidently conscious, and something more she said, but the words were inaudible. Husband and wife watched the clock as intensely as Mrs. Carson had watched it the night before.

Ten minutes to nine! The retreating pulse quickened under the doctor's touch. The lips moved.

"William!" was faintly audible to the bent ear.

Five minutes to nine! The "change" was perceptible.

"Yes, William!"

There was another pause—a burr—the clock's note of warning;. There was a rattle in the throat of the dying woman.

"Coming, William!" was gasped out audibly.

Nine!

A last leap of the pulse—a last flicker of the eyelids—the "call" was obeyed.

Mrs. Carson, wraith-haunted, spirit-summoned, was of the dead!

The Piper's Ghost: A Legend of Elvet Bridge, Durham

CHAPTER 1

In the red annals of war few more romantic passages occur than those which recount the story of Charles Edward Stuart, the Young Pretender. It is a story of blind infatuation, alike in leader and adherents.

On the five-and-twentieth day of the hot month of July, 1745, with heart burning hot as the month, the sanguine man of five-and-twenty summers landed near Moidart, with little money and few men, in the vain hope to drive out the Guelph, and replace the Stuart on the throne of England. Round the standard raised at Glenfinnan rallied Scotland's rebellious chieftains with their clansmen; others joining on the southward march. Victories were gained, towns taken, and further success might have followed prompt action; but the prince wasted precious time in idle ceremonies, giving his enemies a chance to collect and concentrate forces. From Manchester, which he entered Nov. 29th, he departed with a reinforcement of 300 men on December 1st, to return on the 8th of the same month worn and dispirited: a council held at Derby having peremptorily insisted on retreat.

Thence dates a story of disaster which we need follow no farther than Clifton, a village within a short distance of Penrith, where a sharp skirmish took place in the effort to cover the retreat of the cavalry over Clifton Bridge. This was done successfully, the troops advancing under the Duke of Cumberland being repulsed with loss.

When the sharp contest was over it was too dark to distinguish the slain who filled the surrounding ditches; whilst the retreat towards Carlisle was pressed on with such haste that the dead were left unburied, the wounded unattended, in the bitterest of bitter weather.

Amongst the latter was a piper named Dugald Macpherson, who had followed his chieftain with the blind devotion so characteristic of the old Scottish clansman; and in whose breast the gallant young prince stood second only to the "Macpherson."

Sounding the pibroch of the tribe, he was struck down almost at the outset, but not before he had seen one of his stalwart sons fighting by his side cleft through the brain by the same sabre that was next turned against himself.

Scarcely could he have seen the elder brother's flashing claymore deal vengeance on the destroying horseman, than trampling hoofs beat out his own sense of pain or anguish.

Rain was falling heavily when Dugald, recovering consciousness, found himself lying in one of the many pools of water which the bad weather and worse roads had provided, providentially, as it were, for the stanching of open wounds. He was stiff and sore, as much from the bruising hoofs which had passed over his prostrate body, as from the sabre-cut in his shoulder, the haemorrhage from which had long ceased. It was too dark to distinguish more than shadowy outlines, and only the moans of dying men broke the stillness.

Where were the skirling bagpipes of the Scots' Army? How was it their shrill music was inaudible? What sounds could pierce the silence like the blast of the warlike pipes? Had his clansmen been defeated, that he was left to die like a dog?

"It maun e'en be sae, foul fa' the red-coated Southrons! Gin Lord George, (Lord George Murray, headed the Macphersons in this skirmish), had keepit the grund, the chief wad ne'er hae left his auld piper Dugald in siccan a plight as this! They maun be miles awa e'en noo, or I wad catch the skirl o' the muckle pipes in ilka sough o' the wind. But whar be her ain pipes?"

As he thus muttered, rather than spoke, he made a circuit with his right arm on the miry earth, and found his treasured bagpipes within his grasp.

He clutched the bag as a prize; but his sudden exclamation of delight was checked, for in that wide sweep of his arm his fingers had grasped a kilt and philibeg, and like a lightning flash came the recollection of seeing his youngest born struck down like a log by his side; and the glad ejaculation terminated in a groan.

With an effort he raised himself into a sitting posture, his left arm being too painful to use, and drew himself closer to the dead Highlander.

Once again he put forth his hand into the darkness, but it was to feel anxiously and carefully over his garb and accoutrements, and then to grasp nervously the cold hand, which something more akin to instinct than recognition had told him was that of his son, his brave Allan.

"My bairn, my braw Allan! Eh, but this will be a waefu' tale for thy mither at hame. Oh, that sic an auld worn-out stump as mysel should be left, and the tough green sapling be cut down in its prime. Yet wherefore should I lament? Hasna' he befallen whar a Macpherson should fa', in the thick o' the fight, wi' his face to the foe! Shame on ye, Dugald, for a doited auld body, lamenting when ye should be proud that ye'r ain bairn shed his blood for his chief an' his prince, the bonnie Prince Charlie!"

The poor piper drew his sleeve across his eyes, and set his face with stern resolution to exult in his son's glory. But it would not do; the father overpowered the warrior, and big drops rolled down his weather-beaten, blood-stained cheeks, across one of which was an ugly gash.

Grey dawn was creeping up the east, raw and chilly as dawn ever is (whatever poets may sing to the contrary), and with the dawn came the instinct of self-preservation. But the old man's first care was for the ghastly remains beside which he knelt.

"What can be dune; I canna gang awa' an' leave my fair-haired bairn to the corbies and hoodie craws!"

He had already arranged the young soldier's plaid around the head as a decent covering; and now—for he was a stout, brawny man, in spite of his sixty years and aching wounds—he strove to draw the body from the roadway to a hollow in the broken ground close by, which he might deepen with his claymore, and cover with mould and stones.

Bloodshed was no new thing to Dugald; but had it been, the fate of his son would have closed his ears and eyes to the sounds and sights of that limited battlefield. He saw only his dying boy! He had found a sheltered nook between two boulders, had hollowed out a cavity to receive the corpse, and, with infinite pain to himself, had drawn it almost to its resting-place, when a labourer from the village drew near.

There was no need to ask help. The rude but kindly peasant, seeing how he was employed, and how unfit for his pious task, came to his assistance. He had a spade over his shoulder, and with that soon deepened the shallow grave, and covered the dead from sight.

Dugald proffered his son's dirk and sporran as remembrancers; but the man thought he offered payment, and shook his head, sturdily declining the gift.

"Nay, nay, aw canna tak pay for only doin' ma duty. Besides, aw moight get into trouble wi' them things. Who knows!"

In the pre-occupation of his hand and mind the sound of rapidly advancing cavalry had not arrested Dugald's ear, but now the well-known sounds of martial music were borne on the wind—not the familiar drone of the pipe, but the whistle of the fife, the roll of the drum, the breath of the bugle, all telling him of enemies at hand.

The friendly labourer thrust a lump of cheese and an oat-cake into the piper's hand (he had previously bound up the wounded: shoulder with the laced neck-cloth of a dead officer), and decamped hastily, lest his very friendliness should be his own death-warrant.

Dugald was thus left to shift for himself.

But, first, he must secure his bagpipes, dear to him almost as his own life. He gathered the instrument in his arms like a living thing. Nearer came the troops. Whither should he flee?

In danger, thought is rapid. Stealthily as a cat, and as swiftly as his condition would permit; he bent his steps to the river side, keeping close to the thick-set hedge.

As the first horsemen came in sight, his head disappeared below the level of the bank, and he lay crouched beneath the shadow of the sheltering arch long before they gained the scene of the last night's conflict.

What cared the stern Duke of Cumberland for dead or dying not of his own army? But these *were* his soldiers with a few exceptions, and Dugald heard hasty orders given for the interment of the dead, the removal of the wounded to the village, and for the custody of some ten or twelve wounded prisoners.

Dugald's heart beat quicker. What if Sandy, his firstborn, was among these? Better he lay in the bloody grave with Allan: than fall into the merciless hands of the English commander!

No fear, Dugald, thy son is already marching towards Carlisle! And yet there is an English officer wounded nigh unto death, who re-members well the face of him whose vengeful claymore left him but one hand. A hand to hold the reins, but never a one to wield again the sabre, which had cut down father and brother both before your Sandy's eyes!

Colonel Philp has a memory, but no conscience. Pray God, old man, that thy surviving son fall not into that man's hands hereafter!

Though a company of men had been told off to clear the ground of dead and wounded, and though the former were buried with, scant ceremony, it was a work of time; and every moment seemed trebled to the piper, who was liable to discovery at any instant. Besides, his wounds were painful, and, hardy as was his nature, he was not made of cast-iron.

Long after the last footstep had crossed the bridge, Dugald hesitated to leave his place of concealment lest some straggler should confront him. At length he crept out, and, keeping: behind the tall hedge which skirted the road, soon left the village in the rear, at once widening the distance between himself and friends or foes alike.

Avoiding the high roads, he struggled on until almost nightfall, when, faint with hunger and pain, he stopped at a poor cottage in a bye-lane. Children were playing in front, and a woman sat knitting on the doorstep. He was a ghastly object—the blood unwashed from his face, the bright hues of the tartan disguised with mud, his very gait betokening his unfitness to proceed.

The woman rose as he advanced. Though his speech was almost unintelligible, his condition was not.

At the hasty summons "Grandfather," an old man came forward, helped him into the cottage, and into the seat in the chimney corner which he had just quitted.

Oat-cake and a bowl of milk were set before him, and then there was some whispering. One of the children was despatched, somewhere, to Dugald's alarm.

He, however, had no cause for fear. The child speedily returned with his father, a sturdy, good-natured looking man, coarsely habited.

Fresh whispers! "Some poor Jacobite body; do you think Dr. Kendal would come and dress his wounds if ye went and. told him?" and "Mayhap he would!" was their sum and substance; and then the husband departed.

The hospitable woman, whom her husband had called Nanny, moving about quickly, brought water and washed the gore and mud from poor Dugald's face with as much gentleness as if she had been a practised nurse, and he a one hour's child.

Soon the husband returned, and with him Dr. Kendal from the neighbouring borough of Kirkland, a man who stood well in. his profession, but was more than suspected of strong Jacobite proclivities.

At all events he came readily, dressed and bound up the piper's wounds as readily, although he suspected payment was altogether out of the question. But no, Dugald Macpherson was not a poor man, he tendered a gold piece in return for the service rendered; which Dr. Kendal refused as steadily as the peasant had refused the gifts offered in the morning. All the doctor would take in fee was news of Prince Charlie and his movements; for posts were few and newspapers still fewer at that time than the present. Humble as was the accommodation of the cottage, a bed was found for the stranger.

Refreshed by the night's rest and a breakfast of milk and porridge, Dugald quitted the hospitable roof at an early hour, after depositing the rejected gold coin in the grandfather's snuff-box. To have remained longer would have endangered the safety of all concerned. To harbour a Jacobite was no slight offence.

He sought to return to Scotland; but the route was unknown, ;and soldiers were everywhere.

Travelling by unfrequented roads, stopping at farms or hovels, he found himself in the heart of Weardale, and once amongst the hills seemed to breathe more freely.

Amongst the dalesmen hospitality seemed the law. At West Gate a farmer opened his doors to him; and again near Stanhope a bluff yeoman named Hodgson sheltered him for some days.

Christmas was fast approaching, snow lay thick on hill and dale, travelling was next to impossible, even to men acquainted with the intricacies of the fells. But the yeoman and his daughter Hannah, whose Christianity was practical, treated the wandering piper as an honourable guest, not as a poor refugee. He was pressed to remain, and Hannah ventured to hope his shoulder would be well enough by Christmas Eve for him to pipe for the dancers at their yearly gathering.

"Naething wad gie me mair pleasure, my bonnie lassie, but I fear the poor piper maun gang awa, lest nae guid come o' his biding sae lang wi' ye."

"Hout, man! King George will ne'er send into the dale after a solitary piper; at all events, not while the snow lasts," quoth Farmer Hodgson heartily, "so make your mind easy, friend, and be ready to pipe away when Hannah and the lasses are ready to foot it with their sweethearts."

But rosy Hannah, a plump damsel of nineteen, had more sweethearts than one. That is, she had one whom she avowed, Luke Raby, the son of a neighbour, a frank hearty fellow of two or three and twenty; and one other whom she discountenanced.

The latter, Simeon Crawlaw, was an ill-conditioned, pettifogging lawyer, who had wriggled himself into the good graces of the local landed proprietors, so far as to become their agent :and collector. In this capacity he stood between the Rabys and their landlord, a very thorn in Luke's side.

Joe Hodgson's farm was his own; had come to him from a long line of ancestors, and Simeon Crawlaw coveted his broad pasture lands and well-stocked byres quite as much as he coveted possession of the hazel-eyed, ruddy-lipped maiden to whom they would descend.

As may be expected, there was not much love lost between the two suitors. Luke Raby, as the successful candidate, could well afford to be magnanimous to his rival, whom in his heart he thoroughly despised; but that Hannah's rejection had stirred up the malice that lay, like an evil sediment, at the bottom of the lawyer's heart, and he retaliated her refusal upon the elder Raby in a series of petty annoyances, which irritated the young man almost to exasperation.

Joe Hodgson, whose massive frame was a fit casket for the large heart within, had declared for "a fair field and no favour." "You see. Lawyer Crawlaw, Hannah has no mother, and is all the child I have; I don't thwart her inclinations in little matters, and I'll be hanged if I do it in a great one. And the choice of a woman's husband Is a great one, I take it."

" But, Mr. Hodgson, Miss Hannah is so devoted to you, so ready to fall in with your plans, so obedient to your wishes, that a word from you, I'm sure—"

"Hout! hout, man!" interrupted the farmer hastily, "no word of mine shall bar the bairn's free choice. I should be a scoundrel if I made my girl's love for me a reason to break her heart. At the same time I've no objection to your trying your luck, and may the best man win."

The best man had won, and Simeon Crawlaw was yet smarting under his recent discomfiture, when news spread through Weardale that the Pretender had abandoned his design of marching on London, and that the Duke of Cumberland and General Wade were rapidly advancing from different points to cut off his retreat to Scotland.

In no period of great political excitement did party feeling run higher than during what is now known as the Jacobite rebellion. Into remote districts rumour spread like thistledown upon the very winds; oral intelligence, quite as reliable as the printed broadsides, circulated by pedlars and chapmen, the travelling stationers of the time.

Discussions, dissensions, and heart-burnings followed every acces-sion of news; but as any open demonstration in favour of the Pretender was sure to be succeeded by imprisonment and fine, if nothing worse, discretion became the better part of valour, and men communicated by signs or spoke in *equivoque*. Informers flourished, and prisons were gorged. Knowing the aptitude of both Joseph Hodgson and his presumptive son-in-law to speak freely and from the heart, Mr. Crawlaw held it wise to dissemble, and hide his humiliation under a show of patient resignation, the better to scrutinize their movements, and lie in wait like a beast of prey until some incautious word or act should lay either open to suspicion, and so feed his revenge.

Not that either the yeoman or Hannah's lover had a taint of Jacobinism, but they had both a tendency to take the weaker side; and on this characteristic he hoped to trade.

No news of the occupation of Penrith or the skirmish at Clifton had reached Hope House, when Dugald Macpherson, faint with cold and hunger, sought shelter and food at that door whence never poor suppliant was sent uncheered.

It was not necessary to ask if he belonged to the proscribed Jacobites. His dress, his tongue, his wounds declared him a fugitive from the rebel army. He had lodged in the outhouses of people who dared not admit him within their good stone walls. But for his wounds, this would have been little privation to the hardy Highlander. But straying out of the track, now regaining it, every mile had been lengthened into three or more. Once or twice he had plunged into snow-drifts, from which he only escaped as by a miracle, and altogether these hardships had told upon the old man.

Joseph encountered the wet and haggard piper on the threshold, and without a question asked or story told, bade him "Come in for God's sake," brought him into the glowing kitchen, seated him in the ingle nook, ordered the maids to set bread, cheese, and ale before the famished wanderer, and bade him "fall to with a will!"

Hannah's charity was as active as her father's. She hunted up some of his disused clothes, in which the old piper might attire himself whilst his own were dried and cleansed, and laughed heartily at the figure he cut in garments unfitted to him in every way.

She doctored his wounds too with some skill; but, indeed, Dr. Kendal's dressing had left little to be done, and when the farmer begged the piper to remain, they were healing rapidly.

Thankful for their hospitality, but unwilling to bring his host into danger, he hesitated; but when Joseph Hodgson made light of the risk, and Hannah seconded his invitation with so winning a smile, what could the old man do but remain, in spite of his prescience of evil to result?

And there he might have remained in shelter and security undisturbed but for the prowling habits and keen scent of Simeon Crawlaw.

Few stand on the ceremony of knocking at the door of a farmhouse—or did, in those unsophisticated days; so when the lawyer walked unannounced and uninvited into the farmer's kitchen, which Hannah and two able assistants were transforming into a Christmas bower with holly and evergreens, no one was surprised save the sly fox himself.

For the presence of Luke Raby he was prepared; but who was this kilted stranger, who stood as erect as if he were an earl?

The plastered face told of recent conflict; the pipes on a side-table told his calling; but the port and bearing of this man as plainly told he was no common strolling piper, picking up pence at fairs, or wakes, or wayside inns. He was evidently the piper to some distinguished tribe or clan; and if so, a man of sufficient mark amongst them to be worth hunting down, and his entertainers with him.

Here was a rare chance!

His greeting was, however, as oily as if he would fain smooth the lives of all present.

"Ah! Miss Hannah, how do you do? I vow you are always employed for the good or pleasure of your friends, and you look as fresh and bright as the holly in your hand."

"You should have said the ivy, Mr. Crawlaw. Holly is sharp and prickly to handle, its berries are poison; the clinging, yet supporting ivy, verdurous in summer as winter, best portrays Hannah to my thinking," said her lover, with a glance of mingled tenderness and admiration.

"We speak as we find, Mr. Raby," retorted the lawyer, with marked emphasis. "The ivy may have clung round you. I, though wounded by the holly, can admire its beauty, while confessing it dangerous."

"I hope you don't think *me* dangerous, Mr. Crawlaw," said Hannah, with flushed cheeks, as she leapt lightly from the oak settle on which she had been mounted.

"Dangerous to a man's peace of mind. Miss Hodgson," replied he, in an undertone meant for her ears only.

Hannah looked distressed. "What can the old rascal be saying now?" muttered Luke between his teeth, hammering at a nail as if he wished his rival's head in its place, and coming down the ladder without more ado.

Mr. Crawlaw changed the subject. "You have not introduced me to your Scotch friend here."

"Oh, Mr. Macpherson—I forgot!" She repaired the omission. Mr. Crawlaw struck up a conversation with the piper, intending to draw him out; but the canny Scot wits as wary as his interlocutor, and he made no new discoveries.

He, however, did his best to seem friendly, assisted the trio to festoon the whitewashed walls, and would fain have helped to adjust the huge mistletoe bush, had not Luke Raby entered a protest, as a breach of privilege.

But he only remained long enough to set them at ease. When they adjourned to decorate the panels of the best parlour, he took his departure, on the plea that he had business with a near neighbour; promising, however, to make one of the festive party on Christmas eve, a promise he meant religiously to fulfil.

"I wish, hinny, you had not asked that man," said Luke, when he was out of hearing. "He will be a sad spoilsport."

"It was not I who asked him; it was father," answered Hannah. "I would as soon have a toad hopping about the floor. But, Luke, dear, is it not best to be civil to him?"

Luke, with some reservation, admitted it was.

"Yon's a fause loon, lassie, or my auld e'en deceive me; there's muckle mischief under that gleg tongue," suggested Dugald.

"What, Lawyer Crawlaw!" exclaimed Hodgson, entering the room. He had patted from him at the gate, and coming in overheard the last remark. "Nay, the man doesn't show at his best here; Hannah knows why; and if he does bear an indifferent name elsewhere, that's the fault of his calling, I reckon."

"Aweel, it's nae business o' mine; but it's dootless aye best to beware o' uncanny folk," replied the cautious piper, with a sideway nod, as expressive as his words.

Chapter 2

Christmas Eve had come. So had the guests, for a rapid thaw had cleared bye-ways and made open roads passable if not pleasant, and Christmas gatherings at Hope House were by no means to be despised.

Long tables were literally loaded with good things in all the ponderous prodigality of old-fashioned hospitality; and their preparation had kept the house in a bustle for a week or more. Game laws were stringent, but keepers were friendly; so hare and pheasant made as goodly a show on the board as goose and turkey. Huge joints of beef and mutton, flanked by brawn and Yorkshire pie, were matched with corresponding piles of vegetables, with stoups of home-brewed ale to wash all down. Then followed plum-pudding and plum-porridge, mince-pies and tartlets, creams and syllabubs, apples, pears, nuts, such dried, fruits as were accessible, home-made wines, and other dainties.

Appetite and mirth honoured the welcome and graced the feast.

The piper, in his picturesque costume, sat at the board an honourable and honoured guest; but indeed, the whole scene had made a study for a painter, sparkling and glowing with light and colour. Dark-haired Hannah, dispensing smiles and hospitalities, so bountifully, shone in her ample dress of richly-flowered taffeta and jaunty cap, but as one rose in a blooming parterre; whilst the young men of the party rivalled the feminine portion in their display of lace on ruffles and neck-cloths, of Bristol-stones in buckles for shoe or knee, and full tints in the deep-flapped vests and long wide-skirted coats they wore, even if their elders toned down the whole with more subdued drab and brown. Polished silver and pewter flickered with faint reflections from candles in tin sconces on the embowered walls, or in the extemporised chandelier suspended from the huge beams o'erhead; but they twinkled feebly in the warmer glow of the fire on the open hearth, where the Yule log, blazing on a bed of pit coal, sent out showers of bright sparkles, and lit up every beaming face, every cleft and cranny of the ample " house."

But even feasting has an end. A clearance being made, the elders retired to the quiet parlour to play cards and backgammon, or discuss dangerous politics in whispers; whilst Dugald, primed with a stiff dose of whisky-punch from a mammoth punch-bowl, gathered his pipes into his arms once more, and struck up a reel that brought the dancers to their feet in all haste.

In the good-humoured contest for places, couples came incontinently under the mistletoe bough, and coy damsels submitted to be kissed, in deference to indefeasible right; though the grace with which the concession was made depended much on special caprices and individual likings.

Up to a late hour Mr. Crawlaw had not put in an appearance; to the great relief of young Raby and Hannah, both of whom expressed as much in a confidential moment.

Dance followed dance. Not tame quadrilles, through which the staid dancers glide without an effort, but dances which required good limbs, good breath, and strong flooring.

In the midst, Mr. Hartley, an elderly man, a partner in a Weardale mine, who had only just arrived, called the beaming host aside, and asked several questions in quick succession; questions of import in the sequel. "Hodgson, did you not expect Lawyer Crawlaw here?"

"Certainly," was the answer.

"When was he here *last?*"

"On Monday evening."

"Monday! Hm! Quite two days. How long may our friend the martial piper have been with you?"

"About a week."

"And Crawlaw saw him?"

"Yes! But why put me through this catechism? You do not do it idly, I am sure!"

"Idly! No, by heavens! Friend Hodgson, there has been an encounter between Cumberland's advance and Charles Edward's rear; and this Scotch piper is a fugitive. Your liberty is endangered by your harbouring a rebel."

"Hout, man, common charity—" interjected the blunt farmer, to be in turn interrupted.

"Yes, yes! I know all that, as so, no doubt, does that knave Crawlaw. But what does the government or its tools care for common charity? Common charity will hardly save us from the common hangman in these ticklish times. You must get the piper out of the house with all speed, not less for his safety than your own."

"But why this haste Hartley?" interrogated the yeoman, as in a mist.

"Well, I met the lawyer on his way to Durham with exultant mischief in his winking eyes; and from a word he dropped I feel assured he has gone to turn informer. He has never forgiven your daughter's preference of a younger and better man. Faugh! I hate the sneak!"

Loath as Joe Hodgson was to turn the piper forth on Christmas Eve, a hunted man, he felt the absolute necessity of giving him a chance of escape ere the hounds of the law were on his track.

No time was to be lost. Mr. Hartley returned to the glowing kitchen, where blind-man's buff had superseded dancing. A hint sent Hannah to her father. Luke Raby quickly followed, as by inspiration.

Another hint, and Dugald left the merrymakers, taking his cherished pipes along with him. He was warned that he was in peril and must escape. Fortunately, the snow was almost gone, and footsteps could not be tracked in the thaw. Luke Raby volunteered to be his guide through the mazes of the dale. Once beyond, he must assume the character of an ordinary wandering piper, so as to lessen suspicion.

"Dinna greet, my bonnie lassie," said Dugald, as tears sprang into Hannah's eyes. "Dinna greet on Christmas Eve. I wad rather hae streekit my auld limbs under the mools wi' my ain Allan, than hae brought trouble and sorrow to hearts sae kind and leal. An' I fear the warst is not ower."

A hasty parting, and Dugald, with sad forebodings in his heart, left Hope House with his young friend. The square stone building looked darker, from the contrasting light which streamed from doors and windows, and the sounds of laughter fell sadly on the ears of both.

To Luke Raby every winding of the dale was familiar. Keeping near the high road, yet away from it, he led the piper steadily on, though over-ways only passable by a mountaineer. As they left Wokingham in the rear, the distinct beat of hoofs was audible: then followed the murmur of voices. Raby drew the piper into the shadow of a dense planting by the road-side, whilst the horsemen passed.

Voice and figure betrayed one to be Simeon Crawlaw, whilst the conversation of all three, carried on in the loud tones of semi-intoxication, assured them that his companions were constables, and that Mr. Hartley's friendly warning had come not one moment too soon.

Hitherto they had proceeded with caution, lest a sudden turn of the road might bring them in contact with the suspected informer and his coadjutors. Now they pushed on.

Two miles further the highway to Hexham crossed the path they had trod.

"Here we part, good Dugald," said Luke, kindly; "I must return' in haste, lest I should be missed. Keep to the road straight before you; it leads direct to the North. In two hours you will be out of the jurisdiction of Durham, and may cross the borders ere pursuit be possible; even if it be thought worth while to pursue, which I much doubt."

Dugald gave his proffered hand a hearty grip.

"Fare ye weel," said he, "and tak wi' ye an auld man's blessing, for yersel and yon winsome lassie. Ye'll wed ere it be lang, and then may yer bairns grow up as guid as yersels! I can wish ye nae better, I'm thinking. God bie wi' us a'. Should Prince Charlie win his ain, Dugald Macpherson may hae it in his pooer to requite his freends."

How strangely is the web of life mingled! These men parted, never expecting to meet again. How little the most far-seeing can tell whither his next step will lead!

Let us however, follow Dugald, as he strode along through the mire, the mist, and the darkness.

His heart was heavy as the road he travelled, where the half-melted snow yet lay in knee-deep rats, in which one leg would dip with sudden jerk that might have dislocated looser joints. But Dugald lived before the days of Macadam, and took the had roads as matters of course.

Pondering on the fate of Scotland and his sons, he reached a point where the road was crossed at an acute angle. Hesitating, he turned to the right, where he saw signs of habitation. It was Gorecock Hall, and he had turned when he should have gone forward. Yet he walked on with long strides. Beads again, crossed, still he kept to the right, and went wrong. When he hoped to have reached Northumberland, he was passing Neville's Cross, nearing the city from which he should have fled.

And now he met drunken men, who had not slept off the night's carouse, some who wished him a merry Christmas, others who, when asked the road, jeered at his strange garb, or spoke morosely. All, however, eyed him strangely.

At length he found himself in the heart of Durham when its inhabitants were casting off the dreams of night.

That was no safe abiding place. Crossing the Market Place quickly as he could, he stepped boldly through Claypath Crates, and on up Gilliesgate.

A city watchman, armed with a formidable billhook, going to report himself after his last round, perceived him, and summoned him to "Stop in the King's name."

To stop was to be taken! An alley offered an escape. He darted into its dim obscurity. The watchman gave chase, shouting as he ran.

Dugald dashed headlong forward—the way led to the river—there was a sound of rushing waters—the river was a flood—the path covered and crumbling—the stream lapping the foundations of the houses;—another unconsidered step—the man was in the swollen stream, struggling for his life.

He was a swimmer, but the unexpected plunge deprived him, for the moment of his senses.

As he rose to the surface, he struck out. But the swirling waters bore him on. The most powerful swimmer could not have stemmed that torrent. How, then, could an aged man, whose shoulder yet was stiff with a recent wound, hope to escape?

Instinctively he had clung to his bagpipes. They fettered his right arm, but they also helped to buoy him up. He floated, drifting with the stream.

Fortunately every available spot was lined with people striving to recover from the flood such household goods as had been washed from other homes.

Elvet steps were filled with excited men (and women too), provided with poles and ropes.

As the whirling eddies swung the piper round, still washing him onwards towards Bishop Pudsey's many-arched bridge, a simultaneous shout arose from the occupants of the steps—"A man in the river!"

Just then a mass of driftwood struck him on the head. It stunned but saved him. Another instant he would have been under the arch, and lost.

It drove him nearer to the steps, a noosed rope was flung round his body, and he was drawn to land.

Senseless and apparently dead he was carried up Elvet steps, by rough-looking but tender-hearted men.

"Poor fellow, he's gotten a drop ower much ower night at sum Kirsmas feast, and stumbled ower inter the river," surmised one.

"He'll not get fu' agen in a hurry when he gets ower this tout," remarked another.

"Tak care o' the man's bagpipes," bawled a woman. "He'll want 'em gin he does come round."

Where should he be carried?

By this time the city watchman, whose sudden chase had had so disastrous a result, came upon the scene. "Carry him to the gaol, the governor will best know what's to be done with him," said he of the billhook, with a voice of authority not to be questioned.

The gaol was then the North Gate of the city, defended by sally-port and portcullis, the latter rusting in its grooves from disuse. It had been rebuilt by Bishop Langley about 1417, and was a fine specimen of the strong architecture of the period. It divided Saddler Street from the North Bailey. The portcullis, which had been raised quite a century, fell suddenly, during some alterations in 1778, stopping the road until workmen with saws and axes cut it to pieces. The gaol itself was not destroyed until 1820, when a more modern building was erected on its site.

When the watchman, therefore, ordered Dugald Macpherson to be carried to the gaol, he suggested the most accessible place, and when the bearers hurried with their senseless and dripping burden along Elvet Bridge (which, of course, extends far beyond the actual stream) and up the Maudlin or Magdalen steps (so called from a Magdalen chapel which once stood there) into Saddler Street, they took the nearest route to the gaol.

The governor was a man of some humanity for his vocation, and so, notwithstanding Dugald's questionable guise, all then, known appliances were used for his restoration.

The blow he had received in the water had, more than his immersion, given a shock to his system, following as it did months of hardship, excitement, and pain.

He recovered, it is true, even whilst the Christmas bells were ringing; but brain fever supervened, and there was but rough tendance in the gaol.

Leaving him, therefore, to rave wildly of his Allan and Sandy, of Bonnie Prince Charlie and his chief; of bagpipes and bloodshed, condemning himself and others in his delirium; let us return to Hope House, and see how all things fared with the good yeoman on that Christmas Day.

Though Luke Raby retraced his steps with the vigour and activity of early manhood, leaping over impediments which would have daunted a less resolute man, he found that Crawlaw and his myrmidons had reached the farm before him.

They were armed with warrants for the arrest of a Scotch piper called Dugald Macpherson, suspected of being in open rebellion against the reigning sovereign; and of Joseph Hodgson, yeoman, for knowingly harbouring the same.

But the piper was nowhere to be found, and, as may be supposed, no one knew more of him than that he was an itinerant piper earning a precarious living by attendance at dances and places of entertainment. His departure was accounted for on the plea that he was anxious to be in readiness for another merry-making the following day at Bishop Auckland, and as that was a goodish step he had asked permission to retire early.

In the absence of proof the constables were forced to retire, their search-warrant having resulted in nothing but discomfiture to themselves and their leader, Mr. Simeon Crawlaw, who had endeavoured to hide his share in the transaction by entering the house alone to reconnoitre, leaving his followers at some distance from the gate with instructions not to advance for some time. He walked into the midst of the mirthful party with assumed ease and affability, greeting Hannah and her father with apparent cordiality as of old.

But forewarned is forearmed. Mr. Crawlaw was questioned as to the cause of his late arrival; but no word or look betrayed their knowledge that his excuses were fictions. They were equally on their guard when the constables presented themselves.

Of course their entrance and errand spread dismay and confusion, so genuine that suspicion was disarmed. Mr. Crawlaw became suddenly fussy, as if desirous to justify his friends, dexterously cross-questioning the domestics in his apparently officious zeal to prove non-complicity. And he did prove more than he desired.

All he elicited was, that a poor piper, half-famished, and wet with floundering through snowdrifts, who had been hurt in a drunken brawl on his way from St. John's Chapel, had been taken in by the master, and kept out of charity, because he would not have turned a dog out into the snow; and that when the snow was going he stayed to play for the dancers, there having been no chance to get a fiddler.

The men insisted on a rigid search of house and outhouses; and finding nothing, went away swearing at their want of success.

Joe Hodgson could not, however, be churlish to anyone on Christmas Eve, and as the men buttoned their long, heavy overcoats to depart, he called them into the lesser kitchen, and regaled them with cake, cheese, and hot ale.

"Better luck next time," said one of the men, as he raised the wooden bicker to his lips, a toast the discomfited lawyer echoed in his heart.

Luke Raby had returned in the height of the search, and having taken the precaution to change his muddy boots for the shoes previously worn, was seen helping Hannah to allay the fears of her friends as if he had never been absent.

So far, so well.

Such visitors as lived at a distance from Stanhope remained the night, and Christmas Day passed cheerily enough. The yeoman's heart was too generous to harbour suspicion of Crawlaw; and concluding that the arrival of the officers so closely upon the lawyer's heels was a mere coincidence, he decided that Mr. Hartley's unconcealed dislike of the agent had led him to draw false conclusions, and so dismissed the matter from his mind, with a hope that the piper was fairly out of reach. He was consequently as jolly as if no warrants and prisons ever existed, and made fun for the young people with all the zest of thorough enjoyment.

Luke Raby, however, had a deeper insight into his defeated rival's heart. He had too often felt through his father what the man's petty malice could effect, and how he never lost an opportunity to goad or wound those who chanced to offend him, to question the verity of Mr. Hartley's statement; even supposing he had not seen and overheard the agent and officers of justice on the road. Not wishing to disturb Hannah, whom he loved dearly, he kept his fears to himself, and strove to appear as gay as the rest.

His father's farm lay on the other side of Stanhope, two long miles from Hope House; and when, at a late hour, he took leave, promising to see her again on the Sunday, he lingered as lovers do, but uneasily, and embraced her with a fervour so unusual that the girl rebuked him laughingly, saying,

"Why, Luke, you might be parting with me for ever."

"My darling, I trust not; but these are strange times, and God only knows!"

"Well, I shall expect you on Sunday; so mind you are here. Goodnight." So, extricating herself from his clasp, she tripped into the house, and he strode homewards, vainly striving to cast off despondency.

He was not at church on Sunday morning, and Hannah returned home alone, more pettish than anxious, having no knowledge of impending evil. As she drew near home she met Tibby, her old nurse, wringing her hands in sore distress.

Pettishness gave place to bitter anguish. Father and lover, both were on their way as prisoners to Durham Gaol!

CHAPTER 3

Simeon Crawlaw's suspicions had been lulled, not stifled. His sharp, blinking eyes had noticed Luke's hat and cloak, hastily thrown down on a chair in a back room at Hope House when the search was over, and close by his long riding boots, not merely wet with mud, but thickly flecked with *unmelted* snow. They had been evidently used very recently, and on untrodden roads.

Bearing this in mind, and forgetting the "goodwill to men," which every steeple rang out that Christmas Day, he once more betook himself to Durham Gaol. But the governor, after giving his orders concerning the resuscitated Dugald, had gone to spend the day with friends in a livelier and more odorous locality; and would not be back until the following day. So Mr. Simeon had to bridle his impatience and wait until the morrow.

Meanwhile he repaired to the Half Moon, at the corner of Elvet, to refresh himself after the manner of men; and found the pathway obstructed, and the rooms filled with people talking volubly about the flood, and—the Highland piper who had been rescued at Elvet steps just as he was being carried away by the stream.

Here was news! He listened, questioned carelessly, and came to the conclusion that Mr. Macpherson was the man; and if so had dropped as it were into his very grasp. At all events *he* was snug in prison; that was something gained.

After an interview with the governor and an identification of delirious Dugald, once more he trotted to the mayor to make smother deposition, and obtain an extra warrant for the arrest of Luke Raby, with what success we know.

The blow fell heavily. In those days prisons were little better than graves, so few escaped who once entered their noxious precincts, loathsome to the senses, loathsome to the soul; and for suspected Jacobites there was more law than justice.

Still Joseph Hodgson had a brave heart, and seeing Luke Raby wince as they passed under the North Gate to the strong door of the gaol, followed by a noisy crowd, he said—

"Hout, lad, never be cast down! They can prove nought against thee, and charity's no crime. Keep up thy heart! We all be blithe at home again by New Year's Day."

"Amen!" responded Luke, with a fervour which expressed his doubts.

They were not at home on New Year's Day. Delays occurred before they could be brought before the chief magistrate, and then they were hauled back to prison to await their trial at the next gaol delivery; Joseph Hodgson for harbouring, Luke Raby for aiding and abetting, the escape of a known rebel.

There was no concealing the animus of Crawlaw, informer and accuser, now; indeed, so transparent was it, that the mayor checked his protestations of loyalty, and declared that had the guilt of the prisoners rested on his unsupported testimony, he should have dismissed them at once. But the gaoler who had listened to the ravings of the piper rescued from the river had given evidence which compelled their detention. Then first the yeoman and Luke Raby learned the extent of their own and Dugald's misfortune.

In spite of the magistrate's stern rebuke, Simeon Crawlaw returned home exultant. "Mistress Hannah would have leisure to repent her hasty choice *now!*"

But Hannah did *not* repent. She loathed the mean wretch more intensely than ever; whilst the misfortunes of father and lover increased her devotion to them seven-fold.

Mr. Hartley was a true friend to her in her distress; not only giving wordy solace, but active assistance. He engaged a good legal firm in their behalf, and bespoke able counsel. Moreover, he overlooked the accounts of the farm-bailiff, and gave such general supervision as kept things in order at home.

She, poor girl, spent much of her time with old Mrs. Raby, who, like her husband, refused to be comforted for the loss or her son.

Time went by, sorrow in the farms—sadness in the gaol!

Even Joe Hodgson's brave heart sunk under the influence of his confinement. There was little or no separation of untried prisoners, and their days were spent among criminals of the worst description.

In about a month the piper was brought into their midst sorely changed by fever. His shaggy locks had been cut or shaven away, and a thick grisled stubble was rising on his poll like a beard a fortnight old.

There was little light in that cramped and stifling prison room. At first the piper saw only a number of strangers; but his eye lighting on Mr. Hodgson and Luke Raby, who advanced to greet him, his start of recognition was accompanied by a quick spasm of pain over his bronzed face.

"Wha wad hae thocht o' meeting ye in siccan a place as this? It canna be for gieing food and rest to a sinking auld man that ye hae been brought hither. Guid guide us! I had better hae died wi my Allan than lived to see sae sad a day. Wae's me! wae's me!"

He had begged for his pipes, and brought them with him. At once he began a wild lament that filled the prison walls, seeming to gather consolation from his strain.

As the days went by, his old spirit came back to him. He played lilts and strathspeys, and the more reckless prisoners, clearing a space, danced roughly to his music.

At times he vented his feelings in "Charlie is my darling," "Blue bonnets over the Borders," "Wha wadna fecht for Charlie," and other equally patriotic airs. At first the gaolers stopped his Jacobite tunes with threats to take away his pipes; but after a time they ceased to trouble themselves, being probably glad to have the cheerless monotony of their own prison-life broken by the inspiriting melodies.

His pipes had a good effect in rousing the prisoners sinking beneath their own individual sorrows, or lapsing into moodiness from lack of occupation. The very prison walls, cut and carved with rude devices of ships and flowers and animals, told plainly how time lagged even with men whose days were numbered. Dugald therefore was to such men as a beneficent spirit, and many were the blessings he received from lips which were more apt to curse than to bless.

At long intervals Hannah was permitted to visit her father. These were painful interviews. There was no privacy. Even her presence could not restrain loose tongues and coarse jests; and both Luke and he shrank from her introduction into such a den. Mr. Hartley was ever her kind attendant, but even he was unwilling to prolong her stay.

The day of trial came at last. The court was crowded; for both the prisoners had many friends; whilst the lawyer had a still larger number of "good haters," open and secret.

We have no space to report the trial, we can only give results Joseph Hodgson was found guilty of harbouring the rebel Dugald Macpherson, and Luke Raby of aiding and abetting his escape; but as no proof of "guilty knowledge" was forthcoming, and as they had already suffered some months' incarceration, and were known for loyal subjects, their punishment was remitted to a fine, heavy, it is true—but still a fine, and within their means.

Dugald Macpherson was not likely to escape so readily. His course had been traced from Clifton Bridge, and there was little doubt but the gallows would be his doom.

In the course of the proceedings it transpired that he had lost a son in the skirmish near Penrith; and had a second in the Pretender's army.

On the mention of his sons, Dugald became very excited, spoke vehemently, and could not be restrained. Thereupon one of the counsel present rose and said, "Then, my lord, it would be this prisoner's other son, Sandy Macpherson, whom I saw hanged at Carlisle with a number of like rebels, when the Duke of Cumberland re-took the town. I recognise the resemblance between father and son."

Dugald clutched at the rail before him, his face and throat worked convulsively. "What! Sandy, my Sandy, Sandy Macpherson hangit like a dog!" he shrieked more than spoke, and dropped down in a fit.

He was removed insensible, and sentence was deferred.

Judge and jury alike pitied the old man, whose last hope was so rudely snapped.

When an hour later he was brought back for judgment, he looked round vacantly, seemingly unconscious of his situation.

He was condemned—not to the gallows, but to be imprisoned for life, a sentence by many there thought far too lenient for a *rebel*, and there were undertoned mutterings of Jacobite tendencies in the presiding judge.

He was simply a man and a father, and could feel for the Scotch piper in his misery.

Dugald was taken back to his prison-cell, but henceforth he became inane and imbecile. He would have occasional flashes of reason, but rarely. His sole delight was to finger his pipes, and to play martial or melancholy music as his moods alternated.

Dugald's sad condition tempered the rejoicings at Hope House on the release of Mr. Hodgson and Luke, the close intercourse in prison having created a strong feeling of attachment to the piper, who bore up so bravely under his own misfortunes, and was ever so ready to lighten the load of others.

Simeon Crawlaw had little reason to rejoice in his revenge. He was openly hooted at as an "informer," his clients left him, his agencies were taken from him; he removed to a distant county, but odium followed him whithersoever he went; he sank deeper and deeper into poverty, and died in the Fleet Prison.

Before he left he had the mortification to see Hannah and Luke married, while yet the trees were red and russet; and to hear the good wishes which followed them from rich and poor. Mr. Hartley was there, and gave the bride away.

Ere the week was out, the young couple visited Dugald in the prison, by special permission, and many times afterwards.

He knew them, and appeared gratified, but seemed to be no longer troubled by his position. He still clung to his pipes, and so solaced himself and other hearts more keenly alive to die sense of imprisonment. And who can tell how much good he unconsciously effected? Discipline was relaxed in his favour, and when the following autumn young Mrs. Raby's first born was baptised by his name he was permitted to visit the farm and pipe for the company.

Whether his scattered wits were recalled by the scene or the company, they could not tell; but his senses were restored in the short visit.

The return to prison after that brief taste of freedom and fresh air was too much for him; he sank into sadness, ceased to play his pipes, and lost his strength rapidly.

A gaoler had been well bribed to let the family at Hope House know if any change for the worse came over him. On Christmas Eve they thus learned that he was dying, and hastened to the poor piper's bedside in that stone cell, which even the money they gave freely for the purpose could not make comfortable.

He was sinking fast when they saw him; but rallied, asked for his pipes once more, began to play "The King shall hae his ain again," and dropped back dead as the cathedral bells rang out the Christmas peal in honour of the birth of that great King who breaks the prison walls and sets the captive free.

But the piper never left the precincts of Elvet Bridge whilst a stone of the prison was left standing.

From the riverside, up Elvet steps, along the bridge, and Magdalen steps, under the North Gate, and into the gaol his spirit was seen to pass every Christmas Day morning; and every midnight his pipes might be heard in the prison cells, playing his Jacobite airs, even when Jacobinism had died out.

The gaol came down, and now not a vestige of the old prison remains to mark the spot which had for so many decades been, haunted by The Piper's Ghost.

St. Cuthbert's Cup: A Legend of Hell-Kettles, Darlington

CHAPTER 1

Hugh Pudsey was Bishop of Durham. Whether he was son or nephew of King Stephen is not decided; but it is certain that he lived in stormy times, and that stormy work attended and succeeded his translation from the Treasury of York to the Bishopric of Durham. The Conquest was a wrong of too recent date, and the rule of the intruders too oppressive for the Saxon monks of St. Cuthbert's shrine to welcome readily the Norman prelate nominated by their Norman king. His youth (he was but twenty-five), his secular life and conversation, the freedom of his morals (he had then three natural sons), his extravagance in dress, were all raised in objection; and as the monks at that time held the right of election, they might have set him aside in favour of one of their own body, if either Prior or Archdeacon, the rival candidates, would have waived his own claim to the Episcopal chair.

Nor did he find that chair exactly cushioned with roses; at all events thorns were plentiful, and sharp enough to make him restless and uncomfortable. Shortly after his own installation, the election of a new prior, in 1154, gave him hopes of quiet rule, for Prior Absolon was a man of inferior capacity and attainments, and too weak to resist strong hand or strong mind. But his hope was short-lived. Within the year Henry II. had succeeded Stephen on the English throne, and with all his mother's wrongs burnt in his brain, he was not likely to look favourably on Stephen's *protégé* enthroned in the North, with a large body of feudal retainers to maintain his princely state.

Whether as a measure of annoyance, or of precaution against a possible foe, Henry commanded the prelate to render a return of the lands within his diocese held on military tenure, their occupation and values. To this Royal edict Durham owes the remarkable *Boldon Book*, (so called from the place where the survey was commenced—Boldon), still extant amongst its archives—the doomsday-book of the palatinate. This was on the marriage of the Princess Maud, and the pretext that of levying an aid.

Whatever was the king's true motive for desiring such return the effects were anything but prejudicial to the bishop, who thus became more intimately acquainted with the condition and resources of his province. It drew him into closer relations with the knights and barons, and found clerkly work for those monks in whom inaction begot disaffection.

How he dealt with his contumacious monastics may be told in few words. On one occasion he surrounded the Durham convent with a military cordon, and starved them into submission; on another destroyed their fish reservoirs, and later killed all their cattle in Bearpark.

Nevertheless, Durham owes much to his energy and public enterprise. He restored the borough of Elvet (destroyed by Comyn, the Usurper), built Elvet Bridge, and completed the City Wall, and gave the inhabitants their first charter.

But he listened to tattlers and mischief-makers, and these made him irritable, distrustful, and finally impelled him to build himself a palace on the very verge of his palatinate—at Derlyngton—on the banks of the Dare (or Skerne).

Whilst these erections were in progress he was in progress too, that is, he, a man embroiled with his sovereign, embroiled with his ecclesiastics, travelled in state with a large retinue to and fro to superintend and urge forward the works he had in hand; caring little how much he oppressed the Saxon franklins and serfs the feudal laws compelled to do him service. Posterity profited, but his subjects groaned under their bondage.

Amongst the secular vassals of the church none bowed more reverently to St. Cuthbert's prelate than Lord Eustace De Eden, of Castle Eden; none held him in less regard than did Sir William De Turp, who held adjoining lands in Eden Dene, and did knight's service to Eustace as his superior lord.

He was a stern, dark-browed, discontented man, was William De Turp, a man soured by disappointments, to whose lot had fallen land, but not the wealth to turn his barren acres to account, or maintain a Norman retinue sufficient to awe his Saxon *feors* and slaves into abject submission.

The death of Stephen had driven him from court, to the less congenial atmosphere of his own Thorpe,(farm or grange, together with the village surrounding or attached thereto), where, but for occasional quarrels with warlike neighbours, his knightly armour seemed likely to rust.

Dame Elinor, his wife, was a mild, gentle woman, and it might seem at first glance they were unfitly mated. But in her presence his stern brows relaxed, and his moods softened. She offered no opposition to the will of her lord, and so they came not into collision. She was, as ladies of her rank were, the directress of the household; her daughters, Matilda and Emma, plied their rapid bobbins in the production of tapestry, or twirled the distaff amongst their bowerwomen to spin yarn for the websters of Durham to weave into cloth for the family.

Dame Elinor was accomplished as the times went, having in a Norman convent learned not only to read and write, to embroider and spin, but to play the zithern and illuminate the missal she had herself transcribed; and more, she had learned to feed the hungry, shelter the houseless, and heal the sick and the wounded. And what she had learned she transmitted to her daughters, alike by instruction and example. They, however, differed in many respects; Matilda, with the dark eyes and hair of her father, had inherited also his lofty port, his ambitious longings, and pined for restoration to the courtly scenes of which the minstrels sang, and from which she in the fullness of her maiden bloom was excluded.

The brown-eyed Emma had few desires beyond the limits of their home and the beautiful dene. She was quiet and unobtrusive, and pious to superstition. This was not wholly due to the influence of the monks of St. Cuthbert, for though they were busied in building the chapel of St. James on the land in the dene, granted by Robert de Brus, and confirmed to them by charter from Eustace de Eden, and consequently drew largely on the hospitality of the surrounding proprietary, the few who cared to brook Sir William's surly welcome were of the class more inclined to join him in feasting and drinking than in fasting and prayer.

But in a natural recess, at the farthest extremity of the dene, lived Godric the Hermit, near enough to hear the roar and wash of the sea, yet sheltered from the fierce blasts which sometimes swept up the valley, behind the projecting rock, in a cleft of which his rude hermitage of wattled boughs had been constructed. Near and far had spread the fame of the holy man; pilgrims and devotees came by land and sea to ask his prayers, his blessing, and his counsel; and it was his influence which had moulded the plastic mind of Emma to higher and holier aims than those of mere earth.

Barely, in those lawless times, did women above the peasant class venture far abroad unattended; but the tide of battle had hitherto swept other lands than those of the secluded dene, while for common marauders the castle was too strong and well-guarded, and the Thorpe possessed little to repay a raid. So, in negative security, Emma was wont to pass to and fro unaccompanied by other than Getha her maid, save on those rare occasions when Matilda or Dame Elinor herself sought the cell of the good hermit for confession or consolation. There was little to distinguish the two damsels as they threaded the mazes of the wooded dene, or followed the common pathway by the stream, enveloped in long-hooded cloaks, save the texture of the homespun cloth, and the rich brooch which secured that of the mistress at the throat.

But when the cloak was laid aside, and revealed the closely-fitting, open-sleeved tunic of embroidered linen, above the green woollen kirtle which drooped to the very shoes, the richly-ornamented pouch suspended from her gold-buckled girdle, the abundant hair which hung behind in two thick plaits far below her waist, contrasted strongly with the homely robe of Getha, long and loose, confined round the waist by a plain band of leather, and marked at once the difference of their rank and birth.

From the first dawn of womanhood Emma's wont had been to bring the pious anchorite such offerings in the way of eggs, honey, barley cakes, or fruit as would be most likely acceptable to one whose diet was spare to abstinence, and whose daily wants were supplied much as were those of Elijah by the brook Cherith. Little knew she that the stern ascetic never ate the eggs until addled, nor the cakes until mouldy. And for two or three years the budding maiden tripped lightly on her errands of charity and devotion with single-minded purpose; then when the bud blossomed into sweet seventeen, another element was introduced, another motive was superadded.

Her dress required more adjusting for the walk, and as she neared the hermitage her step was less firm, her colour came and went, her glance strayed timidly but expectantly, and within her breast was a faint fluttering as of the wings of an imprisoned dove.

We have said that many penitents and pilgrims sought the saintly

Godric's cell; and one spring day, when the sun was high and the dene was vocal with the songs and twitterings of pairing birds, and the infant leaves were feeling their way into the sunshine, Emma and Getha were startled by seeing a light skiff moored within a short distance of the hermitage.

******

The entrance to Castle Eden Dene in these days is much too confined to admit a boat—what it may have been so many centuries back is another matter.

******

Fain would she have retreated within the shadow of the woods until the boatman should have gone his way; but ere she could make her will known to her companion, the door of the hermitage opened, and she stood within a few paces of a well-formed, clear-eyed youth, whose length of cloak and length of yellow hair betokened him a Saxon, whilst the texture of the one and the golden fillet which bound the other bespoke his rank at least equal to her own. He had stooped in order to pass through the low doorway; but raising his head, an exclamation at once of surprise and admiration burst from his lips—he had not dreamed to see so fair a sight in that lonely place.

Their eyes met, and those of Emma fell abashed before his earnest enquiring gaze, whilst the quick blood flushed her face with the crimson veil of modesty, and her prompt hand drew closer the sheltering folds of her hood.

Rebuked by the action, the young man withdrew his ardent gaze, but not before his sudden exclamation had brought the hermit to the door also. Perceiving the maiden, and guessing the cause of her confusion, Godric advanced a step or two to meet her, saying, "Benedicite, my daughter; pass within with thy handmaiden. I will hear thy errand *anon.*"

With one deep reverence to him and a second to the rude symbol of Christianity carved above the entrance, Emma obeyed, followed by Getha, who, turning to have another glance at the handsome stranger, overheard Godric say, as if in continuation, "And do thou, Alan, turn thy bark swiftly homewards, the winds will rise ere long. The sea-birds seek the land, and thou wilt need all thy strength to reach thy haven ere the storm comes on. Go, with my blessing to speed thy oars!"

"Nay, good father, thou art surely mistaken; the breeze has scarcely strength to ring the bells of yonder hyacinths; though I mind me it blew aside the folds of thy fair penitent's hood, revealing a vision of beauty to my unprepared sight. Holy father, cometh the sweet lady often to her shrift? And wilt thou not tell me what name to remember her by?"

"My son, my son, said I not ere now this would be a day of peril to thee? Go thy ways, whilst thou may. Ukillus de Hoton would scarcely care to hear that his beloved son had looked with fascinated eyes on the child of William de Turp. Go, and the blessed St. Cuthbert be thy shield."

Alan had been slowly (very slowly) loosing his tiny craft from her moorings, his thoughts running in rapid unspoken commentary on the hermit's words—"Peril! I fear me no peril greater than from those soft brown eyes!" But at the name of the damsel's sire he started. There was not much cordiality between the Saxon thane and the Norman knight.

"William de Turp!" he exclaimed in surprise; "William de Turp! I ever heard his heiress was dark and tall, and commanding as her imperious father. This maid seems timid and gentle as a cushat-dove. Her name, good father, her name?"

"She is the younger born, my son; I myself baptized her Emma, and, as thou rightly sayest, she does resemble the dove. But we waste words, and time; and thou hast none to waste. Pray to the saints to guard thee on the sea: thou wilt have need of prayers. *Pax vobiscum.*"

The swift current of the Eden bore the frail skiff rapidly inward to the open sea, though the tide was on the turn, and breakers were advancing. The wind, too, had changed; the distant sky looked threatening; but Alan, the son of Ukillus, had been blinded to the aspect of the weather by that one brief glance from Emma's dove-like eyes.

Emma had withdrawn the inquisitive Getha from the open doorway before her ears had caught much more than the: stranger's name; and assuming her young mistress to be as curious as herself, she decided in her pique to keep the information a secret.

During the absence of the holy man, Emma had laid her simple tribute of wild flowers gathered in the wood, blue hyacinths, sweet lilies of the valley, the purple orchis, the red-crane's bill, before the shrine of St. Cuthbert; and her short shrift over, Getha's prolix confession was austerely abbreviated by the hermit, who bade them hasten homewards, nor loiter by the way.

"Repeat thy *Aves*, *Paternoster*, and *Credo* tonight earnestly, if ever thou didst in thy life. Pray, too, for the souls of all who Are dear to thee, my daughter," said the holy man, with more than his wonted solemnity. "I hear the first pantings of the storm wind, and I must to my knees, for I know that I shall hear more than the shriek of the whirlwind. Evil spirits are let loose, and the foul fiend himself heads his demon host. The Holy Virgin will protect innocents like thee, my pious child, but woe betide those whose path he crosses, whilst evil passions rage within their breasts!"

Chapter 2

Struck by Godric's solemn warning, the two girls sped onwards; but ere they had compassed half the distance, the hermit's prescience was justified. At first a low moaning filled the shrinking woods, then with a sob and a shriek the blast came on and tore the budding branches and tender leaflets from the trees, which swayed, and writhed, and groaned, and tossed their arms abroad like human beings in extremity. The sky darkened, the rain came down, the torrent chafed and roared, their path was impeded by fallen boughs, and ere they reached the uplands and the Thorpe, their thick woollen cloaks were drenched, their long robes torn by the beating brambles.

At the first hut in the hamlet they rested a few moments to wring the wet from their garments and recover breath, and fain, would Getha have remained by the serfs peat fire, but Emma, fearing her good mother would be anxious, rejected the suggestion that Mildred, the thrall's wife, or Osric, his son, might be sent on with an assurance of safety.

"They are dry and sheltered—let them remain so. We cannot be in worse plight than we are," answered she, with a consideration as rare in those times as in ours.

They found the Thorpe in commotion.

Two sea-fowlers, Edred and Oswy, driven from their occupation, had remained near the cliffs to watch the progress of the hurricane. They had seen a boat with a single occupant, tossed and driven by the winds and waves like a leaf upon the waters; nearer and nearer it came with every roller; though the oarsman strained and fought against the raging sea-horses with their manes of foam. But they raced with him to the rocks, and beat his bark to splinters, casting him forth that they might devour him too. He was young and strong and nervous, and still fought for life with the billows. He grasped a rock, its shiny surface slipped from beneath his hand; again and again he strove, and at last maintained his grip. As he raised himself, clinging to the weedy boulder whence the next billow might wash him away, he heard the sound of a human voice from the cliff above.

At the risk of his life, Edred the fowler descended in wonted manner, secured a second rope round the half-drowned man, and, aided by his fellow above, contrived, with such assistance as the poor fellow could himself render, to land him safely on the cliff. There he sank exhausted. Between them they bore him away, until meeting a serf with a load of peat in his ox-cart, they removed part of the load, and carried him in the rude conveyance to the Thorpe, certain of Dame Elinor's approval.

Torn and drenched as were his clinging garments, they told he was of no mean order, and Dame Elinor—her pity for his helpless condition no doubt enhanced by his youth and comeliness—ordered fresh garments and a bed to be prepared, and busied herself about his restoration, the preparation of hot possets, and the dressing of cuts and bruises inflicted by the pitiless limestone crags; not forgetting to reward the brave men to whom the stranger owed his life.

In these active duties of matronly humanity. Dame Elinor almost forgot her own anxieties; but, as the senseless youth revived under her care, came back with redoubled force the consciousness that daughter and husband were both abroad exposed to the raging storm; whilst darkness was fast gathering over the hearth.

So, when Emma and Getha reached the Thorpe, the hall door stood open, and, hurrying down the path, came several men with torches and horn-lanterns in quest of them.

Now was Dame Elinor perplexed. Fain would she have sent the serfs on to scour the country, and light the homeward footsteps of her lord; but his moods were capricious, and he might resent as prying interference any tracking of his movements, even though his own security demanded it.

Expressing her doubts to Matilda and Emma, each of whom gave a different opinion, she was overheard by Oswy the fowler, who, being a freeman, held the dread knight in less awe than did his own slaves. The man roughly but kindly volunteered to scour the neighbourhood with Edred, as if on an errand of their own, and should they encounter Sir William, render him what service he required, for the sake of his good lady.

The night wore on. Matilda and Emma had retired, the latter thoroughly worn out, and wondering if the rescued man were the same she had met on Godric's threshold.

The curfew sounded; torches and candles were put out, the .servants crept to their straw beds in the dark, yet Dame Elinor was still a watcher for her lord. She still kept a taper burning on its spiked candlestick, but its rays were jealously guarded and scarcely afforded a glimmer whereby to con the missal she vainly attempted to read. The crickets chirped monotonously on the hearth, mice left their corners to feast on crumbs and fragments amongst the rushes on the floor, the grey owl hooted from the barn, bats flew against the horn windows, which trembled in the blast, that, piercing every crevice, shook the tapestry on the dais, and the mastiff in the garth, (enclosed land near a dwelling; a courtyard), howled ominously between the lightning flashes and peals of thunder which disturbed his canine dreams. And still Dame Elinor was an anxious, fearful, solitary watcher.

In the fresh beauty of the springtide morn, Sir William, hawk, on hand, and hound at heel, had gone forth with such attendants as he could boast, to join a hawking party assembled at Castle Eden by Lord Eustace. But all things went ill with the knight, Bishop Pudsey was there, and Robert Fitzmaldred, Lord of Raby, and his proud betrothed, Isabel Neville, of Brancepeth, were also among the guests, and my lord's jester did not scruple to twit De Turp on his scant retinue and their faded apparel. Then his mare cast a shoe, his hawk stooped not true to the quarry, and was not easy to reclaim, and Motley's coarse jests thereon were greeted with approving laughter.

In angry mood when far afield he dismounted, cast the reins to Bertrand his page, gave the falcon to her feeder, bade them "back to the Thorpe," then whistling his hound, strode moodily away in an opposite direction to chew the cud of his own bitter and wrathful reflections, heeding not, caring not, whither his footsteps led.

Wild, rugged and little cultivated was the east of Durham then; bleak moors, intersected with limestone rocks and picturesque ravines through which the mountain streamlets sought the sea, with some dark patches of primeval forest; oak and ash, elm and beech, and here and there a sombre group of pine to tell of seed sown by Norseland invaders.

William de Turp was far from Eden Dene when he plunged into one of these thick woods as if to hide himself and his gloomy thoughts from mortal eye, regardless that not the spring; leafage but gathering clouds made the shrouding darkness. Meanwhile he strode on, chafing, fuming, scowling, and uttering fearful maledictions on himself and the untoward fortunes which made him a fair mark for a fool's shafts. The storm broke in its fury, but to the raging storm within his breast it was

115

but as the echo of a battle-song. He heeded not the crashing boughs, the drenching rain, the blinding lightning, the pealing thunder; the elements were at war with earth, but he was at war with. God!

Lupus, his hound, crouched and whined, and slunk behind his master as in abject terror. He turned and with a curse kicked the poor brute. At once the forest seemed ablaze, the thunder rattled overhead, and a whirlwind rushed with terrific shrieks through the wood.

In the prolonged flash he beheld a tall figure leaning complacently with folded arms against the bare straight trunk of a lofty pine, where his eye had discerned no one the instant before. A lordly-looking man, with hawkish nose and lip sardonically curled, his hair and eyes black as midnight, the latter glowing beneath cavernous brows like coals of fire, his eyebrows (like two modern notes of interrogation) the slant lines meeting in the middle, then rising in a sudden arch from the curve of the brow towards the temples. It was a face to remember and dread. His dress was fearful as his features. From head to heel he was clad in what seemed black, but it was shot with a lustrous sheen of crimson, and its hue alternated with every movement. A drooping crimson plume was bound to his black cap by a huge carbuncle, whilst a second flamed on his sword-hilt, and a third clasped his cloak at the throat.

William de Turp, startled involuntarily, sought his sword, a movement answered by the strange knight with a mocking laugh, which seemed echoed in every avenue of the wood.

"So," said he of the crimson plume, "thou art at war with fate, and knowest not how to better thy fortunes!"

"Who art thou? and what dost thou know of me, or of my fortunes?" demanded Sir William, imperiously.

"Men call me variously. To thee I am thy friend of the Fiery-plume; and I am here to serve thee. Strike hands upon the offer!" and the dark speaker put forth his hand.

"I accept nor friendship nor service from strangers," rejoined De Turp haughtily, rejecting the proffered hand.

Again the mocking laugh rang through the forest, and a strange thrill ran through the knight's veins.

"Wait until Leo the Jew forecloses his mortgage, and thy lands and tenements pass from thee and thine for ever. But perhaps as Bishop Pudsey and his shavelings find seventeen *marks* to release Eustace De Eden from the grip of the Jew, thou lookest for like priestly aid in *thy* extremity?" suggested the fiery-plumed stranger with a leer.

"Now, the foul fiend seize Lord Eustace and the drivelling monks likewise, if that be true!" exclaimed the baited man impetuously.

"All in good time, my friend; but it is true as that thy bond and his alike fall due on Friday, and that thou art unprepared. But I owe these men no love, and would serve *thee*. Thou and I are near of kin."

"Of kin? I know thee not!"

"But I know *thee*," and the black eyes twinkled like fiery stars. "I know thou wouldst feed daintily, carouse merrily, drink wines, not mead or cider, have a full purse and a full retinue, with mettled steeds and costly raiment, wouldst vie with the baron thou servest, and have thy revenge on Leo, the Jew of York."

"*I would give my very soul for all thou sayest!*" broke, impetuously and vehemently from the white lips of the knight.

"Give me thy hand upon the bargain, and thou shalt have all—and more than thou dreamest," said the tempter.

"If thou canst redeem thy pledge, here is my hand. But what dost thou require in lieu?" and he held out his hand, which the other gripped, replying with strange emphasis:

"No more than thou hast *proffered*, I have set my seal upon the compact. We are friends henceforth."

A scorching pain seemed to sear the palm he held, and when released the impress of his hand was redly marked on that of William De Turp. A nameless horror thrilled through the man's brain, for the first time conscious with whom he had to deal, and the awful nature of his contract.

Again that hideous laugh rang out, blue lightnings played amid the trees, and heaven's artillery rattled overhead. Heavy drops—not of rain—stood on William's forehead; and he who had braved the storm erewhile trembled at the new significance it bore.

"Nay, man, take heart, and give the Devil his due; he ever keeps his word," said his gruesome interlocutor, fitful flashes of bright crimson lighting up his robe and the three carbuncles, which seemed to flame in the darkness as he moved. "Take a draught of my wine; it will give thee courage man, and, *keep the cup*; it is my gift to thee."

A love of wine was William de Turp's besetting sin, nor food nor drink had passed his lips since morn; his throat was parched, his limbs were faint; a fragrant aroma floated from the cup; he could not resist the temptation; but taking the proffered vessel drank long and heartily, and as he drank seemed to become another man.

The cup or vase was of greenish blue glass, curiously constructed and ornamented. It narrowed bottle-wise at the neck, but round it ranged two rows of trumpet-shaped tubes, their slender tips closed, their wider ends opening like gaping mouths within.

"Mark well that cup, and guard it well; each lobe upon its surface is a horn of plenty. Dost thou lack wine, the upper row will give thee choice of vintage. Dost thou lack gold, or gems, or help, or counsel, seek them from the lower tubes. It is a gift of price, and will not lose its potency *until it finds its counterpart*: for it has a counterpart, fashioned by the same hand, but endowed with other and opposing properties. *Thou* art scarce like to meet its fellow. It is in safe keeping, and whilst thou keepest thy home from monkish intruders thy prize is secure. Farewell, my *friend!*"

He of the glowing eyes and fiery plume was gone; and but for the charmed cup within his clasp, and the burning mark on his right hand, William de Turp had thought the whole a dream.

Chapter 3

With the dawn the household was astir. The patient night-watcher sought the rude pallet of the wrecked youth, subordinating her private troubles to the sacred duties of hospitality. She found him stiff and sore with his bruises, feverish, restless, yet unable to rise. No question had been made of his name or condition; but when in reply to his enquiries he was told that he was under the roof of William de Turp, a troubled look settled on his face, across which flashed a sudden gleam of joy, as bright as it was transitory.

"Thy mother, good youth, will be anxious for thy safety. The men who brought thee hither wait in the lower hall, and would convey to thy home assurance of welfare, if such be thy desire and the distance within compass of willing feet. They bade me say thus much to thee."

"I thank them and thee, good lady. I have no mother, but Ukillus de Hoton will be full of apprehensions, which only the presence of his son Alan can allay. I must depart at once."

Better than the gentle dame did Alan know that the roof of William de Turp was no safe shelter for his father's son; and though Elinor felt bound as a Christian woman to press his stay until recovery, she yielded to his judgment, and her compunctious visitings were tempered by a sense of relief when in a hastily-constructed litter Oswy and Edred bore him from the Thorpe.

Other hands besides Dame Elinor's had helped to place his bandaged head and bruised limbs in the least painful position.

It was Emma who brought the softest cushion, it was she whose kerchief, steeped in scented waters, was pressed to his nostrils, and wiped the dew from his brow when he fainted on removal; it was she who undertook to bear assurance of his safety to the hermit; it was she to whom his last and most intense look of gratitude was directed, and the responsive blush on her fair cheek gave him more strength than all Dame Elinor's simples.

Who can tell whether accident or design left the maiden's kerchief in the litter? Who save a lover could tell how oft that kerchief, through weeks and months to come, was pressed to the lips of Alan.

Men might be cast in sterner mould in those days than in these, but they were men nevertheless.

The sun was high in the heavens, and the midday meal was waiting (to the intense disgust of the cook), when William de Turp entered his own hall, darker, sterner, gloomier than his wont. He bore no question even from his favourite Matilda, and when affectionate Elinor would have examined his scarred hand, he cast her off impatiently, muttering something of "hurt by a falling bough," with a gruff curse for "curious women."

None cared to ask whence came the vase of wondrous workmanship which he placed on the board at his right hand; or whence the mysterious dumb black servitor who displaced Bertrand as cupbearer and page to the knight. But there were secret murmurings in the household, and from gossiping Getha to the meanest swineherd all marvelled why from the night or the great storm Lupus avoided his master's presence, and when called came reluctantly, whining and cowering.

Friday—the day dreaded by Dame Elinor and her daughters, who knew just enough of the mortgage to Leo, the Jew of York, to make them wretched—came, and with it came the Jew, mounted on a sleek mule, accompanied by a sumpter-mule, and guarded by four or five stout fellows who seemed more ready to give blows than to take them.

Dame Elinor and Emma were weeping together in her chamber at the sad prospect before them, and Matilda pacing the floor with clenched hands and angry hectic cheeks, when Getha came with hasty step to say Sir William demanded their presence in the great hall. Serfs and domestics were there before them, and there stood Leo the Jew, his customary cringe mocked by an air of secret triumph. Sir William, with a scowl upon his brow and a strange light in his eye, strode impatiently to and fro.

Waving the ladies to their seats upon the dais, and assuming his own, he said, "Leo of York, I owe thee thirteen *marks*, is it not so?"

"Thou dost," answered the Jew, briefly.

"And thon hast a mortgage on my lands and tenements for the sum?"

"I have."

"Thou knowest that money is hard to come by, Leo, that I have had losses and mischances—what grace wilt thou give me? If I pay thee part, how long wilt thou forbear to press for the remainder?"

"Not a day—not an hour! so help me Moses! Haf I borne the costs of a journeys from York to wait? Nay, nay, I must, haf de monish or I foreclose."

William de Turp made a signal to his black mute, who with a *salaam* left the hall.

"Will not Hugh Pudsey, or his monks of St. Cuthbert, pay the costs of thy journey when they release thy bond over Eustace de Eden with seventeen *marks?* Eh! Jew?"

The Jew stood aghast! "How knew you of mine transactions with your lord? Hath treachery or sorcery revealed it?"

The knight's answer was a scornful smile. The mute placed a brass-bound casket on the table, which none remembered to have seen before. From it he took a handful of gold, and counting down thirteen *marks* on the board, said loudly, "I call all present to witness I pay these thirteen *marks* to Leo the Jew of York, in release of a bond he holds, since he will not give me grace '*for a day, for an hour,*' and now, Jew," said he in a changed tone, "hand me the mortgage, and the release, and take thyself and all thy belongings from my land ere the sun be an hour older, or I will hew thee limb from limb, and cast thy accursed carcase to the hounds."

Astonishment and fear fell on all, for the knight's poverty was no secret. The usurious Jew gathered up the gold, gave the lawful quittance, and without a second bidding hurried off to keep his appointment with Sir Eustace de Eden and the monks of Durham, more in fear lest the Sabbath of his race should find him trafficking than he was of the grim Sir William's threat.

That a half-drowned man, rescued from the waves, had received a night's hospitality under his roof, was too slight a matter to attract attention in the knight's mood, and the stranger's name and lineage did not then transpire.

Besides his hereditary land around the Thorpe, William held the manor of Oxenhall, near Darlington, under the Bishop of Durham. Under his tenure he had a horse-mill, and was quit of multure and service to the bishop's mills, but his tenure bound him to certain services, such as ploughing, sowing, and harrowing fixed portions of the prelate's land, finding labourers in harvest-time, maintaining a horse and dog for the chase, and caning the Bishop's wine. And seeing that four oxen were required for that service, not only must the quantity of wine have been considerable, but the roads in a deplorable condition.

Other terms in the feudal tenure under which Oxenhall was held necessitated the frequent presence of Sir William at Oxenfields, now that the bishop's palace was in course of erection; and the only surprise evinced when he, accompanied by the mute, departed the following morning for Derlyngton, was that they were mounted on mettlesome steeds, black as Hamed's face, which had entered the Thorpe stables in the night none knew how.

If his errand was other than peaceful, none guessed it. But it so fell out that neither Leo the Jew nor the *marks* he had been paid ever found their way back to York. As he neared Northallerton, he and his escort were attacked by a band of armed men on sable steeds, their leader having fiery eyes and a crimson plume, and his companion a *cowed wolf* for his crest, (a seal of William de Turp bears a wolf *passant*, the tail cowed between the legs). The battle was to the strong, and but one of the Jew's men escaped with life enough in him to tell the tale.

William de Turp rapidly grew rich and powerful; a band of retainers well mounted and caparisoned gathered round him at Oxenhall; those who had jeered and sneered at him in his poverty were well content to hunt or hawk with him, to feast and drink with him in his prosperity. If wondering whispers were circulated concerning the source of his wealth, they were silenced by the remark that the knight had been a new man since he had discharged his debt to the Jew. How that had been discharged none were prepared to say.

A new man, certainly; but scarcely a better man. As his wealth and power increased, as neighbouring knights and barons sought his friendship and alliance, he grew more saturnine and gloomy. The cloud never lifted from his brow; the wine he drank so freely from his singular cup never warmed him to geniality, but inflamed to fierceness, and many were the lawless deeds he and his retainers did under its influence.

The Thorpe would have been well-nigh deserted had not Dame Elinor and Emma preferred its quietude to the noisy grandeur of

Oxenhall.

Not so Matilda; she was born for command and admiration; and whilst her mother and sister sat calmly spinning or stitching by the banks of the Eden, she queened it at her father's side amongst barons and noble dames on the banks of the Dare. Isabel of Brancepeth, whose gecks and scorn of William de Turp had borne such strange fruit, was the first to take the beauteous Matilda under her wing— a precedent rapidly followed by others. Minstrels sang her praises, knights splintered lances in assertion of her loveliness; and more then one put forth his claims to her hand. Amongst these the gallant Adam de Setoun shone conspicuously, and it was not long before Matilda herself betrayed her preference for her brave and courtly suitor.

In Matilda's lofty presence Emma's modest charms were little appreciated; but she seldom cared to quit the retirement of the Thorpe, and the heiress shone without a rival.

But deep in the recesses of the intricate dene Emma herself had lost her heart. Lost her heart and taken another in exchange.

Faithfully had she borne the rescued Alan's message to the hermit, and heard with echoing pulses his devout thanksgiving for the youth's safety.

"I had warned the son of Ukillus that that was a day of peril to him, and much I fear me that the peril is not past." And as he looked upon her kindling cheek he added, "I foresaw also peril to thee and thine; and in the visions of that night of storm discerned that *more than mortal* foes menaced the peace of thy house."

"Surely that brave but hapless youth can be no foe, good father!" she cried uneasily.

"Not a willing foe, my daughter, but the Saxon and the Norman are foes by birth, and thy sire holds his at bitter enmity. But tell me of thy sire. Hath aught befallen *him?*" And as he put the question he crossed himself devoutly and began to mutter an *ave,*

"Naught of evil, good Godric. He came not home until the storm had passed, and the young Saxon (she sighed) was far on his way homewards. But he brought with him a rare drinking-vessel, and a black slave, and—money to pay his debt to Leo of York."

"How acquired, thinkest thou? Men give not such things readily."

"We know not, holy father. He was more reserved even than his wont, and bore no question."

The white-bearded hermit shook his head. After a few moments' silent prayer he took from his girdle a small amulet.

"Take this blessed relic, my child; it is one of St. Cuthbert's beads, (fossils from the black-slate at Lindisfarn: *entrochi*), wear it ever about thy person, and here (from a recess in his cell he brought a flask) is holy water, sprinkle the threshold of thy chamber night and morn. Desire that Dame Elinor come hither."

It so happened that when next Emma and Getha came in sight of the hermitage, Alan, the son of Ukillus, was loitering near the doorway, showing few traces of his battle with the billows; a fine stalwart man of some three-and-twenty summers, whom either Saxon *thane* or Norman baron might have been proud to own as son.

The recognition was mutual; their greeting constrained. The first natural expressions of thanks and sympathetic enquiry over, silence ensued. But Getha, stumbling over a stone, shook the eggs out of her baskets, and the laughter of the young couple at her dismay did more to break down the barrier of reserve than half-a-dozen formal meetings.

From that time their devotions took another turn, and before long confessions were made—but not to the venerable Godric; and Getha simpered, kept a discreet distance, and as discreetly kept silence; wisely or unwisely time would show.

Difference of lineage was forgotten, or if remembered, the fears so engendered but made their stolen meetings in the dene more precious; though many were the tears Emma shed on her pillow over the secret she dared not reveal to her mother—for fear of her father's anger.

CHAPTER 4

Time sped on with its freight of human joys and woes. Seldom did William de Turp return to the Thorpe. Never but once did he set foot in his wife's chamber, and then, catching sight of the crucifix suspended by Godric's advice over the bed-head, he ran from the room with his hands clutched in his grisling hair, uttering a sharp yell—half-groan, half-shriek.

So, too, when he had dismounted at the hall door, he withdrew himself with a shudder from Elinor's embrace, and, pointing to the cross worn upon her breast, sternly bade her remove that symbol of superstition.

Bearing in mind the anchorite's injunctions, she did not dare to lay the cross aside, but concealed it within the folds of her upper garment; and the knight henceforth held aloof from his wife, even as Lupus still crouched and held aloof from him.

After a time he appointed one of his Norman vassals, named Rupert, *chatelain* of the Thorpe estate in his absence, deposing Nigel, the old steward, and assigning the new governor honourable place for bed and board. This man became an incubus on the household, serfs and *feors* groaned under his exactions and outrages. Dame and daughter shrank from his coarse familiarity. Complaint to Sir William was useless. His sole remark was, "Tush, tush! women are fools," accompanied by a scowl and a curl of the lip that forbade further remonstrance.

After his advent Emma's walks in beautiful Eden dene were restricted, her pious visits to the anchorite few and far between, meetings with Alan all but impossible. Whithersoever she turned she was sure to encounter the dark-browed *chatelain*; he seemed to dog her footsteps, and his free looks terrified her. Only in the privacy of her chamber was she secure from his detested presence.

The anchorite had long seen the growing attachment of the two young people, seen it with apprehension as to its results, but asceticism had not strained all the human blood out of his heart, which beat warmly beneath his iron jerkin; and pity mingled with his fears. He had been spiritual guide to both from childhood, had mortified his own flesh to spare theirs, and now, at Alan's entreaty, he left his cell, and, Walking barefoot many weary miles, sought the mansion of Ukillus to break the intelligence and obtain his sanction.

What arguments he used it boots not to know; suffice it that the Saxon *thane*, though at first irate that his son should seek to wed the child of his direst foe, the man who had usurped his father's house and lands, softened at length, on the assurance that the maiden was pure as she was lovely; and that Godric would undertake to bend William de Turp to assent also—if Allan marred not all by his impatience.

"It is not meet that a devotee of Heaven should busy himself with marrying and giving in marriage; but I have a mission to accomplish, a soul to rescue, and your young loves will strengthen me to battle with the powers of darkness," said Godric, raising Alan, who had prostrated himself at his feet in humble thanks.

Alan insisted on rowing the aged hermit back to his cell.

About a mile from the outlet of the Eden, they observed two men, one of whom was dangling from the cliff by a rope. "See," cried Alan, "I owe yon men a life; yet, strange enough, they seem to think the obligation theirs, not mine. More thankful to have done me service than willing to be thanked."

"Their grandsire, boy, was *thrall* unto thy grandsire when these lands were his, and in giving freedom to the *thrall* he gave gratitude to his descendants. *He cast bread upon the waters and thou hast found it after many days."*

A signal from the younger fowler caused Alan to quicken his strokes.

They found Emma and Getha resting on a stone by the hermitage, the former wrapped in thought, the latter idly flinging pebbles in the stream. Emma started to her feet, joy chased disappointment from her face, as Alan sprang to her side, and, undeterred by the presence of either Getha or the anchorite, clasped to his ardent breast the beloved maiden, now his own by a father's sacred sanction.

It was long since they had met. On all sides there was much to be asked and answered. Emma told that her gentle mother, anxious at her pallor and dejection, had won her secret from her only to greet it with a flood of apprehensive tears. She told, too, how Black Rupert watched and haunted her; of his repulsive demeanour towards herself; of his oppressive rule; of the terror he inspired. Here Getha, in a voice subdued by fear, put in, "There is something awful and uncanny about him. The hounds whine when he goes nigh them, and two unbaptised babes have disappeared from the Thorpe since he came."

The hermit looked troubled. "Leave me," said he; "painful vigils, penitential prayers, and mortification of the flesh can alone enable me to conquer." Then extending his hands in benediction, he said, "Blessings be on both of you, my children, and St. Cuthbert guard you from your foes;" then abruptly entering his cell, he bolted close the door as if to shut out the world with them, and before they left the spot they heard the scourge in self-inflicted penance on the bare shoulders of the saint.

If ever Emma had needed protection through the Dene, Alan felt that it was necessary now. With one arm round her in affectionate guardianship, his ready sword in his right hand, and Getha close in the rear, he bore her company.

More than half the distance was traversed; when a sudden exclamation from Getha caused Emma and Alan to look up. Gleaming through the thicket above, they saw the evil face and eyes of Rupert leering down upon them with inexpressible malevolence. Alan darted forward, a fallen bough intercepted him; when he reached the spot the man was gone, but the echoes of a low laugh floated through the dene. Not until they reached the Thorpe did Alan quit his charge, and then with all a lover's lingering loathfulness to part.

Hastily retracing his steps to the boat, discarding the beaten track, bounding over one impediment, clearing another with his sword, he was suddenly beset by three or four men, who sprang upon him unawares. But his sword was out, and he was skilled in its use. Setting his back against an oak, he battled desperately, inflicting wounds with every stroke. Odds, however, will triumph over skill; he had received more than one flesh wound, when, with wild shouts, two men, armed with quarter-staves, came to his assistance. One of the ruffians fled. The others soon lay bleeding and disabled on the trampled ground.

A second time was Alan indebted to Edred and Oswy for safety.

There had been some love passages between Oswy and Getha, and seeing these men (known to be creatures of Rupert) skulking about the path she had taken with her mistress, love took alarm. He called his brother, and they followed in time to save, not helpless women, but a brave man, sorely beset.

Before the week was out, a mounted escort arrived with a peremptory summons for Dame Elinor and Mistress Emma to join Sir William at Oxenhall. To their terror, Black Rupert joined their escort.

They found Oxenflelds in a bustle of preparation. On Christmas Day Matilda was to wed with Adam De Setoun, and but three weeks were wanting of the term. Much did Dame Elinor marvel whence came the costly silks, and furs, and jewels, so lavishly provided, not only for the bride, but for herself and Emma, and she shrank with secret dread from the suggestions of her own heart, as the warnings of Godric pressed upon her mind, coupled with the fitful moods of her lord, alternating as they did between savage sullenness and intemperate frenzy.

Even Matilda was not so blinded by the unwonted magnificence of her new surroundings as to shut her eyes altogether on the strangeness of their acquirement. Nor could she shut her ears to the whisperings of her attendants. In shoeing her palfrey, Wybert the smith had gruffly wondered where Sir William and his new followers got their horses shod, for none of them came to *his* smithy; and hazarded a remark that "*horse-shoes* mightn't fit *their* hoofs." The dyers and websters of Derlyngton commented with equal freedom on the hues and texture of Hamed's oriental attire, and the changing tints of black and crimson in that of De Turp's chief companion, a tall knight with a crimson plume, more than hinting that no human hand made the loom they were woven in.

Then the fierce revelry and discordant laughter of her sire and his new associates appalled her. She shrank and left the banquet hall when potations from his charmed cup made him fitter for the orgies of demons than for the presence of a pure woman.

In the privacy of their chamber, Matilda confided these rumours and her own vague misgivings to Emma and her mother; also that Adam de Setoun, anxious to remove her from such scenes, had pressed forward their marriage; and at the instigation of some holy man had fixed Christmas Day for the ceremony; overruling her father's opposition.

******

On Christmas Eve, evil spirits are said to lose their power, nor regain it till Christmas Day be past.

******

Almost in the first hour of their arrival at Oxenhall, William de Turp took poor Emma to task on the sacred secret of her heart. He was seated beneath the canopy at the upper end of the supper table, his family and most distinguished guests ranged near, when, after he had quaffed deeply from the strangely-fashioned cup the turbaned Hamed offered on his knee, he broke forth:

"Soh! daughter Emma, thou hast dared to exchange love-vows with a Saxon, and he the son of thy father's foe! By this cup I swear thou shalt not wed him. Nay, weep not, girl, nor hide thy face; thou shalt have a husband ere long—but he must be of my choice. How say ye, noble friends; is the damsel likely to lack wooers?" and he roughly pulled aside the veil she had modestly drawn down to hide her tears and blushes.

There was an uproar of gallant oaths and flattering protestations; but loudest of all, and backed by glances which made her flesh creep, were the cries of devotion to the beauteous Emma from a dark knight in a varying suit of crimson and black; and the equally saturnine Rupert, who to her surprise was honoured with a seat above the salt.

******

The salt-cellar separated the distinguished guests from their inferiors and the domestics. It was placed midway down the board.

******

At once abashed and indignant, she rose from her seat and fled from the hall, followed by her mother and sister, and pursued by her two dread admirers, who nearing her seemed arrested by some invisible power, as she glided beyond the reach of their outstretched hands, and left them to exchange sinister glances of baffled rage. In after time she ascribed her escape to the amulet and cross she wore together.

Her father's intention so openly declared, coupled with the rumours afloat that Sir William had sold himself to the Powers of Darkness, filled the souls of wife and daughters with dread. Fain would they have sought aid from the saintly hermit, but lacked a messenger.

At length Getha found one in Bertrand, the discarded page. A few words written in Latin, on a slip of parchment, by Dame Elinor, were confided to his care, and under pretence of an errand to the Thorpe for some feminine gear, he was permitted to pass the warders.

He had not spared the spur, but midnight had long passed when be reached his destination. To his surprise and awe, he found the holy man, though it wanted but a week of Christmas, doing penance standing up to the neck in the stream before his cell, and wrestling as it were for victory over an unseen adversary. Hours elapsed before his austere vigils were ended; and Bertrand chafed with impatience.

"Bid Edred the fowler hither, and do thou return to thy mistress, and say Godric bids her 'Trust in God, and fear no evil!'"

Within the hour Edred the fowler was speeding with sure foot over moss and moor, through mire and wood, to Alan the son of Ukillus; and swifter still, as winged by love and fear, came Alan to the hermit's cell.

"Stay thou without," said Godric to Edred, admitting Alan, and closing door and shutter after him.

The cell was bare; the same stone serving Godric for a pillow and a seat, the bare floor being his bed.

Touching a stone in the wall, it revolved, disclosing a recess filled with strange matters. Godric thence lifted, with pious reverence, a greenish-blue glass vase peculiarly ornamented, *the counterpart of that in William de Turp's possession.*

"My son," said he, "mark well this holy relic. It was *St. Cuthbert's Cup,* How it came to unworthy me is not for thee to know. Suffice that it possesses rare qualities. The foulest water placed therein is purified, more aromatic and refreshing than the richest wine. Each separate open lobe pours forth a subtle power to strengthen and *revive a failing virtue.* And greater power than this it hath. Now, mark me! The father of the maid thou lovest, on the night of the storm which wrecked thy skiff, when nursing wrathful thoughts, fell within the power of the Evil One." Here both crossed themselves devoutly. "Blinded by his own fierce passions, he was unwittingly lured by the

Demon to barter his soul for worldly gain. Satan proffered him a cup, to all outer seeming the counterpart of *this*, but opposite as was the source whence it came. From every open mouth some grievous lust, some mortal sin is fed; it too turns filthy liquids into fragrant wine, but the draught maddens and corrupts. With the first draught William De Turp lost the right to his own soul. Nay, more; in his madness he has devoted the pure virgin thou wouldst wed to the Demon he serves."

Alan started: "Now, heaven forfend this should be so! Is there no remedy, good father?"

"Ay—an thou be prudent! Take this cup, obey the instructions on this scroll, and all will go well, but falter not, whatever should appal thee. I have been loath to surrender St. Cuthbert's Cup for so sinful a man, but to save a human soul is work for an angel. May it be weighed in the Divine balance against my sins!"

Besides the wedding festivities, those of the church and the season had commenced. The Bishop's new palace at Derlyngton was all astir with guests. Prior Absolon, and such of the monks of Durham and Finchale as could tolerate their secular prelate for the good cheer he provided, mingled with the barons and knights he drew around him. The houses in Oxen-le-fields and Darlington were bright with holly and ivy; the poorest hut had its Yule-log lit with a brand from the last Christmas fire.

From the palace of the bishop and that of the Neville's, from the hall of William de Turp, provisions were distributed, so that the meanest hind or serf should feast on the day of the blessed Nativity. Fires blazed in the streets and the frozen fields, and oxen were roasted whole, whilst barrels of ale were there for whomsoever would. And in the lordly halls the boards groaned with good things.

At Oxenfields spacious lists had been erected for Morris-dancing and mumming, for football, wrestling, and other rough pastimes, and at either end raised seats had been erected for William de Turp and the bridal party, and for the bishop and his friends. The Abbot of Misrule and his rough followers swarmed everywhere.

It was the third day of the sports—Christmas Day, 1179, the bridal-day of Matilda de Turp and Adam de Setoun. In a joust the previous day, the bride's father had been thrown from his horse. The slight hurt he received served as a pretext for absenting himself from the wedding ceremony; but when the gay cavalcade returned from Derlyngton Church, where not only Ralph the Vicar, but Prior Absolon and the bishop himself assisted in binding the pair together, he seemed blithe as the best, and, for once, the moody puckers were smoothed from his brow.

He of the crimson plume was within the lists, Black Rupert, and a score of William de Turp's fiercest followers; but men jestingly said they seemed to have no relish for peaceful Christmas games, and had, one and all, the look of beaten curs. Nor was Hamed so brisk as his wont.

As the bridal party approached, Emma, holding her sister's veil, caught sight of a Saxon gleeman close beside her father's seat, and a flush of joyful recognition flashed across her face.

"Wine, wine, to drink health to the bride and bridegroom," cried the knight.

Hamed was not at hand; but the Saxon gleeman held to the knight what seemed his charmed cup. "Why, how is this, knave?" said he, as if amazed that other than the mute should bear his drinking cup; but— he raised the cup to his lips and drank.

There was a stir amongst his troop. He drew his left hand across his brow as if to recall some scattered thought. At that instant Hamed thrust *his* vase before William. The two cups had come in contact! An unearthly groan seemed torn from him of the crimson plume.

"Heaven and earth!" exclaimed Sir William, starting to his feet, St. Cuthbert's Cup still in his clasp. "What new sorcery is this? Are my senses leaving me?"

"Nay, rather coming back, Sir Knight. Drink again, I pray thee, drink!" said the Saxon gleeman.

De Turp hesitated, looked from one vase to the other, at the imploring eyes of the mute, wavered in his choice, when the gleeman (or rather Alan) began to chant solemnly—

Place this cup to the living lip,
The sins of the past from his soul shall slip;
Place this cup to the dying lip,
The soul shall escape from the Devil's grip;
Keep it close to the lip of the dead,
While centuries three shall be fully sped,
That soul shall be freed from the taint of sin,
And Paradise open to let it in!

The knight listened, raised St. Cuthbert's Cup again to his parched lip; again drank freely.

As he did so, Ralph the Vicar from behind poured a chalice of holy-water into the demon's vase.

It split to shivers on the instant with a sound that rent the air. A yell burst simultaneously from the shrinking mute and from the Crimson Knight. All nature seemed convulsed. The sky darkened, thunder rattled overhead, blue lightnings played and quivered on the ground, the earth within the lists shook, rent, then emitting sulphurous fumes, rose high above the tops of houses, tower or steeple. Then, breaking in the centre like a crater, swallowed up the Foul Fiend and his demon troop.

Black Rupert and Hamed disappeared at the same time.

Men were affrighted, women and children shrieked and ran for their lives. Bishop and monks told their beads in fear and trembling. The bride clung to her husband, Emma to the strong arm of Alan, and Elinor, throwing herself at the feet of her husband, murmured, "Saved, saved!"

All that Christmas Day the earth remained high above the tree tops. At noon the following day it sank, but where had been green pasture were four large round pools, filled with brack and sulphurous water; water no animal would drink, no housewife could use to wash an infant's face, or cleanse the household linen, or mix with the bairn's porridge, since it curdled milk. Few cared to pass those pools after dusk; and the evil name of Hell-Kettles clung to them.

St. Cuthbert's Cup made William de Turp indeed a better man. Thankful for his deliverance, he grew grateful to the agent, and ere a month had sped gave Emma to Alan with a blessing, in the presence of Godric the Hermit and Ukillus the Saxon. For her dower he gave (Matilda, his heiress, and Adam de Setoun confirmed the grant) "one toft in vill of Hedene, and twenty-four acres of land. Twelve acres free of all service except that due to the king from one ox-gang in Eden," as witnessed many noble names.

In his penitence he gave by seven several charters grants of land to the Chapel of St. James, in Eden Dene.

St. Cuthbert's Cup was guarded with religious care, and in William de Turp's dying hour it was held to his lips by his daughter Emma.

Nor did their pious care end with his death. Herself and Alan, by turns "kept the cup to the lip of the dead" until the very earth closed over his mortal remains and the cup likewise. And so they left it with him in his grave within the precincts of St. James's Chapel, in Eden Dene; and on his tomb was carved the text:

Joy shall be in Heaven over one sinner that repenteth, more than over ninety-and-nine just persons which need no repentance.

Edred and Oswy had been well cared for; and by the time Alan's son Walter was born, Getha was the wife of Oswy. Nigel, the steward, and Bertrand, the page, had been reinstated, the knight's great care having been to make restitution for wrong.

The monks of St. Cuthbert are no more. The chapel of St. James is gone; whether destroyed by time or the more ruthless hands of man is not known; but the torrent still flows to the north of the rains, and on the banks of the little dene, through which it falls, a workman, in 1775, digging here, came across a skeleton, with a vase of thick greenish-blue glass adorned with remarkable tubes, to which a fragrant aroma still clung, placed to the mouth of the skull. And Hell-Kettles may still be found in Oxenfields, three miles south of Darlington.

The Fairies' Cradle

CHAPTER 1

In the south transept of the large and venerable church of Houghton-le-Spring may be seen the mutilated effigy of an armed knight, who bears a shield upon his left arm, whilst his right hand touches the hilt of the sword suspended from his girdle. Before the stone was removed to its present location, the cushioned head rested in a recumbent position on an altar tomb within the same arm of the crucial edifice. The lower limbs are gone, but once they lay there in their mail, crossed as befitted a knight who had fought in the Holy Wars; and strange stories were afloat that ever on the eve of St. Barnabas the image was covered with a dewy sweat, as if the very stone sympathised with the agonised soul of the man who lay in dust beneath.

The armour the knight had worn in life, which hung suspended over the monument, creaked and groaned in unison, while the rigid face grew livid and mobile as the moonlight rays shot through the narrow lancet windows upon it. Time has closed the lancet windows, banished the armour, destroyed the tomb, defaced the scull-capped figure, as if eager to blot that man and his deeds from memory; but the minstrel and the historian who have fought with time to rescue Sir John-le-Spring from oblivion, and have won the victory, point to this relic with warning fingers.

Some of these chroniclers suppose that the Le Springs gave their name as an affix to the parish of Houghton; but it is much more likely that the first of these Norman intruders took his surname (when surnames were rare) from the chalybeate springs within his limestone manor, and that Sir John's parental ancestor was known as Henry-of-the-Spring, simply to distinguish him from some other proprietary Henry in the locality. This same knight Henry-le-Spring (or L'Espring) had married about the year 1264, Mary, the daughter and heiress of Roger Barnhard, High-Constable of Durham. He carried his wife to his fortified manor-house close by Houghton burn, and there in process of time she became the mother of two sons, Henry the elder (of whom genealogists make no mention), so named after father and grandfather, and John, born five years later, whose baptismal name was given in grateful remembrance of the monarch who (ever ready to bestow what was not his own) had granted the manor of Houghton to his courtier Henry.

It might have been that the very name had a taint in it, for John-le-Spring had scarcely passed the age of whipping-top, caylys (nine-pins), and ball before his envious disposition broke out in open resentment of his brother's priority of birth, and consequent advantages, real or imaginary. He hardened his soul against the gentle teaching of his lady-mother, and scorned the holy precepts of the good monk, Robert Kellaw, who came at times over moor and hills from Durham to see what progress the boys made alike in their Latin and religion. But the piety and learning of the young monk made less impression on John than did the pride and gorgeous state of Bishop Beck in his visitations. The latter appealed to the eye, the former to the understanding, and his senses were open if his heart was closed. He longed for wealth, for the power and luxury it gave, and inwardly chafed more and more that the patrimony would descend to his brother, in right of primogeniture, whilst he must be content with a portion of his lady-mother's inheritance.

It was in no spirit of emulation that he strove to cope with Henry in his manly sports and games before the down was well tinted on his chin. He would ride and wrestle, and combat and tilt with him, until long practice made him equal in skill, if not in strength. Those were rough times; a man's own arm was needed to protect his life, and blows came readier, and had more weight than words. So the good old knight, when not doing feudal service in the battlefield, was well pleased to watch and direct these contentions at home; but his brow would cloud, and his voice stop the contest when he saw that John grew fierce and savage in the fight, and took advantages not in accordance with Sir Henry's code of chivalry.

Much of the land which is now open moorland or cultivated ground was then thick forest, peopled with red-deer, wild kine, and foxes. Roads were few, and primitive as the vehicles which traversed them; but horses' hoofs and peasant feet trod pathways to shorten distance between castle and Thorpe, grange and hamlet.

Like other gentlemen of his time. Sir Henry-le-Spring filled up his peaceful leisure with hunting and hawking, his lady joining with him in the latter sport, though she and her bower-women preferred shooting conies (rabbits) with bow and bolt to the rougher sport of the chase. The sons followed where the sire led, though John turned on a scornful heel when Henry sat down to read a book, borrowed from Father Robert, or the Rector of Houghton. He was never far to seek when there was a living creature to pursue or to destroy.

It fell out that in one of their hunting expeditions, when Henry was about six and twenty, the two brothers had the good fortune to rescue a fair maiden from the attack of a fierce red bull. She was a distant relative of the noble house of Neville, a visitor at Brancepeth Castle, separated from her own party by a wilful palfrey, and driven farther into the forest by the bellowings of the wild bull, which tore up the turf and snapped the lower branches of the trees in his progress towards her. The infuriated beast, maddened, no doubt, by its scarlet housings, had already ripped open the palfrey's side, and lowered his horns for an attack on the lady, when a thrust from a stout hunting, spear arrested him, and he turned his fury against his assailant, only to be staggered by a second thrust on the other flank. The blood flowed, but the wounds were not vital, and the rage of the savage bull was terrific.

The brothers were themselves in peril. At length, with well-directed aim, Henry drove his spear right to the heart of Taurus, and with a snort and a quiver he fell to the earth, dyeing the bracken crimson with his blood.

The Lady Isolda had a fair face, and fair revenues, and when her gratitude and that of her friends eventuated in a treaty of marriage with Henry, John had much ado to conceal his rancour, for he coveted both the damsel and her gold. But it had been Henry who had disentangled her from her dead palfrey—Henry who had sprinkled her unconscious face with the water John had brought in his casque; and when sense returned, and the light of reviving life came into her pure grey eyes, Henry's arm supported her, and in the deep brown eyes bent over her she saw love leap as it were out of the windows of his soul to light up hers once and for ever.

Another pair of brown eyes were also fixed on her, but with admiration of another type, from which she shrank abashed, and the eyes, like the uncovered locks, had a redder glow in them. The face was more delicately chiselled, but the lips were fuller, and there was a deep dimple in his chin which might attract others, but not her.

It is needless to tell the many crafty arts by which John strove to oust his brother from Isolda's heart and woo and win her for himself, or his bitter anathemas when his treachery was revealed upon their marriage morn by Ursula, Isolda's nurse, whose fidelity he had endeavoured to corrupt. His pride took fire at the disappointment and exposure. Without a word of farewell, and with but one attendant, he took horse, and, vowing "never to return until he could rule where he had been ruled," bent his steps southward. He was barely twenty, and had not yet won his spurs; but, having resolved to join the crusaders and set distance between himself and Durham, he crossed over to France, and took service in the train of a noble knight preparing; to start for the Holy Land.

No doubt his mother mourned her absent son, and not the less so that he went away with discontent in his breast; but father and brother alike looked on war as the only true path to distinction, and priestly training had strengthened the current belief that through the Holy Land lay the soldier's road to glory and salvation.

If Isolda missed him, it was with thankfulness. She possessed an amulet, the gift of a Syrian *emir* to her grandsire, which enabled her to test the truth of those around her, and it gave her reason to mistrust *him*. He would have come between herself and Henry, and on her doting happiness she could not have brooked intrusion. Five years elapsed before their only child, a baby-girl, came to brighten up the dull Manor House. No marvel that her birth furnished excuses for unwonted festivities. Between Dame Ursula and Lady-le-Spring ensued a generous rivalry which should do most honour to the young stranger; but the good nurse, by virtue of her functions, was mistress of the ceremonies to such visitors as were admitted to the lady's chamber; one of the bowerwomen dispensing the *caudell* (spiced drink) and groaning cake to the gossips of the village who thronged the lower hall.

There was little privacy then, even for the sick; the lady's chamber being also a reception-room, the bed (only separated by curtains from the rest of the room) often serving as a seat by day. In this room, too, at the foot of the bed, was the huge carved coffer in which was kept money and valuables, and against the wall a bulky cabinet to match. Here she would assemble her maidens for spinning or embroidery after the noontide meal, and here receive her private friends, and thus did Lady-le-Spring in her bower.

The Lady Isolda was an orphan, and the few friends she had were denizens of Northumberland. No little surprise, therefore, was excited when the Lady Isolda summoned her husband to her bedside, and said to him, in a low, sweet voice, "Henry, I have a dear friend, the tried counsellor of my mother; if not adverse to my lord's will, I would fain invite her to the christening feast."

"Be it even as you list, sweet dame; the mother who reared so gracious a daughter cannot have had evil counsellors. But how is the lady known? and whence shall I summon her?"

"The Lady Bell lives in retirement, Dame Ursula alone has the clue to her retreat, she will convey our wishes."

Henry-le-Spring bent his bearded lip to his wife's brow. "It is a strange request, fair Isolda, but so submissive and discreet a mate should have all her lord's trust. Be it even as you list."

Within the chamber was a cage containing a pair of pet carrier doves, which had come with the Lady Isolda's gear on her marriage. Ursula was summoned by her lady's silver whistle. At a signal she took one of the doves from its cage, fastened Isolda's amulet (a jewel of pearl and emerald, shaped like a lily-bell) beneath its wing, and opening the narrow casement let the bird fly, Henry-le-Spring standing by the while.

The sun was setting when the bird went forth; the shadows of night had closed on the Manor; the drawbridge was up, Lady-le-Spring had herself, as was her nightly duty, seen all outer doors locked and barred, and taken charge of the keys; seen the fires covered, sent the servants to bed, and had the candles brought back to be extinguished safely in her presence.

A night-lamp was hung on its crotch in the Lady Isolda's chamber, and the last goodnight was being said by Henry to mother and babe, when there came a flatter of wings at the narrow window, and a tap on the panes.

The dove had returned weary, with a lily-of-the-valley in its beak, and the amulet shifted to the other wing.

"The Lady Bell consents, I know the token; Henry, dear lord, goodnight." Isolda turned a well-satisfied head on her flock pillow (feathers came into use later), whilst her lord, lighted by a foot-page with a lantern, trod the long stone passage and left her to repose; not, however, without some stirrings of curiosity anent the lady-friend of whom he had heard nothing before in all the five years of their marriage.

CHAPTER 2

The child had been born whilst the March winds were blowing, sad the eighth day appointed by the church for the baptismal rite happening to fall on New Year's Day, the 25th of that month, (New Year's Day, Old Style, fell on Lady-day), the triple festival called for more than common rejoicing. Lady-le-Spring had doubled the weekly dole of bread distributed each Friday to the poor, Sir John had promised to all comers ale and beef *ad libitum* at the christening, and huge fires were laid down on the open ground beyond the drawbridge to roast sheep and oxen whole. Henry-the-Reeve (who held two ox-gangs of land of twenty-four acres each), besides gathering manorial-dues of hens and eggs, acted as Sir John's *locum tenens*, sending messengers hither and thither, ordering and countermanding in all the importance of office and the occasion.

The warrener and his men came in laden with venison, hares, and rabbits. The falconer and his mate brought home the heron and moor-buzzards, struck by the falcons of Sir Henry and his son. Trout were fished from the burn, and salmon from the Wear. Will Milby, who paid 10s. a year for his malting and brewery, was heard to say over his steaming vats he "hoped there would be a fresh baby at the manor every year, and he should go rent free."

More grain was sent to the miller than the water-mill would grind, and Ralph Hodgson was despatched to Durham to bring from Elmete (Elvet) bread and provisions beyond the range of home produce.

★★★★★★

Doubtless as here the assize of bread was held, here would other merchandise be sold—and the present name be a corruption of Ell-mete—an ell-measure.

★★★★★★

Not even the wedding had created such a commotion. Lady-le-Spring seemed to forget her years, so active was she amongst her bower-women and handmaidens. Her shrill silver whistle was heard, now here, now there, the floors were swept under her superintendence, the long-table and benches were cleansed, fresh rushes strewed on the floor of the great hall; perfumed napery was drawn from the coffer, the *dressior* or sideboard adorned with plate and Venetian glass; and her own hands relieved the anxious cook in the preparation of confections and composite messes, the very names of which are expunged from our modern cuisine. Even the poor little turnspits looked at the cooks with languid eyes from between the bars of their revolving prisons, and with outstretched tongues and plaintive yelps seemed to ask if the roasting would never be done.

Indeed, but for Dame Ursula, the sick lady, nay, even the little stranger about whom all the fuss was made, had like to have been overlooked and neglected in the commotion.

A gay procession swept up the aisle of the large church. Lady Neville as chief sponsor, in a richly-embroidered robe, presented the babe to the rector, whose cope and chasuble were gorgeous to behold, and there was no lack of gallant knights and fair dames; but the Lady Bell, about whom the young mother had seemed so anxious, delayed her coming.

The bells pealed merrily, as the sacristan and his mates vigorously plied the ropes, and little Mary, who had cried lustily (a sign of grace) during the ceremony, was being carried in state from the church to the Lady Isolda's litter, beneath a spreading sycamore, as a courtly cavalcade made its appearance on the bridle-path from Hetton.

There was a general pause and a murmur of surprise amongst the mounting party at the church gates.

Isolda pressed her husband's hand as he gallantly helped her into her litter, and whispered "Henry, the Lady Bell." At the hint he stepped forward with doffed beaver, to greet his unknown guests with courtesy befitting their evident rank and his wife's friends.

Foremost rode the Lady Bell and three attendant knights in complete armour. The lady, of graceful but diminutive stature, rode a milk-white palfrey; above her kirtle of snowy white she wore a closely-fitting tunic of pale green, with a gauzy veil and head-dress of like hue. The housings of her palfrey were also green, sprinkled with many coloured flowers. As variously hued were the garments of the damsels in her train, but all wore tunics and head-gear of bright green. The fashion of the robes was varied in their singularity, their texture was delicate, and not a lady in the manorial party could so much as name their fabrics. A single diamond, clear as a dewdrop, or her own bright eye, glistened on the lady's forehead, her only jewel.

Of the three knights, one, mounted on a coal-black steed, had armour of a strange pattern equally black and shining; the second, on a bright chestnut, wore a suit of polished steel elaborately wrought; the third, mounted on a dappled-grey, was clad in a suit as bright as silver but of a darker hue; yet each wore a scarf of the lady's colour—green, and each esquire and foot-page had also a scarf of green crossed over his dusky brown doublet.

The Lady Bell bent gracefully in acknowledgment of Henry-le-Spring's salute, then in a voice low and sweet, yet clear and shrill as wind rushing through a crevice, she said, "We are somewhat tardy, good sir, yet we trust we are in time to pay our respectful devoir to Sir Henry-le-Spring and his lady, to yourself and Lady Isolda, no less than to bless babe Mary who has brought us hither."

Henry bowed, and she continued, in introduction, waving her lily hand towards the knights on the chestnut and grey chargers, "My brothers, Sir Ferris, from the Cleveland Hills, Sir Plumbius, from the depths of Weardale, and here," she touched the black knight's glove, "My brother. Sir Carbo, who has a home with me here and there beyond the narrow limits of a palatinate, and is as welcome everywhere."

A gleam of fiery eyes shot through the bars of his visor as she spoke, and so warm was his salute to Henry that his heart kindled responsively as he led them to his father. Sir Henry.

Genial and courteous was the host, right noble was the feast; and if the royal peacock with its plumes outspread did not grace the board, a snowy cygnet did, (it was customary to send these birds to table with a covering of their own plumage). There were soups, and fish, and game, and poultry, solid joints; and dainty messes, pates, and blancmange, and manchets of the finest wheaten flour.

Ere the guests were seated, bowls of scented waters were handed round wherein they washed their hands, drying them with graceful motions in the air; and when the practised carver, with no more than a finger and thumb on the meat, dismembered poultry or sliced ham and beef, the viands were handed round, each gentleman shared his platter with the lady next him, and fingers and daggers did duty for those luxuries of the future, forks and table-knives.

And how those fourteenth century gentry did feed! And how Sir Henry-le-Spring and Lady Mary did press their hospitality! And how the haughty Ladies Neville and Belasyse looked askance and whispered their scornful "who?" and "whence?" as they marked the dainty abstemiousness of Lady Bell, whose slight repast was washed down by no stronger liquor than pure water in a tiny crystal cup supplied by her own foot-page. Even Dame Laton exchanged glances and shrugs across the board with Dame Isabell-de-Wessington and her husband Robert, and in the curiosity excited the blind minstrel in the chimney corner twanged his harp and sang his lays of love and war, as little heeded as the iron dogs which kept the burning brands together on the hearth.

But we linger too long over the feast. Let us leave the old knight and his jovial companions to quaff their wine, and with the father follow the Lady Bell and her stalwart brothers from the dais of the escutcheoned hall to the tapestried chamber of Lady Isolda. Fatigued with the exertion of the day. Lady Isolda received her guests reclining on her couch; but Dame Ursula was in high feather, and with little Mary in her arms moved with smiling face from group to group, as proud and mindful of her charge as of the largess which found its way to her ample pocket.

The two dames stood before the cage of the carrier-doves. Ladies Neville and Belasyse arranged the pieces on a chessboard, all seemingly engrossed in conversation, yet listening with ears and eyes open to all that was passing. Rowland Belasyse, a handsome, curly-headed seven-years old urchin had slipped from his lady-mother's side, and clinging to Dame Ursula's kirtle, kept close to the wonderful baby, round which Lady Bell and the three strange knights clustered. As Henry entered she was clasping round the infant's throat, by a chain of fine filigree, a gold amulet, strikingly similar to that worn by his wife, chanting the while in a thin piping voice—

Guard, Mary, the gift of thy friend Lady Bell,
'Twas wrought in the East with a magical spell;
It has virtues thou wilt not for years comprehend;
Unerring, 'twill show thee the foe from the friend.
The pearl will turn black and the emerald white
If danger but threaten by day or by night.
It endows thee with powers to come and to go,
Unseen as the wind, and unheard as the snow;
But holiness, cleanliness, purity, thrift
Must be hers who would dare use so potent a gift;
And seven, and seven, and seven again
Are mystical numbers to strengthen the chain.
And the babe we endow in our cradle must lie
With the stars for its watchers, its canopy sky.

There was a deep hush in the room as the Lady Bell's white kirtle gave place to the bright mail of Sir Ferris and Sir Plumbius, and clear metallic voices followed her reedy pipe—

Time will come, and need will be,
Then remember me—and me.
From our hills we press to aid—

These, our tokens, smiling maid.

Each fat little hand closed over something—Henry could not see what. The Black Knight then touched the baby's brow, smoothing the curls of Rowland Belasyse with the other hand; and in tones hollow as if they came from the depths of a pit, he said.

Babe and boy, I bless ye both.
Looking to a plighted troth;
And my gift on both bestow—
Lapse of years its worth will show.
Rowland, you my token take;
Thine for this fair damsel's sake.

The Lady Bell pressed her tiny hand on that of Lady Isolda, "Farewell! health, peace, and happiness to thee and thy brave husband; remember thy duly as wife and mother, Lady Isolda, and doubt not the fulfilment of ours. Sir Henry, the sun is westering, we crave your leave to depart."

There was a rush to the window to watch the cavalcade cross the drawbridge 'mid the loud hurrahs of the feasting crowd beyond; and then another rush to see the gifts bestowed with so much parade. And then, what a murmur of disappointment and contempt!

One little fist held a piece of ironstone—the other merely a scrap of lead ore.

Lady Neville turned up her nose, "So much for Lady Isolda's friends !"

"Come hither, Rowland; what marvellous boon has that black knight bestowed on thee besides his prophecy?" cried Lady Belasyse, derisively.

The boy displayed a torque of a black substance, in the polished sheen of which a lambent flame seemed to play—perhaps caught from the rays of the setting sun.

His mother would have taken it, but the boy held it fast.

"It is baby Mary's as well as mine. I must take care of it, and when I am a man I will wear it in my casque, and fight to defend it, as a true knight should."

"That's my brave boy! And so you shall! and let those who dare take it from you!" was the exclamation of Sir Hervey Belasyse, who had entered the chamber in time to hear the colloquy.

And the boy did keep the token, as carefully as Lady Isolda preserved the despised pieces of ore; he with a precocious sense of chivalry—she with a knowledge that they were fairy gifts.

CHAPTER 3

Years sped, during which no message of affection or enquiry came from the Crusader. A stray palmer or two sought shelter under the hospitable roof, and repaid their entertainers with current reports of his knighthood, of the bravery of Sir John, and the fluctuating fortunes of the Christian arms. Then Europe rang with the news that the Soldan had wrested Acre from the soldiers of the Cross, and driven the Crusaders out of Syria like flocks of worried sheep. But still Sir John came not, and the old people mourned him as dead. In vain Isolda and Henry strove to comfort Lady-le-Spring. She felt that if not dead he was a prisoner, and under the terrible supposition (for Oriental dungeons were awful things) the mother drooped and died.

Meanwhile Isolda's child grew in strength and loveliness. It is true both the Henries were disappointed that no boy came to transmit their name and honours to posterity; but that did not prevent the black-eyed beauty becoming the pet of the household. She was winsome and engaging as her mother, fearless, and truthful as her father; and, as her character developed with years, displayed a precocity of intelligence and information not to be accounted for either by the book-lore supplied by good Father Robert or the housewifely instruction of mother and grandmother, or Dame Ursula to boot. Then she escaped the ills of ordinary children, or felt them lightly. If she so much as cut her finger, the blood stopped instantly, and no cicatrice was left. If she fell, where another child would have dislocated a limb, she got no more of a bump than would teach her caution.

Those wise in such matters attributed it to fairy guardianship, and strangely enough, twice had she disappeared overnight, only to be found the next morning in a singular oblong hollow at the top of a green mound or cairn fully three miles from the Manor House, in a field near the angle of the Eppylynden (Eppleton) and Houghton Lanes, on the way to Hetton, called by tradition the Fairies' Cradle. To this spot the superstition of the time attached the belief that whosoever slept therein at midnight would be under the protection of the fairies, whose subterranean palace lay beneath, and free to join their fairy revels on the grassy mound. But tradition also added that only the pure in thought and deed could lie therein with safety, and woe betide the incautious wight who, with an evil or revengeful thought in his heart, ventured even so far as to step upon the haunted *tumulus*.

So the country people kept aloof from the spot after dark, and no ploughshare was ever drawn within a goodly circuit of the mound.

The first of these disappearances occurred when Mary was but seven months old. Henry-le-Spring, his wife, arid child, with their attendants, were returning from a visit to Brancepeth Castle; and notwithstanding Isolda's remonstrance, some unaccountable vagary prompted him to travel through the October tinted woods and over the moors of their own demesne in preference to the more beaten and traversed highroad through the City of Durham.

At that period much of the county was uncleared forest; and Bishop Beck underwent a heavy penalty some years later, for daring to despoil the woods and use the timber for smelting purposes. It was also unsafe to travel unguarded. Therefore the attack of armed men on their escort shortly after they had passed Hetton and Eppylynden was no uncommon incident of a journey.

The contest was sharp and well disputed, plunder being the apparent object; but in the end the robbers were driven off, leaving two of their troop dead on the ground.

During the conflict the shrieks of women were unnoted, but it was then discovered that Lady Isolda lay in a deep swoon, and that the infant had been carried off from the litter. The confusion that ensued was indescribable. Horsemen dashed hither and thither, but in the dusk pursuit only ended in failure, and the return of the disconsolate couple to the manor without their child.

Leaving the women in safety, Henry and his followers set forth to renew his quest, and were returning dispirited in the dappled dawn, when they overtook an old peasant woman, with a basket on one arm and the recovered child, wrapped in a rich green mantle, on the other.

She said she had been gathering mushrooms on the Fairies' mound, where they grew thick, and to her surprise found the babe fast asleep in the hollow. She knew it was Mary-le-Spring, because she had been wakened out of her sleep by the fight, and a wounded man was then lying in her hut, who said the bairn was gone.

Surely the good woman had mushrooms in her basket, and the man found in the hut was one of Sir Henry's own retainers. There could be no doubt of her veracity. Questioned farther, she said, "Only ill-folk need fear the little-folk, and mushrooms grew thicker there at sunrise than anywhere about. And that fine green robe was on the bairn, none of *her* spinning." The old mushroom gatherer had cause to bless the child-finding, a double dole being henceforth hers, with wood and wool to keep her warm for the winter. Isolda and she agreed in supposing that the "little folk" had rescued the babe from the ruffian who had carried it off, either from revenge or to claim a ransom.

The second event happened shortly after Lady-le-Spring's death, while Sir Henry and his son were at the court of King Edward. Her godmother. Lady Belasyse was at the Manor; Rowland, a fine boy of fourteen, was about to take service under Sir Henry, as was the custom, and was there also.

It was Mary's seventh birthday. Rowland had renewed his acquaintance with the playful damsel, and was proudly vaunting to Ursula, by the great hall fire, the noble deeds he meant to do in her defence when he was strong enough to wield his father's sword and battle-axe. "Where has the doughty squire of dames left the fair damsel he intends to champion?" asked Lady Belasyse, who had overheard him.

The inquiry sent him off to peer and peep into all the nooks and corners of the irregular mansion, from the very battlements to the buttery, where she had been last seen helping to distribute the week's dole. But as the boy's cry, "Mistress Mary! Mistress Mary, where art thou?" rang through the corridors meeting: no response, an alarm was given, and the search became wilder and wider.

There was weeping and lamenting in hall and bower when night fell, and the daughter of the house was still to seek. But comfort came to the Lady Isolda at midnight with a tap at her window and a piping chant, which Lady Belasyse and Ursula mistook for the wild March winds careering round the mansion, and beating at the casement:

The Fairies' Cradle is soft and green,
There little Mary lies at rest,
Lulled to repose by our Fairy Queen,
Safe as bird in its downy nest.

What she is dreaming lip may not tell;
What is learning her life will show:
The foster-child of the Lady Bell
Fearless lies where the daisies grow.

Thither, at Isolda's instigation, the domestics sped in all haste, their torches flaring in the wind—Master Rowland, at his own urgent entreaty, one of the foremost. It was he who, when the men hung back, pressed up the mound as if he had been storming a fortress; he who, finding the maiden there, wrapped as before in a thick green mantle,

145

uncovered her face and wakened her with a kiss upon her warm, white forehead.

Mary's own account was, that as she gave the old mushroom gatherer her dole of bread, a pretty white rabbit, with pink eyes, frolicked before the buttery-hatch. She tried to catch it, but it ran round the buildings, she following; then it crossed the drawbridge, and led her on, and on, forgetful of distance, until her little feet were weary, and when it disappeared in the hollow on the mound, she just lay down to rest on the soft grass, and forgot everything.

If Lady Isolda pondered over this in silence, Lady Belasyse rated the bairn in good set terms, and Ursula followed suit; but Mary bore their chiding meekly, and when Rowland found her weeping in the garden by herself, he consoled her with promises to take her part when he was older.

The Le-Springs' returned from court, but not to the continuous calm they had anticipated. The Scotch King Baliol, exasperated by King Edward's mortifying exactions, broke loose from fealty. His chieftains crossed the borders, and carried into England's northern counties terror and confusion, burning and destroying all before them. In vindictive frenzy, Edward summoned an army for retribution, and the warlike prelate, Anthony Beck, rousing the vassals of his palatinate, joined him on his march, with a contingent of 1,000 foot and 600 horse, amongst whom were Sir Henry-le-Spring and his son. Rowland Belasyse followed as the younger one's foot-page.

The old man fell in the first conflict. At the terrible massacre of Berwick, an arrow shot from a factory occupied by Flemings pierced his brain, and he dropped from his saddle dead. Exasperated, Edward ordered the building and its brave defenders to be given to the flames, and the cruel mandate was carried into effect, but the savage holocaust could not restore the father to his son. Henry himself, throughout the campaign, seemed to bear a charmed life. Alike in Berwick and Dunbar, the silver owls upon his sable surcoat were so many targets for the shafts of the enemy; but the arrows seemed to glance from his armour, the battle-axe which splintered his casque, spared his skull; and he came back safe in life and limb to clasp his loving wife and child.

Rowland Belasyse was not quite so fortunate; he was brought to the Manor with an ugly wound in his shoulder, received whilst assisting in the removal of Sir Henry's body, and aggravated by neglect. But Dame Ursula and Isolda were skilful chirurgeons, and it healed much sooner than the wound in his heart from Mary's pitiful eyes, child though she was.

"My husband, I do not find the woollen doublet thou wert wont to wear under thy buff-jerkin?" said Isolda, with unwonted anxiety, after a careful search amongst the warrior's mails.

"There was something in the lining which chafed me under my armour; I bore it during all the heat of battle, but after our fight at Dunbar, in my irritation cast it from me. I think I gave it to a poor wretch who was half-naked."

Isolda looked blank.

"Nay, do not look so grave, dear wife," he continued. "What matters the loss of a garment when thou hast got thy goodman back unscathed. I would have given every robe in my mails, could I have brought our good sire home as safely."

Isolda's white arms clasped his neck, "Henry, in that cast-off garment lay thy safety. I had sewn my *amulet* within its lining in my fear for thee. It was perchance that which chafed thee. Alack! that I did not avise thee of my precaution."

Much did Isolda grieve in secret over the loss of the amulet, regarding it as an evil omen.

Two more, years ran their course, and Mary, progressing towards her teens, grew in grace and beauty. The ordinary ailments of childhood had passed her lightly as dew from a roseleaf. She was tall and stately, and at twelve, the black-eyed, black-haired maiden had the port and bearing of fifteen, with the purity and innocence of a babe. She had learning and knowledge never imparted by the good monk, who had been her father's tutor; the flowers on her tapestry seemed to vie with those of the garden; she spun a finer thread than any maiden in the district; music seemed to flow from her fingers as she touched the lute; and the villagers she visited on errands of mercy used to say there was comfort in her voice, and healing in her touch. She had not lain in the Fairies' Cradle for nothing.

There was another call "to arms" when William Wallace drew his sword for Scottish freedom; and neither Sir Henry nor Rowland were likely to lag behind.

And now did Isolda anew lament the loss of her precious amulet. Fain would she and her daughter have pressed him to take Mary's, but he would not hear it. "Only cowards need charms," he said proudly. "A soldier's best amulets, are a good conscience, a good cause, a good sword and shield."

Rowland Belasyse, now his esquire, was as doughty at nineteen as his leader at thirty-eight, and kissed away Mary's tears when she urged him to wear her fairy gift, if her father would not. But he was willing to exchange rings with her before he went to the war, and to take her promise to love him ever and be his wife one day. And in Isolda's bower, disordered with hasty preparations, father and mother ratified the contract (those were days of young betrothal), the latter smiling through her tears, as memory brought back the prophecy of Sir Carbo and Sir Plumbius, those knights of faëry.

How are victories won by kings? Ask the widows and orphans whose dead lie unburied on the battlefield, for kites and corbies to batten on! Ask the widows and orphans whose cries and lamentations are heard when the loud pibroch and the clashing cymbals are mute; heard when the roll of the drum, the whiz of the arrow, the crash of the battle-axe have ceased to madden the pulses of men and make them savages! Ask Isolda and Mary-le-Spring how Edward the First won the battle of Falkirk, and achieved his victory over Wallace? Ask the young esquire who came back wounded nigh unto death, leaving his chivalrous master under the crimsoned turf of Scotland!

CHAPTER 4

Still no tidings of Sir John. An inheritance waited him, yet he came not to claim it. Fain would King Edward have laid his royal paw thereon; but Bishop Beck resented interference with a fief of his church, and the barons of Brancepeth and Belasyse openly resisted the spoliation of the widow and orphan. Little did Edward dream the thorn Sir John-le-Spring had long been in his side, or the ample reason he had for confiscation, or he would have clutched and kept Houghton in spite of bishop and baron.

So Lady Isolda and Mary remained the virtual owners of the manor, Sir John's death taken for granted; and Rowland Belasyse, when long convalescence left him no longer pretence to linger at a lady's apron strings, bent his footsteps homeward. But the turreted Manor House was to him a casket enshrining a priceless gem, and occasions were not wanting when either alone or with his lady-mother he came hither to assure himself of its safety.

Fain would he have had the gem in his own keeping, and he urged upon Lady Isolda royal precedent for early marriages, and Mary's premature development in mind and person. The mother would hear no word of marriage until Mary should be at least eighteen; and Mary knew no higher duty than obedience.

The lady had cause to repent her decision at a time when neither Rowland, nor Sir Hervey Belasyse, nor yet the Lord of Brancepeth were at hand to take her part. Every scattered limb of the martyred Wallace had had a separate tongue to call Robert Bruce into the field; and Lady Isolda's friends were with Sir John Warrenne across the borders, stopping the tide of freedom with the bodies of slaughtered men.

Lady Isolda was busy with her maids, apportioning their tasks, and Mary (sad at heart, for her amulet foreboded evil), under the instructions of Father Robert, was assisting him to illuminate a rare manuscript, when the clatter of hoofs on the drawbridge, and a loud blast on the horn at the gate, caused them both to look from the oriel.

An armed man, arrayed in black and silver (the colours of the Le-Springs), attended by a bodyguard, loudly demanded admission in the name of *Sir John-le-Spring!*

The monk rose. "Let me deal with this, dear lady. Unless Sir John be alive, which I misdoubt, this must be a robber's feint to gain entrance for plunder."

The hall door stood open; he descended the steps, and, approaching the gate, held parley through its small grated window, whilst Lady Isolda and Mary, amongst the white-faced maidens, held their breath in dire expectation.

"Who art thou, and what is thine errand? "

"I am Robert Lascelles, esquire of Sir John-le-Spring, and I come to take possession of his Manor of Houghton-le-Spring, with all revenues pertaining, to hold in his name until it be his good pleasure to appear in person."

"These are not days to take a stranger's word for proof, Robert Lascelles," answered the monk; "produce thine authority."

To the astonishment of all, the black-browed stranger drew a slip of parchment from the pouch at his girdle, and passed it through the grating. It was a legal authority, signed and sealed by Sir John-le-Spring, for the bearer, Robert Lascelles, to take possession in his name. Father Robert, who had himself instructed the brothers in penmanship, could well attest the crabbed signature, but it might be a forgery. Back he went to the grating, whilst mother and daughter, clasped in each other's arms, shuddered with dread.

"Sir John-le-Spring has long been dead to his family, if not in fact. In the name of the Church, which is bound to protect the widow and orphan, and in the name of the Lady Isolda, I ask some further token, before—"

He was interrupted by Robert Lascelles. "Bear that token to the dainty lady, and bid her remember *the wild bull of Brancepeth*;" at the same time a small glove, richly embroidered with seed pearls, was thrust rudely in the monk's face.

It was the missing glove of the Lady Isolda, stained with the blood of her palfrey! John-le-Spring had drawn it from her hand in her swoon, the better to chafe her fingers, and had kept it with a constancy worthy a better love.

There was no further question of authority. The gate was thrown open, and Sir John's claim admitted.

At once Lady Isolda gave orders for refreshments to be served in the great hall, and seeing the free looks Robert Lascelles cast upon Mary, dismissed the maiden to her chamber. Then turning to her brother-in-law's agent, she said, with an effort, yet still with dignified calmness, "This demand is somewhat sudden and untoward. What space of time is permitted for the collection of my personal property, and the arrangement of my private affairs, before I and my daughter retire. My home and lands in Northumberland have been laid waste by the incursive Scots; I shall seek refuge with my cousin, Lady Neville, for a brief space. I trust an escort of our old retainers will not be denied me."

"The Lady Isolda and Mistress Mary are expected to retain their positions in the Manor House." There was a covert sneer on the man's face which cast a doubt on his bland words.

"I thank Sir John, but I have ample means, and prefer to retire," was her quiet but resolute reply.

"Pardon me, Lady Isolda," rejoined the agent, his sinister smile spreading, "Sir John's commands are peremptory. You cannot be permitted to quit the mansion."

"Cannot be permitted!" exclaimed the monk and lady in a breath.

"No! By Henry-le-Spring's will, made and signed on the heights of Falkirk, on the eve of the battle, under presentiment of death, and entrusted to a friend. Sir John, if living, was appointed sole executor of his estate, and guardian of his daughter Mary."

Isolda's eyes flashed. "This is a conspiracy. My dear lord made no such will, or Rowland Belasyse would have known it."

"This must be looked into!" cried Father Robert.

"As you will," said Lascelles, with a contemptuous shrug. "There is the document," throwing it across the table.

The will was brief, but decisive; and in all faith and brotherly love gave stringent powers to Sir John over all which he possessed, either in his own right, or in right of his wife, in trust for his beloved daughter.

It was duly signed, attested, and sealed with the arms of the Le-Springs'. So far as Robert Kellaw saw, there was no disputing it. The two attesting witnesses had fallen at the siege of Stirling; and much as he and the distressed widow might doubt a deed so long held in abeyance, they were not in a position to disprove it.

Not since the tidings of Henry-le-Spring's death had reached his widow had so sad a scene been witnessed in Lady Isolda's chamber, when the good monk, whispering pious words of comfort, led her thither, lest she should swoon in the presence of the intruders. Yet the gleam of exaltation which shot after them from Robert Lascelles' sinister eyes had been unseen. It was Isolda's memories of John-le-Spring which assured her heart of treachery and fraud.

Henceforth the Lady Isolda might regard herself a prisoner, seldom breathing the fresh air beyond &e range of the Manor garden. Did she cross the drawbridge even, for Sunday or Saint-day service at the church. Robert Lascelles was at her elbow, and his presence marred her devotion; while so free was his manner towards the shrinking Mary, and such were the roistering habits of his followers, that at length she began to wish even for the advent of John-le-Spring as a safeguard from insult.

But what of fairy gifts? Had the amulet lost its power? Lady Isolda's own talisman was gone; but had it remained she might have scrupled to use it. Under the priestly influence of Father Kellaw, she had begun to doubt the lawfulness of accepting aid from ethereal beings beyond the pale of the Christian Church; nay, even to fear lest they should be but the specious delusions of Satan. Yet, had it been otherwise, maternal love would not have permitted her to purchase immunity for herself by leaving Mary unprotected in the den of the wolf.

"The King is dead! Long live the King!" John-le-Spring is back, the ruler of his ancestral home! What treason had he committed that had kept him from showing his face whilst the long-armed vengeance of Edward I. could be dreaded?

At all events the monarch's breath was scarcely gone ere Robert Lascelles, with scant ceremony, announced the arrival of Sir John to Lady Isolda and her daughter. The new lord had the same foxy hair and beard as of yore, the same sensuous mouth; but the eye was more shifty, the voluptuary more marked in the smooth face; and ever and anon he would start and glance over his shoulder, as if he feared a spectre stood behind him.

He was marvellously gracious; but it was soon apparent a new persecution had commenced. He renewed his advances to Isolda, offering to obtain a dispensation from the Pope for their marriage. Prisoner though she was, Isolda turned a deaf ear to him, and in this Father Kellaw supported her. Sir John fumed and swore, and would fain have kept the monk out of the Manor; but somehow there was a drop of craven fear in his heart, and he, a vassal of the Church, dared not defy it openly, for reasons known only to himself and one other.

The death of Edward and the dispersion of the army brought Rowland Belasyse back, panting to embrace Mary as his wife after his more than Jacob's probation. Picture his dismay when Sir John refused to ratify the contract agreed to by his brother; and, moreover, asserted that Mary had consented to espouse his faithful follower, Robert Lascelles!

Old Ursula had hobbled into the hall during this colloquy, and contrived by a meaning shake of her palsied head to give a denial to Sir John's assertion. Damped, but not despairing, Rowland mounted his steed in a mist of passion and perplexity. He turned his head as he crossed the drawbridge to see Lady Isolda, pale and tearful, wave her kerchief to him from the oriel in her chamber.

Wrapped in thought, his horse was left to take its own course. It took the road towards Hetton. The last dwelling in Houghton was past; there was no human being in sight. Did his ears play him false, or was that his Mary's voice calling him by name? Was that her touch upon his arm?

"Rowland, my beloved, it is Mary speaks"—and lo! Mary rode beside him, paler, thinner, but lovely as ever.

In an instant he had dismounted, lifted her from her palfrey, and, straining her to his breast with impassioned ardour, covered her crimsoning face with kisses. Then followed a shower of questions, interrupted by fresh kisses and answers, in which Mary told all the wrongs and indignities she and her mother endured. "My amulet frees me to come and go," she said; "yet I cannot wander far lest I should be missed, and I cannot leave my mother to suffer alone; and she will not use it to escape."

"She would be less than a mother if she did, sweet Mary."

"But I am safe, perfectly safe, Rowland. I have slept thrice in the Fairies' Cradle since I was seven years old, once when I was seven months old, and again at fourteen, and lastly this year at twenty-one, and each time the Fairy promise of protection was insured for seven years."

"Protection! and yet in the grasp of your smooth-faced wretch of an uncle!"

"Yes! Rowland, safe! They may annoy, may threaten, but they cannot harm me. I only fear for my mother, who has not such security."

She opened a basket suspended from her saddle, and let forth a carrier dove. "See, Rowland, that bird will bear hither my messages to thee; and if thou be willing, my amulet also. It is not maidenly to meet thee here alone, but shielded by that talisman thou mayst enter the Manor boldly so long as thy purpose be pure; and with the Lady Isolda thou mayst concert some plan to free us. But thy horse must be left with a trusty attendant at a safe distance, since apart from the wearer of the talisman horse or garment will be visible. Yet, Rowland, know thou canst not come unseen into *my* presence. I have been free of the Fairies' Guild since my first dream in their Hetton Cradle, it would task a potent talisman to veil my eyes."

Those were not days when strong men made light of unseen spirits, or magic spells. He felt the truth of all she uttered, as he knew her incapable of falsehood; and longing for any mode of access to the home she brightened, assented to the transfer of the talismanic lily-bell.

"And now I must depart, ere the sun goes down," she whispered, breaking from his clasp. "The amulet confers invisibility, but not the power to lower a drawbridge, cross a moat, or pass through barred doors."

He lifted her gallantly to her saddle, and after a lingering farewell they parted, and as she vanished she murmured the spell—

Safely come and safely go,
Unseen as wind, unheard as snow.

Chapter 5

In changing owners the Manor House changed its character. Sir Henry's invited guests had been of the nobility and chivalry of the North; the casual guests who sought his hospitality, of every grade, but mostly the indigent poor, and for these last there was ever a warm welcome in coming, a filled wallet and a whole garment at departure. Sir John entertained other guests, and a different feeling; he wore no robe of charity to cover his sins; perchance he held that the Paynim blood he had shed absolved him from all other Christian duties.

He converted the peaceful mansion into a fortress, placed sentinels at every outlet, and on the turret; oppressed his tenants and vassals with his exactions; and lavished ill-got wealth in luxury and riot.

One by one the more noble of Lady Isolda's bower-women left her service, scared by the bold manners of the knight's companions. Sir John would fain have replaced them with creatures of his own, but the lady was firm, and preferred waiting on herself, with a maiden or two from the village as aids. Dame Ursula was getting old, and could barely hobble on her crutched stick from room to room. But she kept the maids in order, and guided the household thriftily, now Lady Isolda refused to preside, and to the maids' chamber Ursula was better than bolt or bar, for rude men not afraid of God were somehow in awe of her; yet she was no shrew, and had but a feeble voice. But she was motherly, and the coarsest of these men remembered, perchance with remorse, mothers and *grandames*, dead or far away, and slunk abashed from her rebuke.

The third Christmas spent at the Manor by its new master terrified the women. Feasting and wassail, Yule-log and holly-bush, mimes and minstrels had been of old. But now the license of games and mummeries, indecent jests and buffoonery, beyond even the ordinary coarseness of the age, drove the ladies from the hall, amidst peals of laughter from Sir John and his worthy associate, Robert Lascelles. Something of this .had been the previous Christmas. But now the mirth grew uproarious, until the noise penetrated to Isolda's chamber. Then, in their cups, the worthies quarrelled, and swords were drawn, the man taunting his master with an unfulfilled promise.

"I tell thee, knave, I broke no promise. I said thou shouldst have the wench an' thou couldst win her."

"Win her I sayst thou? I have no dainty words for dainty misses. I have hot blood, and am for hasty wooing. But not even a midsummer sun could thaw such an iceberg. Were she once my *wife* I could bend her to my will. But Sir John-le-Spring grudges his niece's dower to his old comrade!"

"Now, by the fiend, thou liest! An' thou wouldst have the girl, take her. I have heard a woman shriek ere now, and will not bar thee."

Once more the swords were sheathed, the red hands clasped in amity, cups were drained to the success of the foul compact, and the drunken men-at-arms hiccoughed their approbation, as Robert Lascelles, heated with wine and passion, rushed from the hall.

But there were old retainers of Sir Henry, whose blood had long boiled with indignation, who put their hands upon their swords with meaning looks.

In the Lady Isolda's bower there was calm—and a visitor, with such happiness as that visitor could make. Ursula had gathered the maids round their own chamber fire, and whilst sipping spiced ale, kept them alive with old-world tales. They took no note of the impetuous step which passed their door to stop at the Lady Isolda's.

"Who knocks?" was the answer from within, as a dagger hilt rapped loudly on the oak.

"A messenger from Sir John," was the reply. Robert Lascelles was sober enough to know that he was on the wrong side of a barrier almost as strong as a girl's will.

There was a whispered conference in the room.

"It is a late hour. I will hear the message on the morrow."

"It must be heard tonight, should the door be forced for its delivery!"

Lady Isolda hesitated. Her friends, Ralph Neville and Hervey Belasyse were away at Westminster, her husband's will, which left herself and a child, penniless in the hands of his brother, bound her fast. She could but temporize until deliverance came.

"Let him come," was whispered in her ear, by the invisible friend at her side, who had crossed the ice-bound moat to spend his Christmas with his betrothed.

The wooden bolts were one by one withdrawn. Robert Lascelles stalked in; his eyes bloodshot, his face inflamed, his purpose black as his sable suit. Lady Isolda stood between him and Mary.

"Your message. Sir!"

"My message? This. I am to have Mistress Mary to wife an' I can take her! I have waited long enough, been flouted oft enough, but by St. Oswald I wait no longer. Stand aside, good dame. Mistress Mary goes with me tonight, will she, nil she!"

He had thrust Isolda aside as a reed, and put out his other arm to clutch the loathing Mary's waist—all at once his arm relaxed nerveless; his face blackened; his lips parted; his eyeballs glared; the grip of a muscular but unseen hand was on his wicked throat, another on his shoulder, he was thrust backwards through the doorway, and hurled out against the opposite wall of the corridor. There was a heavy fall, a groan, and silence.

The door was closed against intrusion, but it might as well have stood open. No one came to see how so good a comrade fared. No shrieks had been heard, and the jest went in the hall that he had won a mistress easily.

An hour later he crawled to his own chamber, a beaten cur; ashamed to face his mates and tell a story none would credit; his wicked purpose shaken for the time—but only for the time.

As he foresaw, he was jeered and bantered when he told of an unseen hand grasping his throat, even when he bared the blackened marks. "Thou'st had a drunken fit, man; or a tussle with the foul fiend himself. It's like enough," cried Sir John, with a mocking laugh.

"Ay, like enough," exclaimed another; "the Devil will have his due some day, and there's his sign manual across thy weasand as a token."

"He'll have his due of thee, then, John-de-Weardale, and Sir John-le-Spring too, maybe, but he finds not me in your company; and mark me. Sir John, better face the foul fiend than me an' ye pay not what you owe, and send the girl to my hold in the Cleveland hills before the year goes round."

"I tell thee to take her, man; take her! Sure thou'rt not afraid of a wench?"

The baited man's eyes glared. Sir John, reckless from his last night's riot, stretched his hand as appealing to those around him. "An' seem'st he not the very devil now? Good friend Robert, I never look to see a blacker fiend than thou."

"Then look to thyself, or forget not to pay thy bond!"

Robert Lascelles and his troop were gone. Their departure lightened the load of three heavy hearts. Rowland Belasyse, who, unseen, had remained to guard those so dear to him, reported the quarrel, and strengthened Lady Isolda's belief that Sir John detained them illegally, and that the man Lascelles held the secret.

Somehow, Sir John seemed to breathe more freely when his prime minister was no longer at his elbow, and the ladies were treated with less discourtesy. However, Isolda soon found this to imply a renewal of Sir John's importunities, and her temporary satisfaction ended. In her indignation she threatened to charge him before the bishop with forcible and fraudulent detention.

"Hard words, my lady, break no bones! Bishop Beck has but just 'scaped the regal lion's paw. He will hardly dare meddle with Sir John-le-Spring just yet, even should the birds of the air carry your charge. I have given you the chance to be mistress here once more. *Now*," and he ground his teeth, "I will bring a mistress over you."

Sir John took horse and rode away, leaving John-de-Weardale as his deputy. In less than a fortnight he returned, a lady riding by his side, whose robes of costly material were made in the very extreme of fashion; her amber silk under-skirt had a deep frill or flounce, the crimson upper robe swept the ground a yard behind her as she walked, her open hanging over-sleeves drooped almost to her knees; an embroidery of gold and pearls bordered each garment, and her shoes likewise embroidered, almost doubled the natural length of her feet, so long were the pointed toes.

The compression of her waist in leathern stays made her movements stiff and rigid; then her eyebrows had been trimmed, her cheeks painted; her hair (as could be seen through its golden net) dyed; and from her hat, with brim curving upwards on either side, a flowing veil depended. On the simple-minded ladies, who were called into her presence as though she were a queen, this extravagant display made no impression; their minds were too full for envy, and the robes sat so ill upon the wearer admiration was impossible.

With this woman, Dame Maldred Fitzmaldred, came a bevy of bowerwomen, free of look, loud of voice, coarse of manner. To make room for them. Lady Isolda's maidens were dismissed, and the chamber she had called her own since she entered it a bride was usurped by the haughty leman of Sir John.

When the household keys had been ungraciously demanded, Lady Isolda had charged Dame Ursula to surrender them to Lady-le-Spring, supposing this to be Sir John's wife; and in that supposition prepared unmurmuringly to resign her private apartment also.

The return of John-de-Weardale, after temporary absence, dispelled the illusion. There were foul charges and recriminations, oaths and maledictions, drawn swords and bloodshed in the hall, spurred horses dashing out over the bridge—and for what? A vile woman who had left one paramour for another—the poor esquire for the wealthy knight!

It was a dastardly and insolent deed to flaunt his shameless victory in the very face of the man he called friend, and under the cover of his own roof-tree. Had Sir John yet to learn that such wrongs ferment like yeast in the breasts of men, or that the most deadly foe is he who has been friend; or did he hold a charmed life, that thus he braved their vengeance? The imprisonment of Bishop Beck had made Sir John bold. Father Robert had been long excluded from the Manor; and but for the freedom to come and go conferred on Mary's amulet by Rowland, the poor imprisoned ladies would have been solitary indeed.

With him came glimpses of old happiness; and Maldred's petty malice fell innocuous. She had ousted the ladies from their chamber, and transferred them to an incommodious apartment with bare stone walls, rude beds, straw mattresses, rough chests for clothes and other women's gear; but coming intrusively to pry into their privacy, she stood aghast to see the transformation there. Tapestry, fresh of tint and texture, hid the grey stone; a bell-shaped canopy o'erhung a bed inlaid with ivory, and covered with a silken quilt of green and gold. A cabinet of strange device and rich in floral carving appeared to mock her wonder, and on the floor was the only carpet in the mansion.

Straightway she hurried to Sir John, and in a rage accused him of cozening her. Then summoning the household to the work, transferred the priceless furniture to her own use. Marvel of marvels, after a sleepless night on a hard couch, she woke to bare walls, a rush-strewn floor, and furniture of common wood. Back came the solid fittings of Isolda's time for her own use; back went the rude plenishing to the insulted ladies—and lo! all bright and glorious in hue and shape again, they filled that ugly room with beauty.

She impounded their wardrobes, dealing out linen and woollen raiment such as the peasants wore, and said that silken robes were not for dependents; but no sooner were the garments donned than they assumed fresh shape and texture, falling in graceful folds, and mocking art to imitate.

"Mother, the Lady Bell is still our friend, you see. Her lily wand has done this," said Mary, at this second transformation.

"Love, my child, may well convert a prison to a palace; and a modest wearer stamps her impress on her garb. Still, for thy sake, I would that St. Cuthbert sent us deliverance. It is sad to see thy maiden bloom wasted in these walls."

And deliverance was coming, albeit not so swiftly as the lady craved. And Maldred, wearied of ineffectual attempts to lower their dignity or lessen their self-respect, perplexed and defeated, left them at rest while she plotted fresh mischief.

CHAPTER 6

Months went by. Sir John appeared besotted. His leman cast a glamour over him, and made the bad man worse. He left his helpless relatives in her unfeeling hands; lavished his means to gratify her whims; spent in dress and costly indulgence thrice his income; and, as though the Manor House was not spacious or sumptuous enough, built a summer bower within the garden bounds, and fitted it with luxuries from foreign lands, plunging himself in debt.

It so happened that Rowland Belasyse swam across the moat one bright May-day, when the drawbridge was raised, and passed invisibly on to the Lady Isolda's room, heedless of the fact that the water dripping from his garments left a wet track along the floor, scaring the men and maids who, in their wonder and alarm, raised a cry of witchcraft, a cry remembered well by evil Maldred. Rowland had brought good news. Bishop Beck was dead, and their friend Robert Kellaw had been elected bishop in his room. From him they might hope for the succour denied elsewhere. And let it not be thought Rowland Belasyse had been inert or tame in his betrothed's cause. He and his steed had galloped from keep to castle, from castle to court, to stir up friends in their behalf. But the will of husband and father, powerful in life, was powerful from the grave; and those barons who might have interfered were too intent on checking kingly exactions to embroil themselves with a neighbour.

But deliverance came when hope was gone.

One of Sir John's retainers, the bridgeward, fell sick, and was left to die. untended, like a dog. Old Ursula heard talk of him in the kitchen, and telling Mistress Mary, the pair sought the wretched loft where the sick man lay. Mary passed a cooling hand across his brow, and the magnetic touch appeared to check the fever. Ursula concocted healing messes, and between the twain the man in time recovered. Anxious to show his gratitude, he questioned Ursula if Mistress-le-Spring would not be too proud to accept a trinket from a poor man-at-arms. It had come to him, he said, in an old doublet a good knight threw to him as he lay stripped and bleeding on the field of Dunbar. He had kept it in remembrance of the unknown knight.

Ursula's old eyes brightened. She saw in the trinket the jewel her mistress had lost, and rejoiced at its recovery, although she knew not all its properties. She recovered it not one whit too soon.

Sir John and his leman finding all efforts to humiliate Isolda and Mary fruitless—no menial task seeming to rob them of their native dignity—and feeling either their purity a rebuke, or a sense of insecurity crossing their conscious brains, began to long for their death. With the evil-minded to think is to do.

"Hast thou no skill in herbs, Maldred, to rid us of these meek-faced minions? I hate them!" and Sir John hissed out the words.

"Aye, marry have I, and the will to use them," was the quick response, as the woman's evil eyes glittered with satisfaction.

Isolda wore her regained treasure on her arm. That day, as her fingers touched the meat served on a solitary trencher for their midday meal, her hand stopped midway to her mouth. The pearls had turned intensely black, the emerald white. There was danger at hand! "Poison at last!" The exclamation and accompanying gesture checked Mary's hand also. The trencher was emptied from the window, A favourite staghound of Sir John's snapped at the meat, and died in agony within the hour.

A Barbary ape brought home by Sir John shared the same fate the following day. One by one their household animals died; but the ladies lived and throve. The recovered amulet removed all difficulty in procuring wholesome food from the buttery unknown.

The consternation of Sir John and Maldred may be imagined but no remorse entered their breasts. They only chafed with very fresh defeat.

It was June the 11th, the eve of St. Barnabas. The air was hot and oppressive. The perfume of flowers and scented herbs wafted through the open casements of the summer bower where Sir John and Maldred were regaling themselves; spending the hours in wanton dalliance as they concerted a plan to accuse their captives of witchcraft, and so bring on them the awful judgment of the Church.

They might plan, but their long-tried victims were beyond their reach. The previous day Rowland had borne away the carrier dove. It had flown back with Mary's amulet beneath its wing. Ursula, feigning an errand to the village, persuaded Hugh, the grateful bridgeward, to lower it for her exit. Close behind her trod unseen her ladies with such valuables as they could carry. At the church they stopped, and entering the open doors, knelt in thankful prayer.

Rowland had horses nigh at hand, with a litter for the good dame whose feeble limbs had already been overtaxed.

To avoid observation, they took .an unfrequented bridle-path well screened by trees. Barely were they in the covert, when a band of Shevalds, a new tribe of devastating robbers from the hills, dashed at full speed along the road they had just quitted.

Rowland had a precious charge with him, and dared not linger, but a man was sent back to watch the movements of the suspected desperadoes.

On they rode without pause in a straight line for the Manor House. The drawbridge was up, but at the cry, "For Cleveland And Weardale!" as at a signal, the man Hugh lowered it, and the horsemen crossed unopposed.

"With his leman in the garden bower," was Hugh's gruff .answer to a question from the leader of the band.

Drowsy with wine and the heat of the June day. Sir John lay with his head on Maldred's shoulder, her wanton arms around him, dreaming of no intrusion, no mishap. Suddenly the curtains were rent from the doorway. The woman gave a shriek. Sir John awoke, two well-known men with gleaming swords and gleaming eyes were close upon him. His hand involuntarily sought his sword; but swords are not for sensual ease, and his was missing. Guilt had made a craven of the knight; he begged for mercy, begged it from the men he had taunted and mocked. But they were as hungry wolves above a fallen leader. With every blow they struck they called a deed of blood or treachery to mind, and as they let out life through bloody doors added soul-tortures to his death-agonies.

Bloodshed and pillage in the lovers' bower, bloodshed and pillage in the mansion, the clash of swords, the shrieks of women, the groans of men, and flaming banners crimsoning the sky! Hark! "Belasyse to the rescue!" Le-Spring's retainers rally. Through fire and smoke they drive the Shevalds back, as Rowland and a motley force of men-at-arms and peasants dash in and turn, the tide.

One man with a woman in his arms fights his way to his horse, calling his men to follow, and at their head dashes across the bridge, leaving the rest to their fate. Surely that was John-de-Weardale with the faithless Maldred!

The Shevalds had retreated, but now there was another foe to fight, a fierce untameable foe, that licked up blood like water, and made mammocks of masonry.

Little of the Manor House was left when the fire was subdued. But Robert Lascelles, the assassin of Sir John-le-Spring, lingering after his comrades were gone, to dart from chamber to chamber for the fair prize he had reckoned on, had found himself a prisoner; Mistress Mary beyond his reach; himself denounced a murderer by the shrieking Maldred ere she had been carried off.

He was at once transferred to Durham Castle. There he was condemned to the rack. The very sight of the horrid machine opened his lips; and what a confession was his! It was he who had attacked the travellers and carried off the infant at Hetton, bribed by Sir John, who envied his brother's inheritance and happiness. Hotly pursued, he threw the babe into a hollow on a hillock, regardless of its fate. He had fought with Sir John when, under a feigned name, the traitorous knight had leagued with the Scots, headed incursions over the borders, and laid waste Isolda's lands. But it was Sir John himself who at Falkirk Bridge had struck his brother down with his own hand.

The will, said to be Henry-le-Spring's, was a vile forgery. A reprobate friar had been bribed to draw it up, and amongst them the false signatures were added. His brother's signet had been stripped from his dead finger by Sir John on the field of battle.

Here was a category of crimes to stain Sir John withal. Yet Lascelles was executed, being taken red-handed; whilst Sir John was buried in Houghton Church, and someone—it is said a woman who had once loved him—put a monument above his grave, and paid for masses for his soul.

Nor did John-de-Weardale escape. Bishop Kellaw, incensed at the ravaged of the Shevalds in his diocese, vowed their extermination, and put his brother in command of a strong force to hunt them down. One of these soldiers killed John le-Weardale in Holy Island, whither he had fled for refuge.

Whether the fairies helped at the restoration of the Manor, history does not say, but it was ready for a grand wedding-feast long before Sir John's monument was carved.

It is said that Lady Bell and her train re-appeared on the occasion; that Mary's bridal robes, the envy of maids and matrons, were from fairy looms; that the wee guest's shrill piping voice recalled the christening feast, and reminded Rowland and Isolda that fairy gifts were not fallacies. As Sir Plumbius and Sir Ferris had predicted, "time and need" had come, and the hills of Cleveland and Weardale had sent men and steel to the rescue. And Rowland was told that Sir Carbo's flame-lit token was Mary's best dower to him. He would find the solution of the riddle if he dug deep enough below the clay of Hetton. Sir John had no children and no will, and Mary was heiress of the Manor, and the Fairies' Cradle too.

Rowland Belasyse did not take possession of Houghton-le-Spring undisputed. The monks of Durham would fain have recalled it as a lapsed fief; but the new law of Mortmain stood the young couple in good stead. Then King Edward issued a precept to the bishop to "levy £20 of the goods of John-le-Spring, deceased, owing to Philip Morgan and others of the company of merchants trading to Florence." It was a goodly sum then, and Rowland paid it with reluctance; feeling that the merchandise had been for the woman who, but for the Fairies' amulet, had compassed his beloved Mary's death.

Centuries have passed since fairies danced visibly round their Hetton Cradle, but long after they had disappeared the unshrived soul of Sir John showed its agony of remorseful guilt in beaded drops of sweat, which oozed from the carved image on his tomb on each anniversary of his red death—St. Barnabas' Eve, while a lurid haze filled the south transept, and the candles on the altar burned blue and dim. He had shed a brother's blood, and by man was his blood shed; he had robbed the widow and orphan, and he left neither widow nor child to lament him.

The very armour hung above his tomb Sir Ralph Neville tore down and carried off; and if Sir Ralph had to restore the armour and do penance for the sacrilege, it was but that it too might bear witness against the dead in the groans which came from the creaking coat of mail each St. Barnabas' Eve.

My Will

I was seriously ill; there could be no mistake about that. Dr. Godfrey had pronounced my symptoms alarming, and he was not the man to cry "wolf" before the wolf was in sight.

From a tour in the Highlands I had brought back to our home, in Cheyne Walk (besides Anna my gentle wife, and Gilbert our high-spirited son) an intolerable, persistent cold, the result of too many baths of Scotch mist.

This I had neglected in the bustle of getting Gilbert off to school again, until it settled into acute bronchitis, attended with inflammation of the lungs.

The first note of alarm was sounded when Godfrey, our family surgeon (Dr. Godfrey we called him by courtesy), intimated to my poor distressed wife that he should like to consult with Sir James Ponder on the "case."

"Then you think Mr. Leslie is in danger, doctor?" put Anna, interrogatively, looking up at him with white and anxious face.

"Well—a—" and the doctor tapped his chin reflectively with three fingers. "The symptoms are not altogether so favourable as we could wish; and—a—it might be altogether more satisfactory for all parties if we had an additional opinion."

The "additional opinion" did not place matters on a much more promising footing.

"A sound constitution" was all on which Sir James relied to enable me to "pull through."

The second note of alarm was an intimation from Dr. Godfrey that it "might be as well to telegraph for Gilbert to return home without delay."

The final blast came from my old friend Matthew Sharp, when he asked me if I did not think I ought to make my will, and otherwise put my affairs in order.

I had known Matthew Sharp at least twenty years. When I married Anna he was groomsman, and he had stood godfather to Gilbert, who was now a sturdy lad of sixteen. He was a solicitor in Chancery practice, and had offices in Furnival's Inn, though his house was in Sloane Street, pretty near to our own. His son Albert had been sent to school along with Gilbert; visits between the two houses were frequent and *sans cérémonie*, and altogether we were very intimate friends indeed.

"Do not regard me as a bird of ill-omen, my dear friend, for this suggestion," said he, sitting by my bedside, stroking the Marseilles coverlet with one hand and looking across the room, not at me; "but it is always best to be on the right side—to be prepared for anything, in fact."

"Then you think me in a bad way, Sharp?" I murmured, feebly, in response, feeling as if he had given the sands of my life a shake in the hour-glass of time.

"We—ll—well. You know bronchial attacks are treacherous things; and as I said before, it is always best to be on the right side the hedge."

"Certainly," was my sighing assent.

"You have signed too many leases to be frightened by a sheet of parchment; and are not silly enough to fancy you are signing your death-warrant in signing a will," continued he, still smoothing away at the quilt.

It was late in autumn. There was a good fire burning in my chamber, the temperature of which was regulated by thermometer. A shaded reading-lamp on a small side-table served to light Matthew, who sat with one knee crossed high over the other, as a support to the book which he used as a desk. As he sat by my bed-head, the blue damask curtain partially screened him from me, but I heard the scratching of his pen, and life seemed to ebb with every dip of the ink.

I devised all my real and much of my funded property to Bertie, on the attainment of his majority, with a suitable provision for his minority; my dear wife to have £300 *per annum*, for her sole use and maintenance for the term of her natural life, and the use of my real property until Bertie came of age. I also left her sole executrix.

Sharp, or his clerks, must have sat up all night; for before eleven o'clock next morning Matthew was there with the will all ready for signature.

Sir James Ponder and Dr. Godfrey were with me at the time; so Matthew sat in our morning-room with Bertie, who had arrived an hour before, fortifying him with all the platitudes of conventional friendship against the severe affliction which seemed inevitable, and comforting himself with wine and biscuit.

The doctors had barely left my room, accompanied by my anxious wife, when the lawyer entered—not, however, before he had caught Dr. Godfrey by the button-hole, on the staircase, and asked him to remain in the house to witness the will he was about to read over to me.

"In any case I should remain, Sir; our patient approaches a crisis. I hope you will not excite or weary him," answered the surgeon, as he went on.

I was too ill to pay much attention to the will, with its multitudinous "aforesaids" and "hereinafters." but the general tenor seemed all I had desired.

In the presence of Dr. Godfrey, Barton, our housekeeper, Annie and Bertie, I signed it; the two former being the attesting witnesses. And, notwithstanding my friend Sharp's assumption to the contrary, I did feel as though I were indeed signing my death-warrant.

I think Anna felt so too, for she hurried from the room, and I heard a sound of suppressed sobbing outside the door.

The effort tried and exhausted me. Nurse cleared the apartment. Dr. Godfrey remained downstairs. Mr. Sharp went away, carrying the will with him.

I might have died in signing that document; at least the bitterness of death seemed to have passed in the signature of the last sheet, with its formal renunciation of all my earthly possessions. Nothing troubled me—a sort of mental syncope followed; I lay listless and spent, my mind a blank. It may be I fell asleep.

If so, I slept ten or twelve hours. Anna was moistening my lips with brandy on a feather when I opened my eyes on drawn curtains and subdued lamplight.

At all events I cheated the two undertakers who had quarrelled on the steps of Don Saltero's coffee-house for the prospective right of burying me; and I got better.

I had, however, a long fight for it; and I think I had a fair chance of being spoiled by Bertie and his mother during the tedious months of convalescence.

Matthew Sharp was profuse in his congratulations; and I wonder now I did not detect the ring of base metal in them.

I certainly did think he changed colour and appeared fidgety when I remarked casually one evening, while shuffling the cards for *bezique*,

Anna playing and singing Longfellow's "Bridge" meanwhile—

"I say. Sharp, you were right, you see. Signing a will is *not* signing a death-warrant. I think I was an ass to leave a matter of so much import to the last moment; however, I am a living ass, and so am worth two dead lions. And now I am glad that you have my will all right and safe."

"Oh, yes, I have it safe enough, and it's a duty off your mind," said he, taking up his cards and considering them more irresolutely than usual.

Bertie had gone back to school, the domestic wheels ran in the old ruts, and the will I had made passed from my mind altogether.

Months went by placidly. Summer came in full force, and Londoners, to avoid the fate of traditional blackbirds "baked in a pie," were scattering hither and thitherto cool themselves with sea or mountain breezes. Having had a sufficient dose of mountain mist to serve us for one while, we pitched upon Scarborough for our summer retreat, and packing began in earnest.

Then it was my will was recalled to my memory in an odd way.

I had not an overburdened mind, never overburdened my stomach, and as a rule slept well and dreamlessly.

We went to bed at our usual hour, everything being in readiness for our departure on the morrow.

The night was intolerably hot, and possibly that might make me restless. Be this as it may, I awoke in the middle of the night from a confused dream, a voice—that of Anna's dead father—wringing in my ear, "Look to your will!"

I jumped up in bed. There was no one in the room. Anna's breathing told she was sleeping calmly.

With an amused smirk and a shrug of my unsuperstitious shoulders I lay down again, and soon dosed off; only to dream again, and this time more vividly.

I seemed to stand in front of our red-brick house in Cheyne Walk, yet not I myself, in the flesh, but in the spirit; and, gazing on it, beheld Anna and Bertie, both in deep mourning, at an upper window. As I looked I saw the dark building shudder, totter, and fall with a terrible crash, burying wife and son both in the ruins, despite my own frantic efforts to save them.

As I wakened, startled with the noise and the fright, I heard the same voice crying peremptorily, "Look to your will!"

August though it was, I shook as with an ague. My dear Anna was still composedly sleeping. I hesitated to disturb her in the face of a fatiguing journey, but I got out of bed, washed my face, walked about the room, and endeavoured to shake off, as so many superstitious cobwebs, the eerie sensations creeping over my otherwise practical self.

At length I succeeded, or thought I did, and once more stretched my long limbs between the sheets. Sleep again closed my eyelids, only to be rudely re-opened. Again my disembodied self seemed to stand gazing on our old habitation; wife, or rather widow, and son stood mournfully at the window; she clasped her hands imploringly towards me, and screamed as the house rocked and swayed, then fell as before with a hideous crash and a cloud of dust; and as I rushed forward appalled, a ghostly shadow of her father stood by my side, sternly and rebukingly pointing to the ruins as he peremptorily repeated. "Look to your will!"

This time I awakened Anna. A sort of shuddering horror was upon me. I could scarcely describe to her my triplicate dream for the nervous tremor which shook me. I seemed to hear the echoes of that exhortation floating away in the distance.

I need hardly say my fear was contagious, even before its cause was made known, her own hasty surmise hovering between illness and burglars.

Woman-like, Anna's faith in dreams was more developed than mine.

"Three times repeated," she murmured, "and with such a variation! I tell you what, Gilbert, that dream is not to be slighted." Then, mother-like, her thoughts ran off at a tangent to her son—"I wonder if Bertie is well. I will write first thing in the morning."

"Oh! Bertie's all right. If anything is wrong, it is the will I made when I was ill. There may be some flaw in it. I will run across to Sharp's in the morning and ask him to look over it carefully; and perhaps get counsel's opinion upon it. I shall have plenty of time."

So that was disposed of, and we tried to sleep again, but we had been thoroughly aroused, and an hour or more elapsed before oblivion steeped our senses. Then we somewhat overslept ourselves, and breakfast was delayed.

As a rule, I linger at the morning meal, sipping coffee and *Times* paragraphs alternately.

I hurried over both. Nevertheless, when I reached Sloane Street I was too late for Sharp. He had been gone to the office ten minutes. I hesitated. Should I defer my visit to the lawyer's until our return? "Look to your will!" seemed to drift like a breeze through the doorway of the hall.

I looked at my watch. A hansom was passing; I hailed it; promised the driver a fee for speed, and was soon tearing away towards Furnival's Inn in hopes to catch the lawyer and our train both.

The clerks made such desperate efforts to appear busy on my entrance that I felt sure the mice were playing in the absence of the cat, without the announcement, "Mr. Sharp has not yet arrived, sir."

Twenty minutes at least elapsed before Matthew, smug and speckless, put in an appearance.

"Your cab will have outstripped my omnibus; besides which I was stopped by a wearisome client in the gateway," explained he, as he ushered me into his comfortable private office, important with a law library and japanned boxes, supposed to hold title-deeds, &c.

"And now what can I do for you?" he asked—

Washing his hands with invisible soap,
In imperceptible water.

I rarely went to his *office*, save for business.

Notwithstanding the haste I was in, I could not plunge into my errand at once. I felt there was something ridiculous in confessing that I had been brought thither by so intangible a matter as a dream. After some preamble I blundered out—

"Well, the fact is, Sharp, I dreamed last night that there was something wrong with that will of mine; I wish you would just go over it; perhaps get counsel's opinion to see there is no flaw in it."

A curious expression stole over Matthew's face as I spoke, then he broke into as curious a laugh.

"You don't mean to say that you, Gilbert Leslie, rode here posthaste spurred by—a dream—a mere dream?" and he chuckled outright; "and that you would throw away cab-fare and counsel's fees for anything so absurd? I really gave you credit, Leslie, for more common-sense."

I felt somewhat nettled by his reception, even though convinced I should have laughed at anyone else who had been similarly swayed by a nightmare, and I think I answered rather snappishly,

"It is no imputation on common-sense to have a hastily-concocted will examined for security. I want no litigation over my grave; and should scarcely rest there if my neglect brought trouble to my dear ones."

"Oh! well, if you take that view of the case, you may be right. I will do as you wish. But—" and he glanced at a solid marble timepiece on his chimney-piece—"I thought you were off to Scarborough this morning?"

"So we are, and I have no time to lose."

I snatched up my hat and was off. But, though the attendant hansom dashed along dangerously, and Annie had a four-wheeler loaded with luggage waiting at our door, and stood herself on the step ready to get in, we reached Euston Square fully ten minutes after the train had started.

I felt myself looking foolish a second time that morning; and what with my restless night, the heat, and the hurry, was not in the most amiable of tempers. I am afraid I swore at my own folly, in allowing myself to be sent such a wild-goose chase by a dream.

Annie was more philosophic than I.

"Never mind, Gilbert," said she, pleasantly. "On a mere journey for pleasure, one day sooner or later will make very little difference. Let us leave our luggage in the booking-office until tomorrow. Travelling by this precise train is not a matter of life and death."

Not a matter of life and death? How little we mortals know the slight threads on which the issues of life and death depend!

Before night the whole town rang with the terrible news of an awful collision between *that precise train* and a luggage-train, in which carriages were smashed to splinters, and human beings sent out of life, crushed and gashed, and others back to life maimed, disfigured, shaken.

And we might have been among those, but for the dream which Sharp held in such derision.

A telegram in a late evening paper brought Matthew himself to Cheyne Walk, in a state of excitement and agitation, and with a face white as his own spotless shirt-front. The telegram had given no list of the injured, and believing us to have been passengers, he was too anxious to sleep until he had ascertained the worst.

So he said: and certainly his mental disturbance was peculiar—even "ascertaining the *best*" as Annie remarked, "did not seem to compose him."

He had evidently received a great shock, from which he could not recover. Was too restless to remain to supper, but tossed off a glass of brandy-and-water hastily, and rushed away to "relieve Mrs. Sharp's mind." I have since put another construction upon his agitation that night.

Be sure our thankfulness at escape did not allow us to forget the dream which had mainly procrastinated our journey. But we were inclined to put a new interpretation upon it, and regard it as a means to save our lives, rather than as indicating any irregularity in my will; especially when Matthew Sharp assured me he had gone carefully over the document and found it perfect in all respects—the best and clearest will he had ever drawn.

We went to the seaside; but not to Scarborough, and not until we recovered from the shock and horror which every fresh and pictorial representation of the terrible catastrophe had served to renew.

In about a week we found ourselves at romantic Ilfracombe, with nothing to do but enjoy ourselves thoroughly. In order to do this completely, I hired a small yacht, in which we, and a friend or two we met there, spent many delightful hours.

We had been in Ilfracombe about a fortnight when I experienced a recurrence of my memorable dream, in its complete form.

I was not likely to treat the warning lightly now. Both Anna and myself felt it boded evil.

A sailing party had been arranged for the day, but at the risk of offending our friends, I countermanded my orders for the yacht; would neither sail in her myself, nor permit my friends to venture that day. I was unmercifully chaffed, but I stood it well; and all the more stolidly when the freshening breezes got up into a gale, and the waves ran in with white crests.

Moreover, I relinquished the yacht, feeling a sense of danger in its possession.

A few nights later my dream troubled me again. I am a good swimmer, and it had been my wont to bathe every fine morning. I resigned my sea-bath with a sort of feeling that superstition was setting a seal on all my pleasures; but I never thought of obeying the dream-voice's injunction, "Look to your will," until it was repeated, when I had no pleasures to surrender from which danger could possibly threaten.

Then it was we gave up our lodgings, and returned to town, much to the astonishment and perturbation of Barton and the maids, who were deep in the mysteries of "autumn cleaning."

Leaving Anna to find her way through a labyrinth of inverted chairs and bundled-up carpets, I went at once to Sloane Street. I found Sharp's house in like condition. "Master and mistress at the seaside. Gone to Tenby for a month."

The next day saw me pass under the archway of Furnival's Inn to my friend's office, where I had a conference with his managing clerk. He knew nothing of the will. Mr. Sharp had his keys with him, and must have it in his own keeping. He would communicate with his governor; and gave me his address that I might do the same.

Letters brought only the unsatisfactory answer that he would see me on his return; but quite six weeks elapsed before he did return, and I grew restless and worried by delay.

Then he was necessarily overcrowded with business. If I called at his office he was either engaged, or out, or busy, or had an appointment; or had some shuffling excuse. At one time he had left his keys at home, at another was taken ill as he unlocked his private safe; and finally, he told me he had mislaid the will when he had it out for examination, and could not find it; but as soon as he had got over his crush of work he would have a thorough search for it.

"You need be under no apprehension," he said. "You are in good health, and even, if you were not, you could make a fresh will, if that did not turn up in the meanwhile."

"So I can," returned I, with the office-door in my hand, "and I think I shall take your advice."

And I did. I went straightway to Messrs. Shrewd and Cleare, solicitors, in Bloomsbury, and gave instructions for a fresh will. My dream had been latterly very troublesome, and I could not rest with "Look to your will!" perpetually ringing in my ears.

Moreover, I was so haunted with the reiterated idea of a something wrong with the will, that I assented to Mr. Shrewd's proposition to commence legal proceedings for the recovery of the former will from Sharp.

There had been a coolness growing up between the families, dating from our return from Ilfracombe, and extending even to Bertie and his schoolmate Albert Sharp, and now the rupture was complete.

I need not follow the sinuosities of the law in the struggle to recover the missing will, during which Sharp took an affidavit that it was lost; had been abstracted from his desk.

Suffice that it was recovered.

Something wrong with it?

I should think there was!

Sharp had substituted his *own son's name for that of our Bertie, had reduced the sum left to my dear Anna to a mere pittance, and put in his own name as executor and residuary legatee* in place of my wife's. That will would, indeed, have brought down my house—have made them beggars.

We had obtained possession of the precious sample of roguery through a sneak of a clerk who, smarting under some real or fancied wrong, turned upon Sharp, and sold his services to Messrs. Shrewd and Cleare.

Had it not been for Anna, Sharp would not only have been struck off the rolls but placed in a criminal dock. I was so exasperated at the treachery of the man I had known and trusted from boyhood.

His submission had been abject. His wife went pleading to mine— and she, kind creature that she is, forgave him for the sake of their daughters and son, whose whole lives would be blighted by their other's disgrace.

She thought he had had a lesson to last his lifetime.

I was not so sure of it; but I let Anna have her way, and left him to the whip of his own conscience.

But we held no contact with the Sharps in future.

Bertie was recalled from school, and sent to Cambridge.

I read my new will over myself carefully, and then submitted it to counsel to make assurance sure. I was never more troubled with dreams of anything "wrong" in that testament; and I never afterwards signed any document, no matter what, without first reading it myself.

Judgment Deferred

CHAPTER 1: ON BOARD THE "BEGUM"

A trading vessel—the *Alcestis*, from Bahia to Liverpool—found the *Begum* drifting helplessly as a log on the billows. Yet she was a stout ship, well rigged, and seemingly in good condition. When the lookout sighted her, Captain Somers changed the course of the *Alcestis* to come within hail of the apparently disabled craft. But only the scream of the curlew answered the loud "Ship, ahoy!" though the cry was thrice repeated.

Under the conviction that something was wrong with the silent vessel, he still bore down upon her. As they neared, his glass told him that the boats were gone from her davits, and that the man at the helm was the only visible creature on deck.

"Ship, ahoy!" again pierced the stillness. A handkerchief fluttered for an instant above the helmsman's head, and a faint echo seemed to come across the water.

A boat was lowered from the *Alcestis*. As the men pulled steadily towards the mysterious stranger. Captain Somers, who was himself in charge, saw that the figure-head was a woman, and next read her name, *The Begum*.

Cries of horror burst from the lips of the boarders at the sight before them. Captain, mates, and a couple of seamen lay gashed and dead upon the deck, where pools and rivulets of blood lay black and festering; and, sad as anything to see, a fine hound stretched in their midst, killed, no doubt, in the defence of his master.

The man at the wheel—by his garb a passenger and a gentleman—was the only living thing aboard, and he had fainted as Captain Somers stepped upon the deck, apparently from exhaustion caused by wounds.

The sun was broiling hot, and the stench from the exposed bodies was pestilential.

The first care of Captain Somers, after the restoration of the survivor, was to commit the slain reverently to the deep, and next to make such disposition of his own crew as would hest enable him to take the *Begum* in tow, and so preserve the sound teak-built ship and cargo for her owners.

Some hours elapsed before the rescued man was able to throw any light on what was a manifest tragedy. When he did relate the story it was with shuddering horror and many pauses, yet with strange and almost studied precision.

"My name is Stanhope—Alfred Stanhope. I went to India with my parents when a mere child. They have been dead several years. I was summoned from India to take possession of a fortune, inherited and bequeathed to me by a relative; and after winding up my affairs in the Presidency, I embarked on the *Begum* with my private secretary, Oliver Craven. The *Begum*, Captain Manners, was bound from Madras to London, with a cargo of rice, silk, sugar, and spices. There was also specie on board, for consignment to English bankers. Myself and secretary were the only passengers. There was a sufficient crew to work the ship with ease, had Captain Manners been so minded.

"We had baffling winds at the Cape, and our voyage was protracted—not, however, to any alarming extent; yet Captain Manners harassed his seamen with fatiguing duties, which I, a landsman, regarded as excessive. I may be in error, having no knowledge of seamanship. On the plea that provisions ran low, the men were put on short rations, and the allowance of grog was diminished. I am not prepared to say it was not a necessary precaution, but the consequences were terrible!

"A spirit of discontent prevailed. We had called at Madeira for fresh fruits and water. One or two of the men sought leave to go ashore. It was denied, and denied harshly. I ventured to remonstrate with the captain; was told to mind my own business; he was master of his ship, and would do as he chose.

"One glorious morning, about a week ago—I have lost my count of days, but it was the 4th of August—I sat writing in my cabin, Selim, my dog, coiled on the rug at the open doorway. There was a trampling of feet overhead. He gave a low growl, sprang to his feet and rushed on deck, the first to hear the mutterings of the storm and the plashing of the red rain.

"The slumbering mutiny had broken out. I reached the deck un-

175

armed, to find sailors and officers in fierce conflict, and my secretary, in the very midst, endeavouring in vain to quell the strife. Poor Oliver paid the penalty of his rashness. My faithful hound, rushing forward to defend him, fell a sacrifice at the outset. Before I could seize a cutlass, or strike a blow in self-defence, I felt the sharp sting of a bullet through my arm, and almost simultaneously a blow from a marlinspike stunned me.

"I must have lain senseless an hour or more. I recovered to find myself stiff and sore, in a pool of blood, amidst silence profound and terrible.

"It was some time before I attained full consciousness of my awful situation. The *Begum* had been abandoned by her mutinous crew, and I had been left for dead—among the dead.

"I managed to creep to my cabin and obtain a draught of brandy. Fortunately, the bullet was embedded in the muscles of my left arm, and I contrived to extract it with my penknife. Doubtless, I did it clumsily; but I did it, and, moreover, plastered and bound the wound."

"Had I not better examine it?" asked the surgeon of the *Alcestis*, rising, and coming forward.

"It is not necessary, sir," answered Mr. Stanhope, waving him back somewhat stiffly; "the wound is healing."

The surgeon coughed slightly, as he retired disconcerted, and Mr. Stanhope resumed:

"I discovered that the ship had been plundered, my cabin ransacked, money and valuables carried off. They had victualled their boats well. I could find no provisions beyond a few biscuits and a little water."

"I thought rice and sugar were part of the cargo?" suggested Captain Somers.

"Yes; but I was too weak and unskilled to procure them."

"Humph! they would be in the hold, and neither East India sugar bags nor rice bags are made of cast iron!"

There was a world of contempt for a land-lubber's imbecility in the captain's tone.

"The ship tossed and drifted at the will of the wind. My situation was horrible. If I went on deck the open eyes of the dead men seemed to follow me. If I went below I could signal no passing vessel. On the second day I resolved to throw the bodies overboard. I shudder as I think of the result." (He did shudder, indeed.) "Round the corpse of Oliver Craven, my secretary, who deserved a better fate, I wrapped a piece of canvas, and as well as I was able, having one arm disabled, dragged it to the side and pitched it over. There was a downward plunge, and then—"

"Some brandy for Mr. Stanhope, he is fainting."

Mr. Stanhope rallied, again waved back the officious surgeon, and continued:

"The canvas had slipped, and Craven's head and shoulders rose and fell with every wave that lapped the vessel's side, and life seemed to look out of the wave-washed eyes, from which salt tears ran down the white cheeks. It was an awful sight, yet it fascinated me. If I turned away, I was certain to look back, and as certain to see Craven's pale face and glassy eyes before me."

Mr. Stanhope drew his hands across his own as if to shut out the sight.

"Two days more, and a couple of friendly sharks rid me of the horrid spectacle. But not of that on deck, and I had neither strength of body nor will left to cast another corpse into the sea. Even poor Selim had to lie where he fell.

"In all that time no vessel hailed us or hove to. I saw sails in the distance, but what signal I could make was unheeded. I felt abandoned even of Heaven, and gave myself up as lost. Whither the sepulchral ship was drifting—into what solitary sea, I knew not.

"The sleepless nights spent below were haunted by visions of the scene on deck. Prayer seemed frozen on my lips, and morning found me at my post at the helm, with reality before me and my own certain fate in contemplation. The very sharks appeared to multiply and grow more ravenous as they followed steadily in our wake!

"When you found me, Captain Somers, I was on the verge of madness. My debt of gratitude to you will never be cancelled."

The statement made on their arrival in port to magistrates and shipowners by Mr. Stanhope, though precisely the same in all points of fact, was still more concise. He had recovered somewhat his composure, and told his tale with quiet gravity, and with none of the nervous tremor which had marked and broken the first narrative.

Yet he must have suffered greatly, his hair and unshorn beard being white as foam when he was picked up, though he gave his age as twenty-eight, and in answer to surprised inquiry said that on the morning of that fourth of August his hair had been dark brown—a statement borne out by the reddish light in his cavernous eyes. He looked much older; but no doubt an Indian sun, as well as his terrible experience, were accountable for that.

He was apparently a man who had his feelings well under control, yet no effort could hide his perturbation and reluctance to revisit the *begum* for the purpose of collecting his own papers and property; as also the luggage of his unfortunate secretary, of which he offered to take charge for transmission to the friends of the murdered man.

Of everything in the shape of money or jewellery, cabins and bodies had alike been despoiled; how Mr. Stanhope's watch had escaped them was a marvel. The owners of the *begum* were prompt in their offers of cash for immediate use, but Mr. Stanhope had with him letters of credit, which had escaped confiscation, and which were duly honoured.

The story found its way into the newspapers of the time, 182—; and had he been so minded, Alfred Stanhope would have been pushed into notoriety. But this seemed repugnant to his feelings. He said, curtly—

"I decline to be made the hero of a tragedy." And again: "My own business requires my presence elsewhere."

Those who would have feted and lionized him were disappointed, and whilst one half pronounced him sensitive, the remainder voted him haughty and imperious.

His stay in Liverpool ended with the official inquiry. That terminated, Mr. Stanhope sent on his luggage by carrier, and ensconced himself in a corner of the Royal Mail coach for transmission to London. It was a glorious day in September, but he shivered, though he was wrapped in a long, straight, fur-lined cloak which reached to his heels, and in which he shut himself up as in a sentry-box. The very sealskin cap on his head had flaps to cover his ears, and had there been another to cover his mouth, he could not have been more silent and self-contained.

A chirrupy little man on the opposite seat made sundry attempts to draw him into conversation, but failing, turned his attention to more sociable fellow-passengers. Not even when they stopped to change horses or alighted for refreshment was he more accessible. He ate and drank of the best, and paid freely, but his taciturnity increased, if possible, as they neared London. For a man about to take possession of an estate, his cogitations seemed to be of the gloomiest. It might be his past experience led him to fear legal thorns before the full-blown rose could be plucked, or, it might be, a feminine rose as thorny.

If so, he troubled himself in the one case unnecessarily. His credentials were indisputable. Recent investigation had already established his identity, and Messrs. Falconer and Robb, of Verulam Buildings, solicitors under the will, both remarked, "Mr. Stanhope's resemblance to his late uncle," so no impediments were thrown in his way; and he took possession with as little delay as the law permitted, confirming Messrs. F. and R. in their position as solicitors to the Stanhope estate.

Alfred Stanhope was by no means a poor man when he left Madras. His uncle's will had superadded money in the bank, money in the funds, and house property in town, to the old entailed mansion in Warwickshire, with its well-wooded and extensive grounds.

"I understand you have not visited Stanhope Court since you were quite a child," said Mr. Falconer to the new owner, as their travelling carriage passed through the lodge gates, and swept under a long avenue of limes, from which the leaves were beginning to fall.

"Not since I was five years old. My father and uncle quarrelled at the time, and afterwards held aloof. They were only reconciled when my father was about to sail for India some four years later."

"Your memories of the place will consequently be very dim," observed the lawyer.

"Very. I remember only an irregular building, large rooms, and gloomy passages, with a gallery of grim pictures, of which I was half afraid. But I have not to be told that its foundation was laid in Tudor times, and its latest addendum was when George the Third was king. I have memories, too, of a kennel of yelping hounds and a stud of hunters," continued Mr. Stanhope, half questioningly.

"Your memory does not deceive you," said Mr. Falconer. "The late Mr. Stanhope was an inveterate fox-hunter, and you will find stables and kennels much as he left them."

"Shall I? Then I shall make a clean sweep of the whole lot. Send them to auction before the week is out!" was the abrupt and somewhat acrimonious retort.

"Indeed! Then you are not a sportsman?" interrogated rather than asserted Mr. Falconer, with uplifted eyebrows.

"Not an English sportsman, certainly. He who has hunted the antelope, with the cheetah for his hound, and the tiger, with an elephant for a steed, will not care to ride pell-mell over hedges and ditches to witness the worrying of a fox!" And Mr. Stanhope's lip curled unmistakably.

"You speak of the hunting-field with all the force of familiarity, until really, Mr. Stanhope, I can hardly realise that you left England so young," observed the solicitor, in some astonishment.

He was put down by the Anglo-Indian's haughty sarcasm—

"Men who read, sir, need not travel the world for information on such topics."

"True, true!" assented his interlocutor, with the mental rider— "Hang his impertinence! He is as haughty as if he were the Great Mogul."

The haughtiness subsided into sufficient condescension, when stepping from the carriage he entered the wide hall, hung round with sportsmen's trophies, and, passing between a double file of servants, acknowledged their cheer of welcome, and the salutation of butler and housekeeper with almost the first smile Mr. Falconer had seen upon his face.

Chapter 2: At Stanhope Court

"Hush! The place strikes chilly as a vault!" muttered Mr. Stanhope, as the cheering subsided. Then aloud to the curtseying housekeeper (a buxom dame), he said, "I trust you have large fires, Mrs. Hudson. I have never been warm since I set foot in England;" and he visibly shivered under his fur-lined cloak, though there was an ample fire burning in the hall at the time.

"Yes, sir, in all the rooms. Mr. Falconer gave particular instructions, after our dear old master's funeral (how you do shiver, sir!) that the place should be kept well aired, and I trust you will find everything satisfactory."

"As satisfactory as English skies and heavy English masonry will permit, I daresay."

"Do you think the conjunction of an Indian bungalow and an English sky would be more satisfactory, Mr. Stanhope?" put in Mr. Falconer, with a sort of dry chuckle.

"It would be lighter, and brighter, and scarcely colder, sir," answered Mr. Stanhope, in a tone which "put down" the little, wiry, bright-eyed solicitor for the second time that day.

The housekeeper came to his relief. "Your chambers have been prepared, gentlemen, and dinner will be served in an hour—unless, Mr. Stanhope, you would prefer to go over the house at once."

Mr. Stanhope deferred the necessary tour of inspection to the morrow, and both gentlemen were shown to their rooms to refresh after their journey.

There were cheerful fires in bedrooms and dressing-rooms; and as the flames danced and flickered, they were reflected in well-polished furniture of dark mahogany, and swing-glasses in oval frames. But windows and tall four-post bedsteads were draped with dark velvet hangings, loaded with silk lace and deep bullion fringe; and doubtless to the man reared from boyhood amongst the lightsome fittings of bamboo and gauze, their heaviness was oppressive. He had declined the assistance of a servant, and now, instead of dressing, paced the room with his hand at his throat, panting for breath, and muttering in gasps, "What is the matter with me? The very air of the place might be tainted; it seems to stifle me. I can hardly breathe. But I must overcome it, if I would enjoy the good the gods have sent me."

The faint baying of a hound from the distant kennels smote his ear. He turned ghastly white, even to the lips.

"My God! what was that?" He sank into an armchair before the fire, in absolute faintness. "What a fool I am!" he murmured. "It is one of those infernal fox-hounds. I'll have none of their yelping about the old court."

He had thrown his cloak aside and sat there, a white-headed, white-browed man, with a dark skin, a massive forehead, a long, but not straight, nose; a straight upper lip, a close mouth, broad jaws, full rounded chin, and deep-sunk, red-brown eyes, that seemed to pierce the very fire to question it, so keen and searching were they. Yet, at times, they were furtive and stealthy as those of a panther; at others restless and timorous as a fawn's. Indeed, the entire face was one of many meanings, many expressions, and though Indian life, and the fearful tragedy aboard the *Begum*, had blanched his locks and lined his young face prematurely, there was no question he was a handsome man of fair proportions, on whom reserve and hauteur sat not ill.

He was still asking its secrets of the fire, when the second dinner bell rang. He started up, drew his hand across his brow, and flung his open palm outward, as if he threw something from him.

"I will brighten the dull place before I bring *her* here," was the burden of his thoughts, as he hurried his *toilette*.

A respectful servant was in waiting to conduct his new master to the dining-room. This was a long, lofty, dark-panelled apartment, with well-worn carpet, and three windows, across which ruby curtains hung in folds as massive as the antique chairs and tables. Between each window was a mirror reflecting the lights from its own candelabra, and the flames from the sputtering wood fire on the open hearth opposite, and—that which was the most conspicuous thing in the room—a full-length picture of a stalwart man, in a scarlet hunting coat, buckskin breeches, and top-boots. His one hand rested on the neck of a bay mare, a hunting cap and whip were in the other, and by his side stood a long-nosed, tawny fox-hound.

As the picture caught Mr. Stanhope's eye he gave a perceptible start, and for an instant held his breath; but only for an instant. Coming forward, he apologised to Mr. Falconer for being a few minutes beyond time, and then turned to survey the painting more fully.

"My late uncle's portrait, I presume," said he;

"Yes," responded Mr. Falconer, "and, but for his sixty years and florid complexion, a marvellous likeness of yourself. Your grey hair assists the resemblance. It is astonishing how family features are transmitted from generation to generation."

Judkins, the old butler, with the freedom of long service, here struck in: "If I may be so bold, I would say as Mr. Stanhope here is more like to our old squire than to his own father; at least as I remember him before he went to Indy, three an' twenty year ago."

"Ah, that would be when my father and uncle parted in anger, never to meet again. Judkins, what wine have you there ?"

The subject was waived was not resumed. The picture had, however, a strange fascination for the new owner of Stanhope Court. Whenever he lifted his head his eyes sought it furtively, but with a look in which pain and pleasure mingled.

When the meal was over and the servants dismissed, the twain drew nearer to the fire, wine-glasses were filled, cigars lighted, and in the midst of the fumes they talked of many matters, mostly connected with the estate and the late fox-hunter's will.

"And you have no idea what was my uncle's motive for leaving Oliver Craven so substantial a legacy as two hundred pounds a year?"

"Not the slightest. Mr. Robb drew up the will, but received no instructions which gave a clue either to his reasons, or to the young man's connections or antecedents. He was simply described as 'Oliver Craven, sometime secretary to my late brother Alfred, in Madras, and now secretary to my nephew Alfred.' Our late client, though a jovial, social being amongst his fellow-sportsmen, was close and reserved in all personal and private matters. Have you no suspicion?"

"None. Craven came to India, bringing with him a whelp from the same litter as that in the picture"—pointing upwards with his cigar—"and a letter to my father, urging, as a special favour to himself, that he would push the fortunes of his *protégé*—a namesake, whose parents had been friends of his own. This was seven years ago. The young man said he had no recollection of his father, and that he was then in mourning for his mother. He served us with faithfulness and intelligence, and I lament, deeply lament, that he should have been so tragically cut off from the enjoyment of my late uncle's well-meant bequest."

"Of course, the money reverts to you in consequence of his death?" said the lawyer.

"I do not intend to touch it. I gather from letters and a miniature I found amongst Craven's luggage that he had been long engaged to a young girl in his own rank. I shall seek her out, and make the annuity over to her."

"My dear Mr. Stanhope, this is, indeed, noble—"

"It is justice, sir, not nobility," interrupted Mr. Stanhope, rising. "I will leave you to your, wine, Mr. Falconer. I am unused to your mode of travelling, and must plead fatigue as my excuse for retiring early."

Mr. Falconer heard him address a servant in the hall.

"What dogs sleep on the premises—within the house, I mean?"

"Well, sir, there's Snap, the bull-terrier, an' Grip, the mastiff, an'—"

"Turn them all out before you go to bed, and see that no dog crosses the threshold again, as you value your place."

"Strange!" murmured the lawyer. "Fancy a nephew of old Noll Stanhope with an antipathy to *canis*. The old sportsman would have disinherited him could he have foreknown it."

"Strange!" echoed the chorus in the servants' hall. "Turn them animals out! Why, its enoof to make t' old master turn in his coffin!"

They might not have thought it so strange could they have seen through their closed eyelids and chamber-doors the stranger sight of their new master, in slippered feet and dressing-gown, in the dead of the night, wandering about the deserted rooms below, and holding his light to the portraits in the picture gallery, as if to print them on his memory!

The formal tour of inspection took place the next morning, the housekeeper and butler acting as guides. They, no less than Mr. Falconer, were surprised at the tenacity of Alfred Stanhope's memory.

"He was such a little thing when he ran about the place last, and his nurse frightened him with that grim picture in the black frame."

They were in the picture gallery at the time.

"It is a grim picture. I can scarcely look upon it without a shudder even now," said he, in answer to the housekeeper's remark.

"No doubt recent events have given it force," observed Mr, Falconer. "The fierce, murderous eyes of Cain and the imploring ghastliness of the stricken Abel must be like realities to you."

Like realities, indeed!" echoed Mr. Stanhope, in an undertone, as he turned away with a face scarcely less ghastly than that of the painted Abel.

There was a second portrait of his uncle, with the inevitable canine pet, close to the doorway; and by its side one of Alfred Stanhope's father, both taken in their. prime. But he merely paused to note the resemblance between the brothers ere he stepped across the corridor (lighted at one end by a wide mullioned window, emblazoned with the Stanhope arms), and into the library.

Here he drew a deep breath, and sat down, as if to look around.

The door by which he and his attendants had entered lay behind him, in the extreme corner of the wall at his right hand. On the same side was the fireplace, originally open, but which had been closed in beneath the massive carved shelfless chimney-piece with glistening Dutch tiles, and fitted with a modern grate—that is, modern a century ago. The heat of the bright fire in the sweeping semi-circular grate shone on the polished tiles, and radiating, glowed afresh on the brass fender and equipments, and on the margin of polished oak-floor left bare by the square Turkey carpet. An immense mullioned window confronted the fireplace, and through the ermine and gules of its stained *escutcheon* the morning sun fell in ruddy patches upon the solid centre table.

A ponderous *escritoire* held possession of the wall at his back, and before him stood open the chief door of the apartment, covered with crimson baize, spangled with brass nails, and through its two-foot *vista* he saw its duplicate closed. An army of old books, in good but dingy uniforms, were ranged in rank and file on shelves, which left no inch of spare wall uncovered. New books there were apparently none, and the place had the aspect of hasty furbishing up; yet, as Alfred Stanhope surveyed it from his high-backed armchair, a smile of satisfaction swept over his weary-looking countenance. He rose.

"Mrs. Hudson, I will thank you to have another table brought in, and let *tiffin*—I mean luncheon—be served here. In future, unless I have more than one guest, I shall take my meals in this library."

"Very well, sir, your wishes shall be attended to," said the housekeeper, as her master left the library, with Mr. Falconer in his wake; but turning to see her own amazement reflected in the butler's rubicund face, he clasped her uplifted hands with the exclamation, "Laws, Mr. Judkins, how tastes do differ to be sure! When did old master ever put foot in the library, I wonder?"

"Well, Mrs. Hudson," replied the butler, sententiously, "what's one man's meat's another man's pison. Old master liked dawgs, and hated books; the new master hates dawgs, and maybe likes books. It's all one to me, if he don't put a padlock on the cellar door, and turn all the old servants adrift."

Alfred Stanhope did not turn his uncle's household adrift. But he made a clean sweep of kennels and stables. Hounds and hunting-stud went under the hammer, and all superfluous trainers, grooms, and stable-boys were dismissed with pensions or gratuities.

An open hand will atone for a close mouth and many eccentricities; and so, on the whole, Alfred Stanhope grew in favour with his dependents, though he preferred the companionship of books to that of fox-hunting squires, and sat shivering over the library fire, instead of warming his blood with a brisk canter in the crisp autumnal air, and started like a woman at the report of a gun or the bark of a dog.

Chapter 3: Old Papers

These were no railways to whisk people hither and thither, without notice or preparation, at the date of this narrative. Letters and messages did not fly on wings of steam and lightning. People and business went on in an easy jog-trot fashion, and no one then thought the world too slow or felt themselves the worse. Then newspapers were too dear, and too few, to find their way daily to every breakfast table; and their news was not always of the newest.

Thus it happened that when Mary Lloyd, schoolmistress, of Lupus Street, Pimlico, picked up a fragment of newspaper which had done duty as wrappage to a pupil's luncheon, and read thereon a report of the "inquiry into the mutiny and abandonment of the *Begum*," the inquest was over, and the survivor of the massacre quietly established at Stanhope Court.

Poor girl! It was well for her that it was Saturday, and that her scholars had separated for the week; well that she was alone when the direful paragraph met her eye, and felled her as with a blow from an unseen hand!

Her little maid-of-all-work, dish-washing in the regions below, heard the scream and fall, and rushed to her assistance, wiping her hands on her coarse apron as she ran.

Their lodgers were out, and the small domestic was at her wits' end, but she had sense left to raise the head of her young mistress from the uncarpeted floor, using work bags for pillows, while she ran for water to sprinkle her with.

As Mary revived, the tender-hearted maid replaced the side-combs which had fallen from the dark-brown ringlets, and looked ruefully at the tall Spanish back-comb which lay shivered on the floor. But she never doubted the truth of the explanation that the fall arose from sudden dizziness caused by over-fatigue.

Two music pupils, coming an hour later, found her' stretched on a sofa with her hair disarranged, "looking white and awful," and went home with their lessons deferred through their teacher's illness.

"Oliver Craven killed! Oliver dead! Her Oliver—her good, true Oliver, for whose sake she had kept single all these years; to whom she should have been married this very month! Could she ever bear to look again on the wedding-dress he had sent her, which was even then being made up? Oh, that she had listened to his pleading seven years back, and kept him in England—her husband, her own, her Oliver! Yet how *could* she marry whilst her poor paralyzed mother claimed her care? How burden him with such a charge? How stand in the way of his advancement?"

So ran Mary Lloyd's conflicting thoughts as she lay on that chintz-covered sofa in her semi-scholastic back parlour in Lupus Street, with one hand over her tearless eyes and burning brow, holding together the head that seemed ready to split, and the other over the heart that seemed just as ready to break, in its desolation.

And she *was* desolate.

At the death of her father she inherited little besides a good education, a loving heart, strict integrity, a resolute will, and the charge of a paralyzed mother. He had insured his life for three hundred pounds, and with that and their tolerable stock of furniture, Mary Lloyd, with no relatives to assist or oppose, before she was eighteen took the house in Pimlico, let a portion to lodgers, and converted the remainder into a "School for Young Ladies." Had she waited twenty years she might have dubbed it an "Establishment."

It was during the settlement of her father's affairs that she met with Oliver Craven, clerk to a solicitor in Lincoln's Inn Fields. He was struck at once by the fearless energy of the young girl, and her untiring affection for her helpless mother. Of her beauty I think he only discerned that hers was the beauty of goodness; yet she stood above the common height, her limbs well-proportioned, her head erect on a somewhat full throat, her brow was broad and reflective, and if her nose was not classical, and her upper lip was somewhat stiff, the lines of mouth and chin were tender in their . curves, and she had the very mildest of dear grey eyes.

The concern he had evinced for her friendless position, the desire he had shown to serve her, created an interest in Mary Lloyd's breast for Oliver Craven, and love was not far behind. He was her sole confidant, her sole counsellor in the many trials which beset her progress, and when he announced Oliver Stanhope's offer to send him to India under good auspices, a very earthquake seemed to rend them asunder and shatter the temple of her hopes.

But when her lover proposed to remain in England at the risk of his patron's displeasure her negation was final.

"I will wait for you, dear Oliver," she said, "any number of years, but I will not destroy your prospects, nor can I burden you with the care of my mother, and so a double duty compels me to say 'Go.'"

And now that he was no more, for the first time she questioned the basis of her decision. It was she who had sent him to India; she who had been the cause of his death!

All that day and the next her mind was racked with torturing agony. With the Monday came her pupils and her duties, and in their obligatory performance the strain relaxed little by little, the violence of grief and self-accusation subsided; but the wound in her heart was unskinned, the void unfilled, and "Oliver! Oliver!" seemed written in red on every lesson-book, or slate, or copy she touched.

She substituted black crape and bombazine for the delicate Indian silk in the dressmaker's hands, and "the loss of a friend" was the answer to all inquiries.

A week later, a letter with a black seal, from Messrs. Falconer and Robb, made her formally acquainted with that which she already knew, and with the further fact that Alfred Stanhope, Esq., made over to her his right of succession to a legacy of two hundred pounds *per annum*, bequeathed by the late Oliver Stanhope to his young *protégé*, Oliver Craven, knowing her to have been his secretary's affianced wife.

Her wound bled afresh, and now she wept. Had Oliver but lived, how happy might they have been with such an assured income! Then she doubted her right to accept it, and after some correspondence, the solicitors, at the instigation of their client, assured her that she had no alternative—the deeds were already executed. If that was a fiction she was not lawyer enough to know it.

Her grateful letter of thanks was duly forwarded to Mr. Stanhope; but much as she wished to thank him in person, no interview had as yet taken place.

Yet such a meeting could not be far off, since, in a fit of very unusual confidence, he had told Mr. Falconer that he had been so much attracted by the miniature amongst Oliver Craven's papers, and the good sense of Miss Lloyd's letters, that he purposed making her acquaintance as soon as the first tumult of her grief had subsided. And Mr. Falconer having but a low opinion of woman's constancy, duly confided to Mr. Robb that he thought Stanhope Court would not be long without a mistress.

The last swallow had departed on his African tour, with the nightingale close in his wake; the green woodpecker laughed his loudest as old October gripped the trees with firm hands, and shook to the ground their crimson foliage; and along with the rustling leaves down went the hard dinner of the nuthatch from his claw, to be pounced upon by the merry squirrel gambolling at the roots of the oak, and stowed away for leisurely digestion.

The month was dying in a flood of gold and purple splendour when its last sunset glories fell on the escutcheoned window of Stanhope Court library, and flecked with black spots and great crimson patches the papers spread on the oak table, and the warmly-clad figure bending over them.

Alfred Stanhope raised his head, and, as his eye rested on the exaggerated *escutcheon* tingeing his papers, he cast himself back in his chair with a sigh of utter weariness; and, looking upwards at the window, murmured sadly: "Always the same; always those great red quarterings falling athwart my hands, staining my books and papers as if with great blotches of blood. It affects my sight; and but that all the crazy antiquaries in the county would cry out upon me, I would remove it. And then the motto mocks me with its '*A Deo et Rege!*' Well, well, '*familiarity breeds contempt.*' I shall grow indifferent in time."

The old *escritoire* was open, and he was apparently going over its contents to destroy or conserve at his pleasure. The paper before him went with a toss into the waste basket, as he laid his left hand on a packet of letters, yellow with age, and tied round with a faded ribbon. They were addressed to "Oliver Stanhope, Esq.," ill ft cramped female hand, but no dated post-mark gave a clue to their antiquity or order, so he took up one haphazard.

He had taken it up listlessly enough, and paused with it half un-
folded in his hand to ring his bell to have the fire replenished; but
whatever he found therein—when the footman came to learn his
pleasure—he sat with the square discoloured sheet held tightly in
both tremulous hands, poring over it with eager eyes, too absorbed
to note the entrance of the man or heed his twice-repeated query.
But glancing prematurely at the signature, he started to his feet with
an exclamation so sudden and vehement, that the servant went back
to his fellows and said, with much commiseration, that "Master must
have had a sunstroke or something in India, for he sure never could be
right in his head. What with his fancies that dogs were growling when
there was never even the ghost of a dog within the park palings, an'
his shivering over the fire, an' starting and bouncing only to frighten
honest folks, he never could be right in his upper storey."

The man had jumped to a false conclusion; his master had as clear
a head as any in the shire; but he had made a discovery such as would
make any man leap to his feet and cry out, if he had a spark of feeling
in him.

It was the old story of woman's weakness and man's depravity he
read in those letters—the story of a silly girl caught in the toils of a
dashing blade, allured from home, her scruples silenced by a clan-
destine marriage, afterwards repudiated as informal when satiety or
jealousy needed a pretexts to cast her off, and brand her child with
illegitimacy.

The dashing blade had been Alfred Stanhope's sporting bachelor
uncle; the disowned woman had signed herself—*Margaret Craven*.

CHAPTER 4: MARY LLOYD

November was but three days old when a knock, which made
Mary Lloyd's heart beat, came to the door of the "Ladies' Seminary"
in Lupus Street. It was Thursday, and her holiday afternoon, on which
she only gave music-lessons. The last of her music pupils had gone
home, the square piano was closed, and she sat down in her dead
mother's rocking-chair by the fire to muse on her utter desolation—
desolation of heart and home; a void not to be filled by her pupils' love
or the respect of their friends.

The face, paler and thinner than of old, was not improved in tone
by her black dress; but what she lost in colour she gained in gravity
and repose.

The little maid handed in a black-edged card, and before Mary could well decipher the inscription in the waning light, the visitor had followed his pasteboard into the dim room.

The man was so muffled in a long fur-collared cloak and a cashmere shawl worn over throat and mouth, as if to guard both from damp, that all she could discern besides was a mass of white hair, a dark skin, and a pair of searching eyes that seemed to look her through.

"Candles," she whispered to the maid, as she rose to receive the stranger.

The girl retired, closing the door behind her.

There was a momentary hesitation, caused apparently by the gentleman's reluctance to speak before the servant, during which Mary Lloyd contrived to spell out the card in the firelight. A smile of pleased surprise crossed her face.

"Mr. Stanhope," she said, advancing, "this is, indeed, an honour I did not expect. How pleased I am at this opportunity to express my—"

He stopped her with a deprecatory wave of his hand.

"The honour. Miss Lloyd, is mine."

What was there in the motion, or the tones, which came thick through the muffler to make her start?

The maid brought two mould candles in tall brass candlesticks, and placed them on the table.

"Will you not remove your wraps, sir; the room is warm?"

"After the heats of India, I find all rooms cold."

The door again closed. The girl's heavy step was heard to go downstairs. He loosened but did not remove his shawl.

"You wrote to me. Miss Lloyd, for a miniature and some letters of yours found amongst the effects of my late secretary?" There was a huskiness as of deep emotion in his voice as he added: "I have brought them with me."

Mary could scarcely trust herself to speak.

"Thank you, sir; you are very kind," was all that issued from her quivering lips.

"But"—he laid a packet on the table—"pardon me, I am most reluctant to surrender them. I have looked at your semblance until the image is painted on my brain and heart. I would not wrong the memory of your lover; yet time—"

She rose, with an indignant protest on her lips.

"Mr. Stan—"

The next syllable was inaudible. The lips parted; but she stood motionless and rigid, unable to utter a word.

He had unclasped his cloak to get at the packet, and the shawl had fallen aside.

As she confronted him with eager, open eyes, and gasped, "*Oliver!*" he, too, started to his feet, and caught her fainting figure ere she fell.

She had made her discovery prematurely.

If kisses, showered on lip and brow and cheek, could vivify a swooning woman, surely his might have brought her back to consciousness; but she lay white and helpless in his arms so long he was fain to place her on the chintz-covered sofa, and look around for some restorative. A common bottle of smelling-salts stood on the mantelshelf, telling its tale of frequent need. Its application ere long brought back the colour to her cheeks, a faint sigh stirred the curl that had fallen across her face; her eyes opened, to rest on the grey-haired man kneeling by her side with anxiety, love, and dread striving for mastery in his countenance.

As the soft light came back to her eyes, he drew her head once more to his shoulder, and placing his hand on her mouth lest she should scream, whispered:

"For God's sake, Mary, darling, command yourself; it is Oliver, your own Oliver, who bids you be calm and cautious, as you love him."

She had thrown one arm around his neck, and was sobbing as if her heart would break, saying, in broken gasps between her sobs:

"They told me—you were—killed—I—I—Mr. Stanhope—he—I—do not—understand—they—the lawyers—he—oh, Oliver! Is it indeed you?"

"Yes, darling, yes—your own love come back for his sweet wife. You will be my wife, Mary, will you not? You will let nothing part us, will you ?"

Kisses did duty for punctuation as he spoke, and Mary, in bewilderment and bliss, could only kiss him back in answer. The sea had given up its dead to her, and she in fullness of joy and gratitude was dumb.

In his face love and joy seemed dashed with a shadow of distrust—some haunting presentiment of evil appeared to contract his thoughtful brow as if with pain.

The maid in the kitchen waited impatiently a summons for the tea-tray. They sat, oblivious of common things, side by side on the sofa; she with her head on his throbbing breast lulled in a delicious calm; he, with his arm gripped round her waist, as if some powerful foe were about to wrest her from him.

The treacherous calm was soon broken.

"Mary," he whispered, as if the nodding *mandarins* on the mantelshelf were listening, "Mary, I have a strange tale to tell you, but first I want your solemn promise—your oath—to be my wife in the face of everything and anything."

"You have my promise, dear. You know my *love*; if that cannot suffice, what oath could bind me, Oliver?" She looked up proudly as she spoke.

"Hush, darling, not so loud! You must not call me Oliver, I am Alfred—Alfred Stanhope now."

"Alf—what? I do not understand."

"Do not look so strangely, Mary! I have a confession to make. Nay, darling, do not shrink from me. What I have done, I have done for your sake. Nay, listen! It is not so bad, after all.

"Mary, my love, I need not tell the dreadful story of the mutiny; you know it. But, dearest, Mr. Stanhope was the one killed. I, your Oliver, was wounded and left for dead. As I dressed my own wounds with lint from his medicine chest, it flashed across my mind that he had not a relative to take his estate; that no one in England had seen him from a boy, and that if they had I bore a strong likeness to him. By his death I was deprived of an appointment, and if ever I got home could only wed you to poverty. Mary—Mary, darling, the temptation was strong! I resolved to personate him—to be Alfred Stanhope to all the world but you. I knew all the intricacies of their affairs from my own mother; knew all the family traditions; I could not fail. I threw his corpse overboard, and then—"

"Then, Oliver Craven, after sufferings that should have taught the falsity of your policy, you took false oaths, before God and man, to magistrates and lawyers; and thought that I, the child of a Christian clergyman, would be an accomplice in your fraud. Better the deepest poverty than such dishonour."

She had gradually loosened herself from his clasp, and now stood before him erect, with indignation and shame burning in her else calm eyes. She seemed transformed, and he sank cowed before her.

"Mary, Mary, forgive and pity me! If I erred, it was for you. I would make you mistress of Stanhope Court, close the sad volume of your drudgery here, and fill your life with all that luxury or love could give."

"Had you come back to me an honest man, without a shilling in the world, I would have been proud of you, and love would have dignified drudgery. But now—" She crushed her face up in her hands in anguish unsupportable.

In vain he tried to move her. At length: "Mary," said he, in lower tones, "I am not the impostor you think. I made a discovery three days back which staggered me and nearly drove me mad. Had I not proclaimed myself Alfred Stanhope, I might yet have claimed the estate in my own right. *Oliver Stanhope was my father—*"

"Your father?"

"My father, dear one. Whether his marriage with my mother was legal or a vile cheat I have yet to ferret out and prove to clear her name. But I *shall* do it some day, I *know!*"

He would have taken her in his arms again, but she held aloof and begged him to depart. He was abject in his entreaties. Then fear lest she should denounce his fraud took hold of him—the quiet woman so like a pythoness with scorn.

But he mistook her.

"Go, sir. No eloquence of yours can move me from my sense of duty. You have done me a wrong in opening my eyes this day. Dead, and buried in the everlasting sea, I mourned and worshipped you; living, the master of Stanhope Court, I can only strive to forget you. You have dropped your identity; I shall not recall it. Your secret is safe with me."

Hearing the outer door bang, the maid came upstairs to find Mary Lloyd on the hearthrug senseless, and the fire out.

She called loudly to the lodgers, and with their help the prostrate schoolmistress was carried to her bed.

Haggard, careworn, wretched, Oliver Craven—Mr. Stanhope—went back to his ancient mansion to envy the very lodge-keeper who opened the gates, his smiling wife and chubby children; went back to cower and shiver over his library fire, to hear the yelping of imaginary hounds, and fancy uncle, father, and cousin lurked behind him in the shadowy comers of the large room; to feel all the agonies of remorse deepened by failure; to feel his life bleak and barren henceforth. Himself a dry twig, having neither root, nor sap, nor leaves, fit only for the burning; scorned, contemned, despised by her for whom he had periled his own soul.

During all that week he ate little; drink much he dared not, lest he should babble and betray himself. Then, to fly from his very self, he mounted a blood mare he had retained, and dashed helter-skelter over the park, leaving his groom far in the distance, and coming home hours afterwards with his horse in a lather, to dine in solitary state.

He wrote a guarded letter to Mary Lloyd, signing only "Stanhope;" and again a second, but no answer came. Her silence struck him with a greater chill than her indignation. He posted up to town. In spite of the weather, which tried him severely, he began to take long walks, into the circuit of which Lupus Street was sure to come every half-hour.

There was something unnatural in the silence of Miss Lloyd's house for a school. No string of little misses issued forth at noon with bags and slates; no little faces peeped surreptitiously over the wire-blind; there was no echo of music-practice heard in the quiet street.

A light in an upper window at night—a doctor's gig calling morning and evening—filled his soul with agony and apprehension. The doctor's groom, thinking no wrong to take a fee like his master, let out that a young lady was "lyin' ill of brain fever, an' not like to get better."

Truly Mr. Stanhope's punishment had begun. What would he not have given for the right to penetrate to the sick room, and minister to the poor creature he had himself stricken down?

He introduced himself to the doctor, and then introduced a noted physician; laid Covent Garden Market under contribution, and sent in anonymously jellies and chickens sufficient to supply a household of invalids.

Youth and a sound constitution triumphed. In January, Mary Lloyd re-collected her scattered flock, and having aged years in those two past months, set herself resolutely to work as an antidote to care.

And now she wrote to Mr. Stanhope to reject emphatically the use of Oliver Craven's annuity.

It was in vain he urged that he owed her reparation, even if she persisted in rejecting him, and that Oliver Craven's money belonged of right to her. She returned for answer, "I can be silent without a bribe;" accompanied by the deed-of-gift torn in pieces.

"Firm as granite—and as silent, I know—is the rock on which I have wrecked my hopes," said he who to the world and to us is henceforth Alfred Stanhope. "But I will prove to her that I have legal right to bear my father's name, and to sit in his ancestral home; and I will make my name known and respected beyond a, *posse* of fox-hunting squires."

Chapter 5: At the Bar

Att. that year a demon of unrest seemed to possess Stanhope; he returned at last the calls of such county people as were not inveterate sportsmen. The Court was surrendered to upholsterers, and Mrs. Hudson rejoiced in preparations for the reception of guests to enliven the gloomy mansion. Women angled for the interesting man with the prematurely grey hair, burning eyes, aristocratic hearing, and fine estate; yet there was not a member of the Warwickshire Hunt but grieved over the degenerate scion of a race whose stud and pack had been the boast of the shire for centuries.

He visited, and was visited. He overlooked his estate himself, went and came, searching the registers of all the out-of-the-way churches in and about Doncaster, where Margaret Craven had met Sir Oliver Stanhope at the races; and he found time also to resume his law studies, and the examination and docketing of old papers.

Yet the shadow never lifted from his brow, and warmth never seemed to penetrate his chilly frame. To Mr. Falconer he had explained that he had been premature in addressing Miss Lloyd, who was not cast in the common mould; and that she had rejected alike his suit and settlement as insults. So true—and jet so false in everything!

So it got bruited abroad that Alfred Stanhope's gloom and eccentricities grew out of a love disappointment; and even his own servants accepted the story, his valet having somewhat to say of a miniature worn round his master's neck, and kissed and gazed at in supposed privacy.

And so the months went on to the anniversary of the day when Oliver Craven and Alfred Stanhope changed places. The glorious sun poured in through the library window, and, as usual, the red quarterings stained floor and table as if with pools of blood; at least, so the nervously-sensitive man deemed. But he had just made the discovery of a *fact* which closed his eyes to fancies.

An old, worn register of the marriage of Oliver Stanhope and Margaret Craven, spinster, performed m the parlour of the Clifford Arms, Skipton, by John Knowles, Clerk in Holy Orders, and witnessed by Martha and James Cragg (the innkeeper and his wife). The letters were imperative demands for money by the said John Knowles, in consideration of his having falsely denied his priesthood to the young wife some two years earlier, at the bidding of the said Oliver, which demands were attended with threats of recantation unless further bribed to hold his peace.

At the precise moment when Alfred Stanhope was thanking God for one load taken from his heart, Mrs. Hudson ran to the butler in his pantry, white and trembling.

"Oh! Mr. Judkins, I declare I've just seen Oliver Stanhope and his dog walk from the picture gallery, and cross the corridor to the library door!""

"Nonsense, Mrs. Hudson! You're dreaming."

"I tell you I saw him; people don't dream in broad daylight. I mean him when he was young. He looked as if he had walked out of a picture frame. I declare I trem— Hark! what's that!"

The ferocious barking of a dog. was heard from the library; servants, mindful of their master's interdict, rushed thither to remove the intruder. Opening the first door, sounds of scuffling were heard to mingle with the bark; a groan, a fall, and—stillness.

They found their master extended in a fit on the floor, the red lights from the window staining his face and hands, which still grasped the precious certificate.

His neck-cloth was loosened; water was dashed over him, still he did not revive. A groom, with some knowledge of veterinary matters, drew a lancet from his pocket, and bared his arm for blood-letting, exposing a terrible scar. There was another on the throat.

As he plunged in his lancet he said, "Them's oncommon like dog-bites, them be. No wonder th' squire hates 'em mortally."

The bleeding doubtless saved life, and the groom pocketed his reward; but Alfred Stanhope left the court shortly afterwards, and seldom returned to it—never in the autumn.

He took a house in Cavendish-square, and chambers in the Temple, and after the necessary study and formulas emerged a full-blown barrister, to the surprise of all his circle. He had turned to active work to shut out troublesome thought.

To Mary Lloyd he sent duplicate copies of all documents which attested his birth, and implored her, seeing indeed he was a Stanhope, to receive him once again. What tears, what anguish it cost her to deny him, how she wavered, he never knew; he only read her brief "I cannot," and crushed the letter up in a paroxysm of mute agony.

Had he needed briefs they would have been as rare as the dodo; he was rich and fashionable, and they came to him in shoals. Perchance after the first start his sound early-acquired legal knowledge, his acumen, and terse, trenchant eloquence might, in a measure, account for this. He rose rapidly, passing older and less influential men on the road, until his fiftieth year saw him appointed to a vacant judgeship. Envy and congratulations followed him to the bench.

Ah, little knew his foes or his flatterers of his haunted life, of the fits which grasped, and shook, and worried him, when August suns were bright and fierce! Little knew they of the miniature and marriage certificate worn together close to that man's heart. In the twenty years which had elapsed since he took possession of Stanhope Court, society had discussed and forgotten many romances more recent than his, and match-making matrons had given him up as impracticable for very many years.

His appointment was yet new, when in the Autumn Assizes he sat on the bench, for the first time, in a large seaport town within his circuit.

Amongst the names on the charge-sheet Judge Stanhope noted those of James Smith and Owen Nicholson, accused of piracy, mutiny, and murder on the high seas. There were a number of counts in the indictment, some of which dated back more than twenty years. A mate, who had turned informer, was the chief evidence against them.

The judge was observed to flush frequently during this trial, and to make several efforts to taste the water in a glass before him, yet to put it down ere it reached his lips.

The piracy was the more recent offence. The prisoners, with others not in custody, had taken forcible possession of a *barque,* to which they were attached as able-bodied seamen, had put the captain and officers ashore in the *Antilles,* and, hoisting the black flag, had committed outrages enough to hang them three times over.

It is with James Smith our story lies. Under the *alias* of John Jackson, he had formed an item in the crew of the *Begum.* He was now indicted for that, with others not in custody, he had, on the 4th of August, 182—, in the spirit and act of mutiny, murdered, or connived at the murder, of Captain Manners and certain other officers of the said *Begum,* together with one Oliver Craven, a passenger.

The prisoner pleaded "Not guilty;" but the evidence of the informer was too strong to be shaken. The jury, without leaving their box, declared the man guilty on all the counts. At this stage the judge, who was evidently ill, appeared scarcely able to proceed with the case.

As he put to each prisoner in turn the question whether he had anything to say in arrest of judgment, the court was electrified by the change which came alike over the prisoner at the bar and the judge on the bench.

"Ay, my lord, I have this to say, that I am *not guilty* of the murder of Oliver Craven, and that *you, Oliver Craven,* sitting there alive, to judge other men, know it! And I accuse you, my lord, in spite of wig and gown, of the murder of your master, Alfred Stanhope, as was our passenger on the *Begum!*"

His words rushed like a torrent of lava through the breathless stillness of the court; and the very officials, who pressed forward to check him, themselves fell back at the wave of his brown hand, and his impetuous speech.

"Ay, ay, my lord," he cried, "for all so grand as you sit there, I know *you* and you know, me. Didn't I see you steal up the companion-ladder and shoot Mr. Stanhope down with his own pistol? And when your master's dog sprang upon you, and would have worried you, didn't I shoot the brave beast through the head to save the life of the sneaking cur as wasn't worth it? And if we left you aboard to take your chance, what better did you deserve? Who made the men discontented first? You, Oliver Craven! I call God to witness I tell no lie!"

The officials rushed forward to stop him, but at this juncture a low growl was heard in the court. All eyes were turned to the bench, towards which the prisoner pointed with an excited gesture, and a quick—"See! See!"

The impalpable form of a man, who might have been Judge Stanhope's younger brother, stood by his side, fitting a halter round his neck; and there, too, a tawny foxhound crouched, in act to spring.

Horror fell upon the court.

The face of the judge purpled, foam issued from his mouth and flecked his scarlet robes, and from his black and gaping lips came a sound more like a bark than aught human.

He fell forward, snapping at those who would have supported him.

The court was adjourned; the sentence of the prisoners deferred.

But the judge was carried from the court to die in his robing-room—according to doctors—of hydrophobia, the virus of which must have been for all those twenty years lurking in his veins.

Can we say that judgment had been deferred in his case? If so, it had been pronounced at last—and executed!

In a will made many years before, he had left Stanhope Court and all which it contained to Mary Lloyd. But the quiet maiden lady refused to administer, and the place—with its evil reputation of being haunted—passed to strangers.

A Dour Weird

(A dark or hard fate or forecast)

Chapter 1: Foretold

"Lassie, beware how ye wed! Ye will hae walth o' wooers, for weel the bees ken whar to find the honey; an' amang them I see a braw Cummerland lad handin' a pleugh, but ye aye turn awa'. Ah, weel! A dour weird lies before ye, an' ye choose wrang. Again I hear the sound o' the pipes; see the fluttering o' the tartan, an' anither braw chiel wi' dirk an' claymore, an' the front of a Wallace—an' from *him* ye turn *not* awa'! I hear, too, the clash o' swords, the roar o' battle. Ah, lassie, I daur na tell ye a' I see. But there's a leal an' true guidman for ye, there are brave bairns, an' ye sall die on your ain bed under your ain roof, an' yer ain flesh an' bluid sail close your auld e'en. But, mark ye, lassie, gin ye quit Cummerland ye sall never see your bonnie face in the Eden again, never sit on your father's hearth-stane mair, an' whar ye were born ye will na' be buried. I wad tell ye mair, but it is na' weel to ken a' the weird ye maun dree."

Thus spoke, with impressible tone and varying expression, Margery Grant, the noted Scottish spae-wife, to Susan Gray, of Wetherall, whom she had met casually on the bridge over the Eden, and, as if impelled by some resistless power, had clasped by the wrist and drawn out of observation to the water-side, where Corby Castle towered high above them.

It was the shadowy hour when day weds night, and the young heart is most susceptible of outer influences. Shadows of rocks and trees deepened in the watery mirror beneath, in which a single star was looking for the new moon, and a faint breeze went like a whisper through the woods, as the mysterious creature, muffled in a shepherd's plaid, threw into the stream of the girl's life a fateful stone to ruffle its surface for evermore. The whole countryside stood in awe of Margery,

199

who, by sprinkling water from a holy well on the sick, cured disease, who held the key of the future in her grip, and yet never blighted man or beast with the glance of an evil eye. No wonder, therefore, that Susan's natural awe was intensified by the accessories of time and scene; which gave dramatic effect to the witch-like crone's tones and gestures, and impressed her voluntary communication on her young hearer with all the force of revelation.

She was but sixteen at the time, as bonnie a lass as any in Cumberland; frank, fearless, and independent; a girl after Farmer Gray's own heart; but a change fell upon her that night, and that old sybil made or marred her fortune. For Susan Gray was born in the last century, when Superstition walked boldly through the land, sat in high places, and had his strongholds among the mountains of the North. The picture drawn of the "braw chiel wi' the front o' Wallace" haunted her imagination. She had longings to see the world whence came the fine visitors to Corby Castle; and had in her mind an ideal not to be approached by any Cumbrian lad she met at Carlisle fair or market.

People—there are people everywhere—said she was too proud and independent; but when the croakers prognosticated that "Pride would hev a faw," the farmer answered briskly, "Then independence wull pu her up agean. I'se held my awn, an I mean te deu, and Susan wull ho'd her awn too, or I's mista'en." At one-and-twenty she was a study for a painter, in her full dark skirt and short linen over-gown. Her bust was full and round, her form erect, her head well poised, her step springy; health tinged her somewhat high cheeks and shapely arms, the hair braided smoothly beneath her linen cap was brown, only one shade lighter than the bright, dark, steadfast eyes which so plainly had a will in them.

By this time, however, her father had begun to think a little less independence might be quite as satisfactory, as one after another wooer was sent adrift with a hole in his heart, to sink or swim, until only one remained. Reckless Bob had enlisted, Stephen Heskett consoled himself with Dinah Bleckett, Watty Carel made her cousin Tib his guidwife. Only Dick Dalton, of Stainbrig, still hung on her footsteps, and loitered in the kirkgarth on Sundays, sighing if she spoke to another, reddening if she smiled on him—six feet of shyness! Dame Gray, amongst her many duties on the farm, yet found leisure to lament Susan's lost chances. Bell, her youngest sister (who had more than an eye on Dick Dalton), twitted her openly, until her father asked her if she meant to remain single all her life, or to take up the crooked stick at last.

At this she only tossed her handsome head, and with a light laugh replied, "Mappen, (may happen, probably), I may."

It was the very fear of taking the crooked stick that had kept her single; she was by no means so unconcerned about the future as she assumed to be. As she sat by the light of the peat fire in winter, or by the open door in the long summer evenings, ginning the wool from her father's sheep, or knitting his long grey hose, her soul was filled with anxious longings to see the "braw chiel wi' the front o' Wallace." How could she make choice between swordsman and ploughman unless she saw a chance of both? Now and then an officer on his way to Corby 'Castle addressed her with familiar admiration, but only "the uniform was braw; and the expected soldier-laddie had not made his appearance.

As the time went by she began to think she might as well make up her mind to sit up at night after the old folk and Bell had gone to bed, and when next she saw Dick Dalton's wistful eye looking in at the curtainless window, to open the door to him, and to acknowledge him her sweetheart in old Cumberland fashion. He would have a better farm than theirs when his father died, and that he loved her well she knew.

Still the forecast of the "dour weird" made her hesitate. What if she waited until St. John's Eve, and tried her fortune, as other lasses did, before she decided? Midsummer was close at hand.

With Susan thought resolved itself into action; but when St. John's Eve came, and she prepared to question fate, tales of terror and mischance to venturous maids whose timidity overcame their courage flashed across her brain, and her heart beat fast with superstitious dread. Still her purpose held. Unknown to human being (for that was imperative) she provided in secret for the silent midnight supper, which her pre-ordained husband was expected to partake with her, either in the flesh or the spirit.

At noon she prepared this with an impromptu attempt at divination, profoundly credited in the North. Whilst shelling peas, she found a pod containing the mystic nine. This she suspended over the doorway, watching eagerly for the first male foot that should cross the threshold. She helped her mother with the cookery as if in a dream. Presently a child's cry was heard, and little Alick Carel came into the kitchen with blood on his face and frock, sobbing aloud. He had fallen and cut himself.

It was nothing disastrous, but Susan, blanching and trembling, stood motionless, until restored by the asperity of Mrs. Gray's renewed command, "Git a piggin o' waiter an' wash the lal bairn's feace, an' dunnet stond theear like a fuile."

The water was brought, the little fellow bathed and soothed, but Susan did not regain her composure. What might the blood portend? It was an ill omen in any case, though she knew no one whose name began with A. C.

Strong and hearty as she was, her forebodings so unnerved her that she was allowed to retire early to rest on the plea of sickness (her fast unbroken as a condition of the midnight incantation), with no farther remark than the bantering chance hit of her father, "Thou snafflin', tnou'st niver due for a sowdger's wife, gif thou tworn seec at the seight of a drap o' two o' bluid."

She preserved silence by counterfeiting sleep when Bell came to bed. But there was little thought of sleep. For the first time within her memory, she lay awake counting the time by heart-beats more than by the drowsy clock below.

Long after the last stroke of eleven had died away, she slipped warily from her sleeping sister's side, dressed quietly in the moonlight, and stole downstairs, her face whiter than the muslin kerchief which covered her heaving bosom. Her first care was to rouse the fire, kept alight on the hearth by the "gathering peat." Then she spread a home-spun, grass-bleached cloth on the three-legged table, laid on it bread and cheese, and the "dumb-cake," mysteriously baked by herself for the awful ceremony, a jug of ale, two drinking horns, two wooden platters, and two knives. After placing two stools at the table with fingers trembling at their own daring, she drew back the thick wooden bolt, pulled the door open wide, and took her seat at the board five minutes before midnight, with her pale face turned towards the door.

Her breath seemed to thicken, and her heart to beat louder with every pulsation of the pendulum behind her, whilst the effort to maintain rigid silence became insupportable.

Afraid to look at door or window, her eyes wandered from the glowing fire to the rafters. She counted involuntarily the pendant hams and flitches, the oat cakes in the cratch, the platters and mugs on the shelf; but at the first stroke of *twelve*, her eye was arrested by a man's face at the window—*not* Dick Dalton's.

Before the last stroke ceased to vibrate, a Highland soldier in full costume presented himself in the doorway, and receiving no answer to his first free salutation, "How's a wi' ye the nicht?" doffed his plumed bonnet and bent his tall shoulders to enter.

Fain would Susan have fled, but fear glued her to the seat. Had she indeed evoked from the spirit world this "braw chiel" to share her charmed repast? "Are ye expectin' the guidman, lassie, that ye sit by your lane sae late?" questioned he advancing.

Susan's lips were compressed as much by resolution as terror.

"Are ye freightened, my bonnie doo, that ye sit there a' in a swither? Ye need na, lassie; Archie Cameron is no the chiel to harm man or woman, save at the word o' command, an' on the field o' battle."

He drew his lofty figure up proudly as he uttered his own name. Like a flash, the initials struck her as those of Alick Carel; so, too, came the swift thought that here was "the front o' Wallace," and the warm blood rushed to cheek and brow only to retire, leaving her pale as before. That this was mortal man had no place in her thought.

"The guidman's unco late," he resumed, "but maybe, lassie, it's a sweetheart ye're waitin' for, an' ye did na' luik for a stranger. But neither guidman nor sweetheart wad grudge bit an' sup to a tired sodger-body wha's lost his way in the mirk."

He had seated himself opposite to her, and did not see, as she did, pressed against the small panes of the window the face of Dick Dalton almost as ashen as her own.

"Gin ye canna speak, or daur na speak, gie me a sign that ye hearken till me, an' that I am welcome to sup wi' ye."

Terrified as much by the sight of Dick Dalton at that unwonted hour as by the apparition before her, she bowed her head from sheer inability to hold up. Taking it as a sign of assent, her visitor helped himself plentifully to the cake and cheese, poured out a horn of ale, and before drinking, nodded to her, saying heartily, "Here's till ye, my bonnie lassie; wussing ye a kind guidman, an' suin!"

Quite three parts of an hour had fled, when, pushing aside his platter, he rose, and drawing nearer, said, "Mony thanks, my bonnie lassie, for your hospitality, for ye *are* bonnie, gin ye hae no that muckle to say. Gin the guidman had bin at hame, I wad hae asked for a night's lodgin', an' a hantle o' bracken for a bed; but ye are a' alane, an' a maiden's guid name is suin tint, so Archie Cameron wull aye march awa', lest he sould rob a guid an' fair lassie o' her best tocher. A dirk wadna wound mair than those bright e'en, an' I'll ne'er forget this night, nor thee, puir dumb lammie. An' noo, tak' this ae kiss fra' Archie Cameron to keep him in mind."

As he stooped to touch her reddening forehead with his lips, a groan and a rush outside were audible. Susan's overstrained nerves gave way. She dropped from her seat in a swoon as the handsome Highlander started after the retreating figure of despairing Dick Dalton.

The cloth and its contents, dragged from the table when she fell, and the clatter of falling wood and delf, roused the household. Alegar, and burnt feathers restored her to her senses, but no explanation would Susan vouchsafe: maidenly shame and superstitious dread alike kept her silent.

★★★★★★

Alegar—what we call vinegar was formerly made from sour ale, and called alegar; it was only vinegar when made from wine.

★★★★★★

The farmer and his dame from their box-bed in the adjoining room had overheard a man's voice and step, and congratulated themselves that Susan had opened the door to Dick at last. When Dick held aloof, and kept silent, not caring to witness or proclaim the supposed triumph of a rival, they, just as sapiently concluded that the brief courtship had resulted in a lovers' quarrel, which they looked for time to heal.

The girl's secret preyed upon her. No neighbours spoke of a Highland soldier seen in the village. No Scotch regiment had been quartered in Carlisle. The mystery strengthened her belief in the supernatural.

Every wave of the golden hair, or glance of the clear blue eyes, every feature of the manly face, or motion of the stalwart form impressed upon the retina, had left only the conviction of a phantom drawn thither by a potent spell. Would the living man ever appear?

She grew fitful, restless. Weeks, months rolled on. The sight of little Alick made her shudder. Dick Dalton, his jealous fever over, again hung at her heels, but no Archie Cameron came wooing to Wetherall.

She took to wandering by the Eden after the kye were milked and her work done; and gossips meeting her on the bridge smirked to think that it lay midway between her home and Stainbrig. It was there, however, that Margery Grant had planted a thorn in her breast, and inchoate yearnings to meet and further question the wise woman prompted these twilight rambles.

It fell out that one evening as she stood by the water side, within the shadow of the bridge, knitting mechanically, and looking dreamily into the stream, asking herself if it were right that leal Dick Dalton should be set aside for a cantrip ghost, the fateful old crone touched her on the shoulder.

"Weel, Susie Gray, an' hae ye no made your choice yet?"

Susan started, the witch-like woman had come upon her so stealthily, the grey plaid in which she was wrapped leaving her outline dim and indistinct in the twilight.

"Ah, no, dame, but," Susan's voice sank to a whisper, "I've seen the wraith o' the Hielan' sowdger." Then she poured into the wise woman's ear the secret she had kept from her own friends, nay, almost from her own heart, that she was in love with the ghost she had invoked. Not that she said so, but it needed no witch to infer so much from her eagerness to overleap the present and pry into futurity.

Margery's reluctance only made Susan more eager; but when, with a motion as if she washed her conscience of the consequences, and a "Weel, lassie, wilfu' is aye waefu', ye maun gang your ain gate," she proceeded to unfold certain spells and incantations to bring the future husband near, Susan shuddered, the remembrance of St. John's Eve having lost little of its terror.

The witch warned even while she instructed, but her own faith in the diablerie she taught was more powerful than argument.

Susan had, however, been brought up reverently, and the dread of doing that which was unholy, coupled with fears for the result, stayed her hand for many days.

Yet, impelled to tempt fate by something stronger than her reason, one Friday, about the middle of September, she rose at midnight, took an apple from her coffer, knelt down in the darkest corner of the room, and *stuck in the apple nine pins,* muttering in a voice too low to awaken Bell—

I stick thur pins i' ma luive's heart,
I wish ilk pin may pruive a deart,
T' gev him nowther rest nor peace
Till he cum to me an' bring release:

... commencing the incantation with the first pin and ending with the last. Then she wrapped it up and hid it amongst the clothes in her kist.

Cold dew stood on her forehead, and she trembled so violently as she crept into bed that Bell awakened and asked in some concern if she was ill.

Day after day went by, but no lover, save the inevitable Dalton, came near the farm, yet Susan seemed wilfully determined to read her riddle her own way.

It was the season for laying in the winter stock of fuel. The peat had been cut, dried, brought home, and stacked with all the importance of a harvest; and all being done, there was a festive gathering for fun and frolic in the farm kitchen, as was wont on Halloween.

It was the night for spells and cantrips, open or concealed. Nuts were burned in pairs on the hearth, apples pared, and the unbroken rind thrown over the shoulder to indicate the true love's initials; boiling lead poured into water to reveal his occupation. As Susan poured her lead, it shaped itself into what the general voice called a scythe-blade, but what she herself held to be a sword.

Afraid to do her spiriting alone a second time, she prevailed on Bell to leave the party by stealth, and "sow hemp-seed" round the byre while she made the circuit of the barn on a like errand; an act supposed to need swift limbs and steady nerves; and never had she felt her courage at so low an ebb.

The night was gusty, the oaks and elms creaked and groaned, the trailing pendants of the ash swept like dishevelled tresses on the wind, dark clouds scudded across the sky, and through the changing rifts the moonbeams fell in fitful rays. It was an eerie night for such spells, to those who held that evil spirits were abroad to do the hests of man.

The fortune-seekers had not quitted the noisy kitchen wholly unperceived. At a sly hint from the farmer, Dick followed; and, after hesitating which way to take, turned to the left, lured by the flutter of a petticoat.

He ran, overtook the flying damsel, caught her in his strong arms, bent his head to inflict the penalty—and lo! he touched the lips of Bell. If he muttered an oath at the disappointment. Bell never betrayed him. It is certain she returned to the house radiant, accepting the omen in its fullest significance.

It was long before Susan re-appeared, and then in a state of extreme agitation. Twice had she made, in expectant trepidation, the circuit of the barn, one side of which abutted on the lane, fenced off by a low wall of unhewn stones. As she ran past for the third time, scattering imaginary seed, and with her head turned over the left shoulder, repeated the formula—

Hemp-seed I sow, hemp-seed I hoe.

. . . . an unsuspected listener leaped the wall, saying—

"Gin ye hae fand a tongue for siccan a Halloween cantrip, lassie, Archie Cameron wad be a fuile to miss siccan a chance!"

A sudden gleam of moonlight fell on his face and plume, the flying maid felt that she had again raised the spirit that was a fate to her, and with an apprehensive scream fell prostrate in his path. When she came to her senses the Highlander was sprinkling water on her face from a tiny beck close by, whither he must have borne her. He knelt upon the turf, his arm supported her, and the well-remembered voice strove to allay her apprehensions with the assurance that he was no wraith but solid flesh—a living and breathing man.

Whether she was spell-bound or only faint she knew not: she could neither rise nor call out; the effort she made to free herself only inducing a tighter clasp.

"Nay, lassie, ye dinna gang till ye tell me your name, an' your faither's name, that I may ken wha to speer for. I hae thocht mair an' suffered mair ower the white-faced dumb lammie I supped wi' o' St. John's Eve than I wad care to thole again. I hae been like a hen on a het girdle for mair nor three weeks, an' hadna orders come for the Seventy-First to garrison Carlisle, I maun e'en hae deserted, sin' I could get na leave o' absence, an' I couldna bide langer awa' frae ye ony gate."

Susan thought of the apple in her coffer, and assigned to witchcraft that which was due to the more subtle power of first-sight love.

He held her fast. "Your name, my canny lassie? What do they ca' ye at hame? Wunna ye speak? Hae ye lost your tongue agen? Ye had fand it a wee syne. Tell me your name, or I maun kiss it frae your lips."

Afraid lest he should put his threat into execution, she stammered out, "Susan Gray;" at the same time struggling for freedom.

"Susan, my fluttering doo, I'll gie ye liberty noo, but ye ken I cam to mow the hemp-seed ye were sowin', and so hae guid right to mak' your lips my ain."

A kiss fell upon her lips. The strong arms released her; and in a swirl of undefined emotions she fled into the house without even a response to his "Guid nicht!"

Dalton, coming to seek her, saw her break from a soldier's arms, and remembering the supper scene he had witnessed, turned back sharply, to devote himself to Bell for the rest of the evening, in the very revenge of jealousy.

Her lover's paraded defection was lost upon Susan, whose usually firm mind was almost shaken from its balance by the daring act of the night, and its mysterious climax. Man or ghost, the soldier had been drawn thither by spells too powerful to resist, and how far they had been lawful she dared not think. Surely she had not been tempting the devil to her own destruction? Surely the uncanny witch-wife had not beguiled her into the clutches of the foul fiend, and so brought the "dour weird" upon her! In shuddering dread she retreated to her room, and kneeling on the white boards by the bedside put up an involuntary prayer for mercy and forgiveness.

Moreover, she resolved to take Dick Dalton into favour at once, little as she cared for him, and so blot the Scotch soldier from her memory for ever.

Alas! for her resolution. Dick Dalton perversely kept away from the farm, and Corporal Cameron contrived to accost her in Carlisle market on the Saturday; to he the frequent bearer of messages from his captain to the hospitable owner of Corby Castle, and, his road lying past the farm, to scrape acquaintance with William Gray himself.

In less than a fortnight he was not only at liberty to open the gate and walk into the house, but was welcomed to the ingle nook, as news-bringers from the outer world were welcomed in places and times remote from post and press.

Nevertheless, the November sky did not lour more darkly, nor the Eden swell and foam with chafing rains more threateningly than did Farmer Gray with wrath, when some six weeks later Archibald Cameron asked leave to marry his eldest daughter, having her full concurrence.

He spluttered and famed with impotent rage, ransacked his Cumbrian vocabulary for invectives wherewith to batter the inauspicious wooer, and made it quite sufficiently apparent that his "*veto*" was decisive.

The corporal had, however, taken too many hard knocks in his time to mind hard words; and if the imperative farmer had a dominant will, the canny Scot was blessed with a cool temper and tenacity of purpose.

Susan, standing by the open door with the hood of her grey duffel cloak drawn over her head, as a protection from the weather, heard every word of the colloquy, her heart beating time to her father's temper. Her breath came with a quick gasp as Archie's last speech fell on her ear.

"Ye may as weel keep your breath to cool your parritch, farmer; what maun be, maun be, an' ye canna wipe oot Archie Cameron from your bairn's weird as ye wad rub the ruddle fra a sheep's back. An' lang ere I pit a foot ower your doorstane, I hae seen our bonnie Susan an' myself kneelin' thegether i' th' kirk, before the meenister, as man an' wife. Nay, man, ye need na' laugh sae scornfully! Ye wunna be gifted wi' the second-sight, but before Heaven, I hae seen this mair than ance or twice, an' a fated weird is stronger than will of man or maid. Fare ye weel, farmer, ilka ane maun gang his ain gate."

"Dinna greet, Susan lassie," whispered Cameron, interrupting his soothing words with kisses quite as consoling, ere they parted in the lane. "We maun bide a wee; your father may change his mind ere lang. He canna fight against predestined love like ours. So gang ben oot o' the rain, my ain love, an' aye put your trust in an o'er-ruling Providence."

The passionate tears had burst like a thunderstorm and were gone. And now broke forth speech as passionate, born of love and self-will, in which she avowed her determination to be his in spite of father or mother, or even fate itself. She stood erect before him, a hand in each of his, her upturned eyes flashing, responsive to the calm resolution in the eyes looking so far into the depths of her own.

Her father met her on the threshold, and enforcing his will with a leathern bridle, which he laid across her shoulders, using words that fell harder than blows, so crushed out the last spark of obedience.

When the "Kersmus cairdins" came round, and the huge "Yule log" blazed and crackled on the wide hearth, mocking the feeble rush-lights in the tin sconces amongst the evergreens on the wall, Dick Dalton sat once more among the players, but only Bell supplied the hot ale, and Dick's jubilant mirth, like his lovemaking to her, was somewhat overdone.

★★★★★★

In the humblest Cumbrian cottage, even where a board laid across the players' knees has to do duty for a table, cards are played at Christmas time.

★★★★★★

Susan was gone! She had married the soldier against her father's will, and he had discarded her: driven his favourite daughter forth with furious threats of violence if ever she should darken his doors again.

As she fled from his frenzied wrath through the blinding snow to seek shelter and protection in her husband's quarters in Carlisle, she was haunted more by her mother's piteous tears than by her father's denunciations. Surely, the "dour weird" had already begun to fall.

CHAPTER 2: FULFILLED

In Archibald Cameron's large frame was a large heart, and he cherished, well as he could, the woman who had left home and friends for him. But a soldier's wife finds more thorns than roses in her path, even in times of peace; and Susan, on a baggage wagon, or tramping for miles on foot with a babe in her arms, cast many a regretful glance back towards her comfortable Cambrian home; and her wonderings if Dick Dalton had taken a wife to Staneley farm were much more frequent than her steadfast husband might have approved.

Years passed; wandering, restless, adventurous years; years fall of hardship, sufferings and trials, of all but repentance; for Susan had a good husband and did not repent. Archibald was promoted. Sergeant Cameron's wife wrote home to her mother a long, proud letter abounding with love for her husband, but asking no forgiveness, expressing no contrition. Yet the letter told that she had named her fourth son William, after her father, and that she never forgot her home friends in her prayers, as she still loved them all dearly.

That letter was never answered and no second was ever written. The affection thus tacitly rejected by those she had left now concentrated on the dear ones around her. The love kindled so mysteriously never flickered or died out; she was devoted as a wife and mother, as frugal, industrious, and heroic as the partner of a soldier's fortunes should be.

Cameron himself, a compound of religion and superstition, a man of iron will, held a tight rein over his family; even Susan's will yielding to his, although she did resist the curb at times.

But for a soldier's wife, she was singularly fortunate in her domestic relations, and old Margery's prophecy slipped from her memory.

Each son joined the regiment as he stepped out of boyhood, Willie, her golden-haired Willie, entering the ranks at the very commencement of the Peninsular War. His brothers were tall and stalwart like the sergeant; Willie, her latest born, was of slighter build, and in his face she saw a reflex of her mother's. Thus it was that apprehensions of the "dour weird" stirred in the secret depths of her soul, quickened no doubt by the subtle instinct of maternal love. These apprehensions were strengthened by a change which came over her husband. He became gloomy and silent, his "religious exercises" took a more sombre tinge; yet, underlying all was a pitiful tenderness towards his family, which showed some deep feeling at work.

Five finer or braver men were not to be found in the ranks of the Seventy-First Highlanders when they landed in Portugal, in the August of 1808, but only Archibald and Willie came unscathed from Vimeira. As the season advanced, their retreat, hungry, ragged, and shoeless, over mountain snow or through drenching rain, told upon all—most on the boy. Susan herself seemed endowed with supernatural strength; she had water for the thirsty, bandages for the wounded, consolation for the dying.

Christmas came, pitiless, fearful; and Susan, contrasting the misery of their condition with the Christmas hearth by the silvery Eden, began to realise the truth of the witch-wife's forecast.

During a brief bivouac, Susan made her way from the baggage towards a small, ill-conditioned fire, round which Archie and their sons were grouped, sharing its little warmth with many comrades.

She found her husband sitting gloomily apart, his eyes fixed, intently fixed, not on the fire, but on the space beyond, with the strange, unearthly aspect of one who walks in his sleep.

"Archie, my man!" said she, wonderingly, "Archie!" laying her hand upon his shoulder.

To voice and touch he was alike insensible.

Presently he rose, muttering as if to himself, "Four! four! ken ye wha'a the fourth" He turned his bonnet, reversed the position of his plaid, still keeping his eyes fixed on vacancy, "E'en as I thocht, e'en as I thocht"

The words dropped slowly from his rigid lips, accompanied by that short upward and downward shake of the head which confirms ill fears.

Experience had told Mrs. Cameron that a visitation of second sight was upon her husband, and although an indefinable sense of horror and dread crept over her, as she stood with clasped hands and drawn breath watching him, she dared not attempt to rouse or disturb him until the vision had passed.

His sons and one or two comrades rose from their places on the ground, and drew closer as spasm after spasm convulsed his face and herculean frame. At length his limbs became rigid, then relaxed, and with a sigh of infinite relief he sank upon the ground exhausted, murmuring, "Not a', not a'—thank God! for puir Susie's sake."

Susan, kneeling by his side, chafed his rugged hands in hers and peered anxiously into his face with the question, "What have you seen, Archie?"

"Dinna ye ask, guidwife, dinna ye ask. Sorrow comes aye suin enough. I hae had a waefu vision. But I wunna gar ye greet ower suin." And with a short wave of his hand he dismissed the subject.

It was on the fifteenth of January, the eve of the memorable Battle of Corunna, when he referred to it again. Sir David Baird's troops formed the right horn of the human crescent extending between Betezos and the heights of Corunna, waiting for the morrow. Susan, as usual, moved about actively amongst the emaciated men, ministering to their wants with the feeling that common misfortune was kinship.

The night was closing in when Archibald caught her by the hand, saying, in low tones, "Susan, ye hae aye been a guid wife, an' a guid mither to the bairns, an' I wad ill like to part frae ye without my blessing to comfort ye when ye are left yer lane."

"Alane! Archie, what dae ye mean?" she gasped, clinging to him with strange premonitory dread, infected by the solemnity of his tone and manner.

"Ah, Susan dearie, ye maun e'en pray for strength. Ye hae muckle sorrow to thole. I hae seen the smoke o' the comin' battle, an' sword an' bullet do their foul work on a' ye love—an' hae seen it for the third time this vara night."

"It cannot be! I'll not believe it!" burst from the poor woman's white lips in all the agony of full belief in his previsions. "*All!* did ye say, *all?*"

"Ay, danger threatens a', an' ye maun take tent, (care), o' your ainsel. But in a' His dispensations, the Lord remembers mercy, an' a remnant may escape. I saw four stark in death, but the face of one was aye turned awa'."

"But yoursel, Archie, yoursel?"

"I turned my plaid as auld seers advise, an' the plaid in the vision was turned also!" was his impressive answer.

Susan wrung her bauds, doubting not the premonition; but over their farewells, and the subsequent parting with her sons, we must draw a veil, such a veil as Susan was bidden by Cameron to hide her emotion with, lest she should damp the courage of his brave lads.

Night—morning—passed. Noon came. The French brought their guns to the front and opened fire. An attack on General Baird's division followed rapidly, and the bloody work began in earnest; the gallant Seventy-First, in spite of wounds, privations, and fatigue, showing they could yet fight and die like heroes.

At no great distance Susan was posted on a rising ground whence she could watch the conflict; ready to tend a dear one if disabled, but with a feverish, anxious, despairing look in her eyes none ever witnessed before. During the heat of the engagement. Sir James Baird was borne past her, his arm shattered by a grape shot.

Eagerly she questioned the bearers. Prompt but terrible was the response, "Sergeant an' three o' the lads down." They had fallen before a charge of cavalry.

Hardly waiting till the tide of battle receded, Susan rushed like a mad woman to the field, searching, with panting heart, amongst the dead and dying, hoping without hope, to find son or husband surviving. The first sight which met her eager eyes was the prostrate form of her darling Willie. He had but just dropped, wounded by a stray shot; but he seemed on the point of expiring.

Tenderly she raised his head, and put a can of water to his blue lips; but, ere a wound could be examined, a party of the enemy's cavalry in full retreat swept like a whirlwind over the field, leaving Susan barely time for the cry of despair with which she threw herself as a shield across the body of her boy. She felt the cruel beat of iron hoofs, then lost the power to feel.

A remnant of their shattered company, searching the field at the close of the battle, found the poor creature as she lay gasping, an arm and leg broken, a gash on her forehead, bruised in every limb; They raised her gently, and bore her carefully as haste would permit to one of the transport ships in the harbour, for not one man in the corps but respected the motherly wife of Sergeant Cameron.

Rough as was army surgery in those days, she bore the setting of limbs and the dressing of her wounded forehead with unflinching fortitude: anxiety for her beloved ones over-riding bodily pain.

Her tremulous inquiries were at length set at rest—But how? God help her! Hers was indeed "a dour weird." Husband and three sons had been found in one heap, *dead*. Of Willie, her youngest born, there was no trace, but there was little hope that he survived. There were men too disfigured by trampling steeds for recognition—he might be one.

How she endured her mental and physical agony was a marvel to the rough men around her. She gave no demonstrative utterance to her sorrows, but it is no doubt they retarded her recovery.

Months elapsed before she was able to quit the hospital to which she had been consigned on landing at Deal; and then she found herself cast upon the world, homeless, friendless, and almost penniless.

An old piper of the regiment named Rae, a Paisley man, got a memorial drawn up, which Colonel Cadogan endorsed and forwarded. But great is the inertia of circumlocution! No pension, no recognition of any kind came to the stricken heroine, the wife and mother of heroes. Susan Cameron was left to drift, one of England's many martyrs to martial glory.

She was herself too independent to persist in importunities. For the same reason she scorned in her distressed widowhood to crave help of the relatives who had disowned her when a cherished wife. Had Colonel Cadogan remained in England, Susan's case might not have been overlooked, but all things conspired against her. In May the colonel and Piper Rae also were included in the draft from the Seventy-First sent back to the seat of war.

Ere they started, the friendly old piper bestirred himself to raise a subscription amongst his comrades for their sergeant's widow. The money was given freely, and pressed upon her as a farewell token of respect, else her native pride had certainly ignored her poverty, and prompted its rejection.

Susan, in humble but sombre widow's weeds, watched the two frigates sail from Deal harbour, bearing with them her only friends, and as the hulls sank below the horizon she felt her heart sink with them. A friendless, childless widow, with enfeebled frame, and shattered constitution, she was realising in all its force the "dour weird" which had followed her choice of a husband. Yet, keenly as she felt her situation, there was no looking back with regret to Dick Dalton.

She was more engrossed in contemplation of Margery Grant's prophecy, and her own slaughtered husband's second-sight previsions, like Pandora's box, there was Hope at the bottom. What had been true in part, might be true in all. Cameron's eerie vision had shown but *four slain*. Where was the fifth, the lad whose corpse had not been found? Might not he be the one of her ain on whose breast her dying head was to pillow?

Nerved by this hope she bent her steps northward, a woman Aged by afflictions, not years. Her small store of money she sewed in the lining of her stiff bodice, keeping a small reserve for use, and too poor to pay coach-fare, took her way on foot to Edinburgh, hoping to find a welcome amongst her dear Archibald's friends.

Pass we over the long and weary journey, the perils of the road, her expedients to pay honestly, yet without money, for temporary accommodation at wayside farm or inn. Her knitting pins were bright with use, and her rapid fingers far outstripped her poor lame limbs on the homeward journey.

A June sun was blazing in the sky when the footsore wayfarer turned into the bye-lane which led from the Carlisle road to Weatherall and Stainbrig, impelled by strong yearnings towards the place of her birth and the home friends from whom she had been so long estranged.

Alas! for the revisitor! What found she? A grave in the kirkgarth, where slept her mother. A new wife on her father's hearth; Bell reigning in the Dalton farm. Change everywhere, the saddest in herself, to whom no old friend stretched out a hand in recognition or greeting.

Sad and sick at heart she laved her heated brow and feet in the little beck whence Corporal Cameron had baptised her to himself on that fateful Michaelmas eve; then, without a sign, she turned her back for ever on Cumberland and all that it contained.

Her funds were low when she reached Edinburgh. But Susan's unconquerable spirit was not the one to flag at her journey's end. Of Cameron's relations she found but one, a far-awa' cousin, a shopkeeper in the Luckenbooths. Here kinship was a passport; she was welcomed hospitably for her dead guidman's sake, poor though she was.

It was not in Susan's nature to outstay her welcome. Her first conversation with Dugald Cameron convinced him she had not come to be a burden. If her misfortunes and sufferings excited benevolent sympathy, much more did her independence win his esteem. From a friend of his she obtained, at a nominal rent, a small cottage at the foot of Salisbury Crags, which her well-hoarded money just sufficed to furnish with absolute necessaries. These comprised a camp-bed, a three-legged table, a couple of chairs, a low stool or two, a kist for meal, and another for clothes, a girdle for bannocks, platters, pots and pans. To these she added a spinning-wheel and a small stock of poultry.

And now began another phase of Susan's eventful life. A kindly word dropped here and there by Dugald Cameron soon found the sedate soldier's widow purchasers in Edinburgh for her eggs and chickens. Then, while her hens clucked, her knitting-pins twinkled, and her spinning-wheel hummed, and for some years she held her head bravely, a woman who, but for the injuries she had sustained, would have been in the prime of life and activity.

But the "dour weird "had fallen heavily. In the twenty-three years of her wandering life, the horrors she had witnessed, the shocks she had received, the heats of India, the snows of Corunna, had told on her constitution, and at forty-three she bore the stamp of another decade. She had exchanged a stirring, gregarious life for monotony and solitude. The drowsy hum of her wheel, and the *tic-tic-tic, tic-tic-tic* of her knitting pins filled up no vacuum, but followed in low undertones the sorrowful or anxious train of her thoughts from the bloody battlefield, where husband and sons were lost, to that speculative region occupied by her boy Willie, and that one word, "missing;" her anxious unsatisfied yearnings only giving poignancy to her desolation.

She had lived about three or four years at St. Leonards, when an unexpected stone was thrown into this continuous current of thought, breaking it up into whirling eddies.

With a basket of eggs balanced on her head, one fine spring morning she bent her steps towards Edinburgh, busily knitting a blue worsted overall by the way, as was her wont. Where the wall of the King's Park skirted the high road there was a stile for ingress and egress.

Seated on this was a poor feeble creature, whose age, computed by wrinkles and decrepitude, must have been nearly a hundred, gasping and struggling in the tearing grasp of an asthmatic cough. Her plaid and mutch were displaced, her grey hair straggled over her face and neck, her skirts were torn and bedrabbled. She had evidently passed the night on that inhospitable bed, too weak to pursue her journey.

Susan's compassion was stirred. "Mother," said she (her Cumbrian dialect had worn itself out in her long march over the world), "you seem weary and faint; drink this." She had unslung the canteen she still carried camp-fashion when she went abroad, and presented a draught of milk to the parched and palsied lips. "Are you far from hame? Can I help you?" proffering oat-cake from her wallet as she spoke.

The poor creature munched it eagerly, murmuring between each mouthful, "Eh! woman, but ye're gude an' kin'! but ye dinna ken wha ye hae gien your awmous, (alms), to, or may be ye wad hae left the feckless auld witchwife to die her 'lane. Sair worn am I wi' my lang journey ower mair than ninety miles o' life, an' hame canna' be far awa'. But wha cares a bodle gin Margery Ghrant dies by the roadside, wi' a stane for her pillow, or amang the green rashes o' a festerin' pool?"

Susan recoiled with a start. "Margery Grant!" Could this be the same who had spaed her fortune full five and twenty years before? If so, she who had then foretold the "dour weird" was surely the one to lift the veil now and set anxiety at rest.

"Ay, woman! Margery Grant! Does the name sting thee? It's like, noo ye ken me, ye grudge the bit and drap that hae keepit the life in the auld doited body. Weel, weel, it's muckle time I won hame."

"Nay, Margery, if the fortune ye telled me lang syne did set my silly head running on soldier laddies, ye aye warned me to beware how I wed. There is no fleeing from fate, and I had more than one token. But truly the 'dour weird' ye foretold to the thoughtless lass on the banks o' the bonnie Eden has been a dour weird indeed!" and Susan shook her head mournfully.

The old woman strove to rise. Mrs. Cameron helped her to her feet. .Margery put her hand to her forehead with a gesture indicative of recurring memory. "Eh, woman, but I mind it a noo. Ye ken, I spake o' a sweet drap o' comfort i' th' grands o' th' bitter cup. But I trow it's weary waitin' at mirk midnight for the sun to rise."

A deep sigh testified Susan's assent.

Loath to leave the decrepid old crone to perish from neglect, she took her basket on one arm and Margery on the other, and retrod the path to her cottage, with a hasty resolve to shelter the forlorn castaway, whose word had so deeply influenced her life.

Margery's tottering steps made progress slow. The neat cottage once reached, Susan seated her charge on a low chair by the ingle, with a corner of her plaid fanned the gathering peat on the hearth to a glow, and, putting some sowens, (oatmeal steeped in water), into a saucepan, soon set a smoking bowl of porridge before her charge.

Susan never did things by halves. The morning was advancing, and her errand could not bide. As a safeguard against fire, she put the old spae-wife in her own bed, left, food and drink within reach, mounted her basket and again set off towards the city, the grateful thanks of a rescued fellow-being lightening her load.

Housed, warmed, and fed, Margery Grant recovered, and Susan was no longer lonely. Then she had to work for two, so had less time to brood over the past, and faith in Margery's hopeful previsions kept her up wonderfully. Indeed, she had need of some mental support, the persecution which followed the old fortune-teller appearing to cast its shadow over her protectress.

That which should have been her highest honour only aroused credulous suspicion; the slight halt in her own gait, the knowledge (gathered in many lands) of strange herbs and simples, her style of dress (the wallet and canteen to wit), all marked her out for the shafts of ignorance and superstition, which, in time, made themselves felt; and the "twa witches thegither," as the country folk dubbed them, sank to extreme poverty. Through this Mrs. Cameron struggled nobly, asking no alms, accepting no aid, though penury sat down by her side with sharp threatenings to put out the fire, and sweep out the meal kist.

Five or six years had passed, when Margery, quick to note her friend's despondence, roused like the flickering of a spent candle, and stood before her, the embodiment of an ancient sibyl, the fire of prophecy in her eye and on her cheek. Pressing one withered hand on the other's shoulder, she spoke in earnest tones—

"Susan Cameron, look up! Dinna fash yoursel' wi' care for the future. Ye hae been to me as the widow of Zarepath to Elijah, and fear not that *your* cruse o' oil shall fail or your meal be spent in the barrel, till the Lord sendeth his blessed rain on the earth. An' it's comin' Susan, comin'; I see the sma' wee cloud that comes to shed on the dry wilderness o' your existence the tender rain o' new life. Susan woman, ye shall be fed, an' clothed, and see yer ain when these auld limbs lie under the mools. I see your gowden-haired Willie comin', comin', but he's far awa' yet, an' there's sma' glint o' gold in his pouch, or in his locks."

Susan started to her feet in awe and expectation. Margery uplifted a finger to bespeak attention.

"Hark, did ye no' hear the rustlin' wings, and the weird voice o' the angel o' Death callin' the auld witch-wife to rest? Hark!"

The upraised hand dropped, the fiery eye dimmed; the glow of inspiration on her cheek faded to a dull grey; the frame collapsed, and that which Susan caught ere it fell was but a relic of Margery Grant.

In the old woman's leathern stays was found gold enough to bury her and leave a surplus, doubly acceptable to Susan, whom starvation and rheumatism alike held in their grip. It enabled her to make her house once more weather-tight, and to renew her stock of meal and fuel. Yet she missed her old companion sadly, and would gladly have gone on working and pinching for both to have kept the helpless old woman in the ingle nook.

As moons and seasons waxed and waned, and even years rounded bringing no tidings of her missing son, her heart at last began to fail, and with it her energy. Twelve long and weary years had worn out hope, and the "dour weird" pressed heavily.

Sea and land were bathed in the glowing light of a July midday sun. Sheep and cattle sought the shade of rock or wall or tree. Grass and leaves alike seemed fainting with the heat. Susan Cameron sat with doors and window open, inhaling the breath of the honeysuckle she had trailed round the porch in memory of her old home; knitting but slowly, heat and old memories overpowering need.

Her fingers moved mechanically, her eyes looked out on parched pasture land, distant heather and grey rock. Then came into the scene a poor crippled emaciated wayfarer, toiling painfully along, his forehead bandaged, his arm in a sling; his form bent with fatigue or disease, not age. There was just so much shape and colour left in his rags as told he had been a soldier.

The soiled red jacket caught her eye like magic, set her pulses in a strange flutter, and roused all the woman within her. No matter his regiment; he was a soldier, and in distress, and that was sufficient claim on her sympathy. Might not her own boy be a wanderer somewhere!

She had put down her work and risen to meet him ere he approached, and faintly, as one at the last gasp, implored "Drink and food, for the love of God."

Susan's heart was too full for speech; she pointed to the wooden bench outside the cottage, and soon held to his parched lips a bowl of meal and water.

"Here, my poor fellow, drink this. It may serve to keep life in you, and it is all that war and an ungrateful country have left the soldier's widow either for herself or others."

He had taken the bowl eagerly in both hands. As he raised his head and the vessel in the act of drinking, his eyes encountered hers, the tones of her voice fell familiarly on his ears.

The bowl dropped. With one wild cry, "Mother!" he put forth his arms; Willie was gathered to the loving heart which had longed for him, hoped for him, prayed for him through twelve unanswering years; the bandaged head rested on the motherly breast where his golden curls had nestled in infancy.

Here was new life for Susan. She laughed, wept and caressed him by turns. But the growing pallor on his face warned her that emotion was overpowering him. With one strong effort of will her demeanour changed, there was dread as well as affection in the quiet care with which she led him to old Margery's cushioned seat, and, having revived him with a fresh draught of her only beverage, ran, despite her lameness, to her nearest neighbour, to procure with her last coin food

219

and whisky, and to dispatch a bare-legged callant to her friend in the Luckenbooths.

The stimulant might not have been loyally dutiful to King George, but it did good service to his loyal subject. His faintness passed away, and the soldier rallied sufficiently to partake the first substantial meal he had had for days.

After a sound sleep on Margery's comfortable pallet, evening found him another man. Wan and emaciated he was, certainly, but the dust was gone from shoes and garments, a needle had drawn the rags into place, his face was washed, his wounds were dressed and re-bandaged; happiness lit his blue eyes, which followed his mother's every movement with a restful satisfaction not to be described.

See Susan stroking his wasted hand as she sits on a low stool by his knee, endeavouring to trace in the worn features of her recovered treasure the fine boy she remembered.

"Ah, Willie, dearie, want and wounds are sair disfigurers. I see little of the golden-haired laddie I left in his blood on the fatal field of Corunna!"

"I have brought back my heart, dear mother, and my hands to work for you, when I grow strong again. But consider what I have endured since then."

And what had that been? He had roused from a temporary stupor to find himself covered by what he deemed the mangled corpse of his mother; had dragged himself away to a place of safety; a party of the enemy crossing the field had carried him off with them; and for two years he had endured the miseries of a French prison. Then he was exchanged. Could learn no tidings of his family save "death, death." Believing himself alone, he re-entered the army, was sent with his regiment to Canada, was tomahawked by an Indian at Fort Erie, and only escaped scalping through a timely musket-shot which brought down his savage adversary.

His wounds cured, he was draughted from the intense cold of Canada to the intense heat of the West Indies. Had an attack of yellow fever. Wounded and diseased, was at length permitted to exchange into a regiment returning home. Shortly afterwards the regiment was disbanded, and without pension or remuneration he was cast adrift, a crippled beggar, one of England's incongruities—its glory and its shame.

This is but a condensed outline of the wanderer's story, told less connectedly, and with details which made his mother shrink and shudder. The moon was rising as it drew to a close, and silent thanksgivings were rising from Susan's heart as she caressed the straggling curls the scalping knife had spared, when a quick light step was heard on the threshold, and the callant she had sent to their kinsman rushed in crying out, "Braw news, Meestres Cameron! braw news!"

Close at his heels came Dugald Cameron puffing and blowing, out of breath, but waving a paper in one hand, his bonnet in the other.

Speech was impossible, he thrust the paper into Susan's hand, tossed his bonnet across the kitchen, grasped Willie by both hands before he could utter a word of congratulation, altogether in a state of excitement very foreign to douce Dugald Cameron.

It was a document from the War Office. Unknown to Susan, her staunch friend Dugald had for years worried the powers that be (as he said "like a collie-dog at the heels o' a flock o' sheep") until he forced recognition of her claims. That paper confirmed the right of Sergeant Cameron's brave widow to a liberal pension.

Thus was her joy crowned!

Tears of gratitude fell from Susan's eyes that night as she opened her kist, and drawing thence with much solemnity Sergeant Cameron's well-kept Bible, laid it reverently on the table before their son.

"Willie, my boy, let us both return thanks for doubled mercies. For me, I thank God heartily that my long-lost boy is given back to be the comfort of my old age, a token that my 'dour weird' is past."

Their hands met and clasped over the holy book.

"My own Willie!"

"My dear mother!"

That clasp was for life. There was no more parting until the grey-haired woman laid her dying head on the breast of her son in after years.

The White Woman of Slaith

Chapter 1

Superstition dies hard, and who shall say that when Superstition dies, his twin sister. Veneration, will not droop and languish over his bier? But nowhere does superstition linger longer than among the fisher-folk of the far north. The men who "*go down to the sea in ships, and occupy their business in great waters,*" not only "*see the works of the Lord, and His wonders in the deep,*" but they leave behind them ashore women sensitive as barometers to every change of wind and weather, keenly susceptible of all that may affect the husbands, and fathers, and brothers who risk their lives that they and others may live. And they also leave behind them children to be influenced by all they hear and see, and to catch up and transmit every eerie whisper that may fall from their elders.

So from generation to generation the wind has had voices for the fisher-folk that the trading townsman could not hear, and the wreathing mist has held shapes the city matron could not see; voices and shapes of awe and mystery, powerful to bless or ban.

Such may have been the "White Woman of the Wreck," of whom the hardy fisher-wives of Slaith to this day speak in undertones, lest the very utterance of her name should bring the ill-omened spirit amongst them.

Yet only once has she been seen within living memory, and a grey-haired woman keeps the record in her heart.

Far back, when Hilda Sanderson's grandfather was a boy, when the fishermen's huts were not perched here and there upon the rocks to be out of reach of the tide, but looked out from beneath the cliffs on a fair expanse of sand and shingle and a land-locked bay, was the White Woman seen for the first time, and *in the flesh,*

Rude and uncultivated as are the fisher-folk of Slaith in these our times, civilization is yet making its mark on the young; but in those bygone days the dwellers on too many of our coasts looked upon all spoils of the ocean as their legitimate right. So at Slaith, when a fierce north-easter ravaged the coast and kept yawls and cobles at home, the storm would bring as sure a harvest as was won from the deep on those moonlight nights when the herring-boats were out. And notwithstanding the abundance of coal in the wild region around, frequent wrecks made wood the common fuel; it was plentiful, and cost nothing but the gathering and stowing away.

Never had come storm to Slaith at once so productive, or so disastrous, as that which spread its lurid banners over the sky one September evening more than a century ago, warning the busy fishermen to put back and haul their craft high and dry upon the beach for safety. Only one boat, which had set sail in advance of its fellows, disregarded the storm-signals of the sky and pursued its course, whether in recklessness or confidence is not known.

The purple clouds gathered over the crimson glare, the wind came howling up, driving blacker masses of cumuli before it, and night set prematurely in over land and sea.

The village, sheltered on the north and west by a steep, stern ironstone cliff, which spread its protecting arm far out to sea in a formidable reef or "neb," was all astir. Men and women gathered on the beach intent on hauling up the boats, securing nets and tackle, and speculating what luck the sea had in store for them, as it broke in foam and froth on the hard rocks and ran in almost to their feet.

Yet, mingling with the crowd and these speculations, came one short-skirted fishwife to the beach with wildly anxious eyes, and hands pressed on her throbbing breast, for Robert Blackburn's boat had not come back with the rest, and it held her husband and her boys. Only the youngest clung to her woollen skirt, and added, with his questions, to her fears and agony.

As the waves leapt up to meet the vivid lightning darting from the clouds and dancing on their crests, she could discern through the blinding rain a disabled ship struggling amid the billows, and she felt how little hope there was for her husband's coble in a gale before which so large a vessel was driving to destruction.

Yes, driving helplessly on towards the neb, and never a boat or a hand put forth to the rescue, though the minute gun boomed in solemn appeal above the roar of the elements; though shrieks and cries for help were borne in by the wind as the doomed vessel was hurried nearer and nearer to its fate; and though the lightning flashes revealed the white figure of a woman lashed to the broken mainmast, and hapless sailors clinging to the bowsprit and rigging.

Nearer ran the ship to the outlying reef, and nearer to a crowd of stalwart men who knew the coast, were inured to danger, and lacked neither strength nor courage to risk life or limb in saving life—but only *the will*. True, the danger was imminent, the risk great, the men had families dependent on their lives, and—if none were left to tell the story of the wreck, better luck would be for the village. So cries and shrieks fell on deaf ears. Not even the piteous adjuration "For God's sake!" which came with strange distinctness across the waters as the vessel struck, had power to move a man. Maggy Blackburn ran from one to another beseeching pity for the lady and the helpless crew, as they might hope for aid in like straits, as *her* husband and sons might be needing aid even then!

Sullen silence, or gruff admonitions to mind her own business were the only response. Even the women turned away, the greed of gain, the hope of spoil, stronger than womanhood.

Morning dawned on a cold, gray sky, a receding tide, a placid sea, a fishing village nestling under ragged cliff, with a long reach of smooth sand between the cottages and the narrow strip of boulders and shingle, and the outstretched arm of the Neb, looking innocent as any other benevolent protector.

It dawned also on smoke uprising from cottage fires kept alive during all the storm and tumult; on a sea and beach strewn with wreckage; on men and women wading into the surf to bring ashore boxes and bales within reach of arms or boat-hooks; on boats, well manned, steering among the rocks and shallows, or even into deeper currents around the Neb, to pick up jetsam and flotsam before the coastguard or the lord of the manor should come on the scene with a legal claim.

It dawned on the half-naked bodies of drowned sailors swaying hither and thither with the undulating waves, or lying disfigured among the rocks, among weeds, and tangle, and inquisitive lobsters black as undertakers. It dawned, too, on a tall, slim woman in a white clinging garment, her head and shoulders wrapped in a grey shawl, from beneath which her fair hair had fluttered and lay in wet, loosened tresses on the sand, where the tide had landed her and the broken mast together. Landed only to lie there unnoted and unregarded, although when the sun kissed the pale lips and eyes they opened to life light and warmth, and perchance a hope of deliverance thrilled through the half-insensate form.

It came not until too late. Maggy Blackburn and her boy retreating to their hut when the ship struck, had spent the intervening hours in weeping for the dear ones they never expected to behold again; and not until the sun was fairly up, and the boy had cried himself to sleep, did she venture forth to see the devastation night, and storm, and pitiless men had to answer for. Far along the beach, away from the busy knots of wreckers, she found the White Woman lying, to all appearance, dead. A compassionate tear fell on the pale upturned face, and a word or two of pity dropped from the rough fishwife's lips—in her own grief sympathetic.

As she spoke, a pair of lovely blue eyes slowly unclosed and rested for an instant on her own in mute thanksgiving.

With a cry of surprise, Maggy strove to loosen the bonds which held the frail form to the mast. In vain! Loving hands had tied them too securely, and the wetted cordage would not yield.

She had no knife. Rising to her feet she put her hands to her mouth and sent a loud halloo across the sands for help. Again and again she called. Her call was disregarded. A large cask was being rolled over the grating shingles.

At length an answer, prefaced by an oath, was shouted back. "Mind thy own business, Maggy Blackburn, an' let th' woman be."

But Maggy, tender in the hour of her own dreaded bereavement, stooped to whisper, in ears which might or might not be conscious, the nature of her errand; and ignoring the belief that ill-luck follows the restoration of the shipwrecked to life, she sped along the sweep of sand to her own home for a knife, lest a churlish refusal might meet her on the beach, where knives were in active use.

Blackburn's cottage was mounted on a ledge of rock above the rest of the village, and was less accessible, and though Maggy was strong and swift of foot, swifter-footed Death outran her. *He* had severed invisible cords, released the struggling spirit. It only remained for Maggy to release a stiffening corpse, bear it reverently beyond reach of the tide, and compose the dead limbs for burial, woefully wondering the while who would perform the like office for her Robert and his boys.

Intent on her melancholy occupation, absorbed in her own anguish, she heeded not the noisy group near the neb quarrelling over their spoil, until a loud "Halloo" arrested her attention. Turning round, she saw a young fisherman's hand pointing seawards, and some instinct prompted her to fall on her knees with uplifted voice and hands. She felt rather than knew the distant sail for their own.

Robert Blackburn and his sons were safe, though their boat had sustained some damage. They had found a haven close at hand on the first outbreak of the tempest.

But what of the good ship that had gone to pieces on the neb?

What the billows had spared the wreckers had industriously stowed away in secret caves and cellarage, till scarcely a spar remained afloat to tell the mournful story. And after the White Woman and the sailors washed ashore were buried in the sands there was rejoicing and carousal. "That was a lucky day for Slaith," they said, as they sat round fires supplied from the timber of the wreck; "drowned folk were not likely to dispute possession of their harvest, and no man living had put in a claim."

And as the "last lucky day," it was remembered and spoken of with regret as the winter nights drew on; and of all the good ships lost on our northern coasts, not one went ashore at Slaith that had not sailed from it. No more luck of the kind came in their way. Even the take of fish grew scanty and precarious; and a rumour got about that a supernaturally tall woman in a long white clinging robe, whose head was muffled in a grey shawl, was sure to stand like a beacon on the uttermost point of the neb whenever a storm was brewing, and with the motion of her white arms in the air warn approaching vessels of their danger; and that she had been seen to finger the nets as they hung outside the huts to dry, when they would break like tow and let the fish escape.

Certainly the nets were always under repair, and the boats; and when the weird white figure was seen on the neb, like a wreath of mist or spray, there would be apprehensive whispers in the village of the White Woman of the Wreck, and a sense of ill-luck spread its gloom and discontent over Slaith.

It made itself felt in envious antagonism to the Blackburns, who somehow seemed to prosper where others failed, and to be thriving better without a share of the great wreck's cargo than any of those whose cellars had been filled with her merchandize and stores. Silk had mildewed, casks had leaked, and fruits had been damaged by the sea-water.

"Nothing, however, seemed to go wrong with the Blackburns," was said with a grumble, not only at the firesides, but openly to Maggy and Robert both; and they were so often twitted with being "above their neighbours" in more than their dwelling, that as the ill-feeling spread, whilst the seasons went their round, the elder and younger Blackburns alike ceased to grumble at the extra distance and rugged path to their abode, since it kept them apart from ill neighbours.

A year had almost gone by since the day of the great wrecks when Robert Blackburn lamed his foot stumbling over a coil of cable on the beach, at the same time that his two up-grown sons lay tossing on their pillows in the burning arms of fever.

A sad and anxious week this for Maggy, watching her sick, with only Cuthbert, a lad of thirteen, to run to and from the distant apothecary, hew her wood, or draw her water.

His brothers had been three days in bed when he was sent in the early morning for water from the beck-spring. The village lay asleep at the foot of the rock; the boats, which had not been out over-night, were hauled up high on the beach—that beach which seemed to have narrowed so considerably; and a thick haze rested on the slightly heaving sea.

Something of this crossed the boy's mind as he came down the hill with his pail, and noted the high-water mark left by the receding tide.

Suddenly he beheld—as if she came out of the very mist—the tall White Woman of the Wreck glide over the sands and shingle, and touch the stern of every boat as she passed, with one omission—that of his father; and then with a sweep of her long arm towards the line of cottages, glide away silently as she came, leaving Cuthbert so dazed he could scarcely find words to tell his mother what he had seen.

"Not a word to them inside!" she said, as she met him on the threshold. She, too, had seen the White Woman from her own door, and her heart sank lest Betty Rae's ill-savoured words should be true and their own luck indeed be on the turn. What if the omen should be to them, and her sons be taken from her?

Private forebodings did not, however, stifle her goodwill to others. Cuthbert was despatched to the awakening village with the intelligence, and a word of advice for the men not to go to sea that day. Her messenger was greeted with incredulity and scorn. The Blackburns were not in favour, Maggy's motives were suspected, her story disbelieved.

"Are our wives to have empty creels because Maggy Blackburn's men-folk are laid by and canna work?" asked Peter Rae, the man who twelve months before had bade Maggy "Let the woman be!"

Cuthbert went back with a laugh ringing in his ears, and a hint that his mother had picked a convenient time for ghost-seeing.

Nevertheless, her message had not been wholly thrown away, however much her motive might be suspected. There was an absence of ordinary alacrity in preparing the boats for sea, and a disposition to talk rather than work. One old fisherman, with a weather-beaten face, whose name was Sanderson, declared that neither he nor his sons would put out to sea that day. "Better lose a take of fish than a' our lives, an' there's no kenning what mischiefs afloat if th' White Woman has been seen."

There was a sneer at the Sandersons. Nevertheless, one or two young fellows held back at the last, and a yawl or two sailed without the full complement of hands—the Raes for one.

It was a memorable day for Slaith.

When the sun reached its meridian, sea and sky were all aglow like molten gold, and the women on the shore, led by Betty Rae, laughed the stay-at-homes to scorn as they themselves went about their household ways panting with the unprecedented heat.

Maggy was thankful when a breeze came landward with the returning tide and through the open door to fan the flushed cheeks of fever; and not she only. But with the breeze came a little cloud out of the distant wave, and deepened and darkened and spread as the breeze swelled and mounted to a gale, and the long rollers of the advancing tide swept in on the shore, mounting higher and higher, and breaking on the neb as though trying their strength on the rock and disputing its right to bar their progress.

The Sandersons said they saw the tall White Woman on the shore waving her long arms and beckoning to the waves. Calling all hands to help, they drew their own coble and the Blackburns' higher and higher up the beach, now alive with frightened fishwives wading in the surf to secure cables and tackle, nets and creels, hitherto supposed to lie beyond the highest tide.

But on came the rushing water, on and on as the daylight went, on and on in the darkness of night, white-lipped and roaring. Then there was a sudden stir within the cottages, as the water crawled in at the open doors and put out fires on the hearth.

A sudden stir, with glancing lanterns and flaring torches, to bear the infant and its cradle, the grandmother in her chair, and household goods anyhow up the rocky pathway to security; a stir all too late and too hurried in the darkness to save all of life or property. The whole shore was invaded by the sea.

Morning broke on desolation. Weeping women and children up

on the cliffs looked in vain for their homes down below. The village had been swept from the sands.

The two cobles had held to their moorings and were but little damaged; of the picturesquely grouped cottages only ruins mingled with weeds and tangle were visible. No four walls were standing that were not, like the Blackburns', perched on the cliff.

There ran at last a shuddering reminder through the shelterless crowd that it was the anniversary of the "great wreck," as Betty Rae was missed from their midst, and a bundle of blue and red that had once been a woman was found amidst the debris of the Raes' dwelling. And as hour after hour, and day after day went by, and never yawl or coble came back to tell the secrets of the night or of the devastating storm, the homeless women, whose orphaned children clung wailing to their skirts, in their own agony envied the lot of Maggy Blackburn, whose men-folk were spared to her. And not a few remembered that, of all the village, she alone had shown compassion towards the White Woman of the Wreck.

Slaith—the original Slaith—was gone; homes and people: and the White Woman was seen no more by that generation.

Chapter 2

A new Slaith arose. Not immediately, and not on the sands. In spring and autumn the sea had possession of the old site at flood-tide. Of the bereaved families who had found refuge in holes and caves among the rocks, some wandered inland; others, who had means or a man left, began to build cabins here and there on the irregular hillside. Buxom or energetic widows attracted husbands from other stations on the coast. There were marriages and intermarriages, notably between the Blackburns and the Sandersons. Even Raes' only surviving son (the one who had stayed ashore), having wherewith to purchase a new boat—secret spoil of the great wreck—had not far to seek a wife, who scouted the suggestion of ill-luck.

The new village rose under other auspices. The patriarchs of Slaith would have no wreckers in their midst, the awful visitation of the White Woman of the Wreck serving as a deterrent, so long as an eye-witness remained to verify the story he handed down to future generations.

So long as Cuthbert Blackburn, the last survivor of the great storm, sat in the chimney nook, and related to his listening grandchildren how, with his own young eyes, he had seen the white woman with the grey shawl cut away from the broken mast to be buried; and how, a year after, to a day, he had beheld the shadowy form of the dead and buried woman, but tall as a ship's mast, glide over the sands, shake a threatening hand at the village, and touch the stern and sails of every foredoomed boat; the listening children would edge closer to each other, look fearfully around, and hold their breaths with awe.

And so long as the old man could totter about, with the wind playing amongst his grey locks, never a Blackburn or a Sanderson was known to bring other than a legitimate cargo ashore, although smuggling was openly connived at by people of note and respectability on the coast and inland.

But when the old grandfather was laid to rest, the White Woman might have been laid to rest also. She had lapsed into the airy region of tradition, and, in the daily duties and anxieties of fishermen's lives, the very awe her name had inspired was fast dying out. And no wonder. Seventy years had almost rounded their circuit since the sea made its obliterating inroad upon Slaith. Cuthbert's youngest grandchild, Hilda Sanderson, was a blooming maiden of eighteen—golden haired, fresh coloured, firm of foot, and round of limb—as ready to wade in the surf as a water nymph; and she carried on her shoulders the wicker fish creel, suspended by its strap across her forehead, with a grace peculiarly her own.

Eighteen. And nine years had gone since she, her grandfather's pet, had, for the last time, wandered with him on the shore, and drunk in his never-failing recital, as, with his stick, he pointed to the end of the Neb where the ship went down, marked out, as on a map, every detail of the scenes he had witnessed, and cautioned her, as she hoped to prosper, never to form a friendship or have any dealings with a Rae.

Eighteen—and the youngest representative of the Raes had come a-wooing to her!

During his lifetime Cuthbert Blackburn's own children, in obedience to his behest, had held aloof from the Raes. But his grandchildren had felt his interdict a hardship; since avoidance of the Raes meant (to the lads at least) exclusion from companionship and from such sports and games as called for numbers, and of which one or other of the two Raes was almost sure to be leader.

Certainly Hilda's brothers held out the right hand of fellowship to Stephen Rae almost over their grandfather's grave, but surreptitiously, and no one at home was the wiser.

Hilda, seeing the lads together, put in a protest in memory of her grandfather, and their cousin, Robert Blackburn, set his face against the new friendship; but all to no purpose. He himself had, in time, to go with the stream or be left in a minority. And even Hilda, when she grew old enough and strong enough to be sent to the beck for water, was not sorry to find a stronger arm ready to carry the full pail down the hill in her stead.

The Blackburns' cottage no longer looked down from an elevation on the village. It now stood with the Sandersons', almost in the front rank, with a sea-wall as a protection; at the edge of the rock on a higher level the Raes had built, and their footpath to the beach skirted the tumbling mountain stream; and so it came about that, without design, Stephen was so often at hand to do her a service.

That he proffered his services might be due to her pretty face; that she accepted them might be set down as much to the careless, matter-of-fact, yet masterful manner in which he had possessed himself of her pail in the first instance, as to his black eyes and curly head.

He was five years her senior, and the girl of fifteen, taken by surprise, submitted with something akin to fear in her breast, following him down the steep path with an eerie misgiving of evil to come, and answering his few brief remarks with mere monosyllables. She scarcely said "Thank you" as he set down the pail almost at her own door, and, without waiting even for those curt thanks, proceeded on his way to the beach with a net over his shoulder, whistling as he went.

His shadow darkened the cottage window as he stooped to set down the pail.

"Who was that?" asked Maggy Sanderson, looking up from her washtub.

"Stephen Rae, mother," she answered, half afraid of a rebuke.

"And what brought thee with Stephen Rae? Thy gronfeyther Blackburn would have given thee a word of a sort had he seen thee wi' one o' them folk, for a' they be better off than ourselves."

Hilda was conscious of this.

"I could not help it, mother. He took up the bucket, and was off with it down the hill before I could get out a word."

"Weel, lass, it was neighbourly; an' if thou didn't throw thyself in the lad's way, thou'rt noan to blame." And the energetic woman made the soapsuds fly as she rubbed away at a blue guernsey, and went on saying: "Will and Cuddy say we ha' no' right to cast up to Peter and Steve what their great-gronfeyther was, an' that thy gronfeyther's tale was half superstition an' half prejudice, an' that it's time old animosities died out. May be it is. Me an' thy feyther have talked it over mony a time; an' though it did look like a judgment when old Peter was drowned, as his forbears were afore him, thy feyther said that, forbye a bit o' smuggling, nobody knew aught again him. An' it's noan Christian-like to turn a cold shoulder to the lads, seeing they're so good to the poor mother, though they do come of a bad stock. But surely, lass, thou needn't stand still while I talk. You might have had them potatoes peeled by this time, an' ready for the pot."

The bustling matron's reproof was not ill-timed. Hilda's knife went round the roots somewhat mechanically and slowly. She was thinking more of her mother's speech than of her occupation. It was a tolerant reversal of all preconceived notions and old beliefs—a doubt thrown on Grandfather Blackburn's theory of ill-luck as the White Woman's legacy to the Raes—a blow struck at the roots of prejudice and Superstitious fear.

She hurried over the potatoes; set them to boil, and with them a dish of silvery fresh herrings, then carried the basket of newly-washed clothes to the beach, and spread them out on the shingle to dry, strewing pebbles over them to keep them down.

But all the while her mother's speech was in her mind, and consequently Stephen Rae: a conjunction Maggy Sanderson had scarcely contemplated.

When next she, on her way from the spring, in her pink half-gown and blue woollen petticoat, was overtaken by Stephen, much of her eerie dread had disappeared, and something of girlish shyness, which kept her tongue-tied, had taken its place.

Whatever her mood, if he chanced to overtake her on her way from the spring, he was certain to possess himself of her pail, and carry it down the hill, no matter what other burden he might have, and he was seldom empty-handed.

And he always stepped on briskly in advance, as if to show that, though willing to serve her, he had no desire to obtrude in the way of conversation. After a time she caught herself admiring the manliness of his bearing, the careless ease with which he bore the brimming pail down the rugged path, nor spilled a drop, though, it might be, a cable or a net was slung across his shoulder; and she was prone to contrast his black curls with her brothers' red locks. At such times she would take herself to task and resolve to avoid him as her dead grandfather had enjoined. But she could neither shut her eyes nor her ears, and she found herself looking and listening for his step, and when he was not there feeling a sense of disappointment which made her angry with herself.

Her brothers had long rallied her on her sweetheart, heedless of her angry disclaimer, and her cousin, Robert Blackburn, had provoked her even to tears with his bitter taunts of barefaced impropriety in running after one of the Raes. But neither her brother nor Robert would accept her challenge to fetch water in her stead. Robert tried it for a week or ten days, but he soon found the task incompatible with his daily duty.

She was nearly seventeen before she would admit to herself that Stephen was more to her than a friend, and quite seventeen before he claimed a higher privilege.

He had watched her step by step on her way to womanhood, noted her modesty, her industry, and made himself sure of a place in her heart before he asked for it. Nay, he might have waited longer still had he not seen Robert Blackburn haunting her like a shadow, with all the facilities which cousinship and adjoining dwellings could give.

She had now to take her part with the women on the narrowed beach in unloading and preparing the fish for market and the curing-house: and as he saw red-haired Robert always at her side to lighten her labours, and was conscious she had avoided him of late, he had a salutary reminder that he might dally a little too long.

Accordingly he loitered on the path by the beck, and saw more than one damsel fill her pail and cast coquettish glances his way; but Hilda came not. He saw her busy on the beach, or leaning over the sea-wall in conversation with her brothers or Robert; but she scarcely looked towards him, and only nodded when he called to her.

In fact, she was avoiding him, fetching water when the boats were out or preparing to sail, having taken herself to task with a will.

Stephen was not easily baffled. He had gone down to the shore in his sea-boots and sailing gear, and was helping Peter to make all trim aboard the yawl, with an eye on Sanderson's cottage, when he suddenly professed to have left something at home, and set off in a hurry, leaving Peter, the two men, and the boy to get all right and tight without him.

He did not slacken his pace until he was fairly out of sight; then he stepped along at leisure and, where practicable, on the soft turf. Hilda was some paces in advance, toiling along in the hot sun with her empty pail as wearily as if it had been filled to the brim with lead.

The spring gushed cold and clear from the rock in a sheltered nook among heather and hart's-tongue fern, a few paces from the beck to which it was tributary, and here Hilda seated herself on a stone in a drooping attitude, sighed heavily, and clasped her knees with both hands as if forgetful of her errand.

A hand upon her shoulder made her start. She turned, and met the gaze of Stephen with eyes that sank before the new light in his.

"Where have you hid yourself, Hilda, the last fortnight? I had a fairing for you, and had never a chance to offer it."

"I do not want a fairing. I—I would rather not have it," faltered she, going alternately cold and hot, as he pulled a gay silk kerchief from his pocket and proceeded to tie it under her chin, saying as he did so, "Yes, you do, and will give me a kiss for it." And holding her face between his two hands, as if to look how her new head-gear became her, he lifted it up to meet the kiss he had ready for her lips.

Her modesty took fright. Never before had he by act or word overstepped the bounds of propriety. She struggled to free herself.

His arm was around her, but the clasp was that of tenderness, not power.

"Nay, Hilda," said he, "I have brought you something more than a fairing. I have brought you a true heart and honest love, and I want yours in return. And now, my lass, how is it to be?"

Hilda was not a fine lady to swoon in her lover's arms, but she had been caught in a melancholy mood, and she certainly grew sick and dizzy, half doubting her own happiness, half dreading the evils her grandsire had prognosticated. She was, however, too honest to keep him very long in doubt, and had coyly given him back his kiss, when a loud halloo farther down the beck reminded him that the tide was on the turn, and that Hilda's pail was still empty.

Home went Hilda in a sort of a dream, to be taken sharply to task for loitering; but Hilda's ears were impervious to sharp words since the magical sweetness of love had been breathed into them. It was not until the bright kerchief on her head attracted her mother's eye that she was awakened from her trance of new delight.

"Where did thee get that thing?"

There was not a colour in the silken square so brilliant as that which flushed her face as, with a sudden flash of recollection, her hand went up to her head. She had forgotten her adornment in thinking of the giver.

There was no longer hope of concealment.

"Steve Rae gave it me for a fairing," she faltered.

"An' what business had thou to take fairings from Steve Rae? Pull the thing off this minute. What would Robert say if he saw thee wearing aught that had come through Steve's fingers?" "It's naught to Robert what I wear," jerked out Hilda, conscious that her cousin had assumed a right of dictatorship not conceded by herself; but she removed the offending headgear nevertheless.

When the boats came in the next morning with a great take of fish, the goodwife was too busy to think of the "fairing." And by the time Maggy Sanderson bethought to broach the matter to her good man, as he smoked his long pipe in the nook, their two sons were in Steve's confidence and prepared to do battle in his behalf.

It was not so tough a contest as Hilda had expected. Her father puffed away, asked for a sight of the kerchief, turned it over, held it to the light, felt its texture, and with the air of a connoisseur decided "that were noan bought at a fair, and it's never been smuggled in thy time or mine, Maggy."

"I only hope he came by it honestly," suggested Maggy, with an expressive jerk of the head.

"That I'm sure he did!" put in Hilda promptly, resenting the impeachment of her sweetheart.

"So am I," supplemented Cuthbert. "Peter and Steve overhauled everything when their father was drowned, and they came across lots of queer things stowed away in a sort of cellar in the rock, that had never seen daylight in their memory, or their mother's either—a mouldy box of women's tackle amongst the rest. It fell to pieces as they moved it, the fastenings were so eaten away with rust. They thought it had been in the water. I'll be bound the kerchief came out o' that."

"Mebbe so, Cuddy. When I were a lad, folks told queer tales of the old Raes and what they had in hiding holes. But I've heard naught again the lads, though they do come of a bad crew. And as for Steve, if it were not for Robert—"

Here both Cuddy and Will launched out in praise of Steve; the end being tacit permission for Hilda to retain possession of her fairing, and to wear it openly with her best clothes on Sundays, greatly to the chagrin of Robert Blackburn, who counted over his savings with a rueful perception of their inadequacy to compete with Stephen Rae in the way of love-gifts.

Certainly a countess might have envied Hilda that Oriental kerchief worn by the fisher-maid in all simplicity, its value to her being only estimable as a token of Stephen's love.

Had she known whence it came, or by whom it had been worn, she would have cast it from her with a shudder. Blissfully ignorant, she walked from church, with Stephen by her side, in a flutter of pride and joy, damped—but only for the moment—by the sight of Robert Blackburn's mournful aspect as he leaned over the low parapet wall, looking drearily out to sea.

"Happy the wooing that's not long a doing! When's it to be, Hilda, lass? There's our Peter married, and Bet—it's quite time thee and me were spliced."

Steve was lying at full length, chest downwards, on the shingle, as he spoke; his elbows buried in the smooth pebbles; his upturned chin resting on his brown palms, his black eyes fixed on the face of Hilda as she—the week's work over—leaned against the stern of a boat turned keel uppermost.

"I don't know," answered Hilda, irresolutely. "Mother says there's no room under Peter's roof for me. Two sons' wives And their mother on one hearth would make it too hot for the men."

"Aye, aye, like enough. But there'd be room enough for thee and me on our own hearth, dearie. I know where there's a snug cottage to be had, so you've only to say the word, and by the time the banns are out, there shall be a home ready for us. What dost say? Shall I put up the banns next week?"

"Ask father. I don't mind," replied Hilda, shyly.

"Do you mind trying on these? You see, Hilda, when a fellow has made up his mind it's best to have everything ready," and he held up a massive wedding ring and keeper, the latter of usurious workmanship, though neither was new.

He had her hand in his clasp, had slipped both rings upon her finger, and was raising himself to snatch a kiss, when she suddenly started to her feet, with her eyes fixed on the point of the neb, and the startled cry, "What's that?" The evening shades had been deepening unheeded whilst they lingered on the beach, but there on the summit of the bleak promontory she beheld a shadowy shape which thrilled her soul with fear. "What is that?"' she repeated in a whisper, pointing with her finger as she spoke.

"What? Where?" questioned Stephen, in perplexity.

"That figure on the neb?"

"I see nothing but the mist and spray. We'd best go in. The wind's rising, and we're like to have a rough night of it."

A rough night it was, but Stephen laughed at her belief that she had seen the White Woman, and said he knew the thing had never been more than mist and foam and fancy; he thought she had had more sense than to believe old women's tales.

His masterful manner kept her silent, but she could not conquer her impressions; and though she carried the two gold rings sewn in her bodice, and loved him, if possible, with a deeper and stronger affection, she put off the actual date of her marriage from time to time as if afraid to venture.

Robert Blackburn had something to do with this. Never a stormy night came but he protested he saw the White Woman hovering about the neb, but as "nothing came of it," and no one else saw more than a wreath of mist, the village laughed him to scorn, until he held his peace and kept his previsions to himself. Yet neither Hilda Sanderson nor Hilda's mother joined the coarse mirth at his expense.

Steve had taken a pretty cottage, had fitted it up to receive his bride, not only with common appliances, but with one or two rare old things brought from some secret hoard, a rarely carved coffer among the rest; had put up the banns and waited impatiently for her to fix the day. And as she put it off and put it off from time to time, for no earthly reason but that she "was afraid," he began to grow jealous of Robert Blackburn and his influence.

On Peter's marriage there had been some talk of having a new yawl built; and now it lay at its moorings on the beach; the finest and largest craft that had ever belonged to Slaith.

In proof of goodwill, and the better to bring Hilda to reason, the Rae brothers offered to take the Sanderson brothers into partnership, an offer Cuddy and Willy were only too glad to accept, having long aspired to something beyond their father's coble.

Their generosity overpowered Hilda; banished Maggy's last objection; the wedding-day was fixed; they were to be married on the Sunday.

On the previous Thursday the yawl, called the *United Brothers*, was to make its trial trip, an extra man and boy completing the crew with Peter as master.

That morning early Hilda wakened with a shiver. She had dreamed that Stephen placed the wedding-ring and its keeper on her finger, when the White Woman came between them and plucked it off. There was no more chance of sleep. The very moonlight streaming through her lattice seemed to mock her. For the first time the atmosphere of the narrow room seemed to stifle her.

To breathe more freely and shake off her fears she lifted the latch of the front door and stepped across the path to the sea wall.

Was she still dreaming, or had her fancy conjured up a ghost to haunt her? There, in the pale moonlight, the lofty, ethereal form of a woman robed in white, with a hood or shawl of misty grey was slowly making the circuit of the *United Brothers*, one shadowy hand gliding over the smooth surface of the hull, the other touching mast and sails and rigging, one by one. Too much appalled to scream, Hilda gasped for breath. Her head swam. She clutched the low wall for support. Another moment and the weird figure was gone.

Back to her bed she crept, stunned and terrified. A sort of stupor bound her senses. Then she slept so heavily, the shrill voice of her mother rebuking laziness could scarcely rouse her.

Once awake all the terrors of the night came back to her. Her first impulse was to seek her brothers and Steve, tell them all she had dreamed and seen, and implore them not to launch the new yawl that day.

Her brothers listened and looked one at another in doubt. Peter Rae frowned, and asked her how fishermen were to live and keep their families if they stayed ashore when their wives had bad dreamt. He scouted the idea that it was anything more than a dream.

Her appeal had more effect on Steve, to whom she clung in entreaty, though he too held that she was the dupe of her own fancy. Her pale face and tearful eyes unnerved him. He was half inclined to hold back, and induce the others to put off the trial of the new boat until after the wedding.

She saw her advantage, and to clinch her argument reminded him that Robert Blackburn had seen the White Woman, more than once.

Jealous Steve set his teeth sternly.

"Oh! Robert Blackburn! There, that's enough, my lass. I want none of Robert Blackburn's hand on our tiller, and shall not wait his breath for a fair wind. You'd best go up to our house and have all put to rights for the wedding; and remember you're mistress there till I come back, or, if I never come back." He said this with his ordinary lightness; drew from his pocket a curious necklet, with a heart-shaped locket, clasped it round her throat as a wedding gift, and with a hearty kiss said she was to wear it for his sake. But he would hear no more of keeping back the boat, either for Robert Blackburn or the White Woman, whilst the sky was clear, and wind and tide in their favour.

Wind and tide in their favour. The *United Brothers* slipped her cable, set her helm, spread her brown sails to the breeze, and with all her nets in readiness, breasted the dancing waves as if proud that the antipathies of generations were at an end, and she bore the proof.

Wind and tide in their favour. A peaceful twilight. A promising nightfall. Only a low mist creeping over the waters. Women and children sleeping calmly as the waves.

What was that?

The invisible hand of a hurricane shaking the windows and doors of Slaith. Billows battering, and breaking over the seawall in foam. A blacker midnight never roused a population to wait in fear and trembling for the mom.

And there, on the extreme point of the neb, the only thing distinctly visible in the darkness, clearly outlined, stood the White Woman, slowly and majestically waving her arms as if in exultation.

Other eyes than Hilda's saw, other hearts than Hilda's sank with apprehension.

The swift storm was over; the turbulent wreck-strewn sea was at rest. One by one the fishing-boats came home, some laden, some empty; all in sorry plight, and all late.

All? No, not all. Robert Blackburn had piloted old Sanderson's coble safely mid the rocks and shallows. But what of the *United Brothers*?

There was never a wedding-day for Hilda. Brothers and betrothed had sailed together and sunk together, and with them had perished all her hopes.

Grey-haired as her own mother, she wept as she recalled too late her grandfather Cuthbert's warning for all of his honest kith and kin to "steer clear of the Raes," and bitterly reiterated that her "dream had indeed come true—the White Woman had torn her wedding-ring from her finger!"

"Aye, and wrecked the last of the Raes and those who dared to claim brotherhood with them," cried Robert Blackburn remorselessly. "You knew the White Woman's silent curse lay on those who let her die unaided, and the good ship go down with every human soul for the sake of spoil. Yet you suffered Steve Rae to adorn you with finery from the wreck, and bind you to himself with the rings his forbear Peter Rae cut from the dead woman's fingers. You did not know it? You knew they were never honest gains, and the Raes were a bad lot. You had better have been content with a poorer mate and a good name."

"I shall never mate. Poor or rich, good or bad, I shall take no man's

name," said Hilda, with a shudder.

She kept her word, and, keeping it, has kept alive the dread of the White Woman of the Wreck among the fisher-folk of Slaith.

Larry's Apprenticeship: An Irish Fairy Legend

CHAPTER 1

"Ah, sure, an' did I ever tell ye how the M'Canns came to be carpenters?"

This query was put by Margaret M'Cann (an old, valuable, faithful, and warm-hearted Irish servant of my mother) to myself and youngest brother, who were seated—myself on the kitchen fender, and he on a low stool—listening to her *true* stories of banshees and leprechauns, in both of which she was a stout believer.

She had just told us of the wailing banshee she had herself seen and heard on the river bank, and of a leprechaun in his red cap and miniature suit of green; and she had borne with perfect good humour our ridicule and banter over her credulity, when she put the sudden question, "Did ye know, then, how the M'Canns came to be carpenters?"

"I never knew they were carpenters," said I, with a light laugh.

"Why, Margaret, I thought all your family were farmers," cried Fred, with an assumption of prior information.

"Them's the Quin's, Master Fred. They are all farmers, to this blessed day; an' the M'Canns were farmers too, an' had a fine holding amongst the Wicklow mountains, just a trifle beyant Enniskerry, till Larry M'Cann (my grandfather that was) met with an adventure amongst the Good People."

Here Margaret, being a devout Catholic, crossed herself.

"Good People! Oh, I suppose you mean fairies," was my amendment.

"Sure, miss, an' I do; but we never speak of them but as the Good People. It's onlucky."

"Oh, that's only in Ireland," suggested Fred, with a droll wink at ma. "In England, you may call them anything you like, and they won't mind it one bit."

"Are ye sure now, Master Fred?"

"Certain. But, Margaret, what had the fairies to do with Larry M'Cann's carpentering?"

"Well, I'll tell ye, of coorse, as it wor towld to me, when I was a slip of a colleen no bigger than yez."

And Margaret settled herself on her chair with all the importance of an old story-teller.

"Ye mast know that Larry was as fine an' strappin' a lad as ever stepped over the daisies. It was he that could handle a flail or a plough, or dig the praties, or stack the hay in the haggard. And when he went to chapel on a Sunday in his best frieze coat, with the ends of his bright handkercher flying loose, an' his caubeen cocked rakishly on one side, sure an' weren't all the girls in Enniskerry in love with his blue eyes an' yellow hair, an' weren't half of them dying to have him for a bachelor?"

I presume we listeners looked mystified with the word "bachelor" so applied, for Margaret explained, "That's what you call a sweetheart, miss."

"But Larry, though not consaited, laughed with one girl, an' joked with another; an' whenever he went to Dublin, or Phoenix Park, or the Strawberry-beds, could take the flure with the best, an' have the purtiest girl for a partner—an' troth it's he that could dance a jig—but he never thought of takin' a partner for life, or of offerin' himself as a bachelor, till he met with Kitty Quin, an' her black eyes made a hole in his heart at wanst. He was nigh six-an'-twenty when he met her. It was at a pattern at the Seven Churches of Glendalough, an' sorra a bit could he mind his prayers for looking at her as she towld her beads so piously, without seemin' to think of the bachelors or her own pretty face at all.

"Well, I heard grandfather say that, though he was as bowld and impident in his way with the lasses as any lad in Enniskerry, his knees fairly knocked together, an' his heart went all in a flutter before he could bless himself, when Michael Quin tuk her by the hand, an' comin' towards him, said, 'Larry, here's our Kitty come back from Aunt Riley's;' an' when Larry was too dazed to speak, went on, 'Have yez got a dhrop in yer eye, man, that yez cannot see the colleen, or has Dublin made her so strange ye don't know her agin?'

"What Larry said he niver remembered, but he felt as if he hadn't a bit of heart left, and his words tumbled over each other like stones rolled downhill. He knew he had blundered out somethin', for Kitty's cheeks went red as the roses on her print gown. She put out her soft little hand with a smile that showed two rows of teeth as white an' fresh as hailstones; an' she said modestly as a nun, 'I'm glad to see any of my owld friends again, Misther M'Cann.'

"He had sinse enough left to take howld of the hand she offered; an' sure he must have given to it a hearty grip, for the roses grew on her forehead to match her cheeks, an' she drew it back hastily.

"Larry, however, kept close to the brother an' sister; and when the prayers were over, an' the people began to enjoy themselves, an' the dudeens an' the whisky went round to warm the hearts an' the toes, then Larry plucked up his courage an' asked Kitty to tak' the flure with him.

"Now Kitty was either shy, or her Dublin manners made her too proud to dance at a pattern, so she made excuses. Michael, who had kissed the whisky-jar very lovingly, would not have his friend said 'no' to; and so, to *keep Mike in a good humour*, she consinted to dance a jig with Larry.

"Sure, an' it was then he must have won her heart; for they went back to Enniskerry together, an' she let Larry put his arm round her waist, jist to *hould her on the car*, bekase of the bad roads, an' stale a kiss when he lifted her down at Farmer Quin's garden gate. An' from that out Larry followed Kitty like her shadder.

"But Peter Quin farmed more than two hundred acres, an' Larry's father only held a hundred an' twenty, an' that's a good differ, Master Fred. Then Mike an' Kitty wor all the childer Peter had, whilst Larry's brothers—God be praised!—were as thick on the flure as rabbits in a run: wheriver ye turned yez' might tumble over a pig or a gossoon.

"Troth, an' it wasn't long afore the neighbours began to look on Larry as Kitty's bachelor, an' one decaitful ould fellow, who had himself an eye to Kitty's bit of money, gave Peter a hint that Larry was coortin' the lass for the love of her fortin'; tho' sorra a bit had Larry M'Cann so dirty a thought as that same.

"Peter had a temper that was always on the simmer, an' it biled over at wanst. By some ill luck Larry showed his face at the Quins' door before it had time to cool, so Peter thrated him to a thrifle of his tongue, the mane blackguard.

"'Div ye think Kitty, the illigant darlint, is for such a poor spalpeen as yez?' he shouted. 'She that's been eddicated in Dublin, an' hez booklarnin', let alone manners, an' a fortin' to the fore! But it's the fortin', I'm thinkin', yez looking for wid one eye, an' the girl wid the other, Misther Lawrence M'Cann,' he said, with a sneer an' a turn up of his ugly nose.

"'It's well for yez, Mr. Pether Quin, that yez Kitty's father, or, by jabers, an' it's showin' ye the taste of this blackthorn I'd be,' said Larry on the instant, kaping it down with an effort. 'Ye may kape your dirty money, bad cess to them as put the black thought of me into yer heart, if ye'll only put Kitty's sweet little hand into mine wid a blessin'.'

"You may be sure, miss, as they did not whisper; an' hearin' a row, Mike ran from the barn into the slip of garden fornent the house to join in the fun. He was jist in time to hear his father repate his insult, an' accuse Larry of wanting Kitty's hundred pounds; an' then Mike fired up, an' took his friend's part like a Trojan."

"And what's a Trojan, Margaret?" asked Fred demurely, with another sly blink at me.

"Whisht, Masther Fred, an' don't be afther interruptin', or we'll never get to the Good People at all," said Margaret, ignoring the question.

Thus admonished, Master Fred allowed the story to proceed.

"But Mike could not bring his father to reason, even though he offered him a dhraw of his pipe. More by token, he himself was unwillin' to let his sister marry a man who had neither house nor furniture of his own.

"'It's not for the likes of her to lay her head undher a father-in-law's roof, an' have her childer runnin' over a flure that is not her own,' said Mike. 'I'd say nothin' agin the match, Larry, if ye had but a farm or a house of yer own, or even the bits of things to make a house dacent for the lass.'

"Larry went away with a very sore heart, miss, you may be sure, for he'd set his very sowl upon Kitty Quin.

"An' sure an' that was the black morning for Larry! Turnin' a corner of the quickset hedge on his way home, who should he come across but Kitty with a basket of ripe strawberries on her arm, an' she lookin' more temptin' than the fruit.

"Kitty had a tender drop in her heart, and seeing that he was sad, she set herself to discover what it was about; and didn't she regret her curiosity in another minit?—for he poured out all his love and his sorrow like a great gushin' stream, and held her hand as if he was drownin', an' only that could keep him from sinking quite.

245

"Taken by surprise, Kitty dropped her basket, an' would have fainted outright, had not Larry put out his arm an' caught her, and that brought her to her siven senses.

"Poor Larry *mistook* her faintness for a sign of her affection, an' in his joy kissed her sweet lips over an' over again. But Kitty soon told him the differ.

"She said she had only fainted from the heat. She was sorry he had mistaken her friendship for a warmer feeling; but though she was ashamed her father should have suspected him of a mercenary motive, she could not encourage his hopes. She should niver marry without her father's consint; an' besides, her bringin' up had made her unfit for a farmer's wife, an' so she had determined—yes, determined was the word—niver to marry any man who had not a good trade in his hands that would be a livin' either in country or town.

"Every word that Kitty said fell like ice on Larry's hot heart, and he reeled home as if he had had lashins of whisky; and when he got there, he took the whisky to drown his sorrow till he wor drunk in arnest.

"There was nobody to tell him of the battle in Kitty's breast between love and pride, nor how she had crept into the house by the back way, and shut herself up, all alone in her room, to shed tears like a February cloud over the very mischief she had done, and the pain in her own breast.

"Sure, all the fun and the frolic in Larry's nature were murthered that black mornin'. He went about the farm without a smile on his lip or a sunbeam in his eye, an' his mother would have it the boy was bewitched.

"Even Father Maguire noticed his altered looks, and his careless dress when he went to mass on the Sundays, and the good priest did his best to set matters straight, but all to no use, miss.

"Peter Quin was sorry when his temper was off, but—small blame to him!—he still thought she might do better than go to the M'Canns' to be undher a mother-in-law, and work like a slave for all Larry's younger brothers.

"As for Kitty, before the feel of Larry's kiss had gone from her lips, the colleen was angry that he had taken her at her word; but she fed her courage with pride, and put a calm face on, though her heart was all in a tempest of throuble. An' sure, miss, there's many and many a girl does that, although you are too young to know it, and I hope never will."

Here Margaret looked at me soberly, as if giving a leaf out of the book of her own experience.

"One fine June morning, when the roses were in full dhress, an' the air had the smell of flowers an' new-mown hay, Larry went to St. Patrick's Market to sell a cow that had gone dhry.

"Three weeks before, and that same Larry would have sung or whistled every foot of the road, barrin' he met a traveller and stopped to give him the time o' day, or exchange a joke. But now he kept his hands in his pockets, his chin hung on his chest, an' his mouth was as close as a miser's purse. He had a sup of whisky before he left the house, to keep his heart up, but for all that he looked as melancholy as the cow he wor drivin'.

"He had barely got a couple of miles beyant Peter Quin's farm, which lay in his way to Dublin, when he heard a thin weak voice callin' to him, like the wind through a keyhole.

"'The top o' the morning to you, Larry!'

"'The same to you, misther,' answered Larry, slowly lifting his eyes, an' then rubbin' them to clear the cobwebs away; for straight across the road was a gate where niver a gate had been before, an' sittin' cross-legged on the topmost bar was the queerest old man Larry had ever seen.

"He was no bigger than a two-year child, but his face was as wizen an' wrinkled as if he was four hundred. He was dressed in an old-fashioned coat an' breeches as green as the grass, had shining buckles in his shoes, and on his head a bright red cap. By all them tokens Larry knew that the little old man was a leprechaun, an' his mouth began to wather for some of the goold he knew the old gintleman must have hid in the ground somewhere about, an' his heart began to thump. But Larry was not the boy to be afraid, so he put a bould face on when the leprechaun, with his head cocked on one side and a knowing twinkle in his eye, said to him—

"'That's a fine baste yez drivin', Larry.'

"'Troth, yer honour, an' ye may say that same,' replied Larry, doffin' his caubeen an' scrapin' his foot, for he thought it best to be civil.

"'An' so you are dhrivin' the cow to market bekase she's lost her milk; an' ye mane to ax sivin pound tin for her!' said the leprechaun with a comical chuckle.

"'Bedad, an' I am!' exclaimed Larry, opening his eyes, and slapping his thigh in amazement, 'an' sure it's the knowin' old gintleman yer honour is!'

"'Thrue for you,' said the leprechaun; 'an' may be I know, besides,

247

that Larry M'Cann's goin' to the bad for love of the purtiest girl in Wicklow! But pluck up a speerit, Larry; don't be cast down. It's I that owe Pether Quin a grudge this many a long day, for his maneness in chatin' the fairies of their due. Niver a fairies' dhrop (milk left as a propitiatory offering to the Good People) is to be found in Pether's cow-house or dairy; and niver a turf or a pratie, or a cast-off coat has he for a poor shivering beggar or omadhaun (idiot), bad cess to him! An' so, Larry, I mane to befriend yez, for it's yez that have the warm heart and the open hand, an' we'll back thim against the cowld heart and the tight fist any day!' an' the leprechaun plucked off his red cap and swung it over his head, as if in high glee.

"Larry, with another scrape of his foot, thanked the green-coated old gentleman, an' asked him if he meant to show him where to find a pot of goold.

"'Ay, an' that I do; but, Larry,' an' here he looked slyer than ever, 'the fortin's in your own right hand, man, an' it's I that mane to tache ye to find it there.'

"Larry opened his great brown hand, an' turned it over, an' looked in the broad palm.

"'Divil a bit I see of a fortin' there,' says he.

"'Whist!' says the leprechaun. 'Go on wid your baste, an' when ye meet a man wid his breeches knees untied, an' his coat tails down to his heels, an' a wisp ov straw in his shoes to kape his toes warm where they peep out ov his stockins, an' a caubeen widout a brim, then ye'll know the man that'll bid for yer cow, an' give ye nine goolden guineas for her, not dirty notes.'

"'Nine guineas! bedad, an' that's more than—' Larry stopped short.

"The leprechaun was gone, an' the gate gone, an' the poor cow walked on as if she had never been stayed."

"Perhaps she never had," suggested Fred.

"Now, Masther Fred," said Margaret, "if ye interrupt me agin wid yer roguish doubts, I shall stop, an' ye'll never hear how it all ended."

"Go on, Margaret," urged I, and Margaret obeyed.

CHAPTER 2

"Larry's surprise an' the leprechaun's promises drove the thoughts of Kitty out of his head, an' he stepped toward Dublin with something of his ould lightsomeness; when just as he crossed the canal bridge he saw Kitty Quin standin' on her Aunt Riley's doorstep in Clanbrassil-street, dressed as illigant as a lady, an' lookin' as grand an' as proud as a queen.

"Well, Kitty's face went crimson, an' Larry's heart gave a great leap; but she just made him a stiff kind of curtsey, an' the door bein' opened, went in without a word.

"'Thim's Dublin manners, I suppose,' thought Larry, as he went on, with his heart aching worse than ever; while Kitty watchin' him from behind the window-blind as far as she could see, felt the tears rowl over her burnin' cheeks, an' then wiped them off angrily, as if ashamed of her natural feelin's, an' blamed herself for being silly.

"Larry hardly knew how he got to the market, but sure enough there he met that same identical man the leprechaun had towld him of. An' more by token, he made Larry a bid for the cow. He bid eight pound ten, but Larry heartened beforehand, stuck out for nine guineas; and sure he took Larry into a public-house that stood convanient, and took out of his breeches-pocket an owld rag tied round wid string to sarve as a purse, and there an' thin counted down the nine goolden guineas. Then he asked Larry to have a dhrop an' a dhraw' to seal the bargain.

"Larry's customer called for the whisky, an' offered Larry his own pipe. So the boy had both the dhrop an' the dhraw, an' then they had another dhrop and a dhraw; an' Larry remembered no more till he found himself lyin' on the grass, wid the stars shinin' out in honour of Midsummer-eve, an' a rushin' in his ears as of a great sea.

"Then he heard a rustle as of leaves, an' a mighty whisperin', an' lifted himself on his elbow to look about him, an' there he saw hundreds of little people no more than a span high, dressed in all sorts of queer outlandish fashions. But all the little men had coats of green velvet, and leaves of green shamrock in their hats; whilst the ladies had scarves of green gauze as fine as cobwebs; an' shamrock was wreathed round their hair, which shone like goold in the moonlight.

"They were all in commotion, running hither an' thither, howlding long discoorses, an' appeared to be in some sort of throuble or difficulty.

"Presently he saw in their midst the loveliest little creature the light of his eyes ever flashed on. She was sittin' in a silver-lily of a car, an' drawn by seven-and-twenty grasshoppers, three abreast. She had a wand in her hand, on which a crystal dewdrop twinkled like a star, an' Larry knew at wanst they were all fairies, an' she was their queen.

"Then, miss, as they drew nigher to him, Larry heard that one of the old fairies lay dead, an' that they wanted a coffin for the berryin'.

But sorra a coffin could they get, for fairy coffins must be made by mortals, or the dead fairies never lie at rest. An' that was what the council an' the confusion wor about.

"Soon Larry heard the fairy queen say in a voice for all the world like the chirp of a cricket, 'But who shall make the elf's coffin?'

"All of sudden at least fifty of the Good People laid howld of him an' cried out like so many bees humming, 'Here's Larry M'Cann, here's Larry M'Cann! it's he will make the coffin.'

"'But he never handled a saw or a plane in his life; he cannot make a pig-trough, an' how will he finish a coffin fit for an elf?' said one of the Good People.

"'Sure, thin, an' it's we that must tache him,' answered another.

"With that the fairy queen touched him on the forehead, as lightly as if a leaf had dhropped there, with her shining wand, an' it flashed before his eyes till they seemed to strike fire; an' before he could cry out, or ask a saint to purtect him, he felt himself goin' down, down, down into the very earth itself, an' it's lost he thought he was for evermore.

"Troth, an' Dublin Castle's but a mud cabin in comparishun with the palace Larry was in when he came to his sinses. The walls were brighter than sunshine or rainbows, an' goold, an' silver, an' prechus jewels were plentiful as praties. There was gardens with trees an' flowers, the likes of which were never in all Ireland, an' the birds were all crimson, an' green, an' laylock, an' sang sweeter than thrush or nightingale. He seemed to see all this at once, an' many a curious thing beside which I disremember, and amongst it all the Good People were as busy as bees in a hive.

"Almost the first thing he saw was the dead fairy lying on a bed of Indian moss, under a delicate silken quilt, with a tiny wreath of lilies-of-the-valley on his head, forget-me-nots all about him. There was a fine bird-of-paradise singin' over him so soft an' sweet, it charmed the very sowl of Larry. There were fairies watchin' the corpse, but sorra wan of them was sobbin' or cryin', an' sure that same bothered him; for ye must know, miss, when a pious body dies in owld Ireland the keening women come an' lament over the corpse, with wailin' and cryin.'

"It was not long he was left to stare about him. One of the Good People put an inch-rule into his hand, an' set him to measure the corpse, an' sure that same came as natural to him as hoeing the cabbages. Then he was taken to a fine fairy workshop, where everything was as nate an' orderly as if it had just been claned. There was piles of wood of all sorts, an' one owld brownie towld Larry their names; and there was lots of bright tools, an' another wee owld fellow towld him their names; an' then two or three showed him how to use them. Then they gave him the wood an' the tools, an' he made an illigant little coffin as aisily as if he had been at the thrade all his life.

"The dead corpse was lifted in by the moorners as never moorned, an' Larry fastened, down the lid as cliverly as any undhertaker in Leinster.

"As the funeral percession, wid the coffin in the midst, moved away to the fairies' cimetry, the owld brownie who first took notice of Larry said, 'Very nately put togither, Larry M'Cann; sure an' ye're a credit to your taichers. Take your wages, man, an' go.' Larry put out his hand an' stooped for the glitterin' purse that wor held out to him, an'—whist!

"He was lyin' on his back, with his curly head on a hard stone, undher a big tree, wid the mornin' sun shinin' full in his face, Powerscourt Falls tumbling in foam down the great high rocks, that frowned above him, leapin' over big boulders, an' rushin' away wid a roar undher a little wooden bridge just beyant.

"Larry rubbed his eyes, sat up, an' rubbed them again, an' sure the more he looked about him the more he was bothered.

"'Begorra, an' this is a quare thrick to be sarvin' a man,' says he, as he scrambled to his feet, wid his bones as stiff an' sore as if he had been beaten with a shillaly. 'Is it meself I am, or somebody else? an' whare have I bin? an' by the powers, how did I come here at all, at all? Is it dhrunk, or dhraming, or aslape I am this blessed minnit? Be jabers, the Good People—'

"Larry stopped, an' crossed himself, an' bethought him of his wages, an' all that was in his grip was dead leaves!

"But he gave a great jump, and cried out, 'Plane laves, bedad; an' it wur fairy goold, an' that iver turns to laves! An' it's a plane tree I'm lyin' undher! Musha, but that's a rare joke!'

"In another minute his heart sank, an' he thrimbled with fear lest he had been paid for the cow in fairy goold too, an' should find only yellow leaves in his pocket. But, faith, the nine bright goolden guineas—not dirty one-pound notes—were solid and safe.

"The sun was dancin' brightly on the waters as Larry hastened along the narrow footpath by the stream, an' turnin' sharp off before he reached the foaming waters of the Dargle, mounted the crooked

251

an' dangerous way up the steep banks to the high road, wondering why the Good People couldn't have laid him down under a roadside hedge, or in a green field, instead of carrying him out of the way intirely to Powerscourt Falls. It was all a mystery an' a dhrame to him, an' as he went along he kept repeating, 'A fortin' in my hands, the owld leprechaun said he'd be afther showin' me. Sure, an' mightn't it be somethin' moore thin the *plane laves* he meant? Ah, Kitty, my darlint, if I'm sivin days owlder since ye saw me last, I've sarved an apprenticeship that's made me more than sivin years wiser.'

"From the day he saw Kitty at the pattern, Larry M'Cann had taken to savin' his money. It was kept in a crock hid under the thatch of the barn, an' there he went quietly before he put a foot on the kitchen floor. Takin' seven one-pound notes an' ten shillins out, he put the nine guineas in, an' took to his father the price he had fixed on the cow.

"'Where have ye been, ye vagabone, all this blessed night?' cried old M'Cann, as the broth of a boy put his bright curly head in at the door.

"'All night, father, all night, did ye say?' cried Larry, bewildered; for ye see. Master Fred, he thought he had been a week with the Good People.

"'Yis! all night; for isn't the sun shinin', an' this the blessed Midsummer-day, ye spalpeen? Is it dhrunk ye are before the dew is off the daisies? Ah, Larry, Larry, me lad, it's the wrong way yez goin' ever since Kitty Quin showed ye the cowld shouldher; bad cess to the whole lot of them! But where's the price of the baste? If ye were dhrunk, sure ye'd sinse left to take care of that.'

"Aye, an' sure when he found he had not been more than a night with the fairies, he had sense enough left to keep his own saicret. His mother said a mighty change had come over Larry, but sorra a guess had she where it came from.

"He put the potheen aside when it came his way, an' took to the farm so kindly, he went about his work whistling, and did as much in one day as he had ever done in two. Then he went an arrand to Dublin with the car, an' brought back a lot of carpenter's tools, an' some dale boards. He put them in an old shed that was tumblin' down, unknownst to anyone but his brother Pat. Then he put a door on the pigsty to kape the pigs out of the house, an' persuaded his father to have the holes in the mud-floor of the kitchen filled up; an' conthrived somehow to make the farm dacent and comfortable, with odd bits of improvement here an' there.

"Amongst it all, he an' Pat got the crooked walls of the shed to stand upright, an' mended the thatch, an' put the door again on its two hinges, an' put a lock on the door, widout a word to father or mother. An' then, sure, he contrived to put up some sort of a carpenter's bench, after the patthern in the fairies' workshop. More wood was got, an' troth, one mornin', to her surprise, Mrs. M'Cann found a new dale table, an' a dresser, an' an aisy-chair in her kitchen, the like of which wasn't in all Enniskerry.

"'Sure an' its illigant, it's fairy work!' said all the neighbours.

"'Thrue for you; it is the fairies' work,' said Larry, with a sly wink at Pat; an' Pat, knowin' what he had seen, an' nothing of the fairies, burst into a loud laugh, an' let out that Larry was the workman.

"No neighbour was more astonished than Larry's own father an' mother. They knew nothing of Larry's friend the leprechaun, nor his fairy taichers; they said the blessed St. Joseph must have put the knowledge in his head, an' called the boy a rale born genius.

"Other farmers' wives envied Mrs. M'Cann her fine dresser, on which a set of new wooden platters an' bickers were ranged, with here and there a bright-coloured crock for show; an' they came beggin' of Larry to make the copy of it for thim. So, sure, an' it came about that soon Larry had so much of his new work, be was forced to tache two of his brothers the trade, an' build a proper workshop; and Farmer M'Cann had to set the gossoons to work on the farm instead of lounging about an' propping up door-posts all the day.

"But niver a bit did Larry go near Kitty all this time, though many a longin' look did he cast that way when he passed Peter Quin's gate. If they met at mass, he just gave her the time o' day, as any other friend might do; but though his very heart was bursting with love, he kept it, like his other saicrets, to himself.

"As for Kitty, there were plenty of bachelors after her, either for herself or her fortin'; but she never got the feel of Larry's kisses off her lips, an' cared more for a glance of his blue eye than for all the bachelors in Wicklow.

"She knew she had sent him away with her proud words, but she would have given all her goold for a whisper of love from him now he had taken her at her word, and seemed to forget her intirely. She just went paler an' thinner, an' when the next Midsummer roses were red on the bushes, they were only white ones on Kitty's cheeks.

"Mike and Larry had been fast friends all the time, an' many a job of work Larry did for him on his own account, but sorra a nail would he drive for Peter Quin. It was Mike who let Larry into the saicret that owld Corcoran the agent was after Kitty, an' that she sent him about his business with a sharp word agen his desait in slandering a better man—maning Larry.

"A smart young shopkaiper from Dublin had made her an offer besides, an' even set Molly Mulroony the Blackfoot to thry an' persuade her."

"What's a Blackfoot, Margaret?" we asked, in a breath.

"Sure, an' a Blackfoot's a matchmaker, a woman as goes between shy lovers and helps the coortin'.

"Well, then, as Larry never went to the whisky shop, nor to Peter Quin's, Mike found his way to the busy carpenter's shop. He used to ask a power of questions about the work in hand; for I must tell ye, Larry had been so well taught by the Good People, he could turn his hand to cabinet-work as well as rough carpentry.

"About this time, Mike saw Larry and Pat workin' early an' late over furniture not meant for the farmers or gentry about; an', for a wondher, Larry never said a word who they were working for. But Pat, the sly rogue, let out as a great saicret that it was for Larry's own house, agin his weddin'.

"'Whare is the house?' says Mike.

"'At Bray,' says Pat.

"'An' who's the sweetheart?' says Mike again.

"'Arrah, now, an' that's jist what meself don't know,' says Pat, in reply.

"Mike went with his news straight to Kitty, who, with bare arms an' tucked-up gown, was makin' butter in the dairy, though she did despise a farmer's life.

"Down went butter an' butter-mould, an' Kitty into the bargain, an' Mike had much ado to bring her out of her faint.

"Kitty,' says Mike, when they were all by themselves, "sure an' ye didn't care for Larry, did ye? I thought ye didn't, as ye trated him wid scorn and contimpt, and Larry tuk to the dhrink with the heartbreak.'

"'Oh, don't, Mike dear, don't! Throth, an' it *was* my own pride an' consait that druv Larry away, an' it's I that have had the heartbreak ever since.'

"'Be me sowl, an' it must be a new sweetheart, an' a cliver lass, that set him agin drink an' made him turn carpenter! Och, Kitty, I'd sooner ye'd had Larry M'Cann than the biggest lord in the land;' an' Mike took out his pipe—his unfailing consoler—for a dhraw an' a think; an' Kitty, having no such consolation, he left her sobbin'.

"The next day was Sunday, but Kitty was not at mass. Mike, howiver, was there, an' Peter, an' Larry, as fine as a Dublin tailor could make him.

"'How's Miss Quin?' asked Larry purlitely of Mike, as they walked home together.

"'Throth, an' she might be better,' answered Mike; an', says he, quite abrupt, 'Whin's this weddin' of yours to come off, Larry?'

"'It's not settled,' says he; 'I've not got the lady's consint yet.'

"'Not settled, an' her a lady, an' your house taken, an' your furniture made! Bedad, this passes me intirely!' An' Mike looked hard at Larry, an' Larry looked at Mike, and whatever they saw they shook hands, an' Mike flung up his shillaly an' caught it again, and danced every foot of the way to their own gate.

"'Mebbe ye wouldn't mind comin' in for a bit, as Pether's stayed behint for confession,' says Mike, with a grin. An' in they went together.

"Dinner wor bein' laid in the kitchen, but Kitty was in the parlour.

"'As ye're not very well, Kitty, I thought I'd betther bring a docthor to see yez,' says Mike, openin' the door, with a quare twinkle ov his eyes.

"'A doctor!' says Kitty, starting to her feet, growing crimson an' then white as Larry stepped into the room, an' Mike discraitly shut the door upon them, an' being weak she might have fainted again, but Larry caught her in his arms—an' she got better.

"Dinner waited for Peter, and Peter waited for Kitty; but Mike towld him that Kitty was ill an' the doctor was wid her, an' they couldn't be disturbed. But Peter wanted his dinner, an' grew impatient; an' then Mike towld him that as he had been to confession, Kitty was at confession too, an' that Larry M'Cann was her confessor.

"Sure, Peter was thunderstruck; but he had sinse to see that Larry M'Cann, the thrivin' young carpenter, was another sort of a man from the Larry M'Cann who worked on his father's farm with scarce a thought of payment; an' Mike soon got his father to give his consint with a blessin'.

"The praist followed the doctor in less than a month, but the praist this time was Father Maguire.

"The day before the weddin', Larry took Kitty down to Powerscourt Falls, an' there sittin' with his arm round her slender waist, on the stone under the plane tree where his head had lain, he towld her all about the leprechaun, an' his own apprenticeship to the fairies.

"An' that was how the M'Canns became carpenters."

Fred and I tried to convince Margaret that the leprechaun was the result of her grandfather's morning dram, and that under the influence of further potations he had strayed in safety from the road down the precipitous path to the Dargle, and so on to the Falls; and there sleeping, had dreamt of the fairy funeral.

But Margaret was not convinced; and a few years later the faithful creature died, as firm a believer in fairies as when she told us the story of Larry's apprenticeship, and the fortune he found *in his own right hand*.

The Fate of the Fosbrookes

Though possessed of no actual patent of nobility, the Fosbrookes of Fosbrooke Manor held their heads as high, and were as proud of their long pedigree, as any baronet in the county. And with good cause; so many intermarriages with right noble dames were emblazoned on that roll, so broad were the acres over which the squire held manorial and territorial sway, so fine a specimen of Tudor architecture was his grand old mansion, that the lord of the manor it represented might well be pardoned if he boasted the blue blood which had come to him through successive maternal veins, and forgot that he held no other lordship.

The Fosbrookes of Fosbrooke, however, were not given to boasting. They had been squires of the land for so many generations that their position was assured, and needed no trumpet-tongue to proclaim it. I am myself a Fosbrooke, and perhaps inherit the old leaven, if I inherit nothing more.

For it happens, I am but the descendant of a degenerate and disowned Fosbrooke, who struck a deadly blow at the family pride, and my name—neither Rupert nor Reginald, but blunt, plain John, Barrister-at-Law—may be found on the lintels of a door in the Inner Temple; and three months ago Fosbrooke Manor was known to me only through tradition.

My grandfather's grandfather, so I have been told, was the squire's second son, and destined for the army in accordance with established precedent. But he, Rupert, had no mind to gird a warrior's sword upon his thigh. He had watched the family portraits grow warm and life-like under the hand of Gainsborough; had gone with the artist into the woods and terraced gardens, in quest of fitting backgrounds; and, lingering by his side, the longing grew within himself to be a painter, and reproduce on the lifeless canvas the loveliness of life and nature. Unknown to squire or dame, their son sketched by Gainsborough's side; and he, proud of his art, fostered the youth's enthusiasm, all unwitting of mischief.

Thus it chanced that when the rising painter returned to the metropolis, after a prolonged stay in the ancient Manor House, he left behind a pupil longing to emulate his master, as well as a group of pictures in the oaken gallery.

Then it was discovered that Rupert dabbled in pigments; but so long as he only handled his brush for amusement, he might copy the old pictures on the walls, group together cottage children, or case a groom in armour from the staircase, and transfer to the panels of his chamber his crude imaginings of art, with no further token of disapprobation than the contemptuous laughter of his father and brother, who regarded a fox's brush as a trophy, but a painter's as the mere tool of a craftsman. Yet the very taunts and sarcasms which followed the young laggard in the hunting-field, the unsportsmanlike shot in woods or stubble, drove him for refuge to the solitude of his own chamber, and for solace to the art condemned by those around him.

But not until Rupert declined to be a soldier did opposition culminate, and wrath grow fierce. In vain did the good mother plead with son and sire; in vain did Reginald urge his brother to renounce his degrading pursuit as a slur on their ancient lineage and escutcheon, holding up the army as the only outlet for a Fosbrooke.

Rupert was as persistent as his elder brother, as resolute as his father was vehement; all argumentation ending with the same resolve, "I will *not* lay down my paint brush for a sword."

"Then, by heaven I'll make a bonfire of your painting rattletraps! No son of mine shall spend his days in daubing canvas to disgrace us all!" cried the old squire in his wrath.

Presently there was a great blaze in the courtyard, that seemed to flame again in the dark eyes of Rupert, who stood in the doorway with knitted brows and folded arms, a fire kindling in his heart as all his treasures went to feed the holocaust.

His lip curled. "Ay, burn them, an' you will; I shall be a painter notwithstanding."

"You paint no more in Fosbrooke Manor, Master Rupert," replied his father, with decision. "There is your commission, take it or leave it. But if you leave it you quit Fosbrooke at once and for ever. See, then, if brush or sword be best to fight your way with."

"You may cast the commission among the burning rattletraps," retorted the young man proudly. "I'll none of it. You have kindled a fire to destroy, and it will die in ashes; but the fire of genius is unquenchable, and that creates."

"No weeping, madam," shouted the squire, as Dame Fosbrooke's kerchief went to her tearful eyes. "Let him carry his genius elsewhere. He paints no more under this roof. And look you, sir," he called out to Rupert, who was following his distressed mother, "if ever you put a living foot on this threshold whilst I'm above ground, I'll have you pitched out neck and crop, you ungrateful whelp!"

Reginald stood apart, but made no sign of interposition. Rupert turned. "At your bidding, sir, I go. Fosbrooke Manor in now no place for me. But, living or dead, I shall come back to my home some day, and none shall say me nay when next I paint beneath its roof."

He sought his sorrowing mother, and clung to her embrace, but, proud and persistent as his kin, tore himself away. In half an hour he was on the road to London, with nought but what his steed could carry, and his mother's tearful blessing.

Squire Fosbrooke closed the chamber of his degenerate son, and the avenues of his heart. He made a will in which he utterly renounced him, and thenceforth woe betide the luckless wight who dared to speak of Rupert in his hearing.

He had been his favourite child, the son of his age—a posse of girls had come between Reginald and him—and the wrench made in a moment of anger set his heart-strings quivering for ever. But a Fosbrooke of Fosbrooke was never known to yield where the family honour was concerned, and silence as of the grave closed over Rupert's name within the shadow of the manor. If ever a whisper reached the mother's ear that he had found a welcome in Gainsborough's studio, the whisper never had an echo from her lips. The squire, once bluff and hearty, grew stern—the blow he had dealt at his boy had fallen on himself.

Nothing was heard of Rupert for many years. His sisters married and went their several ways to distant homes. Reginald alone was left. Then he took to himself a wife, and grandchildren ran in and out of the tapestried rooms with a pleasant patter on the oaken floors, and climbed the old squire's knee, and won smiles from the sad-eyed grandmother, who sighed so heavily as she watched their childish gambols.

The seasons came and went. It was the tenth anniversary of the day on which a prejudiced father drove forth his son (as stubborn as himself) to shape a future in an untried world. Ten years since Rupert, with the double fire of genius and obstinacy in his eye, rode away down the long beech avenue without one backward glance at battlements or mullioned window to stir the deeper emotions of his soul and change his purpose.

Squire Fosbrooke and his heir had been out with the hounds since dawn. The London carrier's waggon creaked slowly along a bye-lane to the back of the great house, and there surrendered a square, unwieldy, flat packing-case, over which conjecture wasted itself, until the white-haired dame, yielding less to the curiosity of her grandchildren, and their mother. Lady Annabel, than to some unconquerable impulse within herself, gave orders for the forcing of the lid. Whatever lay within was covered by A thick cloth, on which was inscribed in bold characters:

"Rupert Fosbrooke's Addition to the Family Portraits."

The elder lady blanched to her very lips. With gesture rather than word she ordered the removal of the cover the while the children crowded round in wonderment, and Lady Annabel drew herself up disdainfully.

There, limned by no tyro, the discarded son of the house looked out from the canvas, older, manlier, nobler than of old, palette and brushes in hand, a fine boy's head before him on an easel; and by his side, with fingers lightly resting on his shoulder, A woman lovely as a painter's dream. No need the written legend to declare that Eupert's wife and son were also there portrayed, or that his had been the artist hand.

"Rupert Fosbrooke, Maud his wife, and Rupert his son," read Reginald's eldest boy. "Why, grandmother, who are they?"

"Your uncle, and your aunt and cousin, child," sobbed the bereaved old lady in broken accents, whilst the servants drew respectfully apart and whispered beneath their breath. Lady Annabel plucked her children away, saying:

"Uncle and aunt, forsooth! They are neither kith nor kin of mine, boy. No common painter's doll-faced wife claims affinity with me!"

"Lady Annabel," said the elder, gathering up her form, "Rupert Fosbrooke is my dear son. I never disowned him. I will not disown the fair mate he has chosen. He would never stoop to one unworthy."

"Stoop! He had sunk to the portrait-painter's level ere he wedded his master's niece. I heard so much, madam, when I was last in town." So saying, Lady Annabel swept away to give her little ones a lesson in pride of birth, and obliterate, if possible, the pictured relatives from remembrance.

Lady Annabel was no favourite with the old servants, and dark-eyed Rupert had been.

Reverently they obeyed Dame Fosbrooke's behest, and carrying the picture into the long dining-room, set it upright against the tap-estried wall by the side of the carved buffet.

As the squire entered with a troop of hungry hunting friends, the picture caught his sight. For a few moments he stood gazing upon it with changing colour and breath that came and went; then, raising the whip he held, he struck at the figures fiercely, whilst he demanded hoarsely who had dared to brave him thus; and bade the servants haul it forth and burn it.

There was a bonfire blazing in the yard whilst the squire and his friends supped, and Lady Annabel looked on with stern satisfaction from an upper window. But the packing-case alone was burned. The picture itself had been quietly smuggled into the closed chamber of the artist, and the good dame's secret was well kept; not for fee or re-ward, but for love of Barbara Fosbrooke and her youngest born.

Four years Dame Barbara kept that secret, along with others, in her heart; and then, lying on her deathbed, she broke the long silence and prayed that Rupert might be summoned to close her dying eyes.

It may be that the squire was likewise wearying for a sight of his discarded son, and only lacked a pretext for his recall, for he was no longer obdurate. No doubt in his hidden soul he had long repented his hasty orders anent the picture, and blamed the too obedient ex-ecutants of his will. With barely a show of hesitation he consented, but Reginald and Lady Annabel, too crafty to demur, too proud to own a painter for a brother, threw obstacles in the way. "There was no clue to the vagabond's whereabouts."

From a locket worn concealed the feeble mother produced a tiny slip of paper. It held Rupert Fosbrooke's name and address. Here was an unlooked-for revelation. Annabel and Reginald exchanged glances.

"Ah! this implies correspondence. I presume, sir, you had no knowledge of any communication with my brother."

Once this would have been a spark on tow. It passed unheeded. All the squire seemed to hear was his wife's appeal for haste; which his own voice seconded on her account, he said. Himself wrote a hurried letter of recall. At once Reginald became officiously active. He despatched a trusty messenger with the missive; so trusty, that he failed to return before the dame's ears were closed to any message he might bring.

Days went by. The white-haired squire paced the corridors as anxiously expectant as the sick lady in the state bed. But the shifty or irritable answers of Reginald to her enquiries had aroused suspicion of treachery.

As the end drew nigh, she insisted on being carried to Rupert's chamber as the only chance of seeing the face of her lost son.

They thought her mind was wandering. Her meaning was clear enough to them all when her chair was placed in front of Rupert's picture, which yet bore the mark of the squire's whip across its surface.

Not more eagerly did Barbara Fosbrooke's filming eyes trace the well-remembered lineaments of her banished son than did those of the old squire, in whom affection had seemed so long dead; whilst Reginald and Annabel looked lost in amazement.

Life's fire relit in Barbara's wan features as she gazed: strength came to her anew. She kissed the squire's brown hand as the other dashed from his eyes the fast-gathering tears; and then marking the scowl on Reginald's swart face as he slunk behind her chair, she lifted up her withered right hand, and extending it towards the picture, said impressively, in a voice which seemed to have gathered preternatural strength for the effort: "Rupert, my son, I call and thou dost not answer; I have longed for thee and thou dost not come. But thou shalt come, and thou and thine be masters of Fosbrooke when treachery has done its worst. I cannot die in my bed for lack of thy presence. But if there be treachery, let those who kept thee back answer it, for never shall a Fosbrooke die in his bed till the lost be recalled, and younger and elder join hands in love and friendship under the old rooftree.

"And mark you, Reginald! my curse shall cling to him who dares destroy or disturb the picture I have preserved and cherished, the solace of my old age."

The flickering flame was spent. Barbara Fosbrooke fell back in her chair; and there, with the painted eyes of son, grandson, and daughter-in-law fixedly set upon her, she closed her own for ever.

He "would never set living foot in Fosbrooke Manor again" was the verbal message said to come from Rupert: and the old man winced as he listened, for the words were his own—never forgotten, it seemed, by either. He had no doubts of the messenger's fidelity; no thought of duplicity in his eldest-born. He accepted the answer as final; made no second attempt at reconciliation; never again mentioned Rupert's name. But from that hour a change fell upon him. All his old sports were neglected. Reginald might hunt and shoot, and fill the manor-house with roistering squires: he kept himself aloof, and would pace the long corridor between his own chamber and Rupert's by the hour together, not seldom turning into the unused room and lingering there alone with his regretful memories.

The servants said he was bewitched; and Reginald threatened to burn Rupert's picture in earnest, since it seemed like to turn his father's brain. And no doubt he would have carried his threat into execution but for an appalling incident which made the very room and all within a terror to him.

The only sport to which the squire had clung was angling. It was quiet, and all noise and bluster had, as it were, died out of his life. Reginald strode in and about with heavy tread and resonant tones; *he* came and went as silently as the silver hairs fell from his thinning scalp; and sat in the shade of the alders and willows by the moat side, heedless of the flight of time. At first his youngest grandson bore him constant company, and fished by his side with a willow-wand for a rod, prattling in boy fashion, with or without reply.

One memorable evening, as Lady Annabel was about to retire for the night, and the housekeeper bore a lamp before her along the corridor, they saw a pale light streaming under the closed door of Rupert's room: then there was a moan, and a fall.

Both women screamed; Reginald and a troop of servants rushed up the wide staircase. The latter hung back when told the cause of alarm, but Reginald dashed open the door and found, as he had expected, his father lying senseless on the floor.

But where was the light the pair had seen? There was only the lamp in the housekeeper's hand! And the servants whispered among themselves.

The squire was raised and after a time revived. But he would give no explanation as to what had caused his swoon.

From that night, however, he would have no companion when he went to fish; sending his grandson back, kindly but peremptorily. He assigned no reason; and when the child cried, his lady mother encouraged him to disobey. His grandfather drove him back; but one day when so dismissed, he refused to depart, and then the squire gave up his sport altogether, warning the boy not to go near the moat alone.

The warning was disregarded. Before many days had gone, a slimy and dripping form was drawn from the moat, and Lady Annabel, wringing her hands, accused the old man of having murdered her boy. And the squire turned mournfully away—but answered her never a word.

A month or more elapsed. Squire Fosbrooke came not to the breakfast-board. House and grounds were searched. He was found at last, lifeless, before the painting of his banished son.

Reginald, now Lord of the manor, shut up the room once more, and kept the key. It was a needless precaution. From the time that Mistress Hope, the housekeeper, had confided to the steward that Rupert the painter had died in London the very night the old squire was found senseless before his picture—from that time superstitious awe locked the door without a key. The old squire, and he alone, would approach it night or day.

His death there confirmed the evil repute of the chamber, and Dame Fosbrooke's dying words were repeated under breath through house and village.

Mistress Hope having long rebelled against the rule of Lady Annabel, retired on the pension left by the squire.

In less than a couple of years Reginald Fosbrooke was pitched clean over the neck of his hunter, and Lady Annabel was left a widow, to reign supreme at the manor during the three years of the heir's minority.

Then the steward followed Mrs. Hope to London, and, though late in life, they made a match of it. They did more: they rescued Rupert Fosbrooke's wife and son from the poverty into which they were falling.

When the picture scheme of reconciliation had failed, Rupert grew bitter and angry with himself for having made the advance. But when, through Mrs. Hope, he heard of his mother's death, and the haughty answer Reginald's messenger had conveyed to the manor as from him, grief and vengeance alternated in his breast, and in the turmoil he could not paint, and disappointed his patrons. A brain fever set in, and he died execrating his brother Reginald, and threatening to haunt him and his until the wrong was righted.

Maud, the unfortunate painter's widow, though too proud to appeal to her haughty sister-in-law, was not too proud to accept the home made for her and her son Rupert by the faithful steward and his wife; who, in their turn, felt it only an honour to devote to the service of a Fosbrooke the money they had saved in other Fosbrooke service. They lived to see the younger Rupert married, and impressed on him for his descendants this record of family history and estrangement, coupled with the doom hanging over the elder branch of the family; insisting that in some secret manner every fatality which befell a Fosbrooke had been mysteriously foretold or provisioned within the haunted chamber of the discarded son.

So the story was handed down to me, with an addition of casualties by flood and field which had carried off the Fosbrookes, either in infancy or age, and which were only to be averted when the elder Fosbrooke extended the right hand of fellowship to the younger, and Rupert's heirs became masters of the manor.

My grandfather believed this implicitly. As for myself, I was born in a sceptical and practical age, and have had to fight my own way so sturdily, I have had no leisure to waste on the ghostly traditions of bygone ancestors in a remote manor-house.

So it might have been to the end of the chapter but for a combination of fortuitous circumstances which, to say the least, were remarkable.

Chapter 2

My friend Stretton, the solicitor, of Clement's Inn, to whom I owe whatever success I have made, came to my chambers in the Temple one summer day in unusual haste for him, and handed me a lengthy brief and a stiff retaining fee, saying: "There, run your eye over that! If you can talk the jury over to give our clients a verdict, your fortune's made!" and he gave me a quick tap on the shoulder.

I had taken up the paper languidly. "Myers *v.* Fosbrooke."

With a quickening thrill I ran my eye rapidly over the brief and soon made myself master of the contents.

The client I was called upon to defend was Charles Fosbrooke, of Fosbrooke Manor: our opponent, the plaintiff, a neighbouring landowner. The cause simply this.

Three of the squire's children had been drowned by the upsetting of a small skiff on the moat. He at once vowed no more lives should be given up to its greedy waters, and set about its drainage. In so doing he unavoidably diverted the current of a small watercourse known as the Fosse-brook, to the alleged detriment and damage of the plaintiff's property.

Had the plaintiff not being litigious the case might have been compromised at the outset, when the squire offered compensation to Sir Joseph Myers.

By a strange coincidence, a letter lay open on my table before me, containing overtures from the opposite side, wherein my supposed hereditary antagonism to the Fosbrookes of the manor was openly relied on as a reason why they should retain me as counsel, and I rejoice to hold their brief.

It is possible to have too low an estimate of human nature. Why should I, John Fosbrooke, exercise such gifts as I possessed in order to oppose my own distant kin, who had never done me a personal wrong.

I had just declined the plaintiff's brief, when Mr. Stretton put his head in at the door. I showed him the letter and my reply.

It remained for me to prove black was white, or to suffer a nonsuit. There is something in the old adage that "*blood is thicker than water.*" I resolved to do my utmost for our client, in spite of dead-and-gone feuds. I threw myself into the case, ransacking legal records for points and precedents.

A day or two had elapsed. Leaving the Temple in the forenoon I encountered Stretton in the gateway, just as I was turning into Fleet Street. He caught me by the button-hole and invited me to luncheon with him. As I hesitated, a light basket-phaeton containing a gentleman and lady, with a small page in dark livery behind, drove under Temple Bar and stopped in front of us.

"By Jove!" exclaimed Mr. Stretton, and almost before the words left his lips the page was at the horse's head, and the gentleman, whose eyes and hair were black as my own, and who struck me as a disagreeable likeness of myself—but not a bad-looking fellow on the whole—had jumped out, throwing the reins to the lady, as lovely a young brunette as it had been my fate to meet, with eyes as soft and melancholy as her companion's were eager and fiery.

With barely a word of apology to me, he drew the solicitor aside and began in a hurried voice I could not choose but hear.

"What's this your clerk tells me, Mr. Stretton? Do you know into what hands you have committed our case? This Mr. John Fosbrooke—"

"Is a very rising young barrister—could not be in better hands," interrupted the lawyer imperturbably.

"He claims kinship with the Fosbrookes of Fosbrooke, sir. There is an old feud between his branch of the family and ours. You must withdraw the brief at any cost. He will ruin our cause. In my father's name I insist on the withdrawal of the brief!" This in answer to Mr. Stretton's visible protest.

I thought it quite time to interfere. As haughtily as himself I stepped forward. "Mr. Reginald Fosbrooke, I presume."

His bow said, "Ay, and who on earth are you?"

"Your brief, sir, and my retaining fee shall be in Mr. Stretton's office in less than twenty minutes. There is no need to withdraw the case—I throw it up." And I turned on my heel under the archway. I met my clerk on his way to dinner and sent him back flying for the offending brief and Stretton's cheque, which lay unchanged in my drawer. I had heard Stretton's remonstrance as I went, and the other's annoyed response.

I had barely taken three steps after my clerk, when a crash and a shriek called me back. Reginald Fosbrooke was lying stunned on the pavement, the page was scrambling to his feet, a bystander had caught the affrighted horse, the carriage-wheel was crashing in collision with a cab, and the lovely occupant was in imminent peril.

Darting forward, I managed to extricate the lady from the phaeton before the plunging animal had made a total wreck of it.

She seemed as lifeless as the man on the ground. My clerk was back by this time. Shouting to him to bring a doctor to my chambers, and to Stretton to have his prostrate client conveyed thither, I hurried forward with the insensible girl in my strong arms, and placed her in my own chair. The couch had soon another occupant.

"This will be quieter than a shop," I whispered to Stretton, "and we can keep the crowd out *here*." He nodded a sort of dazed assent.

Before a doctor reached us my charge had revived. And then her distress over her "dear brother," her "dear Reggy," was pitiable to witness.

I did my best to console her, and to assure her that her brother was not dead, only stunned, and would doubtless recover shortly; and, as she turned her liquid eyes in thanks on mine, I felt there was one Fosbrooke who could never be my enemy.

A couple of hours went by before Reginald Fosbrooke gave a sign of returning animation. The doctor had muttered something of concussion of the brain, and internal injury, from the horse's hoof; insisted on quiet, forbade removal, and, aside to Stretton and me, suggested telegraphing to friends.

Barbara—I could almost have guessed her name, had not the injured man murmured it, as she knelt beside him in sobbing agony—caught the suggestion and remarked simply—so simply that I am sure the doctor thought her wits were wandering—"There is no need:

they will already know of this catastrophe at home."

They must have had a telegraph of their own, swifter than that of science! Surely enough, before the close of the afternoon Squire Fosbrooke—who must have been on the road before our message was despatched—stood by the side of his eldest son, and clasped my hand with grateful earnestness as that of a stranger, saying he was glad he had found him alive. He was a grave, dignified, but not haughty man, preternaturally old, and bent beneath the heavy burden of inexorable fate.

He and his daughter took possession of my chambers with many courteous apologies for turning them into a hospital; apparently unconscious that they were indebted to more than a chance namesake. Only the patient knew my antecedents; and when, at the close of the week, he recognized me as his involuntary entertainer he grew irritably impatient to be removed.

The doctor shrugged his shoulders, his gentle sister shed tears, his father, Mr. Stretton, and myself remonstrated. The heir of Fosbrooke was wilful.

He was borne thence with the tenderest care; but barely had he crossed the threshold than violent haemorrhage set in, and only a lifeless body was carried into the neighbouring hotel. A broken rib, displaced, had lacerated some internal organ.

Mourning did not arrest the law-suit. The squire, ignorant of Reginald's prohibition, wrung my hand at parting, and said he was sure his cause was in good hands. I had gone with them to the station, possibly drawn thither by the grateful thanks in Barbara Fosbrooke's every tone and gesture. Then it occurred to the squire that I might better understand how the case stood between him and Myers if I went over the grounds and tracked the Fosse-brook; and he asked me to follow them down in time for his poor boy's funeral.

I went back to my chambers musing. Two strange events had come to pass. I, the descendant of Rupert the discarded, had been invited to the manor. Moreover, I was in love with Barbara.

The Manor House was a magnificent pile with a background of waving woods. Perhaps it was the presence of undertakers, and a crowd of funeral guests with mourning robes and faces, made me feel the interior so gloomy in its grandeur, notwithstanding the faint smile of Barbara and the courteous reception of Barbara's mother.

Was it chance that assigned to me, the latest comer in the crowded mansion, the apartment at the end of the corridor? I had followed the servant mechanically, my mind filled with Barbara's greeting, and not his apologies; but my rapid survey of the hastily prepared chamber set me thinking.

A label outside the oaken door showed that it was set apart for "Lawyer Stretton's friend." The hurried and bewildered servants had no conception that they had shown Rupert Fosbrooke's representative into Rupert's room.

If I had had a doubt it was dispelled by the sight of a large picture reared against the wall, from which three faces seemed to look at me through a veil of dust.

I have not an atom of superstition in me—at least I had not then. It was rather with reverence than awe that I sacrificed my cambric handkerchief to the restoration of the picture. Then I was struck with the resemblance between my ancestor and myself; and wondered if any of the many assembled relatives would perceive it: never thinking how little was known of the faces I was scanning so minutely.

Yet I think my appearance at the dinner-table did excite some curiosity, if furtive glances and whisperings were any index. Sombre dresses and long faces spoiled the meal for me. I was glad when I found myself back in my room in front of a wood fire kindled at my request; and, taking advantage of the double doors, took out a cigar to make myself at home.

There was a suggestiveness of damp and rheumatism about the heavy velvet-hung four-post bed. I declined its invitation, preferring to wrap myself in my travelling rug and stretch my limbs on an antique couch at right angles with the hearth. A second cigar sent me to sleep, to dream of Barbara. I awoke shivering, with an uneasy impression of a hand laid on my shoulder to arouse me. The fire was almost out, the candles quite, but there was a light in the room, and—yes I in the very midst of that light stood Rupert the Painter, palette and brush in hand, painting away at a picture on his easel.

I rubbed my eyes and gave myself a shake. The artist was still at work, and I saw the picture growing under his brush. It was an Alpine scene familiar to myself. Now figures appeared upon the canvas toiling up the snowy ascent. The artist looks round at me, and back at his canvas. I see delineated a broken rope, a shivered alpenstock, and a figure slipping and falling headlong into a terrible crevasse.

Again the artist turns his head, and his dark eyes transfix me. The canvas is blank. Again the brush is plied. Judge, jury, counsel, take their places. I see a brother barrister of long standing addressing the court, see him painted out; and my very counterpart stands out in my very attitude in my most eloquent mood. I see the effect on the faces of judge and jury; it is cheering. The artist turns round and smiles. Picture, painter, easel, light are gone! I am shivering in the dark, with barely a ray of moonlight straggling in through the windows.

I give myself another shake, say I am an arrant fool, conclude I have been dreaming, and compose myself to sleep again.

Convinced, when I awaken in the morning, that I have been dreaming, I say nothing at the breakfast-table of my broken rest, not caring to excite either alarm or ridicule.

As Stretton and I return to town in the express the day after the funeral, I elicit from him that the squire has another son, now travelling in Switzerland, to whom, of course, the heirship will descend. After that, I fear Stretton has but a stupid companion to the end of the journey.

My survey of the moat, converted into a shrubbery, and the track of the watercourse in dispute, did not tell in my client's interest. Nevertheless, I went into court with a conviction I should win, although I scouted the idea of being influenced by a dream.

And I was successful. The case was dismissed as litigious and vexatious, and when I shook hands with our client, he insisted on my returning with him to the manor, and said I did honour to the name I bore.

Other cases kept me in town until the end of term. Then I, John Fosbrooke, availed myself of the squire's invitation, and was welcomed; Mrs. Fosbrooke offering many apologies for my being thrust into an unused room on my former visit. I protested I was perfectly satisfied, and thought it a pity so commodious a chamber should be left to me and the spiders.

The lady sighed, and said no more. This time I occupied the adjoining room, smaller, but well kept, and less antique in its appointments.

The squire took to me amazingly, and Barbara's heart opened to me. I hesitated how best to disclose my ancestry and propose for the sweet girl, when the whole fabric of my future was shaken by a telegram from Switzerland.

Charles Edward Fosbrooke had perished in the ascent of the Simplon. I was staggered, and the whole family were overwhelmed. It was no time for love proposals.

I volunteered a journey for the recovery of the body; saying that I knew the precise spot in which he was lying. This involved explanation of what I called my dream.

"Dream! It was no dream," cried Barbara and her parents, simultaneously.

"But who are you?" demanded the squire, rising to his feet, "who have seen the spectral painter of our house? Rupert Fosbrooke never reveals the future save to one of his own near kin."

My answer and its effect may be imagined. An avalanche could scarcely have overwhelmed them more completely. The old squire, his eyes suffused with tears, held out his hand to me.

"This is no time to perpetuate feud," said he. "Fate is too strong for us."

Need I add that I went to Switzerland and recovered the remains of the last heir of the elder Fosbrookes.

But ere I took my departure, unknown to the family I spent a night in the haunted chamber, still inclined to be sceptical. I came out next morning converted. Once more the mountain scene was painted before me, but I saw myself and guides recovering the lost, and the means employed.

Another picture was painted before me, and then the artist seemed to fling brushes and palette aside, and vanish with a benediction.

★★★★★★

I stood with my now acknowledged relatives by the grave of the squire's last son, and saw his tears fall fast on the coffin-lid before he turned away, and grasping my hand, called me with a sigh, the heir of Fosbrooke Manor.

I could hardly realise it then. I can realise it now, as I stand amid a perfect bower of bloom and perfume, in a pretty country church, and clasp the hand of Barbara before the altar, in that bond which for ever reunites the severed branches, and averts the fate of the Fosbrookes.

And this was the last picture shown to me—now a Fosbrooke of Fosbrooke, a picture of love, and peace, and goodwill.

A New Leaf

Chapter 1: The New Secretary

There was a new inmate at the Hall. Squire Appleton, J.P., finding that increasing years did not add to the elasticity which once made business a pleasure, had engaged a young fellow from London to keep accounts, overlook matters on the estate, carry on business correspondence, and relieve him in many odd ways; in short, a kind of clerkly factotum, though his duties were by no means onerous, and he was by courtesy dubbed a secretary.

The servants' hall had, of course, somewhat to say on his appointment. What did the squire want with a secretary? His father had done without one, and his grandfather before him. And if he must have a secretary, why not engage someone from Leigh or Manchester, instead of a fop of a fellow from London, whom nobody knew anything about?

From this it will be seen that Mr. Alfred Lawrence had not made a favourable impression in the lower domestic circle. Still, opinions were divided; and if heads grown grey in the Appleton service were shaken disparagingly, the maids one and all pronounced him "charming," and the "*bow-idol*" of a fine gentleman."

Naturally these conflicting opinions drifted beyond the limits of the park palings, and if they reached the pretty cottage of the pensioned-off ex-housekeeper, no wonder. She had two fair granddaughters who, in their vocation as dressmakers, had many errands to the hall. Then, Mrs. Lane herself was on friendly terms with her successor, and, moreover, attended the same dissenting chapel as did Mrs. Bridoake, the lodge-keeper's wife, and piety by no means precluded gossip, or closed Mrs. Lane's ears to the commentaries afloat.

Moreover, she had an interest in listening, for Mr. Lawrence had endeavoured to ingratiate himself in the good graces both of herself and her grandchildren whenever an opportunity occurred to render himself agreeable, or display his fascinating person in :the vicinity of the cottage.

This was a rustic building, in a bye-lane leading to the high road between Leigh and Tyldesley, over which ivy clambered to the very chimney tops, curtained the transom windows against intrusive sunbeams, and in summer disputed possession of the trellised porch with the green fringes of the purple-blossomed tea plant. A strip of garden lay between the cottage and the road, effectually screened from observation by a tall privet hedge. From the low wooden gate a path of variegated pebbles, arranged in quaint devices, led to the broad step beneath the porch, and to the green door resplendent with a bright brass knocker. It was a knocker for ornament, not use, since it spoke but in whispers, and fully one half the callers at the cottage ignored the knocker altogether, walking in *sans cérémonie,*

A narrow passage divided the seldom-used parlour from the "house"—a sort of compromise between a kitchen and parlour; the stone floor and shining cooking range being suggestive of the former; the rug, the worn Turkey carpet, chimney ornaments, solid mahogany furniture (transfers from the Hall), and an air of spotless nicety, being equally suggestive of the latter.

In this room, one autumnal afternoon, when the new secretaryship was but a few weeks old, Mrs. Lane sat near the fire, a picture of primitive neatness. Her closely-fitting dress of dark merino had neither trimming nor ornament; a white spun silk kerchief was pinned closely down over the bodice, and her grey hair was banded down under a cap of plain white net, enlivened only by tiny loops of white satin ribbon interspersed within the close border.

At an ample work-table, placed close to the ivy-curtained window for the benefit of the light, sat Jessie (a bright pink bow at the throat relieving her dark merino dress), a wilful, wayward beauty, early spoiled by the foolish flatteries of a silly mother. Ruth, her plainer sister, sat there at work likewise, linen cuffs and bands her sole adornment. She had come at a more ductile age under her grandmother's care, and had grown up gentle and retiring, with a shade of gravity upon her face scarcely in consonance with her nineteen years. Indeed, there were people who spoke of her placidity as melancholy, but they must surely have been mistaken.

Mrs. Lane, fresh from meeting, and from Mrs. Bridoake (and surely with some mysterious prevision in her mind), had come to the conclusion of a homily on worldly-mindedness and sin in general, with a special application to the new secretary in particular, denouncing him as a specimen of the typical "pitch," and warning the girls to shun all communication with him if they would escape contamination.

Ruth stitched and listened passively.

Jessie—who had formed her private estimate of Mr. Lawrence—contrasting him with her own sweetheart, much to the disadvantage of the latter—stuck the pins into the pattern she was adjusting with an impatient click, and handled her scissors as if longing to cut up her grandmother's sermon along with her work.

"Depend upon it, girls, he is a bad man: he went to church last Sunday for the *first* time, and then *fell asleep!*" The iniquity of this untimely nap was expressed more by look and tone than words.

"Well, if the stupid old rector preached, I scarcely wonder," said Jessie, apologetically.

Mrs. Lane raised her hands. "Jessie, you shock me! If a man went to worship his Maker, or hear the gospel in a right spirit, no dull sermon would send him to sleep." Jessie was silent under the rebuke; and for a little while nothing was heard but the rustle of silk and lining, the sharp crunch of the scissors, the faint click of the needle.

"We have reason to be thankful all men are not like him! Look at Reuben Isherwood. *He* would not spend his money in cigars and perfumery, or waste his time in frizzling his whiskers and flirting with the girls!" burst triumphantly from the old lady as the result of long cogitation.

Ruth broke her needle, and rose to replace it.

"I wish he did," thought Jessie, with a sigh; *she* did not regard these delinquencies as very flagrant.

"Ah! Jessie, you have reason to be proud of Reuben; he will be a husband to esteem. Very unlike that scrapegrace at the Hall," continued the grandmother.

"Very!" murmured Jessie with another audible sigh, which somehow seemed to be faintly echoed by her sister Ruth.

With an innate consciousness that Mr. Lawrence was just the individual to catch a foolish girl's fancy, and with marvellous want of tact, Mrs. Lane thus held him up to constant reprobation, contrasting his vices, real or imaginary, with Reuben's known virtues. She hoped thereby to prevent Jessie from wavering in her choice under the seductive influence of a plausible tongue and a handsome person: the very hope proving her fear. For Ruth, she knew her precaution was unnecessary. Her sister had long dubbed her "a little old maid; "she held all would-be suitors at such a distance, whilst at men of the Lawrence stamp she did not care to glance. Her heart was a mystery, a woman's heart so often is; yet, though no love-light was ever seen to sparkle in her eye or leave a bloom upon her pale cheek, there *might* be a "graven image" somewhere shrined for secret worship.

With Jessie, Mrs. Lane overshot the mark. She was fond of finery, and of admiration, so that when Reuben left Leigh to enter into a draper's shop in Fishergate, Preston, she pined for attentions he was no longer at hand to render. He was moreover a plain man, without dash, or pretension, and in his absence the stylish secretary shone resplendent.

"I don't see why grandmother should say such dreadful things about Mr. Lawrence; he is quite a gentleman; and I'm sure half the girls in Tyldesley are in love with him. The new curate isn't half so handsome. I wish Reuben was more like him, and had such white teeth and such beautiful black curls. I hate brown hair!" (Reuben's hair was of the obnoxious colour.) Thus from day to day Jessie would talk to herself; and so from, time to time, as she met this fascinating Mr. Lawrence, their intimacy grew closer.

This admiration became more outspoken, and was couched in language which cast honest unsophisticated Reuben's love-making into the shade. Gratified vanity more than affection had tied her to her country lover, and Mr. Lawrence was an adept at loosening such bonds. In spite of Reuben's weekly letters, Jessie gradually forgot her fealty to him, and Mr. Lawrence deliberately ignored his in another quarter.

Two months had passed since Mrs. Lane's antagonism to the foppish secretary had first broken out in words. It was midwinter. The tea plant fringe upon the porch was worn to threads, and the tall privet hedge, now a mere network of fine stems from which the leaves had dropped, ceased to be a screen between road and cottage.

Possibly that was the reason why one of the young dressmakers, seated close by the window—of course for the benefit of the light—raised her head so frequently from the bodice she was stitching, and glanced across the strip of garden.

Was Jessie expecting someone? Most likely, for as one or two passing figures loomed dimly through the leafless hedge, a keen glance of scrutiny followed each.

The ground was soft with recent rain, and footsteps were inaudible; but presently a masculine shadow went by, and there was the sound as of a light switch whisking away the few lingering leaves.

The quick blood leaped to Jessie's very temples, tingled even within her silent thimble, as she looked out furtively; but, artful young damsel, she was as reticent as her thimble.

Giving herself time to still the tell-tale pulses ere she spoke, she observed, as if deliberating, "Ruth, I think now the rain is gone I had better step over to Leigh, and match Mrs. Heap's dress with velvet and buttons myself."

"I thought you gave Dixon a bit of the silk, with a message to Mrs. Arrowsmith."

"So I did, but if Dixon should stay too long at the Boar's Head, he may forget my message altogether. It will most likely rain again tomorrow, and if he *should* forget, and Mrs. Heap's dress not be finished in time—"

"We should certainly lose our best customer," said Ruth, completing the sentence.

"And half Tyldesley would follow her," added Jessie, as with a slight toss of her shapely head, she left the room and speedily re-appeared attired in a well-fitting mantle and most becoming bonnet.

"How pretty you always look!" exclaimed Ruth admiringly; "and what a colour you have got, to be sure!"

"We should both look prettier if grandmother would only let us dress like other girls. I'm sure we are always as prim as Quakers. It's a wonder anyone trusts us to make a dress tastily or fashionably!" and there was quite a grievance in her tone.

"Nay, Jessie, we only dress as befits our station, and I think grandmother is quite right in saying we had better be neat than flaunting."

"Now, don't you begin to preach too! I've quite enough of it from her!" exclaimed Jessie, petulantly; "you are as prim as she is."

Ruth had risen, and was moving towards the easy chair in which Mrs. Lane sat dozing by the fire. Jessie stopped her. "Now, don't disturb grandmother out of her sleep. You can tell her where I am gone when she wakens, just as well. Good afternoon."

Jessie was off. As the front door snapped in closing, Ruth snatched a scrap of silk from the large work-table, and ran hastily down the pebble-path, after her sister. The wooden gate had just closed behind her.

"Stop, Jessie!"

She turned angrily. "Why do you follow me? Cannot I leave the house without being watched like a child?"

"You were going without the pattern—here it is," said Ruth apologetically, though not without marked surprise.

"Oh, so I was. Thank you. Now run in, or you will take cold." (Was that sisterly thought, Jessie, or only one more item in the sum of growing artifice?)

Ruth turned—but so did the lane into the Tyldesley road close by; and during that brief colloquy over the low gate she had caught a glimpse of a loitering figure just at the curve.

"Who is that?" she murmured, as she slowly retrod the short path to the porch. "Who is that? Surely not the squire's new secretary! It was like his figure. Could he be waiting for Jessie? Oh, I hope not! Yet she seemed so unusually anxious to get out. And why was she afraid of being watched? Oh, if grandmother only suspected such a thing, how angry she would be! And what would Reuben say? She never met *him* clandestinely. Grandmother ought to know; but I hate mischief-making, and, after all, I may be mistaken. Our Jessie could never be so false to Reuben as to meet that man in secret after all grandmother's cautions. Poor Reuben!"

These and like ruminations occupied Ruth's mind long after her return to the window seat and her sewing. She stitched and thought, thought and stitched; and started like one from a dream, when Mrs. Lane, waking from her nap, asked—

"Where is Jessie?"

"Gone to Leigh for Mrs. Heap's trimmings." Ruth's voice hesitated; lurking doubt of her sister's real errand twitched at her truthful tongue.

"Gone to Leigh without my knowledge! Ruth, was not Dixon commissioned to bring those trimmings?"

Mrs. Lane was a strict disciplinarian, and her exclamation implied that Jessie's offence was of magnitude.

"Yes, grandmother; but she said he might get drunk and forget."

"Forget!"—(How much was comprised in that word!)—"Dixon has been a carrier for twenty years, but I never knew him drink enough to confuse his memory. Drunk or sober, he does his business. But, Ruth, I have had my eye on the silly child for some time, and am truly uneasy about her. Have you not noticed how slight a pretext has served for a reason to call her out and neglect her work at home?"

Ruth acknowledged she had.

"Then she has grown restless and discontented, and is neither so frank nor good-tempered as she used to be. There is something the matter, I am sure. Mrs. Bridoake gave me a hint to look after her as we walked from chapel yesterday, and said that that man, Lawrence, had been seen hanging about the cottage. But I should not like to accuse Jessie of disobedience to me and inconstancy to Reuben on mere suspicion."

Now, Ruth, is your time! Ruth was silent—she could not make mischief.

The old dame lapsed into silence also, and took counsel with, the ruddy fire.

The brief daylight gone, a lamp was lighted, tea prepared, and kept sputtering in its bright pot on the hob, whilst the toast on a brass footman, equally bright, frizzled and spoiled before the fire, waiting for the absentee.

When patience was exhausted, Mrs. Lane pronounced a tremulous grace, and the meal was partaken in very ominous silence, whilst the deepening shadows without were only equalled by the deepening shadows within.

As Ruth proceeded to clear away the cups and saucers wheels were heard outside: they stopped before the gate, and then a heavy foot blundered up to the door. Without the ceremony of knocking, Dixon, the red-faced carrier, presented himself, a huge bunch of holly, a small parcel, and an item of intelligence he had never been instructed to carry.

Chapter 2: Sowing the Wind

Ruth's eyes had not deceived her. The switch on the wintry hedge had been a signal to Jessie, and Mr. Lawrence himself waited her approach at the bend of the lane in not too amiable' a mood. Profoundly impressed with his own superlative attractions, he was apt to bestow his favours on admiring maidens, not doubting their gracious acceptance. Fluttering here and there, displaying his elegant person to the best advantage, he had made many a silly girl's heart ache because he "meant nothing."

But now he did mean something; having resolved to take a desperate leap into matrimony, moved thereto by the double charms of Jessie's purse and person, he chafed at all delays.

"I wonder if that girl expects me to cool my heels under the dripping trees all the winter waiting for her? If her country bumpkin did it I shall not, pretty as she is. Unless she make-up her mind today I shall try my luck in another quarter. My face and figure should sell for a good round sum. Still, I think this is a safe card. Let me see."

The soliloquizing secretary flicked his hoots with his cane, debating his own value as a marketable commodity.

"Let me see! I must *marry* her, that's clear; yet is it worth while running the risk—(What risk?)—on £190 and chances? Um—ah, she's deuced pretty. What if that swain of hers should turn up this Christmas? Well, I must cut him out, that's all. As luck would have it, he won't know me. Ah, she's coming at last!" muttered he, as the gate opened and the graceful figure presented itself. "What does that Methodistical sister of hers want now?" he cried with an impatient slash of his cane. "Always a spy at hand! Ah, my sweet Jessie, my winter rosebud, I was in despair. I feared the old dame was keeping your bloom to herself." And then the gallant gentleman raised her hand to his lips very impressively.

"Grandmother was asleep. I had to invent an excuse for coming. And oh! Alfred"—(it had got to that)—"I am so afraid Ruth saw you." He offered his arm, which she took unhesitatingly. They walked on towards Leigh.

"And what then, my charming Jessie?" he asked, with a pressure of her arm. "Why should you be afraid of her? Will you not be your own mistress immediately?"

"Yes; but—." And Jessie heaved a deep sigh—it may be of contrition.

"But what? She is not the arbiter of your destiny. Give yourself at once to me, and you will escape the tyranny you now endure."

Another sigh. He had talked of home tyranny until the girl fully believed herself a victim.

"Jessie, can you not trust the intensity of my love?"

"Yes, Alfred; but, then, I have been thinking I ought not to—to listen to you. You know I am already engaged to—to—"

"Oh, ah! to a country counter-jumper—so I have heard."

He dropped her arm, and pulled his perfumed black whiskers, in profound disparagement of his rival. Jessie blushed. The sneering epithet had somehow lessened her estimate of Reuben's calling. She hesitated, stammering out—

"I meant to say, Mr. Lawrence, that though—well, I have been promised to—to—Mr. Isherwood for a good many years, and cannot well run off my word. He would break his heart."

Mr. Lawrence laughed.

"Break his heart! A man who is content to see you twice a year!"

"But he has only two holidays, Mr. Lawrence," she said, deprecatingly.

"Then he's worse off than a schoolboy! But what are holidays to a man in love? *I* should take French leave, and the first train, if I had a governor without a conscience."

"But Mr. Lawson is a very kind master, Reuben says."

How Alfred Lawrence started!

"What is the matter?" asked Jessie.

"Oh, nothing, nothing; but if you prefer this draper's assistant, who has most likely forgotten you in his long absence, and may even now be making love to his master's daughter—"

"Mr. Lawson has no daughter," interrupted Jessie. "He had a son, who nearly ruined his father with his wickedness, and then ran away."

Her companion took several steps in silence.

"Miss Lane, I have no desire to force your choice, or to enter into competition with this Mr. Isherwood. If he be likely to break his heart, Alfred Lawrence will not break *his*. There are other young ladies on whom my attentions will not be thrown away."

It was far from the speaker's intention to be taken at his word. Her hesitancy had taught him his advantage. He played with her vanity, her jealousy, her impatience of control, and urged the injustice of keeping an engagement made ere either of them knew their own minds, placing Reuben ever in a false light, until at length he argued her out of her better feelings. She became convinced that the perfumed being by her side, on whom she saw so many damsels, both in Leigh and Tyldesley, cast longing glances, must be infinitely superior to homely Reuben, for whom nobody cared but herself. So, finally, she promised her ardent admirer to place herself and her little fortune in his hands, with or without Mrs. Lane's consent, as soon as she could command it; but never a benignant star looked through the murky evening sky on the ratification of the compact.

She would be of age on New Year's Day, and her own mistress. She did not come to this decision readily. There were scruples to be overcome, qualms of conscience to be stifled; yet, when Dixon passed the pair on their lingering way homeward, his keen eyes, accustomed to pierce the darkness, saw the arm of Mr. Alfred's light overcoat crossing the shoulders of Jessie's black mantle in loving clasp. And *that* was his item of news!

A bombshell bursting on the hearth could scarcely have created greater consternation in Mrs. Lane's quiet home. She was a truly good woman, kind to all within her sphere, but, as I have said, was a strict disciplinarian, and intolerant of deception. Rigid in morals and manners, she held it a duty to be "instant in season" and out of season; and this caused her to be considered harsh by more persons than Jessie, whose awe of her aged relative had latterly somewhat abated—thanks to her new friend's training.

When Dixon was gone, Mrs. Lane and Ruth compared notes. Then the old lady posted herself on the window-seat, to await the transgressor's return. The moon had risen when the offenders reached the gate; and if she did not hear the protestations, promises, and appointment for the next interview, she saw the close embrace at parting. Indignant, she confronted the flushed and excited girl, ere her excitement had time to cool down, in the shadow of the porch.

"What is the meaning of this?" Jessie's fluttering heart stood still for an instant, and her tongue was mute. "How is it, girl, that you, the promised wife of one man, thus meet in secret and suffer the caresses of another?"

"I could not help it, grandmother," she faltered. "He overtook me in the lane, and would kiss me when he went away."

"Do not add falsehood to disobedience, Jessie," remonstrated Mrs. Lane, leading the way into the house. "No man kisses a modest girl against her will. Modesty will awe even the profligate. Are you grown so shameless that you set my counsels at naught, and, in defiance of propriety, meet this man, and walk with him at nightfall, with his arm around your waist?—a man, too, of whom nothing is known!"

Jessie stood at bay.

"Nothing known! Then it is not for lack of tale-bearers." And her head went up with a toss.

Ruth's head was bent so closely over her work that she lost the glance which pointed this retort.

"Ill news flies fast," continued Jessie, advancing into the room, at the same time throwing back her loosened bonnet strings with a jerk; "and he cannot be a bad man of whom nothing evil is known. Besides, the squire *must* know all about him; and what satisfies Squire Appleton might satisfy us."

"You simple girl! a man may be a good secretary (or clerk, for he is little more), yet be a worthless vagabond; and such I have an instinctive belief is this Lawrence. It would be a deep sorrow to me if you were entrapped in his meshes." And the good old woman resumed her seat by the fire, with a grave, sad face.

"I don't see—"

"No, child," interposed the elder woman, "you do not see, but the people at the hall do. There is something mysterious about him. He has been three months there, and never once had either a letter or anyone to call on him, much as he brags of his London friends."

"Then he has no sweetheart anywhere else, that's clear," thought Jessie.

"And," put in Ruth, "it is thought that his name is not really Alfred, for all that his clothes are marked A. L."

"It does not take much to get gossips *thinking*. And pray what set that afloat? I suppose that meddlesome Mrs. Bridoake had a hand in it."

"It was noticed, no matter by whom, that whenever Tony, the page was called sharply in his hearing, he started and turned as if to answer. Even the squire remarked it, and his excuse was 'he had a brother named Tony.'"

"And quite a sufficient reason."

"But not a reason, miss, why you should defend him, allow his embraces, or meet him in secret. A maiden who is engaged should hold herself as sacred as a married woman. How can you answer this to Reuben?" demanded the grandmother.

Jessie hung her head, and muttered something inaudible.

"Reuben trusts you implicitly," said Ruth, sadly, "and it is a fearful thing to trifle with a true heart. I hope you are not deceiving him."

Jessie snapped her up sharply: "Mind your own business! What should a little old maid like you know of either true hearts or false ones?"

Mrs. Lane interposed: "Ruth is right. If you are playing Reuben false, he must be informed. It is evident this is not your first meeting with Mr. Lawrence, and flirtations of this kind are so discreditable, I cannot suffer a worthy man to be imposed upon."

"You can tell him what you please; fancy will supply the want of fact."

Mrs. Lane *bethought* herself she knew nothing beyond that evening's indiscretion.

"Jessie," said she, "you are bold and disrespectful tonight.. We are all in an untoward frame of mind. Go to bed now. We may reason quietly tomorrow. If there be more in this than girlish imprudence, however painful the task, I shall acquaint Reuben Isherwood when he comes on New Year's Eve, whatever be the result, and I will put up special prayers in your behalf."

And so the pious old lady did, little foreseeing how mysterious,. how awful would be the answer.

All the following week Jessie thought proper to assume a fit of sulks as the best cover to her real feelings. She was not so heartless as her flippant tongue suggested, and did not brave the just indignation of her relatives, or conceal her treachery from Reuben, without many a sharp pang. But the tempter contrived to be often at her elbow, and kept her constant to him, regardless of Reuben. She assumed, too, an air of injured dignity; with or without pretext went out, leaving so much work on Ruth's hands that the Christmas festival proved no holiday to *her*. But for the evergreens and holly decorating the walls, and the good things sent in so abundantly from the Hall, she would scarcely have recognised the season. Not, however, being a gadabout at best of times, and now in no mood for visiting, she made no complaint, but stitched on, hoping to have her hands at liberty for the New Year—that New Year so full of presage for all.

CHAPTER 3: "FROM THE DEAD"

The year drew to a close tearfully. Reuben was hourly expected. So was Mrs. Bridoake, for it was the Watch-night, and neither she nor Mrs. Lane would have thought of letting in the New Year outside the precincts of Ebenezer Chapel. Mrs. Bridoake was coming to take tea, and lend the old lady her arm afterwards, for it was a goodly distance.

Ruth had just completed her preparations for the birthday festival of the morrow—that New Year's Day to which Jessie looked for emancipation from one thraldom only to shackle herself with another. But Ruth, possibly depressed by the weather, her dread of Reuben's reception by her sister, and the threatened disclosures, moved about even more soberly than her wont. She had set the tray for an early tea, when Mrs. Bridoake came hurriedly up the path. As she was behind time her flurried aspect escaped Ruth's attention.

She was the bearer of strange tidings.

"Ruth, Where's Jessie?" (Christian names come pat from country people.)

"In her own room. She has only just come in."

"An' yo'r gran'mother?"

"Laying her things out ready for chapel. The rain will not keep *her* at home."

"Aw should think not! But what's a' this stir abeaut Jessie's wed-din'?"

"Jessie's wedding!" echoed Ruth, turning pale, and dropping her hands on the tray, where the cups and saucers rattled like castanets. "Jessie's wedding!"

"Yo' didn't know? Th' banns wor axt in Leigh Church, for the first toime, yesterday."

"What is that?" asked Mrs. Lane, coming into the room.

Mrs. Bridoake repeated her news. The old lady looked, displeased.

"Reuben ought to have let me know," said she, gravely.

"Reuben! It's noan Reuben," cried Mrs. Bridoake. "I wish it war. It's that clooas-peg, Lawrence—Squire's new *secatary*."

Mrs. Lane groaned, and stood aghast.

"Poor Reuben!" murmured Ruth, with a pitying sigh.

Jessie was hastily summoned downstairs. She came, singings with an open letter in her hand.

"Jessie," said Mrs. Lane, sternly, "what is this I hear? Is it true that you intend to marry that coxcomb, Alfred Lawrence, without even asking my consent?"

"Yes," answered Jessie, faintly, nervously biting her nails the while. "It was no use asking your consent."

"And so, knowing my strong objections to this underhand stran-ger, you heartlessly break faith with an upright man who loves you well—who even now may be on his way hither, believing you true to him. Oh, Jessie!"

"Break faith, indeed! If Reuben loved me as well as you all seem to think, he would not stay away months at a stretch; nor is he on his way now. There is his letter." And she tossed it contemptuously into her grandmother's lap.

"Thank God! There will then be time to soften the dreadful blow to him. It will break his heart. Oh, Jessie! how could you serve poor Reuben so?" cried Ruth, with streaming eyes.

"Look you, Ruth, everyone seems to care more for Reuben's hap-piness than mine. I don't think we should suit each other one bit; and, as you seem so much concerned about him, why not take him yourself, and try to piece his heart if it should break? But I want my tea!" So saying, she took her seat, as if dismissing the subject from her mind.

If that was more than a random shaft, it was a cruel one; it went home. The warm blood surged upwards, crimsoning throat and forehead with a sudden flush, leaving Ruth's fair face whiter than before. Fortunately, the deepening twilight shielded her from observation; and as she turned in silence to light the lamp and pour out the tea, both Mrs. Bridoake and her grandmother interposed. In the strong emotions of the hour hospitality was all but lost sight of, though the meal was unusually prolonged. In vain Mrs. Lane reasoned and expostulated with her wilful grandchild. Both waxed warm, and words ran high. Twice Mrs. Bridoake reminded the incensed old lady that it was almost chapel time before she essayed to move; and even then something seemed to fetter her movements, as if she had a reluctance to quit the house which she could not overcome. Going, she turned at the door, excited by Jessie's reiterated assertion—

"I shall be of age tomorrow, and have a right to please myself."

"Yes, to begin a New Year and a new life of sorrow together! And, mark me, girl, I shall alter my *will* with the New Year. Not one penny of my hard-earned savings shall that man have to squander in sinful vanities."

"We don't want your money; Alfred has plenty of his own, and there will be mine. He has a rich uncle in London.—(Uncle, indeed! Ah, simple Jessie!)—You can alter *your will* tomorrow, if you like."

"I shall! We will all turn over a new leaf with the New Year. But, remember, Jessie, disobedience cannot prosper. You will live to rue your folly bitterly."

With a reproachful, sorrowing look both girls remembered throughout their lives, she took Mrs. Bridoake's proffered arm, and went out into the night and drizzling rain, as she told her companion, "to intercede at the Throne of Grace for the wilful child rushing headlong to her own destruction." Could she have pierced the shadows of that night, would she have gone on?

Silence fell on the house and on the sisters after her departure. Ruth had cleared away the tea-things during that long altercation, and now sat down by the fire. Jessie, after a while, went out into the porch, and there was presently a hum of voices. In about half-an-hour Jessie bolted the door and came back, looking very blue and cold.

"The rain is over and the moon shining; I think it is freezing," she remarked, as she stirred the fire, and seated herself opposite to her sister.

"I hope not; it would make the roads so dangerous. I wish grandmother was back," said the other, anxiously.

"We need not expect her on this side midnight; and I am sure I don't want her, if she comes in no better humour to let the New Year in. A nice birthday I am likely to have!"

Ruth made no response. She was gazing at the fire, thinking of the "might-have-been," and, perhaps—who knows?—of the "might-be;" thinking of the sorrow in store for a true-hearted man, and longing for power to assuage it. After a time she trimmed the lamp, brought forth her Bible, and sat down to read, with her back to the door and window. Jessie sat opposite, with her head thrown back, a mingled look of scorn and defiance gathering on her face. Hour by hour was told by the American clock on the wall. As its wiry pulses vibrated under the stroke of midnight came the sound of Tyldesley Church bells, with far-off echoes from Leigh, to welcome the new-born year.

"I wish you a happy New Year, Jessie," said Ruth, advancing to kiss her sister.

But Jessie was not conciliatory: she took the proffered kiss with an ill grace, saying, as Ruth resumed her seat—

"It won't be either you or grandmother who will make the New Year happy for me." And she looked down on the hearthrug in sheer dissatisfaction with herself.

Something—she never knew what—after a long silence caused her to look up. *Behind her sister's chair, with her warm shawl pulled awry, her plain black satin bonnet crushed, its white lining and primly-quilled cap specked with blood, stood her grandmother with pale face and finger up, as if she said, "Beware!"*

Jessie screamed, and started to her feet. The figure did not move.

"Oh, grandmother, what is the matter? How did you get in?"

Ruth, alarmed, rose, her eyes following the direction of her sister's. She saw *nothing*, and said so.

"Not grandmother, covered with blood?"

"Nothing !"

Jessie crossed the hearth hastily. The figure was *gone!*

"Oh, Ruth! Ruth! that was grandmother's *ghost!* I know it was. Something dreadful has happened."

"Perhaps it was grandmother herself, trying to frighten you. It is almost time she was at home."

"She could not get in; I *bolted* the door."

Her alarm was infectious. Both girls ran screaming to the door; with trembling hands undid the bolt, and rushed out, only to fall over each other on a pavement like glass. Scrambling to their feet with equal haste, but more caution, they ran across the road to the lodge.

As they reached the gates Mrs. Bridoake came hurrying down, the road, using her umbrella as a staff. She was *alone*. Descrying them in the moonlight, she cried out, "Oh, lasses, yo'r good, pious grandmother has fawn deawn th' chapel steps, an' hoo's killed!"

It was even so. That was a night of accidents, and as such remembered through a wide district for many years.

Freezing as it descended, the sleet had covered the ground with, a treacherous glaze. Stepping out of chapel unprepared, Mrs. Lane, with several other persons, fell. They were bruised, no doubt, but she never rose again in this world. Fatally prophetic had been her own words. Whilst the echoes of her last prayerful "Amen" yet lingered in the little chapel, she had passed at once through its portals and the portal of Death, to "begin a new life with the New Year."

Chapter 4: New Revelations

The sudden blow fell heavily on both girls—heaviest on Jessie, the violence of whose grief admitted of no consolation. Her last words to the dead had been those of ungrateful self-assertion. Her grandmother's parting words had been well-merited rebuke and auguries of evil. To her, and her only, had the phantom shape appeared, in the very instant of dissolution, even as she sat nourishing thoughts of disobedience and wrath. Ever before her seemed to stand the bleeding figure, with disordered dress, and warning finger up; and in her remorseful mood the conscience-stricken girl felt constrained to obey it. She refused to see Alfred Lawrence, and wrote kindly to Reuben Isherwood. Still she had not courage to confess her breach of faith, and the wrong was never righted. Of the apparition (which filled the gossips of the Hall and neighbourhood with consternation and amazement) he was informed later, and by another hand.

One ghastly circumstance, over which public comment was loud, must not be forgotten: neither inquest nor funeral had stopped the reading of the "banns" in due course; and though at the third reading a voice had been heard to cry, "I forbid!" no one had entered the vestry to record an objection. An unknown voice went for nothing in the ear of the law; but there were ears in the congregation on which it fell like a solemn protest from the dead.

No *new will* had been made. Jessie's moiety under the old one was just £200; so, besides being her own mistress, the new year had made her mistress also of nearly £400 in hard cash. It was not likely Mr. Lawrence would resign her now. Again and again he presented his speckless person at the cottage-door; but as the transparently leafless hedgerow betrayed his approach, and town manners taught him the use of a knocker, Jessie was warned from the window-seat, and Ruth was prepared to deny his entrance.

Could Reuben Isherwood have appeared at this juncture, I might have had a different story to relate. As it was, Mr. Lawson, his employer, continued seriously ill; and Reuben, being now manager, where he had formerly been only assistant, duty, as well as gratitude, kept the conscientious young man at his post. Jessie's demonstrative grief, as, might have been expected, wore itself out. More powerful even than the memory of her grandmother's warning spectre was the spirit of vanity in her own breast. She became disgusted with her own red eyes and mottled face, and ceased her lamentations, since she found that tears destroyed her beauty. Every fresh consultation with her looking-glass made her long to air herself abroad, if only to show how well she looked in her new mourning.

"I cannot be expected to stay at home for ever," she argued, first with herself and then with her sister, who could only acquiesce in an observation so self-evident.

Going out, however, involved chances and mischances.

Besides his duties at the desk, Mr. Lawrence had frequent business out of doors, and a not too curious master; so he contrived, by watching, to waylay Jessie in her walks, when he brought his subtle influence to bear on her instability and avowed affection for himself. Her resolution wavered, and before a month had flown, or the crispness gone from her crape, he had regained his old ascendancy over her. There was no secrecy in their intercourse now. He did not scruple to call at the cottage, although Ruth testified her displeasure by carrying her work into another room whenever he came. The warning of her grandmother's ghost he "pooh-poohed," as the offspring of an excited imagination, treated the coincidence as accidental, and ridiculed the importance she attached to the "angry words of an old woman." She withstood Ruth's arguments better than his banter. In vain her sister strove to wean her from her infatuation, and pleaded the cause of the absent lover. Opposition only strengthened wilful Jessie's resolves.

Once more the wedding day was fixed. The announcement was made to Ruth one stormy day in March, when the wind moaned round the house, the tree tops bent their heads at every gust, and the loosened ivy beat like angry whips against the casement. It was not a choice season for such a communication, but the subject filled Jessie's mind, and a slight incident called it forth. The carrier's cart went by. As it passed, the flapping tilt-cover burst its bonds and showed a shivering woman seated amongst the boxes and parcels. It was no uncommon thing for Dixon to give "a lift" to a tired child, or tramp, or market woman with her basket; but whilst the cart stopped, and one of two men walking with the sturdy carrier by the horse's head ran to help him in securing the rebellious tarpaulin, they saw that his present passenger was none of these. Only her head and shoulders were visible, but they belonged to a stranger, young, pale, with a miserable face, and a respectable bonnet.

Very trivial circumstances awaken interest and comment in remote country places. Curiosity and imagination were brought to bear on the carrier's unwonted passenger. The long discussion drifted to the night when he carried thither unwelcome news as well as Mrs. Heap's trimmings. With that, Alfred Lawrence came on the carpet, and, the subject once broached, transition was easy. Ruth was deeply grieved.

"Going to be married! and *so soon*, too, after grandmother's shocking death!"

There was a long pause.

"Have you ever apprised Reuben of your changed sentiments and intentions?" she asked.

"No. I have left his letters unanswered; that is all. I have not opened the two last. There they are."

She took two letters from her work-basket, and threw them across the table to her sister.

"You can answer them if you like."

"*I* cannot answer them! But, Jessie, common honesty forbids that you should marry one man with your engagement to another uncancelled. Only write and tell him. Reuben is too much a man to maintain a claim to a woman's hand without her heart."

"Indeed, I shall not. You can write and tell him if you like. I think he will know quite soon enough."

"Quite too soon for his happiness. Poor Reuben! I wish his trusting heart could have been spared the pain you will inflict."

"I wish so too," replied Jessie, sobered—for the instant only. She resumed, carelessly: "But it can't be helped. We never did suit each other. And I say, Ruth, if you are so *very* anxious to spare his feelings, why not take pity on him yourself, as I said before? Your sober ways would just suit each other."

"Heartless!" exclaimed a voice from the doorway. The girls

dropped their work, and started to their feet as if electrified. The crimson flush had not paled from Ruth's forehead, or from the tips of her round ears; and large drops stood in her eyes ready to fall. There, in deep mourning, stood Reuben Isherwood, tall and erect—mingled pain and scorn visible in his expressive face. All that had once been homely in his gait was gone. He stood there, a man either sister might have been proud to love.

What had Reuben overheard?

He had overheard *all*—had seen his unopened letters tossed to Ruth like waste paper—had heard her plead for him—had heard the insidious taunt—seen the quick flush and swimming eyes, and was startled by the double revelation.

True, he did not come wholly unprepared. Mrs. Bridoake—present on New Year's Eve—had, like a good wife, taken counsel with her husband, and the twain decided that Reuben Isherwood ought to know he was being jilted. They were no great scribes, however; and, before a letter was concocted to their satisfaction Jessie's penitence and seclusion disarmed their indignation. The proximity of the lodge to the cottage made it a post of observation; and, keeping a sharp look-out, Mrs. Bridoake saw signs of a reaction. The result was a long letter from Mrs. Bridoake, not too well spelled or indited. It told the story of Mrs. Lane's death—of the apparition (in which they thoroughly believed), and of Jessie's fickleness—a story which her prolonged silence confirmed. Had she but opened Reuben's letters she would have read—first, his demand for a refutation, and next, his bitter renunciation, and resolve to see her no more.

A strange errand had brought him to her presence now.

As Jessie stood before him, silent and abashed, he said coldly:—

"Miss Lane, I am not come to upbraid you—you have made your own choice—so be it! Whatever feelings of tenderness or pity I retained, you have yourself dispelled. You were queen of my heart—you have been deposed from your throne never to be reinstated."

Could this be Reuben—homely Reuben? And what did he mean by pity?

"As you have just said, we should *not suit* each other—Ruth." He gently took her trembling hand. "I came hither to save your sister from a great wrong. From my heart I am sorry for her!" he continued.

Jessie started. "A great wrong!—sorry for her!" What could he mean? She would not seem afraid—she would brave it out.

"Who called you to interfere with my affairs, Mr. Isherwood?"

"Who should interfere if not I? But that is past, Miss Lane," he added gravely. "I will trouble you to walk to Appleton Hall—there you will learn. You might incline to doubt my unsupported testimony."

Testimony! against what, or whom? Should she decline to go?

As she hesitated Reuben put in, "Do not keep the squire waiting. It is for your own sake."

Shivering with sudden fear, she hastened to equip herself; but even then paused before her glass to re-adjust her crape bonnet more becomingly. Ruth was ready also. She knew from Reuben's manner something urgent and important called for their presence; indeed, he had said as much. A lad opened the gates. Grinning from ear to ear, he said, "Mother's oop at th' Ha'—there's foine doin's yond'." The wind blew keenly—the trees tossed wildly; but something keener than the wind smote Jessie's thoughtless heart with a sudden dread, as Tony, the page, met them at the open door, and, with a significant smirk and leer, ushered them into the Justice-room, and Reuben whispered, "I would gladly spare you both the pain, but duty is imperative."

There were assembled servants and tenants, whom swift-winged rumour and swifter-footed curiosity had brought together in a short space of time. There, too, was a strange, rough man, and half-fainting, on a chair by his side, sat the pale, lady-like woman they had seen in the carrier's cart. There, too, was Lawrence, shrinking, crestfallen—all his jauntiness gone. And there, too, sat Squire Appleton, no longer the easy master, but the *Justice*, stern and uncompromising.

"Jessie Lane," said he, "your grandmother was long a faithful servant of our house; I respected her highly, and for her sake I am sorry for the circumstances which render your presence here necessary."

Someone else *sorry*! But for her grandmother's sake, not hers. She felt faint, and grasped Ruth's arm.

"Mrs. Lawson," said the Justice, addressing the pale woman, "will you repeat to this young person that which you have deposed on oath to me? Tell her who that fine gentleman is." And he looked towards Alfred Lawrence.

"He is *my husband*, miss—Anthony Lawson."

Jessie put her hand to her side, and held her breath. Tony, close by the door, tittered audibly. The woman spoke with an effort.

"We were married five years ago. Here is the certificate,"—producing a paper. "He took me to London. He soon ran through my bit of money, and left me in ill health, with two children, chargeable to the parish. We were in Islington workhouse till we were passed on to

291

Manchester, more than a year ago. Only last December the guardians ferreted out his father, and old Mr. Lawson, a better man than his son, has kept us ever since."

"An' a pretty hunt we've had to find the rascal, under his new neame," interrupted the warrant officer, by Mrs. Lawson's side. But, thanks to that gentleman (nodding towards Reuben), we've got him safe now; an' I *rayther* think he's wanted i' Preston fur somethin' *more* than wife-desertion. He looks chapfallen enough neaw—dunnot he, miss?"

Indeed he did. "An' would yo' believe it, miss, that them whiskers an' curls wer' red afore he dyed 'em?" A laugh, instantly suppressed by the squire, went round the room. Jessie had fainted. When she recovered she was in the housekeeper's room with only Ruth and Mrs. Bridoake.

"Where is where is—?"

"Reuben?" suggested Ruth.

"No—Alfred."

"On his way to prison—the villain!" blurted out Mrs. Bridoake, "and aw hope they'll keep him theer. Aw've had my suspicions o' eawr foine *secataty* for some toime, and reet glad aw am that I let 'em eawt to Mr. Isherwood, or a pratty mess you'd ha' been in. Why, who dun yo' think the chap is? Who, but that theer vagabon' lad o' Mr. Isherwood's measter, who robbed his feyther an' ran away from whoam nigh ten years sin'."

Jessie shuddered.

"Aye, yo' may weell shiver. Miss Jessie; but yo' may go deawn on yor bended knees an' thank God it's no waur. What if he hadno bin fun' eawt till a week further on?"

What, indeed? Well might her grandmother come back from the other world to warn her of peril! And to think she had despised that solemn warning! As the swift thought flashed through her mind, Jessie bowed still deeper her bent head, and covered her face with both hands, as if to hide her shame and suffering. Reuben came in with the housekeeper at this moment. He looked compassionately on the drooping girl, so long cherished as his future wife, and felt how keen must be her humiliation. He was a man of fairly developed intellect, and fully developed heart; and though his love had gone at one fell swoop, with his esteem, the bitterness of a broken trust remained.

"This is no season for reproaches, Jessie; your own sufferings will teach you to feel for mine," he said, with enforced calmness. "But an explanation is due to you and to Ruth also. You asked who called for my interference. I will tell you. It is too mysterious and remarkable an interposition to be passed over lightly." (He spoke to attentive listeners, though Jessie never raised her head.)

"The room I occupy in the house of my employer was once the chamber of his profligate son, Anthony Lawson. Over the fireplace still hangs a coloured portrait of him, which has never been removed. One night last week, as I sat ruminating on Mrs. Bridoake's story of your faithlessness, of the perfumed and bewhiskered fellow who had supplanted me, and cursing my own folly in yielding my heart to a pretty face without a sterling quality to ensure happiness—(Jessie sobbed aloud)—I must have fallen asleep and dreamed—I can account for it in no other way—your grandmother appeared before me, pale, very pale, bleeding from the temple, and very sorrowful. She raised her arm—pointed to the portrait—her lips moved—she said 'Lawrence' distinctly and impressively; then melted slowly away, her finger still pointing to the picture. I suppose I wakened—for I must have been asleep—with the word 'Lawrence' in my ears and the vision fresh in my memory."

"It wur' no dream!" stoutly advanced Mrs. Bridoake.

"Oh, grandmother! dear grandmother!" broke from Ruth; while Jessie, choking with sobs, rocked on her chair in agony.

"Dream or no dream, "continued the young man, much moved by Jessie's deep distress, "I was bewildered. All at once the character of Lawson flashed across my mind, coupled with the name of 'Lawrence' in the letters of your true friend, Mrs. Bridoake. The initials A. L. were identical. The clue once found was easily followed. His heartless desertion of a young and confiding wife and his two helpless children had exasperated his father beyond measure. I believe Mr. Lawson's illness arose from mental disquietude on that score."

"No doubt," said Ruth, quietly.

"With the consent of father and wife, the guardians were at once communicated with, and a warrant issued. Mrs. Lawson came hither for identification. She was too weak to walk, and we brought her on from Leigh in Dixon's cart. We have reason to be thankful the discovery was made before he added another to his many victims. Squire Appleton has not yet had time to look into his accounts."

Jessie Lane never held up her head in Tyldesley or Leigh again. Her story, and that of her grandmother's re-appearance from the other world, filled the mouths of gossips far and wide. She shrank alike from sneers and sympathy. Soon she went away amongst her mother's relatives in Bury, wiser, and, it is to be hoped, better for the sharp lesson she had had. She did rue her folly bitterly, as her grandmother had predicted.

Nor did Ruth remain very long at the old place—nor did she live to be a little old maid, stifling in her bosom a love she might not own. Mr. Lawson took his manager into partnership; and before twelve months were gone Ruth was in Preston, filling up the void in Reuben's heart and home—gentle and quiet as ever, but with no unnatural gravity shadowing her young face as heretofore. Her love had leapt from her heart to her eyes—they beamed with affection; and though many years have passed, neither she nor Reuben have yet regretted the "new leaf" which the squire's secretary and Jessie's wilfulness had turned over for them.

The Plainbury Mystery

Plainbury Castle had been long without a master. The earl, despairing of peace and rest in this life, had, it was said, sought both in the depths of a black pool in the recesses of his own woods. Yet there were not wanting hints and intangible rumours that rest in that watery bed was none of his own seeking; and from the day when he was carried thence, swollen, blue, and oozy, to be deposited on the table of the great hall, a fearful shadow of suspicion seemed to invest the countess as with a mantle. The dead earl's few aristocratic friends dropped from her like leaves from a decaying tree; even the ranks of her own less scrupulous set thinned.

How much she felt each defection could only be surmised. Oaths and curses were ready to her lip as to those of her lowest groom, and these fell in venomous showers at every rejected invitation, every deliberate cut in the hunting field. Her brow contracted with a perpetual scowl, and if her heart were only as wrinkled as her forehead, it must have been corrugated indeed.

She was a woman of strong bad passions, and every line of her wicked face showed it. Yet she had been a beauty in her time, a beauty with a haughty step and a dominant will, when her lord married her—or rather when the Lady Matilda Hanley married him; for never did eagle pounce on a devoted lamb more surely than she in her thirtieth year swooped down upon the Earl of Plainbury, and obtained from the infatuated nobleman unparalleled settlements. She was not without an ample dower, but every acre, every jewel of her own, was secured to herself most stringently.

He was a quiet man, of studious and retired habits, with a strong religious bias; and much society marvelled that he, of all men, had been caught by one whom more worldly men were content to dance, ride, boat, flirt, bet with, but did not care to marry.

The recluse life he had led was in her favour. There were no kind friends to enlighten him on the Welsh mountain where they met, and they were engaged and married before society awakened from its dream of astonishment.

And then his dream of astonishment began—a long, terrible nightmare, the culminating horror of which was a dark pool in a dense wood.

The earl was gentle as a woman; the countess bold, horsey, profane; in defiance of her lord filled the castle with strange guests, who drank and smoked in the drawing-rooms, played cards and dice through the night, and made the proud home of his ancestors a hot-bed of riot and sin.

Not all at once be it said; an oath hurled at a loitering postillion during the bridal tour was his first rude awakening. His next painful surprise was Lady Matilda's disregard of the Sabbath and all religious ordinances. Then followed his knowledge of her gambling and drinking propensities to fill his pious soul with horror, all the greater that her imperious will overrode his, and held him down as if with a spell.

Once, before his voice was utterly silenced in the household, he roused to the level of his own worth and duty. But then she had not reached the crowning-point of her assumption. This was when their only son and heir, Lionel, was old enough to observe and mimic the manners and language of the new guests who came in the train of Lady Matilda from the hunting-field and racecourse, or the new Brighton Pavilion.

Convinced that Plainbury Castle was no home for an innocent child, he resolved to sacrifice his own parental yearnings, and bear him away to a purer atmosphere. Perhaps had the lady's motherly instincts been stronger, her opposition might have borne down his. As it was, she gave a tacit consent to the little Lionel's removal; but all those preparations for her son's comfort or appearance which mothers of any rank love to superintend, she left to the forethought and affection of others. And much to the disgust of Anne Wilton, his nurse, when at mid-day the travelling chariot stood at the Norman entrance, and the old servants ranged in the ancient hall shed tears at losing their young master, as if heaven's purity went out with him, the boy had to be led to his lady-mother's bedside to say farewell, and to bear thence as strong an impression of her concern lest he should spill on the silken coverlet the chocolate she was sipping, as of the hasty parting kiss, in which irritability strove with lazy languor.

A college friend of Earl Plainbury's, the Rev. Lucas Woodward, held a living in one of the loveliest dales in Derbyshire.

He was a man worthy of his high calling, and was as worthily mated. The good pair, full of pity for a babe so much worse than motherless, consented to receive the young viscount to rear and educate with their own children.

Lionel was a fair-haired, dark-eyed boy, with his father's sensitive tenderness and his mother's strong will. He had a broad open forehead, and there was a dimple in his chin, but there was a resolute set in his childish lip when, in his seventh year, he and his nurse Wilton took up their abode at the picturesque parsonage, and the little lord became one of the good clergyman's family.

These characteristics had only deepened when to the well-developed, well-trained youth of fifteen, still sharing the studies of the rector's sons, came the sad intelligence of his loving and estimable father's death. It was Lionel's first great sorrow, and he bowed beneath it. Not even the caresses of little Mabel Woodward, the sunbeam and darling of the household, could rouse him from his grief.

She came and stood by his side as he sat with his head buried in his arms on a table in the rector's study, and as heavy sobs broke from him all the sympathy of her nature was roused. She was an affectionate, auburn-haired maiden of twelve, with brown, loving eyes. They were fall of sorrow for him who had been to her as a brother. Long she watched him in silence, then her soft arm stole round his neck, crushing unreproved his carefully-plaited cambric frill, and she whispered in his ear such consolation as her pitiful child-heart prompted. "Don't cry so, Lionel dear; you can stay here always now, and my papa and mamma can be your papa and mamma too; and I would like you for a brother better than Fred or Lucas. Don't fret so, Lionel dear, you make me cry too."

But his tears only fell the faster. He was old enough to know that the mother he had visited once a year was a very different being from the mamma of whom the Woodwards were so proud; and though he knew he was now Earl of Plainbury, what was the new honour to him, so dearly purchased? What cared he for dignity or title if the kind, sorrowful face he was wont to see every month would never smile upon him again; if the gentle voice, so eloquent in the cause of virtue and religion, should never more respond to his welcome, or bestow advice or blessing upon him again.

The Rev. Lucas Woodward had been summoned to the funeral as well as his young charge, and it was after the solemn obsequies, and prior to the reading of the late earl's will, that I, Thomas Skinner, of the Cathedral Close, Plainbury, made my first bow to the new earl in my official position as lawyer to her ladyship.

Why she had selected me I know not. Possibly because I had the chief practice of Plainbury. Still, I think she would have sought her business-man farther afield had she known how much I sympathized with her disappointed husband, and that I held it as a sacred duty to the dead, in the execution of her orders, to stand between her and any injustice her lawless inclinations might prompt.

No effort of memory is needed to recall a single incident of that day, or the library in which the will was read. Black cloth hid books and shelves, and draped the oriel window; the large oak table was dark almost as its sable cover; busts and statues were veiled and shrouded; the huge fireplace (from over which the painted semblance of the dead man was conspicuous in its black frame) seemed to lack a fire, though it was June; the mourning garments of the assembly gave a pallor to their faces, and added to the funereal aspect of the solemn scene. The countess herself, robed in a scant, short-waisted dress, so loaded with crape that the ostensible silk was a mere suggestion, sat (with little delicacy) in the late earl's chair by the table, her still magnificent black hair banded under the hideous cap, then the badge of widowhood.

Lionel, the young earl, with a face white as the broad -hemmed frill round his throat, was seated on the opposite side of the table, one hand holding fast that of his reverend protector. I myself, with sundry papers before me, occupied the side of the table between mother and son, and we thus confronted alike the noble friends of the deceased, seated in a broken semicircle, and the upper servants standing by order of the countess in two sombre and sorrowful groups on each side the door.

Mr. John Stiff, of Lincoln's Inn, being solicitor to the late earl, was, of course, present *pro forma*.

Knowing as I did that the will in my hand, which left the countess sole administratrix and executrix, and sole guardian of her son in his minority, had been drawn up by me that year under the dictation of her ladyship, and signed by her lord in a spirit of resignation which I had mistaken for cowardice, I shrank from the task imposed upon me. I fumbled among my papers, wiped my spectacles, lost them, coughed, and opened the parchment so deliberately that the impatient lady gave a smart tap on the table with her fingers as a reminder. Thus admonished, I cleared my throat, and went through my unpleasant duty as frigidly as though I had not been consigning the young earl and his estates into perilous keeping.

As I read, I noted that a smile of triumph crept over Lady Matilda's countenance. It flushed a deeper red, her eye kindled its she looked on the astonished listeners and their contracted brows, and her haughty head raised to its highest. I saw, too, with pain, how the young earl shrank closer to the Bev. Mr. Woodward, their clasped hands having a more convulsive grip, and as I completed the last folio I heard audible murmurs from servants and others disappointed of legacies.

There had been two enigmatical auditors in the room, whose demeanour had somewhat puzzled me. These were Sir James Tarleton, the late earl's bosom friend, and his lawyer, Mr. John Stiff. The former held a gold snuff-box jauntily in his left hand, from which he took long pinches at every pause I made. The latter crossed his knees, leaned back in his chair, his left elbow cradled in his right hand, his chin reposing on the left, the index-finger on his cheek-bone—a placid, stolid listener.

The puzzle was at an end when the triumphant countess, rising proudly to dismiss the assembly, was politely requested by Mr. Stiff to resume her seat.

She bridled, cast upon him a withering look of inquiry, and stood confronting him with a look which, plainly as words, questioned his right to interfere.

But she absolutely paled and sank into her chair, when he produced *another will*, dated one week later than that which I had just read.

An excited murmur ran through the assembly. Mr. Stiff raised one hand to impose silence, Sir James Tarleton closed his snuff-box with a snap, returned it to his waistcoat pocket, looked steadily at me, then glanced significantly from my lady to the boy, and thence at the pale portrait over the fireplace, as if there was a sentient witness.

And thither the boy's eyes followed his, to remain fixed in sadness until recalled by a sharp exclamation from Lady Matilda, who started from her chair only to reseat herself, with teeth set and hands folded tightly as if to hold her passion in.

Mr. Stiff had read in clear, impressive tones as strange a preamble as ever opened will. The last will and testament of Frederick, Earl of

Plainbury, set forth that "having been coerced by his wife, Lady Matilda, to sign a will adverse to his own inclination, and the well-being of his dearly-loved son and heir, Lionel, he had submitted solely from motives of policy, that he might with more secrecy and security revoke that or any other former will, and do his duty alike to his son and his dependents."

Again a murmur like an electric thrill ran through the room.

The document went on to confirm Lady Plainbury's settlements, and to surrender Plainbury Castle to her sole use until her son's marriage or majority, provided always she left that son unmolested in the hands of his guardians, Sir James Tarleton and the Rev. Lucas Woodward, whom he also appointed his executors. With the exception of sundry legacies to friends and servants, all personal property whatever was secured to Lionel. Finally, the will provided that these faithful servants should be retained so long as it was their own wish and that of the executors.

As clause after clause fell distinctly on the ear, the baffled countess purpled with passion-her lips were closed, her hands clenched rigidly, her eyes blazed fiercely, she breathed alone through her panting nostrils; and when at its close the servants, who had expected instant dismissal, gave an involuntary shout, she strove to give utterance to her impotent rage, and in the effort fell forward in a fit.

For some months the good people of Plainbury had been troubled in their minds to penetrate the *incognito* of a certain mysterious Dr. Mendoza, who came—no one knew whence—and settled amongst us. He was a tall, dark, handsome, but not inviting man, whose age might be fifty—more or less. His skin was olive, his hair and piercing eyes black as midnight, his eyebrows, which almost met, grew upwards at a sharp angle, his lips had a sardonic curl, his form was lank but sinewy, and his long thin fingers terminated in long-pointed nails, like talons. He spoke broken English, interlarded with scraps of so many tongues that it was impossible to determine his own. Some said he was a Polish Jew, others an Italian, or a Spaniard, or what was then in worse odour—a Frenchman.

No matter; the Countess of Plainbury consulted him—her carriage was seen at his door, and curiosity brought him general practice. But no curiosity ever fathomed his secrets. He was close as he was skilful. He made no friendships, visited nowhere, save at the castle.

Instructed by the countess, he was present at the inquest on the drowned earl, and also at the funeral and the reading of the will.

It was he who raised the fallen woman, administered restoratives, bore her to her chamber, and remained in attendance during the fever which supervened. He introduced a dark gipsy-like woman as nurse, excluding Lionel and all others from the chamber on the plea of contagion, but not in time to prevent whispers floating through the household, concerning the fearful mutterings of Lady Plainbury in her delirium: whispers which hardly dared shape themselves into the ugly word they suggested.

On her recovery, an inventory was taken, certain cabinets and receptacles were sealed up in my presence, and the young earl was borne away by his guardians to spend a few weeks at Tarleton Court prior to his return to Derbyshire.

I cannot accredit the countess with a particle of maternal affection, yet their departure stirred her to fury, which she vented on all things animate or inanimate within her reach; and ere she sobered down, instructed me to institute proceedings to set aside the second will and obtain the custody of her son.

It was vain to argue with a woman inflamed alike by rage and brandy. I obtained the opinion of counsel. She refused to be guided, and threatened to employ another solicitor unless I proceeded at once.

I shrugged my shoulders, and let the mad woman have her way. Of course she lost.

Years passed, those years in which the castle was virtually without a master, and the Plainbury estate, through those unfortunate settlement deeds, was, in a measure, under the control of the countess.

The consequences soon became apparent. Neglect and misrule set their destructive claws on everything. Two or three of the old servants endeavoured to maintain order indoors and out "for the credit of the family" and for the sake of the young earl; but setting at naught superiors whom the countess barely tolerated, their underlings were seldom amenable to order. Oppression followed extravagance, and labourers and tenants grew alike discontented.

The executors and Mr. Stiff did what they could to keep matters straight; but they were distant powers, and Lady Matilda was a present and very evil one. Her widowhood seemed but an excuse for fresh licence. Blacklegs and courtesans were her only guests; stay—Doctor Mendoza came and went at will, and had rooms in the castle itself.

The young earl I saw at intervals. He visited his mother from time to time, and on these occasions generally strolled into my office, either for a chat, for information respecting tenants, or in hopes to correct current gossip. At first Sir James or Mr. Woodward bore him company; but as he neared manhood these visits became more frequent, and were often made alone. His school and college vacations were spent alternately at Tarleton Court and Darley-Dale Rectory, in society very different from that which polluted his natural home.

He was a fine-grown specimen of England's young nobility, with well-developed whiskers, light wavy hair, and a downy moustache above his firm lip; he had a feminine chin and quick dark eyes, which lit with fire or softened with shadows like a clear lake beneath a sunset sky, as indignation or pity moved him.

They were sad enough when he stepped into my well-warmed office in the quiet close, one March morning, when he was about twenty. Throwing aside his fur-collared cloak as he sat down, I saw that his left arm was in a sling, and his hand wrapped in a white kerchief, on which a spot of blood was visible.

"Has any accident befallen your lordship?" I asked hurriedly.

"No, Mr. Skinner, I thank you; not an accident by any means—a wanton injury!"

I echoed his words with. amazement.

"Yes. It is, however, less serious than it might have been, but for timely attention." He saw I looked curious, and proceeded. "I arrived at the castle last night unexpectedly, and unattended, save by my valet and groom. I regret I cannot say to my surprise, but certainly to my sorrow, I found the house lit up as if for a carnival. Some time elapsed before I obtained admission. The man who opened the door was a stranger, and far from sober, and soon I found that his fellows were in little better condition. They had helped themselves freely to the wine and dessert, of which the remains yet strewed the table and floor of the dining-room."

"Shameful!" I ejaculated, not knowing what else to say—the case was, as I well knew, so common.

"You may well say so, Mr. Skinner; it *was* shameful. But I wish I had seen nothing worse," said the young nobleman sadly. "On inquiring for Ghrimes, I was told that the old butler had been dead and buried a fortnight. The housekeeper, I ascertained, was in her room. I found Mrs. Trowbridge sitting by her fire crying bitterly. She threw up her hands in lamentation:'Ah, my dear young master, what a house is this for you to come home to!' and then assured me her authority over the domestics was at an end, and whispered that she had retired to her room like a fox run to earth, for safety, lest interference should place her by the side of Ghrimes. I was too much annoyed at the time to take in the full import of her words; but, Mr. Skinner"—he looked full at me—"of what did Robert Ghrimes die?"

The question took me unawares. It was an awkward question to answer, under all circumstances. The butler's death, though not sudden, had been, to say the least, mysterious.

"Well, it was generally considered he had taken something that disagreed with him."

"Disagreed with him?"

I think his lordship saw the *equivoque*; he literally looked me through.

"Why was I not informed? A faithful servant is not to pass to the grave unheeded."

"No instructions," was my excuse; but I saw that did not satisfy him, and not caring still further to disturb his peace with my own vague suspicions of foul play, I recalled attention to his own hand.

"Ah, to be sure!" he ejaculated, roused from a fit of perplexed musing. "That was done in my own mother's drawing-room," and he heaved a deep sigh. "I found her surrounded by eighteen or twenty people she had entertained at dinner. And such people, good heavens! I know that scant feminine robes are not yet banished from aristocratic circles; but there I what paucity of bodice, paucity of sleeve, paucity of skirt, and airiness of material! I felt as if so many nude statues would have been more delicate. True, one or two of these *ladies* had gauzy-looking scarves floating over their bare shoulders, but the majority seemed to think paint and patches ample covering for their charms. I had just left a pure, modest girl and a chaste matron in the peaceful sanctuary of their tasteful home, and the contrast struck me painfully."

"Miss and Mrs. Woodward," thought I to myself, though I merely bent my head to show I was listening.

"Of the men, some wore scarlet coats, buckskins, top-boots, and spurs, just as they had come from the hunting-field, in marked contrast to the pumps, pantaloons, dress coats, frilled shirts, and white cravats of others. The room was well lighted with lamps, and candelabra, and dotted with tables of all sizes, devoted to sets or couples of card players. At one of these sat Lady Matilda" (he did not say "my mother") "in a purple velvet dress, with a pile of guineas, and, I blush to say it, a glass of brandy-and-water close beside her. All the players were drinking, and the fumes of spirits struck my nostrils not less painfully than the rattling of dice and the jargon of quarrelsome gamesters did my ears. It was not a scene, sir, for a nobleman's mansion, and I no doubt expressed my indignation in strong terms."

"And no wonder, my lord," said I, though I added no word to expose the orgies in which those gambling dinner parties were wont to terminate. I should have done no good, and only added to his sense of degradation.

"At my first word of protest the inebriated partner of the countess jumped to his feet with a face scarlet as his coat, and threatened with foul oaths to horsewhip me for my interference."

"And you?" I asked, bending forward.

"I called a couple of servants and ordered the expulsion of the brute."

"Quite right. And then?"

The room was in an uproar. My mother, livid with passion, and, I fear, not in a state to control her own actions, snatched her glass from the table and dashed it at me. It shivered on the hand I raised to protect my face."

I could not suppress a shudder.

"A tall dark man in a loose black robe had interposed to quell the riot. He was one of the few sober men in that disgraceful company. Though too late to prevent the injury, he did efficient service. He dismissed the company, called a dark, handsome, foreign-looking girl from the fireside, and as one having authority, put the countess under her charge; and, to my surprise, Lady Plainbury, though still quivering with excitement, submitted to be led to her chamber without a word."

"So I suppose."

The earl darted a quick glance at me, but did not interrupt his narration.

"This tall, thin individual—this man in authority—promptly produced a case of instruments, summoned Mrs. Trowbridge, extracted the broken glass from my hand, bathed and bound it; and, seeing me faint from loss of blood, administered a restorative as potent as his influence over her ladyship, and, so far, I am his debtor," said the earl, haughtily; "but"—and here he paused—"my business here today is not to lay bare our domestic sore, but to ask you, as Lady Plainbury's man of business, *who* is this Doctor Mendoza who was present at the reading of my dear father's will, who assumed the right to attend the countess in her illness, and exclude all but his own creatures, whom I find domiciled with his niece in the castle, exercising a subtle and mysterious power over every member of the household, and of whom

Mrs. Trowbridge, with many dark hints, bade me beware lest I should share the fate of my lamented father and poor Ghrimes? Who is this man, and what can be the nature of his influence on our hearth?"

"I am as ignorant as your lordship," was my answer.

Whatever were my own private theories respecting the doctor, I did not think it wise to foster in Lord Lionel's mind suspicions which I felt it would be impossible to verify, and the incautious airing of which might lead to disastrous results.

I therefore made light of the old housekeeper's fears and warnings. Lord Lionel's death would only serve to dispossess the doctor's patroness and induct a stranger, so I assured him his life was in no manner of danger from malpractices. Of his *heart* I was not quite so sure.

He smiled and said "*that* was in safe keeping," shook hands with me, and departed.

That was on the Tuesday.

On the Friday I saw him again.

"I came out for a drive," said he, "to shake off the fascination of a pair of black eyes, which seem to follow my movements and haunt me everywhere."

"Ah, ah, my lord, your heart is not so secure as you thought," was my light rejoinder; "but is it fair to ask who owns the bewitching black eyes?"

"No fear for my heart, Mr. Skinner," he replied; "neither black eyes nor blue can bewitch me. Still, I must own the doctor's niece Mizpah has a pair of orbs which dazzle me. I feel almost spell-bound within their range."

"Much, I should think, as a mouse under the eye of a cat, or a bird for which a snake has opened its jaws," suggested I, drily, as a sort of hint

"Possibly," assented he, and I thought I was understood.

That afternoon's post bore a private letter to Mr. Stiff and another to Sir James Tarleton, with an intimation that the atmosphere of Plainbury Castle was not good for Plainbury's Earl.

Posts were slow things in those non-railway days, and I had reason to congratulate myself on my prevision and forethought, when on the following Monday Mrs. Trowbridge's grandson (a deep little fellow that), watching his opportunity to find me alone, handed me an incoherent note from the good housekeeper. It ran thus:

"For God's sake, Mr. Skinner, get our young lord out of this wicked house. They are drugging him or something to make him stupid, and marry that awful doctor's awful niece. I just feel as if the doctor was a devil and she was a witch. As for my lady, she is just under the doctor's finger and thumb. I think *you* can guess *why*. Do save Lord Lionel. He is too good to be the prey of these wretches."

Chapter 2

A pretext was never wanting for a visit to the castle, and ceremony had been buried with the late earl.

I found Lord Lionel, the present earl, lying on a sofa, languid, listless, heavy, with the black-eyed Mizpah by his side singing seductive songs, and showing off a graceful figure as she accompanied herself on a guitar. Her dress was foreign, picturesque, and sufficiently modest to meet his fastidious taste. Neither the countess nor any of her guests were present.

I saw the danger of the situation, and broke in upon it.

"My lord, can I trouble you to step with me to Farmer Wilton's? The old man is in some difficulty respecting his daughter, your sometime nurse, and is anxious—if you will so far condescend—to see you."

This was partly a fiction, but the ruse was successful. In the fresh air, out of sight of those intense eyes, out of reach of doctor or mother, his frame and mind recovered its elasticity. His hand was still in the sling; but I did not share his belief that loss of blood had made him languid and inert.

Again he observed to me the strange influence Mizpah's eyes possessed over him, and plainly said he thought Dr. Mendoza and his mother had laid their heads together to entrap him into a marriage with the girl. She was by no means the sort of woman he should love; but, somehow, when with her he was not himself; and no sooner did her eyes rest upon him than he felt as though he were her slave. And yet—and yet, his heart was far away.

"In Derbyshire?" I presumed.

"In Derbyshire," he assented, and the subject dropped.

The first dinner-bell rang before we returned to the castle. The countess graciously invited me to remain. Before the second course was served, a post-chaise and pair drove Sir James Tarleton to the front entrance, and I knew the young earl was safe.

Sir James tapped his snuff-box significantly, but no stray glance betrayed any intervention of mine. He, however, professed to be in hot haste, declined refreshments, and in less than an hour bore his ward away.

Six weeks later Lord Lionel was hastily summoned to the sick-bed of his mother. The Augean Stable was cleansed. Doubtful women and more doubtful men were gone. The castle was quiet; servants went about their business in an orderly manner, and the young fellow remarked to Mrs. Trowbridge that the change was most satisfactory.

Five days elapsed before he saw me, and then he seemed perplexed with doubt. I had gone to the castle to inquire after the health of the countess.

Halfway down the beech avenue, on my way home, I met the earl; he turned and strolled with me as far as the gate. The air was laden with the perfume of hawthorn and lilac, freshened by a light breeze which had sprung up after a slight shower.

I noticed that he drew his hand across his forehead more than once, as if he would throw off some oppressive feeling.

"Has your lordship experienced any return of the languor which attended your last visit to Plainbury?" I asked carelessly.

He smiled.

"You are as great a necromancer as the grim man who hovers round my mother's bedside, and occupies the suite of rooms adjoining; the very apartments"—and I saw his hands clench nervously—"of my honoured father. Yes," he added, after a brief pause, "I came out into the fresh air to see if I could throw off the inertia which is fast creeping over me again."

"Has the glamour of Miss Mendoza's presence aught to do with it?" and I cast a sidelong glance at him as I spoke.

He crimsoned to the very brow.

"I fear so. And yet, sir, I am not in love with the girl, and would avoid her were it practicable. But we seem perpetually thrown together. Her large dark eyes look into mine, or follow me with the pathetic devotion of a dog's. I am called upon for little acts of courtesy which bring us into continual contact. Her thanks are spoken in low and seductive tones, and I somehow seem to lack strength to resist her blandishments. I am half mad with myself at my own weakness. In her presence I seem as if under the influence of some intoxication."

I know I looked grave. I took of my spectacles, and wiped them fidgetily.

"My lord," said I, respectfully, "I am a man of mature age, in whom your lamented father placed confidence. I thank you for yours. It removes from my tongue the embargo of disparity in position, and leaves me free to caution and advise. Be on your guard. Miss Mendoza plays for a coronet, and is a most consummate actress."

"I feel assured of it," was his response. "Nay, more, the countess is lavish in her praise; and her malady, whatever it may be, is evidently heightened by the morbid desire that I should make this Mizpah my wife."

"And you?"

"Mr. Skinner, I am already engaged to one whose artless purity forbids a thought of Miss Mendoza."

"I am glad to hear it, my lord. Has the countess been informed of your engagement?"

"She has not. I feared to irritate her, having Dr. Mendoza's assurance that any excitement might prove fatal."

"H'm!"

We had reached the extremity of the avenue. The lodge-keeper opened the gate to let us pass. I kept silent until we were beyond earshot.

"May I ask the nature of her ladyship's illness?"

"Indeed, sir, I am not sufficiently informed to tell you. I hear of inflammatory action, of heart and nerves and brain in a critical state, yet not all the perfumed flowers and pastiles in her chamber can overpower the smell of brandy, and Mrs. Trowbridge assures me her dietary is not that of an invalid."

"Yet she is dangerously ill?"

"So I am given to understand." But his tones were not those of conviction.

"Are you satisfied with Dr. Mendoza's treatment?"

There was a sharp contraction of brow as he gave involuntary expression to a secret thought.

"As much satisfied as if his Satanic majesty were in his place!"

"I am not sure but he would be as safe an inmate," was my significant addendum, which called forth one of those rapid searching glances which showed him on the alert. "Perhaps, my lord, you would like to have the additional opinion of Dr. Overton? He is a reliable authority."

"Thanks for the suggestion. I will walk with you into the city and see him myself."

I observed that as we walked on his step and bearing regained its firmness and elasticity, his voice became stronger, his eyes less heavy. He confessed himself invigorated by the exercise.

Remembering Mrs. Trowbridge's troubled note, without a seeming purpose I elicited from him that Dr. Mendoza and his daughter had a kindred passion for rare perfumes—that his sleeping-room was odorous with flowers of Miss Mendoza's selection; that the coffee she poured out at breakfast was delicious, and singularly exhilarating; that the cup she insisted on handing to him after dinner, though equally pleasant, had quite another effect: he grew dreamy, melancholy, and sentimental. I advised him to breakfast in his own room, on any plea he liked, to decline coffee after dinner, and to drink no wine the doctor or his niece did not patronise.

"This is a terrible implication, Mr. Skinner," said he.

"No matter; caution can do no harm. Dr. Mendoza is not to be trusted. By-the-by, is Sir James Tarleton aware of your presence here, my lord?" I asked, as we were parting at Dr. Overton's gate.

"I should think so. I wrote to him the day following my hasty arrival; though, strange to say, I have not yet had an answer."

"Indeed. I suppose your lordship's letters go in the general bag from the castle?"

"Certainly. How else?"

"Well—a—you see lawyers are instinctively cautious," I said adding, drily, "I think Mrs. Trowbridge could find you a much surer conveyance."

He took the hint. Jim, Mrs. Trowbridge's grandson (a lad seemingly hanging at her heels for the sake of stale pastry and confections), became his courier and mine. But letters to Sir James and to the Rev. L. Woodward were on their way before the Earl of Plainbury and Dr. Overton stepped out of the latter's gig at the great door of the castle.

Dr. Overton confirmed my suspicions: Lady Plainbury was simulating illness. No woman who drank brandy as she did could be in perfect health; but all beyond this was feigned, for some occult purpose. And he held that Dr. Mendoza was in the plot. Nevertheless he put on an air of grave profundity, and expressed his perfect faith in Dr. Mendoza's skill—whilst within Dr. Mendoza's hearing. But as the latter, with his long-flying foreign black robes and sardonic face, hovered about the English practitioner from the time he entered the patient's room until he closed the carriage door upon him with his own lank long-nailed hand (looking, for all the world, like an evil spirit or a big black bird of ill omen), no chance of private word or sign to the anxious young earl could he get.

He paid two more visits to be similarly baffled.

I met him after the last on one of our many bridges, and being; old friends, he confided his doubts to me.

Meanwhile, Mrs. Trowbridge, in obedience to my secret instructions, removed Miss Mendoza's too odorous flowers from the earl's chamber and dressing-room; prepared his breakfast and carried it to him with her own hands, and saw that no food was tampered with on its way to the dining-room. Her love for her young master made her vigilant, regardless of self.

For a day or two the earl was on his guard, but, unfortunately Dr. Overton's timidity lulled his vigilance to sleep. Then, as I afterwards learned, some misunderstanding had grown up between, himself and his distant betrothed, widening almost to a breach; and laying him dangerously open to the seeming devotion of an accomplished beauty close at hand. His mother, too, who apparently lingered in an alarming state, artful as when she spread her lures for his unsuspicious father, cajoled him with professions of penitence and piety, with sad regrets for a wasted life, interlarding all with sly insinuations that Mizpah had been her good angel, and the blessing she would be to a husband she loved, and so on; not failing to wind up with the self-depreciatory remark: "If I had been a better mother, Lionel, no doubt you would have trusted my choice of a wife for you; as it is—ah, well, dear, I fear I must die without that satisfaction. Yet, Mizpah adores you, I know."

There was a constant harping on the same string in that shadowy perfumed chamber where a seemingly dying mother lay, and his filial instincts were strong as his duty. There were music, and perfume, and the witchery of thrilling eyes and love-subdued tones in the drawing-room; and the earl was impressionable. There was an irritating something in the letter-bag every morning, and he had a spice of his mother's spirit. And then everywhere and over all was the subtle doctor—whether as a pervading influence or a palpable presence, with his winged black robes, keen eyes, his slant brows, incomprehensible smile, and few but well-weighed words.

Many a man has married a woman for whom he cared little, piqued by a slight from one for whom he cared much; and there is no knowing how far these combined influences might have worked upon the earl to conquer his resistance, had I not met Dr. Overton on the bridge when I did.

I took my way to the castle, ostensibly anxious about the countess. Jim, my swift-footed messenger, had preceded me. Instead of going round by the carriage road, I took a short cut through the woods.

310

To my surprise I found that the woodman'a axe had been busy here, many fine trees had been felled, and the number marked for destruction was incredible.

"H'm!" said I to myself. "What does this mean? A gambling debt? This must be put a stop to, my lady."

The pool where the late earl's body had been found lay on one side of the path, and strangely enough, without any appointment beyond notification of my intended route, the earl and I met on its brink. On all other sides the reedy pool was shut in by copse-wood, pendant willows, and larger trees, whose overreaching branches cast their green shadows on it even at noon.

His lordship was standing in deep thought, gazing into the depths of the sullen water, as if to penetrate its unfathomable secrets. He wore a bottle-green coat, and as the path wound, I did not see him until close upon him.

"A fearful place this to be brought to by a friend at midday," was his salutation to me.

"A still more fearful to be brought to by an enemy at midnight," was the retort I would fain have unspoken soon as said, he was so swift to take my hidden meaning.

"Mr. Skinner, you speak in parables. You seem to bold the clue to a terrible secret," said he, in much agitation.

"My lord," I answered, with a solemnity which attested my truth, "I hold no clue. I hold theories, suspicions, which some day will be at your service—not now."

He was urgent; I was firm. I had another purpose before me now. It required some little tact to break to him Dr. Overton's conviction that his own mother was partner in a nefarious plot, and was no more in a dying state than he or I, and still more to induce him to wait quiescent the arrival of his legal guardians. At first he was incredulous. "Absence of adequate motive," was his objection. "Why should a lady of high birth plot to wed him to an adventuress?"

"It is not always easy to trace the secret springs of action, but here is duplex thought. By your marriage with Miss Mendoza, the countess hopes to retain power, influence, and income *here*, which she would surely lose by your marriage with any other lady."

"I see," said he, with contracted brow.

"Then," and I paused, "the scheme is Dr. Mendoza's, and the countess acts under pressure."

"Pressure! What pressure?" and two fiery sparks seemed kindled in his eyes.

"Ah, my lord, that is part of the mystery which has hung over Plainbury Castle so long."

I had given him food for thought. If he looked miserable as he stood over the pool, he looked still more wretched as we emerged from the wood, and took separate paths to the castle, and I was at a loss to account for his very haggard countenance. I was not then aware of his estrangement from Miss Woodward.

As I passed the Crown Hotel on my way home I saw an elderly clergyman and a young lady alight from the northern stage coach. She wore a gipsy hat, trimmed with pale blue, a soft grey dress and blue velvet spencer, and I thought she had the sweetest face I ever beheld.

In the clergyman I recognised the rector of Darley-Dale; and before I could approach to make myself known. Sir James Tarleton came down the steps of the hotel, raised his hat with graceful courtesy, took her little hand in his, and said: "Miss Woodward, I salute you."

I stepped forward and was introduced. We entered the hotel together. After a little light chat a chambermaid conducted Miss Woodward to her room, and we three sat in solemn conclave, previously despatching Boots with a summons to the earl. We compared notes. I related all that I knew, with a running commentary; and they related that which I did not know.

It appeared that the earl had been engaged to Miss Woodward with the full consent of both guardians more than a year, and were on the point of marriage when he was called so hurriedly to a "dying mother."

Of course, he left abruptly, promising with all a lover's ardour to write daily, and exacting the same promise from Mabel. She wrote and he wrote, their letters of course crossing on the road. But his were so strange, and grew so cold, and then so flippant, every post brought only torture to the troubled girl. Then came an anonymous letter from a "well-wisher," whom she took to be Anne Wilton, telling her that Lord Lionel was making fierce love to a beautiful lady staying in the castle, and was likely to marry her; and was not worthy of Miss Woodward's affection.

But for the change in his own epistles this had been innocuous.

It was shortly followed by my communication, and the next post bore a confused incoherent epistle from the earl, accusing his true little love of inconstancy, perfidy, and no one knows what.

I had suggested possible tampering with letters, and this missive of his (the first posted by Jim) almost confirmed the suspicion.

They heard also from Sir James Tarleton, and at his wish Mr. Woodward, with his daughter, had joined him here to bring matters to a crisis.

We were at dinner when Lord Plainbury was announced.

We rose.

"Mabel!"

"Lionel!"

There was an impulsive rush towards each other, a pause, a stop midway—the meeting was painfully embarrassing to both.

We old people, however, soon cleared away the mist, and dismissing them to an inner room to feast on love and kisses, resumed our dinner and laid out our plans.

At five o'clock I took Miss Mabel under my wing to show her our ancient city, whilst the three others whirled away to Plainbury Castle in Sir James's barouche, taking up Dr. Overton on their way, and avoiding the main entrance both to park and castle.

Lodge-keepers and porters opened their eyes wide as the gates and doors; but they alighted, and allowing no time for signals, hastened to the "sick chamber" swiftly but silently.

The earl was not expected home until nightfall. It was his habit to knock. Now he turned the handle and threw open the door.

My lady, jolly and comfortable, sat in a loose *negligé*, with wine and cards before her, at a small table. Dr. Mendoza was her partner. Her face was flushed and merry. She was winning. A laugh and an oath were arrested on her lips by the sudden opening of the door. Picture her consternation!

Miss Mendoza looked up from her tambour frame by the window, and a cloud, as of night, settled on her brow.

Even Dr. Mendoza was, for the nonce, disconcerted.

The interview was brief, stormy, but decisive.

Sir James, stepping forward, said, with a low bow of mock courtesy:

"Permit me to congratulate your ladyship on your speedy recovery."

She started to her feet in a fury, grasped a decanter by the neck, and would have hurled it at the baronet, but Dr. Mendoza clutched her wrist with one of his claws, and forcing it from her held her in her seat with a whispered "Be calm; you vill ruins all!"

But calm she was not; and her rage found vent in language not to be repeated. Dr. Mendoza simply watched, and glowered on the intruders.

At the first lull, the earl, with a face white with agony and shame (for the mother lost to shame), and a voice tremulous with agitation, said, with deliberation:

"Madam, you are anxious that I should marry. I am perfectly willing. My guardians are also agreeable."

Miss Mendoza flushed. The countess looked as if she felt she had been too precipitate.

He continued, and not a syllable was lost:

"This is Saturday. On Monday I propose to marry Miss Mabel Woodward, a young lady whose modest worth I know, and whose love I can trust. You can hand these forgeries to your *protégée*, at leisure;" and he laid a packet of letters on the table.

Again Sir James spoke.

"With our ward's marriage your ladyship's dominion here ceases. He will wish to bring his bride home immediately. You will therefore retire to your dower house."

Her ladyship's eyes blazed with ferocity.

"Retire! Make way for that parson's brat! By—— I will not, if a legion of devils come to drive me forth!"

But it is not pleasant to follow her ravings or her threats. It was not pleasant to look on the dark mocking faces at her elbows.

The next morning being Sunday, Miss Woodward and her father attended the cathedral service, sitting with the earl.

From my seat I saw them enter, her gipsy hat and muslin dress bringing a sense of freshness and purity with them long unknown to the Plainbury pew.

"From battle, and murder, and sudden death—"

The verger whispered me—

"Wanted, sir, outside."

A groom was in waiting with a led horse. He touched his cap.

"My lady wants you, sir, immediate."

I was ushered without ceremony into her ladyship's chamber, where I found her in bed, playing *ecarte* with Dr. Mendoza.

I had a thorough repugnance to this man, who always seemed to me like some foul bird of prey, and felt a shudder as I saw his claws on the cards and the counterpane.

Though it was barely noon, the countess was inflamed with wine. He was as ever—sober, wary, and watchful.

It was some time before I could ascertain wherefore I had been called; and on the Sabbath too. Her ladyship wished me to draught out her will; but between brandy and cards (in which she wanted me to join) hours elapsed before her instructions were complete. Dr.. Mendoza, to my annoyance, sat with his eyes on her face as she dictated. She gave and devised all moneys of which she might die possessed to her dear friend Dr. Mendoza, all landed property or buildings not entailed to him, with reversion to his niece, to whom she also bequeathed her private jewels, plate, &c. I was to have the will ready for signature on the morrow.

The sun was setting as I shook hands with Mrs. Trowbridge at the hall door. Dusk was gathering as I passed the lodge gates at the end of the long avenue, deepening with every step I took. Shadowed by umbrageous trees, I went on absorbed in thought. As I turned a corner beyond the limits of the park, rapid hoof beats caused me to look up.

The sky was red, angrily red.

"The castle is on fire!"

It was Lord Plainbury who called to me through the gloom below, as he and Sir James rushed past at a gallop.

I hastened back, followed by eager crowds from the city, to render what aid I could; but the flames, which had broken out in the chamber of the countess, held their own, and rendered little back but blackened stone and charred timber.

Pictures and other valuables had been rescued; but the countess and Dr. Mendoza were both missing. One of the servants had seen him flying as with expanded wings along a burning corridor with a burden in his arms; and hence a rumour spread that he was the Evil One, to whom Lady Plainbury had sold her soul, and that he had carried her off at last. Miss Mendoza disappeared mysteriously the following day, and then, not unnaturally, she was set down by the vulgar as a witch.

How had the fire originated? The countess was still in bed when I left, half stupid with brandy. A servant who had borne candles to the room swore to a violent altercation between Mendoza and his lady, followed by a scream, only disregarded because so common. Had draperies or counterpane been set alight by accident, or had the man murdered her and set fire to the bed to hide his crime? The will I had draughted made that doubtful. In any case the bed was utterly consumed, and not even a charred cinder remained of the wicked beauty.

But there had been a depredator at work—half-consumed cabinets, locked and sealed, had been forced open: were empty, of course.

And before news of the fire reached London, a tall, dark man, presented a cheque for many thousand pounds at her ladyship's bankers. Her gambling proclivities being known, it was cashed at once. The cheque was a forgery. The man gone.

Then I laid my theories before Sir James and the young earl, to remove the reproach of suicide from his father's memory. I maintained that after the signature of the late earl's first will, the countess and Mendoza had compassed his death to get possession and control; that the villain had stupefied him with narcotics, in that state plunged him in the pool, and so inquiry was baffled; that he held some inculpatory agreement *in terrorem* over her; and that Ghrimes had overheard something which made *his* removal necessary to their safety.

Still, these were but theories, and they did not prevent the restoration of the castle, or a very happy bridal there in the autumn. But the Plainbury Mystery remains a mystery to this day.

The Shadow on the Blind and Other Stories

Mrs Alfred Baldwin

Contents

The Shadow on the Blind   321

The Weird of the Walfords   340

The Uncanny Bairn   356

Many Waters Cannot Quench Love   372

How He Left the Hotel   380

The Real and the Counterfeit   385

My Next Door Neighbour   400

The Empty Picture Frame   415

Sir Nigel Otterburne's Case   428

The Ticking of the Clock   442

The Shadow on the Blind

Harbledon Hall had stood empty for seven years. For seven years no smoke had issued from its chimneys telling of the cheerful hearth within, no voice or laughter had been heard under its roof, no footstep coming or going across its threshold. A straggling growth of ivy and Virginia creeper, that covered the walls and veiled the windows, made the front of the house look forlorn and neglected, as the face of a sick man who has grown a ragged beard during a long illness. The window-sills were green with the drip of rain from the spouts choked with decaying leaves, and the brickwork was stained with dark patches of damp. The birds had built their nests undisturbed in every gable and projection of the roof, and in the wide chimneys, secure from danger of being smoked out of their comfortable quarters.

And within the house, though man had withdrawn his presence from it, other tenants were in possession. Rats and mice held revels in the empty rooms and passages, that resounded with the patter of their feet, the squeak of their voices, and the nibbling of their teeth. In the dead of night, bold as they had grown, they scared themselves by catching in wires that set bells ringing and echoing through the house, and an army of rats would rush helter-skelter down the great staircase, bounding over one another's backs in their panic, as we see them depicted in illustrations of the famous history of Dick Whittington and his cat.

If desolation reigned in Harbledon Hall, its gardens were returning to a state of savage nature, and the rank growth of weeds choked and overtopped the flowers and shrubs. No seeds had been sown, no lawns mown, no hedges clipped or tree or bush pruned, in seven long years, and the once orderly gardens had become a tangled thicket, where the fairy prince might seek the sleeping beauty. A bramble had sprung up by the sundial, and, clasping it in its thorny arms, threw its branches about it, effectually hiding it from the light of day. The stone basin of the disused fountain had become a nursery of young frogs, that hopped, swam, and croaked undisturbed, and nature was endeavouring to re-establish her sway where man had withdrawn his cultivating and restraining hand.

It was a radiant day in June. The hot sun poured down on the tangled overgrowth in the gardens of Harbledon Hall, the birds were in a perfect riot of song, and a south-west wind rocked them on the bough. Even the old house on such a day wore its least sombre aspect. One could imagine there had been happy household life within its walls, and it was possible to conceive that they might again resound to the laughter and voices of children at play.

Some such thought as this must have entered the mind of an elderly gentleman driving in an open carriage with his wife, a pale grey-haired lady, seated beside him. Mr Stackpoole was a cheerful, energetic man of sixty years of age, of strong likes and dislikes and sudden impulses. As he caught sight of the wide front of Harbledon Hall with its red gables glowing in the sun, its confused mass of creepers almost hiding the lower storeys from view, he told the coachman to draw up at the iron gates at the entrance.

'This is a very picturesque house, my dear; I should like to have a look at it,' he said to his wife; 'it may be the kind of place we are in search of,' and he alighted from the carriage as nimbly as a young man to read the notice painted on the weather-stained board fastened to the gates. 'For admission to view these premises, apply to Mr Judd, sexton, by the church.' Mr Stackpoole returned to the carriage and bade the coachman drive to the church, the tower of which they could see embowered among trees, apparently not more than a quarter of a mile distant. As they drove he continued, 'I like the look of the place very much. I am sure I could do something with it. I should just enjoy setting to work upon it to call order out of chaos, and in six months I would undertake to effect an entire transformation in the house and grounds, and make it one of the prettiest places in the neighbourhood. What do you think, my dear? Hey?'

The frail-looking elderly lady thus addressed made but a faint rejoinder, and her husband's sanguine enthusiasm by no means communicated itself to her. Harbledon Hall was the sixth old house Mr Stackpoole had taken a fancy to in the last ten years, and fallen out of love with as quickly, after exercising his ingenuity in putting it in perfect order and living in it for a short time. It was his diversion, now that he had retired from business and had nothing particular to do, to hunt up old country houses, put them in thorough modern repair and working order, live in them just long enough to induce his wife to hope that he had pitched his tent finally, when the demon of unrest would break out in him once more, and he was off again on the old quest.

This hunting of houses, catching them, and then letting them go, that he might pursue game of the same kind elsewhere, was naturally more entertaining to Mr Stackpoole than it could be to his wife and daughter. But the elder lady was patient and philosophic, and when her daughter said petulantly, 'Oh mamma, what a shame it is that we have to be dragged about the country like this! We have not been a year in this lovely house, and papa is tired of it already, and looking out again for some tumbledown old place to put that in good order, and leave it too, I suppose!' Mrs Stackpoole would reply, 'Never mind, Ella. Papa must do as he thinks best. The excitement and interest he finds in frequently changing house are necessary to him now that he has done with business; and remember, my dear, he has no home occupations to pass the time as you and I have.' But Ella Stackpoole was now married and settled in a home of her own, and the only other child, a son, was stationed with his regiment in Malta.

Therefore it was that when Mr Stackpoole became suddenly interested in the appearance of Harbledon Hall his wife was unable to feel any enthusiasm on the subject. Their last home had been in Cornwall, where, after six months spent in its most westerly corner, Mr Stackpoole discovered what everyone else had always known, that he was in a decidedly rainy part of England. He could scarcely have been more astonished at the quantity of rain that fell if it had been in Egypt, and he fled to London to make that his headquarters while he looked about for an old house to suit his fancy in the drier county of Surrey.

And on this bright June day he and his wife were driving through the fair country, house-hunting, and the more dilapidated a house looked, provided that his experienced eye saw capacities of improvement about it, the more attractive it appeared to Mr Stackpoole, as affording wider scope for his particular form of genius. His was a costly hobby, and strangers reaped the benefit of his lavish outlay on houses he perfected, tired of, and left so soon.

Mr Judd, the sexton, was found without difficulty, for indeed he was a conspicuous object, sitting in a large armchair by his cottage door reading the newspaper, and taking an occasional sip from a glass of cold brandy-and-water that stood beside him on the window-sill. He was a person of dignity in the village, accustomed to waste his own time and that of others, but Mr Stackpoole hurried him off to the carriage as soon as he had found the keys, and compelled him to unwonted activity. 'The garden be a wilderness, sir,' said the old man, opening one of the great iron gates, 'and it's four years since e'er an inquiry was made about the place.'

'It wouldn't be to everyone's taste, you see; it'll need a considerable outlay before it is fit for habitation,' said Mr Stackpoole complacently as he stooped to disentangle a briar from his wife's skirt. 'Who were the last tenants, and how long did they live here?' he said, turning to the old man and asking two questions at once.

'Sir Roland Shawe and his family had it last, sir. They took the place on a twenty-one years' lease, and they left uncommon sudden when it had five years and more to run. There was a deal o' talk about what made them leave i' that way,' and Judd opened wide the front door as he spoke, and they entered a large, lofty hall, smelling mouldy as though there were vaults below.

'Folks did say there was reasons more'n what they's own up to, for a large fam'ly to turn out all of a sudden, as if they was running away from the plague,' and the old sexton looked mysterious, and as though he longed to be questioned on the subject. Mr Stackpoole, however, was too much interested in pacing the length of the dining-room to notice any hints he might throw out.

'My dear,' he said to his wife, who was resting on the low window-seat, 'we will have the whole of this oak floor polished, and Turkish rugs laid down at intervals.'

'That was what we did in our house in Cumberland,' said Mrs Stackpoole gently, 'and if you remember you were not pleased with it when it was done;' then, turning to the old man: 'You were going to tell us why Sir Roland Shawe left so suddenly.'

'Forbid, ma'am, as I should say definite why he left, not knowing for certain,' said Mr Judd, swelling with importance as he spoke. 'I never believe more'n 'alf o' what I hear, and puts no faith in tales, whether master's or man's. But by what I can make out—and old Jemmy Judd can see through a stone wall as fer as most folks—I should say as ghosts was at the bottom of the whole kick-up.'

Mrs Stackpoole smiled at the old man's mode of expressing himself, and then looked anxiously towards her husband, who laughed heartily, and they left the dining-room for the upstairs regions, which he was impatient to explore.

'They fled before ghosts, did they?' said Mr Stackpoole, still laughing at the idea. 'If the house is supposed to be haunted I should like it all the better for its reputation,' and he swung open the door of a large, low room, with a deep projecting chimney-place and wide window letting in a flood of sunshine.

'This is certainly a very cheerful aspect,' said his wife, stepping to the window and looking out upon the wild garden enclosed by ragged yew hedges; 'there is nothing ghostly about this room, at all events!'

'Pooh! Ghosts indeed! Those who believe in them deserve to see them,' said Mr Stackpoole contemptuously. 'If we take the house this shall be your morning-room; you'll get plenty of sunshine, which is a great thing for you; and if I like the room under it I will have it done up for a business room for myself.' And they wandered from cellar to attic of the big house, Mr Stackpoole delighted with the possibilities of the place, and noting in his pocket-book the dimensions of the chief rooms and of the entrance hall.

'At all events I shall enquire on what terms the place is to be let,' he said, after spending two hours in energetically inspecting the premises, and as he slipped five shillings into Mr Judd's expectant palm, 'By the way, I have not asked who is the landlord?'

'The landlord, sir, be a many and not one,' and the old man named a well-known city Company to which the property belonged.

'I've rented from landlords, landladies, and trustees, but never yet from a Company: it's all one to me, and I'll see their agent in town tomorrow.' Then Mr Stackpoole took a farewell look at the room on the ground floor, immediately under the cheerful room at the head of the stairs that he had assigned to his wife's prospective use, and decided that it was exactly adapted to his requirements. After which they threaded their way back to the gates through the neglected maze of the garden.

'And how do you like the look of Harbledon Hall?' he asked his wife as they drove away; 'what do you think of the old place?'

'I confess that it does not impress me very favourably, though it is a handsome, well-built house, and might be made very comfortable, no doubt. But it struck me with a kind of chill.'

'So would any place, my dear, that had been shut up for seven years. I feel it in my back now; I wish it may not mean an attack of lumbago for me.' Mrs Stackpoole smiled at the literal interpretation of her words.

'I don't mean that kind of chill, but a sort of depressed foreboding feeling that I have never had before in any of the houses that you and I have been over together, and their name is legion.'

'Why, Anna, you don't mean to say that the old sexton has frightened you with his silly gossip! It was merely some nonsense or other he had made up to increase his importance. If I take the place I shall put in an army of workmen at once, and when next you see it, with good fires drying the rooms, windows bright and clean, and painters and paperers at work upon it, it will look very different, I can assure you. Any house that has been uninhabited as long as Harbledon Hall wears a forlorn look, but for all that I see the possibilities of it, and I could make it the prettiest place we have lived in yet.' And Mrs Stackpoole felt certain that her husband would take the old house.

The following day, when Mr Stackpoole saw the Company's agent, he was surprised at the very moderate rent asked for the house. Whether he wished to take it on lease or as a yearly tenant, the sum demanded was small enough to arouse suspicion in the most unwary.

'Why do you ask such a low rent for a fine old place like that?' he asked.

'It is so much out of repair from standing empty so long, I suppose the Company is willing to submit to a certain loss for the sake of having it inhabited again.'

'But with such a tempting low rent, how is it that it has not been taken long ago?'

'There have been any number of applications for it.'

'Indeed! The old fellow in charge of the keys who showed me over the house yesterday said that no-one had inquired about it for four years.'

A peculiar expression passed over the agent's face, but it was not one of surprise.

'He said so, did he? I've had plenty of enquiries.'

'He certainly said so. He was a talkative old man and anxious to impress us with the idea that Sir Roland Shawe left Harbledon Hall suddenly, some considerable time before his lease was up, in consequence of an absurd notion that the house was haunted. Now, personally, I care nothing about it, but my wife is sometimes nervous, and I thought I would ask you if you know anything of any unusual circumstances connected with his leaving so abruptly.'

'Judd is a chattering old fool! Did he tell you anything definite about it himself?' asked the agent.

'Nothing whatever, but he said some nonsense about ghosts driving them away from the place.'

'Of course there was an absurd story that got about at the time. It was some hocus-pocus about a magic lantern, I believe, got up by the young fellows to frighten the servants, with pictures of a skeleton on a sheet hung up somewhere or other. The whole thing was a stupid practical joke, only too successful, for the scare spread to the ladies of the house, and of course Sir Roland had to leave; they made the place too hot for him,' and the agent laughed uproariously. 'I remember all about it now that you ask me. The young Shawes got up the panic for their own purposes. They found the country too slow for them, they wanted to live in London, so with the simple apparatus of a magic lantern and a sheet they frightened the family back into town, and got what they wanted. Naturally Sir Roland used not to speak of it when he found it out, for no-one is proud of being made a fool of. And now, my dear sir,' he said, with an air of great candour, 'you know as much about this childish folly as I do myself. It has been magnified into something wonderful, till we've had that tempting property on our hands for all these years in consequence.'

Mr Stackpoole was pleased and amused with the agent's frank explanation of the basis of Mr Judd's mysterious allusions, and he and his wife laughed at it together over their dinner in the evening. Mrs Stackpoole was now willing that her husband should take Harbledon Hall, which he did as a yearly tenant, with the right of taking the property on a lease if at the end of three years he felt inclined to prolong his stay.

Then began the delightful bustle that Mr Stackpoole's soul loved —the drying, warming, painting, lighting, decorating and furnishing of the house, the taming and reclaiming of the garden; the stubbing up of old lawns and laying down of new turf; the clearing and re-gravelling of weed-grown paths. Such an army of workmen was engaged that Mr Stackpoole calculated that in less than five months the house would be ready to go into, and the gardens be looking clean and bare in their winter tidiness. 'It must be finished by the middle of December,' he said, 'that I may keep Christmas here with my family; and if every man has done his work well, and is out of the house by the twelfth of December, I will give each a bonus on his wages and a Christmas supper to you all.'

No wonder that the workmen caught something of Mr Stackpoole's enthusiasm, and that every time he brought his wife to see what was going on she was astonished with the progress made. All their friends were informed of the lucky find of the old house in Surrey, and invitations were issued long before for a series of entertainments, dances, and private theatricals they intended to give at Harbledon Hall in the following January, when their daughter, Mrs Beaumont, and her husband would be staying with her parents.

Shortly before Mr and Mrs Stackpoole removed into Harbledon Hall they were dining out one evening, and after the ladies had left the room and the gentlemen had comfortably rearranged their chairs and were seated at their wine, Mr Stackpoole began on his favourite theme, the furnishing and repairing of the old house. As most of those present had frequently heard him on the same subject before, he was not much heeded, and prosed on without interruption till a tall, bald-headed gentleman opposite to him caught the words Harbledon Hall and at once became an attentive listener.

'Harbledon Hall did you say? Do you mean the old gabled, red brick house, three miles from Mendleton? I hope no friend of yours is thinking of taking it.'

Mr Stackpoole smiled. 'Not exactly a friend of mine, though probably I know him better than anyone else. I have taken Harbledon Hall myself, and intend moving into it in December.'

'The deuce you do!' said the bald gentleman, setting down his glass. 'I don't know why it should surprise you,' said Mr Stackpoole. 'Surprise me? Certainly not. Only I thought that the house was empty and likely to remain so.'

'Surely it has stood empty long enough—seven years. It requires an immense deal doing to it, of course, but I took a fancy to the place, and am putting it into thorough repair, introducing the electric light among other modern improvements; in fact I am sparing no expense. Do you know anything about Harbledon Hall?'

'I used to do. Sir Roland Shawe, the last tenant, is my brother,' and the bald-headed gentleman spoke in a dry and uncommunicative manner. But a hint was not enough for Mr Stackpoole.

'Then you are the very person to tell me about an absurd story I have heard—it had something to do with a magic lantern, I believe, some kind of scare the young people got up to pretend there were bogies in the house, and frighten their parents back to town, where they preferred to live. You see, I've heard all about it, and I only want it corroborated by a member of the family,' and he laughed heartily, as though it were the best joke in the world. But the gentleman opposite him grew grave to severity and said, 'I am unable to understand your allusion to a magic lantern performance which is supposed to have tried my brother's nerves, and absurd is the last word applicable to the circumstances under which Sir Roland was compelled to leave Harbledon Hall.'

'Then I must have been misinformed,' replied the undaunted Mr Stackpoole, whose curiosity was now thoroughly aroused. 'As I am about to live in the house, will you not tell me the real circumstances, that I may be able to contradict the foolish stories that one hears?'

'Why should it be necessary for you to contradict gossip on the subject? Sir Roland never mentions it. It is possible that some time you may learn for yourself why my brother left the house; then I think you will be satisfied that he acted wisely, and if not, I should be sorry to prejudice you against Harbledon Hall.' And the gentlemen rose to join the ladies, and Mr Stackpoole remained in a state of mystification. Evidently something had happened to drive Sir Roland Shawe and his family from Harbledon Hall, with which neither old Judd nor the agent were acquainted. What could it be? For himself, so long as it was neither rats nor drains, he did not care, but with his wife it was different. If she had an inkling that there was anything uncanny about the house, she would refuse to go into it at the eleventh hour, or, if she went, would make a point of seeing a ghost the very first dark night.

But she must hear no silly talk about it. Any ghosts that former inhabitants of the Hall had imagined they saw was when they went about the house starting at their own shadows by the dim light of oil lamps. The electric light would put all that to rights. It was the best cure for such preposterous folly, and in its illumination Mr Stackpoole felt that he should be more than a match for all the powers of darkness.

But shortly after meeting Sir Roland Shawe's brother an odd coincidence happened that drew his attention again to the subject of their conversation. Mrs Stackpoole had written to her son at Malta telling him that his father had taken an old house in Surrey with which he had fallen in love, how beautifully he was fitting it up, that they expected to keep Christmas in it, and that it was at Harbledon Hall they hoped to welcome him on his return to England. In reply Jack wrote:

So my father is again on the wing. Well, this time I am glad he
is taking you to a thoroughly accessible place, and not to Corn-

wall or Cumberland. But is the old house he has taken a fancy to not far from Mendleton? I suppose there can't be two Harbledon Halls in the same county, but it is odd if it is the house of that name that I have lately heard something about. There was a young civilian out here for his health—he has gone to Egypt now—and he told me that his uncle, Sir Roland Smith, or some such name, had been fairly driven out of an old house in Surrey by ghosts. I'm sure he called it Harbledon Hall, and he said that his uncle was not in the least a nervous man, but it was more than he could stand, and he had to leave. I wish now that I had asked him all about it, but he was such a dull chap, nothing he said interested me, so I lost the chance of learning particulars. Don't be timid, dear mother. Let me tackle the bogies when I come home; I should enjoy nothing better.

Mrs Stackpoole did not like this at all. It produced an eerie and creepy sensation, and her husband took care not to increase her discomfort by telling her of his conversation with Mr Shawe.

'It is odd, my dear, very odd,' he said, in his most cheerful tones; 'and we are obliged to admit that, somehow or other, someone or other received some sort of a fright at Harbledon Hall. Nothing can be more vague, yet that is all that is known about it. A pity the whole silly business was not inquired into on the spot, for of course it would admit of a perfectly simple solution. Very likely one of the maids had supped rather more heavily than usual on cold pork, and in a paroxysm of indigestion walked in her sleep; someone saw her in her white nightgown, took her for a ghost, and got up a scare—for it is always easier to cry out than to investigate. And there you have the history of a ghost story in a nutshell, my dear—in a nutshell.'

The workmen were punctually out of Harbledon Hall on the day agreed upon, and as punctually received their pay and Christmas supper, and the house was ready for the reception of the new tenant, with the good wishes of all who had helped to prepare it for him. Mr Stackpoole arranged that his family should arrive after dark, that he might surprise his wife with the electric light in every room and passage, and introduce her to her new home under its most cheerful and attractive aspect.

As they approached the house both Mrs Stackpoole and her daughter exclaimed with delight, and Ella said it was too pretty to be real, it was like something on the stage. From every window, from the basement to the garrets, streamed the pure radiance of the electric light, undimmed by curtain or blind, sending shafts of light far into the surrounding darkness. From the porch the white light illumined the drive like a cold sunshine, and showed every pebble on the ground and every twig on the bare boughs.

'There, my dears,' said Mr Stackpoole triumphantly, as he led his wife and daughter into the brilliant hall; 'this is how modern science drives away foolish fears of darkness by turning night into day. No-one could be nervous or afraid of ghosts in a house like *this*.'

'No, indeed, the thing would be impossible,' replied Mrs Stackpoole, her daughter, and son-in-law in confident chorus.

Christmas was kept with much festivity at Harbledon Hall, and it was impossible to say who was most delighted with the house the host or hostess, or the guests under its hospitable roof. Each was charmed with his own room, but Mrs Stackpoole's morning-room was the general favourite, and afternoon tea was frequently taken there in preference to the more stately drawing-room. The grandchildren played in the empty rooms upstairs on rainy days, and every evening watched the miracle of lighting the house with the electric light with breathless interest. They regarded grandpapa as a light-producing wizard, so that something of awe was mingled with their wildest frolics, and they did not dare to open the door of his own particular room, which was respectfully called the study, though its principal use was to smoke in, or to take a quiet nap in before dinner.

It was the end of January, and the Stackpooles were daily congratulating themselves on their good fortune in meeting with a house so perfectly suited to their requirements, when they wound up their festivities with a fancy ball. Several young people were staying in the house for the occasion, who were to depart the day after the ball, leaving their host and hostess for the first time alone in their new home. Numbers of guests were coming from a distance, many of whom had accepted the invitation out of curiosity, as a dance afforded a good opportunity of spending a night under cheerful auspices in a house with the reputation of being haunted.

All their entertainments had so far been successful, but the last was to be the best, and Mr and Mrs Stackpoole threw their whole souls into the preparations to ensure its complete success. The room was charming, the floor perfect, the band that came from town the most renowned of the season. The costumes to be worn were of no special period or country, and the Stackpooles themselves set an example of reckless catholicity in the matter, the hostess being dressed as Queen Elizabeth, and her husband as an Admiral of the Fleet of today, while Mr and Mrs Beaumont figured respectively as a Japanese lady and Spanish matador! By the time that the guests had arrived, clad in the garb of all ages and countries, the ballroom appeared to contain such a motley throng as only the Day of Judgement could bring together. Here an ancient Greek danced with a Swedish peasant, and the Black Prince with a female captain of the Salvation Army, and there a clown and a nun waltzed gaily past Mahomet and a ballet-girl.

The electric light was a greater novelty then than it is now, and the guests were loud in their admiration of the fairy-palace appearance of the house as they approached, and of its brilliance within. Mr Stackpoole was as delighted as a child with a new toy, and led his friends about showing them how, by merely turning a button on the wall, he could plunge a room in darkness, or flood it with radiant light.

Dancing was kept up with great spirit till the small hours, and as the clock in the hall chimed a quarter-past three, the old house resounded to the half sad and wholly romantic strains of a waltz by Waldteufel. The guests who came from a distance had begun to depart, and Mr Beaumont stood in the porch laughingly seeing Lady Jane Grey and Flora Macdonald into their carriage. Just then a maid gave a message to one of the footmen for Mrs Beaumont, who sat fanning herself near the door of the ballroom. 'If you please, nurse says Master Harry won't go to sleep till he sees you, ma'am.'

'Tell nurse I will come directly,' and, excusing herself to the lady who sat next to her, she slipped out of the room. In the hall she met her father as he was entering his study.

'I'm going to put this miserable encumbrance by,' he said, smiling and flourishing the admiral's cocked hat, which he had gallantly carried the whole evening to his great inconvenience.

'And I am on my way to the nursery to see little Harry,' and Mrs Beaumont ran upstairs, singing softly to the sweet music that came floating from the ballroom below. Mr Stackpoole laid his hat on the table, and looked at the clock on the mantel-piece. 'A quarter-past three! I'm tired, and the young people ought to be. Heigh-ho! I'd rather give ten dinners than one dance,' and he sank into a low chair by the fire, yawned profoundly, stretched his legs out before him, and closed his eyes. Sleep fell upon him instantly, and for a few minutes he was lost in its depths, light and sound had ceased to exist for him, his brain was steeped in silent darkness.

Mr Beaumont still stood in the porch, the servants had returned to the house, and he was alone. It was a mild winter's night. He flung a cloak over his shoulders, and stepped into the open air. 'I shan't be missed for five minutes,' he said to himself, 'while I smoke a cigarette,' and he walked briskly along a broad path some thirty yards from the house, from which he had a perfect view of Harbledon Hall. And very pretty its cheerful brightness looked against the dark background of star-set sky. Brilliant rays of light shot from the undraped windows, and those that had the blinds drawn down showed the outline of objects in the room thrown upon them in shadow, as clearly as from a magic lantern.

Involuntarily, he raised his eyes to the window of Mrs Stackpoole's sitting-room, and stood rooted to the spot. Two figures as clearly defined as silhouettes were visible on the pure square of the blind the shadows of an old man and a young man struggling together. From the shape of the heads, George Beaumont saw that they wore wigs, and there was the clearly-cut shadow of the ruffles at the wrists, and the younger and taller man wore a large Steinkirk with laced ends round his neck. At first he thought that they were guests dressed in the costume of the early Georgian period, though how they had gone upstairs into that room, or why there was a deadly struggle between them, he did not know.

But wonder and speculation were swallowed up in terrified interest as he watched the course of the brief conflict. The elder and shorter man, who stooped considerably, appeared to be unarmed, and seized the younger man by the throat, when he shook himself free, stepped quickly back, drew his sword, and, plunging forward on his right foot, ran his opponent through the body. He staggered backward and fell out of sight below the level of the window, and there remained only the shadow of the younger man in clear profile on the blind. He stood for a minute looking down, and George Beaumont had time to observe the finely cut features of a total stranger. Then he wiped the blade of his sword, turned, and walked away, and his shadow passed out of sight, leaving the window blind a blank, luminous square.

Indoors at the same time Mr Stackpoole had been waked from his short sleep by a sound in his wife's sitting-room overhead, and he sprang to his feet with every faculty concentrated in listening. A noise as of chairs pushed back and upset on the polished floor, and a scuffling of feet as though two men were struggling together. Then a moment of silence, a loud stamp, and a heavy fall that seemed to shake the ceiling, followed by deep groans. 'Good God! What can be the matter!' cried Mr Stackpoole, and he rushed out of the room into the hall. The front door stood open, though the inner glass doors were closed, and neither his son-in-law nor any of the servants were there. He stopped to call nobody, but ran upstairs to his wife's room as his daughter came downstairs from the storey above with a white and terrified face.

'Oh, Papa, someone has just frightened me so, but whoever he is he is in there! I saw him go into Mamma's room a few minutes ago, and I'm so glad you've come, for I dare not follow him,' and without asking her of whom she was speaking, Mr Stackpoole flung the door wide open and rushed into the room. No-one was there. Not a chair or table displaced, and the electric light illuminating every corner of the room forbade the possibility of anyone being in hiding.

'It is the most extraordinary thing!' he exclaimed, wiping the moisture of terror from his brow as he spoke. 'I would not have your mother know of it for the world!'

'Have you seen him too?' said his daughter faintly.

'Seen whom, child? Seen what? No, I've seen nothing, but I've heard enough to last me my lifetime. God forbid that I should hear it again!' and he looked about the room and under the table, fairly stupe-fied with amazement.

'He passed me on the stairs just as I came out of the night nursery,' said Mrs Beaumont, anxious to tell her experience without waiting to hear her father's. 'A tall young man ran quickly by me dressed in a blue coat, with ruffles at the wrists and a great laced cravat and a wig tied with ribbon at the back. He carried a long thin sword in his hand. At first I thought it was Arthur Newton, who wore a powdered wig like his this evening, but I remembered his coat was black, and that he left early. When I saw his face it was a stranger's, and he looked cruel and passionate. I followed him till I saw him go into this room and shut the door after him.'

'Then where the devil is he now?' said Mr Stackpoole. 'This is some miserable practical joke, but I'll get to the bottom of it and be even with them yet—I'll get to the bottom of it!' and as he spoke the door that he had taken the precaution to close burst open, and his son-in-law entered in his matador's dress, pale and breathless, as if the bull had turned and given him chase. 'Oh, George, have you seen him too?' said his wife. 'Did you hear anything?' asked Mr Stackpoole. 'Sit down, man; you are trembling like a leaf.'

'There were two of them, an old man and a young man, in this room a minute ago! In God's name, who were they, and why did you not stop them before murder was done?' he said excitedly.

Mr Stackpoole grew quiet and self-collected at the sight of his son-in-law's agitation. 'Pull yourself together, George, and tell me what you mean. There is something up tonight that needs explaining.'

'But where are they? They were in this room, and if you were with them you must have witnessed what happened, or if you only came upstairs this minute, you must have met the young man leaving the room. The old man will never stir again,' and he lifted the tablecloth and looked under the table.

'How come you to speak confidently of who was in this room a few minutes ago, when you were downstairs all the while?' asked Mr Stackpoole.

'I was smoking a cigarette in the garden after seeing the Westons off, walking in the broad path, when I looked up at mamma's sitting-room window and saw the shadow of two men on the blind, shown up by the electric light as clear and sharp as in a magic lantern. I saw their profiles perfectly, but I did not know their faces. They wore wigs tied behind, and ruffles at their wrists, and the younger, taller man, as I saw by the shadow, had a laced Steinkirk round his neck. They struggled together, and the old man grasped the young man by the throat. But he tore himself free, drew his sword, and ran him through the body, then moved away, and left the blind a blank sheet of white.'

'Good God! And I heard it all in my room below, the struggle and the fall, and deep groans!' said Mr Stackpoole.

'And I met the young man—if it was anything human—he passed me on the stairs!' said his daughter, seizing her father by the arm. 'Oh, papa, Harbledon Hall *is* haunted; people were right about it! Do let us leave this dreadful place tomorrow!' And the concluding notes of the Waldteufel waltz sighed through the house as she spoke.

Mr Stackpoole shook his head. 'I don't know how that is to be done, for your mother must not be frightened. For heaven's sake try to look as if nothing had happened. We shall be missed downstairs; I'll go, and you two must manage to bid our guests goodnight decently, and not to alarm those who remain till tomorrow. We must rouse no suspicions. George, fetch Ella a glass of champagne, it will do her good.'

'Oh, don't leave me alone!' cried Mrs Beaumont like a frightened child. 'Then I'll send wine up for you both,' said her father, 'and mind, you must follow me directly.'

Mr Stackpoole rejoined his guests, who had not missed him, and had begun the last dance with as much freshness and enjoyment as though it were the first in the evening. At length all the guests had departed except those composing the house party, and the ladies retired, leaving the gentlemen to have a smoke in the billiard-room.

'You don't look very well, Beaumont,' said a young man dressed as a Tyrolean peasant, as he lit a cigar and looked up at his friend's pale face.

'It's nothing, only waltzing makes me giddy,' and he mixed himself some brandy and soda.

One by one the guests bade goodnight and left the room, till there remained only Mr Stackpoole, his son-in-law, and Mr Liston, a gentleman with very long legs, wearing tights that displayed them to advantage.

'Did your father-in-law know when he took Harbledon Hall that it was supposed to be haunted?' he said in a low voice to Mr Beaumont. Mr Stackpoole happened to hear the question and replied to it himself.

'We heard some foolish gossip on the subject, for of course no place stands empty so long without legends being invented to account for the fact. But I am not the man to listen to vulgar chatter. I took the house, and have been highly delighted with it.' And Mr Beaumont could only admire his father-in-law's admirable self-possession.

'Just so, and the electric light is the true cure for the supposed supernatural. Of course you know how suddenly Sir Roland Shawe left the place?'

'Oh yes, we've heard all about that,' said Mr Stackpoole, forcing a laugh.

'Do you know, I doubt whether you have heard *all* about it; at least if you have, you must be a cheerful sort of person if you can laugh at it,' said Mr Liston.

'Why, of course the whole thing was a foolish practical joke, something connected with a magic lantern, if I remember rightly.'

'Magic lantern! I never even heard the word mentioned. No; if you care to hear the truth about it, I think I can tell it you. I've lived in the county all my life, and I know the story of Harbledon Hall by heart. I only wonder you don't. I should not tell it you now if I thought it would make you nervous; but since you've put in the electric light, and done up the house in such cheerful modern style, the whole place is changed, and anyone might enjoy living here.'

'Let us hear the story,' said Mr Stackpoole abruptly.

'I see I've roused your curiosity. The story goes that some hundred and fifty years ago there lived in this house a certain father and son who hated one another like the devil, and it is needless to say there was a woman in the case and a fortune at stake. The old man must have been an uncommonly bad lot, and he is said to have grossly insulted the young lady his son was about to marry, having in the first instance proposed to her himself and been refused. The two men had a deadly quarrel about it in this very house, and the upshot was that the son, mad with passion, ran his father through the body, and killed him on the spot. There, I shan't say anything more about it, if it is too much for you,' said Mr Liston, struck by the blanched faces before him.

'Go on, go on,' said Mr Stackpoole.

'Well, one winter's night, now eight years ago, as Sir Roland Shawe was coming home late, walking across the garden, he looked up at a window on the first floor where a light was burning, and he saw on the blind, in clear outline, the shadows of the old man and his son struggling together, and he saw the young man run his father through the body with his rapier.'

'I cannot bear it! I cannot bear it!' said George Beaumont, pale as death, and looking ready to faint.

'You could but say that if you had seen the grim shadows yourself. It certainly is a horrid story, and though I can't say that I believe in ghosts myself, I can offer no explication of the details I have given you. Sir Roland believed it, and he was a clear-headed, matter-of-fact sort of person. Other members of his family, too, saw and heard unaccountable sights and sounds that night. One of his sons who was sitting up late for his father, met the shadow of an evil-looking fellow dressed in a blue coat and wearing a powdered tie-wig, hurrying along an upper passage, carrying a naked rapier in his hand.

'And Lady Shawe was waked by a sound in the room next to hers, which was the room where the shadows were seen on the blind—a sound of struggling and upsetting of chairs, followed by a heavy fall and deep groans. Now, if only one person had thought he had heard or seen unaccountable things, Sir Roland would have made the best of it and stayed on at Harbledon Hall; but, by Jove! when three rational beings are each an eye- or ear-witness it becomes intolerable. Whether you believe in ghosts or not, you can't put up with a thing like that!'

'By Heaven, you can't, that's true!' said Mr Stackpoole, wiping his moist brow. 'And now, Liston, that you have told me this, I'll tell you something in return. I and my family leave Harbledon Hall tomorrow for the precise reasons that drove Sir Roland Shawe out of it eight years ago.'

'Never!'

'As sure as I'm alive we leave here tomorrow! I must find some reason for our sudden flight, but go we must, and I cannot have my wife alarmed.'

'I would not spend another night in the house for the world!' said Mr Beaumont.

'But, my dear Mr Stackpoole, I hope that nothing that I have said leads you to make this extraordinary resolution. Your imagination is excited by what you have heard; there cannot be any cause why you should leave this charming place that you have just fitted up to your own taste,' said Mr Liston soothingly.

'The story you have told us has only helped to explain what we already know. I'll tell you that this very night, not a couple of hours ago, in the blaze of the electric light and with the house full of company, Beaumont, my daughter, and myself have seen and heard the sights and sounds that drove Sir Roland Shawe out of Harbledon Hall; and we leave tomorrow—or rather today, for it is nearly six o'clock now—never to spend another night under this accursed roof!' and Mr Stackpoole's voice shook as he spoke. 'I have only to request,' he added, 'that you will treat this communication as confidential, for neither Beaumont nor I shall care to speak or to be spoken to about what has occurred tonight.'

Where was Mr Stackpoole's intelligent curiosity on the subject of ghosts, and what had become of his courage? The one had been satisfied and the other daunted, and he had not the slightest desire to remain and investigate the mystery.

At late breakfast Mrs Stackpoole was shocked by the appearance of her family. It would have been difficult to say which was most pale and haggard, her husband, her daughter, or her son-in-law. They made the poor excuse that late hours did not suit them and that dancing knocked them up, and she told them that they looked like young children who had been to their first pantomime the night before. When the last guest was gone Mrs Stackpoole saw that there was something seriously amiss with her husband, and was at a loss to account for his changed humour.

'My dear, we will go up to town with George and Ella,' he said, with quick decision.

'Impossible,' replied his wife calmly. 'You, of course, will go if you like to do so, but I really cannot.'

'Oh, do come with us, mamma? You know how much papa wishes it,' said her daughter.

'Yes, do come with us,' urged her son-in-law with unwonted ardour, 'it is so long since we met,' forgetting that they had spent the last month together.

Mrs Stackpoole laughed. 'There is evidently some deep-laid plot among you to hurry me off. Well, if you will be any the happier for my coming with you, I will do so, though it is most inconvenient to leave home in this sudden way,' said the good-tempered lady.

And they travelled up to London that day, never to return to Harbledon Hall. Mr Stackpoole so managed it that his wife did not know the reason for so soon quitting the most delightful house they had ever lived in. He preferred that she should attribute it to his restlessness and caprice, anything rather than that her nerves should be shaken by hearing the truth.

He consulted a fashionable physician, first giving him a hint that he wished to be ordered to the South of France immediately, and the hint being taken he told his long-suffering wife that Dr Blank had recommended him to go at once, and in two days they were *en route* for Marseilles.

Mrs Stackpoole was used to her husband's impulsive, angular movements, so that it did not greatly disturb her; but when a week later he said that he had decided to give up Harbledon Hall and to look for a place somewhere in the eastern counties which were as yet untrodden ground, she shed tears of present disappointment and prospective fatigue. When the much enduring lady had dried her eyes and her husband had enumerated to her in detail every reason but the real one for which he was leaving their beautiful home, she said, 'My dear, if I did not know better, I should be forced to believe that you too had seen the ghost that frightened Sir Roland Shawe out of Harbledon Hall eight years ago!'

The Weird of the Walfords

On a Summer's Day in the year 1860, I, Humphrey Walford, did a deed for which I should have been disinherited by my father and disowned by my ancestors. I laid sacrilegious hands on the old carved oak four-post family bedstead and destroyed it.

Alone I could not have accomplished the work of destruction. The massive posts, canopy, and panels would have resisted my single efforts; but I compelled two reluctant men to lend me their aid, and by the help of saws and hatchets we reduced the whole structure to billets of wood such as one might kindle a cheerful flame with in the parlour grate on a damp summer evening.

It was a bed with a history to me so unspeakably melancholy that I had resolved when I was my own master I would destroy the gloomy structure, and rid me of the nightmare-like feeling with which the sight of it never failed to inspire me.

The bed itself was upwards of three hundred years old, carved in oak grown on our land, while the heavy dark-green hangings, faded and musty-smelling, dated only from the time of my great-grandfather Walford. I have the dimensions of the huge hearse-like thing by heart. It was ten feet long by eight feet wide, and ten feet high; and when as a small child I was brought to see my young mother die in the recesses of the vast bed, I looked up at its tall posts with something of the awe with which I should now regard the loftiest tree.

For three centuries this bed had been the cradle and grave of our family. Its heavy drapery had deadened the sound of the first cry and the last groan of the generations of Walfords who had been born or died in Walford Grange. In its solemn depths the newly-wedded brides of the family lay the first few nights in their new home, till the wedding festivities were ended, and the squire and his wife began their everyday married life by occupying a less stately but more comfortable bed. I knew the history of the gloomy old piece of furniture as family tradition had preserved it for three centuries. Ten Squire Walfords had either died in that bed or had lain on it after death awaiting their burial. I was the eleventh squire dating from the epoch of the bed, and I would neither die in it nor be laid upon it after my death. And to make sure of this there was no way but now, in my youth and strength, to fall upon it with hatchet and saw and utterly destroy it.

I did not fear death more than my forefathers, but I resented being bidden by family tradition and custom to die in a given spot. I rebelled at having a definite place assigned to me to lie down in and die—a place so fraught with dismal associations as the ancient, hearse-like bed. I could not endure to think that, wander wide as I would, I must return to this bed of death at last, and here, among stifling pillows and heavy curtains, end my life precisely where it began.

Must this ghastly horror of my childhood be the goal towards which I tend? When I am sailing on mid-ocean, the ship ploughing her way through the furrows of the sea, shall I only be speeding, sooner or later, towards this dismal bed? When I climb mountains and breathe the keen air of the heights, is it but to end in the exclusion of light and air? Must every step I take, every journey I make, be but a stage on the road that ends in the stifling pillows of this bed of death? No, a thousand times no, and I brought my axe down on the footboard with a crash.

How vividly both the dead and living who had occupied this ancient bed rose before my mind's eye! Here had lain Ralph Walford, killed in the Civil Wars, fighting for the king, and his wounded body was brought home and stretched on what had been his bridal bed to await his burial. And here died Squire Ralph's young widow, who, a short time after her husband's sad homecoming, gave birth to his posthumous child, and never again left this ill-omened bed till they carried her out feet foremost. Ralph Walford's brother Heneage, the next squire, thought to make the old bed festive with gold and crimson hangings, to forget that his brother's corpse had lain on it, his orphan child been born in it, and his widow died in it, and by the upholsterer's wit to convert a hearse into a bridal bower.

Brighter times came to our family with the Restoration. We had spent our blood and treasure in the king's cause, for which he did not suffer us to go unhonoured; for shortly after his joyful restoration his gracious majesty was travelling within ten miles of Walford Grange, and, the weather proving stormy, and there being no other Royalist house of consideration near, he made shift to pass a night under the roof of his faithful servant Heneage Walford.

My father often told me the history of that memorable visit, as ii had been handed down from generation to generation. How gracious and witty was the king's majesty, how merry and light-hearted, as little troubled by the murder of his royal father and the heavy misfortunes of his house as by the brave lives lost and families impoverished in his cause!

Squire Heneage was as loyal a man as ever drew sword for the king, yet he was heard to say that it was a cursed day for him when his gracious majesty honoured him by being his guest, for it turned his wife Mistress Johanna's head, and she was never again the woman she had been. She grumbled and bemoaned herself that the king had not knighted her husband, so that she might have ruffled it a step above the squirearchy. But one abiding comfort remained with her from the royal visit. And this was that both at coming and going the king had saluted her, and she ever after prettily described the royal manner of kissing, which she affirmed to differ from that practised by ordinary men. Mistress Johanna's serving woman, Anne Grimshaw, said that the king had saluted her too; but this her mistress would not hear of, and when she appealed to Squire Heneage he set the vexed question at rest by giving his opinion that, judging it as a matter of probability, it was more likely that a vain woman should lie, than that his sacred majesty should kiss Anne Grimshaw, who had a foul face of her own.

If I have somewhat enlarged on the fact of the king's visit to Walford Grange, it is not so much on account of any tokens of his royal favour that he was pleased to bestow on my ancestors, as because he lay in the best chamber, in the great oak bed with its brave new hangings. But the king was tormented by terrible dreams, and woke in the morning haggard and weary, as though he had been ridden by witches. And that I attributed to a malign influence in the hearse-like bed itself, and with that I crashed into it afresh.

I had long promised myself this fierce destructive joy, when I in my turn should be master of Walford Grange. My father had died in this bed three years ago, and I had been travelling in the south of Europe ever since, urged partly by the restless curiosity of youth, and partly by the belief that no squire Walford had ever crossed the seas before. Some younger sons and thriftless members of our family, in pursuit of the fortune denied them at home, had ventured into foreign lands, but the head of the house never. My father met any wishes or arguments I advanced on the subject of travel by a statement that seemed to him conclusive—that a man sees enough in his own country that he can't understand, without going abroad to complete his confusion. But now on my return home I hastened to carry out my design on the hated ancestral bed.

What consternation prevailed in the house when it was understood what I was about, and when I and Gillam the carpenter and his man, having stripped the great bed of its drapery, proceeded to take to pieces the panels of the carved oak canopy! Mrs Barrett, the old housekeeper, stood wiping her honest eyes and bewailing my impiety.

'Don't 'ee do it, squire, don't 'ee do it! You may come to know the want of a good feather bed to die in yet! Such a bed as it's been for lyings in and layings out, and I'd hoped to ha' seen you laid in it, like your poor father before you.'

What Mrs Barrett's expectation of life may have been I know not, but she was sixty-five, and I twenty-four years of age.

'My good Barrett, I have determined that this bed shall utterly perish. We will not contribute one more corpse to its greedy maw. But if it be its feathers that you bewail, you are welcome to its pillows to line your nest with, but the bed itself must perish.'

'What, squire, the bed that your great uncle Geoffrey was found dead in, when he'd gone upstairs overnight as well and as hearty as ever man was, and making his ungodly jokes, the Lord forgive him! The very bed as your grandfather lay in two whole years before he died, and all the house heard his groans; and where your Aunt Hester was laid with the water drip, drip from every limb, just as they brought her in drowned from the brook!'

'Yes, my good Barrett, because of these very things the bed must perish.'

Then Gillam began, as he took off his paper cap and wiped his brow: 'If it's as the bed don't seem nateral like to sleep in after so many o' your kin has laid stiff and stark in it, won't you sell it, squire, to them as knows nothing of its ways? That there panel with the berried ivy on it is a deal too pretty a bit of carving to make firewood on.'

'No, Gillam, I shall not sell it. The man who would take money for the bed his ancestors died in, would sell their bones to make knife-handles of. Besides, the bed has existed long enough; it has served my family to die in for ten generations. It's my own property, Gillam; mayn't I do what I will with my own?'

'Ay, surely, squire; there's no law to hinder a man making any fool of hisself as he pleases wi' what's his own. But I sides with the chap as made the bedstead, and I shouldn't like to think as in a matter o' two or three hundred years a bit o' my work 'ud be chopped up for firing.'

'Be under no uneasiness, Gillam; you and I do not live in an age that produces lasting work. Our glue-and-tintack carpentry is not done with a view to posterity.'

'Well, squire,' continued Gillam, returning to his first idea, 'if you won't sell the bedstead whole nor piecemeal, you might give me them panels with the carved ivy on 'em. I could find you some bits o' wood as 'ud burn brighter and better.'

'I don't mind giving you the old ivy carving, Gillam,' I said, 'but only on condition that I shall never see anything more of it, in any shape or form.'

'That's easy promised, sir, and thank you kindly. I'll make it up into something as'll surprise itself.'

Having weakly consented to his request, I saw him lay aside two or three beautiful panels, richly carved with branches of berried ivy, as salvage from the general wreck. If the gloomy horrors of the old bed had not eaten into my very heart, I could never have lent a hand at such a work of destruction. I should at least have saved the footboard with its carving in high relief of Adam and Eve under the tree, a man-headed serpent twining round the trunk, and the branches bending beneath their load of fruit. But I could not look at it without thinking of the dying eyes that had fixed their fading gaze on it, so my axe and saw made havoc of a work of art. When the floor was littered over with billets of wood, and the men were wiping their hot faces, I felt a strange lightness of heart, a comfortable sense of work postponed at length happily accomplished.

'Gillam,' I said, 'there was timber enough in that huge thing to build a man-of-war, drapery to make her sails, and rope enough for all her rigging.'

'Ay, there was a'most;' and, hastily throwing his tools into his basket, he added, sarcastically I thought, 'There'll be nothing else I can help you to pull down or to smash up, squire?'

I soon found that my destructive toil had benefited me in more ways than one. Not only had it freed me from an intolerable oppression of spirit, but it had established for me in the neighbourhood a reputation for eccentricity, which I maintained afterwards at the smallest cost, and found of great service. The carrying out of my long-cherished purpose was regarded as evidence of a wild and lawless disposition, bordering on mental derangement. Night after night at the alehouse Gillam recounted to a breathless audience the story of the scene of destruction at which he had assisted professionally. And it grew in the telling till, without the slightest intention of lying, he added that the squire's rage against the old place was such, that he had been obliged to menace him with the screwdriver to keep him from tearing down the mantelshelf and wainscot.

I was evidently a man whom it was not wise to thwart or contradict. My servants flew at my least word with an alacrity I had not before observed. My bidding was promptly done, my orders were not disputed, and whatever I said was agreed to with servility. While enjoying the sweets of mental health, as my neighbours voted me on such insufficient grounds on the borderland of insanity, I availed myself of the liberty it gave me to speak and act as I chose. Their hasty judgement had made me free of the wide domain of conduct. There was nothing I could do, however extravagant, but was clearly shadowed forth in the destruction of the ancestral oak bed.

I began to grow lonely in Walford Grange. My good Barrett died suddenly, and in my solitude I wanted someone to sit and talk with me in the long evenings, for even the bright wood fire flickering on the hearth could not satisfy all my desires for cheerful companionship. I should not have wished to marry if I had had a brother to live with me, to share my thoughts and occupations, and who would himself marry and preserve the name. But I was the last of the family, and I did not mean to let an ancient race die out.

I began seriously to think of marrying, though whom, I had not an idea, for so far I had not seen the woman I should care to marry, nor could I suppose that anyone looked with an eye of favour upon me. But when a man makes up his mind to marry, and sets out on his travels by land and sea, resolved never to return to his home till he brings a wife with him, it would be hard if he could not effect his purpose.

It happened that I met with my wife unexpectedly, and where I should have thought I was least likely to meet her—in a log house in the far west of America. Her name was Grace Calvert, and she was only eighteen years old, fair and fresh as an unfolding flower, and full of the high spirits and delight of life suited to her age and her free and simple bringing up. I fell in love with her at first sight, and we were married after a short courtship, for I had obtained the object of my travel, and my little wife was wild with curiosity and impatience to see England. She had a most romantic conception of the land of her forefathers, and delighted me by her belief that every village in England contained a church, vast and venerable as Westminster Abbey, and was engirt with hills crowned by frowning fortresses.

Grace had never seen houses built either of brick or stone, and had I not been able to show her a photograph of Walford Grange, it would have been impossible to give her any idea of an object so strange that there was nothing within the narrow limits of her experience with which to compare it. Her imagination was greatly stirred by the picture of the old house. Not a detail escaped her, from the fluted chimneys to the stone seats in the wide porch. The oriel windows, with their diamond panes, pleased my young wife more than anything, and especially she admired the broad windows of the best bed-chamber, in which some two years before I had wrought my destructive will on the ancestral bed. The room was now bare and stripped of furniture, and since Mrs Barrett's death I had kept it constantly locked.

Grace was fascinated with the position of the room, with its large window over the porch, looking down the avenue of limes by which the house was approached, to the open country, and the line of low hills that bounded the horizon.

'That room must be lighter than those on the ground floor,' she said, 'see how the upper storey projects and throws a shadow over the lower rooms. We will make it our sitting-room, will we not?'

The request gave me a strange sinking of heart, and I felt that not even the society of my young wife could induce me to live in the room that had so long contained the hearse-like bed. I temporised with her in a vague manner, neither granting nor denying her request. I begged her to wait till she could see for herself how much better adapted to the comfort of daily life were the rooms on the ground floor than those on the upper storey.

In all her short life, Grace had not been further than twenty miles from the spot where she was born, and I feared lest taking her away from all she loved, and from everything with which she was familiar, might prove too keen a pain.

There was a brief tempest of tears at parting with the dear ones she was never to meet again, but it was an April shower succeeded by smiles. Each outburst of weeping was of shorter duration, and the sunny intervals between them were longer, till in a few days Grace was her bright self again. The excitement of the journey was so overwhelming as to swallow up every other feeling.

We reached our home one November afternoon, as the setting sun looked out through a rift in the clouds, and his level beams lighted up every casement with a red glow. As we drove up the leafless avenue, heavy drops fell from the bare boughs overhead, and Grace, clinging to my arm, said in a frightened whisper: 'Oh Humphrey, that light in the window is not like sunshine! It looks as if your old house was on fire!' and raising my eyes I caught for one moment the full effect of the illusion. But, the sun sinking into his bed of cloud, the red glow faded from the windows and left them dark and dim. 'Welcome, my darling, to your English home!' I said, and I took my little wife by the hand and led her up the wide oak staircase; and before we sat down to our evening meal I had taken her over the house from garret to basement, preceding her, candle in hand, through the darkening rooms.

She expressed unbounded admiration for the house and its furniture, but the old family portraits and pictures excited her utmost enthusiasm, for Grace had never seen anything more venerable or older than her grandparents and the log house in which she was born. When her raptures had toned down sufficiently to allow her to eat a little, and we were seated at supper in the oak parlour, my little wife suddenly said: 'Humphrey, there ought to be a ghost in a house like this.'   .

'Why should there be?' I asked, while I smiled at her extreme gravity.

'Because so many generations of men and women cannot have been born and died in this house without leaving some trace of themselves for us who come after,' and I saw that works of fiction had penetrated into the far west, for Grace had certainly been reading romances.

'I object to talking about ghosts at supper,' I said; 'breakfast is the best time for such conversation, and not a word should be uttered on the subject later than twelve o'clock at noon;' and I rose, and taking one of the candles with me, and holding it so as to throw the light on a dark painting over the mantelshelf, I asked: 'Do you know who that is?'

My little wife looked earnestly at the portrait, with her head inclined dubiously, and with a puzzled expression of face.

'I am not surprised that you do not know who that dark sinister-looking man is, for the backwoods of America are not hung with portraits of Charles the Second. Yes, that is King Charles; and the melancholy cast of his features must be merely an inherited expression—certainly nothing in his nature answered to it—for he passed through grief and tragedy with a light heart. He once spent a night in this very house; we have the tradition of his visit, with many quaint details, preserved to this day.'

'Oh how wonderful to think of it!' said Grace eagerly; 'and would the king sup in this very room where you and I are now?'

'Yes, in this very room, and would you like to know what he had for supper?'

'No, that is not the kind of thing that makes me curious. I want to know how the king looked, how he was dressed, and in which of those solemn-looking old bedrooms upstairs he slept. No doubt you still have the bed the king slept in?'

'No,' I replied with decision, 'that I am sure we have not.'

'Then tomorrow, Humphrey, you will shew me the room the king slept in, and the bed I can imagine for myself.'

The bed she could imagine for herself! My little wife did not know what she was talking about. The next day the event occurred which might have been expected. I was walking in the garden, when Grace came to me, and slipping her hand through my arm, drew me towards the porch.

'You see that large window,' she said, pointing towards it as she spoke; 'that is the one I admired so much in the picture of the house. I have looked out of every window but that, and I fancy the room must be locked, for I cannot open it, so I have fetched you to unlock it for me.'

I walked in silence by her side while she led me into the house and upstairs to the door of the hated room, talking with so much animation herself that she did not notice that I had not spoken a word.

'This is the room,' she said gaily, and she turned the latch of the door to and fro, saying as she did so, 'You see it is locked.'

'I know it is,' I said sullenly.

'Then fetch the key and open it,' and Grace gave the door handle a little impetuous shake.

'My dearest, don't ask me again to open that door, for I shall not do it.'

'Not do what I ask you to do? How cruel of you!' and her eyes filled with tears.

I knew that my young wife thought me brutal, but I could only say 'Anything else in my power I will do for you, only this one thing, this one little thing, I beg you will not ask me to do.'

'If you admit that it is such a very small thing, there can be no reason why you should refuse to grant me such a trivial request,' persisted Grace; 'when I ask you simply to unlock a door in your own house, and you refuse to do it, I can only think that you do not love me, or else that there is some horrid mystery about the room that you wish to keep hidden from me;' and she wiped away a hasty tear, that proceeded rather from indignation than from grief.

'My dear Grace, do not let us be tragic about nothing. There is no secret connected with this room that I have ever heard of, and I love you so much that I cannot bear to see you troubling yourself with absurd imaginations. The fact is this. I have a feeling—call it superstition, what you will—but I have a feeling that would make it very painful to me to open this door and take you into the room. And what pleasure could there be in seeing a bare, unfurnished room, precisely like any other empty room?'

'But I should set about furnishing it at once.'

'Let us come away,' I said, gently removing her dear obstinate hand from the lock. 'I repeat, I have a feeling about that room that would prevent my ever being happy in it,' and, I added lightly, 'Don't let my Eve spoil our paradise by longing after the forbidden fruit.'

But Grace said quickly, 'It was not Adam who forbade Eve to eat of the fruit. If it had been, I can't see that there would have been any great harm in disobeying him.' And we said no more about the locked door, but a cloud had come between us, and the unalloyed sweetness of our first happiness was lost.

One day, a few weeks after this folly, when I was beginning to hope that my little wife had forgotten her curiosity, I saw from her constrained and uneasy manner that something had happened to disturb her.

'My dear Grace, you certainly are not happy this morning—will you not tell me what ails you?' I asked.

Her voice trembled and her face flushed as she replied. 'Humphrey, I did not think you could tell me an untruth.'

'My child, what do you mean? We are playing at cross purposes. Be so good as to explain your meaning, that we may not misunderstand each other for a moment.'

'You told me that the big bedroom you keep locked was empty.'

'So it is,' I said, growing impatient at this childish scene, 'but what is the untruth I have told you?'

'Why, the room is not empty. I can prove what I say.'

'The room not empty! Nonsense! I keep the key, and none but

myself has entered it these two years.'

'How can you persist in such an untruth, Humphrey? I am not ashamed to confess that I looked through the keyhole I wonder I did not do it before—and I saw in the middle of the room, between the door and the window, an enormous old bed. I could only see the two foot-posts, but they went up to the ceiling, and the footboard was high and richly carved, and the curtains a gloomy, dark green. So you have deceived me about the room, and I am afraid there is some secret connected with it that you dare not tell me. What ails you, Humphrey?' and my wife rose with a terrified exclamation, for I thought I was fainting, and all the life seemed to have gone out of the air.

'Grace,' I said, when I had shaken off the sense of oppression, 'let us go at once to that unlucky room, and settle this preposterous dispute. You say that the room has furniture in it—I say that it is empty. We will see which of us is right, and then we will never mention the subject again;' and I asked my wife to come with me and assure herself that the room was, as I said, absolutely bare and unfurnished. My hand shook as I turned the key, and, flinging the door open till it strained on its hinges, we entered the room together.

Grace shrank back with a low cry, and covered her face with her hands.

'Where is it gone to, the great bed that I saw standing on this very spot? I cannot have been deceived. Oh Humphrey! why do you play me such cruel tricks? You terrify me.'

'My little wife,' I said, assuming an air of cheerfulness I was far from feeling, 'this comes of what I must call your overweening curiosity. If my dear girl had been content to let me keep this door locked, she would not have grown so curious that her little brain is almost turned, and she has taken to seeing housewifely spectral illusions of domestic furniture. Depend upon it, what you think you saw was nothing but the creature of your own imagination, that has dwelt so long on the idea of furnishing the room that you have only to peep through the keyhole, and, hey, presto! the thing is done, and beds and tables start forward at your bidding. But henceforward you can enter the room as often as you like, only we will not live in it, and I will not have it furnished.'

This appeared to satisfy Grace, and though I could not fully persuade her that the great bed she had seen when she peeped through the keyhole was an illusion begotten of curiosity and a lively imagination, yet with the door of the room unlocked, she felt that she had some control over any tricks I might play her in the future.

I was deeply disturbed by what she had told me. I had not breathed a word to my wife about the destruction of the ancestral bed. Mrs Barrett was dead before we were married, and I had changed my servants since her death, and, as we saw nothing of our neighbours, Grace could not have heard from anyone of the ghastly old bed, which nevertheless she had accurately described to me.

I could never tell her the truth now. It would shake her nerves, and impress her with the idea that there was something weird about the house. I wished I had not destroyed the old bed. Better far that she should have known the gloomy reality than behold a presentment of it that was neither an embodiment of memory nor a vivid picturing of it from imagination. I tried if I could summon up a like hallucination, but in vain. Though my memory of the ancient bed was perfect, and every detail stamped on my mind, never could I call it up before my external vision, however earnestly I tried to do so.

Grace completely regained her accustomed cheerfulness, and in the spring was busy making a thousand little preparations for the expected arrival of an infant, which was to surpass any yet born into this world. I could hardly believe the gentle obstinacy of my wife, when, after all I had said about the empty room, she asked one day if she might not make it into a nursery.

'Do you not remember, dear, that I said we would not furnish that room?' I said.

'Oh, of course, not furnish it; a nursery needs no furniture; but it is much the most cheerful and sunny room in the house.'

And again I had to appear inhuman and refuse my little wife a trivial request.

One morning as I sat in my room busy with my accounts, Grace came to tell me that she was going to drive to the county town, some eight miles distant, for a round of shopping, such as her soul loved. I said that if she would wait till the next day I should be able to take her myself, but she tapped the barometer on the wall, that had stood for some time at 'set fair', and assured me it would rain tomorrow, and that she must avail herself of the fine weather today. So away drove my self-willed darling, nodding a gay farewell as the carriage drove away from the house.

Grace returned late in the afternoon in the best of spirits, bringing with her an enormous package such as none but a country woman, or one, like my little wife, from the far west, would dream of bringing with her in an open carriage. It must have broken the coachman's heart to drive with it through the streets of the county town.

'What in the name of wonder have you brought home with you?' I asked.

'Ah!' she said, laughing, 'it is a trial for your curiosity now! Anything else you may ask me I will tell you, only I cannot let you know anything about this mysterious package.'

'Then have it put out of sight,' I said, 'or depend upon it I shall find some hole in the wrapper to peep through. You ought to know what a devouring passion curiosity is.'

As the unwieldy bundle was carried upstairs, its cover slipped aside and revealed a pair of black oak rockers. But I said nothing; Grace should tell me her little secret in her own way, and at her own time.

We thought ourselves the happiest creatures in the world when our little son Heneage was born. The gloom that brooded over the house from the death of many generations was lessened by the joy of birth, and my young son's life was like the sprouting acorn that sends up its vigorous shoot through the earth, fed by the fallen leaves of a hundred autumns. On the third day of our happiness my wife sent for me, and told me she had a very pretty surprise for me.

'I can tell you all about the big mysterious package now. It was a beautiful old-fashioned cradle that I bought in Carlyon from a man called Gillam, who keeps an old furniture shop here. I fell in love with it at once, for I knew how well it would suit this house with its old oak. Gillam said he could swear it was old work; in fact, he said it was originally part of a fine old bedstead a poor mad gentleman in the neighbourhood actually destroyed in a fit of frenzy, but he was lucky enough to secure a portion of the wreck, and made it up into that cradle, and baby looks lovely in it. I'm afraid I gave a great deal of money for it, but one does not meet with such a beautiful thing every day:' and the nurse removed a screen from before the cradle, that its beauties might burst upon me suddenly and with the more effect.

Cold drops stood on my brow as I recognised, in the high sides and head of the cradle, the carving of ivy branches and berries I had so madly given Gillam when I destroyed the old bed.

'I thought you would have been so pleased,' said Grace, disappointed by my silence as I stood spellbound, my eyes following every line of the hatred carving. 'I thought you would have been so pleased to see baby in a cradle really worthy of him.'

But I could not speak; I was oppressed by a sense of coming doom.

'It is very unkind of you,' said Grace. 'I had prepared a pretty surprise for you, and instead of being pleased, you stand and sigh and look as if you saw a ghost. Nurse, take baby out of his lovely cradle; we must get him a common wicker thing to lie in instead!' And the nurse did as her mistress bade her, and lifted little Heneage from his cradle of death, for while we talked the child had slept his feeble life away.

I have no memory of what happened day by day during the few weeks following. It was my one consuming fear that my wife too should die. Six weeks after our child's death I carried her downstairs, and this was the only progress made towards recovery. She remained at the same stage of convalescence, made wayward by grief, with shattered nerves, and so weak in mind and body that I dared not thwart her in anything. As the dim, sunless days of autumn drew on, my little wife said to me as though we had never spoken on the subject before: 'I want the big empty room furnished for my sitting-room, Humphrey. I shall have a little sunshine there sometimes to cheer me in your dismal English winter, and it will amuse me to furnish it.'

As I looked at her white wishful face, I felt that nothing mattered to me now, and I said, 'Do exactly as you like, dear, in everything,' and she was too listless to thank me.

But the work of transforming the sombre room into a bright *boudoir* proceeded rapidly, for Grace said with a shudder, 'I will have no more old oak furniture.'

My little wife always went to extremes, and now, in her antipathy to old oak, she filled the room with tawdry chips of furniture, chairs made of gilded match-sticks tied together with ribbons, that must sink into feeble ruins if a cat so much as jumped on them.

I entered into all her little fancies, and feigned excessive admiration of each fresh idea she had on the subject of decoration. I did her bidding, even to placing her couch on the very spot where the hated bed had stood. Thus was my resistance broken down, and I, who three years ago had tried by sheer physical force to thwart destiny, was now unconsciously working to bring about its fulfilment. It did not tarry long.

One gloomy November afternoon, Grace lay on her couch covered with soft shawls, and the window curtains were drawn back to give as much light as possible. The glow of the setting sun illuminated the room, and lent a more living hue to the grey pallor of her face.

'How like the day when I first came to Walford Grange!' she said; 'the sun is setting with the same fiery light. Do go into the garden,

Humphrey, and see if the windows are aglow with red light as they were then.' And I left her to do as she asked me.

Seen from the garden, the house looked precisely as it had done on the day of our homecoming. From garret to basement every window glowed red in the light of the setting sun, as though from fire within. Everything that my eyes rested on was as it had been a year ago. Grace and I only were changed—changed in ourselves and changed to each other. I felt impatient of the changeless aspect of nature and of inanimate things around me, and I entered the house, now dark in contrast with the twilight without, and returned to my wife's room with a heavy heart.

'The house looks as it did when you first saw it,' I said. 'Till the sun sank behind the hill, the windows were lighted up with the same strange effect of fire that you noticed a year ago,' and I threw a fresh log on the embers as I spoke, sending a bright train of sparks up the wide chimney. 'Shall I light the candles?' I asked, turning towards my wife's couch; 'the room is growing dark.' But there was no reply. I was speaking to the dead.

In vain I had baulked the old bed of its prey, for there on the very spot where it had stood for three centuries and generations of my ancestors had died, the wife of the last of the Walfords lay dead.

I buried my sweet Grace by our little son, and on the night of the funeral, alone in my desolate home, I conceived the idea of freeing myself for ever from the horror of darkness that had fallen on Walford Grange. I sent every servant away. I would have the house and my sorrow to myself.

When I was assured that I was alone in the house, I went rapidly from room to room in a strange exultation, speaking aloud and flinging open doors and windows till the cold night air rushed through chambers and passages, and curtains and hangings flapped in the wind.

'When I destroyed the old bed of death,' I said, 'I thought to restore joy and brightness to Walford Grange. But I should have destroyed not it alone, but the room in which it stood, and the very house of which it formed a part. Never more shall man dwell in this house glutted with death. Never more shall the voice of the bride and bridegroom be heard in its chambers, or footsteps of children be heard on its stairs. Never more shall fire subdued to harmless household use be kindled on its hearth, but fire untamed in its ferocity shall devour the accursed pile.' And I seized the burning log from the hearth and threw it on the couch where Grace had died.

Carrying a lighted brand, I sped from room to room of the doomed house, leaving in each a fiery token of my presence, and then, descending the wide staircase, where flickering shadows were past from every open door, and the silence was broken by the crackling sound of flames, I let myself out into the darkness, closing the heavy door behind me with a crash.

On through the cold damp air I ran, the moon through a rift in the clouds guiding me by her fitful light, till, drawing her shroud around her, she left me again in darkness. Not once did I turn to right or left or look behind me till I had gained the summit of the hills that bounded the valley. Then I stood and turned to take a last look at the home of my fathers. Just then the moon, issuing forth in cold splendour from her bed of cloud, shed a solemn lustre far and wide. And I saw for the last time the house of my birth, the cradle and grave of my race, and every window from basement to garret glowed with fire, no mere reflected glare, but red from the raging fire within, and keen flames darted from the casement of the room above the porch.

I stood long to watch the fire of my own kindling, till when a sudden burst of light and leaping splendour of flame showed me that the gabled roof had fallen in, I shouted, took off my hat, and waved a last farewell to Walford Grange.

The Uncanny Bairn
A Story of the Second Sight

David Galbraith owned a compact estate in East Lothian which he farmed at a considerable profit. The land had passed from father to son for a couple of hundred years. It had always yielded a good livelihood to the owner, but never had it been so highly cultivated or produced such abundant crops as under David Galbraith's liberal and skilful management. The oats and potatoes grown on his farm commanded the highest prices in the market, and his root crops were superior to any in the district. The large, solidly built stone house in which generations of Galbraiths had lived and died stood in the midst of the property, sheltered by a belt of trees on rising ground from the sweeping east wind. And the labourers' cottages, equally well constructed to resist the gales that blew across the Firth of Forth, were models of decent comfort. The livestock on the farm was well fed and cared for. The whole property bore evidence to the wealth, thrift, and intelligence of its owner.

And David Galbraith's wife was well-to-do and thrifty like himself. She too was the child of a Lowland landowner and farmer, and brought her husband no inconsiderable tocher, while her industry and housewifely accomplishments might in themselves have served as a marriage portion. She too, like her husband, came of a douce Presbyterian stock, worthy, upright folk, holding by the faith and practice of their forbears; orthodox and thrifty, worshipping as their fathers had done, and hauding the gear as tightly, nothing doubting but that to them was especially assigned not only the good things of this world, but also of that which is to come.

Galbraith did not marry till he was a middle-aged man. But he had long had the cares of a family on his shoulders without its pleasures to lighten the burden. He was the eldest of six orphan sisters and brothers, to whom he had acted the part of a father. And it was not till Colin, the last and youngest, had left Scotland for a sheep run in Australia, with money lent him by his brother, that he felt himself at liberty to marry. But now that his pious duty towards his family was fulfilled, David Galbraith did not hesitate to take to himself a wife in the person of Miss Alison McGilivray, a lady of some five-and-thirty years of age, with large hands and feet, small grey eyes, high cheek-bones, and a complexion betokening exposure to a harsh climate. She was well educated and intelligent, and in talking with her servants and poor neighbours, commonly fell into the comfortable Lowland Scotch that her father and mother had taken a pride in speaking.

Only one child was born to David and his wife in the ample home where there was space, maintenance, and welcome for a dozen. Yet this one was a son, and the Galbraiths were not doomed to die out. The boy was christened Alexander, after his two grandfathers, both of whom were Alexanders, so that there was no chance of dispute as to which side of the house should have the naming of the child.

And a poor, wee, frail child he was, apparently inheriting nothing of the strength and vigour of the Galbraiths and McGilivrays, nor did he resemble father or mother in feature. He seemed a little foreigner that had come to stay with them for a while, and often in his feeble infancy he bade fair to depart and leave his parents childless. The shrewd bracing winds, that were life and health to them, nipped and shrivelled him. He took every ailment that was to be had, and when there was nothing catching in the neighbourhood, he would originate some illness of his own, severe enough to have shaken the constitution of any but a seasoned weakling like himself. The Lowland farmer would hang over the cradle of his waxen-faced baby, holding his breath for very fear as he looked at the puny thing, and would say, dropping into broad Scotch, as his wont was when strongly moved, 'Wha wad ken this for a bairn o' mine, sae strang and bonny and weel set up as the Galbraiths have aye been?'

But the babe won through the troubles and perils of his sickly infancy, and at six years of age had grown into a delicate slip of a child, with an interesting pair of grey eyes in his pale face, and a bright spark of intellect in his big head. The family doctor, to whose unceasing care Sandie owed his life almost as much as to his mother's devoted nursing, forbade his parents to attempt anything in the way of systematic education till the boy was eight or nine years of age.

'Canna ye be content to let weel alane,' he would say, 'and bide till

357

the bairn's strang and healthy before ye trouble him to read and write? Gin ye set his brains ableeze wi' letters and figures, ye'll just be burnin' down the house that's meant to be the habitation of a fine soul; gin ye wad haud your hands aff it, and leave it alane!'

And little Sandie did very well, though unable to read or write till long after the age at which the children of his father's labourers could spell out a psalm, and sign their names in a big round hand. But the child had a memory such as must have been commoner in the world before there were books to refer to at every turn than it is now, and his mind was stored with fairytales and old border ballads that his mother and his nurse told or sung to him in the winter evenings. But Mrs Galbraith and Effie were careful never to tell him stories of a weird or ghostly nature, for the doctor had impressed upon them before all things that Sandie must never be frightened. 'For gin the bairn be frighted he will na sleep,' said the astute mistress to the maid, 'and ye'll just hae to sit the lang mirk evenings by his bed, while ye hear the maids daffin' by candlelicht below, or walking wi' their laddies; but gin ye never let him hear o' ghaists and wraiths, he'll just sleep like a bird wi' its head under its wing; and whiles ye'll be able to leave him and hae a crack wi' your neebors like ony ither body!'

Though mother and nurse, actuated by different but equally strong motives, kept all knowledge of the supernatural from the child, there came a day when his father accused them both of poisoning his mind with stories of witches, warlocks, and ghosts, and making an uncanny bairn of the boy.

When Sandie was seven years of age, a lean and overgrown child without his front teeth, and any comeliness he might possess existed only in his mother's eyes, a strange circumstance happened that greatly perplexed and distressed his parents. One cold afternoon late in October Mrs Galbraith told Effie to take a pudding and a can of broth to an old and very poor woman, called Elspeth McFie, who lived in a lone cottage a mile from the farm, and Sandie was to go with her for the sake of the walk. The trees were already stripped by the autumn gales, to which a dead calm succeeded, and a cold fog had crept up from the sea and brooded over the bare fields, settling on the naked boughs in chilly drops of moisture. The careful mother wrapped a plaid round the boy, and bade him run as he went, to keep himself warm. Away sped Sandie along the high road, driving a ball before him, running after it to send it flying again with a dextrous blow of his stick, till his pale cheeks glowed with exercise, and he overshot his mark, ran past old Elspeth's cottage, and had to be recalled by Effie.

'Ye maun pit the basket in her hand your ain sel'', she said, as she led the reluctant child into the dark close room where the old woman sat shivering by the fire, spreading her skinny hands over the dying embers. But Sandie held back, and neither threatening nor coaxing would induce him to move a step nearer to Elspeth, so that, stigmatising him as 'a dour limb', Effie was obliged to set the basket on the table herself.

'It's just a pudding and a few broth that Mistress Galbraith has sent ye, for she's aye mindfu'o' the puir,' she said, as she set out the can and bowl before the old woman. Elspeth looked with a bitter smile at the good things spread before her.

'It's a' verra gude sae far as it gaes, but gin I'd been the rich body, and Mistress Galbraith the puir carline, I wad hae sent her a mutchkin' o' something stronger than mutton broth. Does she no warm her ain thrapple wi' a drap whusky hersel'?'

'For shame, Elspeth! Ye maun just tak' what's sent ye and be thankfu'!' said Effie sharply; and turning to Sandie, who stood gazing intently at the old woman, 'What ails the bairn that he canna tak' his eyes aff your face? It's no your beauty, I'm thinking, Elspeth, that draws him sae!'

The ill-favoured old woman cackled to herself, displaying a few yellow tusks, the last survivors of a set of teeth that had once been as white and strong as Effie's.

'It's lang since man or bairn looked at auld Elspeth wi' sic a gaze. What does the bairn see in an auld wife's face? Ye suld look at the lasses, Sandie, lad,' and Elspeth stretched out her lean arm, caught the boy by the wrist, and drew him towards her. She was a hideous old woman, and in the gathering twilight, when the red glare of the embers shed a glow on her harsh features, she appeared positively witchlike. Sandie suffered himself to be drawn close to her as one who walks in his sleep, with wide-open eyes void of expression, and then stood opposite her for a moment pale and silent. Before either of the women could speak, the child's voice was heard.

'What for ha'e ye bawbees on your een, Elspeth McFie, and a white claith lappit under your chin?' Old Elspeth dropped Sandie's hand and sank back with a groan. 'Effie, Effie, hark till him! The bairn has the second sight, and he sees me stricket for the grave, aye, and ye'll all see it sune! I feel the mouls upon me a'ready! Tak' him awa', tak him awa', he's an awesome bairn!' and Sandie quietly put on his cap and went out into the could mist. Effie followed him, and relieved her fright and agitation by speaking sharply to the child.

'For shame of yoursel', Sandie, to fright an old woman wi' gruesome words that ye never heard from your mither nor me!'

'But what for suld Elspeth be frighted? There were bawbees on her een, and a white claith round her heid, and I just tauld her aboot it; and gin I see the like of it on your face, Effie, I will tell ye!'

'My certie! but ye'll be brent for a warlock gin ye read folks' deaths on their faces, and ye'd best haud your clavers!' and Effie said no more, but thought much on her way back to the farm. She was sure that Sandie did not know the meaning of his own words. He had never seen a dead body, and he did not know how a corpse is prepared for the grave, and he certainly had no information on the subject from books, for he could not read. And the appearance he described on old Elspeth's face did not seem to frighten him. He had gazed at her from the moment in which they entered the cottage till they left it, but with wonder and interest rather than fear. The fright was for Elspeth McFie and herself, and as she watched the child, unconscious of the death wound he had given, bounding along the road still playing with his ball and stick, Effie shuddered with vague and nameless fears.

That night at supper Effie told her fellow servants of Sandie's weird words, and they took counsel together whether his mother should be told about it or not, and they decided only to speak to her if anything untoward happened to old Elspeth. It was on Thursday that Effie had been sent to Elspeth McFie's cottage, and she resolved to go there again on her own account on the following Sunday afternoon. Her native superstitions were strong upon her, though she had never imparted them to her young charge, and she drew near to Elspeth's cottage with a boding heart. It scarcely surprised her when she entered to find old Elspeth lying dead on the bed, with coins on her eyes and a white cloth bound round her head, precisely as Sandy had seen her on Thursday.

Two women were in the room with the dead, eager to tell how Elspeth had taken to her bed on Thursday evening, refused bit or sup, and had died early that morning. Effie trembled, but merely hiked of what old Elspeth had died, for three days before she seemed in no likelihood of death. But the only account the women could give of her sudden death was that she appeared to have had no illness at all, and that she had said, 'I'm no a sick woman, but a dying, and I maun gae!'

Effie hastened home to tell her mistress everything, repeating faithfully every word that old Elspeth and Sandie had said on the previous Thursday. And Mrs Galbraith listened with a white and awestruck face.

'Ye'll just say naething about it, Effie; it'll be a sair prejudice against the poor bairn, and stand in his way, gin folks think Sandie has the second sight.' And Effie did not think it necessary to mention that every servant in the house was acquainted with the result of her visit to old Elspeth's cottage. But she hinted that if she continued to wait on such an awesome bairn, that might see the death tokens on her face any day, and fright her into an early grave, her wages should be raised in proportion to the danger of her service.

When Mrs Galbraith told her husband of Sandie's ghastly remark, its tragic result, and the child's unconsciousness in the matter, he disguised the fears that possessed him beneath a bluster of wrath, and rated her and Effie soundly. 'It stands to reason that the bairn canna speak o' what he does na ken, and you and Effie, but mair likely Effie than you—for I was used to think you a woman of sense—hae been telling Sandie auld wives' tales about the second sight, till he thinks it a fine thing to practise what ye've taught him, and the auld doitered fule Elspeth dies out o' sheer fright in consequence, and ye maun see for your ain sel' what your ain folly has brought about!'

But Mrs Galbraith protested that neither she nor Effie had ever uttered a word about the second sight in the boy's hearing. And David, who in his heart believed his wife, though he did not deem it consistent with his dignity to own as much, abruptly ended the unpleasant affair by saying peremptorily, 'I'll no permit the bairn to be tauld any mair ungodly superstitions and auld wives' tales. Effie may gang to the deil and Sandie sail be wi' me in his walks and rides and I'se warrant ye'll hear naething from him but what he learns fra' me, guid sense and sound doctrine.'

And Effie was dismissed to her own great relief, and from that day forth Sandie became his father's outdoor companion, to the visible benefit of his health and spirits.

But no-one was so really alarmed at Sandie's uncanny remark and its consequences as David Galbraith himself. His grandmother, a Highland woman, had had the second sight, and his father had told him how she lived to become the terror of her family. Her premonitions of death and calamity were unfailingly true, and the spirit within her never enlightened her as to how the impending evil might be averted.

She was simply the medium of announcing approaching doom. What if her ghostly gift had descended to her grandson, a barren heritage that would make him shunned by his kind!

Poor Alison Galbraith, finding her husband irritable and unreasonable on the subject of Sandie's weird speech, sought comfort in pouring out her fears to their minister, The Revd Ewan Macfarlane, who gave ear to her with as much patience as could be expected from a man whose chief business it was in life to speak and not to listen.

He drew the very worst inference from what he heard. 'It's a clear case o' the second sight, and I canna but fear that there may be waur to come. When the uncanny spirit lights on a body there's nae predicting what its manifestations may be, and for aught that we ken it may be you or me that Sandie'll see the death tokens on neist. And if ye continue to bring him to the kirk, I wad request that ye'll no let him sit glowering at me, for though sudden death wad doubtless be sudden glory to me, it wad no be consistent wi' the dignity of a Minister o' the Free Kirk that he suld be harried untimely into his grave by an uncanny bairn, that wad hae been burnt for a warlock in times gane by. And if I was spared such a sair visitation, the bairn might yet be permitted to wark a certain perturbation of spirit in me, that wad cause me to curtail the word of God, and bring my discourse to a premature end, to the grievous loss of them that hear. And, Mistress Galbraith, let me tell ye, ye'll fa' into disrepute wi' your neighbours gin Sandie sees bawbees on your minister's honoured een, and aught came of it to his prejudice!'

In the following spring David Galbraith's youngest brother Colin returned, after an absence often years, to spend a few months with his relations in Scotland. His industry had been prospered in Australia, and he was in a better position than he could have attained by any exertions of his own in the old country. He and his nephew struck up a warm friendship together, and it was a pretty sight to see them golfing on the links at North Berwick, the strong man accommodating his play to that of the puny boy by his side, and restraining his speech so that not a word fell from his lips but what was fit for a child to hear.

One day when they had played till Sandie was tired they sauntered down to the beach, Uncle Colin to sit on the rocks smoking his morning pipe, his nephew to perch beside him and amuse himself with the shells and seaweed that abound there. Presently Sandie grew weary of sitting still, threw away the handful of shells he had picked up, and proposed that they should go further along the sands to where the children were bathing. 'And gi'e me your hand, Uncle Colin, and I'll tell ye something while we walk that I canna just understand mysel'. I've seen an unco' strange thing; I've seen your house in Australia!'

'Hoot, mon! what havers are ye talking? Ye've been dreaming!' said Uncle Colin cheerily.

'Na, I saw it. It was no dream; I ken weel the difference between dreaming and seeing. Your house has na slates on the roof, like our house; it was theckit like a hay-rick, and it had a wide place round it covered with another little theckit roof, and windows like big glass doors opened on it. And there was fire all about, and tall grass all ableeze, and sheep rinning hither and thither frighted, and a man with a black beard and a gun in his hand ran out o' the house and shouted: "O'Grady, save the mare and foal! If they're lost, the master will never forgi'e ye!" What ails ye, Uncle Colin, that ye look sae gash?' and the boy looked up in his uncle's face with wonder.

'It's no canny to see such a sight, Sandie! What do ye ken o' bush fires? And ye've never seen a picture of my house; and who tauld ye that my groom is an Irishman named O'Grady? I've tauld naebody here, and the man with the black beard is my Scotch shepherd.'

'There was no need to tell me onything about it, Uncle Colin, for I saw it a'; but if the man at the door hadna shouted O'Grady, then I suld na hae kenned his name.'

Colin made a poor attempt at laughter, that he might hide from the child how shocked and startled he was. But as soon as they reached home he told his brother about his son's vision, and heard from him in return the story of Sandie and old Elspeth. A few days later Colin Galbraith received a telegram from his head shepherd informing him of the heavy loss he had just sustained from a very serious bush fire, and both he and David were convinced that Sandie was an uncanny bairn.

Colin returned to Australia immediately afterwards, and as he parted from his brother and sister-in-law he said with a melancholy smile, 'If ony mischance befa's me, ye'll ken as sune as I do mysel'. Your awesome bairn will see it a', and ye may tak for gospel aught tauld ye by ane that has the second sight.'

One fine afternoon, some three weeks after Colin had sailed, David having just then no particular work to keep him on the farm all day, proposed for a great treat to row Sandie to the Bass Rock. Oatcutting would shortly begin, and then he would not have a spare hour from morning to night. But today he and his son would enjoy a holiday together, and Sandie was to take with him the small gun that his father gave him on his last birthday, for he was now nine years of age, and high time that he set about learning to kill something or other. All the latent boy seemed developed in the delicate child by the possession of the small fowling-piece, and he blazed away at the rats under the hay-ricks and at the sparrows on the roof, to the peril alike of the poultry and of the bedroom windows. 'Mother, mother, I'll shoot ye a gannet and mak' ye a cushion o' the down!' he shouted in wild excitement as he set forth on the expedition.

Mrs Galbraith stood on the doorstep watching her husband and son leave the house together, David a stout, tall man in the prime of late middle life, red-faced and grey-haired, and Sandie a lanky lad with pale freckled face, but with more vigour in his step than the fond mother had ever expected to see. He carried his gun over his shoulder and strode along by his father's side, glancing up at him frequently to try to imitate his every look and gesture. David Galbraith was fond of rowing, and as it was a very calm day he dismissed the man in charge of the boat, and taking the oars himself said it would do him good to row as far as the Bass Rock and back again.

The sea was like a mill-pond, a glassy stretch of water with here and there a wind flaw wrinkling its smooth surface. There was not a wave that could have displaced a pebble on the beach, and masses of olive-green seaweed floated motionless in its clear depths. To the left, high above them, stood the ruins of Tantallon Castle, bathed in August sunshine, its grey walls taking warmth and colour from the glow of light that softened and beautified its rugged outline. Before them the sullen mass of the Bass Rock towered above the blue water, circled by countless thousands of sea birds, the glitter of whose white wings was seen as silvery flashes of light, from a distance too great to distinguish the birds themselves.

They were near enough to the shore to hear voices and laughter borne over the water from the grassy enclosure before Tantallon Castle, and lowing of kine in the pastures, and as they neared the Bass Rock these sounds were exchanged for the squealing of wild fowl and the clang of their wings. To Sandie's delight he was allowed to shoot from the boat, which he did with as little danger to the birds as to the fishes, and the only condition his father imposed was that he should fire with his back towards him, 'till your aim is mair preceese, mon'. Though it soon became evident even to the sanguine Sandie that he would bring home neither gannet nor kittiwake, it was a rapturous delight to be rowed about the island by his father, who told him the

name of every bird he saw, and pointed out their nests on the precipitous face of the rock. Then David rested on his oars, and the boat
scarcely moved on the still water while Sandie ate the oatcake and
drank the milk provided for him by his mother, and his father took a
deep draught from his flask till his face grew crimson.

'Father, gi'e me a drink, too,' said Sandie, stretching out his hand.

'Na, na; ye'll stick to your milk-drinking till ye ha'e built up a
strong frame, and then ye may tak' as much whusky as ye wull to keep
it in guid repair.'

And now the boat was turned landward once more, and they soon
lost sound of the clang of the sea birds' wings, and the lowing of kine
was again heard, and David rowed slowly past the rock of Tantallon.
Sandie had fallen silent, and sat leaning his arm on the gunwale of the
boat looking into the limpid water, dipping his hand into a soft swelling wave, and scattering a shower of glittering drops from his fingers.
Suddenly he ceased his play, and kneeling in the bottom of the boat,
clung firmly to the side with both hands, leaned over, and gazed intently in the water. His father, who was always on the alert where his
son was concerned, at once noticed the change that had come over
him, rowed quicker, and said cheerily, 'What are ye glowering at, mon?
Did ye never see a herring in the sea before?'

Sandie neither spoke nor stirred, and David took comfort in thinking that after all the lad could see nothing uncanny in the water; it was
just some daft folly or other he was after, best unnoticed. But when
Sandie did speak it was to utter words for which he was unprepared.
'Father, I see Uncle Colin in the water wi' his face turned up to me,
and his een wide open, but he canna see wi' them.' And the boy did
not raise his head, but continued to gaze into the water. Drops of
sweat broke out on Galbraith's brow, and he lifted the dripping oars
high in the rowlocks and leaned towards Sandie, his red face now as
white as the boy's.

'Whether it's God or the de'il speaks in ye, I dinna ken, but ye'll
drive me mad wi' your gruesome clavers! Haud up, man! And fling
yoursel' back in the boat, where ye'll see naething waur than yoursel'.'

But Sandie did not stir. 'It's Uncle Colin that I see floating in the
water, lappit in seaweed, and he's nae sleeping, for his een stare sae
wide,' and Galbraith, who would not have looked over the gunwale of
the boat for his life, with an oath plunged the oars deep into the water
and rowed with furious strokes.

'Ye've struck the oar on his white face!' shrieked the boy, and fell back crying in the boat.

A heavy gloom settled on the Galbraiths, and this last hideous vision of Sandie's they kept strictly to themselves. They did not seek counsel of their minister or of anyone. They were certain that Colin was drowned. It was a mere question of time when they could hear how it had happened, but hear it they assuredly would. And Sandie, too, was gloomy and depressed. 'The bairn has frighted himself this time as weel as others,' said his father, 'and sma' blame to him. But I would rather follow him to the kirkyard than that he suld grow up wi' the second sight! It may ha'e been a' varra weel in a breekless, starving Hielander a hundred years ago, but it's no consistent for a well-fed Lowlander in these days o' trousers and high farming. How is Sandie to do justice to the land and mind the rotation of crops if he goes daft wi' the second sight?'

The oat harvest was plentiful and got together in fine condition, but neither David nor his wife had any heart to enjoy it. They simply lived through each day waiting for the tidings that must come. Nor had they long to wait. A month after Sandie's vision David read in the newspaper of the safe arrival of his brother's ship at its destination. It reported a prosperous voyage with but one casualty during its course. On the twenty-fourth day after sailing, a passenger booked for Sydney had mysteriously fallen overboard in perfectly calm weather and was drowned. The gentleman's name was Mr Colin Galbraith, and his sudden untimely end had cast a gloom over the ship's company. So far the newspaper report, which, brief as it was, was all that David and Alison could ever learn of their poor brother's fate. They carefully compared the dates, and found that Colin had been drowned three days after Sandie had seen the vision of the body in the sea.

'I winna tell the bairn that puir Colin is dead,' said David gloomily.

'Ye'll just tell the bairn he's dead, but you'll say naething of drowning.'

'Ye maun do as ye think best, but I canna mention puir Colin's name to him.' And it was from his mother that Sandie heard of his Uncle Colin's death. He listened gravely and thoughtfully to the tidings. 'Aye, it was him that I saw in the water.' And that was all that he had to say about the death of his favourite uncle. He asked no question and made no further remark.

From this time forward a great change came over David Galbraith. From being wholly matter of fact and little inclined to believe more than his senses could attest, he became credulous and superstitious. He trembled at omens, and was unnerved for his day's work if his dreams overnight were unpropitious. He disliked being out on dark nights, and cast uneasy glances over his shoulder as though he heard steps behind him. At times when he was riding he thought that he heard someone following hard on his heels, and he would gallop for miles and reach home, horse and rider both in a sweat of fear. And Sandie, the unconscious cause of the evil change in his father, mutely wondered what had come over him.

David scarcely let the boy out of his sight, though his society was a torment to him, and he was always wondering what would be the next shock he would receive. Unhappily he tried to restore tone to his shaken nerves by drinking, and the habit grew quickly on him to his good wife's great distress. And times were now so changed that Sandie was often more frightened of his father than his father was of him. Mrs Galbraith proposed sending Sandie to stay with some relations of her own at Linlithgow, thinking that it would do her husband good to have the strain of the boy's constant society removed for a while. But he would not hear of it, and merely said, 'The bairn sall bide at hame. It's my ain weird, and I maun dree it.'

Some two years passed by in which Sandie had no visions, and grew steadily healthier and stronger and more like other boys of his age, so that his mother began to think they should make a man of him yet. But though his father noticed the physical improvement in his son with pride, nothing could persuade him that the dreaded gift had departed from him. In vain his wife tried to convince him that there was no further cause for anxiety. He shook his head and said, 'Ye'll no get rid of an ill gift sae lightly. It's a fire that burns low, but it'll burst out into flame for a' that.'

In the third summer after Colin Galbraith was lost at sea, on a lovely summer evening Mrs Galbraith sat at the open window, knitting and smiling placidly, as she watched her son at work in his little plot of garden watering the tufts of pinks and pansies. She laid her work in her lap, and her eyes followed his every movement with quiet pleasure. Sandie would make a good gardener. There was not a weed nor a straggling growth in his plot, all was neat and trim. And the flower beds were prettily bordered with shells he had collected on the beach at North Berwick.

He was gathering a posy with fastidious care, and his mother knew that it was for her, and thought to herself that if he had been uncanny in time past, he was a good boy, his heart was in the right place. But something disturbed him in his work. He rose from stooping over the bed, dropped his flowers to the ground, and Alison thought he was listening to some far-away sound, till a change that passed over his face showed her that she was mistaken. Sandie was not listening, he was seeing. His face grew pale and his features pinched, his grey eyes were fixed while the colour faded out of them till they were almost white, and he shuddered as though a cold wind blew over him.

Mrs Galbraith rose silently, and assured by the deep breathing of her husband, who was sitting in an armchair by the hearth, that he was asleep, opened the door softly, left the room, and hurried into the garden. There in the sunshine, surrounded by summer sights and summer scents, stood Sandie, a very image of midnight terror. His mother laid her large warm hands on his shoulders, and gently shook him.

'Sandie, Sandie, if you're seeing again, for God's sake say nothing to your father! He canna bear it; ye'll tell me,' she said in a frightened whisper.

The boy gave a sigh, passed his hands over his eyes, and staggered as though he were dizzy. Alison grasped her son firmly by the arm. 'Come awa'! If your father wakes and goes to the window he'll see us; come awa'!' And she hurried the boy through the warm evening sunshine that had suddenly grown cold and dim to her, and led him to a retired part of the garden.

'And now what was it that ye saw?' And looking at her with a strange expression of fear and compassion, Sandie said, 'I saw my father lying on the road at the foot of the steep brae by Sir Ewen Campbell's gates, and his een were shut, but for a' that he was the same as Uncle Colin!'

The self-controlled, unemotional Alison Galbraith gave a smothered scream as she listened to her son, and seizing his arm in a passion of fear, with a grip like a vice, said 'Elspeth McFie was right when she called you an awesome bairn! What for has God in His wrath given me such a child?' and she shook him off, and left him alone in his confused misery.

If David Galbraith had not been overcome with drink that night, he would have seen that something terrible had occurred to agitate his wife. But when the drunken fit was spent he noticed that she looked white and ill.

'Alison, woman, you keep too close in the house,' he said; 'ye should walk to the sea and breathe the caller air, to bring the colour back to your cheeks.'

The following Friday was the corn market at Haddington, and David Galbraith, sober, shrewd, and business-like, set out to attend it, bent on driving a hard bargain. Alison stood at the gate as he mounted his horse to wish him good luck, and to add a word of wifely admonition as to the advisability of not drinking too much whisky before the return journey, and 'Ye'll no be late coming home the night, Davie?'

'There is no night at this time o' year, Alison.'

'And ye'll mind to come by the level road. There's the steep brae beyond the Campbell's gates, and I'd rather ye gave it a wide berth, and came by the long road.'

'Not I, woman! Do ye expect me to mak' a midnight ride a mile longer just to avoid a brae that I ken as weel as my ain doorstep? Kelpie'll be sober, douce beast, if his master's not, and he kens every stane on the brae. Ye'll go to bed and leave the house door unlocked for me,' and David gave his horse a touch with the whip and away he trotted.

Alison stood till the sound of hoofs had died away and then went back into the house with a boding heart. Sandie returned from school at noon in high spirits, and asked his mother's leave to bring home a schoolfellow to play with him in the afternoon. It was wonderful how his spirits had rallied since his vision of a few days before. It seemed as though his body had now grown strong enough to shake off the ghastly influence entirely. But his mother was shattered both by memory and apprehension.

A dreadful restlessness possessed her as night drew on, and after the shouts of the boys at play were over, and silence fell on house and garden, she slipped out unnoticed and walked in the twilight to the beach. It was high midsummer, when in those latitudes the sunset lingers on the western horizon till in the east the vigorous dawn breaks to quench its lesser light. The crescent moon hung low in the sky over the gently murmuring sea that glimmered mysteriously in the diffused twilight, and the brown rocks loomed dark above the water. A time and a place to suggest eerie feelings to the most unimpressionable. But Alison's whole mind was so filled with apprehensions of approaching doom that the scene had no effect upon her—she scarcely noticed where she was.

The fear that possessed her was an inward fear, neither suggested nor increased by the aspect of familiar things. She did not meet a soul in her restless wanderings. As she opened the house door on her return the clock struck twelve. Oh, when would David be home? He was seldom later than midnight. Alison needed no light, and creeping softly upstairs she entered Sandie's room, and drawing aside the curtain, by the solemn twilight of the northern night she saw his sleeping face calm and peaceful as an infant's. Did she grudge him his untroubled slumber, that she would rather have found him awake and oppressed with terror as herself?

While she stood listening to the beating of her own heart, that sounded louder than the breathing of her child, she heard the first distant sound of approaching hoofs, and as they rapidly drew nearer she recognised Kelpie's familiar steps.

'Thank God, he is safe home!' she said, and lest her husband should be displeased to find her sitting up for him she hastened to her room and lighted a candle. The horse had stopped opposite the house, and David had had time to dismount, but he had not opened the gate. Someone might be detaining him there. Yet there was no sound of voices to be heard, only Kelpie impatiently striking the ground with one of his fore feet. Alison looked out of the window, but could see nothing for the high wall. As several minutes passed and still her husband did not come, and the horse stamped with increasing impatience, she slipped downstairs out of doors and across the garden to the gate. So deadly a fear lay upon her spirit that when she flung the gate open and saw Kelpie standing riderless on the dusky highway she felt no surprise, only an assurance that Sandie's vision was about to come true.

'Oh, Kelpie lad, your master's no far to seek!' she said as she led the trembling, sweating beast towards the stable yard. Then, without calling up any of the men, just as she was with uncovered head, Alison Galbraith sped through the dusk and silence of the summer night.

'The steep brae by Sir Ewen Campbell's gates! The steep brae by Sir Ewen Campbell's gates!' she said to herself as she ran, and when the dark firs and high wall bounding the park came in sight her limbs almost gave way beneath her. Then she reached the great iron gates between granite pillars, and in the twilight she caught sight through their bars of the black avenue within, and heard the wind sigh in the boughs. Alison pressed her hand to her heart and urged herself on. Now a bat cut its zigzag flight through the air and startled her. The white scut of a frightened rabbit shone out in the dusk as it flashed across her path in search of a friendly burrow, and her echoing steps woke many a sleeping bird and set it fluttering with fear.

The next turn in the road would bring her to the foot of the brae, and to something that she dared not name that she knew was waiting for her there. She closed her eyes for an instant as she rounded the curve of the road and clenched her hands. Then the soft silence of the summer night was broken by a wailing cry, and Alison Galbraith fell senseless on the dead body of her husband.

David was sober that night, but as he rode through the mirk lanes the old horror had overtaken him. He thought that he heard a horseman following hard upon him, and clapped spurs to his beast and galloped down the hill, at the foot of which Kelpie slipped on a rolling stone, threw his rider heavily to the ground, and he neither spoke nor moved again.

Alison Galbraith did not long survive her husband, and her death took place without Sandie having any intimation of its approach. He never had vision or prophetic foresight again after his father died. The weird gift departed from him with his weakly childhood, and he grew up robust and stout, thriving and commonplace as his forebears. Sandie is even a better farmer than his father before him, and is in a fair way to solve the problem of how to make two blades of wheat grow where only one had grown before. He has married a wife, practical and matter of fact as himself, and their sons and daughters are as guiltless of imagination as they are of any touch of the uncanny.

The burly Lowland farmer can never be induced to speak of the second sight, even to his most intimate friends. In the early days of their married life his young wife ventured to ask him about the visions of his childhood, of which she had heard. But he silenced her with such severity that she did not again dare to approach the subject, and she will never know whether the stories of her husband's uncanny childhood are wild legends or plain truth.

Many Waters Cannot Quench Love

Did I not know my old friend John Horton to be as truthful as he is devoid of imagination, I should have believed that he was romancing or dreaming when he told me of a circumstance that happened to him some thirty years ago. He was at that time a bachelor, living in London and practising as a solicitor in Bedford Row. He was not a strong man, though neither nervous nor excitable, and as I said before singularly unimaginative.

If Horton told you a fact, you might be certain that it had occurred in the precise manner he stated. If he told it you a hundred times, he would not vary it in the repetition. This literal and conscientious habit of mind made his testimony of value, and when he told me a fact that I should have disbelieved from any other man, from my friend I was obliged to accept it as truth.

It was during the long vacation in the autumn of 1857, that Horton determined to take a few weeks holiday in the country. He was such an inveterate Londoner he had not been able to tear himself away from town for more than a few days at a time for many years past. But at length he felt the necessity for quiet and pure air, only he would not go far to seek them. It was easier then than it is now to find a lodging that would meet his requirements, a place in the country yet close to the town, and it was near Wandsworth that Horton found what he sought, rooms for a single gentleman in an old farmhouse. He read the advertisement of the lodgings in the paper at luncheon, and went that very afternoon to see if they answered to the tempting description given. He had some little difficulty in finding Maitland's Farm.

It was not easy to find his way through country lanes that to his town eyes looked precisely alike, and with nothing to indicate whether he had taken a right or wrong turning. The railway now runs shrieking over what were then green fields, lanes have been transformed into gas-lighted streets, and Maitland's Farm, the old red-brick house standing in its high-walled garden, has been pulled down long ago. The last time Horton went to look at the old place it was changed beyond recognition, and the orchard in which he had gathered pears and apples during his stay at the farm, was now the site of a public house and a dissenting chapel.

It was on a hot afternoon early in September when Horton opened the big iron gates and walked up the path bordered with dahlias and hollyhocks leading to the front door, and rang for admittance at Maitland's Farm. The bell echoed in a distant part of the empty house and died away into silence, but no-one came to answer its summons. As Horton stood waiting he took the opportunity of thoroughly examining the outside of the house. Though it was called a farm it had not been built for one originally. It was a substantial, four-storey brick house of Queen Anne's period, with five tall sash windows on each floor, and dormer windows in the tiled roof. The front door was approached by a shallow flight of stone steps, and above the fan-light projected a penthouse of solidly carved woodwork.

On either side were brackets of wrought iron, supporting extinguishers that had quenched the torch of many a late returning reveller a century ago. Only the windows to right and left of the door had blinds or curtains, or betrayed any sign of habitation. 'Those are the rooms to be let, I wonder which is the bedroom,' thought my friend as he rang the bell for the second time. Presently he heard within the sound of approaching footsteps, there was a great drawing of bolts, and after a final struggle with the rusty lock, the door was opened by an old woman of severe and cheerless aspect. Horton was the first to speak.

'I have called to see the rooms advertised to be let in this house.' The old woman eyed him from head to foot without making any reply, then opening the door wider, nodded to him to enter. He did so and found himself in a large paved hall lighted from the fan-light over the door, and by a high narrow window facing him at the top of a short flight of oak stairs. The air was musty and damp as that of an old church.

'A hall this size should have a fire in it,' said Horton, glancing at the empty rusty grate.

'Farmers and folks that work out of doors keep themselves warm without fires,' said the old woman sharply.

'This house was never built for a farm, why is it called one?' en-quired Horton of his taciturn guide as she opened the door of the sitting-room.

'Because it was one,' was the blunt reply. 'When I was a girl it was the Manor House, and may be called that again for all I know, but thirty years since, a man named Maitland took it on a lease and farmed the land, and folks forgot the old name, and called it Maitland's Farm.'

'When did Maitland leave?'

'About two months ago.'

'Why did he go away from a nice place like this?'

'You are fond of asking questions,' remarked the old woman drily. 'He went for two good reasons: his lease was up, and his family was a big one. Nine children he had, from a girl of two-and-twenty down to a little lad of four years old. His wife and him thought it best to take 'em out to Australia, where there's room for all. They were glad to go, all but the eldest, Esther, and she nearly broke her heart over it. But then she had to leave her sweetheart behind her. He's a young man on a dairy farm near here, and though he's to follow her out and marry her in twelve months, she did nothing but mourn, same as if she was leaving him altogether.'

'Ah, indeed!' said Horton, who could not readily enter into details about people whom he did not know. 'So this is the sitting-room; it's large and airy, and has as much furniture in it as a man needs by him-self. Now show me the bedroom, if you please.'

'Follow me upstairs, sir,' and the old woman preceded him slowly up the oak staircase, and opened the door of the back room on the first floor.

'Then the bedroom that you let is not over the sitting-room?'

'No, the front room is mine, and the room next to it is my son's. He's out all day at his work, but he sleeps here, and mostly keeps me company of an evening. I'm alone here all day looking after the place, and if you take the rooms I shall cook for you and wait on you myself.'

Horton liked the look of the bedroom. It was large and airy, with little furniture in it beyond a bed and a chest of drawers. But it was delicately clean, and silent as the grave. How a tired man might sleep here! The walls were decorated with old prints in black frames of the 'Rake's Progress' and 'Marriage à la Mode', and above the high carved mantelpiece hung an engraving of the famous portrait of Charles the First, on a prancing brown horse.

'Those things were on the walls when the Maitlands took the

place, and they had to leave 'em where they found 'em,' said the old woman. 'And they found that sword too,' she added, pointing to a rusty cutlass that hung from a nail by the head of the bed; 'but I think they'd have done no great harm if they'd sold it for old iron.'

Horton took down the weapon and examined it. It was an ordinary cutlass, such as was worn by the marines in George the Third's reign, not old enough to be of antiquarian interest, nor of sufficient beauty of workmanship to make it of artistic value. He replaced it, and stepped to the windows and looked into the garden below. It was bounded by a high wall enclosing a row of poplars, and beyond lay the open country, visible for miles in the clear air, a sight to rest and fascinate the eye of a Londoner.

Horton made his bargain with the old woman whom the landlord had put into the house as caretaker, pending his decision about the disposition of the property. She was allowed to take a lodger for her own profit, and as soon as Mrs Belt found that the stranger agreed to her terms, she assured him that everything should be comfortably arranged for his reception by the following Wednesday.

******

Horton arrived at Maitland's Farm on the evening of the appointed day. A stormy autumnal sunset was casting an angry glow on the windows of the house, the rising wind filled the air with mournful sounds, and the poplars swayed against a background of lurid sky.

Mrs Belt was expecting her lodger, and promptly opened the door, candle in hand, when she heard wheels stopping at the gate. The driver of the fly carried Horton's portmanteau into the hall, was paid his fare, and drove away thinking the darkening lanes more cheerful than the glimpse he had had of the inside of Maitland's Farm.

Horton was thoroughly pleased with his country quarters. The intense quiet of the almost empty house, that might have made another man melancholy, soothed and rested him. In the daytime he wandered about the country, or amused himself in the garden and orchard, and he spent the long evenings alone, reading and smoking in his sitting-room. Mrs Belt brought in supper at nine o'clock, and usually stayed to have a chat with her lodger, and many a long story she related of her neighbours, and the Maitland family, while she waited upon him at his evening meal.

On several occasions she told him that Esther Maitland's sweetheart, Michael Winn, had come to talk with her about the Maitlands, or to bring her a newspaper containing tidings that their ship had

375

reached some point on its long voyage in safety.

'You see the *Petrel* is a sailing vessel, sir, and there's no saying how long she'll take getting to Australia. The last news Michael had, she'd got as far as some islands with an outlandish name, and he's had a letter from Esther posted at a place called Madeira. And now he gives himself no peace till he can hear that the ship's safe as far as—somewhere, I think he said, in Africa.'

'It would be the Cape, Mrs Belt.'

'That's the name, sir, the Cape, and he werrits all the time for fear of storms and shipwrecks. But I tell him the world's a wide place, and the sea wider than all, and very likely when the chimney pots is flying about our heads in a gale here, the *Petrel's* lying becalmed somewhere. And then he takes up my thought and turns it against me. "Yes," he says, "and when it's a dead calm here on shore, the ship may be sinking in a storm, and my Esther being drowned."'

'Michael Winn must be a very nervous young man.'

'That's where it is, sir, and I tell him when he follows the Maitlands it's a good job that he leaves no-one behind him that'll werrit after him, same as he's werrited after Esther.'

It was the middle of October, and Horton had been a month at the farm. The weather was now cold and wet, and he began to think it was time he returned to his snug London home, for the autumn rain made everything at Maitland's Farm damp and mouldy. It had blown half a gale all day, and the rain had fallen in torrents, keeping him a prisoner indoors. But he occupied himself in writing letters, and reading some legal documents his clerk had bought out to him, and the time passed rapidly. Indeed the evening flew by so quickly he had no idea it was nine o'clock, when Mrs Belt entered the room to lay the cloth for supper.

'It's stopped raining now, sir,' she said, as she poked the fire into a cheerful blaze, 'and a good job too, for Michael Winn brings me word the Wandle's risen fearful since morning, and it's out in places more than it's been for years. But there's a full moon tonight, so no-one need walk into the water unless they've a mind to.'

Horton's head was too full of a knotty legal point to pay much heed to Mrs Belt, and the old woman, seeing that he was not in a mood for conversation, said nothing further. At half-past ten she brought her lodger some spirits and hot water, and his bedroom candle, and wished him goodnight. Horton sat reading for some time, and then made an entry in his diary concerning a day of which there was absolutely nothing to record, lighted his candle, and went upstairs. I am familiar with the precise order of each trifling circumstance. My friend has so often told me the events of that night, and never with the slightest addition or omission in the telling.

It was his habit, the last thing at night, to draw up the blinds. He looked out of the window, and though the moon was at the full, the clouds had not yet dispersed, and her light was fitful and obscure. It was twenty minutes to twelve as he extinguished the candle by his bedside. Everything was propitious for rest. He was weary, and the house profoundly silent. The rain had stopped, the wind fallen to a sigh, and it seemed to him that as soon as his head pressed the pillow he sank into a dreamless slumber.

Shortly after two o'clock Horton awoke suddenly, passing instantaneously from deep sleep to the possession of every faculty in a heightened degree, and with an insupportable sense of fear weighing upon him like a thousand nightmares. He started up and looked around him. The perspiration poured from his brow, and his heart beat to suffocation. He was convinced that he had been waked by some strange and terrible noise, that had thrilled through the depths of sleep, and he dreaded the repetition of it inexpressibly. The room was flooded with moonlight streaming through the narrow windows, lying like sheets of molten silver on the floor, and the poplars in the garden cast tremulous shadows on the ceiling.

Then Horton heard through the silence of the house a sound that was not the moan of the wind, nor the rustling of trees, nor any sound he had heard before. Clear and distinct, as though it were in the room with him, he heard a voice of weeping and lamentation, with more than human sorrow in the cry, so that it seemed to him as though he listened to the mourning of a lost soul. He leaped up, struck a match, and lighted the candle, and seizing the cutlass that hung by the bed, unlocked the door, and opened it to listen.

So far as all ordinary sounds were concerned, the house was silent as death, and the moonlight streamed through the staircase window in a flood of pale light. But the unearthly sound of weeping, thrilling through heart and soul, came from the hall below, and Horton walked downstairs to the landing at the top of the first flight. There, on the lowest step, a woman was seated with bowed head, her face hidden in her hands, rocking to and fro in extremity of grief. The moonlight fell full on her, and he saw that she was only partly clothed, and her dark hair lay in confusion on her bare shoulders.

'Who are you, and what is the matter with you?' said Horton, and his trembling voice echoed in the silent house. But she neither stirred nor spoke, nor abated her weeping. Slowly he descended the moonlit staircase till there were but four steps between him and the woman. A mortal fear was growing upon him.

'Speak! if you are a living being!' he cried. The figure rose to its full height, turned and faced him for a moment that seemed an eternity, and rushed full on the point of the cutlass Horton involuntarily presented. As the impalpable form glided up the blade of the weapon, a cold wave seemed to break over him, and he fell in a dead faint on the stairs.

How long he remained insensible he could not tell. When he came to himself and opened his eyes, the moon had set, and he groped his way in darkness to his room, where the candle had burnt itself out.

When Horton came down to breakfast, he looked as though he had been ill for a month, and his hands trembled like a drunkard's. At any other time Mrs Belt would have been struck by his appearance, but this morning she was too much excited by some bad news she had heard, to notice whether her lodger was looking well or ill. Horton asked her how she had slept, for if she had not heard the terrible sounds that waked him, it still seemed impossible she should not have heard his heavy fall on the stairs. Mrs Belt replied, with some astonishment at her lodger's concern for her welfare, that she had never had a better night, it was so quiet after the wind fell.

'But did your son think the house was quiet, did he sleep too?' asked Horton with feverish eagerness.

Mrs Belt was yearning to impart her bad news to her lodger, and remarking that she had something else to do than ask folks how they slept o' nights, she said a neighbour had just told her that Michael Winn had fallen into the Wandle during the night—no-one knew how—and was drowned, and they were carrying his body home then.

'What a terrible blow for his sweetheart,' said Horton, greatly shocked.

'Aye! there's a pretty piece of news to send her, when she's expecting to see poor Michael himself soon.'

'Mrs Belt, have you any portrait of Esther Maitland you could show me? I've heard the girl's name so often I'm curious to know what she is like.' And the old woman retired to hunt among her treasures for a small photograph on glass, that Esther had given her before she went away. Presently Mrs Belt returned, polishing the picture with her apron.

'It's but a poor affair, sir, taken in a caravan on the Common, yet it's like the girl, it's very like.'

It was a miserable production, a cheap and early effort in photography, and Horton rose from the table with the picture in his hand to examine it at the window. And there, surrounded by the thin brass frame, he recognised the face of all faces that had dismayed him, the face he beheld in the vision of the preceding night. He suppressed a groan, and turned from the window with a face so white, that, as he handed the picture back to Mrs Belt, she said, 'You're not feeling well this morning, sir.'

'No, I'm feeling very ill. I must get back to town today to be near to my own doctor. You shall be no loser by my leaving you so suddenly, but if I am going to be ill, I am best in my own home.' For Horton could not have stayed another night at Maitland's Farm to save his life.

He was at his office in Bedford Row by noon, and his clerks thought that he looked ten years older for his visit to the country.

A little more than three weeks after Horton returned to town, when his nerves were beginning to recover their accustomed tone, his attention was unexpectedly recalled to the abhorrent subject of the apparition he had seen. He read in his daily paper that the mail from the Cape had brought news of the wreck of the sailing vessel *Petrel* bound for Australia, with loss of all on board, in a violent storm off the coast, shortly before the steamer left for England. By a careful comparison of dates, allowing for the variation of time, the conviction was forced upon John Horton that the ill-fated ship foundered at the very hour in which he beheld the wraith of Esther Maitland. She and her lover, divided by thousands of miles, both perished by drowning at the same time—Michael Winn in the little river at home, and Esther Maitland in the depths of a distant ocean.

How He Left the Hotel

I used to work the passenger lift in the Empire Hotel, that big block of building in lines of red and white brick like streaky bacon, that stands at the corner of Bath Street. I'd served my time in the army and got my discharge with good conduct stripes, and how I got the job was in this way. The hotel was a big company affair, with a managing committee of retired officers and suchlike, gentlemen with a bit o' money in the concern and nothing to do but fidget about it, and my late colonel was one of 'em. He was as good-tempered a man as ever stepped when his will wasn't crossed, and when I asked him for a job, 'Mole,' says he, 'you're the very man to work the lift at our big hotel. Soldiers are civil and businesslike, and the public like 'em only second-best to sailors. We've had to give our last man the sack, and you can take his place.'

I liked my work well enough and my pay, and kept my place a year, and I should have been there still if it hadn't been for circumstance—but more about that just now. Ours was a hydraulic lift. None o' them rickety things swung up like a poll parrot's cage in a well staircase, that I shouldn't care to trust my neck to. It ran as smooth as oil, a child might have worked it, and safe as standing on the ground. Instead of being stuck full of advertisements like a' omnibus, we'd mirrors in it, and the ladies would look at themselves, and pat their hair, and set their mouths when I was taking 'em downstairs drest of an evening. It was a little sitting-room with red velvet cushions to sit down on, and you'd nothing to do but get into it, and it 'ud float you up, or float you down, as light as a bird.

All the visitors used the lift one time or another, going up or coming down. Some of them was French, and they called the lift the 'assenser', and good enough for them in their language no doubt, but why the Americans, that can speak English when they choose, and are always finding out ways o' doing things quicker than other folks, should waste time and breath calling a lift an 'elevator', I can't make out.

I was in charge of the lift from noon till midnight. By that time the theatre and dining-out folks had come in, and anyone returning later walked upstairs, for my day's work was done. One of the porters worked the lift till I came on duty in the morning, but before twelve there was nothing particular going on, and not much till after two o'clock. Then it was pretty hot work with visitors going up and down constant, and the electric bell ringing you from one floor to another like a house on fire. Then came a quiet spell while dinner was on, and I'd sit down comfortable in the lift and read my paper, only I mightn't smoke. But nobody else might neither, and I had to ask furren gentlemen to please not to smoke in it, it was against the rule. I hadn't so often to tell English gentlemen. They're not like furreners, that seem as if their cigars was glued to their lips.

I always noticed faces as folks got into the lift, for I've sharp sight and a good memory, and none of the visitors needed to tell me twice where to take them. I knew them, and I knew their floor as well as they did themselves.

It was in November that Colonel Saxby came to the Empire Hotel. I noticed him particularly because you could see at once that he was a soldier. He was a tall, thin man about fifty, with a hawk nose, keen eyes, and a grey moustache, and walked stiff from a gunshot wound in the knee. But what I noticed most was the scar of a sabre cut across the right side of the face. As he got in the lift to go to his room on the fourth floor, I thought what a difference there is among officers. Colonel Saxby put me in mind of a telegraph post for height and thinness, and my old colonel was like a barrel in uniform, but a brave soldier and a gentleman all the same. Colonel Saxby's room was number 210, just opposite the glass door leading to the lift, and every time I stopped on the fourth floor Number 210 stared me in the face.

The colonel used to go up in the lift every day regular, though he never came down in it, till—but I'm coming to that presently. Sometimes, when we was alone in the lift, he'd speak to me. He asked me in what regiment I'd served, and said he knew the officers in it. But I can't say he was comfortable to talk to. There was something stand-off about him, and he always seemed deep in his own thoughts. He never sat down in the lift. Whether it was empty or full he stood bolt upright, under the lamp, where the light fell on his pale face and scarred cheek.

One day in February I didn't take the colonel up in the lift, and as he was regular as clockwork, I noticed it, but I supposed he'd gone away for a few days, and I thought no more about it. Whenever I stopped on the fourth floor the door of Number 210 was shut, and as he often left it open, I made sure the colonel was away. At the end of a week I heard a chambermaid say that Colonel Saxby was ill, so thinks I that's why he hadn't been in the lift lately.

It was a Tuesday night, and I'd had an uncommonly busy time of it. It was one stream of traffic up and down, and so it went on the whole evening. It was on the stroke of midnight, and I was about to put out the light in the lift, lock the door, and leave the key in the office for the man in the morning, when the electric bell rang out sharp. I looked at the dial, and saw I was wanted on the fourth floor. It struck twelve as I stepped into the lift. As I passed the second and third floors I wondered who it was that had rung so late, and thought it must be a stranger that didn't know the rule of the house.

But when I stopped at the fourth floor and flung open the door of the lift, Colonel Saxby was standing there wrapt in his military cloak. His room door was shut behind him, for I read the number on it. I thought he was ill in his bed, and ill enough he looked, but he had his hat on, and what could a man that had been in bed ten days want with going out on a winter midnight? I don't think he saw me, but when I'd set the lift in motion, I looked at him standing under the lamp, with the shadow of his hat hiding his eyes, and the light full on the lower part of his face that was deadly pale, the scar on his cheek showing still paler.

'Glad to see you're better, sir,' but he said nothing, and I didn't like to look at him again. He stood like a statue with his cloak about him, and I was downright glad when I opened the door for him to step out in the hall. I saluted as he got out, and he went past me towards the door.

'The colonel wants to go out,' I said to the porter, who stood staring. He opened the front door and Colonel Saxby walked out into the snow. 'That's a queer go,' said the porter.

'It is,' said I. 'I don't like the colonel's looks; he doesn't seem himself at all. He's ill enough to be in his bed, and there he is, gone out on a night like this.'

'Anyhow he's got a famous cloak to keep him warm. I say, supposing he's gone to a fancy ball and got that cloak on to hide his dress,' said the porter, laughing uneasily. For we both felt queerer than we cared to say, and as we spoke there came a loud ring at the door bell.

'No more passengers for me,' I said, and I was really putting the light out this time, when Joe opened the door and two gentlemen entered that I knew at a glance were doctors. One was tall and the other short and stout, and they both came to the lift.

'Sorry, gentlemen, but it's against the rule for the lift to go up after midnight.'

'Nonsense!' said the stout gentleman, 'it's only just past twelve, and it's a matter of life and death. Take us up at once to the fourth floor,' and they were in the lift like a shot.

When I opened the door, they went straight to Number 210. A nurse came out to meet them, and the stout doctor said, 'No change for the worse, I hope.' And I heard her reply, 'The patient died five minutes ago, sir.'

Though I'd no business to speak, that was more than I could stand. I followed the doctors to the door and said, 'There's some mistake here, gentlemen; I took the colonel down in the lift since the clock struck twelve, and he went out.'

The stout doctor said sharply, 'A case of mistaken identity. It was someone else you took for the colonel.'

'Begging your pardon, gentlemen, it was the colonel himself, and the night porter that opened the door for him knew him as well as me. He was dressed for a night like this, with his military cloak wrapt round him.'

'Step in and see for yourself,' said the nurse. I followed the doctors into the room, and there lay Colonel Saxby looking just as I'd seen him a few minutes before. There he lay, dead as his forefathers, and the great cloak spread over the bed to keep him warm that would feel heat and cold no more.

I never slept that night. I sat up with Joe, expecting every minute to hear the colonel ring the front door bell. Next day every time the bell for the lift rang sharp and sudden, the sweat broke out on me and I shook again. I felt as bad as I did the first time I was in action. Me and Joe told the manager all about it, and he said we'd been dreaming, but, said he, 'Mind you, don't you talk about it, or the house'll be empty in a week.'

The colonel's coffin was smuggled into the house the next night. Me and the manager, and the undertaker's men, took it up in the lift, and it lay right across it, and not an inch to spare. They carried it into

Number 210, and while I waited for them to come out again, a queer feeling came over me. Then the door opened softly, and six men carried out the long coffin straight across the passage, and set it down with its foot towards the door of the lift, and the manager looked round for me.

'I can't do it, sir,' I said. 'I can't take the colonel down *again,* I took him down at midnight yesterday, and that was enough for me.'

'Push it in!' said the manager, speaking short and sharp, and they ran the coffin into the lift without a sound. The manager got in last, and before he closed the door he said, 'Mole, you've worked this lift for the last time, it strikes me.' And I had, for I wouldn't have stayed on at the Empire Hotel after what had happened, not if they'd doubled my wages, and me and the night porter left together.

The Real and the Counterfeit

Will Musgrave determined that he would neither keep Christmas alone, nor spend it again with his parents and sisters in the south of France. The Musgrave family annually migrated southward from their home in Northumberland, and Will as regularly followed them to spend a month with them in the Riviera, till he had almost forgotten what Christmas was like in England. He rebelled at having to leave the country at a time when, if the weather was mild, he should be hunting, or if it was severe, skating, and he had no real or imaginary need to winter in the south. His chest was of iron and his lungs of brass. A raking east wind that drove his parents into their thickest furs, and taught them the number of their teeth by enabling them to count a separate and well defined ache for each, only brought a deeper colour into the cheek, and a brighter light into the eye of the weather-proof youth. Decidedly he would not go to Cannes, though it was no use annoying his father and mother, and disappointing his sisters, by telling them beforehand of his determination.

Will knew very well how to write a letter to his mother in which his defection should appear as an event brought about by the over-mastering power of circumstances, to which the sons of Adam must submit. No doubt that a prospect of hunting or skating, as the fates might decree, influenced his decision. But he had also long promised himself the pleasure of a visit from two of his college friends, Hugh Armitage and Horace Lawley, and he asked that they might spend a fortnight with him at Stonecroft, as a little relaxation had been positively ordered for him by his tutor.

'Bless him,' said his mother fondly, when she had read his letter, 'I will write to the dear boy and tell him how pleased I am with his firmness and determination.' But Mr Musgrave muttered inarticulate sounds as he listened to his wife, expressive of incredulity rather than of acquiescence, and when he spoke it was to say, 'Devil of a row three young fellows will kick up alone at Stonecroft! We shall find the stables full of broken-kneed horses when we go home again.'

Will Musgrave spent Christmas day with the Armitages at their place near Ripon. And the following night they gave a dance at which he enjoyed himself as only a very young man can do, who has not yet had his fill of dancing, and who would like nothing better than to waltz through life with his arm round his pretty partner's waist. The following day, Musgrave and Armitage left for Stonecroft, picking up Lawley on the way, and arriving at their destination late in the evening, in the highest spirits and with the keenest appetites. Stonecroft was a delightful haven of refuge at the end of a long journey across country in bitter weather, when the east wind was driving the light dry snow into every nook and cranny. The wide, hospitable front door opened into an oak-panelled hall with a great open fire burning cheerily, and lighted by lamps from overhead that effectually dispelled all gloomy shadows. As soon as Musgrave had entered the house he seized his friends, and before they had time to shake the snow from their coats, kissed them both under the mistletoe bough and set the servants tittering in the background.

'You're miserable substitutes for your betters,' he said, laughing and pushing them from him, 'but it's awfully unlucky not to use the mistletoe. Barker, I hope supper's ready, and that it is something very hot and plenty of it, for we've travelled on empty stomachs and brought them with us,' and he led his guests upstairs to their rooms. 'What a jolly gallery!' said Lawley enthusiastically as they entered a long wide corridor, with many doors and several windows in it, and hung with pictures and trophies of arms.

'Yes, it's our one distinguishing feature at Stonecroft,' said Musgrave. 'It runs the whole length of the house, from the modern end of it to the back, which is very old, and built on the foundations of a Cistercian monastery which once stood on this spot. The gallery's wide enough to drive a carriage and pair down it, and it's the main thoroughfare of the house. My mother takes a constitutional here in bad weather, as though it were the open air, and does it with her bonnet on to aid the delusion.'

Armitage's attention was attracted by the pictures on the walls, and especially by the life-size portrait of a young man in a blue coat, with powdered hair, sitting under a tree with a staghound lying at his feet.

'An ancestor of yours?' he said, pointing at the picture.

'Oh, they're all one's ancestors, and a motley crew they are, I must say for them. It may amuse you and Lawley to find from which of them I derive my good looks. That pretty youth whom you seem to admire is my great-great-grandfather. He died at twenty-two, a preposterous age for an ancestor. But come along Armitage, you'll have plenty of time to do justice to the pictures by daylight, and I want to show you your rooms. I see everything is arranged comfortably, we are close together. Our pleasantest rooms are on the gallery, and here we are nearly at the end of it. Your rooms are opposite to mine, and open into Lawley's in case you should be nervous in the night and feel lonely so far from home, my dear children.'

And Musgrave bade his friends make haste, and hurried away whistling cheerfully to his own room.

The following morning the friends rose to a white world. Six inches of fine snow, dry as salt, lay everywhere, the sky overhead a leaden lid, and all the signs of a deep fall yet to come.

'Cheerful this, very,' said Lawley, as he stood with his hands in his pockets, looking out of the window after breakfast. 'The snow will have spoilt the ice for skating.'

'But it won't prevent wild duck shooting,' said Armitage, 'and I say, Musgrave, we'll rig up a toboggan out there. I see a slope that might have been made on purpose for it. If we get some tobogganing, it may snow day and night for all I care, we shall be masters of the situation any way.'

'Well thought of, Armitage,' said Musgrave, jumping at the idea.

'Yes, but you need two slopes and a little valley between for real good tobogganing,' objected Lawley, 'otherwise you only rush down the hillock like you do from the Mount Church to Funchal, and then have to retrace your steps as you do there, carrying your car on your back. Which lessens the fun considerably.'

'Well, we can only work with the material at hand,' said Armitage; 'let's go and see if we can't find a better place for our toboggan, and something that will do for a car to slide in.'

'That's easily found—empty wine cases are the thing, and stout sticks to steer with,' and away rushed the young men into the open air, followed by half a dozen dogs barking joyfully.

'By Jove! if the snow keeps firm, we'll put runners on strong chairs and walk over to see the Harradines at Garthside, and ask the girls to come out sledging, and we'll push them,' shouted Musgrave to Lawley and Armitage, who had outrun him in the vain attempt to keep up with a deer-hound that headed the parry. After a long and careful search they found a piece of land exactly suited to their purpose, and it would have amused their friends to see how hard the young men worked under the beguiling name of pleasure. For four hours they worked like navvies making a toboggan slide. They shovelled away the snow, then with pickaxe and spade, levelled the ground, so that when a carpet of fresh snow was spread over it, their improvised car would run down a steep incline and be carried by the impetus up another, till it came to a standstill in a snow drift.

'If we can only get this bit of engineering done today,' said Lawley, chucking a spadeful of earth aside as he spoke, 'the slide will be in perfect order for tomorrow.'

'Yes, and when once it's done, it's done for ever,' said Armitage, working away cheerfully with his pick where the ground was frozen hard and full of stones, and cleverly keeping his balance on the slope as he did so. 'Good work lasts no end of a time, and posterity will bless us for leaving them this magnificent slide.'

'Posterity may, my dear fellow, but hardly our progenitors if my father should happen to slip down it,' said Musgrave.

When their task was finished, and the friends were transformed in appearance from navvies into gentlemen, they set out through thick falling snow to walk to Garthside to call on their neighbours the Harradines. They had earned their pleasant tea and lively talk, their blood was still aglow from their exhilarating work, and their spirits at the highest point. They did not return to Stonecroft till they had compelled the girls to name a time when they would come with their brothers and be launched down the scientifically prepared slide, in wine cases well padded with cushions for the occasion.

Late that night the young men sat smoking and chatting together in the library. They had played billiards till they were tired, and Lawley had sung sentimental songs, accompanying himself on the banjo, till even he was weary, to say nothing of what his listeners might be. Armitage sat leaning his light curly head back in the chair, gently puffing out a cloud of tobacco smoke. And he was the first to break the silence that had fallen on the little company.

'Musgrave,' he said suddenly, 'an old house is not complete unless it is haunted. You ought to have a ghost of your own at Stonecroft.' Musgrave threw down the yellow-backed novel he had just picked up, and became all attention.

'So we have, my dear fellow. Only it has not been seen by any of us since my grandfather's time. It is the desire of my life to become personally acquainted with our family ghost.'

Armitage laughed. But Lawley said, 'You would not say that if you really believed in ghosts.'

'I believe in them most devoutly, but I naturally wish to have my kith confirmed by sight. You believe in them too, I can see.'

'Then you see what does not exist, and so far you are in a fair way to see ghosts. No, my state of mind is this,' continued Lawley, 'I neither believe, nor entirely disbelieve in ghosts. I am open to conviction on the subject. Many men of sound judgement believe in them, and others of equally good mental capacity don't believe in them. I merely regard the case of the bogies as not proven. They may or may not exist, but till their existence is plainly demonstrated, I decline to add such an uncomfortable article to my creed as a belief in bogies.'

Musgrave did not reply, but Armitage laughed a strident laugh.

'I'm one against two, I'm in an overwhelming minority,' he said. 'Musgrave frankly confesses his belief in ghosts, and you are neutral, neither believing nor disbelieving, but open to conviction. Now I'm a complete unbeliever in the supernatural, root and branch. People's nerves no doubt play them queer tricks, and will continue to do so to the end of the chapter, and if I were so fortunate as to see Musgrave's family ghost tonight, I should no more believe in it than I do now. By the way, Musgrave, is the ghost a lady or a gentleman?' he asked flippantly.

'I don't think you deserve to be told.'

'Don't you know that a ghost is neither he nor she?' said Lawley. 'Like a corpse, it is always *it*.'

'That is a piece of very definite information from a man who neither believes nor disbelieves in ghosts. How do you come by it, Lawley?' asked Armitage.

'Mayn't a man be well informed on a subject although he suspends his judgement about it? I think I have the only logical mind among us. Musgrave believes in ghosts though he has never seen one, you don't believe in them, and say that you would not be convinced if you saw one, which is not wise, it seems to me.'

'It is not necessary to my peace of mind to have a definite opinion on the subject. After all, it is only a matter of patience, for if ghosts really exist we shall each be one in the course of time, and then, if we've nothing better to do, and are allowed to play such unworthy pranks, we may appear again on the scene, and impartially scare our credulous and incredulous surviving friends.'

'Then I shall try to be beforehand with you, Lawley, and turn bogie first; it would suit me better to scare than to be scared. But, Musgrave, do tell me about your family ghost; I'm really interested in it, and I'm quite respectful now.'

'Well, mind you are, and I shall have no objection to tell you what I know about it, which is briefly this: Stonecroft, as I told you, is built on the site of an old Cistercian Monastery destroyed at the time of the Reformation. The back part of the house rests on the old foundations, and its walls are built with the stones that were once part and parcel of the monastery. The ghost that has been seen by members of the Musgrave family for three centuries past, is that of a Cistercian monk, dressed in the white habit of his order. Who he was, or why he has haunted the scenes of his earthly life so long, there is no tradition to enlighten us. The ghost has usually been seen once or twice in each generation. But as I said, it has not visited us since my grandfather's time, so, like a comet, it should be due again presently.'

'How you must regret that was before your time,' said Armitage.

'Of course I do, but I don't despair of seeing it yet. At least I know where to look for it. It has always made its appearance in the gallery, and I have my bedroom close to the spot where it was last seen, in the hope that if I open my door suddenly some moonlight night I may find the monk standing there.'

'Standing where?' asked the incredulous Armitage.

'In the gallery, to be sure, midway between your two doors and mine. That is where my grandfather last saw it. He was waked in the dead of night by the sound of a heavy door shutting. He ran into the gallery where the noise came from, and, standing opposite the door of the room I occupy, was the white figure of the Cistercian monk. As he looked, it glided the length of the gallery and melted like mist into the wall. The spot where he disappeared is on the old foundations of the monastery, so that he was evidently returning to his own quarters.'

'And your grandfather believed that he saw a ghost?' asked Armitage disdainfully.

'Could he doubt the evidence of his senses? He saw the thing as clearly as we see each other now, and it disappeared like a thin vapour against the wall.'

'My dear fellow, don't you think that it sounds more like an anecdote of your grandmother than of your grandfather?' remarked Armitage. He did not intend to be rude, though he succeeded in being so, as he was instantly aware by the expression of cold reserve that came over Musgrave's frank face.

'Forgive me, but I never can take a ghost story seriously,' he said. 'But this much I will concede—they may have existed long ago in what were literally the dark ages, when rushlights and sputtering dip candles could not keep the shadows at bay. But in this latter part of the nineteenth century, when gas and the electric light have turned night into day, you have destroyed the very conditions that produced the ghost—or rather the belief in it, which is the same thing. Darkness has always been bad for human nerves. I can't explain why, but so it is. My mother was in advance of the age on the subject, and always insisted on having a good light burning in the night nursery, so that when as a child I woke from a bad dream I was never frightened by the darkness. And in consequence I have grown up a complete unbeliever in ghosts, spectres, wraiths, apparitions, *doppel-gänger*, and the whole bogie crew of them,' and Armitage looked round calmly and complacently.

'Perhaps I might have felt as you do if I had not begun life with the knowledge that our house was haunted,' replied Musgrave with visible pride in the ancestral ghost. 'I only wish that I could convince you of the existence of the supernatural from my own personal experience. I always feel it to be the weak point in a ghost story, that it is never told in the first person. It is a friend, or a friend of one's friend, who was the lucky man, and actually saw the ghosts.' And Armitage registered a vow to himself, that within a week from that time Musgrave should see his family ghost with his own eyes, and ever after be able to speak with his enemy in the gate.

Several ingenious schemes occurred to his inventive mind for producing the desired apparition. But he had to keep them burning in his breast. Lawley was the last man to aid and abet him in playing a practical joke on their host, and he feared he should have to work without an ally. And though he would have enjoyed his help and sympathy, it struck him that it would be a double triumph achieved, if both his friends should see the Cistercian monk. Musgrave already believed in ghosts, and was prepared to meet one more than halfway, and Lawley, though he pretended to a judicial and impartial mind concerning them, was not unwilling to be convinced of their existence, if it could be visibly demonstrated to him.

Armitage became more cheerful than usual as circumstances favoured his impious plot. The weather was propitious for the attempt he meditated, as the moon rose late and was approaching the full. On consulting the almanac he saw with delight that three nights hence she would rise at 2 a.m., and an hour later the end of the gallery nearest Musgrave's room would be flooded with her light. Though Armitage could not have an accomplice under the roof, he needed one within reach, who could use needle and thread, to run up a specious imitation of the white robe and hood of a Cistercian monk. And the next day, when they went to the Harradines to take the girls out in their improvised sledges, it fell to his lot to take charge of the youngest Miss Harradine.

As he pushed the low chair on runners over the hard snow, nothing was easier than to bend forward and whisper to Kate, 'I am going to take you as fast as I can, so that no-one can hear what we are saying. I want you to be very kind, and help me to play a perfectly harmless practical joke on Musgrave. Will you promise to keep my secret for a couple of days, when we shall all enjoy a laugh over it together?'

'Oh yes, I'll help you with pleasure, but make haste and tell me what your practical joke is to be.'

'I want to play ancestral ghost to Musgrave, and make him believe that he has seen the Cistercian monk in his white robe and cowl, that was last seen by his respected credulous grandpapa.'

'What a good idea! I know he is always longing to see the ghost, and takes it as a personal affront that it has never appeared to him. But might it not startle him more than you intend?' and Kate turned her glowing face towards him, and Armitage involuntarily stopped the little sledge, 'for it is one thing to wish to see a ghost, you know, and quite another to think that you see it.'

'Oh, you need not fear for Musgrave! We shall be conferring a positive favour on him, in helping him to see what he's so wishful to see. I'm arranging it so that Lawley shall have the benefit of the show as well, and see the ghost at the same time with him. And if two strong men are not a match for one bogie, leave alone a home-made counterfeit one, it's a pity.'

'Well, if you think it's a safe trick to play, no doubt you are right. But how can I help you? With the monk's habit, I suppose?'

'Exactly. I shall be so grateful to you if you will run up some sort of garment, that will look passably like a white Cistercian habit to a couple of men, who I don't think will be in a critical frame of mind during the short time they are allowed to see it. I really wouldn't trouble you if I were anything of a sempster (is that the masculine of sempstress?) myself, but I'm not. A thimble bothers me very much, and at college, when I have to sew on a button, I push the needle through on one side with a threepenny bit, and pull it out on the other with my teeth, and it's a laborious process.'

Kate laughed merrily. 'Oh, I can easily make something or other out of a white dressing-gown, fit for a ghost to wear, and fasten a hood to it.'

Armitage then told her the details of his deeply-laid scheme, how he would go to his room when Musgrave and Lawley went to theirs on the eventful night, and sit up till he was sure that they were fast asleep. Then when the moon had risen, and if her light was obscured by clouds he would be obliged to postpone the entertainment till he could be sure of her aid, he would dress himself as the ghostly monk, put out the candles, softly open the door, and look into the gallery to see that all was ready. 'Then I shall slam the door with an awful bang, for that was the noise that heralded the ghost's last appearance, and it will wake Musgrave and Lawley, and bring them both out of their rooms like a shot. Lawley's door is next to mine, and Musgrave's opposite, so that each will command a magnificent view of the monk at the same instant, and they can compare notes afterwards at their leisure.'

'But what shall you do if they find you out at once?'

'Oh, they won't do that! The cowl will be drawn over my hue, and I shall stand with my back to the moonlight. My private belief is, that in spite of Musgrave's yearnings after a ghost, he won't like it when he thinks he sees it. Nor will Lawley, and I expect they'll dart back into their rooms and lock themselves in as soon as they catch sight of the monk. That would give me time to whip back into my room, turn the key, strip off my finery, hide it, and be roused with difficulty from a deep sleep when they come knocking at my door to tell me what a horrible thing has happened. And one more ghost story will he added to those already in circulation,' and Armitage laughed aloud in anticipation of the fun.

'It is to be hoped that everything will happen just as you have planned it, and then we shall all be pleased. And now will you turn the sledge round and let us join the others, we have done conspiring for the present. If we are seen talking so exclusively to each other, they will suspect that we are brewing some mischief together. Oh, how cold the wind is! I like to hear it whistle in my hair!' said Kate as Armitage deftly swung the little sledge round and drove it quickly before him, facing the keen north wind, as she buried her chin in her warm furs.

Armitage found an opportunity to arrange with Kate, that he would meet her half-way between Stonecroft and her home, on the afternoon of the next day but one, when she would give him a parcel containing the monk's habit. The Harradines and their house party were coming on Thursday afternoon to try the toboggan slide at Stonecroft. But Kate and Armitage were willing to sacrifice their, pleasure to the business they had in hand.

There was no other way but for the conspirators to give their friends the slip for a couple of hours, when the important parcel would be safely given to Armitage, secretly conveyed by him to his own room, and locked up till he should want it in the small hours of the morning.

When the young people arrived at Stonecroft Miss Harradine apologised for her younger sister's absence—occasioned, she said, by a severe headache. Armitage's heart beat rapidly when he heard the excuse, and he thought how convenient it was for the inscrutable sex to be able to turn on a headache at will, as one turns on hot or cold water from a tap.

After luncheon, as there were more gentlemen than ladies, and Armitage's services were not necessary at the toboggan slide, he elected to take the dogs for a walk, and set off in the gayest spirits to keep his appointment with Kate. Much as he enjoyed maturing his ghost plot, he enjoyed still more the confidential talks with Kate that had sprung out of it, and he was sorry that this was to be the last of them. But the moon in heaven could not be stayed for the performance of his little comedy, and her light was necessary to its due performance. The ghost must be seen at three o'clock next morning, at the time and place arranged, when the proper illumination for its display would be forthcoming.

As Armitage walked swiftly over the hard snow, he caught sight of Kate at a distance. She waved her hand gaily and pointed smiling to the rather large parcel she was carrying. The red glow of the winter sun shone full upon her, bringing out the warm tints in her chestnut hair, and filling her brown eyes with soft lustre, and Armitage looked at her with undisguised admiration.

'It's awfully good of you to help me so kindly,' he said as he took the parcel from her, 'and I shall come round tomorrow to tell you the result of our practical joke. But how is the headache?' he asked smiling, 'you look so unlike aches or pains of any kind, I was forgetting to enquire about it.'

'Thank you, it is better. It was not altogether a made-up headache, though it happened opportunely. I was awake in the night, not in the least repenting that I was helping you, of course, but wishing it was all well over. One has heard of this kind of trick sometimes proving too successful, of people being frightened out of their wits by a make-believe ghost, and I should never forgive myself if Mr Musgrave or Mr Lawley were seriously alarmed.'

'Really, Miss Harradine, I don't think that you need give yourself a moment's anxiety about the nerves of a couple of burly young men. If you are afraid for anyone, let it be for me. If they find me out, they will fall upon me and rend me limb from limb on the spot. I can assure you I am the only one for whom there is anything to fear,' and the transient gravity passed like a cloud from Kate's bright face. And she admitted that it was rather absurd to be uneasy about two stalwart young men compounded more of muscle than of nerves. And they parted, Kate hastening home as the early twilight fell, and Armitage, after watching her out of sight, retracing his steps with the precious parcel under his arm.

He entered the house unobserved, and reaching the gallery by a back staircase, felt his way in the dark to his room. He deposited his treasure in the wardrobe, locked it up, and attracted by the sound of laughter, ran downstairs to the drawing-room. Will Musgrave and his friends, after a couple of hours of glowing exercise, had been driven indoors by the darkness, nothing loath to partake of tea and hot cakes, while they talked and laughed over the adventures of the afternoon.

'Wherever have you been, old fellow?' said Musgrave as Armitage entered the room. 'I believe you've a private toboggan of your own somewhere that you keep quiet. If only the moon rose at a decent time, instead of at some unearthly hour in the night, when it's not of the slightest use to anyone, we would have gone out looking for you.'

'You wouldn't have had far to seek, you'd have met me on the turnpike road.'

'But why this subdued and chastened taste? Imagine preferring a constitutional on the high road when you might have been tobogganing with us! My poor friend, I'm afraid you are not feeling well!' said Musgrave with an affectation of sympathy that ended in boyish laughter and a wrestling match between the two young men, in the course of which Lawley more than once saved the tea table from being violently overthrown.

Presently, when the cakes and toast had disappeared before the youthful appetites, lanterns were lighted, and Musgrave and his friends, and the Harradine brothers, set out as a bodyguard to take the young ladies home. Armitage was in riotous spirits, and finding that Musgrave and Lawley had appropriated the two prettiest girls in the company, waltzed untrammelled along the road before them lantern in hand, like a very will-o'-the-wisp.

The young people did not part till they had planned fresh pleasures for the morrow, and Musgrave, Lawley, and Armitage returned to Stonecroft to dinner, making the thin air ring to the jovial songs with which they beguiled the homeward journey.

Late in the evening, when the young men were sitting in the library, Musgrave suddenly exclaimed, as he reached down a book from an upper shelf, 'Hallo! I've come on my grandfather's diary! Here's his own account of how he saw the white monk in the gallery. Lawley, you may read it if you like, but it shan't be wasted on an unbeliever like Armitage. By Jove! what an odd coincidence! It's forty years this very night, the thirtieth of December, since he saw the ghost,' and he handed the book to Lawley, who read Mr Musgrave's narrative with close attention.

'Is it a case of "*almost thou persuadest me*"?' asked Armitage, looking at his intent and knitted brow.

'I hardly know what I think. Nothing positive either way at any rate.' And he dropped the subject, for he saw Musgrave did not wish to discuss the family ghost in Armitage's unsympathetic presence.

They retired late, and the hour that Armitage had so gleefully anticipated drew near. 'Goodnight both of you,' said Musgrave as he entered his room, 'I shall be asleep in five minutes. All this exercise in the open air makes a man absurdly sleepy at night,' and the young men closed their doors, and silence settled down upon Stonecroft Hall. Armitage and Lawley's rooms were next to each other, and in less than a quarter of an hour Lawley shouted a cheery goodnight, which was loudly returned by his friend.

Then Armitage felt somewhat mean and stealthy. Musgrave and Lawley were both confidingly asleep, while he sat up alert and vigilant maturing a mischievous plot that had for its object the awakening and scaring of both the innocent sleepers. He dared not smoke to pass the tedious time, lest the tell-tale fumes should penetrate into the next room through the keyhole, and inform Lawley if he woke for an instant that his friend was awake too, and behaving as though it were high noon.

Armitage spread the monk's white habit on the bed, and smiled as he touched it to think that Kate's pretty fingers had been so recently at work upon it. He need not put it on for a couple of hours yet, and to occupy the time he sat down to write. He would have liked to take a nap. But he knew that if he once yielded to sleep, nothing would wake him till he was called at eight o'clock in the morning. As he bent over his desk the big clock in the hall struck one, so suddenly and sharply it was like a blow on the head, and he started violently. 'What a swinish sleep Lawley must be in that he can't hear a noise like that!' he thought, as snoring became audible from the next room. Then he drew the candles nearer to him, and settled once more to his writing, and a pile of letters testified to his industry, when again the clock struck.

But this time he expected it, and it did not startle him, only the cold made him shiver. 'If I hadn't made up my mind to go through with this confounded piece of folly, I'd go to bed now,' he thought, 'but I can't break faith with Kate. She's made the robe and I've got to wear it, worse luck,' and with a great yawn he threw down his pen, and rose to look out of the window. It was a clear frosty night. At the edge of the dark sky, sprinkled with stars, a faint band of cold light heralded the rising moon. How different from the grey light of dawn, that ushers in the cheerful day, is the solemn rising of the moon in the depth of a winter night. Her light is not to rouse a sleeping world and lead men forth to their labour, it falls on the closed eyes of the weary, and silvers the graves of those whose rest shall be broken no more. Armitage was not easily impressed by the sombre aspect of nature, though he was quick to feel her gay and cheerful influence, but he would be glad when the farce was over, and he no longer obliged to watch the rise and spread of the pale light, solemn as the dawn of the last day.

He turned from the window, and proceeded to make himself into the best imitation of a Cistercian monk that he could contrive. He slipped the white habit over all his clothing, that he might seem of portly size, and marked dark circles round his eyes, and thickly powdered his face a ghastly white.

Armitage silently laughed at his reflection in the glass, and wished that Kate could see him now. Then he softly opened the door and looked into the gallery. The moonlight was shimmering duskily on the end window to the right of his door and Lawley's. It would soon be where he wanted it, and neither too light nor too dark for the success of his plan. He stepped silently back again to wait, and a feeling as much akin to nervousness as he had ever known came over him. His heart beat rapidly, he started like a timid girl when the silence was suddenly broken by the hooting of an owl. He no longer cared to look at himself in the glass. He had taken fright at the mortal pallor of his powdered face. 'Hang it all! I wish Lawley hadn't left off snoring. It was quite companionable to hear him.'

And again he looked into the gallery, and now the moon shed her cold beams where he intended to stand. He put out the light and opened the door wide, and stepping into the gallery threw it to with an echoing slam that only caused Musgrave and Lawley to start and turn on, their pillows. Armitage stood dressed as the ghostly monk of Stonecroft, in the pale moonlight in the middle of the gallery, waiting for the door on either side to fly open and reveal the terrified faces of his friends.

He had time to curse the ill-luck that made them sleep so heavily that night of all nights, and to fear lest the servants had heard the noise their master had been deaf to, and would come hurrying to the spot and spoil the sport. But no-one came, and as Armitage stood, the objects in the long gallery became clearer every moment, as his sight accommodated itself to the dim light. 'I never noticed before that there was a mirror at the end of the gallery! I should not have believed the moonlight was bright enough for me to see my own reflection so far off, only white stands out so in the dark. But is it my own reflection? Confound it all, the thing's moving and I'm standing still! I know what it is! It's Musgrave dressed up to try to give me a fright, and Lawley's helping him. They've forestalled me, that's why they didn't come out of their rooms when I made a noise fit to wake the dead. Odd we're both playing the same practical joke at the same moment! Come on, my counterfeit bogie, and we'll see which of us turns white-livered first!'

But to Armitage's surprise, that rapidly became terror, the white figure that he believed to be Musgrave disguised, and like himself playing ghost, advanced towards him, slowly gliding over the floor which its feet did not touch. Armitage's courage was high, and he determined to hold his ground against the something ingeniously contrived by Musgrave and Lawley to terrify him into belief in the supernatural. But a feeling was creeping over the strong young man that he had never known before. He opened his dry mouth as the thing floated towards him, and there issued a hoarse inarticulate cry, that woke Musgrave and Lawley and brought them to their doors in

398

a moment, not knowing by what strange fright they had been startled out of their sleep. Do not think them cowards that they shrank back appalled from the ghostly forms the moonlight revealed to them in the gallery. But as Armitage vehemently repelled the horror that drifted nearer and nearer to him, the cowl slipped from his head, and his friends recognised his white face, distorted by fear, and, springing towards him as he staggered, supported him in their arms. The Cistercian monk passed them like a white mist that sank into the wall, and Musgrave and Lawley were alone with the dead body of their friend, whose masquerading dress had become his shroud.

My Next Door Neighbour

Some years ago it was my doleful hap to spend five months as a patient in one of our London hospitals. They were the dreariest months in the whole year, from November to February, when the great city is shorn of its summer attractions, and rain, fog and frost alternately strive for the supremacy, so that I did not lose many outdoor pleasures owing to my illness. My life had been an up-and-down-hill journey, full of varied experiences. I had travelled much and seen many peoples and countries, I had had wealth and squandered it, and now at length poverty and I were fairly face to face. I had only myself to thank for my reverse of fortune, and I could not complain of the result of my own actions. The boon companions who helped me to spend my money forsook me at the approach of adversity, as midges that dance in the sunshine disappear when the sky is overcast.

I could not but admire the symmetry and completeness of my misfortunes. Penniless, friendless, and for the first time in my life, at thirty-five years of age, fallen seriously ill. Health, without which I could do nothing and be nothing, was withdrawn precisely at the time when it was the one thing needful to enable me to retrieve my position. I had wealthy relations, but as I had not cared to know them in my prosperity I had no claim on them in my adversity, nor any desire to imitate the return of the Prodigal Son on the baseless presumption that a fatted calf would be killed for me. I remember it struck me as odd, when the doctor who visited me in my cheap lodgings gave me an in-patient's ticket for the hospital, whose pleasant lot it had been hitherto to bestow, instead of receive favours. But there was no flavour of private charity in the proffered aid. I accepted it as coming from that great impersonal body, the public, towards whom no-one ever felt a burdensome sense of obligation.

The principle on which I had always chosen my friends probably made it easier than it would have been to most men of my education, to pass twenty weeks on amicable terms with the very mixed specimens of humanity that passed through the hospital ward as my fellow patients. If a man pleased and interested me, that was his letter of recommendation. I enjoyed his society regardless of social distinctions. I thought no more of him if he happened to be a duke, or less if he chanced to be a cabman.

Many were the changes I saw during my long stay in the hospital. Some of my fellow patients died, but most recovered and went away, while I remained till the population of the beds had changed repeatedly, and I grew to be the oldest inhabitant and father of the house. Our ward was a long narrow room with folding doors at each end, a large fireplace in the middle, with four high windows at either side, six beds under each row of windows, and twelve beds along the opposite side of the room, making twenty-four in all. The walls were stained a cheerful blue, and hung with engravings of more or less merit, and garnished here and there with texts and mottoes inciting us to be very joyful, or, where that was not possible, to try resignation as a useful work-a-day substitute.

The floor was of polished wood, unrelieved by carpet or rug. The windows opened easily by an arrangement of ropes and pulleys, and ventilators close under the ceiling at the opposite side of the ward ensured a thorough current of air when it was necessary to change the atmosphere. But nothing can prevent the peculiar flatness of hospital air. I never lost the consciousness of it, while the smell of carbolic filled with me loathing. It is supposed to overpower other and so-called worse odours than itself; but to me it seemed merely a substituting of one evil for another.

The illness that kept me so long in the hospital was a surgical case of great interest to the doctors and considerable suffering to myself but gratifying to my invalid's egotism, because it was the only case the kind in the ward, where nine diseases were apportioned among twenty-four patients. To have one all to oneself out of that limited number conferred a certain distinction upon one.

An Anglican sisterhood was in charge of the nursing at the hospital, and splendidly they performed their duties. I think of them still with respect and gratitude. The nurses were strong, capable women, for the most part wonderfully forbearing with ill-tempered and thankless patients. During the time I spent under their care I gained some insight into the trials and difficulties of a hospital nurse's life. I came to the conclusion that, if I were a woman, I would do or be anything that was honest, except stewardess on board ship, rather than nurse sick people for a livelihood.

It is a marvel to me how anyone used to quiet and privacy in his own home when he is ill ever recovers in a hospital, where he has neither one nor the other. But I had such a splendid nervous system that it was only on days of prostration following an operation that I really suffered from living in public, and then I did so acutely. In spite of the screen put round my bed to form a make-believe room to myself, in imagination I still saw the seven faces on the pillows to my right hand and four to my left in the long row of beds. I heard every groan, every impatient exclamation of the weary sufferers, and at night I listened with a frightfully exalted sense of hearing to the long-drawn snores of such of them as were happy enough to be able to sleep.

The crowd of medical students, who accompanied and thronged about the doctors when they made the round of the wards, was in itself enough to kill a sensitive and nervous patient. They clustered like bees round any especially interesting case, and the more hideous the sights they saw, or the details they listened to, the happier they were and the more notes they took. I looked at the dignified bearing and the fine face of the celebrated operating surgeon to whom they were listening by a patient's bedside, and wondered could he ever have been an uncouth lad like so many of his pupils. Could those penetrating eyes, full of the fire of genius, ever have winked at a fellow student behind the back of the great doctor of the day some forty years ago?

I soon became interested in the routine of hospital life, and on those days when I was fairly well and free from pain I should never wish to be better entertained than I was in studying my fellow-patients.

We were a motley crew, surely the oddest four-and-twenty men that circumstances could have thrown together. The changes in our population were so rapid that a bed had scarcely time to grow cold before it was in possession of a fresh occupant. We were of all ages, shapes, and sizes, and of a variety of nationalities; being, I think, at our most representative when our company consisted of Englishmen, Irishmen, and Scotchmen, with a choleric little Welshman, Germans, a Yankee, a Frenchman, a Swede, a Lascar seaman, a Jew, and a Negro. By chance the Yankee on the day of his arrival was put in the next bed to the Negro; but after much nasal vituperation, the arrangement was altered for peace and quiet's sake. We also represented many trades, and had amongst us tailors, policemen, costermongers, postmen, a butler, cabmen, a gravedigger, a sugar refiner, shoemakers, and an omnibus conductor.

We also had some of those mysterious gentlemen of no particular calling or visible means of sustenance, who live at the back of everywhere, that a crowd or an accident brings into the street in swarms, as heavy rain brings worms to the surface of the soil. They are always open to an odd job, when it is highly paid for and not of an arduous nature. They spend their Sunday afternoons demonstrating in the park, clothed in long topcoats and woollen comforters, and never without a short pipe and tobacco, which presumably cost money. Where they sleep at night when they are not in hospital I have no idea.

One of our company, who afforded me much amusement, was a genteel and sensitive young clerk, who had it on his mind to explain to me how he came to be in such a vulgar institution as a public hospital. He was consumed by a haunting dread lest, when he had recovered and returned to his place in the office of Messrs Scrawley and McNib in Lincoln's Inn, he might be recognised in the street and spoken to by one of his fellow patients, a chimney-sweep of too friendly a disposition. 'His face, sir, would be black in the pursuit of his avocation and I shouldn't know him, but he'd see me a mile off and run after me; and if a man in my position is seen talking to a sweep I shall be ruined,' said my sensitive little clerk.

I made a great variety of friends among my fellow patients who stayed long enough to feel some interest in others, as the terrible egotism of their own sufferings abated. I parted on excellent terms with a butler, who taught me the kind of whistle I must give at the area gate when I called to see him after nightfall. A hansom-driver, bidding me goodbye, in the fullness of his heart, offered to take me in his cab down Piccadilly for my first airing after I left the hospital. A thoughtful little German baker with whom I talked metaphysics in accordance with the definition, that, '*when a man talks to you in a way that you don't understand, about a thing which he doesn't understand, them's metaphysics,*' as a parting gift presented me with a list of shops whose bread one would do well to avoid, from the baker's custom of working the sponge with unwashen hands, and I thanked him. A costermonger acquaintance taught me how, when buying fruit off a barrow in the street, to detect the tricks of the trade. In short, I picked up a great deal of information that, if it was not useful, amused me and afforded me a glimpse into the lives of other men.

I had been three months in bed, and was recovering from the effects of an operation, when I became acquainted with a man who interested me more than any other of my fellow patients. I remember the day that he came into the hospital. It was in the first week of the new year, and a nurse had congratulated me on the good luck of having had the bed to the right of mine standing empty for two whole days. Its last occupant had been a dull, heavy fellow, absorbed in the contemplation of his own symptoms and doggedly convinced that he was the head martyr in the universe, unable perhaps, and certainly unwilling, to take part in the courtesies and amenities of invalid life. We did not miss him when he left, and the blank pillow was a pleasanter object to look at than the furrowed, irritable face and bald head that had lain upon it. It occurred to me, how fortunate I should be if the fates should send me an intelligent, sympathetic fellow sufferer in the bed that I had seen so diversely occupied during the past twelve weeks.

The previous night my rest had been troubled, and in the forenoon, between the disturbance of the doctor's visit and dinner being brought to us, I fell asleep. When I awoke I was astonished to find the bed that an hour and a half before had been empty occupied by a fresh patient, looking as comfortable and established as though he had been there a week.

The newcomer was a tall, swarthy-complexioned man of about thirty years of age. He lay on his back with his eyes closed and his head inclined towards me, so that I had a good view of his very remarkable face. That he was not an Englishman I felt sure, though to what country he belonged I could not tell. He was clean-shaven as I thought, but I afterwards found that no hair grew on his face, and a month without a razor did not darken his lip or chin. His skin was of a yellowish-brown, and his straight black hair that covered his ears and lay on his cheek was cut square across the forehead. The nose was large and prominent, the mouth large, thin-lipped, and well-shaped, and the jaw formed a powerful angle from the ear. The length of the face from the eyes to the mouth was greater than is usual, and the finely-modelled long hollow of the cheek gave a melancholy and dignified outline to his countenance. I wondered what he would be like when he awoke, and as I watched he opened his dark eyes, large and set wide apart, with a clear and penetrating expression.

As I looked in his face, that in spite of its smoothness was essentially masculine, and in expression a quaint mixture of shrewdness and childlike simplicity, I said to myself, 'My friend, I cannot offhand assign you to any particular country, but I can date your type of face for you. You have no business at all wandering about in the nineteenth century. You ought never to have stirred from the fourteenth, nor emerged from the pages of Froissart, to which you really belong.'

There was a quiet dignity about the man that forbade me to ask the usual questions that inaugurate a hospital acquaintance, such as, 'What's your name? Where do you come from? And what's the matter with you?' and I waited my time for a favourable opportunity of speaking to him.

When the nurse gave me my dinner I asked her, 'Who is the man in the next bed?'

'A Frenchman; he was brought here while you were asleep.'

'Good,' thought I; 'then I shall amuse myself by rubbing up my rusty French with him. Can you tell me his name?'

'No, I can't remember French names, and besides, he has a string of them, those foreigners always have.'

I reached paper and pencil from the locker by my side and gave them to the nurse. 'Just oblige me by copying his name from the card over his bed and bring it to me, will you?' She did as she was requested, and returning handed me the paper, on which she had written the names Jean-Marie Thégonnec Pipraic. 'Why, the man must be a Breton,' said I, repeating the two last names to myself.

'A Briton! A Frenchman never yet was a Briton, and couldn't be if he tried,' said the nurse promptly, her national susceptibilities rubbed the wrong way in an instant through her misapprehension.

'A Breton, my good woman, a Breton, not a Briton,' said I; 'and a Breton is no more a Frenchman, though he may happen to speak French, than a Welshman is an Englishman, even if he talks English. When did that solemn, dignified, fourteenth-century face ever belong to a Frenchman I should like to know?' and I wished to argue with my nurse concerning racial differences. But she cut the matter short by turning to the new patient and asking him plainly whether he was a Frenchman or what, for an Englishman in the next bed would not take her word for it. Our stranger, who was sitting up with his table across his knees, waiting for dinner, bowed gravely, first to the nurse and then to me.

'I am a Breton, *madame*, and I come from Roscoff, in the *département* of Finistère,' he said in a low, melancholy voice, speaking with a strong foreign accent; and he added with dignified simplicity: 'My name is Jean-Marie Thégonnec Pipraic, but I am everywhere called Jean-Marie.'

'I thought you a Breton from your name,' I said. 'I know your part of Brittany very well. I used to know Finistère and Morbihan from end to end. I once spent a summer there.'

'Does *monsieur* know Bretagne?' said my new acquaintance, with flashing eyes. 'Has he been to Morlaix, Landenau, Quimper, St Pol de Leon, Carnac, Plougastel?' and then followed a torrent of names of places, some on the coast and some inland, just as they rushed into his mind.

'I know them all, my friend,' I said, smiling at his eagerness, 'and when you have eaten your dinner you shall ask me as many questions as you please, and see if I speak the truth.'

'I should not doubt that *monsieur* spoke the truth, but it is wonderful; it is wonderful!'

I noticed that Jean-Marie, as I already called him to myself, devoutly crossed himself on the forehead and on the breast, before and after he took food. I tried to talk French with him, though not always with lucid results, for he had learned French as a second language, and spoke a strange *patois*, while mine, such as it was, had been acquired in Paris. An acquaintance sprang up rapidly between us, founded on my knowledge of the scenes of his childhood, and the places dearest to him in his manhood. And I grew fond of Jean-Marie, so that my heart sank when I learnt how badly the doctors thought of his case. By degrees he told me the simple story of his life.

Jean-Marie Thégonnec Pipraic was the son of a poor fisherman and his wife who lived near Roscoff, on the coast of Finistère. He and his younger sister, Anne—namesake of *La Bonne Duchesse,* who after four centuries is still spoken of in Brittany as though she had been dead but a generation or so—were the only children, and had been brought up in such poverty and hard work as sounded incredible to my pampered English ears. They never tasted meat. Their food was the coarsest bread, with onions and potatoes, and occasionally on festival days a little fish and milk. They rose at four in the morning to make or mend fishing-nets, or to work on the small plot of ground surrounding the hut in which they lived. The father was out fishing every night, and the mother burnt a taper in the window that in calm weather he could see as a glimmering point of light, when his boat was tossing on the water far from shore.

When he came safely home out of the teeth of the western gales that ravage that coast, the pious mother took her children to the church, to thank the Blessed Virgin for her protection. Once when the husband and father had been miraculously preserved in a storm, they made a votive offering of a model of a fishing boat, which was hung suspended, from the roof of the chancel before the altar of their patron saint, in visible token of the mercy of Heaven and the gratitude of man.

But there came a fearful night in autumn when a sudden squall of wind struck the little fleet of fishing boats, and in the dismal dawn, when stormy sea and sky seemed torn together in one grey mist, out of the welter of devouring waves, the drowned bodies of brave fishermen were washed ashore. And among them that of Thégonnec Pipraic, the father of Jean-Marie.

'The sea is cruel on the coast of Finistère, *monsieur*; it makes many widows and orphans; and on winter nights we hear it howling like a hungry wolf at our door. But in the summer it is often still and blue as the sky above, and the little islands are like clouds floating on its surface. In the summer, *monsieur*, the sea is like the love of the *Bon Dieu*; in the winter it is like his wrath, and we tremble before it.'

Jean-Marie was to have been a fisherman, like his father before him. But the mother, dreading lest the cruel sea should take from her her son as well as her husband, moved a short distance to St Pol de Leon, where she found work for herself and little Anne in the fields. Jean-Marie, only ten years old, worked his twelve hours daily as a farm labourer for a trifling pittance; but, as he said, 'the *Bon Dieu* saw that I wanted for nothing. I had bread; I had health and strength; and as I grew older I was able to succour my mother and my sister.'

Jean-Marie saw the *Bon Dieu* in everything. I have never met man or woman with the same childlike faith.

When he was twenty years of age his mother died, worn out with toil and scanty living. Work as they would, the three of them, they could not earn more than enough to meet each day's recurring want. They could not lay by a *sou* against sickness or accident, or afford the weary mother a little rest before she died. Shortly after her death her daughter married a fisherman and went to live on the island of Batzoff, the soil of which is tilled by the women, while the men plough the sea. And there she still lives in many-childed poverty.

'How come you to speak English, Jean-Marie?' I asked him one day when he was free from pain and able to enjoy conversation.

'*Monsieur*, I learnt it from an excellent compatriot of yours, who lived for many years at Carnac, trying to find out the meaning of the great stones there. Monsieur Smitt was like a father to me. I was his servant, I dug his garden and tended his horse and cow, and he taught me to speak his difficult language. For several years I lived with my master. He was not Catholic, *monsieur*; Père Croisac would have it that he was not even Christian, but the *Bon Dieu* had given him a good heart, and the poor prayed for him. I tried to convert my master, and I assured him of the miracles that the holy saints still work in Bretagne. But Monsieur Smitt would not be convinced. He had a way like so many Englishmen—pardon me, *monsieur*, but it is not a good way of jesting at holy things. But in his heart I think my master believed, for he let me go all the way to Helgoet when our cow had cast her calf, and was suffering like a Christian, to intercede with Saint Herbot for the poor beast.'

'I remember Saint Herbot's church perfectly well,' I said. 'He has taken the cattle under his special protection, and I saw tufts of the hair of sick animals laid on his altar by their unfortunate owners, who had come to pray for their recovery.'

'Then *monsieur* must have seen the very wisp of hair from our poor cow's tail that I laid on the altar of the holy saint myself,' said Jean-Marie with animation. 'It was red, with here and there a white hair mixed; *monsieur* could not forget it.'

I was obliged to evade the difficulty by saying that when I visited Saint Herbot's church, the altar was so thickly covered with tufts of goats', horses', and cows' hair that Jean-Marie's lock must have been hidden beneath them.

'And did the cow recover?' I asked.

'*Monsieur*, when I returned from my pilgrimage on the third day the poor beast was dead.'

'What, when you had walked two whole days to lay a tuft of her hair before Saint Herbot? What could the saint be dreaming of?'

'*Monsieur*, the Holy Saint Herbot has two ways of answering prayer for *les pauvres bestiaux malades*. If he judges it best for them to recover, they will get better; but if not they will die,' and as though unwilling further to discuss the saint with an unbeliever, Jean-Marie passed on to other reminiscences.

'When I was twenty-five years of age my master took me with him to Paris; the first time that I had left my native Bretagne. But, *monsieur*, what a thing it was, the people there treated me as if I was a savage. They laughed at me in the street, at my long hair, my wide hat, my excellent *bragous bras*—breeches is your English word for them, *monsieur*, of the pattern that my forefathers had worn since the days of *La Bonne Duchesse*. They jeered at me when I went to mass, and their churches were empty; in Bretagne they are crowded with men. My money was stolen from me, and when I politely asked my way in the street, I was directed to the wrong place. The very children used vile words, and the young girls said things to me that a man in Bretagne would blush to think of.'

One day when we had grown quite intimate, Jean-Marie confided to me the love he had borne to his fellow servant Françoise.

'*Monsieur*, I have never loved but one woman, my Françoise. For five years we ate at the same table, we worked in the same garden, we went to mass together, we prayed together. We were not married because I desired to save a little money first, that my wife might not have to toil as my poor mother had done. *Monsieur*, I cannot tell you whether my Françoise was beautiful or not, but the *Bon Dieu* had given her to me, and I never looked in another woman's face. We were to be married: Monsieur Smitt would still keep me as his servant, and we were to live in a little cottage near him, and he would have another woman for his cook, though my Françoise was still to help in the housework.

'Within a fortnight of our intended marriage our good master fell ill of a fever, and my Françoise nursed him, and took it from him and died. They both died, *monsieur*, my master and my Françoise, and I tried to take the fever from them that I might die too, but the fever had no more power to kill me than fire has to burn the holy saints. And to think, *monsieur*, that we might have been man and wife if I had not loved my Françoise so well. *Monsieur*, this rosary is all that I have that belonged to my Françoise, for she was as poor as the Blessed Virgin herself.'

And Jean-Marie stretched his long, thin arm towards me, and laid on the locker by my bedside a cheap rosary, made of a string of small berries, with a crucifix attached to it.

After the death of his master and Françoise, Jean-Marie returned to the neighbourhood of Roscoff and worked under a well-to-do farmer, who grew great quantities of the onions for which that part of Finistère is renowned. He was an enterprising man, and anxious to find the best market for his produce. Jean-Marie served him faithfully and intelligently, and when he had been with him three years he increased his wages, and as he spoke English he sent him to London, to negotiate for the sale of his onions with English dealers. I was astounded to find how astute my fourteenth-century friend was in business matters. He had made bargains profitable to his employer and to himself, and Monsieur Ploumel was highly satisfied with the honesty and ability of his agent.

And now, on his third journey to England, Jean-Marie was smitten with a mortal illness, and would never return to his native land.

'I have been ill for more than a year, *monsieur*. I know it by the pain I have suffered. But it does not matter; it is over now. I have finished my work. The day before I came into this hospital, I sent to Monsieur Ploumel every *sou* I had made for him, and a draft for three hundred *francs* that I had saved for my poor sister and her children. I have come here to die,' he said, in quiet unemotional tones, as though he were speaking of a stranger.

I listened in silence, for I knew what the doctors thought of his case: that nothing could be done to cure, but only to palliate the disease. Never had there been a more patient sufferer in the hospital. In spite of his mediaeval superstition, Jean-Marie was a most courageous Christian, and put us all to shame. When he was sufficiently free from pain to speak, it was with a gentle courtesy, and no word of complaint or of impatience ever escaped his lips. He was always ready to listen to the egotistic grumbling of his fellow-patients, though he tried, by example and precept, to lift us out of the narrow groove of self-centred suffering.

One day I saw that he was enduring agony. His dark face was livid, and when he could speak he said quietly, '*Monsieur*, these pains are pin-pricks compared with those the Blessed Redeemer suffered for us.'

That night Jean-Marie was very ill, and I lay awake, partly from sympathy with him, partly because his restlessness made it difficult for me to sleep, as he muttered and talked to himself without ceasing. The nurse was in constant attendance upon him, and she said to me: 'His sleeping draught has not suited him tonight; he is terribly restless.'

Between two and three o'clock in the morning I thought that she was again leaning over Jean-Marie. On the opposite side of his bed, facing me, a woman stood wearing a white cap, but not such as our nurses wore, and she was bending over Jean-Marie as though she would kiss him. Then she knelt, holding his hand in hers, and the light in the ward was sufficient for me to see that she wore the costume of a Brittany peasant, with the coloured cotton kerchief on the shoulders, tucked into the bib of the black apron in front. I raised myself in bed, and a nurse, who was sitting by the fire, came to me at once.

'Do you want anything?' she asked.

'Yes; who is that woman?' and I pointed to the figure still standing by Jean-Marie.

'What woman?' she said, looking in the direction I indicated.

'That Brittany peasant woman, to be sure, by Jean-Marie's bedside, talking to him and holding his hand.'

'You have been dreaming!' said the nurse; 'there is no-one there. Lie down and try to go to sleep, though I dare say that poor fellow makes it hard for you to rest.'

I had not been dreaming, though Jean-Marie had, for afterwards he awoke with a little sigh as if he were sorry to return to consciousness, and said in his quiet tones, '*Monsieur*, the *Bon Dieu* has been very good to me. He has sent my Françoise to me in a dream, and I have seen her and held her hand in mine. I am only to suffer three days more, for on Sunday morning at two o'clock my Françoise is to fetch me!' And he laughed to himself, a little laugh of incomparable happiness, and soon afterwards became again delirious.

All Thursday, Friday, and Saturday, my friend grew steadily worse, though the doctors did not anticipate an immediate end of his sufferings. His mind wandered the whole time, and he talked to himself incessantly in Breton. When occasionally he dropped into French, and I understood what he said, he was imagining he was a child again, playing on the sands, or sitting on the rocks with his little sister, mending their father's fishing-nets. I grew feverish with excitement and anticipation of what would happen to Jean-Marie. I had certainly seen his Françoise, and I dreaded her return. But I did not dare confide in either doctor or nurse. My strange experience could only be regarded by them as a sick man's fancy. But my state of nervous excitement was duly noticed and commented on by one of the house surgeons, a pleasant young man who had shown me much kindness.

'What in the world are you exciting yourself about?' he asked me on the Saturday afternoon. 'You haven't had a pulse like this since before your first operation, and you've nothing of the kind in anticipation to account for it now.'

But I could not tell him the truth, because from me it would appear incredible. I said that I had slept badly for several nights past, and that might account for my not being so well as usual. And I wound up with the apparently inconsequent request, 'Do come and see Jean-

Marie at two o'clock in the morning, doctor.'

I spoke so earnestly that the surgeon ceased tapping his palm with the stethoscope he held in his right hand. 'I shall be in the ward at four o'clock under any circumstances, so that unless you have any very good reasons for asking me to see him earlier, your request is absurd. If I could do the poor fellow any good by seeing him, then it would be another thing. And I'm almost run off my legs as it is.'

'But I have a perfectly valid reason for asking you to see Jean-Marie precisely at that hour,' I urged. 'I cannot tell you now what it is, but I will do so afterwards, if you will only come.' And he felt my pulse again, and I knew that he thought I was wandering in my mind.

'Well, well,' he said, good-humouredly, 'if I can wake myself at that hour—two o'clock I think you said—I'll run in and have a look at Jean-Marie.'

About eleven o'clock, when the lights were turned low and all was quiet for the night, Jean-Marie's mind for a short time became clear and tranquil. He was like a man about to set forth on a delightful journey to some place and friends he longed to see; he was full of deep, happy excitement. When the nurse asked him if he wanted anything, his answer was always the same, *'Mon ami,* my wanting days are over, I have everything.' Then he spoke to me. 'I am ready to go when my Françoise fetches me. *Monsieur,* if I may leave to you my rosary I shall be glad. It may be that the *Bon Dieu* will lead you by it to become Catholic,' and he looked wistfully.

'Jean-Marie, I would become anything that would give me your peace and courage,' I said. But I do not think that he heard my reply, for he was again wandering—talking to himself and singing snatches of old Breton songs, that were not unlike Gregorian tones.

'I wish that French fellow would be quiet and let me go to sleep,' whimpered a fretful voice from my left-hand neighbour. 'It is the last night that he will disturb you; have a little patience,' I said.

Midnight had long past, and in due course I heard the church clocks for a mile round strike one, like irregular file firing. I had not long to wait before I should know whether Jean-Marie's prophetic dream was true or not. In the exalted state of my senses every sound in the ward, every footfall of the nurses, seemed unnaturally loud, as I lay watching in the subdued light the old-world features of Jean-Marie. He was lying on his back with closed eyes, his long, brown fingers telling his beads and his lips moving rapidly. Just then a nurse approached his bedside with a dose of medicine so nauseous that the smell of it as it wafted by made me feel ill.

'Must you disturb him to give him that vile stuff?' I asked, as I looked with compassion on Jean-Marie, tranquil for the first time in many hours. 'Doctor's orders,' she replied briefly, and raised the patient's head to put the glass to his lips. He opened his eyes, and I saw by his expression that his soul revolted at the loathsome draught. Then, with the meekness of a little child, he drained it to the dregs.

It was a few minutes to two o'clock, and I was strung up to an almost intolerable pitch of excitement. When a cinder fell from the grate it sounded like thunder, and I started and trembled. Jean-Marie had fallen into a restless sleep, but he no longer muttered and talked to himself. I could hardly believe my eyes, though I firmly expected what I saw—by the side of Jean-Marie's bed stood the same form I had seen three nights ago, the Brittany peasant woman. Her plain, swarthy face was covered with the sweetest smiles, and she leaned her dark head in its snowy cap over Jean-Marie till her cheek almost touched his. My heart beat to suffocation, and I leaned upon my elbow, determined to watch closely. It was seldom that everyone was asleep in the ward at the same time, and the sister in charge and the nurses were certainly awake. Did no-one but myself see the tall figure by Jean-Marie's bed? It must have been full ten minutes that I saw the woman both standing and leaning over him in her quaint dress, and at length she knelt by his side and I heard him say in a low voice of ecstasy, 'Oh, *ma Françoise! Ma Françoise!*' as he sighed away his last breath.

'Nurse, nurse,' I cried, 'Jean-Marie is dying!' And she hastened to him in a moment, as she did so unconsciously passing through the shadowy form that still hovered over him. Just then the door at the end of the ward opened and the house surgeon entered.

'What is the matter?' he said as he saw me out of bed and the nurse feeling Jean-Marie's pulse.

'Jean-Marie is dead—very suddenly; I only gave him his draught half-an-hour ago,' said the nurse. Then I told the doctor as collectedly as I could what I had seen on Thursday night and how Jean-Marie had told me of his dream, which I had seen fulfilled, and of the ghostly figure of the Breton peasant woman that had but that moment faded from my sight. I dared not tell him the night before, but now that there was confirmation of it he must see for himself that it was true, and I pointed to poor Jean-Marie's corpse. He listened with the greatest attention.

'If it had been any other patient that had told me such a thing,' he

413

said at length, 'I should have known that he was delirious, and have ordered ice to his head, and I don't say but that it mightn't be a good thing for even you. Still, when an educated man like yourself is convinced that he has been brought face to face with the supernatural, he is entitled to a hearing. It is strange, very strange. Jean-Marie was a remarkable man; I have never met a patient like him. There is only one thing that I can be sure of in the whole affair, and that is, that I must have you out of this ward the first thing in the morning, or your nerves will be shattered in addition to your other troubles.'

The body of my poor friend was removed before any of the patients were aware that a death had occurred. In a few hours I found myself in another ward of the hospital, surrounded by fresh faces, and I could hardly be certain whether or not I had dreamed the strange story of Jean-Marie Thégonnec Pipraic.

The Empty Picture Frame

It was a wild day in September. An equinoctial gale had raged since dawn, shaking doors and windows, and battering the walls of Eastwick Court. The orchards were strewed with bruised fruit plucked by the rude hand of the wind. The gardens that yesterday, neat and trim, basked in autumn sunshine, today were littered with branches stripped from the trees, and melancholy with uprooted flowers. The paths were cut into channels by torrents of rain, that washed the loose sand on to the grass, where, as the water subsided, it lay in red patches. At sunset there came a sudden lull. The gale fell to a whisper, and the rain ceased. But no flush of light overspread the grey sky. No western glow shone on the sombre walls, or reflected its red light on the rain-washed windows of the old house.

Within doors it was too dark to read or work, and in the enforced idleness of twilight, Miss Swinford laid down her book, and seated herself on a low chair by the fire.

Katherine Swinford was alone in the great drawing-room. As she leaned forward with hands clasped in her lap, watching the bickering flames that played about the logs on the hearth, there was something pathetic as well as dignified in her appearance. The mistress of Eastwick Court was no longer young. Her thick hair was streaked with white, and sundry lines on her brow, and about her clear grey eyes, showed where time's finger had touched her and left its mark. Her features were large but finely formed, her expression firm and self-reliant. Miss Swinford had lived so long alone, mistress of a large property, and a law unto herself in her own domain, that she had acquired the somewhat imperious manner of one who exercises a benevolent tyranny, and has an unquestioned right to be obeyed. She was the only child and heiress of Sir John Swinford who had been dead some twelve years, and she had lost her mother in her infancy.

No-one could have supposed that Miss Swinford, like Queen Elizabeth, was destined to reign alone. She had had as many suitors as the Virgin Queen herself, and they might be classed in three orders. The first, and most numerous, was attracted by the estate to which the lady seemed but the necessary appendage. The second felt the charm of the heiress, and the still greater charm of her wealth, while the third order of suitor was represented by one man only, who loved Katherine for her own sake, and would have sought her for his wife if she had been penniless. No need to tell the story— *'es ist ein altes Liedchen'*—the true love died long ago, and his fever-worn body lay buried in the hot sand of a tropic shore, and Katherine Swinford was still and would always remain Katherine Swinford.

Perhaps as she sat by her lonely hearth in the gathering dusk, she was thinking of what might have been, of the strong arm she might have leaned on, of the children that might have called her mother. She sighed, and rising abruptly, rang for lights. 'This will never do! I shall grow melancholy if I sit by myself in the twilight. It is peopled with ghosts, and with might-have-beens, the worst of all ghosts. I have been too much alone lately. I ought to keep up a succession of visitors. By the way, I wonder why I have not heard from Sir Piers Hammersley. It is ten days since I wrote to him inviting his daughter to come and stay with me.' And an air of bright energy succeeded to her momentary depression, and when the lamps were brought into the room Miss Swinford was looking ten years younger than she had done a short time before.

Sir Piers Hammersley was a cousin of the late Sir John Swinford, and both descended from a common ancestor, Sir Miles Swinford, who lived at Eastwick Court in the time of Charles the First. The Hammersleys were originally Swinfords. But Sir Miles's second son Adam had married an heiress in Cumberland, Anne Hammersley, on the condition that he should bear her name as well as share her fortune. When Adam went to live in the north he took with him his sister Joceline, whose lover Colonel Dacres had been wounded fighting for his king, and died in her father's house, since when she had pined and drooped at Eastwick Court. Joceline was only three-and-twenty years old, and her family thought that absence from home and its tragic associations would restore her to health and cheerfulness. And in this hope she made what was then the long wild journey out of Herefordshire into Cumberland. But no change of air or scene could arrest the decline into which she had fallen. Before the spring came she was laid in the vault of the Hammersleys.

Her sad story and the tradition of her beauty, confirmed by a portrait still preserved at Eastwick Court, had caused her to be remembered both by the Swinfords and Hammersleys, and the name of Joceline had not been allowed to die out in the family. The very reason why Miss Swinford had bestirred herself to write to her father's cousin whom she had not seen since she was a girl, was that his only daughter was named Joceline. Her heart had warmed towards her unknown kinswoman in her loneliness, and she had written asking Sir Piers to allow his daughter to visit her at the house that was the birthplace of the original Joceline. The Hammersleys still lived in Cumberland, and Miss Swinford's letter must have reached its destination the day after it was posted. But she had received no answer to her friendly invitation. She was astonished and almost affronted by chilling silence where she had hoped to meet with a cordial response.

'My cousin Joceline is so much younger than I that perhaps she does not feel very eager about spending a few weeks alone with me,' she argued with herself. 'But at least she should be wishful to see the home of her ancestors, and the portrait of Joceline Swinford, whom she is fortunate if she resembles in personal appearance.'

Here Miss Swinford's soliloquy was cut short by an unexpected interruption. A sound of heavy wheels driving slowly up the avenue by which the house was approached from the high road, and the carriage, waggon, or whatever it was that could be so ponderous, came to a standstill at the front door. 'The storm must have cut the gravel up terribly,' thought Miss Swinford; 'I never heard wheels sound so heavy in the avenue before. Who can be paying an afternoon call so late, just when I am about to dress for dinner!' and the heavy carriage drove slowly away. Immediately afterwards the drawing-room door was thrown open, and Bennet the old butler announced 'Miss Hammersley'. Miss Swinford started with surprise, and advanced to welcome a young and tall lady dressed in black, some fifteen years her junior. She was of a mortal pallor of complexion, with dreamy brown eyes and fair hair, and bearing the most extraordinary resemblance to the portrait of Joceline Swinford.

'My dear cousin! You have dropped upon me from the clouds! I have received no intimation that I should have the pleasure of seeing you today, or I would have driven to the station to meet you myself,' and she kissed her young kinswoman's pale cheek.

'How cold you are, my dear! Come and sit near the fire before you take off your cloak.' And she led Joceline to a low chair, and she sat down by the flickering fire, with her back to the lamp.

'What sort of a journey have you had this stormy day? I'm afraid you had to change trains rather often between Cumberland and our little village station.'

Joceline Hammersley raised her eyes with a strange uncomprehending gaze, as though she were listening to a language she did not understand, and instead of replying to her question merely said, 'I have come a long way, I am very tired.'

'You are not strong, my dear, I am afraid, you look so pale and weary. It is a pity I cannot give you a little of my superfluous strength,' and Miss Swinford smiled kindly on her young cousin. She could not take her eyes from the white oval face with its high marble brow, large dark eyes and heavy eyelids, delicate nose, and small mouth with lips too pale for health. 'It is astounding, perfectly astounding!' at length she said. 'Do you know that you are the living image of our common ancestress Joceline Swinford! You are exactly like the van Dyck portrait in the library! I must show it to you!'

'Oh, not tonight! Not tonight!' pleaded her cousin.

'Very well then, not tonight, but first thing in the morning. By candle-light it might startle you, it would be like looking at the reflection of your face in a mirror. But let me unfasten your cloak for you, my dear.' For her guest was enveloped in a long black silk cloak, with a hood drawn over her fair curls, a quaint garment becoming her so well as to suggest the idea that the pale silent lady was an artist in dress, and studied effects very successfully.

'Do not let me trouble you,' she replied, throwing her hood back upon her shoulders, 'my waiting-woman will give me the help I require.'

'Your waiting-woman! Dear child, what an antiquated phrase! But I suppose odd words and expressions still linger in the wilds of Cumberland. Your maid, yes, I will ring for her, and I will show you to your room, where I am afraid the fire can hardly be lighted yet. It should have been burning all day if you had only done me the honour to announce your arrival beforehand.' And Miss Swinford opened the drawing-room door, when to her amazement her guest with unhesitating step as though she knew her way perfectly, turned towards the old part of the house, that was full of empty rooms.

'Not that way, my dear! You are going to the disused part of the building, that has not been inhabited since my grandfather's time, and belongs nowadays entirely to ghosts and rats. Let me lead you to our comfortable modern rooms, less historically interesting, but better suited to the requirements of a tired traveller like yourself.' And her guest turned to follow her with an expression of disappointment on her pale face. 'May I not see the old rooms?'

'Certainly. I will show you everything, beginning with your own portrait, tomorrow morning. But here is your maid and this is your room; as we dine in half an hour I will leave you now to dress.' And mistress and maid were left together.

Miss Hammersley's maid was no less remarkable-looking than her mistress, with the same extreme pallor, though here the resemblance ended, for the mistress was beautiful and the maid distinctly ugly. Her grey hair was drawn away from her dark bony forehead under a close-fitting white cap. Her eyes were small and black, and her mouth large, with thin compressed lips. Like her mistress, she was dressed in entire disregard of existing fashion, in a dark woollen material, with a deep linen collar and long white apron. At first the sight of a maid wearing a cap that a modern cook would scorn, and an apron suitable in size for a scullion, occasioned rude mirth among Miss Swinford's servants. But their laughter was brief, and succeeded by uneasy fear, for Mistress Galt (as Miss Hammersley called her maid) had queer unaccountable ways, in harmony with her strange and repellent appearance.

The morning after Miss Hammersley's arrival at Eastwick Court, the sun shone brightly on the destruction caused by the storm of the previous day, and the gardeners were busy repairing the damage done by the wind and rain.

When Miss Swinford entered the breakfast-room, her guest was walking on the terrace, dressed in a white close-fitting gown low and open at the front, and her bare neck exposed to the chilly morning air. Miss Swinford hastened to her from the open window, exclaiming, 'My dear child, you will catch your death of cold! Come back and put a shawl over your neck. Is it still the fashion to come down to breakfast in a low dress as my grandmother used to do!' and she led her into the house, and wrapped a soft shawl about her shoulders.

'How cold you are! And the morning air has brought no colour to your face! My dear child, are you always as cold as this?'

'Yes, always,' she replied quietly. Then adding as though speaking to herself, 'yet I am clothed in woollen and sheltered from wind and rain.'

'Drink your coffee, you make me cold to look at you! And after breakfast I will take you upstairs to the library to show you the portrait of your namesake, and you shall tell me if you see the resemblance to yourself which I think so striking. It is an odd coincidence the dress you are wearing might have been copied from that in the picture. But you shall see for yourself,' and Miss Swinford, pleased to have someone to talk to, continued chatting, and did not notice how silent her cousin remained.

After breakfast she took Joceline's cold hand in hers, and led her upstairs. 'The library was my father's favourite room, and I have made no alteration in it since his time. It was there that I last saw your father, and I remember how greatly he admired Joceline Swinford's portrait. He said he should like to have a copy of it, but he does not need that as long as he has you to look at, my dear.' And Miss Swinford flung the door to the library wide open with a triumphant There!'

But she started in astonishment, for over the fireplace, where the portrait of Joceline Swinford had been, hung only the empty frame, its tarnished gilding in sombre harmony with the square of blackened wall that had been covered by the canvas.

Miss Swinford rang the bell impetuously, and ran into the corridor to second its summons with her voice.

'Bennet, Bennet! there is the most extraordinary thing! The old portrait of Miss Joceline Swinford has been taken out of the frame, and carried away bodily! The house has been broken into during the night! Search everywhere, and find out by what door or window it has been entered.

The servants gathered in a cluster round the library door, looking Up at the empty frame with awe-stricken faces, and Miss Swinford sat down and fairly burst into tears. Joceline gently laid her hand on her shoulder, and said in a low voice, 'Do not weep, the picture will be restored to you!' and raising her eyes her cousin beheld the very embodiment of Joceline Swinford's portrait standing beside her. The shawl had slipped from her shoulders, leaving her neck uncovered and in face, attitude, and costume, she was so amazingly like the figure in the missing picture that Miss Swinford started. And the servants, still peering in at the door, looked from the empty frame to the pale lady, and then at each other with indefinable fear.

No trace of the thieves could be discovered. No lock, bolt, or bar on door or window had been tampered with, and the picture was hung so high that whoever had stolen it, must have accomplished the theft by the help of a ladder. The local superintendent of police came to examine the house, and to take down a description of the missing picture from Miss Swinford's lips, and she advertised a large reward for its discovery or for such information as should lead to the detection of the thief. 'The picture will be restored to you,' repeated Joceline. 'I am afraid not, my dear. The stolen portrait of the beautiful Duchess of Devonshire has never been recovered, and how can I hope to get my picture back again, and to unravel the mystery of its disappearance?' Miss Swinford telegraphed tidings of her loss to her lawyer in London, and followed it up by a long letter of instructions. He was to send a description of the missing portrait to all the picture dealers, and an advertisement was put in the papers warning pawnbrokers to detain the bearer, as well as the picture, if it was offered to them. And having done everything in her power to recover her treasure, Miss Swinford remained inconsolable under her loss.

The excitement in the servants' hall was intense, and the physical difficulty of abstracting from its frame a picture hung at such a height was dilated upon at great length. Finally they all agreed with old Bennet when he gave it as his opinion, 'that it was like as if it had been sperited away!'

Only one person in the house appeared indifferent to the prevailing distress and anxiety, and this was Mistress Galt, who went about chuckling to herself with eldrich laughter.

Several days passed in which Miss Swinford did little but lament her loss, and exhaust conjecture as to how the picture could have been so mysteriously removed. But neither search nor enquiry threw any light on the matter. The portrait had vanished, leaving no more trace than if it had melted into thin air.

Her distraction of mind at first prevented Miss Swinford from noticing her guest, as she otherwise would have done. But as she became less preoccupied, she observed in Joceline Hammersley numberless little peculiarities, that, taken all together, convinced her she was unlike anyone she had ever met before. She had none of the ardour and impetuosity of youth, she was silent and reticent. She was ignorant of everyday matters that a child would know, and yet surprised her by considerable out of the way knowledge, and acquaintance with bygone times, though she knew nothing of contemporary history. Her phraseology was often amusingly antiquated. Sometimes too she would misunderstand the plainest language, and require it to be translated into another form before she appeared to grasp its meaning.

'Does your father never take you to London, my dear?' asked Miss Swinford, thinking it a pity that so lovely a young creature should not see more society than her country home afforded.

'He took me thither once on a time when I was but a child, and I call to mind that while we were at our lodging in Whitehall the queen was brought to bed of a son, and the rejoicing thereat.'

'My dear Joceline, you positively must not make use of such an old-fashioned, countrified expression as "brought to bed"!' said Miss Swinford, 'it is only fit for an old nurse! Ladies may have spoken in that way a century ago, but it is purely rustic now. If you must date your visit to London by royal domestic events, you should say you were there when the queen was confined.'

'But that would not be the truth,' replied Joceline, raising her dark eyes and folding her hands in her lap, 'for it was not the queen's but the King's Majesty that was confined in Carisbrook Castle,' and she sighed heavily.

Miss Swinford was confounded. Could it be that her beautiful young kinswoman was mildly deranged? She looked into the dreamy brown eyes fixed upon her, and merely saying, 'I think you have lived too much alone in the country,' lapsed into thoughtful silence.

That night when Miss Swinford was returning to rest and her maid was about to leave the room, she lingered at the door and said, 'There's something I want to speak to you about, miss, but I hardly know how to, for it's about Miss Hammersley.'

'What is it, Dapper? What can you have to say that concerns my cousin?'

'There's something strange about the young lady, miss, and about Mistress Galt too, as she calls her. They walk in their sleep or something as bad. Last night when I was lying awake I heard footsteps, and I got up and opened my door, and crossed the gallery and looked over the banisters, and there below if there wasn't Miss Hammersley and her maid going into the empty rooms in the old part of the house. I saw them quite plain in the moonlight through the big window. They were in their day dresses, they hadn't undressed for bed though it was past two o'clock, and Miss Hammersley was crying and sobbing. They seemed to know their way about the house in the dark as well as we do by daylight! I felt frightened and went back to bed, and it would be a good half-hour before I heard them creep back to their rooms again. I thought I'd better tell you about it, miss.'

'You amaze me, Dapper! It's impossible that they both walk in their sleep. But perhaps my cousin does, and her maid follows her lest she should meet with some accident, or wake suddenly and be alarmed.'

'I hope, miss, that if you hear anything tonight you'll please to get up and see for yourself. I'll put your dressing-gown by the candle and matches, and if you want me I'm a light sleeper, I should wake if you only scratched on the door.' And Dapper retired, leaving her mistress profoundly uneasy.

Many uncomfortable thoughts were suggested to Miss Swinford's mind by what she had heard. She rose and locked the door, that if Joceline walked in her sleep, at all events she would not be startled by her entering the room in the night with wide unseeing eyes. She thought over all her cousin's peculiarities, her strange inanimate expression, her deadly pallor and coldness, her silence and dreamy look, and decided that she was a very likely subject to be a somnambulist. Having settled this painful matter to her satisfaction, Miss Swinford's mind reverted to its favourite theme—the inexplicable loss of the portrait. And she fell asleep to dream that her cousin stood in the tarnished frame over the library mantelshelf, saying, 'I told you that Joceline Swinford's portrait would come back to you!' when she woke suddenly, the clock struck two, and she heard gentle steps in the carpeted gallery.

In a moment she had put on her dressing-gown and opened the door. Dapper had left a lamp burning, and by its light she saw Joceline Hammersley in the gallery on the opposite side of the hall, followed by her maid, walking towards the door leading to the old part of the house.

Miss Swinford hastened along the gallery that ran round the four sides of the hall, till she was close behind the dim figures that had now passed beyond the light of the lamp. Mistress Galt was silent and rigid, but Joceline, pale as death, walked with clasped hands, moaning to herself. They left the door open as they entered the deserted rooms, and Miss Swinford followed unperceived. They passed quickly across stretches of pallid moonlight falling through the dusty windows, alternating with breadths of blackest shadow, opening door after door till they came to a corner room, looking out to the front and end of the house. Then they paused, and Joceline lifted up her face that no moonlight could bleach whiter, and cried, 'It was here that he died! On this spot my love died! Here he lay till they bore him to his last resting place, but far from me! I lie alone in my narrow bed!' and Miss Swinford, terrified, and convinced that her cousin was either a mad woman or a somnambulist, turned and fled.

She did not pause or look behind her till she had locked herself in

423

her room, when she fell half-fainting upon the bed. 'My poor cousin is insane! She has heard the story of the death of Joceline Swinford's lover in this house, and has brooded over it, till with her peculiar temperament it has turned her brain. And that strange woman Galt is her keeper, I see it all now! How shall I get rid of her? I shall become mad myself if we stay together much longer in this old house. How could she know the room in which Colonel Dacres died? I have not told her, and she has not been at Eastwick Court before. It is hateful, it is uncanny!' and Miss Swinford shuddered.

Presently she heard light footsteps once more, and opening the door saw the dim figures of her cousin and her maid returning to their room. They had made a complete circuit of the house, and regained the gallery by means of a disused staircase, the door leading to which was kept locked. When all was once more silent, Miss Swinford crossed the gallery, candle in hand, to examine for herself if the lock had been tampered with. But the door was fastened as it had been for many years, and the paper pasted round it to prevent draughts was undisturbed. Yet there was no other means of reaching the side of the gallery by which Joceline Hammersley and Mistress Galt had returned to their rooms, except by this staircase.

Miss Swinford slept no more that night, and when she closed her eyes, it was only to open them and assure herself that the pale-faced Joceline was not standing by her side.

At length when morning light filled the room, she drew aside the curtain and looked into the garden. She was startled to see Joceline and Mistress Galt standing together under the window. Neither of them wore hood or kerchief in the keen morning air, and Joceline's bare neck looked white and cold as marble. 'She is as like the old portrait as though she were the original Joceline come back from the dead!' exclaimed Miss Swinford.

Mistress and maid were looking fixedly at a spot in the garden, towards which first one pointed and then another, and in the silence of the early morning Miss Swinford could hear every word.

'And I say, Mistress Joceline, that the bowling green lay yonder!'

'Nay, be not so confident. You were here but for a few months when all was sorrow and confusion, while I dwelt here for three-and-twenty years, and till the cruel wars came had great joy and pleasure in my home. The bowling green was by the sundial, and lay to the north of the maze. But that is gone too. All is changed, the very flowers wear strange faces.'

'Shall you not rest, Mistress, since you have seen that which you prayed to see once more?'

'Yes, I shall rest. I shall sleep till we all wake together.'

'Mad! Stark mad!' ejaculated her cousin as she dropped the curtain and turned from the window.

The day proved wet and stormy, and Miss Swinford had to pass the heavy hours indoors with her uncanny guest. She was now so fully convinced of her cousin's insanity that she felt nervous in her presence, and unable to question her about her mysterious conduct. Joceline was, if possible, quieter and more reserved than ever. She looked fearfully ill, at times scarcely conscious, and as though her dark eyes moved with difficulty from one object to another.

'I am afraid you did not rest well last night, you seem so tired,' Miss Swinford ventured to say.

'I have not slept of late, but soon I shall rest again.' And she seemed almost to fall asleep as she spoke. Only once did she show spontaneous interest in anything, when turning over the leaves of a book, she came upon an engraving of the celebrated portrait of Strafford. Then her pale face seemed to radiate light. 'My Lord Strafford!' she exclaimed, 'and yet how unlike, for no picture can give the dark fire of his eye! O noble soul, that gave thy life for thy king, and yet wast powerless to avert his doom!'

At length the tedious day drew to an end. The two ladies were sitting in silence in the drawing-room, Miss Swinford wondering when her strange cousin would depart. She was resolved that she would write to Sir Piers to say that the change back to the bracing air of the north would be beneficial to his daughter's health, when Joceline rose noiselessly and left the room. 'How shall I get through another night with that unaccountable being wandering about the house, asleep or insane!' she thought, looking after her with a troubled expression. 'I cannot bear the strain of her company! It will be long indeed before I invite a stranger again to pay me a visit!' when the door opened and her cousin stood before her pale as a lily, dressed in her black travelling cloak and hood. Miss Swinford rose in amazement. 'My dear, what is the meaning of this! You came unannounced, you cannot surely be leaving me as abruptly as you arrived!'

'I must go, I am wanted,' she said. And as she spoke the sound of heavy wheels was heard approaching the house. An inexplicable fear fell upon Miss Swinford.

'But how shall you travel? You are too late for any train tonight.'

'I go as I came. I shall soon be at my journey's end. Farewell, cousin Katherine, and be of good cheer, the portrait of Joceline Swinford will be restored to you!' Miss Swinford mechanically followed her downstairs, where Mistress Galt was already waiting, and the servants peering over the banisters to watch the departure. Miss Swinford stepped into the porch with her guest, and there stood waiting a huge coach, drawn by four black horses. By the light of the moon, issuing from beneath a cloud, she saw that the coachman was dressed in as antique a style as his mistress, and that his face like hers was deadly pale.

'Farewell, cousin, farewell!' said Joceline, touching Miss Swinford's cheek with her cold lips, 'the missing picture will be restored to its place.' And followed by Mistress Galt she stepped into the coach, in which six persons could have seated themselves with ease. She leaned out of the window, and bowed to her hostess with solemn formality. Then the horses moving at a heavy trot drew the lumbering vehicle down the avenue towards the high road. Miss Swinford, Bennet, Dapper, and a couple of grooms attracted by the extraordinary sound of the heavy carriage approaching the house, stood awestruck watching it depart. Not one of them could have expressed his fear in words, and the terror each felt was the greater for being unspoken. The huge coach rumbled along the avenue, when it turned into the high road, and still they could hear the heavy waggon-like sound of its wheels.

'They have taken the turning to the left!' cried Miss Swinford, the first to break the silence. 'That great carriage and four horses can never cross the Brook Bridge. They should have turned to the right. See if you can overtake them before the road is too narrow for them to turn!' and the grooms ran down a side path that was used as a short cut to the road. The heavy sound of wheels grew duller and more distant, and suddenly ceased. 'Thank goodness they are stopped in time, they will turn now!' said Miss Swinford. But still no sound was heard. Presently the grooms came back breathless with running, the younger of them looking ready to faint.

'You stopped them in time, Landon, I hope?' asked Miss Swinford of the elder of the two men.

'Oh Lord, Oh Lord, ma'am, there's no coach nor nothing to stop! As I'm a living sinner there's nothing but a three mile stretch o'road clear as day in the moonlight, and not so much as a wheelbarrow on it, and neither man nor beast to be seen! That big coach and four's clean gone, same as if it had sunk into the ground!'

'Come into the house, madam,' said Dapper, supporting her mistress, for she staggered as though she would fall, 'and thank God, however they're gone, those white-faced witches are out of the place at last!' And sick with amazement Miss Swinford suffered herself to be led indoors.

When she had recovered herself, she said with her usual determination, 'Dapper and Bennet, come with me into the library, I want you both!' And they followed their mistress in silence. Miss Swinford paused for an instant on the threshold, then opening wide the door all three entered the room. The lamp stood on the table, a cheerful fire burned on the hearth. Everything was in its accustomed order, and Dapper and Bennet looked vaguely about them wondering why they were wanted. But their mistress pointed to the wall above the mantelshelf. From its tarnished frame the portrait of Joceline Swinford looked down on them once more, as though it had never been missing from its place. Dapper screamed shrilly, Bennet gazed open-mouthed, Miss Swinford buried her face in her hands and said in a tremulous voice, 'This is dreadful! What does it mean, what can it mean!'

The next morning's post brought Miss Swinford a letter from Sir Piers Hammersley, at Carlsbad, where he and his daughter were staying, apologising for her letter remaining so long unanswered, but it had been carelessly overlooked and only forwarded to him that day. He was exceedingly annoyed to think how uncourteous he must have appeared. Joceline, too, was as sorry as himself. She hoped that her cousin would renew her kind invitation some future time, to give her the pleasure of making her acquaintance, and of visiting the old home of the family.

Then the strange beautiful girl who had come and gone so mysteriously, whose visit had corresponded with the absence of the portrait of Joceline Swinford, was not her cousin after all! Who then was she, or *what* was she? Miss Swinford believed that she knew who her strange guest had been. But she dared not express her conviction in words. Her friends would have thought her mad. She kept her secret locked in her breast. But she was a changed woman from that time forward, and within twelve months the last of the Swinfords was laid to rest in the family burial place. The old servants still tell the story of the pale lady's visit, and her weird ways, and how their mistress fell into pining health from the very night of her mysterious departure.

Sir Nigel Otterburne's Case

It is thirty years since I completed my career at the Eastminster Hospital. I had passed all my examinations successfully, and taken more than my share of medical honours, when one of our most celebrated physicians, Dr Grindrod, asked me to watch an important case for him, the study of which I should find of the deepest professional interest.

Dr Grindrod's patient was suffering from an obscure form of malaria, contracted abroad, which had developed into an extremely rare form of intermittent fever, with really beautiful complications, such as he had never met with before in all his wide practice. But Sir Nigel Otterburne lived a three hours' journey from town in Hampshire, and when the doctor went to see him it practically took a whole day of his valuable time, which was more than he could afford to devote to any one case. Dr Grindrod therefore proposed that he should see the patient himself once a week, and send down one of the most promising of the hospital students to watch the case under him, and to take minute medical notes of its progress.

I was the fortunate man selected for the work, and was to go into the country with Dr Grindrod, taking with us a couple of our most trustworthy nurses. I can never again feel as important as I did on that first day of August when I entered upon my onerous duty. The doctor and I were met at the station, and driven through lovely country to the Hammel, which was the name of Sir Nigel Otterburne's house. It was a fine specimen of Jacobean architecture, and, externally at least, had undergone but little change for a couple of centuries past. It was a three-storied building, with tall fluted chimneys, and dormer windows in its high-pitched roof. The front of the house was nine windows wide—narrow sash windows with a great deal of framework in proportion to the glass. The front of the house, with its wings to right and left, made three sides of a quadrangle, the fourth side of which was formed by wrought-iron railings, with great gates in the centre.

Leaving the carriage outside for fear of disturbing the patient by the sound of our arrival, we crossed the wide courtyard on foot. The front door was approached by shallow steps, and sheltered by a richly carved penthouse of black oak. Upon the wall between the second and third storeys was a sundial, and the bright August sunshine threw the sharply defined shadow of the gilded gnomon on the figure denoting the hour of four o'clock in the afternoon.

Above the dial a small turret rose from the centre of the roof surmounted by an elaborate piece of ironwork, with quaintly twisted letters N. S. E. and W., and a glittering arrow for a weather-vane.

I was struck by the appearance of the house, at once stately and homely. But I received from it an impression of melancholy which was not lessened when the door was opened by a grey-headed servant, who led us across the panelled hall into a vast and dreary dining-room. It contained nothing in the way of furniture except a long table with a row of high-backed chairs pushed close against it on either side, and a sideboard of carved oak, on which stood a row of silver flagons. A china bowl on the middle of the table, filled with roses and white lilies, made the atmosphere of the room heavy with their perfume. A few gloomy old portraits looked down from their tarnished frames, some with faces austere and rigid as though they had been painted after death.

Dr Grindrod had acquainted me with the details of Sir Nigel Otterburne's case on our journey, and having nothing further to say till we had seen the patient, he stood with his hands behind his back, looking at the portrait of a lady over the mantelpiece, so lavish of her charms that I assigned her at a glance to Charles the Second's period. 'That is what I call a magnificent woman,' said the doctor, waving his hand sumptuously towards the expanse of bare neck and bosom depicted on the canvas. But I should have rather applied the words to the lady who entered the room while he was speaking, and whom he introduced to me as Miss Otterburne. The doctor had told me that Sir Nigel Otterburne was a widower with an only daughter, but he had said nothing to prepare me for the appearance of so amazingly handsome a creature.

I have never met a woman who so completely fascinated and interested me at first sight. Miss Otterburne was not a girl. She was in the ripe beauty of womanhood, and with a most dignified and haughty carriage. She covered me with a glance of her beautiful dark eyes, and curtsied so low that it was almost a sarcasm to a young man like myself. She was tall and slender, of an ivory pallor of complexion, with fine sensitive features, and a mass of dark hair worn high on her head. She was dressed in some soft, cream-coloured fabric, and her sleeves came only to the elbow, displaying to the utmost advantage her beautifully formed hands and arms.

'I promised you, Miss Otterburne, that I would bring one of our hospital students to watch Sir Nigel's case for me,' said Dr Grindrod. 'You must not mistrust Mr Caxton because he is young. He has had experience in the hospital which many older men might envy. He will post to me daily notes of the patient's condition. I shall be down myself once a week, and you would telegraph for me in any emergency. Indeed, my dear young lady, I can assure you that Sir Nigel is in good hands,' and Dr Grindrod smiled, and attempted a light and easy manner. But Miss Otterburne was entirely irresponsive.

'Heaven grant that you may be right,' she said in chilling tones, and she led us upstairs to the patient's room. As she walked erect before us, there was that in her bearing and appearance which reminded me of some distinguished Frenchwoman at the time of the Revolution, and I thought how many a proud head like hers had fallen from its white shoulders under the guillotine.

Sir Nigel's room was dark and dreary, and he lay in a funereal bed with heavy hangings, and I mentally vowed to have him out of it and in a more cheerful room within four-and-twenty hours. If the house did not contain some light, undraped bedstead, I would send to the hospital for one such as we use for our patients.

Sir Nigel Otterburne was in a half-comatose state when I first saw him, and I judged him to be about sixty-two or -three years of age. He was tall and thin, and looking at his face I saw at a glance whence Miss Otterburne derived her fine features. His hair and moustache were thick and grey, and he looked what he was, a soldier. In his lucid intervals there was a dignity and self-restraint in his manner which again reminded me of his daughter. The local practitioner, Mr Walton, was present in the room, a good-humoured, rustic-looking man, more like a farmer than a doctor, but who, if he was unprofessional in appearance, luckily for me had less than the usual amount of professional jealousy.

So far from being annoyed at seeing me installed in the house to watch the case of his distinguished patient for Dr Grindrod, he expressed his approval of an arrangement that relieved him of so much responsibility. But he said nothing before Miss Otterburne, and I saw that she exercised the same repressive influence over him that I felt so strongly myself. But when we were in the dining-room again, and I was receiving my final instructions from Dr Grindrod, Mr Walton said, as he poured himself out a glass of sherry: 'I don't profess that single-handed I could pull Sir Nigel round. I've not had the opportunity of studying malarious fevers. But if you gentlemen succeed in curing the patient, I share the glory of it, and if he slips through your fingers Miss Otterburne cannot reproach me, for nothing could be expected of me where Dr Grindrod failed.' 'Is Miss Otterburne likely to reproach you, if the case ends fatally?' I asked.

Mr Walton looked round to see if the door was shut, emptied another glass of wine before he spoke, and said in a low voice: 'Miss Otterburne is Miss Otterburne, and it would be unprofessional to gossip about any member of my patient's family. Eyes and ears open, and mouth shut at the Hammel, is my advice.'

After Dr Grindrod's departure I went upstairs to make arrangements for my first night in charge of Sir Nigel. A small room leading out of the patient's had been assigned to my use, and I went to the window to look at the view. My eyes never rested on a more peaceful scene. Immediately in front of the house, bounded on either side by its projecting wings, was the great courtyard, with its wide grass borders bathed in sunshine, and beyond the iron palisades and the high gates stretched an expanse of undulating country thickly wooded with trees in their heaviest summer foliage. On the brow of a gentle ascent, some quarter of a mile distant, stood a grey church with an ivy-grown tower, and the evening sunshine was glittering on the weather-vane.

When I had seen the night nurse enter upon her duties, I went for a stroll in the open air, leaving the house by a door at the back of the hall. I found myself in an old-fashioned garden with grass terraces and clipped yew hedges. I thought that I was alone in the garden, when suddenly I caught sight of Miss Otterburne's light dress, white and ghostly in the gathering gloom, and in a moment we were face to face in the path. I raised my hat and stood aside for her to pass, and I felt the blood mount to my cheeks. She might think that I was intruding on her privacy, and following her on her evening walk. Miss Otterburne did not quicken her pace as she passed me. She regarded me with grave intensity. But her eyes were void of speculation, like those of one who was walking in her sleep. I watched her stately figure recede among the darkening alleys, and heard the door close as she entered the house. I felt chilled and disconcerted, why I could not tell; but I would run no second risk of appearing to intrude upon Miss Otterburne.

At eleven o'clock Miss Otterburne entered her father's room to bid him goodnight. He scarcely knew her, yet I fancied that he smiled faintly as she pressed his hand, or it may have been the flickering of the lamplight on his face that I mistook for a smile.

'I trust Sir Nigel will have a tranquil night,' I said.

'His nights are always tranquil,' she replied in measured tones.

'And yet he has gained no strength the five weeks he has lain here.'

'He never will,' she said in the same passionless voice.

'You speak more positively, Miss Otterburne, than any doctor would dare to do. Such an illness as Sir Nigel's is not necessarily fatal. We do not know ...'

'But I know,' and her voice sank to a whisper. 'It is useless your staying here. My father will never leave this house alive.'

'It is wrong to speak so,' I said firmly. 'And if Sir Nigel understands what you say, it must cause him the most exquisite pain.'

Not a line in her white handsome face softened or changed.

'My father knows it already,' she said, and swept from the room, leaving me bewildered by her manner.

I slept but little during my first night at the Hammel. My mind was so much occupied with Sir Nigel's case, that I went frequently to see my patient, and to note any change in his condition, however slight. My obstinacy, too, was roused by Miss Otterburne's assertion that her father would die, by the way in which she ignored anything that medical skill could do for him. Her manner was that of a person expressing a profoundly melancholy conclusion forced upon her against her will, and yet that she believed to be irrevocably true.

'If that man's sentence has not gone forth from heaven, he shall live,' I exclaimed, 'and that handsome, obstinate creature shall be taught that she is not infallible!'

My resolution being made, I tried to sleep, but tried in vain. The profound silence of the country after the roar of London had the same effect upon me that noise has upon those who are accustomed to quiet, and kept me wide awake. And from time to time I was startled by the screeching of owls, sounding like the cries of terrified children lost in the dark.

At length the dawn came, and I rose to go into Sir Nigel's room.

This time he was conscious, and as I felt his pulse he whispered, 'Are they come?'

'Yes,' I replied, supposing that he alluded to me and the nurses. 'We came yesterday, and we shall try to relieve you as much as we can.'

But he sighed impatiently, closed his eyes, and turned his head from me. It was useless to lie down again, so I dressed myself, and the clock was striking four as I opened the window and leaned out to enjoy the freshness of the morning air. To my great surprise, Miss Otterburne also was looking out of her window in the centre of the right wing of the house. I drew back at once, but she had not heard me throw up the sash, and she was not looking in my direction. Her dark eyes were fixed in a trance-like gaze on the entrance to the courtyard, or on the church crowning the grassy slope. She certainly was not looking at any part of the house. She was ghastly pale, and her eyes wore the same unseeing expression that I had noticed in them on the previous evening.

For more than a quarter of an hour Miss Otterburne remained immovable, and how long she may have been at her casement before I saw her I cannot tell. She was wrapped in a white robe, and her dark hair lay in waves on her shoulders, but her face was not like that of a living woman. It seemed probable that I might have two patients in the house to look after. And I felt a distinct sense of relief when at length she withdrew from the window and I lost sight of her.

That day I carried out my intention with regard to Sir Nigel. We moved him into a small bed and carried him to a bright, cheerful sitting-room on the same floor—a room suggesting pleasant, sunny life as clearly as the gloomy bedroom had suggested death. I felt sure that the patient would appreciate the change, that it would prove beneficial to him. But to my disappointment, he did not appear to notice it, and it produced no effect on his physical condition. I heard him murmuring to himself as he lay, 'It will make no difference; it will make no difference.'

It was singular, too, that Miss Otterburne seemed to take no interest in her father's removal to more cheerful quarters. However, I had Dr Grindrod's approval of what I had done, and I was content.

'How do you get on with Miss Otterburne?' the doctor asked me abruptly on one of his visits, when I had been more than a week in the house.

'You might as well ask me how I get on with that picture on the wall,' I replied. 'But I think she is the handsomest woman I ever saw in my life.'

'You do, do you? Hum! Not my style; I prefer flesh and blood,' and Dr Grindrod shot a glance in the direction of the Charles the Second lady, and fell to talking of purely medical matters.

When I had been in hourly attendance on Sir Nigel for a fortnight, I began to realise not only that my patient was making no progress, but that I was making no progress with my patient. I expected no lively gratitude from him. But it would have been pleasant if there had been any token of recognition, either on his part or his daughter's, that I was doing my utmost for him. I imagine that he regarded me as a servant whose attentions were indispensable to his comfort, but with whom he could not be familiar. It did not annoy me, sometimes it even amused me, for I never count a sick man in the category of sane persons, and should no more think myself insulted by an invalid than by a madman. This excuse, however, did not apply to Miss Otterburne, and I was puzzled more and more by her conduct.

Every morning at earliest dawn, if I looked out, she was leaning on her window-sill, gazing with a tragic melancholy, not I am sure at any tangible object, but on something that presented itself to her mental vision.

Not only did I gain no ground with Sir Nigel and his daughter, but the old housekeeper and butler, though perfectly civil to me, were both exceedingly reserved. Sometimes the housekeeper would have a short confab with me on her master's state, consisting on her part chiefly of sighs and head-shakings, and once the butler went so far as to observe, 'Master Raymond will wish that he'd parted friends with his father when he went to India!' So then Sir Nigel had a son, a fact of which I was not aware, and furthermore it would seem that father and son had had some quarrel or misunderstanding.

Meanwhile there was no disguising the unwelcome fact that my patient was steadily sinking. Dr Grindrod approved of all that I did in carrying out his instructions to the letter, but nothing we could do availed to check the downward course, and we racked our brains for treatment and remedies which should keep the enemy at bay. The disease was not running a normal course. Unexpected complications arose at an unusual period in its progress, and how interesting the battle between the force of disease and the power of science became to me none but an enthusiast in the medical profession can tell. I seldom quitted the patient's room. Only when he was sleeping did I venture to leave him for an hour in charge of a nurse while I went for a stroll in the fresh air.

It was just before sunset one evening, when I had been nearly a month at the Hammel, that I closed the front door gently behind me, and crossing the courtyard, let myself out into the park, and made my way towards the church on the grassy slope. I was exhausted and excited, and I walked bareheaded that the cool breeze might blow about my heated temples. I hated to be baffled. I had been so sure of victory, and now defeat stared me in the face. Miss Otterburne would have a melancholy triumph. She would be right after all, and I should be wrong.

I went over every event of the previous weeks in detail. I was satisfied that all that medical science could do for Sir Nigel, at the point to which it had then attained, had been done and was still being done for him. But I reflected with a crushing sense of impotence on the irresistible power of the force with which I was contending. I, a finite being, was measuring my strength against death, the conqueror of man. The contest was hideously unequal. I was sure to be worsted. Even if the patient recovered, it would be at best but a reprieve, and sooner or later he must retrace his anguished steps towards that bourne from whence I was striving with all my strength to turn him back.

I entered the churchyard in the deepest depression of spirit. It was not merely the anticipated loss of my patient that weighed on me; that was but one item in the incalculable total of human misery. In his death I saw the doom of every son of Adam—the death of the whole human race. I was ready to wish that I had died myself before I had embraced a profession which constantly brought me face to face with a terrible elementary fact in nature, with which the utmost skill of man is powerless to cope.

The church door stood hospitably open, and I entered the cool twilight within. Here were tombs of the Otterburnes, from the time when intra-mural burial was a universal custom to the present period, when a memorial tablet or monument is all that is permitted within the church itself. I thought how soon Sir Nigel would be numbered among his ancestors, and be as remote from us who still lived as his own earliest forbears were from him now. Suddenly I heard a deep sigh, and starting, I turned and saw Miss Otterburne close to me, but almost hidden by a great pillar against which she leaned. Her dark eyes were fixed with the wide unseeing gaze which I had noticed in them each early morning as she looked from her window. I spoke to her, and when she heard my voice the pupils of her eyes dilated as though the twilight had deepened round her.

'Miss Otterburne, if there is anything that you wish to say to Sir Nigel, I should advise you to take the opportunity of his next interval of consciousness. It grieves me to be obliged to say this, but I have no choice in the matter. I must tell you the truth.'

'Yes, they will soon come. I know it,' she said with a slight shudder.

I thought that she was wandering in her mind, and, taking no notice of her incoherent reply, I continued.

'I would give my life, Miss Otterburne, if I could prolong the life of one so dear to you.'

But she looked past and through me, as though she were piercing into futurity, and I heard her say: 'When they come you will know that I was right.'

And she glided like a ghost out of the dim church into the amber light of evening. Her manner disquieted me profoundly, and I wished that Miss Otterburne was not so lonely; that her brother in India was at home to take his share of the trouble, and to comfort his sister.

I hastened back to my patient's bedside, and, knowing that it would be impossible to leave him that night, I sat down to copy my notes of the case for my own private use. About eleven o'clock Sir Nigel rallied slightly. I administered a powerful restorative, and sent the nurse to fetch Miss Otterburne at once. As she entered the room, I said: 'If you would like to be alone with your father, I will remain within call outside the door.'

She bowed her head in assent, and I left them together. I remained waiting in my own room, listening to Miss Otterburne's voice distinctly audible in low urgent tones. Then, as Sir Nigel again lapsed into unconsciousness, she spoke a little louder, and I heard her say: 'Father, will you not forgive Raymond?' and then all was silent. I reentered the room, and Miss Otterburne was kneeling by her father's bedside. She had been weeping, and I saw that beneath the armour of pride and reserve there was a woman's tender heart. But my return was the signal for her to depart, and she left the room hastily, as though displeased that I had witnessed her emotion.

I looked at my dying patient with more regret than I should have thought possible to feel for a man who, in his short intervals of consciousness, had always treated me as a stranger. Certainly I had no affection for Sir Nigel, but I was struck by the pathos of the situation. There he lay, needing, like each one of us, both divine and human forgiveness, but unable to ask it for himself or to grant it to another, even when it was his daughter who knelt weeping by his side, imploring pardon for her brother.

Slowly the night passed, and slowly the patient died. I noted the decreasing temperature, the failing pulse, and I applied restoratives which formerly had power to rally him, though now they had lost their virtue. But the heart still beat, and now and then a sighing breath escaped his lips.

There was nothing more that I could do. But that I might leave no expedient untried, I sent the nurse into my room for an air cushion, which I told her to inflate and bring to me. If I raised the patient's head by means of it, it was possible that he might feel a momentary ease, though he would be unconscious of its cause.

I looked at my watch. It was four o'clock, and the grey light of dawn glimmered through the curtains. I wondered whether Miss Otterburne was at her window, according to her strange custom, when the door opened swiftly and silently, and she entered the room as I had often seen her at that hour, clad in a loose white robe, and her dark hair hanging about her shoulders. There was mortal pallor on her face. She did not cast a glance in the direction of her dying father, but exclaiming in tones that chilled my blood: 'They have come, they have come!' she went to the window, drew back the curtains, let in the cold light of dawn, and stood with clasped hands gazing into the courtyard below. I was by her side in an instant.

'They have come, they have come; I knew they would come!' And I heard the effort she made to speak with a tongue that was dry with terror. In the courtyard beneath, directly opposite to the window, was a strange, silent crowd of men, women, and children, looking up at us in the faint morning light with faces of the dead. And though they pressed and thronged each other on the gravel path, not a sound was heard.

I am not a superstitious man, and in those days my nerves were of iron. But I reeled as I stood, and the blood rushed to my head with a singing sound. I saw the dead of centuries ago, and the dead of yesterday, grey-bearded men who fought in the civil wars, young men and maidens who never were contemporaries in this life, and little children, all gazing at us with upturned faces. Miss Otterburne spoke again as one speaks in nightmare, with deadly effort and oppression.

'I know them. I saw them when they came to fetch my grandfather, and when they fetched my mother. Oh, mother! mother! you are there!' And she leaned forward in an agony, and gazed with set and rigid face at a slim form that drifted through the ghostly throng and lifted its sad eyes to hers. By her side stood a tall man in uniform, whose white face I shall never forget, and he solemnly waved his hand towards us. 'Oh Heaven! my brother Raymond is with them!' shrieked Miss Otterburne, and sank on the floor insensible, at the moment that Sir Nigel gave his last groan.

I hastily fetched a cushion and placed it under her head, and then turned once more to the window. But the courtyard was absolutely empty, nor was there a trace of its recent occupation. I could not have been absent from the window a couple of minutes, and the instantaneous disappearance of the ghastly throng shook my nerves fully as much as the sight of it had done. There was not a mark on the untrodden dewy grass. Not a pebble displaced on the broad gravel path that had been so crowded a moment before. On the spot where the tall figure had stood and waved its hand to us a cat was seated, licking her paws, and I heard the fitful chirp of the first awakened birds.

I felt physically ill, and turning from the window I poured out and drank a powerful cordial that restored an artificial calmness to my nerves. Just then the nurse returned. She had not been absent from the room more than five minutes.

'The patient is dead, and Miss Otterburne has fainted,' I said. 'Help me to lay her on the couch.'

I have never in all my experience seen anyone in so deep a swoon. The nurse and I were unspeakably relieved when at length she showed signs of returning consciousness, though I dreaded what she might say when she recovered. I gave her a composing draught which would secure her some hours' rest, and committed her to the care of her maid.

I sent at once for the family doctor, who had seen Sir Nigel on the previous night, to acquaint him with the death of the patient. He was exceedingly inquisitive about every possible detail, and appeared to long for information concerning something he dared not enquire about directly.

'Were there any circumstances of an unusual character attending the death?' he asked anxiously.

'It was the ordinary termination of such an illness as Sir Nigel's,' I replied guardedly.

'And Miss Otterburne, how did she bear the shock?'

'She had a severe fainting-fit, and remained insensible for fully half an hour. She appears to feel her loss acutely.'

Mr Walton agreed with me that I had better remain in the house till the following day, to make the necessary arrangements for the funeral, and to write to Miss Otterburne's relations, with whose names and addresses the butler supplied me, to prevent his mistress from being disturbed. The old man became almost talkative for so taciturn a person.

'The family has died and died till yonder churchyard is full of them,' he said. 'The very soil of it was once Otterburne flesh and blood, and there's no-one left of this branch but Miss Otterburne and the major in India, that's now Sir Raymond. There's a few cousins up in the north, and a widowed sister of the master's, and they'll like to come for the funeral, if it's only to see where they'll be laid themselves when their time comes, for all the Otterburnes are brought here to be buried.'

'Will one of the ladies of the family stay with Miss Otterburne till her brother returns from India?' I said, and as it was the first question I had asked, the old man cast a suspicious glance at me, resumed his uncommunicative manner, and changed the subject of conversation. By noon I had sent the nurses back to London. Then there remained the long afternoon and evening in which to collect my distracted thoughts and to get my nerves into something like order for a return to the active duties of life. I could not for an instant forget the horror of that early dawn. I saw, as clearly as I now see the pen with which I am writing this narrative, the ghostly throng with upturned, dead faces gazing at us, and Miss Otterburne's words and cry still rang in my ears. Whatever the ghostly vision was, we had both of us seen it. If only one person had seen it, and that one myself, I should not have been convinced of its reality. I should have believed that I was subjected to some terrible hallucination. But we both saw it at the same moment. And Miss Otterburne had seen it twice before, and each time under the same ghastly circumstances. There was no doubt that it had been as visible to us as natural objects are. It was no picture conjured up separately in our brains.

I confess that I was so unnerved I could not look out of that window again, nor could I spend my last night at the Hammel in any room at the front of the house. I asked the housekeeper to give me a bed in one of the back rooms. She cast a peculiar glance at me and said: 'You don't care for a room that looks out into the courtyard, and I don't blame you for it. But you need not mind it now, sir; they won't come again till—till they are sent.'

I made frequent enquiries during the day about Miss Otterburne.

But I did not ask to see her, so fearful was I of the effect my presence might have in recalling the horror we had witnessed together. The last thing at night I sent a message to her saying that I should return to town in the morning, and I hoped that she would send for me if I could be of the slightest service to her. But she did not require me, and I retired for the night to a small back room on the second floor.

Sleep was out of the question. I did not undress, but sat smoking pipe after pipe and trying to read, till when the grey dawn came a great terror took possession of me, and I shook like a man in a fit of ague. I scorned myself for my weakness. But the feeling was beyond my own control.

At length, when daylight flooded the room, I threw myself across the bed and fell into a deep sleep which must have lasted for hours, and from which I was awakened by loud knocking at the door. 'Who is there?' I said, starting to my feet, and the knock was again repeated. I ran to the door and opened it. The old butler stood before me pale and trembling.

'Miss Otterburne wishes to see you, sir, in her sitting-room.'

'Tell her I will be with her directly,' and I hastened to make myself fit to enter the presence of a lady, and went downstairs to Miss Otterburne's room, where her maid stood waiting for me with a scared face. She said nothing, but opened the door of her mistress's room. I entered, and she closed it after me.

Miss Otterburne was standing by the table with an open letter in her hand. I should not have known her. Her hair had turned white in the last twenty-four hours, and there was a strange glitter in her eye. She handed me the letter, saying: 'It was Raymond that we saw with them; I knew it.'

I read the letter. It was very short. A few lines written in haste by a friend of the major's to Sir Nigel, telling him of the death of his son, of cholera at Meerut a month ago, and promising all particulars by the next mail. As my mind took in the meaning of it I grew giddy. The room became suddenly dark to me, and I groped for a chair like a blind man. Miss Otterburne laughed, the cackling laugh of insanity, and it recalled me to myself in an instant through extremity of compassion for her.

'Why do you pretend to be surprised? You knew that Raymond was dead as well as I; we both saw him. Oh, he was merry! They were all a merry company; why should we be sad?' and the poor lady laughed in such an awful fashion I could have shed tears of blood to listen to her.

It was the last time that I saw Miss Otterburne. Twenty long years she continued to live at the Hammel in a state of hopeless insanity, dangerous neither to herself nor to others while she was allowed to remain there. But if any attempt was made to take her elsewhere, her frenzy became ungovernable. 'They would not know where to find me,' she would say. 'They can only fetch me from here, and I want the merry, white-faced folk to come for me;' and her anger would subside into dreadful laughter.

Every day in the early dawn she rose to look out of her window into the courtyard. But one morning she failed to do so, and her attendant was thankful to find Miss Otterburne lying peacefully dead, on the twentieth anniversary of her father's death.

The Ticking of the Clock

Elijah Walrond, or Old 'Lijah as he was commonly called, was a small tenant farmer, who, by dint of hard work, hard living, and saving, had contrived to lay by enough money to make a frugal provision for his old age. 'Lijah's wife died the year before he quitted the farm that had been their home for forty years, and when he lost her it was like losing a part of himself. He was never the same man again. It took the heart out of his work when there was no wife to talk it over with; he could not relish the food prepared by a strange hand, and he lay awake at nights in his loneliness, staring into the darkness with tearless eyes. There was nothing left to make life sweet to him, and his seventy years weighed on him like a hundred. Then he asked his landlord to let him off the short remainder of his lease, and he left the farm to live in the white cottage with the big garden down by the common.

His neighbours said that Old 'Lijah would go silly with loneliness all by himself, for he saw nobody and spoke to no-one but the woman who came to clean and to do his bit of cooking. He seldom left the house, and never went beyond the garden, and he had not entered the church since the day of his wife's funeral. The rector of the parish, who had known Elijah Walrond many years, called to ask him why he never saw him in his accustomed place on a Sunday, but the old man would only reply, 'I canna do it, sir; I canna do it! 'Er'd used to go to church with me, and I canna go alone,' and lapse into silence again. There was no-one at home now to care what he did, or whether he was well or ill, so he ceased to strive against stiffness and rheumatism, and crept along with the help of a stick, with bowed shoulders, as though he carried a heavy burden. Old 'Lijah was in a parlous state, both of body and mind, when one day the very best thing that could happen befell him, though it came about through someone else's sorrow.

'Lijah had an only child—a daughter—who some years previously had married a ne'er-do-well of the name of Grove, and lived with him in the north of England, where, after a short career of idleness and poverty, he died, leaving Jane a widow with one little child. Jane Grove had not a farthing in the world to call her own when she had paid her fare to travel southwards to her father, and her sticks of furniture had been sold to pay for her husband's burial, for her honest pride revolted at a pauper's funeral. She knew that her father had left the farm, but in however poor a place he lived now, he would not shut the door upon his daughter, though he had been displeased with her for marrying as she did. But bygones were bygones, and though the mother, who would have welcomed her child, was dead, Jane could cook and work for her father, and make the meanest place seem like home; and good as her intentions were towards the old man, she could not tell—no-one could have told—the kindness she was about to do him.

Jane Grove reached her father's cottage in the grey of a summer evening, weary and footsore with her long walk from the station, carrying her sleeping child in her arms. She inquired from a man whom she met crossing the common where Elijah Walrond lived, and he pointed out to her the little white cottage with the big garden. Slowly she walked up the long, narrow path, with its straggling border of sweet-smelling pinks, wondering that the place was so untidy and ill-kept, till she stood on the threshold of the half-opened door. She tapped timidly, and no-one replying to her knock, she looked into the kitchen, and there sat her father dozing in his chair by the chimney corner.

She was shocked at the change in his appearance. His features were sharp and worn, his hands like birds' claws, and a ragged growth of white beard and moustache covered his once well-shaven face; nor was old 'Lijah as clean as he might have been. His stockings were in holes and his clothes ragged and unmended. It was plain to be seen that he had lost all interest in himself, and that there was no woman to look after him. Jane entered, and quietly seated herself opposite to her father, and her tears fell fast as she took in the meaning of his forlorn and neglected aspect, and whispered to herself, 'Oh, mother, mother!'

When 'Lijah opened his eyes, there sat his daughter on the other side of the hearth, nursing a child on her lap. At first he did not know who it was, and looked vaguely puzzled until he heard her voice.

'It's me, father; it's Jane come to live with you and make you comfortable.'

He did not seem startled, and received the announcement with the most matter-of-fact calm.

'Whatever brings you back i' these parts? It's trouble, I doubt,' and the old man shook a boding head.

'Aye, father, trouble enough it is! My man's dead, and I 'aven't a penny in the world and no home but what you'll give me and this little lad to keep,' and the child, now wide awake, sat up on her lap and looked about him.

'What's that you say about a little lad? You've got a little lad to keep?' and there was a strange stir in the old man's heart as he uttered the words, for he had never had a son of his own, and it had been the great disappointment of his life.

For reply Jane crossed the hearth with her child in her arms, and set him on the old man's shrunken knees—as beautiful a boy of twelve months old as a mother ever doted on.

'Yes, father, that's my little lad as I've got to keep; that's little Peter, your own little grandson; and he's rare good company a'ready for lonely folks. Many's the time he's dried my tears watching 'is pretty ways. 'Old 'im tight, father, for 'e isn't used to old folks, and p'r'haps 'e mayn't take to you.'

No need to tell 'Lijah to hold his little grandson carefully. The touch of the child's firm young flesh, the sight of his golden hair in lamb-like curls, his gentian-blue eyes and moist, innocent breath nourished his old bones, and he felt there was vital warmth in him yet. And when little Peter put up a dimpled hand to grasp his ragged beard, and made pretty baby jabbering, and laughed in his troubled old face, displaying four pearly-white teeth like grains of rice, the frost in the grandfather's heart, that had bound it since his wife died, melted, and he said: 'Jane, if you 'aven't got a penny in the world, your man's left you rich enough wi' a little lad like this! You must bide wi' me—both of you.'

'Aye, father, so we will. But look you how that grey wire beard o' yourn is scratchin' little Peter's face! You'll 'ave to shave it off, and poor mother always thought so much o' your clean chin!'

The ragged beard was duly taken off, and the old man began the trouble of shaving again, and renewed his acquaintance with soap and water, for the little lad's sake; and his daughter washed and mended his clothes, and 'Lijah looked once more himself, but old very old.

'Lijah's whole heart was garnered up in his little grandson, and as the boy grew older it was a pretty sight to see them in the fields together, the child bringing wild flowers to the old man to name, or a bird's egg or nest; but whatever it was he could tell him everything about it, and nothing short of that would content little Peter. For he had a healthy child's thirst for every kind of knowledge, so long as it was not what schoolmasters teach or what comes out of a book, and he was eager after all country lore and old-world word-of-mouth wisdom. It was wonderful how much the little lad learnt from his grandfather about four-footed creatures, from oxen to stoats and weasels, and he could have passed an examination with honours in the names, songs, and plumage of British birds.

The two were inseparable companions, and Peter would rather play with his grandfather, whom he regarded as an overgrown child with bent back and stiff legs, than with any little boy of his own age. Jane Grove would stand on the doorstep and smile as she watched her father and his little grandson set out for a walk hand in hand, perfectly happy and content together. 'They're more like a pair o' lovers, them two, than anything else! Father's like wrapped up in that lad, and don't think o' me exceptin' to eat the vittles I cook and set afore 'im; nor little Peter, 'e don't think o' me neither so long as 'e can 'ave 'is grandad! They're both of 'em civil to me, and that's about all they are, they're so took up with each other.'

When little Peter had stuck to his grandfather like his shadow for five years, he began to be aware that his beloved companion could not see very far, and was shaky on his legs, got tired before they were half across the common, had a habit of falling asleep in the midst of the most interesting conversation about rooks and water rats, and was growing deaf, so that he had to speak loud to make him hear. These things grieved little Peter, and as he could not see the necessity for them he asked his grandfather what he did them for.

'Granddad,' he said, as he walked slowly by his side, having hold of his hand, 'grandad, why don't you run as quick as me?'

The old man smiled delightedly at a question that seemed to him to display little Peter's immense intellectual powers.

'It's seventy 'ears too late, my little lad, for grandfather to go running about like a little dog at a fair.'

'But, grandfather, you know a deal more than me; you'd ought to know how to run ever so fast, and climb the bank and gather blackberries same as me.'

'Aye, so I did when I was your age, but blackberries was bigger then than what they are now. They was worth climbing for seventy 'ears ago, I can tell you! But I'm an old man now, Peter,' and 'Lijah looked down on the child's upturned face that was fresh and clear as a flower.

Little Peter walked on a few paces in thoughtful silence. 'But, grandfather, what makes you such an old, old man?' And 'Lijah laughed with delight at the question. Oh, Peter was a rare deep little chap, he'd get to the bottom of everything if he could.

'It's nothing but *Anna Dominoes* as makes me such a' old, old man, and that's Latin for the 'ear of the Lord. It's *Anna Dominoes*, that's the matter wi' me, little Peter, and nothin' else,' and the child stored up the mysterious words in his tenacious memory.

Not long afterwards Old 'Lijah, who had grown neighbourly again now that he was happy, went one evening, accompanied by his grandson, to spend an hour with his old friend, Farmer Blewitt. The two old men were seated in armchairs at each side of the table, with a tobacco jar and cider mugs, and a small narrow box before them. Little Peter was lying on the hearth playing with a young spaniel puppy, in whose delightful society he was wholly absorbed, till he heard Farmer Blewitt say: 'Let's have a game o' dominoes, 'Lijah; it's many a day since you and me played together.'

Little Peter sat up.

'I don't mind if I do play a game,' said his grandfather.

Little Peter rose to his feet, pushed the frivolous and seductive puppy aside as being likely to interfere with serious business, and modestly, but firmly, approached the table where the old men were beginning their game. He laid his hand on his grandfather's arm, but he did not feel it at first, so he pressed harder.

'Hallo! little chap, what's up?'

'Don't touch none o' them dominoes, grandfather! Don't touch 'em,' said little Peter urgently.

'Whatever's to do with you, Peter? You're onreasonable!' said 'Lijah, with as near an approach to asperity as was possible towards his little grandson.

But Peter was not to be daunted. 'Grandfather, don't you remember that day when I asked what made you such an old, old man, you said it was *Anna Dominoes* as did it all? Don't touch 'em, grandfather, don't touch one of 'em!' and Peter's young face was full of anxiety.

Old 'Lijah and Farmer Blewitt laughed till they cried, while 'Lijah told him what he had said to the little chap in the lane about his age; 'for he's that peart, I said *Anna Dominoes* was the matter wi' me, speaking Latin, and Latin or Greek he'll get to the reason o' things! No, little

446

Peter, these ain't the kind o' dominoes that's made an old, old man o' your grandad; it was the 'ear of the Lord I was speaking on, and when you go to school you'll learn all about un!'

Peter was now an active little slip of seven years of age, never still except when he was sleeping, and not knowing what it was to be tired. He had grown used to his grandfather's increasing infirmities by now, but they irked his restless young body and spirit, and on their walks together, when the old man sat down by the way weary and breathless, little Peter beguiled the time running to and fro as fast as he could, to let off his pent-up energy, after crawling at a snail's pace by old 'Lijah's side.

A few weeks later and little Peter again returned with a child's persistence to the puzzling subject of his grandfather's decaying strength.

'Grandfather, if it isn't the dominoes that does it, do tell me what it is that makes you such an old, old man!'

Old 'Lijah did not laugh at the boy's question now. He felt his life feeble within him, and he did not know what to say in reply that could be intelligible to a child. They were alone in the kitchen, and no sound was heard but the loud ticking of the tall clock, the audible footstep of time. The old man looked into the child's fresh young face as he stood between his knees waiting for an answer, and he smiled feebly, and pressed the firm round cheek with his shaking hand, but he said nothing.

'But what is it, grandfather, that makes you such an old, very old man?'

Then 'Lijah looked up at the tall clock whose loud tick tack penetrated his dull hearing, and it seemed to him as though he had heard it for eighty years, counting out aloud the minutes, hours, days, and years of his whole life.

'It's the ticking of the clock, my little lad, the ticking of the clock, that makes grandfather such an old, old man;' and Peter was satisfied with the reply, and set his young brains to work to find out how he could baffle the evil influences of the clock.

Now the tall case clock was a very big person for a small boy to tackle. He stood six feet without his shoes, with a huge round face behind a pane of glass, and a long front door opening straight into his vitals, and Peter had peeped in on winding-up days, and seen two heavy weights hanging, and the shining brass pendulum swinging to and fro, whose everlasting tick tack had made an old man of his grandfather. Well, never mind, wait till some time when mother was out of the house, and grandfather asleep in the big armchair, as he was nearly all day long now, and little Peter knew what he would do!

Not many days afterwards everything happened as Peter wished, and he looked out of the window to make sure that his mother was at a safe distance at the top of the garden, and there she was, standing with her back to the house, busy pegging clothes on the line, so that no danger need be feared from that quarter. Indoors, too, all was equally favourable to the carrying out of little Peter's deep-laid scheme. Grandfather really was older than ever today. He had not stirred from the big chair since he came down in the morning, and when he was spoken to he said nothing, he only smiled and fell into a doze. He was fast asleep now, and little Peter's heart beat with joy to think what a fine surprise he was preparing for his grandfather. What would the old man think when he felt the stiffness and trembling going out of his legs and back, his eyes growing clear and bright again, and his deafness leaving him? All which would be sure to happen if the clock would only stop ticking.

Grandfather was so fast asleep, with his head leaning forward on his breast, that little Peter was not afraid of waking him. He summoned all his courage to his aid and stepped cautiously up to the great clock, with its menacing tick tack, unlocked its front door, opened it wide, and peeped into the resonant cavern in its inside, with the heavy iron weights hanging and the bright brass pendulum swaying to and fro with its everlasting *tick tack, tick tack*. Then, without giving himself time to take fright at his own daring, he seized hold of the swinging pendulum and, after a brief struggle, held it in his hand, a silent, motionless thing.

Then little Peter loosed his hold, and glanced over his shoulder at the old man, but he was still quietly sleeping. He cautiously seated himself on a stool at his grandfather's feet, waiting to tell him when he awoke how he had stopped the ticking of the clock that made him such an old, old man.

There his mother found him sitting when she returned from the garden, and neither daughter nor grandson could rouse the old man from the sleep that knows no waking. When the pendulum was set swinging once more, the clock began to tick again as though nothing had happened, and it ticked out the minutes till they grew into years, and little Peter became big Peter, and then he understood what his grandfather had meant.

LEONAUR

ALSO FROM LEONAUR
AVAILABLE IN SOFTCOVER OR HARDCOVER WITH DUST JACKET

MR MUKERJI'S GHOSTS *by S. Mukerji*—Supernatural tales from the British Raj period by India's Ghost story collector.

KIPLINGS GHOSTS *by Rudyard Kipling*—Twelve stories of Ghosts, Hauntings, Curses, Werewolves & Magic.

THE COLLECTED SUPERNATURAL AND WEIRD FICTION OF WASHINGTON IRVING: VOLUME 1 *by Washington Irving*—Including one novel 'A History of New York', and nine short stories of the Strange and Unusual.

THE COLLECTED SUPERNATURAL AND WEIRD FICTION OF WASHINGTON IRVING: VOLUME 2 *by Washington Irving*—Including three novelettes 'The Legend of the Sleepy Hollow', 'Dolph Heyliger', 'The Adventure of the Black Fisherman' and thirty-two short stories of the Strange and Unusual.

THE COLLECTED SUPERNATURAL AND WEIRD FICTION OF JOHN KENDRICK BANGS: VOLUME 1 *by John Kendrick Bangs*—Including one novel 'Toppleton's Client or A Spirit in Exile', and ten short stories of the Strange and Unusual.

THE COLLECTED SUPERNATURAL AND WEIRD FICTION OF JOHN KENDRICK BANGS: VOLUME 2 *by John Kendrick Bangs*—Including four novellas 'A House-Boat on the Styx', 'The Pursuit of the House-Boat', 'The Enchanted Typewriter' and 'Mr. Munchausen' of the Strange and Unusual.

THE COLLECTED SUPERNATURAL AND WEIRD FICTION OF JOHN KENDRICK BANGS: VOLUME 3 *by John Kendrick Bangs*—Including twor novellas 'Olympian Nights', 'Roger Camerden: A Strange Story', and ten short stories of the Strange and Unusual.

THE COLLECTED SUPERNATURAL AND WEIRD FICTION OF MARY SHELLEY: VOLUME 1 *by Mary Shelley*—Including one novel 'Frankenstein or the Modern Prometheus', and fourteen short stories of the Strange and Unusual.

THE COLLECTED SUPERNATURAL AND WEIRD FICTION OF MARY SHELLEY: VOLUME 2 *by Mary Shelley*—Including one novel 'The Last Man', and three short stories of the Strange and Unusual.

THE COLLECTED SUPERNATURAL AND WEIRD FICTION OF AMELIA B. EDWARDS *by Amelia B. Edwards*—Contains two novelettes 'Monsieur Maurice', and 'The Discovery of the Treasure Isles', one ballad 'A Legend of Boisguilbert'and seventeen short stories to cill the blood.

LEONAUR

ALSO FROM LEONAUR
AVAILABLE IN SOFTCOVER OR HARDCOVER WITH DUST JACKET

THE COLLECTED SCIENCE FICTION AND FANTASY OF STANLEY G. WEINBAUM 1—INTERPLANETARY ODYSSEYS *by Stanley G. Weinbaum*—Classic Tales of Interplanetary Adventure Including: A Martian Odyssey, its Sequel Valley of Dreams, the Complete 'Ham' Hammond Stories and Others.

THE COLLECTED SCIENCE FICTION AND FANTASY OF STANLEY G. WEINBAUM 2—OTHER EARTHS *by Stanley G. Weinbaum*—Classic Futuristic Tales Including: *Dawn of Flame* & its Sequel The Black Flame, plus The Revolution of 1960 & Others.

THE COLLECTED SCIENCE FICTION AND FANTASY OF STANLEY G. WEINBAUM 3—STRANGE GENIUS *by Stanley G. Weinbaum*—Classic Tales of the Human Mind at Work Including the Complete Novel The New Adam, the 'van Manderpootz' Stories and Others.

THE COLLECTED SCIENCE FICTION AND FANTASY OF STANLEY G. WEINBAUM 4—THE BLACK HEART *by Stanley G. Weinbaum*—Classic Strange Tales Including: the Complete Novel The Dark Other, Plus Proteus Island and Others.

THE COLLECTED SCIENCE FICTION & FANTASY OF JACK LONDON 1—BEFORE ADAM & OTHER STORIES *by Jack London*—included in this Volume Before Adam The Scarlet Plague A Relic of the Pliocene When the World Was Young The Red One Planchette A Thousand Deaths Goliah A Curious Fragment The Rejuvenation of Major Rathbone.

THE COLLECTED SCIENCE FICTION & FANTASY OF JACK LONDON 2—THE IRON HEEL & OTHER STORIES *by Jack London*—included in this Volume The Iron Heel The Enemy of All the World The Shadow and the Flash The Strength of the Strong The Unparalleled Invasion The Dream of Debs.

THE COLLECTED SCIENCE FICTION & FANTASY OF JACK LONDON 3—THE STAR ROVER & OTHER STORIES *by Jack London*—included in this Volume The Star Rover The Minions of Midas The Eternity of Forms The Man With the Gash.

THE CRETAN TEAT *by Brian Aldiss*—The Cretan Teat is a wry and comic novel that interweaves its own fiction with an inner fiction about the discovery of a Byzantine painting of the Mother of the Blessed Virgin Mary suckling the infant Jesus and a fake ikon that becomes an instrument of Nemesis.

www.ingramcontent.com/pod-product-compliance
Lightning Source LLC
Chambersburg PA
CBHW020924020726
47495CB00002B/332